Gurcharan S. Mann

Nov. 17, 1974
Calgary,
Canada

Surjit Lally
26/2176
Jan. '75

ਤੇ ਖਿਆਲ ਨੂੰ ਸੰਭਾਲ ਹੈ

ਤੇਰੀ ਜਿੰਦੜੀ ਨੂੰ ਪਿਆਰਦੇ ਹਾਂ

Duce!

Benito Mussolini in 1921

Duce!

A Biography of Benito Mussolini

Richard Collier

THE VIKING PRESS / NEW YORK

Published in 1971 by The Viking Press, Inc.
625 Madison Avenue, New York, N.Y. 10022

SBN 670–28603–6
Library of Congress catalog card number: 70–157972

Printed in U.S.A.

Originally published in England as *Duce! The Rise
and Fall of Benito Mussolini*

To the Men and Women of Italy
who lived these things

*What I am to Germany, you are, O Duce, to Italy.
But what we are together for Europe, only posterity can
value and decide.*
ADOLF HITLER to BENITO MUSSOLINI,
28 February, 1943

*After all this suffering and all this fighting, all these
tears and all this anguish, all this blood, all this hate,
and all this hopelessness, what must we do?*
IGNAZIO SILONE, *Fontamara*

Contents

List of Illustrations

Duce!

1. 'Rome or Death!'

27–30 October, 1922

It did not seem a night for revolution. At 6 p.m. the rain had set in, driving in furious gusts across the Tyrrhenian Sea, soaking the men in their gleaming black capes as they crouched on straw before guttering fires. Yet on this October night in 1922, beyond the hills that cradled Rome, close to forty thousand men awaited the fall of the city.

All day the men of the Blackshirt Army, shock-troops of the 300,000 strong Italian Fascist Party, had made ready for the March on Rome. From Bolzano in the Dolomites to Palermo in Sicily, more than a thousand miles south, massed cohorts of Blackshirts, hearing the magic word 'Rome', had piled on to trucks, farm-carts and creaking horse carriages. There were Blackshirts bivouacked in brick kilns, Blackshirts camped in vineyards and villas, Blackshirts in barns and byres and wine-cellars. Only three years after 100 men had founded the Fascist Party in a pitchpine hall on Milan's Piazza San Sepolcro, their aims were as piratical as their skull-and-cross-bones banners: to crush their Socialist and Communist opponents and seize the reins of government by force.

In blueprint, their plan was foolproof. At Tivoli, twenty-two miles from Rome, more than four thousand Fascists, camped in the Villa D'Este's sixteenth-century gardens, commanded the source of all Rome's water-supply and electric current. At Monterotondo, fifteen miles north-east, 13,000 Blackshirts from Tuscany were poised to seize the main railway line down the spine of Italy. Westwards at Civitavecchia, the old port for Rome, Blackshirts from Pisa, Lucca and Carrara had another vital objective: the railway spanning the coast. Already Capua, junction for the south, was the target of Blackshirts from Naples.

At dawn on 28 October the Blackshirts of a hundred cities would stand revealed as the enemy within – geared to the swift, silent seizure of post-offices, prefectures, railway stations and military barracks. Within hours, the Fascists would surround the Eternal City and control Italy.

Yet incredibly, at this eleventh hour, the Blackshirt Army was as ill-equipped to perform its appointed task as fourteenth-century mercenaries. The men encamped on this drenching October night, when the thermometer hovered nine degrees above zero, lacked food, weapons, above all directives. Typical was one company, 130 strong, heading for Monterotondo; apart from two machine-guns, only eighty had even the hunting rifles used against bear and wild boar in their native Sabine Hills. From the four columns that made up the March on Rome, not a single heavy gun could be brought to bear against the 30,000 men of the Rome garrison.

In a tradesman's house on Monterotondo's main piazza, the column commander, twenty-six-year-old Ulisse Igliori, a tall blond World War One aviator, confided his worries to his diary: 'Not a lira to hire cars . . . our men are soaked to the skin and have eaten nothing since yesterday.' In the pine-fringed Castello Odescalchi at Santa Marinella, perched on a bluff above the Tyrrhenian Sea, the Marchese Dino Perrone Compagni, a cashiered ex-cavalry officer, was also at work on his journal. Tersely he noted: 'Needs: water, food, money. It is impossible to keep in touch with the High Command at Perugia.'

Ordered to take command of his troops at midnight on 27 October, it had taken Perrone nine hours, driving at top speed over rain-scoured roads to cover the 136 miles from Perugia. The corollary was plain. Any orders to strike hard and fast for Rome would be nine hours old before they reached him – and it was as long since he had even had contact with his fellow column commanders.

Meanwhile, the night was an eternity, the rain teemed, the red earth streamed in rivulets down the gutters. In cold and darkness and mindless misery, 40,000 men patiently awaited the decisions of their leaders – and, even more urgently, arms and reinforcements.

In Ferrara, near the railway station, almost two hundred and fifty miles north of the waiting columns, the rain had stopped. Like hundreds of other Fascists on this night, twenty-four-year-old Carlo Goldoni's task was to search out arms, ammunition and transport. A veteran Fascist, who earned a precarious living as a freelance shorthand-writer, this was old stuff to Goldoni, clad now in the regulation steel helmet and black shirt that was the shock-trooper's battle array. In the three bloodstained years since the Fascist Party opened its Ferrara branch, thirty-two of his comrades had died in clashes with the police, or with rival Socialists and Communists.

The search for arms had been stepped up two nights earlier on the eve of the revolution. At 2 a.m. a three-man raid, led by Goldoni, had knocked up the caretaker of the local cavalry museum, threatened him into silence and stripped the showrooms of what arms there were. But most had proved antediluvian. Their total haul had been three machine-guns, with twenty belts of ammunition between them.

It was then that Goldoni's chief, Italo ('Iron Beard') Balbo took a hand. A lisping, red-bearded, twenty-six-year-old ex-officer, whose good-luck charm was a lock of Lucrezia Borgia's hair, Balbo was one of four chiefs organizing the march from Perugia's High Command and he saw this revolution in terms of blood. 'You must find more,' Balbo ordered. 'We shall yield only when our last cartridge is spent.'

Next, along with two comrades who now crouched beside him, Goldoni had staged a night raid on the 28th Infantry Barracks. Fitted out with sacks like poachers, they had formed a leap-frog chain over the high wall, broken into the armoury, and escaped with twenty muskets and six revolvers. As Goldoni's squad commander commented shrewdly: 'If only forty out of 100 work, it's still a show of strength.'

The score was mounting. But it could go higher yet.

Now, at 11 p.m., under the flaring gas-globes of the railway station entrance, Goldoni saw the man he had been waiting for – Dr Caputo, an old acquaintance, head of the railway police. Motioning the others to silence, the Fascist marched steadily from the shadows towards the lamplight, across the rain-damp forecourt. 'Goldoni?' the police chief called, peering into the murk. 'What brings you here at this hour?'

'I came to pay you a visit,' Goldoni replied, and quietly, professionally, pressed his gun against the policeman's ribs. 'Put up your hands and give me your guns.'

Caputo was flabbergasted. 'Are you crazy?'

'Never mind about that – I have my men outside. Just give me your guns, call your men, and tell them to do the same.'

By now, more Blackshirts were converging from the shadows; Caputo and his seven policemen were disarmed without resistance. For strategic reasons, Goldoni and his comrades had days ago been briefed on the necessity of seizing the key-point early. On this rainy overcast night, the passengers of DD 49, the Trieste-Rome express, were in for an unpleasant kind of surprise.

Promptly on schedule, at 1.08 a.m. on 28 October, the old Pacific engine came pounding out of the night from Padua. Before the train had even pulled up, Fascists were springing aboard, moving swiftly with drawn guns through the dimly-lit compartments. From the outraged bleary-eyed passengers, roused by the cries of 'Everybody out' and bundled unceremoniously on to the platform, they collected another thirty guns. Now, as scores more Fascists arrived, mobile canteens were set up, doling out spartan rations: rolls, mortadella sausage, mineral water. Others got busy setting up the three machine-guns filched from the museum – one in the baggage car at the rear, the second amidships. Goldoni himself helped to settle the third on the footplate alongside Engineer Vittorio Nespoli. As he mounted to the cabin, the two men exchanged a long triumphant handclasp.

Days earlier Goldoni had warned Nespoli: 'Send word when next you're passing through Ferrara – we'll need a train for Rome, we can't go by bike.' Unperturbed, Nespoli had replied: 'It'll be the 26th or 27th.' All over Italy this night, 11,000 railwaymen, loyal members of the Fascist Party, were following this prearranged plan – calmly abetting the local Blackshirts to hijack their own trains.

At 2 a.m., with 120 Ferrara Fascists now aboard, a whistle shrilled. To the strident strains of a brass band, the train began to gather speed. In a packed compartment towards the rear, Carlo Goldoni relaxed, content; tonight, he knew, there would be no sleep, for at the next stop, Bologna, another 400 front-liners were scheduled to board the train. Coach after long lit coach slid by, hammering through the night towards Rome.

In the stationmaster's office at Civitavecchia, Major Arnaldo Azzi of the 16th Infantry Division fumbled with the seals of the bulky envelope. The telegram had arrived shortly before 9 p.m. on 27 October, just as the Director General of Public Security, had warned them three days earlier that it might. It was the message that Azzi and three other commanders on detachment to the railway were waiting for: 'Put order agreed into effect at once. Pugliese.' Now it remained to open the sealed orders already received from General Emanuele Pugliese, Rome's garrison commander.

By the wavering light of a paraffin lamp, Major Azzi studied his briefing. It was an eight-point memorandum but the first proviso stood out diamond-clear:

'In the event of Fascist trains trying to reach the capital you will try by all means of intimidation (to prevent them) excluding the use of arms . . . allowing the train to proceed with any number of Fascists up to a total of 300.

'Once this total has been reached, you will dislocate the line and prevent their proceeding by any and every means including armed force . . .'

King Vittorio Emanuele III brought the clenched fist of his right hand with a smack into the palm of his left – a sure sign that he was worried or distressed. At 9 p.m. on 27 October, pacing his arras-hung study in the sixteenth-century Palazzo del Quirinale, high above Rome, the King was as fearful for the future of his throne as any monarch in Europe.

His face puckered with irritation, gnawing his scrubby moustache, the diminutive King looked without favour at the man who had disrupted both his day and his peace of mind – sixty-three-year-old President of the Council, Luigi Facta.

At six that morning the King had been making ready for a day's hunting on his country estate at San Rossore, over two hundred miles from Rome, when an urgent cable from Facta had arrived in code. Beset by vague unrest, the King had lost all heart for the hunt, and the decoded message did nothing to allay his fears: to 'tranquillize the situation', his immediate presence was called for in the capital. At eight that night, when Facta greeted him at Rome's Central Station, the King told him sharply: 'We'll talk things over at once because I must see things clearly.'

Plainly there was much to talk over, for what Facta proposed to counteract the threat of a Fascist *coup d'état* was nothing less than a state of siege throughout the realm.

Already it seemed a reality. In the Piazza della Pilotta, below the Quirinale, the white horses of 200 cavalrymen bowed their heads beneath the rain, flanking a line of government machine-gun trucks with their revolving candy-striped towers. Barbed-wire entanglements wreathed the Palace itself, and the city's fifteen gates; it was the same on the seventeen bridges spanning the River Tiber. Though the night wind brought the sound of bugles and the rumble of armoured cars, the city streets were deserted. General Pugliese had imposed a 9 p.m. curfew, forbidding private cars, even trams, to circulate.

In his twenty-two year reign the King had received the oaths of twenty Prime Ministers – and rarely had he despised one more than he despised the bumbling Facta. A quiet country lawyer from

Piedmont, thirty years a Deputy, Facta was a man so obscure that, eight months earlier, when he became compromise premier, the Government had issued potted biographies to newsmen who had never even heard his name. Only in Rome's Caffè Aragno, where he daily took a scrambled egg at noon, were his massive white moustaches a familiar sight – moustaches the Fascists loved to caricature in crayon on café tables. Fellow deputies derided him as 'President-I-cherish-the-hope' – because his groundless optimism had made the phrase a stock-in-trade.

For eight long months Facta had cherished one hope above all: that the Blackshirts were bluffing. 'A March on Rome?' he had echoed to his cabinet, three weeks previously, when the Fascists had illegally created their own militia. 'But *I* am in Rome with troops and artillery.' Calling for a map of the Roman fortifications, he assured them: 'I have ordered the guns to be greased.' Although General Pugliese, fearing a *coup d'état*, had submitted a counter-plan a month ago, Facta's Minister of War had not even acknowledged it. Ignored, too, was the sharp pronouncement of General Pietro Badoglio, forty-seven-year-old Army Chief of Staff: 'Five minutes of fire will scatter that rabble.'

Only twenty-four hours before this meeting with the King, the reaction of Facta and his cabinet, as they at last recognized the danger, had been to resign en bloc. Urged by deputies to take a decisive step, Facta had burst into tears, declaring, 'You want a decisive step? Very well, I'll blow out my brains.'

His hands trembling, his cheek agitated by a constant restless tic, the angry little King in turn sought to shift the onus. He told Facta: 'I won't form a government while there's violence in Italy – I can't and I won't. I'll leave everything and go to the country with my wife and son.'

The King disliked responsibility as he disliked most things in life – but now the thousand-year-old House of Savoy, which he cared for above everything, stood in jeopardy. For the most part, the Lilliputian monarch, nicknamed 'Little Sword', was a legend around the Quirinale for the things he didn't like. So tight-fisted that he wore frayed, patched uniforms even on State occasions, his parsimony had enabled him to deposit a sizeable £1,500,000 in Hambro's Bank, London. Grown warped and misanthropic through his lack of inches (he was barely 5 feet tall), as a child he had slept with an iron weight dragging at his legs, yearning to increase his stature. He was the butt of every European cartoonist; one had even shown a visitor peering for him vainly beneath a cocked hat. Now, at fifty-five, he cared for only three things: his stately Montenegrin wife, Queen Elena, his priceless sixty-cupboard coin collection, and his throne.

The King had no love for the Fascists. At his own request, hundreds of officers who had attended party meetings in uniform had been retired or transferred. As recently as 7 October, he had told his Minister of War: 'I don't want these people down in Rome. Take any steps to avoid the danger.' Yet one factor above all unsettled him: of late, the Fascists had been paying court to the monarchy.

On 23 August, their news-sheets had given him discreet warning: 'The Crown is not at stake – so long as it keeps out of the game.' By 20 September came a grudging hint of loyalty: 'We must have the courage to be monarchist.' Three days earlier, at the 24 October Naples congress that decided the March on Rome, 40,000 Fascists had found that courage: the first mention of the King's name had kept the cheer-leaders on their feet for twenty unforgettable minutes.

It was an ironic contrast to the way he had been served by the republican-minded Socialists. The King would not easily forget the rankling humiliation of 1 December, 1919, when he had opened the first parliament following the armistice. As he entered Rome's Chamber of Deputies, 156 Socialist members had risen as one, shouting 'Down with him!' Then, tucking scarlet carnations, symbols of Socialism, into their buttonholes, they had left the Chamber in a body, chanting 'The Red Flag'.

Recently a further complication had arisen to perplex the King: the rivalry of his cousin, fifty-three-year-old Emanuele Filiberto, Duke of Aosta, former commander of the Italian Third Army, father of Amadeo II, who later commanded Italian forces in East Africa. Only a month previously the Duke had reviewed Fascist troops at Merano while a band played Fascist anthems – and tonight he was reported at Bevagna, near Perugia, in close touch with their High Command. To further their cause, he had threatened, if need be, to appeal to the Army and depose the King – a giant step towards civil war.

It was unthinkable that the Army's loyalty to their King should waver, despite their kinship with ex-soldiers in the Blackshirt ranks – yet the scandal could tarnish the monarchy's prestige throughout the world. Frankly, the King had sounded out their Commander-in-Chief, General Armando Diaz. 'What will the Army do?' he asked.

The General had replied soberly, 'Your Majesty, the Army will do its duty – but it would be better not to put them to the test.'

The King had a shrewd idea of what Diaz meant. From the balcony of Florence's Prefecture, where he was dining, the General was that night responding warmly to a demonstration by the Fascists – and it was no lone example. No less than nine generals on the retired list, handpicked for their emotional impact on the Army, had key roles in the strategy of the march.

Nine days earlier, one of them, General Emilio de Bono, and another of the March's organizers, Cesare Maria de Vecchi, had met secretly with the one woman the King feared – his mother, the implacable blue-eyed Queen Margherita. To Bordighera's Park Hotel, where the four chiefs had retired to divide Italy into twelve zones of command, had gone a dinner invitation from the Queen Mother's villa – and the Queen had made no attempt to disguise her sympathies. As they took their leave she had offered them: 'Many, many good wishes for your work – I know your plans have only one end, the safety and glory of our country.' Since then she had not ceased to goad her son as to where his duty lay.

'This state of siege,' the King said thoughtfully, as he gave Facta permission to withdraw, 'must be considered very carefully indeed. We will discuss it again in the morning.'

The audience had lasted twenty minutes, yet still the King was uncertain where his interests lay. Could the Fascists assure the safety of both King and country – or would the monarchy benefit most by declaring a state of siege?

There was nothing for General Ambrogio Clerici to do but to run the errand himself. At 2 a.m. on Saturday, 28 October, the long grey-carpeted corridors of the Palazzo del Quirinale were as silent as a crypt; the King's footmen had gone off duty hours ago. But minutes earlier, the King's junior ADC had woken to an urgent phone call from Premier Luigi Facta. At all costs the President must contact Clerici's chief, General Arturo Cittadini, but could get no reply.

Now, hastening along the deserted corridor, Clerici halted, puzzled. A pencil of yellow light glowed beneath the door of Cittadini's suite. Entering, he found the old General in his nightshirt, peacefully absorbed in a book.

Crisply, Clerici reported that the situation was now as bad as could be. Since the King had appointed no other Premier, Facta still had power to hold Cabinet metings – and at this very moment his ministers were engaged in a despairing all-night session. Within the hour, they had listened, stunned, to an angry diatribe from General Emanuele Pugliese, demanding 'precise written orders'.

The forceful Pugliese had pointed out that to date 26,000 Fascists had been halted without bloodshed on the railway lines north of Rome by 400 *carabinieri*. 'Give me a mandate,' he raged, 'and the Army will re-establish order in all Italy in a few hours. The Fascists will not enter Rome!'

There was no time to lose; all over northern Italy the Blackshirts were striking. At Cremona, where the King's Guards had opened fire, seven Fascists had died. Rovigo's Blackshirts had seized the government press, determined that no proclamation of siege should be printed. In Perugia, Florence, and six other cities they held all public utilities – waterworks, telegraph offices, telephone exchanges.

Now Facta and his Cabinet needed guidance, for reports from many cities like Siena told of Army barracks freely doling out arms and ammunition to Fascist shock-troops.

Abruptly Clerici stopped. He noticed that Cittadini's ornate gilded telephone was as usual on the bedside table – but the receiver was swinging gently off the hook. He made to replace it and his senior stopped him: 'Leave it as it is – and tell Facta you have not found me.'

'But – forgive me – is that wise?'

Cittadini was imperturbable. 'These are His Majesty's orders. He wants his government to perform its duty – but without placing the responsibility for their action on his shoulders.'

The King read the telegram with mounting anger. Beyond the tall windows of his study, it was a bleak morning; despite the shelter of trim boxwood hedges, rain lashed the palms in the Royal Gardens. On the mantel behind his desk an ormolu clock showed 8 a.m. It was six hours since Facta's vain attempt to contact General Cittadini.

The telegram had been despatched ten minutes earlier. It needed no words from Facta to show how the all-night Cabinet session had gone. Addressed from the President of the Council and the Minister of Home Affairs to the provincial military commanders of the realm, it read:

'No. 28859: Council of Ministers has decided proclamation of state of siege in all provinces of the Kingdom from mid-day today relative decree will be published immediately. Meanwhile use all possible means to maintain public order and security of persons and property.'

'You evidently ignore constitutional law,' the King told the

Premier sharply, 'to instruct the military before consulting me.'

Mumbling an apology, Facta thought back gloomily over the night just past – one of the longest and tensest he could remember. It had taken until 3 a.m. to draft the proclamation of the state of siege that he was now presenting to the King. Following this, he had waited five patient hours for a royal summons but the King had remained silent – only the insistence of his ministers had goaded Facta into taking the plunge.

Already he knew that troops up the railway line at Orte, Civitavecchia and other junctions had hacked up 150 yards of track to halt the Fascist trains. What would happen next no man could guess.

Hopefully Facta passed to the monarch the cabinet's draft proclamation: 'Seditious demonstrations are taking place in some provinces of Italy . . . such as to throw the country into the gravest disorder . . . meanwhile the citizens must keep calm and have faith in the police measures which have been adopted . . .' He stood by holding the traditional china cup of fine blue sand with which the signatures of the House of Savoy had been blotted from time immemorial.

But to Facta's dismay the King did not pick up his goosefeather pen. Instead, muttering something which Facta could not catch, he took the decree and locked it in the drawer of his desk. All his doubts of the past night were now resolved. Rumour had it that almost seventy thousand Fascists were ready to storm the city if need be – which spelt nothing but trouble. But along Rome's Corso Umberto at this same hour sped truckloads of local Blackshirts, brandishing the tricolour and crying 'Long live the King!' – which meant that their loyalty was his for the asking.

'President,' he told Facta drily, 'the only thing resulting from a state of siege is civil war. What is called for here is that one of us must sacrifice himself.'

For the first and only time in his career the weak, good-natured Facta found himself capable of irony. He replied poker-faced: 'It is not necessary, your Majesty, to indicate which one of us that will be.'

Nine-year-old Giorgio Bottelli felt a sense of let-down. The strange men who had bivouacked for three days in his grandfather's hotel, the Brufani Palace, Perugia, had departed as suddenly as they had come. Even so it seemed to Giorgio that life at Brufani's could never be quite the same again.

Normally, the old red-brick hotel, perched 1600 feet above the umber-coloured plain of Assisi, was a home-from-home for English tourists, soothed by its shadowy rooms smelling of linseed polish, its deep leather armchairs and maidenhair ferns in brass pots. But three days earlier, when the Fascist general staff moved in, all this had suffered a change. Blackshirt sentries, as lean and dangerous as the daggers they sported, lounged in the pillared porticoes. Beyond the revolving doors, where the head porter summoned horse carriages, machine-guns were set up to menace the piazza. At every window, sandbags obscured the fine view of the rolling Umbrian Hills.

Giorgio didn't know that the Fascists had chosen Perugia for the best of strategic reasons: there were munitions works, meat canning plants, biscuit and chocolate factories, all within a few miles' radius. And if plans went awry, it would be easy to stage a swift retreat north to the valley of the Po. But he had seen the chiefs arrive to take over the library, and was thrilled to think that plans were being finalized there, among the rows of red leather-backed books. He had come to know all of them by sight: Cesare Maria de Vecchi, the pompous walrus-moustached Piedmontese; Michele Bianchi, thin and pince-nezed, who seemed the true diplomat; Italo Balbo, by far the noisiest, with his unkempt red hair. At fifty-six, General Emilio de Bono, with his bald head and white nanny-goat beard, was very conscious of being the senior man, ex-commander of the Army's 9th Corps – though at the rumour of a state of siege he had flown into a most unmilitary panic. 'They'll shoot all us officers,' he was quavering to everyone within earshot.

It was when the Fascists took over the Prefecture at gun-point, soon after midnight on 27 October, that the tension mounted. On Mount Subasio, twenty miles away, a heavy-type cannon was trained on the old hotel. Across the Piazza d'Italia, troops had machine-guns covering every door and window. They viewed impassively Balbo's defiant way of boosting his men's morale – marching them out at two-hour intervals to laugh hysterically at the army for five minutes.

Empty champagne bottles stood discarded, the ashtrays were choked with cigar butts – it wasn't Brufani's style at all, thought Giorgio, more like a G H Q before a battle. Messengers tut-tutted up on motor cycles, floury white with dust like millers. In the lounges and the billiard-room campaign maps showing the positions of Fascist troops were spread out on big mahogany tables. Officers, their faces pinched with fatigue, arrived in autos that had almost jolted to pieces, reported, then left without even gulping a glass of water. One thing seemed certain: these men would never yield up arms until they had reached the pinnacle of power.

Abruptly the mood had changed again. A messenger brought a telegram and General de Bono, ripping it open, was suddenly transfixed. Incredulously, he stammered out, 'It's going to be a play with a happy ending.' Minutes later, following De Bono's hasty parley with the Army commander, the troops were dispersing. Blackshirts went wild with joy, hugging and embracing one another. Hats were hurled skywards; all the bells of Perugia were pealing. The four chiefs made speeches from the balcony to the near-delirious Fascists – then as suddenly as they had come, they piled into cars.

As an uncanny silence settled over the hotel, Giorgio tip-toed towards the library. The little boy wanted to see the very room where his grandfather avowed that historic decisions had been made. Because of the conclaves it had been off-limits for three days. But he was disappointed to find that it looked much as it had always done. A blue scarf of cigar smoke lay trapped in the still air; a clock ticked; on the marble hearth, a telegram smouldered gently.

Giorgio picked it up and smoothed it out. It read:

'No. 23870: You are warned that instructions contained in today's telegram No. 28859 concerning state of siege should not be carried out . . .'

Again and again, Italo Balbo's driver clenched his fist over the Lancia's bulb horn. The klaxon was deafening, but it was all in vain. Despite the rain, the traffic ahead was unending. The roads were choked with men heading for Rome, over the old stone bridges that spanned the Tiber's willow-hung reaches, along the Roman roads of triumphant emperors two millennia ago.

They were coming on foot from the cloud-capped hills, tramping through vineyards turning yellow, startling the flocks of grazing sheep. They were resting where they could – beneath silvery stunted olive-trees, in the lee of stone farmhouses hung with ripening corn-cobs, under hedges white with wild clematis. The lucky ones came by truck, spraying the marchers with tawny-grey water, but only one thing counted now: not to be left behind. It had all happened just as they had known it would: the King and the government had yielded. Nothing could cheat them of their march on Rome.

Rainsodden, cold, lacking hard-and-fast orders, they had put a bold face on it as long as they could. Many would stay put with the columns for thirty-six hours longer, awaiting the signal to march,·

but others, now the siege was lifted, broke ranks and streamed for
Rome. Whatever lay ahead, there was solace in action.

They were in need of solace; most had never been so hungry
in their lives. At Monterotondo, Lieutenant Giorgio Chiurco had
found a rare use for his skills as an intern at Siena Hospital; standing
in as locum, he treated the townsfolk for everything from sprained
ankles to pleurisy, demanding food for his hungry troops in lieu of
payment. Some foraged for themselves; seventeen-year-old Novello
Bartoli and his mates, repair workers from outside Florence, used
wicker apple-baskets to bake the head of a sheep – their first meal
since they clawed cooked pasta from a cauldron with their bare
hands as the march began.

Thousands were students who saw it as a holiday adventure – a
carnival they'd look back to all their lives. With the resilience of
youth they bedded down under the hard wooden benches of third-
class rail compartments, a haversack of hand-grenades as a pillow.
On a packed train rattling south from Ancona, sixteen-year-old
Giovanni Ruzzini, an accountancy student, couldn't sleep for
excitement. When the march was alerted, Giovanni still hadn't saved
enough to buy a black shirt. In desperation he'd sought out the
local dyer's son, posing his problem and handing over his one white
shirt.

Now, though the shirt was still moist with dye, it was at least
regulation black – as martial as his steel helmet, foraged from an
old war surplus dump, which he had wadded out with newspaper
until it fitted. He had just twelve lire (about ten shillings) in his
pocket and one slice of cold roast meat, and he knew that he had never
been happier in his life because at last he was part of the glorious
revolution.

Others were dressed as strangely. One youngster from Arezzo
had to put up with any amount of ribbing; in the heat of departure he
had grabbed up the first garment to hand, his mother's sky-blue
raincoat. But for many uniforms were a luxury. Naples fishermen
marched in black reefer jerseys and pilot caps; farmers from the
Tuscan hills wore corduroy hunting jackets and billycock hats. Those
whose shoes gave out walked barefoot – or fashioned stockings from
brown paper. Most striking of all was a man bedecked with fifty
hammer-and-sickle badges – taken, he boasted, from the bodies of
dead Communists.

Their weapons were as bizarre. North of Rome, Rafael Sanchez
Mazas, war correspondent for Madrid's 'ABC' watched men moving

into battle with museum-piece weapons – some with rifles and muskets, others with powder-loading pistols, old safari guns from Africa, Swiss Vetterli repeaters, obsolete since 1880.

Thousands couldn't have fired a shot. To cow the King's troops they had snatched up any weapons that lay handy – golf-clubs, scythes, garden hoes, tree-roots, even table-legs. One man marched with a dagger in his teeth; another juggled with sticks of dynamite. Some, hailing from towns where the Prefect forbade firearms, carried board-hard lengths of dried salt cod. Federico Antonioli, taking a leaf from Samson and the Philistines, carried an ox's jawbone.

For hundreds it was a split-second decision; there were family problems to be solved. To make it at all, many had mortgaged their winter wool clip or pawned their wives' ear-rings. For Galliano Bruschelli of Siena, the summons was so dramatic that he almost didn't go: at the sight of a courier fishing a red-inked message from a wet boot, his wife, Noemi, almost nine months pregnant, became hysterical. When duty won, she gave premature birth to his son Raul. In Ferrara, a municipal accounts clerk, having word of the march, hastened in to his chief, stripping off his white office shirt to reveal the black shirt beneath. Pressed as to how long he'd be away, he was withering: 'How do *I* know how long? This is a revolution!' At Chianciano, near Florence, a lieutenant attached to the Army remount service, didn't even bother to tell his CO the call had come. Racing from the corral, he scrambled impulsively over the fence on to the railway embankment, flagging down the first train going south.

For the self-employed there was a special problem, but a Ferrara perfumier solved it neatly. Told off for guard duty at the central station, he left a scribbled card in the shop window: for the next two days travelling salesmen could bring their samples to the sentry-box by the first-class waiting-room.

To all who embraced the Fascist creed, Rome was now more than a magnet; whatever their infirmity, they had a rendezvous with history. On a train packed with Blackshirts leaving Grosseto, men gave pride of place to 'Il Cecco', a blind eighty-year-old veteran who, fifty-two years earlier, had marched with Garibaldi. At Monterotondo, orderlies kept a watchful eye on Paolo Petrucci, mortally sick with tuberculosis; despite a fever of 102° he was determined to make it somehow.

Others in the prime of life travelled with a panache all their own. The 'cavalrymen' of Fascist chief Giuseppe Caradonna were riding from Foggia, fifty strong, in fur cloaks and mountie hats, astride sturdy plough horses. From Ascoli Piceno, one wealthy young man was staging a one-man March on Rome – a machine-gun mounted on the bonnet of his Fiat racing car.

More and more were coming by the hour, eager to share the triumph – on bicycles and trucks, in trains and carts, their vehicles plastered with the slogans they had scrawled in charcoal or daubed in whitewash: 'WE DON'T GIVE A DAMN' – 'ROME OR DEATH'. All of them were drawn irresistibly by one man's magnetism, a man who had worked for years to bring their emotions to this flash-point.

His name was as bold as a war-cry on banner and truck and helmet: 'VIVA MUSSOLINI!'

In the baroque crimson and gold Manzoni Theatre, Milan, the house-lights dimmed. Momentarily the globe lights in the four-tier horse-shoe of boxes still glowed. All over the theatre, mother-of-pearl opera glasses flashed into focus, sighting on the jutting profile sil-houetted in a box of the second tier. But the face gave nothing away. Thirty-nine-year-old Benito Mussolini apparently had nothing more urgent on his mind than an evening out with his comely blonde wife, Rachele, and their twelve-year-old daughter, Edda.

Then the darkness thickened, the footlights gleamed and the curtain rustled upwards on the first act of Ferenc Molnar's *The Swan*. As the renowned actress Lina Paoli spoke her opening lines as Princess Beatrice, Mussolini, oblivious of the stares of the audience, struck a pose familiar to all who knew him. His chin propped on his white, almost feminine hands, he stared darkly forth across the theatre like a bulldog peering from its kennel.

Most of the audience on this eventful night knew no more about Mussolini than could have been condensed into a few lines of his rabble-rousing daily paper, *Il Popolo d'Italia*. He had been unknown in Milan until 1912, when, as managing director of the Socialist daily *Avanti!*, he had won fame as a trenchant writer. Few had fore-seen that the man expelled by the Socialists in 1914 over Italy's entry into the war, whose newly-founded Fascist Party had polled less than five thousand humiliating votes in 1919, could have brought Italy in the past week to the brink of civil war.

Nor did they know that Mussolini had been in this same theatre the previous night, along with his mistress of the moment, red-haired Margherita Sarfatti, *Il Popolo's* art critic. For prudence Mussolini had sat well back in the box, out of sight, until an alarmed sub-editor, tracking him down, brought word that Cremona's Fascists had begun the insurrection already – six hours before the midnight deadline. Impassive, Mussolini's first comment as he scanned the cable had been, 'Here we go.' Then, passing back the copy, he ordered, 'Keep this, it may be a historic document.'

Tonight Mussolini's plan was different. He was deliberately appearing in public 'to keep them guessing', as he told Rachele; his tangled skein of intrigue was at a crucial stage. Immobile, his eyes were riveted on the lighted stage until half way through the second act – then abruptly he commanded, 'Let's go.'

Rachele accepted, uncomplaining. She was used to Benito's vagaries, and in any case plays bored her – the family joked that she would feed them on chicory salad for a week running to save enough to see her favourite operetta, *La Duchesse du Bal Tabarin*, for the fifth time. She accepted, too, that it might be days before Benito returned to the third-floor apartment at 38, Foro Bonaparte.

In the second-floor offices of *Il Popolo*, newsmen exchanged meaning glances as the stocky (5ft 6ins) Mussolini strode in – quite how the score stood now was anyone's guess. For days, thought foreign editor Piero Parini, it had been hard enough to get the paper out at all, with Fascist delegates stomping in and out, leaving their hand-grenades in the in-trays for Arnaldo, Mussolini's gentle, bespectacled younger brother, to gather up. Outside, the main entrance was barricaded with rolls of newsprint – and each shrilling of the telephone brought news of another fallen stronghold.

Though his staff could not know it, the revocation of the state of siege had imbued Mussolini with steely purpose. The King was plainly scared and the thought gave him courage. Within hours of the decision, Fascist chief Cesare Maria de Vecchi, an ardent monarchist, known to the King, had been summoned to the Quirinale. 'I want the Italian people to know that I refused to sign the martial law decree,' the King had said, adding: 'Perhaps within a week they will have forgotten it.'

Grimly De Vecchi had assured him: 'Your Majesty, they shall not forget. We shall make them remember.'

As recently as 2.45 a.m. on 27 October, Mussolini had been ready to settle for portfolios in a new government. Now he was resisting all attempts from Rome by De Vecchi and his young aide Dino Grandi to effect a compromise: six ministries in a new government under former Premier Antonio Salandra.

Grandi argued: 'Seventy per cent of the Italians are with us – if we accept and have elections, we'll come to power anyway.' Grandi was one Fascist who stubbornly opposed the March from the outset: a needless revolution might lead to civil war. But Mussolini would have none of it. 'You're a traitor to the revolution,' he cursed Grandi. 'I will not have a mutilated victory.' To the Fascist Party treasurer, Giovanni Marinelli, who also sought to mediate, Mussolini made himself plainer still: 'I won't go to power through the servants' entrance.'

All that night the haggling went on. Again Grandi came on the line, this time calling from the Quirinale office of the King's aide, General Cittadini. He and De Vecchi had talked with the General, and the news was triumphant; the King would entrust Mussolini to form a government. The blacksmith's son was suspicious: 'It sounds like a trap. I want an official cable.' Though Grandi assured him it was genuine, Mussolini was unconvinced.

For secrecy he was taking calls from Rome in the stenographer's padded phone booth, the sweat dribbling down his face and wrists. The paper's agricultural correspondent, Mario Ferraguti, solicitously opened the door to give him air. Mussolini grinned at him cockily and said, 'We'll do great things for agriculture.'

At 3 a.m. Captain (later Admiral) Count Costanzo Ciano, World War One naval hero and a keen supporter of Fascism, was on the line. He sounded harassed: 'Listen, Mussolini, how do you want this cursed telegram from the King to you?' The editor was patronizing. 'I can't understand this difficulty. It's enough if the telegram says: "His Majesty begs you to accept the charge, etcetera" – don't you think so?' Still in the dark, the Admiral asked, 'The unofficial charge?'

Mussolini became steely. 'No, no, dear Ciano, let's be quite clear. Listen: the charge to form the Ministry. That's the way it must be – agreed?' The Admiral assented hurriedly, adding that the King had been 'very close' to the Fascist cause.

'And now we'll pay the King due homage,' Mussolini assured him. 'But don't forget that all the Blackshirts must be down there in Rome, because they must leave the city with the physical sensation that they came in with flags flying – as victors.' Again the Admiral agreed, urging Mussolini to depart for Rome as soon as possible – 'to prevent anything going wrong'. Mussolini was adamant. 'I'll come when I get that telegram – and as I dictated it to you. Good night, Ciano.'

Minutes later, foreign editor Parini noticed that the red bulb was glowing outside Mussolini's door – the warning sign that he was not to be disturbed. In his private sanctum Mussolini was mulling over his plans. He was going to make doubly certain that the telegram came, for now he had three aces up his sleeve. Those ill-armed ragtail cohorts at the very gates of Rome were a potent factor in keeping the government on edge – and no matter how peaceful the settlement, Fascism would still come to power in an aura of violence and heroism. And his editorial for tomorrow's paper, cabled to the Naples bureau, would surely be intercepted in Rome and give them more food for thought.

Frantically, he began scribbling it, as he always did, his see-saw handwriting covering any scrap of paper available – the backs of envelopes, wrapping paper from the delicatessen: 'Victory already appears to be widespread, with the nation's near-unanimous consent, but the victory should not be mutilated by last-minute concessions. It is not worth mobilizing only to arrive at a Salandra compromise . . . Fascism wants power and will have it.'

In an adjoining office, sub-editor Luigi Freddi stood by disconsolately: the night's most burdensome chore was still to come. The one member of the staff who could somehow decipher Mussolini's tormented calligraphy, his would be the job of re-vamping the completed text into something the compositors could read.

At 4 a.m. came Mussolini's summons. The editor was looking pleased. Within hours, when the public read those words, his Fascists would show they meant business with one of the most daring coups the march had yet produced.

One hundred miles south of Milan, in Genoa, the sky was pewter coloured. Under a raking east wind, whitecaps lashed the harbour. In the Piazza Corvetto, journalist Corrado Marchi, glancing anxiously at the sky, hoped the rain would hold off – but whether it did or not he must carry on with the job, whipping up the crowd 300 strong milling beneath the rostrum where he stood.

On this Sunday morning, 29 October, Marchi, a member of the blue-shirted Nationalist party, which, at the eleventh hour, had joined forces with the Fascists, must speak until precisely 10.45 a.m., until all plans had been made ready. Across the square, the sixteenth-century Palazzo Montorsoli housing the Prefecture was barred and silent – but from its upper windows eyes were watching every movement of the crowd.

But on the face of it, there was nothing suspicious to see. Even

The March on Rome

Above. Abetted by loyal railroad workers, Carrara Blackshirts hi-jacked train with machine-guns. *Below.* Headed by troops from Siena, the Monterotondo column streams over Rome's Ponte Salario

The March on Rome

Above. Fêted as Roman victors with flowers and wine

Left. The Fascists devastate remaining Socialist strongpoints like the newspaper *Avanti!*

Fascist chief Gerardo Bonelli, who now gave Marchi the nod from the front rank, was dressed, like all the others, in civilian clothes.

As Marchi began to speak, the first raindrops fell. Turning up his coat collar, he plunged resignedly on: 'Companions of my faith, always ready for King and country, the great hour of the insurrection has come . . .'

Now the rain came in solid sheets, plashing in droplets on his head from the magnolia tree above. Marchi struggled on, his audience applauding damply. The piazza was like a giant wheel from which seven streets radiated like spokes. Above the heads of the crowd, Marchi now saw seven autobuses swing into the square from each one of these streets, parking broadside on, bottling off all access to the piazza. Deftly, the drivers descended and removed the magnetos. For the Fascists of Genoa, H-hour was just six minutes away.

Blocked off by an autobus from the eyes of the curious, eight men slipped quietly through the swing-doors of the Sala Sivori, a pocket-sized cinema abutting on the back of the Prefecture. Their chief, twenty-two-year-old Giuseppe Gonella, a dapper young law student, led his men quietly up the stairs to the circle, heading for a door at the far end – the private entrance to the Prefect's box. Behind it they could hear the naval guard seconded to the Prefecture talking in low tones. Cautiously Gonella went to work with a screwdriver on the bolt, ears cocked for the signal he awaited.

It was 10.45 a.m. Abruptly the sound of tumult smote Gonella's ears. Outside, in Piazza Corvetto, as if on cue, 300 Fascists had turned their backs on orator Marchi, haring through the rain to storm the Prefecture's heavy wooden doors. From a long way off, Gonella heard the crack of splintering wood. Simultaneously, he rammed with all his might at the connecting door, bursting through to ambush the guards from the rear.

The marines were fast, but Gonella was faster. As the first man lunged with his bayonet he skipped it as neatly as a rope, closing his man with a bear-hug. His men closed too. Seven flailing thrashing couples rolled in savage combat down the marble stairs – at the same moment that Gerardo Bonelli, pistol at the ready, crashed in at the head of his troops.

Two at a time, Bonelli scaled the stairs to the office of the Prefect. Gun levelled, he told him: 'Call Rome – Ministry of Home Affairs.' The Prefect placed the call and Bonelli took the phone. 'Everything all right?' he heard an Under-Secretary's query up the wire.

Bonelli, grinning broadly, was to relish this moment all his life as he answered: 'Couldn't be better. This is the chief of the Fascist forces – we've just taken over the Prefecture of Genoa.'

'Arnaldo,' Benito Mussolini urged his brother patiently, 'get a grip on yourself. We must get ready to come out with a special edition.' But Arnaldo didn't seem to hear. At noon on the Sunday, when Benito showed him the message newly-arrived from General Cittadini, his first reaction had been to sit down heavily and take off his pince-nez. Then, as Mussolini repeated the sentence, he abruptly put them on again, leaving the room as unsteadily as if he were drunk.

The telegram was all that Mussolini had ever wanted: 'HM the King begs you to proceed to Rome as soon as possible as he wishes to entrust you with the task of forming a Cabinet.'

Just as he had gambled, his fighting editorial had turned the scales – and within hours the Genoa seizure had proved that even in cities which held out against Fascism the Blackshirts' arbitrary use of power would prevail. Now, at 8 p.m. on the Sunday, he was briefing Arnaldo on the make-up for Monday's edition and preparing for his own 'march on Rome' – in a first-class wagon-lit of DD 17, the 8.30 p.m. Milan-Rome express.

On this rainy night, the newsboys thronged the streets; as Mussolini and his five-man entourage reached the central station he paused for an instant to watch and listen. Their cries were the strident sound of approaching triumph: 'Resignation of Facta Cabinet! Mussolini called by King!' Thrusting towards the train, hands jammed deep in the pockets of his grey raincoat, hat pulled over his eyes, he saw other portents of power: men snatching the newspapers from one another's hands, thousands lining the forecourt, cordoned off by a Fascist guard of honour, his compartment loaded with garlands of flowers. At the door of his coach, engine-driver and fireman, black-shirted, overalls ablaze with war medals, solemnly awaited him.

No man for farewells, Mussolini had just one injunction for the followers staying behind: before dawn, shock-troopers must burn down the offices of the Socialist daily *Avanti!*, once Mussolini's own, for fear they proclaimed a general strike and marred his triumph. Then a band struck up, and as DD 17 slid gently towards Rome, Mussolini remained at the corridor window, blowing kisses.

That whole night was a triumphant progress. To a journalist from Turin's *La Stampa*, Mussolini confirmed that his cabinet list was already drawn up – to include fifteen non-Fascists out of a total of thirty. At Piacenza, Pisa, and Carrara, there were beaming, weatherworn troops to review, and again at Civitavecchia – where the King had sent two cars in case the track was still disrupted. Towards 10.50 a.m., as the train neared Rome, Mussolini was suddenly transfigured as three silver specks fell like falcons in the sun: Fascist aviators from Centocelle airfield were diving to honour him.

As he descended from the wagon-lit, his face was haggard – for nights now he hadn't slept. For his first greeting to the Romans, he wore an attire that was to become his trademark: black shirt into which he had just then changed, morning coat, black trousers, bowler hat, and white spats dusted with talcum, an economy measure he had long ago adopted to hide worn-out shoes.

At 11.45 a.m. he strode stiffly into the ante-room of the audience chamber on the first floor of the Palazzo del Quirinale. Within the day 60,000 Fascists would stream past its portals, tasting their victory. As he advanced to meet the King, Mussolini's never-failing sense of the theatrical was equal to the occasion: 'Your Majesty will forgive my attire – I have come from the battlefield.'

2. 'A Day When All Italy Trembles...'

July 1883 – October 1922

Thirty-nine stormy years lay between a blacksmith's forge at Predappio in the Romagna and the audience chamber of the Palazzo del Quirinale. Born on 29 July, 1883, in the big iron bedstead fashioned by his father, Benito Mussolini seemed from the first a loner, staring at life as at an enemy. For three long years, despite all his parents' cajoling, the child remained obstinately mute – and only an ear, nose and throat specialist in nearby Forlì set their minds at rest.

'It will pass,' he assured them. 'I have a feeling that when the time comes he may even talk too much.'

Outwardly a united family, the Mussolinis differed on one vital issue – a schism which the perceptive Benito saw vividly spelt out in pictures. Above his parents' big double bed, his mother, twenty-five-year-old Rosa, the village schoolmistress, had placed a symbol of her ardent Catholicism: a portrait of the Virgin. But next to it, as if to balance the scales, the handsome moustached Alessandro, three years her senior, had hung a glowering likeness of his lifelong hero – the Republican liberator of Sicily, General Giuseppe Garibaldi.

A heavy, genial, dark-haired man, Alessandro, in deference to his wife's views, had submitted to a church wedding – 'I'm still an atheist,' he excused himself to friends, 'but in love.' Yet the grand passion of his life was his mission as an International Socialist. Under constant police surveillance following a six-month jail sentence for left-wing activity, he needed a permit to travel the nine miles to Forlì. Even his first-born son had been christened after Benito Juarez, the Mexican revolutionary, who sixteen years earlier had executed the Emperor Maximilian.

From the first, the forge, where he sometimes worked the big leather bellows while his father argued politics with his cronies, was a polarizing force to Benito. Hidden below in the cellar, inside an iron box, was the forbidden red-satin flag of the party, brought out once a year on May Day and passed reverently from hand to hand.

Though his mother yearned for him to be a priest, Benito saw his father's lifelong war with authority as headier stuff. To his sister

Edwige, five years his junior, he grumbled once: 'With so many prayers we'll go to heaven, even if we never get on our knees again in our lives.'

Alessandro taught other values. Once during harvest time, an older boy stole Benito's tiny wooden cart of corn cobs, belabouring him unmercifully when he protested. But when Benito, bruised and tearful, ran to Alessandro, the smith was unyielding: 'Men have to defend themselves – not ask for pity. Don't come back to me again until you've licked him.' Brooding, the boy sharpened a flint, pouched it in his right fist, then waded into his enemy like a fury, leaving him bloody and subdued.

It was a gesture any Romagnol would have understood. The arid, silent land sloping to the Apennines bred a harshly independent people, square-jawed and aggressive, long schooled to poverty. One pair of shoes between father and son was commonplace – and so, too, was borrowing bread, oil and salt from neighbours who were in luck. On the stony slopes even wood, the one fuel peasants could afford, was scarce. A bleak proverb expressed the true temper of the region: '*Chi ha freddo, salti!*' ('If you want to get warm, skip!')

The Mussolinis were as poor as any. Despite Rosa's salary as a teacher, the family income rarely exceeded 100 lire a month – and the improvident smith was always good for a loan where Socialist comrades were concerned. In the three-room apartment of a tumble-down palazzo Benito and his younger brother Arnaldo shared a simple maize-straw palliasse in the cubbyhole that was also the kitchen. Lunch was unleavened *piada* bread and vegetable soup, ladled by Alessandro from the big terracotta tureen; dinner was salad. Only on Sundays did the six-strong family, which included Rosa's mother, Marianna, share their one treat of the week: a pound of boiling mutton.

Though Alessandro prophesied great things for his son, Rosa was less certain. From the toddler who had created chaos in the tiny class she held beyond the family bedroom, tugging at the small girls' plaits, he had grown, at eight, into a wild nomadic rural thief, roaming the Romagna plain, more attuned to the stray dogs around the farm than to human beings. Often he spent hours astride an old farm horse in the midst of the swift-flowing River Rabbi, so riveted to a book that only twilight reminded him to head for home.

Taken by Rosa for the good of his soul to the ninth-century church of San Cassiano, he pinched his neighbours with such savage glee he was banished from the aisle. Promptly, armed with acorns and small stones, he shinned up an oak tree, picking off choristers and priests impartially with devastating aim.

Solitary, taciturn, at odds with authority, he was a byword for unpredictable gestures. Once, after gorging himself on stolen cherries, he fell as if in mortal agony in the village street, red juice welling like blood from his lips. As bystanders, convinced that he had suffered a haemorrhage, crowded round him, Ber'to leapt up, sprayed them with cherry juice, then ran fleetly away. Yet on another occasion, spying an old peasant, Filippino, sweating on a spade, he silently took over, dug for hours, uncomplaining, while the old man sat by puffing his pipe.

No coward, he once led a gang stealing quinces – an episode which came close to tragedy when the infuriated farmer let loose with a shotgun. In the resultant stampede, one boy fell and broke his leg – but the stubborn Benito refused to turn tail like the others. Facing the farmer with glowering defiance, he lifted the boy like a sack on to his shoulder and carried him to safety.

His energy, fierce and unharnessed, was proverbial. One village elder, Matteo Pompignoli, always recalled how Benito would press him into service as a timekeeper – standing patiently with a turnip watch to check how long it took the boy to race round the block. 'Two minutes?' Benito would challenge incredulously. 'I *couldn't* have taken so long.' Somehow, even at the age of eight, he was driving himself like a piston engine, determined that he must on every occasion prove himself a super-being. Often, although Benito was two years his senior, it was only the gentle, reflective Arnaldo who kept him from serious scrapes – or sponged away the blood and mire that so outraged Rosa.

Despite her husband's fervent anti-clericalism, Rosa, gentle but indomitable, had the last word. As a nine-year-old who time and again arrived home with both eyes blackened, Benito was packed off to a boarding-school run by black-gowned Salesian priests twenty miles away in Faenza. Typically, he left home with the knuckles of his right hand swathed in bandages. Aiming a piledriver at a youthful adversary one day earlier, he had connected instead with a stone wall.

As the donkey cart jolted along the dusty road, a six-hour journey through yellow autumn fields, Alessandro, in the driver's seat, gave his son eleventh-hour counsel: 'Pay attention to what they teach you, especially the geography and history – but don't let them stuff your head with nonsense about God and the saints.' To his relief, the nine-year-old piped up confidently: 'Don't worry, Papa – I know there's no such person as God.'

Afterwards, looking back to those years, Benito was to rate them as the bitterest of his life. Always beset by a deep-rooted inferiority complex, he revolted at a refectory system which split the pupils into three grades according to wealth – with himself among the third-graders, fobbed off with kitchen scraps at a bare trestle-table.

'It no longer worries me that third-grade children had ants in their bread,' he said years later, 'but the fact that we were graded at all still rankles.'

From this moment until the very end Benito Mussolini was a man in quest of an equalizer, seeking to annul the bitterness of childhood hurts.

He felt an aching nostalgia for the scenes of his infancy: his tame olive-green siskin, twittering in a cage in the kitchen window; the grapes hanging in purple-black clusters in the tiny family vineyard at Camerone; painted carts creaking through the stubble at harvest time; the slow tolling of the heavy iron cowbells. At constant odds with the third-grade teacher, he retaliated to a blow from a ruler with an accurately thrown inkpot. Only Rosa's tearful intervention with the director saved him from expulsion.

To humble Benito's spirit, the priests decreed twelve days of punishment – kneeling for four hours each day on a spiky carpet of maize-grains. If he asked for pardon, the director said, the sentence would be remitted. But Benito was too far gone in bitterness to crave pardon. Though bleeding wounds had opened in his knees after the tenth day, he knelt in silence until the end.

What followed was, to Mussolini's rebel spirit, worse still. Condemned to sleep in the yard with the watch-dogs after another breach of discipline, he scrambled in terror over the gate – leaving a shred of his trousers in the jaws of the swiftest dog. As penance he now spent each recreation break alone, face to the wall, in a far corner of the playground. In the summer of 1894, after stabbing a fellow-pupil in the buttocks with a pocket-knife, he was expelled for good.

Already, at eleven, Mussolini's character was fast hardening into the mould of manhood. Veering between abject self-abasement and overweening confidence, his aim was unwavering: to command attention at all costs. Once during the summer vacation, Rosa, hearing a garbled torrent of words from the bedroom, hastened in to find her son, his face suffused, ranting to the four walls. Was he mad, she queried, alarmed. But Benito, his face softening, at once reassured her: he was rehearsing a speech, 'preparing for a day when all Italy trembles at my words'.

Yet when the occasion demanded, his approach could be mellower, almost hypnotic. Encouraged by Alessandro, he devoured an old battered copy of *Les Misérables*, seeing in the flight of Jean Valjean through the Paris sewers a parallel to his own lonely stand against a world of priests and petty bureaucrats and capitalists. Old people around Predappio would long recall how Benito first gave readings from the book in the strangest setting – in a cowshed, by the flickering light of a lantern, peasants with unkempt beards, brown corduroy coats and broad-brimmed hats squatting absorbed among the oxen, as the childish voice rose and fell, holding his first audience rapt.

At Forlimpopoli Secondary Modern College, seven miles from Predappio, Benito, despite his innate shyness, was overtly bold and audacious. Other boys grumbling at the sour stone-hard bread served at meal-times were content to leave it at that – until the day Mussolini rose to face the rector and denounce it as shameful. 'We're treated worse than in a pauper's hostel,' he charged. As the rector fled, the boys were on their feet; a hail of loaves burst about the steward's head. But Benito, having gained his point, stilled them with one giant leap on to the table. 'Enough!' he commanded, his arms folded imperiously. 'To throw bread is to insult the food of the poor.' When the case was brought before the Mayor, who sampled a slice, Mussolini was vindicated.

Whatever the moment, he was a compulsive attention-getter. At a teenagers' country dance, impatient with the dreamy tempo of a waltz, he shouted for silence, stepped on to the dance floor, and did a Romagnol-style waltz as a whirling solo, a knife gripped in his teeth. At other times, shunning society, he retired to the chapel belfry to read – Bakunin, Zola, Gorki, sombre stories of men at odds with destiny.

One fellow-pupil, Rino Alessio, still recalls: 'Already he was a man among boys.'

It was true in more senses than one. In his teens, a visit to a cheap Forlì brothel left Mussolini feeling 'dirty – staggering like a drunken man' – yet the love of woman's flesh which was never to leave him was now like a virus in his blood. 'I've begun undressing every girl I see with my eyes,' he told Alessio. Already the long series of shabby amours – against trees, on staircases, by the banks of the River Rabbi – had begun its course.

Quick to learn if the subject held him, he still conducted himself as if rules and regulations were for other people. Once, told to write an essay 'Time is money', he left a peremptory note on the teacher's desk: 'Time *is* money – so I'm off to study geometry for tomorrow's exam. Surely more logical?' Though his gall cost him ten days' suspension from classes, it won him fresh adherents among the boys.

For Alessandro Mussolini, 8 July, 1901, was a red-letter day, one to be marked on the wooden wall-calendar shaped like a cribbage-board which hung on the wall of every Romagna farm-house, with slivers of wood pegged in to show highdays and holidays. At last, with an elementary school teacher's certificate in his shabby pocket, Benito was coming home. Yet none, apart from the feckless smith, saw Benito as destined for great things. Rosa, who had set her heart on his becoming a white-collar worker, urged him to apply for the vacant job of Communal Scrivener. Without zest, the boy complied – spending the interim in trudging the miles between Predappio and Forlì Public Library, immersed for hours in the books, before trudging home again under a big black shepherd's umbrella.

Yet whatever Benito's qualifications, his father's constant preaching to priests to burn their soutanes and don workers' clothes did nothing to help his son's cause. The municipality refused him the job.

Incensed, Alessandro bearded the Mayor and Corporation in their own Town Hall. In white-hot passion, inflamed by the local San-giovese wine, he told them: 'You'll be sorry you refused my son a job, but remember – even Crispi couldn't find a job in his own village.'

The town elders exchanged wry glances. They could see no connection between the shabby school teacher, Benito Mussolini, his black cape turning almost green with age, known locally as 'the crazy man', and Francesco Crispi, one of the founders of Italian unity, three times Premier of Italy.

'Your place is not here in this village, boy,' Alessandro comforted his son. 'Go out into the world, take your place in the great fight.'

Though Benito sought to follow his father's advice, he could go no farther into the world than the township of Gualtieri, 100 miles away in the province of Reggio Emilia, where a teacher's vacancy existed at twelve shillings a week. But though the headmaster and the Mayor welcomed him civilly, local bigwigs soon looked askance at Mussolini's offbeat ways. Shunning the houses of the gentry, he spent most of his leisure over a dish of stewed green peppers, arguing politics – a carbon copy of Alessandro's own – in smoke-filled *trattorie*, to the jangling refrain of a barrel-organ.

And few townsfolk cared to have as houseguest a man who washed at dawn, stark naked in the Po – then walked to school barefoot along the railway track, his boots strung from a walking stick like a hobo's bundle, a peasant economy from Romagna days. Sometimes, following a night's drinking, he bedded down with the apprentices on the floor of the local cobbler's shop rather than awaken the hunchbacked maid of his landlady, Signora Panizzi.

By the summer of 1902, Benito had had official word of what his fellow teachers had long since prophesied: that his appointment would not be renewed. The news lent fresh urgency to Alessandro's words: 'Go out into the world, take your place in the great fight . . .' Wiring his parents for the forty-five-lire train fare, he resolved to seek new worlds in Switzerland.

On the morning of 9 July, 1902, en route for Lausanne via Parma, Milan and Chiasso, Mussolini trudged to the station with a close friend, Cesare Gradella. Behind them, carrying his one purchase in Gualtieri, a pair of new shoes, came Signora Panizzi's hunchbacked maid. As the Parma train steamed in, Benito embraced them both, then clambered aboard. The stationmaster's bugle blew and Benito bent from the vestibule opening as the woman handed up the shoes. The train jerked forward, gathering speed, and suddenly, looking down at his friends trotting to keep pace, he stooped on impulse, tossing back the parcel.

Faintly his words drifted back to them through the pulsing of the wheels: 'Keep them as a souvenir! The luck of a Mussolini won't hang on a pair of shoes.'

Within ten days Benito Mussolini had cause to repent that impulsive gesture. His one pair of shoes was in ribbons and his belly throbbed with hunger – in the first stage of his hegira he had existed mainly on apples and baked potatoes. Reaching Switzerland with 2 francs 35 centimes in his pocket, he could find work only as a bricklayer at Orbe, near Yverdon – toiling an eleven-hour day for 32 centimes an hour, carting a barrowload of bricks to a building's second storey 121 times a day.

Now, on Saturday, 19 July, he quit. His shoes had given out and his hands were calloused and bleeding. To make matters worse, his employer literally hurled his 20 francs at him, shouting that it was 'stolen money'.

Buying a pair of stout mountain boots, Mussolini moved on to Lausanne – but soon the one metal object he possessed was a nickel medallion of Karl Marx. For the first time he starved, and it was now that he developed his obsessional life-long hatred of the rich – kindled by his loathing for those who dined in comfort on the terrace of the Beau Rivage Hotel. A pale-faced youngster with glittering eyes, he stooped to snatching bread from a peasant family's dinner-table, bearing it off like an animal to its lair – the wooden packing-case beneath a bridge in which he slept. Within days he was seized on a vagrancy charge. Just prior to his nineteenth birthday, jail doors, for the first but not the last time, clanged shut on Benito Mussolini.

Bitterly, Mussolini was later to sum up his two years in Switzerland: 'Hunger is a good teacher – almost as good as prison and a man's enemies.'

From all these, Mussolini was learning fresh lessons in his compulsive climb to power. On leaving jail, a chance meeting at Lausanne's Café Torlaschi with a group of Italian Socialists revealed that most were bricklayers at odds with their boss. Regaled with spaghetti, Mussolini revealed his militant Socialist leanings and his new-found comrades fixed him up with a job. Within four months of his arrival they had elected him secretary of their Italian Trade Union of Bricklayers and Bricklayers' Assistants. With typical panache, he now signed all his letters,' Benito Mussolini, Bricklayer.'

Now, at demonstrations and strike meetings, he realized for the first time his power over the masses, his ability to play on their feelings like a skilled harpist on the strings – as one man recalls him, 'shaking his fists as if he was trying to claw down an invisible wall between himself and his audience'. No true Socialist, he was in truth what Alessandro had raised him to be, a near-anarchist, anti-Christ, anti-King, anti-militarist, anti-government.

His instinct for the gesture that electrified the crowd was unerring. Facing a Lausanne pastor in a public debate on the reality of God, Mussolini, having borrowed a cheap nickel watch, whipped it from his pocket to announce: 'It is now 3.30 p.m. If God exists, I give him five minutes to strike me dead.' When no celestial thunderbolt was forthcoming, a torrent of applause greeted his blasphemy. But to this brash, tormented nineteen-year-old, the roar of the crowd was already a commonplace – and as needful to him as the panting embraces of the Russian and Polish émigré girls with whom he shared torrid nights. Significantly, the Italian-language *Tribuna* had already dubbed him 'the great Duce (leader), of the Italian Socialists'.

One woman who befriended him and helped him earn a living as a translator was Socialist agitator Angelica Balabanoff, a plump, blond-braided, thirty-three-year-old Russian. Reshaping the world in their image, they spent long evenings over the samovar in Angelica's lodgings, chain-smoking cigarettes -- but soon the Russian girl was aware of a disturbing trait in Benito Mussolini. To her it seemed that his hatred of oppression sprang not from love of the people but from his own sense of indignity and frustration, his passion to assert his ego.

Though Mussolini was a power among illiterate bricklayers, he was still in fact a dirt-poor unknown, his toes peeping through his broken-down boots, and the knowledge galled him. Although the Swiss police distrusted and feared him – twice he was jailed and escorted from the country only to return through another canton – he could find only menial jobs to do. Once he won bread telling fortunes with cards; at other times he was delivery boy for a Lausanne pork butcher, then for the wine merchant, Tedeschi. Sculptor's assistant, grocer's errand boy, window-moulder, machine factory worker – to survive, Mussolini tried them all, devoting his nights to learning French and German, his feet in a box of sawdust to keep them warm.

To Angelica, his constant talk of strength and physical courage was compensation for his own weakness – tangible proof of his longing for personal recognition and prestige. For months she strove to tell herself that she was being unjust, but the day Mussolini passed through Lugano to dine with her friend Maria Rygier, a school teacher, confirmed all her worst suspicions. 'For years he's been sick and obsessed by a sense of inferiority,' she defended Benito in advance, but Maria, who had met him before, found it hard to bottle up her dislike of Mussolini. As she set his macaroni before him, she remarked contemptuously: 'Maybe you'd have preferred chicken and truffles, but you see we're proletarians.'

It goaded Mussolini to fury. 'And why not?' he blazed. 'Before I came here I read the hotel menu. If you only knew what those swine eat and drink.' Maria, too, was furious. 'If you had an opportunity to live like those people you'd soon forget the masses,' she charged.

Mussolini stared out across the lake, his black eyes on fire with anger. 'People eating, drinking and enjoying themselves,' he raged. 'And from here I'll travel third class, eating miserable cheap food. *Porca Madonna*, how I hate the rich! Why must I suffer this injustice? How long must we wait?'

The answer, could he have foretold the future, would have depressed the ambitious Mussolini profoundly. From the November day in

1904 when he finally quit Switzerland, fully ten years were to pass before his name was a household word on the lips of every Italian – the prize that he coveted above all others.

As a private soldier in the 10th Bersaglieri, a rifle-regiment famed for its jog-trot pace and the green cock's feather plumes drooping from round tilted hats, Benito's fame as high-jump champion never penetrated beyond the brick walls of Verona Barracks. As an impecunious (£2 a month) second-grade teacher at Tolmezzo, a mountain town in the north-eastern region of Friuli, he was noted as the master who kept chaos from his classroom only through bribery. Powerless to control his forty-strong class of urchins, he furtively began the day's lesson by doling out sweets from a paper bag.

In truth, the only men to follow his career like hawks were the officials of the Forlì Police Dept, whose dossier, opened in 1904 before ever he returned from Switzerland, grew bulkier by the year. Already a prolific contributor to Socialist news-sheets like *La Lima*, Benito Mussolini was written down as 'violent and impulsive', a man who attacked Catholics and Christianity alike, who jeered at the national flag 'as a rag to be planted on a dunghill' and reviled the Fatherland as 'a Christ-like phantom – vindictive, cruel, tyrannical'.

To the quiet town of Trento, in Austria, where Mussolini in February 1909 moved as editor of *L'Avvenire*, went the injunction: 'He needs watching.' The Trento police took the injunction to heart. By the end of September, when Mussolini was expelled over the border for attempting to 'incite violence against the authorities', his paper had been eleven times banned and he himself had served six jail terms.

Back in Forlì, Mussolini threw in his lot with his father Alessandro, now running a wine-shop on Via Mazzini. Four years earlier, when Rosa had died of meningitis, aged forty-six, both men had been heartbroken. Near-paralysed, Alessandro had sold up his forge, taken a common-law wife, Anna Guidi, and opened the wine-shop. Helping them in the bar was Anna's pretty blonde daughter, nineteen-year-old Rachele.

A shy country girl, who had worked both as goat-herd and farm hand, Rachele had known Benito Mussolini since she was seven years old – years in which she had both feared and admired him. Once when he stood in for Rosa during a vacation from college, she had actually been one of his pupils. As he strode through Forlì's main square, muttering to himself, his eyes rolling, he was an all-too-familiar sight – his tufted beard as black as his flowing cravat or the cape he swathed around him, his shoes held together with strips of wild broom. Yet like scores of country folk Rachele looked on him as godlike for his battle to protect the labourers from share-cropping farmers.

When Mussolini, after flirting with the pretty waitress, told her that he'd marry her on his return from Trento, Rachele only laughed. In any case, Socialists who married in church and baptized their children were often expelled from the party.

It was an October afternoon in 1909 when he called for her, stalking without ceremony into her sister's farmhouse at nearby San Martino. To sister Pina he made his intentions crystal-clear: 'I want Rachele to be the mother of my children – but tell her to hurry, I'm pushed for time.' Forced to break into her piggy-bank and bundle her clothes into a shawl, Rachele didn't even have time to comb her hair. But she wouldn't have had it otherwise. She was irrevocably in love and adored his masterful ways – like the recent evening when she'd partnered others at a country dance and Benito, livid, maintaining an icy silence, had pinched her arms black and blue in the carriage going home.

Now she hastened downstairs to join him, and trudge uncomplaining, without an umbrella, a mile and a half through the rain to Forlì. 'We're a couple of poor devils,' was her only cheerful comment. 'Even the dogs bark at us.'

Both Alessandro and Anna were outraged by the common-law union. With uncanny foresight, father warned son: 'Leave the girl alone – think of what your mother went through because of me. Your politics will bring suffering to you and the woman who shares your life.' Benito's answer was to produce a revolver, avowing: 'Here are six bullets – one for Rachele, five for me.' Dismayed – for Rachele was the eighth girl that Mussolini had thus far seduced – the parents had to give in. Fitted out with matchstick furniture and cracked china, the young couple moved into a tumbledown apartment across a muddy courtyard in Forlì's Via Merenda.

From this unlikely base twenty-six-year-old Benito now embarked on his most ambitious venture to date – reorganizing the federation of Socialist clubs in Forlì electoral district and editing a new 4-page Socialist weekly *La Lotta di Classe* (The Class Struggle), whose circulation never rose above 350 copies. As editor, manager, chief reporter and copy-reader, Mussolini's editorial desk and campaign headquarters was the matrimonial bed – screened off from the main living-room by a dusty curtain.

Though his £5 a month salary doubled his rate of pay, it was a gruelling routine – one which few save the thrusting, dynamic Mussolini could have sustained. Apart from his editorship, he was now the party's leading orator and agitator for the Romagna district. Often, seeking out the farm hands in cowstalls, tool sheds, and barns, along with his nineteen-year-old admirer Pietro Nenni, he tramped thirty miles a day.

More often than not, poverty kept step beside him. If money for food was lacking, Mussolini, editor, became Mussolini, newsboy – sitting in at Damerini's news-stand while its owner took lunch, in return for a free ham-roll. On 1 September, 1910, when his daughter Edda was born, he had just fifteen lire in hand to buy a cheap wooden cradle, trudging home with it on his shoulder. And once, when a colleague called for an urgent conference, Mussolini was constrained to hold it from his bed. Rachele had washed his one pair of trousers and they were drying off in the local bakery.

His interests were few, apart from politics. When the local theatre manager offered him free press tickets, Mussolini refused curtly – for despite his gnawing ambition, he sat only in the balcony, with the common herd, free to guffaw like a peasant when he felt like it. His chief pride was the second-hand violin which hung from a nail above the bed. He had badgered Professor Archimede Montanelli to give him lessons and though the maestro protested he was too old to master it, Mussolini battled on, undaunted – soothing himself with an ear-splitting cacophony of harsh scrapes, sharp squeaks and galloping glissandoes.

A near-teetotaller, with milk and coffee as his staple drinks, his companions knew the danger sign: if he ordered spirits trouble was afoot. Once, deathly-white and fighting drunk on cognac, he staggered home at 5 a.m., awaking nine hours later to find that he had smashed every item of crockery they possessed – mixing bowl, soup tureen, and plates. 'If you ever come home like that again, I'll kill you,' Rachele flared – but Mussolini needed no second bidding. Like a father in a melodrama, he swore on Edda's head to touch spirits no more, and he kept his word.

In truth, his built-in instinct for violence sought more public channels – in direct and dramatic action. Once, when the price of milk was raised, Mussolini, followed by a yelling mob, strode into Forli's Town Hall. 'Either the price of milk is revised,' he told the quaking Mayor, 'or I'll advise these people to pitch you and all your bigwigs over the balcony.' The price of milk went down.

The pace of life was quickening; there was time now for nothing but action. Always a superficial reader, he had advised a fellow-Socialist at Trento: 'Nine pages of a book has to be enough to understand it – the first three, the last three, and the three in the middle.' A man who saw revolution and social change only in terms of violence, he read only those writers who spoke for violence, like Georges Sorel and Friedrich Nietzsche. Often he embarrassed the moderates of the party by preaching an extremism they could never endorse – yet none could deny his ardour and none could curb him. 'Live dangerously,' he told the Socialist Party conference in 1910, and for the next thirty-five years death and violence were to haunt his life.

Italy's imperialist war against Turkey in September 1911, with Tripoli as the battleground, gave Mussolini the chance he sought. 'Before conquering Tripoli, let Italians conquer Italy,' he raged in *La Lotta*. 'Bring water to parched Puglia, justice to the South and education everywhere. On to the streets for the General Strike!'

It was a brief and bloody foray. When the strikers, led by Mussolini and Nenni, tore up the railway lines to halt the troop trains, the cavalry scattered them with unsheathed swords. Undeterred, the strikers ripped up paling fences and battled back; to impede the horsemen, women flung themselves fearlessly in the line of charge. But following a declaration of martial law the strike petered out, and Mussolini, arrested, found himself on trial for 'instigation to delinquency'. Predictably, as his own defence counsel, he turned the courtroom into a theatre, the dock into a stage. 'If you acquit me,' he told his judges, 'you will give me pleasure; if you condemn me, you will do me honour.'

The judges honoured him – awarding him a year, later reduced to five months, in Cell 39 of Forlì Jail. Though few outside the 21-mile radius of Forlì had ever heard his name, Mussolini, still dreaming of destiny, settled to his autobiography. 'I have a wild restless temperament,' he wrote in a blinding moment of self-knowledge. 'What will become of me?'

What became of him was something that nobody save Alessandro, who had died a few months earlier, aged fifty-seven, would ever have credited. Within nine months of leaving jail, the man now hailed as 'Duce' of all Italian Socialists was elected to the Party's National Executive Committee, taking over its ailing Milan-based daily *Avanti!* at a salary of 500 lire per month.

On 1 December, 1912, with Angelica Balabanoff, at his own request, as deputy editor, Mussolini set out to conquer Milan –

leaving Rachele and Edda behind in Forlì. Soon his real flair for bold muck-raking journalism had almost quadrupled circulation – from 28,000 to 100,000. Still under thirty, he was at last beginning to achieve the notoriety that he craved – and even insults from rival journalists were treasured because they took note of him. These he kept in a special folder, rejoicing to find himself described as 'hired tool', 'slimy reptile', 'paranoiac', 'ninth-rate hack', and even 'criminal lunatic'.

'Have you seen,' he burst out one day, as Angelica entered the office on Milan's grey Via Settala, 'how the Russians treated Marinetti?' Angelica shook her head, barely aware that the leader of the avant-garde Futurist movement, Filippo Marinetti, was just then visiting Moscow. But Mussolini, eyes shining, enlightened her: 'As soon as he appeared on the stage to deliver his lecture, the audience began to scream, howl and throw tomatoes at him. How I envy him! I should like to have been in his place . . .'

Shortly after 9 p.m. on Tuesday, 24 November, 1914, almost two years after that strange confession to Angelica Balabanoff, Benito Mussolini got his wish. As he strode down the long aisle of Milan's Teatro del Popolo, in a grimy side-street south of the Cathedral, he ducked, head bent, through a gauntlet of angry fists. Above the raging tumult one chant, monotonous as a drum beat, was clearly audible: '*Chi paga?*' ('Who's paying?')

Barely had Mussolini mounted the stage than a shower of small coins spattered at his feet: a woman screamed shrilly, 'Judas, there is your blood money!' Then her voice was lost as 3000 Socialist delegates rose to their feet as one, screaming abuse: 'Sell-out! Traitor! Assassin!' And again came that steady menacing monotone, '*Chi paga? Chi paga?*'

Pale, dry-mouthed, with a three-day growth of beard, Mussolini glanced in mute appeal at the chairman, Giacinto Menotti Serrati. 'Comrades,' Serrati implored them, 'let him speak!' But his words went unheeded. On this icy night, bent on what they saw as a treason trial, Milan's Socialists were in no mood for reasoned debate. Though one of his supporters at the back of the hall appealed for fair play, no sooner had Mussolini opened his mouth than the crowd began a rhythmic taunt: 'Louder! Louder! Speak up!'

Their angry bewilderment was understandable. On 29 July, five days before the outbreak of World War One, Mussolini, along with other members of the executive, had signed the Italian Socialist

Party's anti-war manifesto, condemning any attempt to drag Italy into a militarist, capitalist conflict. Even if the government declared war, the Socialists were determined to boycott it. Yet incredibly, on 18 October, Mussolini, finding himself alone in the *Avanti!* office, had gone to press with an article committing the entire party to support Italy's entry into war.

Worse was to follow. Nine days before this Teatro del Popolo meeting, while party chiefs were still debating Mussolini's fate, an unknown news-sheet, *Il Popolo d'Italia*, was hawked for the first time on the foggy Sunday streets. Campaigning for direct intervention, the masthead of editor Benito Mussolini featured two martial slogans: 'He who has steel has bread' and 'A revolution is an idea which has found bayonets.' The paper had sold out within the hour.

Now Mussolini sought to explain to his fellow Socialists why he had so swiftly turned his coat – but in vain. More coins rained at his feet, deftly he side-stepped a flying chair. Whistles, cat-calls and boos mingled in one single scream of execration. 'If you proclaim that I am unworthy . . .' came Mussolini's voice faintly, and the response was instantaneous: a thunderous 'Yes!' The unrepentant culprit sought to become the judge. 'I shall have no mercy for those who do not take an open stand in this tragic hour,' he warned them.

Suddenly, enraged by the heckling, he seized a glass tumbler and held it aloft, crushing it until it splintered and the blood ran down his wrist. Passionately he challenged them: 'You hate me because you still love me!' Then, pale and trembling with rage, he strode back down the aisle. 'You have not seen the last of me,' some by-standers heard him grate.

Within sixty days of war's outbreak he had severed his connection with the Socialists, determined that Italy should take part in this war.

On the face of it, it was professional suicide. To his embarrassment, for he was revelling in a bachelor life, Rachele had brought her mother and Edda down to Milan and he had been forced to set up a family apartment. Now there was not only rent to find, but food and clothing for four – and his monthly salary was gone. Returning that night, he told Rachele the grim truth: 'Things are going to be tough.'

Yet his choice had its own harsh logic. Italy's neutrality meant passive spectatorship and Mussolini was temperamentally incapable of that. To an ambitious politician, war offered more scope. And publisher Filippo Naldi of Bologna, whose paper, *Il Resto del Carlino*, spoke for the big landowners, had himself suggested that Mussolini should set up a paper to press for intervention, agreeing to loan the initial capital. All his life indifferent to money Mussolini saw the chance of power and prestige as infinitely precious.

Renting a few garret-like rooms on the second floor of 35, Via Paolo da Cannobio, in the heart of the red-light district, he set up in business with no more furniture than a chair, a desk and half-a-dozen orange boxes. Above the door loomed a sign that bespoke his own mordant humour: 'If you enter, you'll do me an honour; if you stay out, you'll do me a favour.'

Five days after his expulsion by Milan's Socialists, the executive at the Bologna Convention ratified it, banishing him from the party.

The gesture cost Mussolini no sleep. By March 1915, after upping *Il Popolo*'s circulation to 100,000, he had won fresh backers. Anxious that Italy should enter the war on the Allied side without delay, French government emissaries had paid him a 15,000-franc subsidy (then worth £1000) via Charles Dumas, Secretary of the Department of War Propaganda – and regular payments of 10,000 francs followed. Other French agents, like Julien Luchaire of Milan's French Institute, weighed in with donations of up to 30,000 lire.

The man who only two years earlier had counted his supporters in hundreds now numbered them in millions. All over Italy, groups sprang up urging intervention, men who saw Mussolini as their brazen-tongued spokesman. The city streets came alive with them, chanting rhythmically, with linked arms – pale students, bespectacled clerks, brawny labourers – and their shouts had a counterpoint in the harsh cries of the newsboys ducking from door to door – '*Il Popolo d'Italia!*'

'Every time that blockhead Mussolini writes an article the circulation goes up,' a newsvendor told Rachele, who was conducting a spot-check incognito.

Typical of those now rallying to his cause was nineteen-year-old Bologna University law student Dino Grandi, who two days after *Il Popolo*'s founding wrote to him: 'Permit an ordinary young man to express his fullest admiration for your work of courage and faith.' To him, as to a million others, Mussolini replied: 'Dear Friend, we must fight and be pelted if need be.'

These were not empty words. In those feverish months, Rachele always recalled, he often staggered home with his hat stove in, his jacket half torn off. On 12 April, leading a pro-war demonstration in Rome, he was jailed for eight hours – his eleventh and last sentence. A month later, unrepentant, he urged the people to have their way 'by shooting a few dozen deputies in the back'. By 24 May, 1915, when

Premier Antonio Salandra, assured of good booty by the secret Treaty of London, declared war on Austria, millions viewed Mussolini as little less than a prophet.

By late September, Mussolini, donning the grey-green uniform of the 11th Bersaglieri Regiment, was based in the trenches of the Carnia. Nor was he sorry to go; the world's tumult was mirrored in his private life. His love-hate feeling for women had grown so intense that the sight of one enjoying a meal now turned him sick and dizzy; only recently, dining with a pretty dressmaker on the balcony of a Genoa restaurant, he had seized the chafing-dish of fish and hurled it into the sea, following up with the girl's dinner, tearing cloth and cutlery from the table. In Milan he had failed to seduce Leda Rafanelli, an exotic woman novelist who smoked Egyptian cigarettes and made Turkish coffee on a brazier – but he was already involved with red-haired Margherita Sarfatti, his art-critic.

True, he was to marry Rachele in a civil ceremony on 16 December, 1915, but he had, only one month earlier, had a son by Ida Dalser, a dark, intense, beauty-parlour operator whose trade advertisements appeared in *Avanti!* Mussolini, who signed himself 'Your savage lover', had agreed to recognize his son, Benito, legally, but steadfastly refused to marry her – though Ida later claimed that he had done so. A hysterical, eccentric girl – once, to test the efficiency of the Post Office, she posted herself twenty-seven post-cards from the same box – she was beginning to make scenes and Mussolini sought a way out.

Few regiments served under starker conditions than the 11th Bersaglieri. In seventeen months of active duty, Mussolini clung doggedly to rocky trenches offering scant protection against snow, ice and lethal Austrian shellfire. But in that terrible static war, 3000 feet up along the snowy crest of the Alps, Mussolini, as one officer still recalls him, proved a 'modest soldier – almost to the point of wanting to suppress his strong personality and make others forget his political past.'

Though soldiers, even officers, scrambled into his trench to shake the hand of *Il Popolo*'s interventionist editor, he sought few privileges. He shared the same gripes and hardships as the others: nights when the temperature plummeted to below zero and a laggard sentry found his boots freezing to the rock; tormented days when a bitter wind carried the stench of corpses and water was so precious that a man went a month without washing, plagued by bloated lice; hungry weeks when the Austrian guns pinned down the field kitchens, and men in paroxysms of hunger gnawed the straw jackets of their wine flasks; rain-soaked months when water fell from the sky for forty-six days on end, and a soldier had only his boots with which to bale his shelter dry.

But Mussolini accepted it uncomplainingly – almost as if glad to be relieved of decisions. He grumbled with the others when Christmas dinner, 1916, was stewed salt cod – but toiled steadily away at the war diary he sent each week to *Il Popolo*, scribbling by the reeking light of a sardine-oil lamp, a thread from his puttees serving as the wick. On leave, he found it hard to adjust to a soft bed; leaving Rachele to sleep alone,he bedded down on the marble floor of the Milan apartment.

Silent, self-contained, for the most part he kept his dreams of destiny secret, though he was still a law unto himself when he felt like it. Once, when the regiment withdrew from the line for anti-cholera shots, Mussolini calmly ducked the parade and retired to a deserted barrack-room. Then, commandeering four empty beds, he strewed them with notebooks and newspapers and settled comfortably to write his diary.

But while most recognized his worth as a crusading editor, few saw him as a mover and shaker. Only once, in a rare moment of self-revelation did he console his fellow-corporal, Cesare Ravegnani: 'One fine day, I'll be the master of the world – you come to me then and I'll fix things.' Ravegnani, who was to owe almost every job he ever held to Mussolini, proved himself no prophet. 'You big bald hunk,' was his ungrateful reply, 'what rubbish are you talking?'

For Benito Mussolini, the war ended at exactly 1 p.m. on 23 February, 1917, just twenty-three days after his promotion to Lance-Sergeant. Early that year he and the regiment had been transferred to the Carso, the icy limestone range north of the Adriatic, whose rocky basins made shellfire more terrible through flying splinters. At Hill 144 where they held out, Austrian guns, as soldiers' slang had it, 'pinched' more Italians than in any other sector.

Twenty men, Mussolini among them, were in a pit that day, practice-firing a howitzer whose barrel had grown red-hot. The last two shells proved fatal. As it blasted apart, four men died in an instant, ripped to pieces by flying molten fragments; miraculously Mussolini himself was thrown fifteen feet. Second-lieutenant Francesco Caccese who was the first to reach him, never forgot 'his eyes fixed in a terrifying stare, the jaws clamped tight in a desperate effort to hide his pain'.

His body tattooed with forty-four fragments of shrapnel, he was rushed to base hospital with a fever of 103° – metal embedded in his immobile left leg, in his breast, in his groin. Some wounds were so huge surgeons could insert their fists into them. Within a month Mussolini had undergone twenty-seven operations, all save two without anaesthetic; to offset gangrene the flesh was packed with alcohol-soaked swabs. 'I wanted to howl like a crazy wolf,' Mussolini admitted later.

Not until June was he able to resume his column for *Il Popolo* – after fever so intense he had lost all sense of time and place. Once, maddened by an incessant tinkling in his ears, he screamed from the depths of delirium, 'Stop that damned telephone!' He was too far gone to know that it was an acolyte's bell he had heard, as a priest administered the last rites to the man in the next bed.

By August, hobbling on crutches, he was fit to return to Milan, his trench warfare over. From then on he could wear only button (later zip-fastened) boots or his left leg would suppurate.

He had come back to a land divided. One Italy belonged to the six million men he had left behind at the front, men so patriotic they wholeheartedly shared the sentiment inscribed on their field post-cards: 'To die crying Long live Italy, long live the King, is to go to Heaven.' On the home front the picture was bleaker; few civilians had expected the war to enter its third year – a war which the Socialists as international humanitarians still stubbornly boycotted. Hated by many Army generals, who saw them as 'the enemy within', they hit back with rules of their own. To place a wreath on a soldier's grave or attend a military funeral rated expulsion from the party. In the Chamber of Deputies, Socialist Claudio Treves, Mussolini's predecessor as editor of *Avanti!*, minted a slogan which travelled like fire through the ranks: 'Not another winter in the trenches.'

Since thousands of workers were exempt from war-service, they saw Treves's words as rock-ribbed sense.

Back in his Via Paolo da Cannobio garret, Mussolini saw himself as the passionate prophet of every infantryman who had ever slogged to the front with a 60lb haversack on his back. In the last week of October, 1917, he broke down completely and had to be given morphia; Rachele, too, wept silently as she went about her household chores. At Caporetto, in the heart of the Isonzo Valley, the Italian Second Army had broken before the Austro-German push. Under icy pelting rain, one million men fell back for sixty miles without a shot being fired. It was a tragedy that cost Italy 250,000 prisoners, a million rifles, six billion lire of winter clothing.

The anarchist who had once rejected all things military was now a drum-beating King-and-country patriot. At white heat he launched a 'Stand to a Finish' campaign, urging government action against defeatism, martial law in North Italy, the suppression of all Socialist newspapers. To old comrades at the front he wrote nostalgic letters, signing himself, 'Your old bersagliere, almost sawn in half'. Later fully 400 of them claimed to have carried him from the battle-field.

One year later, on 30 October, 1918, when the Italian armies under General Armando Diaz, smashed through the Austrian ranks near the town of Vittorio Veneto, forty-three miles from Venice, millions of servicemen felt that the man who had done most to boost front-line morale in that year of resurrection was Benito Mussolini.

It was a transient glory. Under the secret Treaty of London, Italy had been promised much to compensate her for more than 600,000 dead, almost one and a half million wounded, a war debt of twelve billion lire: fine natural ports on the Jugoslav shore of the Adriatic, the Italian-speaking Austrian colonies of Trento and Trieste, a stake in Turkey. But at the Versailles Peace Conference the austere Woodrow Wilson, twenty-seventh President of the United States, stubbornly refused to recognize a secret treaty which America had never signed – and one which clashed with his Fourteen Points giving self-determination to every nation.

Along with Georges Clemenceau and David Lloyd George, Wilson held meetings to which Italy's Vittorio Emanuele Orlando was not even invited – meetings which denied Italy every claim save Trento and Trieste. Wilson, only recently created a freeman of Rome and presented with a golden model of the she-wolf that suckled Romulus and Remus, was now burned in effigy across the piazzas of Italy.

The backlash was bitter disillusion – with the war and all who had fought it. Each day, in *Il Popolo*'s ramshackle offices, Mussolini listened in scowling silence as the telephone brought news of fresh outrages against the most obvious scapegoats of all: returning front-line soldiers. Bologna bystanders watched aghast as roughs kicked the crutches from under war cripples. In Milan, one veteran, complaining when a tram-car passenger trod on his foot, was set upon by fellow passengers who stripped him of his campaign medals and tossed him bodily into the street. There were even cases of murder. Two officers of the 71st Infantry, knocked senseless outside a Venetian barracks, were jammed into a sentrybox and toppled, to die by inches, in the waters of the Grand Canal.

As the months wore on, one factor was plain: the soldiers could expect no champions among the government ranks. At Milan's Central Station, an officer of the Alpine regiment was set upon by thugs, disarmed, then beaten until his arm was broken. A complaint to the local military commander brought a verdict which was soon a nationwide decree: in future officers on leave should wear only mufti 'to avoid inflaming the populace'.

Soon Italy's 160,000 demobilized officers were malcontents with a vengeance. When Mussolini's bitter opponents, the Socialists, the one party to oppose the war all through, upped their card-carrying members to 1,200,000, Liberal Premier Francesco Nitti, eager to pacify them, granted an amnesty to 150,000 deserters.

But not only officers were targets for Socialist wrath: the priests and the monarchy were fair game too. At Denore, near Ferrara, Socialists who took their cue from the two-year-old Russian Revolution stormed into the church to drape the altar with a Red Flag. When elections brought them control of 2000 municipalities, that same flag replaced the tricolour above most town halls – and in the Mayor's office, the King's portrait, like an errant son in a melodrama, was firmly turned to the wall.

For the rich and the middle-class these were troubled times. Men angry and disillusioned by forty-one months of fruitless war could construe almost anything as a class symbol. In Siena citizens sporting ties or carrying books faced the same hazards as Florentines who wore hats or stiff collars: a barrage of rocks and wine bottles. Motor-cars or fur coats roused a mob to the pitch of lynch-law. At Pegli, a seaside resort near Genoa, where a Socialist council held sway, women holidaymakers were forbidden to dance, wear jewellery or silk stockings – and the lights in every hotel must be out by 11 p.m.

On the rainy Sunday morning of 23 March, 1919, Mussolini took the first steps in the counter-offensive which was to cast him in his long-cherished role of man-of-destiny. In a hot little hall on Milan's Piazza San Sepolcro, a handful of men met as founders of the newly-formed Fascist Party – so styled from the *fasces*, the bundle of elm rods coupled with an axe, bound by red cord, that in ancient Rome had symbolized a consul's powers of life and death. Many who crowded round their leader were men who had tasted those powers and found them sweet – black-shirted, black-sweatered Arditi (shock troops) of World War One, whose combat duty was to storm the Austrian trenches, daggers in their teeth and a grenade in each hand. An insolent élite whose reveillé was a volley of grenades, they had trained with live ammunition from the first – and rated a meat ration whoever else went short.

Their hands clasped over a dagger blade, they swore: 'We will defend Italy, ready to kill or to die.' And Mussolini gave voice to all their bitterness as he told them: 'We will defend our dead even if we dig trenches in the squares and streets.' Yet the party's beginnings were modest. Though *Il Popolo* boasted that 120 had taken part, only fifty-four signed the manifesto. A too-zealous reporter, covering a trade meeting in the next room, had tacked on the names of seventy Lombardy milk wholesalers.

Other branches were swift to follow. By the end of the month, Turin, Genoa and Verona, followed by Padua and Naples; by mid-April, Pavia, Trieste, Parma, Bologna and Perugia. Within two and a half years, 2200 separate groups were exultantly hailing Mussolini as their 'Duce'.

It was not unduly surprising. By 1920 Italy was a land divided, trembling on the brink of civil war. Strike-fever gripped the nation; in the columns of *Il Popolo* Mussolini charted more than two thousand stoppages and walk-outs in this one year. Prison warders, intent on a pay rise, held a pistol to the head of Premier Nitti: if the rise wasn't granted in five days they would turn loose every wrong-doer in Italy. Striking postal workers poured sulphuric acid into packed letter-boxes; the nightly black-out by Rome's electricians didn't even spare the hospitals.

If a priest or an officer boarded a train, the engine men jammed on the brakes and refused to budge. Timetables became obsolete documents; one train from Turin arrived 400 hours late. Even Premier Nitti knew when he was beaten; booked to attend a San Remo conference, he took a closed car to Anzio, then boarded a naval destroyer.

September saw the Soviet-style coup when 600,000 metal workers seized the factories from Milan to Naples; in a month-long lock-in, the Red Flag flew free above 600 silent smokestacks. Lacking credit to purchase raw materials, the operatives had to give in – but government five per cent stock plummeted by seven billion lire.

Still the workers saw it as their victory. When Fiat boss Giovanni Agnelli returned to his Turin office, he passed through an archway of Red Flags; in his office a portrait of Lenin had replaced the King's. Menaced by angry factory-hands, Agnelli took down the portrait and kissed it.

After that, in the hope of propitiating his men, one Milan industrialist openly sported a hammer-and-sickle emblem – in the shape of a diamond tie-pin.

Not only industry was in chaos; the land was a battleground too. Ferrara's 200 Communist unions, dominating the labour market, forced farmers to hire labourers allotted to them without choice, clamping down on the use of machinery. A man who wouldn't comply faced a total boycott – denied food by the grocer, a haircut by the barber, even medical treatment. Often a line of red flags down a hayfield proclaimed that the labourers were harvesting their own share, leaving the farmer's to rot.

Thousands now looked with new urgency to the one campaign headquarters which might right these wrongs: the three dingy offices, with their peeling wallpaper and spavined chairs, at 35 Via Paolo da Cannobio. Though the key-note of signs to the staff was wry humour – 'Reporters are requested not to leave before arriving' – the editor's own quarters suggested the operations office of a banana-republic general. Placidly sipping a glass of milk, he sat with an Arditi's black skull-and-crossbones flag serving as back-drop, a machine-gun in the firing position trained on the door, his desk strewn with grenades, hunting knives and cartridge cases.

Despite his overt calm, Mussolini was still a man seeking the crossroads of destiny. In November 1919 he had for the first time put up candidates for the Chamber of Deputies – refusing even to form a bloc with the blue-shirted King-and-country Nationalists, who were later to merge with the Fascists. The party's star candidate, nominated without even being asked, was conductor Arturo Toscanini, later a staunch anti-Fascist, picked on the grounds that he would carry the Musicians' Union. The result was a disaster. Milan's musicians, irked by the brusque, bristling maestro, boycotted the polls altogether. Against the Socialists' 170,000 the mortified Fascists polled only 4795 votes.

Exultant, the Socialists besieged *Il Popolo*'s office – guarded by barbed wire and twenty-five armed Arditi – convinced that Mussolini was now a spent force. But on the surface the Duce seemed on top of the world. 'If they break in,' he wisecracked, 'I can always bite half a dozen and give them blood-poisoning.' Days later, when six Florentines appeared, confessing they had been paid twenty lire apiece to assassinate him, he mock-grumbled, 'I thought I was worth more than that' – then gave each man 200 lire from the petty cash to save him from walking home. His love of cocking a snook at authority was still a sixteen-year-old schoolboy's. About this time, when *Il Popolo* ran into censorship troubles, Mussolini retaliated with a four-page blank issue, its only items the masthead and a squib: 'Banned – by order of that swine Nitti.'

But those close to him, like Rachele, saw his tension snap like a steel spring. He battled with a terrible conviction that his destiny was to sit on the sidelines and acclaim others, that fate had never cast him as a contender for the laurels. His nails were bitten beyond the quicks, almost to the moons. Once, incensed by a tardy switchboard operator, he tore his telephone from the wall and hurled it through the window, to dangle by its wires above the street.

Arnaldo, now the paper's business manager, suffered as much as any. When he installed a comfortable armchair in Benito's office his brother railed: 'Take it away, d'you hear me? Armchairs and slippers are the abomination of mankind.' Often, too, Arnaldo had to soothe disgruntled staffers: 'Pay no attention – our mother always said that Benito was a monument of rudeness.'

Just as in his youth, he sought release in violent direct action – cycling eighteen miles a day for flying lessons, sandwiching in driving lessons, fighting half a dozen duels. But he had come late in life to all recreation, and despite his dogged determination to excel, he was as clumsy with a rapier as he was behind the wheel of his first Bianchina – even on mountain roads with the engine boiling, he never saw the need to change gear. On his first solo flight, a crash from 120 feet cost him twenty days in bed with a temperature of 103° F – yet he still went on to clock up over 17,000 flying hours.

All through his life to acknowledge defeat was to risk exposing himself to ridicule – the one thing he feared above all. Though he wielded his rapier like a bludgeon, grunting and grimacing, he threw out challenges with the aplomb of a D'Artagnan – fighting under bridges, on the banks of streams, once in a rented room after the seconds had piled all the furniture on to the landing. 'Have spaghetti today,' was the code he had fixed with Rachele to avoid alarming the family, which had grown to include Vittorio, six, and Bruno, two; then, while she looked at the bloodstained shirt in which he fought all his duels, the family handyman, Cirillo Tambara, hurried off to the store for the pitch Mussolini secretly used to glue his rapier to his fencing-glove.

No adversary ever made Mussolini look foolish by disarming him – nor would the Duce ever yield until promised a signed statement that victory was his.

There was much to gall him in this post-war era; for the first time in years he found himself playing second fiddle. In September 1919, the fifty-seven-year-old poet-novelist Gabriele d'Annunzio, at the head of 1000 legionnaires, had defied Woodrow Wilson in the name of Italy to seize the Jugoslav port of Fiume, with its large Italian colony – though the country had given him no such mandate.

A bald-headed, monocled popinjay, whose sensuous imagery extolled the virtues of the superman and free love, D'Annunzio was a flagrant exhibitionist – shopping for forty-eight pairs of lace drawers, pealing the church bells each time he completed a poem, guarding himself with thirty-five watch dogs. But he was also a patriot and a gallant World War One aviator and to his banner, in the fourteen months he held the port, flocked 9000 men of the Arditi stamp, their minds fired by this patriotic freebooting. Outside the limelight, Mussolini was forced to fume in the wings, using *Il Popolo* for a fund drive which reached three million lire – much of which he siphoned off for his abortive election campaign.

But at Christmas 1920, he brightened perceptibly. D'Annunzio had been shelled out of Fiume by the Italian Navy – and his roistering corsairs were happy to flock to Mussolini, the one man who seemed ready to strike a blow for *la patria*. A genius at making over another man's ideas for his own purposes, Mussolini gladly adopted the poet's circus trappings for his own Fascist movement: the tight-fitting black shirt of the Arditi, worn with grey-green breeches and puttees, the black fezlike cap with a black tassel. Adopted, too, was the raised right arm salute of the Roman legionaries, the battle-cry of '*A noi!*' (To us), with which shock troops scaled enemy trenches, the meaningless chant of '*Eja, eja, alalà*', which D'Annunzio claimed was the war-cry of Aeneas and his Trojans.

Young, bold and intolerant, the Fascist action squads swaggered like men to whom conquest was commonplace – as contemptuous as their motto '*Me ne frego*' (I don't give a damn), which a wounded man had scrawled on his bandages. Their anthem was the wartime shock troops' song '*Giovinezza*' (Youth); their weapons were the castor-oil with which they dosed their victims, half-a-pint at a time, and the sturdy nineteen-inch bludgeon called the *manganello*.

Soon thousands of men who craved change and action were coming to emulate them – lured by the glamour of the vermilion wound stripes on their right sleeves, the cherry brandy they swigged as their one-for-the-road, the thunderous cry of '*Presente!*' with which they answered a dead comrade's name at roll-call.

It was a motley army. Some joined under enemy duress; when

Communists invaded his lawyer's office to rip the blue ribbons off his military jacket, Dino Grandi, a contemplative twenty-year-old who had once spent three months in a monastery, drew his revolver to stop them. That same evening, as he left his office, seven shots whistled past him; he escaped only by zig-zagging on his bicycle. A fervent admirer of Mussolini since his defection from the Socialist ranks, Grandi now pedalled straight to Bologna's Fascist Party headquarters.

Other ex-officers met trouble more than half-way. At Casale Monferrato, near Turin, Lieutenant Giovanni Passerone prowled the streets with a tame wolf on a leash, challenging the Socialists either to spit on his uniform – or to fight a duel with him in the lion's cage at the circus.

Some were embittered intellectuals: Verona's Alberto de Stefani, Professor of Political Economy, chosen by his own students to head their protest movement; Alfredo Misuri, zoologist and world authority on the tail structure of the wall lizard, dedicated to working over every Communist who displayed a portrait of Lenin; Rome's Giuseppe Bottai, avant-garde poet, who spoke of the King as 'Comrade Savoy' and spat on the ground when a royal carriage passed.

More were intransigent pseudo-toughs, as crude as the fragments of a grenade. When Sandro Carosi of Pisa visited a pastry-cook's, he always chose his favourite cream cakes by impaling them on his dagger. Nineteen-year-old Ettore Muti, ex-D'Annunzio legionnaire, disdained to ring on door-bells; he announced his arrival at his mother's house with a fusillade of pistol shots. Six-foot Italo ('Big Beast') Capanni, one-time pornographic postcard salesman on the streets of Buenos Aires, later elected a deputy, made the only maiden speech possible for a man short on words: prising a bench loose from its moorings, he heaved it clean across the Chamber at the Socialist ranks. And in Florence, called 'Fascistopolis', the bald, bandy-legged Tullio Tamburini created such havoc among the Communists that *La Nazione* kept a reporter on all-night duty at the General Hospital to record the toll of his victims.

Most unbridled of all these men was Cremona's Roberto ('The Slap-Giver') Farinacci, whose reign of terror in the quiet city of Stradivarius was to endure for twenty-five years. A foul-mouthed, hectoring twenty-nine-year-old, once the railway station's chief telegraphist, he claimed to have forced the 'resignation' of sixty-four Socialist Mayors – keeping a revolver hidden in his sock-suspender for speedier action. But Farinacci didn't stop at the Cremona region;

when a court case was decided against a close friend, he called on the Minister of Justice in Rome and threatened to burn down his house.

As self-appointed vigilantes, sworn to smash the Socialists' power, the Fascists' methods were raw – and often effective. When cattle were starving during a farmworkers' strike at Oca, near Rovigo, local Fascists, seventy strong, staged a four-hour Wild West cattle-drive on horseback and restored them to their owners. Truckloads of Blackshirts scoured the countryside, looting, burning, shooting; by June 1921, the Socialists threw in the sponge. To stay alive, every labourer in the Po valley had enrolled in the Fascist Party. But landlords, too, were made to toe the line. When one wealthy Tuscan dilettante neglected his estates to build up a collection of 2500 song-birds, the Fascists seized almost six thousand acres of his land, forcing him to put it under tillage and hire Fascist labour.

Night after night, householders wakeful behind darkened shutters heard echoes of the bloody crusade; the crack of revolver shots, the tramp of marching feet across deserted piazzas and beneath shadowy colonnades. Florence's Tamburini ordered all retailers to slash their prices by twenty per cent: those who didn't comply saw their cartloads of eggs, fruit and vegetables overturned and trampled in the mire of the market. Soon a familiar sign loomed on many a shuttered shopfront: 'Closed for Daylight Robbery.'

At Adria, south of Venice, the Fascists stamped out alcoholism by forcing every wine-seller to display a pint bottle of castor-oil in his window – a warning of the fate awaiting any man found drunk. In Alessandria, long a city of recidivists, the Fascist chief sent a printed circular to 300 burglars, pick-pockets, and con-men, inviting them to a midnight meeting in a cellar. Faced with the stark alternative – to go straight or be put in hospital – most were glad to enrol at a Fascist labour exchange and take on honest work.

Countless middle-class workers, small storekeepers, students – and indeed the authorities – began to see Mussolini's Fascists as crusaders, superpatriotic idealists who alone could save Italy from Bolshevism. Impressed by its 'patriotic value', the Army's commander-in-chief, General Armando Diaz, ordered the circulation of *Il Popolo* throughout the ranks free of charge. The police were so partisan that when Trieste Fascists stormed the premises of Ignazio Silone's Socialist news-sheet *Il Lavoratore*, police arrived by the truck-load – to arrest the besieged Socialists.

And Mussolini was winning more tangible support. Men like Giacomo Toeplitz, president of Milan's Banca Commerciale Italiana, the power behind the silk and textile industries, were as ready to swell the party's coffers as the Credito Italiano, bankers to the great auto plants, which donated 300,000 lire (then worth £12,000). Milan's Masons, and Secretary-General Gino Olivetti of the General Confederation of Industry, were equally benevolent. By the time the March on Rome was mooted, Mussolini's campaign fund totalled twenty-four million lire – though little enough would be used to arm or feed the troops. Fearful of a reverse, Mussolini held tight to the funds, anticipating a long siege.

But at this stage of his life, he had a more pacific plan in view. A year after moving to roomier offices on Milan's Via Lovanio came the elections of May 1921, when his Fascist candidates won thirty-four seats in the Chamber of Deputies – Mussolini himself polling 178,000 votes. To defeat the hated left wing, the cynical seventy-nine-year-old Liberal leader, Giovanni Giolitti, five times Premier, had agreed to form a bloc with the very Fascists he despised as 'firework men'. Vainly he hoped that Fascist action squads would crush the Socialists, then enter meekly into the Liberal fold. But the Duce's foot was planted on the first rung of power. From November 1920, on seeing the Bolshevik flame flicker out, he had sought to make peace with the Socialists.

'To say that a Bolshevist danger still exists in Italy means taking base fears for reality,' he warned in July 1921. 'Bolshevism is overthrown . . . Fascism is no longer liberation but tyranny.'

He had cause to be fearful. Nourished on violence, even those who had begun as idealists were fast degenerating into bullies – or worse. At Ferrara, Mussolini had angrily refused to walk down the carpet of captured red flags which Italo Balbo had spread before him like a conqueror. Scores of Fascist leaders, like Carrara's Renato ('Little Earthquake') Ricci, were becoming a law unto themselves; to free eight delinquent Fascists from jail, Ricci mobilized 6000 Blackshirts in a yelling reign of terror until the magistrates gave in. In February 1921, Tamburini's men shot a Florentine railway unionist in cold blood, left him lolling in his office chair, a cigarette gummed to his lips.

Now Mussolini struck a blow for peace. In August 1921, in the Chamber of Deputies, he solemnly signed a Pact of Pacification with his enemies. Within hours he had news which left him white and shaken. The Fascists of the north – Ferrara's Balbo, Cremona's Farinacci, Florence's Tamburini – refused to abide by the pact: the Socialists must be wiped out. In a passion Mussolini resigned from the executive. From now on, he declared, he would be a simple member of the Milan branch, no more.

It was a short-lived resolution. Mortified, Mussolini soon saw that he was again in the wilderness: whatever their Duce might feel, his men had switched from an ex-soldiers' movement to one bent on crushing democracy and setting up a Fascist state. To be left in the cold was something that no man with Mussolini's deep-rooted sense of inferiority could stomach: wherever the party was going he must be at the helm. By November 1921, he had made his uneasy peace with the militants.

What followed was a series of swift bloodless take-overs: dress rehearsals for the great coup to come. Three years earlier, control of all public utilities – light, telephones, water – had helped Lenin and Trotsky to seize Petrograd; now Mussolini was taking leaves from their book. Ravenna came first; in September 1921, 3000 dust-grimed Fascists, under Balbo, some of whom had marched over sixty miles, took over the Adriatic city. On 12 May, 1922, it was Ferrara's turn; 63,000 Fascists seized every public strongpoint while Balbo, in the sixteenth-century castle that housed the Prefecture, held the Prefect at gunpoint. Seventeen days later, 20,000 men held Bologna for five days, camped on straw in the colonnades. The point had been made: a city could be taken and held.

In August 1922, when the Socialists declared a general strike, Mussolini gave a sharp ultimatum to Facta's government: either they broke the strike or he would. When the authorities stood idle, the Fascists stepped in to keep railways and trams running, charging no fares. From Taranto to Merano the flames from more than a hundred wrecked Socialist headquarters trembled in the night.

And Mussolini's tone was hardening. On 11 August he declared: 'The March on Rome has begun.' On 19 August: 'The century of democracy is over.' When Gabriele d'Annunzio heard of the plan he declared in horror: 'Rome, Rome, will you give yourself to a butcher?' Premier Facta even suggested that D'Annunzio himself should enter Rome on 4 November, Armistice Day, with a column of crippled ex-servicemen. But when this news was broken to Mussolini at the 24 October Naples Congress, the Duce made up his mind: that bald-headed poet shouldn't steal his thunder again. The plans that had begun in Milan on 16 October, when Mussolini appointed Generals De Bono, Balbo, Bianchi and De Vecchi to plan the march, were now put into effect. The race for power was on.

The post-war chaos, the fear of Bolshevism, the rise and fall of six governments in three years had all combined to help Mussolini, which was why he stood before the little King in the Palazzo del Quirinale at 11.15 a.m. on 30 October, 1922, as Italy's sixtieth premier.

Twelve hours later, in his second-floor suite at the Hotel Savoia, Mussolini held his first cabinet meeting. But first he took time to put the Fascist house in order. At 1 p.m. the long five-hour march past of his troops through Rome's streets began – from the Piazza del Popolo, along the narrow Corso Umberto to Piazza Venezia, up the steep canyon of the Via IV Novembre, at last, in total silence, past the Quirinale, where the King took the salute. Ahead of them marched black-shirted Fascists, who held aloft fluttering palm branches as symbols of their victory.

Their triumph was brief. Angered by reports of wanton destruction, and assaults on Socialists, Mussolini sent a peremptory order to Rome chief Gino Calza-Bini: 'Work with the chief of police to avoid bloodshed.' For the departing Premier Facta, Mussolini ordered a ten-strong Blackshirt bodyguard. 'He has lost a son in the war,' he reminded them sternly, 'nobody touches a hair of his head.' When the stationmaster of Rome's Central Station complained that 60,000 uproarious Fascists couldn't be evacuated within twenty-four hours, Mussolini told him coldly: 'Erase the word impossible from your vocabulary.'

It was a time for reunions too. For Italo Balbo, who arrived at 7 p.m., he had no commands, merely a long, silent embrace. With Dino Grandi, who had done all in his power to avert the march, he was accusing: 'You didn't believe in my star. I can't put you in the government now – the Blackshirts wouldn't like it.' To Giuseppe Mastromattei, his personal observer at Perugia, he seemed in sober mood. When Mastromattei protested that a true revolution called for bloody daggers, Mussolini shook his head silently, vehemently. 'No,' he objected. 'You pay for blood with blood – and I don't want to end up like Cola di Rienzi.'

As he left the suite, Mastromattei recalled the fate of the fourteenth-century Roman tyrant, whose reign of a few months had ended when the mob dragged him, bloodied, through the streets, to hang him by his heels outside the church of San Marcello.

There, in the Hotel Savoia, on 30 October, 1922, no fate in the world seemed quite so remote.

3. 'The Body Between My Feet'

November 1922 – December 1924

With a screech of brakes, the black Isotta Fraschini drew up outside the Palazzo Viminale in Rome, seat of the Ministry of Home Affairs. Almost before the Premier's chauffeur, Ercole Boratto, could open the door, Mussolini had bounded out with Presidential Under-Secretary Giacomo Acerbo at his heels. Taking the stone stairs that fronted the building two at a time, the Duce intercepted the frock-coated functionary whom a porter with silver mace and cocked hat was just then saluting.

On the cold winter air Mussolini's greeting came sharp and peremptory: 'I am sorry that you are not in good health, Signor.'

The bureaucrat, like scores of others in these November weeks of 1922, fell unsuspecting into the trap. 'Your Excellency must be mistaken,' he protested, 'I am perfectly well.'

'Then,' answered Mussolini angrily, his clenched fist coming down on his open palm like the crack of a whip, 'be good enough to explain why you are entering your office at 11 a.m. when the official hour is 9 a.m. Acerbo, take his name – there'll have to be a lot of weeding-out done here!'

A new broom bent on scouring every corner of Italy, Benito Mussolini, President of the Council, Minister for both Home and Foreign Affairs, had started as he meant to go on. Before 8 a.m. on 31 October, striding through the conformist corridors of Palazzo Chigi, where his office as Foreign Minister was located, he had already propped his visiting card, like a veiled threat, on the desk of every absent staffer. By 9 a.m. he was on the line to each of the thirty Ministers and Under-Secretaries who made up his Cabinet: from now on every department would hold a daily roll-call.

Soon the shaken bureaucrats realized that 1922 marked Year I of the Fascist Era – by law all public documents soon bore a double date – and that no hour within the twenty-four was sacrosanct. Once, when a Minister proved untraceable in his office at 2 p.m., Mussolini slammed down the phone, raging, 'What is this bourgeois habit of going to lunch?'

He drove himself as hard. In his first two months of office, he held thirty-two Cabinet sessions, all of them lasting an average of five hours; if he himself reached his desk at 8 a.m. he rarely left it before 9 p.m. Often it was 3 p.m. before he returned to the dingy third-floor apartment he had rented at 156, Via Rasella, for his own frugal lunch – three bowls of minestrone seasoned with pork crackling, prepared by Cirillo Tambara, the family factotum, who had followed him to Rome.

A passion for efficiency seemed to consume him like white fire. Memos and telegrams flowed in a non-stop tide across his desk, to be approved in the margin, 'Good – M.', or struck through in blue pencil. He created a Grand Council of senior officials to advise on legislation, streamlined Italy's cumbersome bureaucracy by firing 35,000 civil servants, and merged the blue-shirted Nationalists with the Fascists. Suppressing the King's Guards created by Premier Nitti, he absorbed his action squads into a Militia for national security – whose oath of allegiance was sworn to the Duce, not the King. As zealous as a traffic cop, he forbade cars to sound their horns, instituted one-way pavements, banished hansom-cabs as antediluvian. And somehow he found time to attend every ceremony from the opening of a new factory to an operative's silver jubilee.

'I want 50,000 Italians working like clockwork,' he insisted, and that is what he set out to get.

His ministers found his enthusiasm contagious. In an effort to balance Italy's budget for the first time in many years, Finance Minister Alberto de Stefani was even sleeping in his office, starting work at 5 a.m. to reduce the current deficit by thirteen million lire. Edoardo Torre, a hustling Alessandria doctor, hired to reform Italy's railways, began the job by hurrying to the station, only to find the Rome express running fourteen minutes late. Promptly Torre fired the driver, hired another from the crewroom, then rode all the way to Rome on the footplate at full speed.

In his first week of office, finding that the railways now paid out 3000 per cent more for losses on theft than in 1915, Torre hit on a novel solution: to ship trunks empty of anything save action-squad men who sprang like djinns from a bottle once the robbers had jimmied the lock. The robberies slumped – and soon, as every tourist never tired of telling, the trains were running to time.

It was the same at all levels. As a tribute to Mussolini's charisma, workers in the national tobacco factory, the Naples arsenal, and Rome's Army and Navy stores, all pledged overtime without pay. Over ten thousand letters a week reached him from citizens offering voluntary work. One man even sought the royal decree to change his three-year-old son's name from Lenin Esposito to Benito Mussolini Esposito.

Only Luigi Pirandello remained unimpressed. Asked for his comments soon after the March on Rome, the famous playwright grumbled: 'All I know is that people who come to power have to eat – and these people, being younger, will probably eat more.'

But his was a lone voice. Most people then gave Mussolini such unswerving loyalty that he could exclaim to a friend with cold certainty: 'I'm not just passing through Rome – I'm here to stay and I'm here to govern. The Italians have got to obey and they will obey – if I have to fight friends, enemies, even myself.'

As Premier, his first speech to the Chamber of Deputies, on 16 November, was in this same vein. On the Socialist benches the members shifted uneasily – long before Mussolini strode in, raising his arm in the Roman salute, they sensed a brooding tension. Already the public benches were packed with Blackshirts, ostentatiously trimming their nails with their daggers. And the Duce's first words to the hushed assembly, as he faced them, hands on hips, his face pale with emotion, were menacing. 'I could have turned this drab grey hall into a bivouac for my Blackshirts,' he told them roundly, 'and made an end of Parliament.'

A cold silence descended on the Chamber, for Mussolini had paused dramatically before adding: 'It was in my power to do so, but it was not my wish.' He waited for the rustle of relief that greeted his words, for he had rehearsed this speech in private for fully three hours. Then he jerked the rug from under them: 'At least, not yet.'

Now, speaking more plainly still, he drove home his point: 'The Chamber must understand that I can dissolve it – in two days or two years. I claim full powers.' That point was taken. Within days, with only some Socialists and Communists abstaining, full powers were granted him by 275 votes to 90.

'I want to make a mark on my era . . . like a lion with its claw,' he burst out to Margherita Sarfatti at this time, 'a mark like this!' And as if overcome by the potential of his power, he scored his nails down a leather chair-back.

But it was not only in Italy that Mussolini was flexing his muscles. At the end of August 1923, General Enrico Tellini and four staff officers, an Italian frontier commission engaged on demarcating the boundary between Greece and Albania, were ambushed and gunned down on Greek soil by unknown assassins. Promptly Mussolini demanded a homage to the Italian flag, the discovery and execution of the killers and compensation of £500,000 – all demands to be met within five days. When the poverty-stricken Greeks could offer nothing more positive than an apology, Mussolini sent the Italian Fleet to bombard and seize the island of Corfu.

For the first but not the last time, Mussolini had pitted himself against the three-year-old League of Nations – convinced that no nation's authority should exceed its armed strength. It was a battle that he won hands down. Only twenty-seven days later, when the Conference of Ambassadors, to whom the League passed the case, had decreed that Greece must pay the levy, did the Navy relinquish Corfu.

As early as November 1922 Mussolini had shown his form in the international field: whatever the means, the Duce and Italy would make their presence felt. As his train steamed into Sion, Switzerland, en route to the Lausanne Conference on Turkey's post-war future, Mussolini, beaming broadly, summoned the puzzled Salvatore Contarini, Secretary-General for Foreign Affairs, to his compartment, along with conference delegate Raffaele Guariglia. Without comment he handed them draft telegrams to be despatched as priority to the French Premier Raymond Poincaré, and the British Foreign Secretary, Lord Curzon.

On this same evening, both statesmen and Mussolini were guests of honour at an official banquet at the Hotel Beau Rivage, Lausanne, – where the Duce, twenty years earlier, had lingered as an embittered have-not, envying the wealthy diners. Due to reach Lausanne forty-five minutes before the others arrived from Paris, Mussolini was to await them at the station.

Now his telegrams announced a high-handed change of plan. Opting out of the banquet altogether, Mussolini sent word that he was leaving his train at Territet, fifteen miles up Lake Geneva from Lausanne – and would be pleased to greet the statesmen at the railway hotel.

No newsman who covered that conference ever forgot the moment when the elder statesmen's private train shuffled into Lausanne station. Peering first in bewilderment, then in anger from their Pullman saloons, Poincaré and Curzon saw no sign of Mussolini. It was M. René Massigli, the Conference's Secretary-General, who broke the news of the Duce's defection. In the hearing of every man present, the harsh-voiced Poincaré burst out: '*Mais où est-ce qu'il est, ce salaud?*' (Where is this bastard?)

Half an hour of angry argument followed – until the delegates, as Mussolini had known they must, gave in. To refuse was to reveal an open breach between the Allies, and the need was to display a united front to the Turkish delegation. In silent fury Poincaré and Curzon travelled on to Territet for their first glimpse of Mussolini – standing stock still in the foyer of the Grand Hotel, clad in an ill-fitting morning-coat with pink linen cuffs, clutching a thick black stick like an Irishman's shillelagh and grinning broadly. Around him like a mobster's bodyguard was a phalanx of pugnacious be-fezzed young Fascists.

As diplomats of the old school, nothing in their thirty years at Whitehall and the Quai d'Orsay had prepared Poincaré or Curzon for this. All through the first meeting in a private room, the Duce's personal bodyguard stood menacingly by with a loaded carbine – and afterwards, the banquet a fading memory, they were forced to dine with Mussolini in the hotel's public restaurant. Their final humiliation was the worst. As the three men left the hotel to return to their private train, a twenty-strong Boy Scout band fell into step ahead. In fuming silence, the gouty Curzon leaning heavily on a stick, the two elder statesmen stumped back to their train to the brassy strains of the Fascist anthem '*Giovinezza*', forced willy-nilly to form part of Mussolini's triumphal march.

Yet after Corfu, Contarini and Guariglia took fresh heart. It was as if, having twice thumbed his nose at the world's powers, Mussolini was now tamely content to follow his advisers' counsel: the traditional Italian policy of alignment with Britain. A shrewd Sicilian, Contarini now briefed his chief of cabinet, Giacomo Barone-Russo, to screen every memo and telegram that passed across Mussolini's desk.

All three had noted, too, the vital chink in Mussolini's armour: his fear of ridicule. 'When I make a gaffe or realize I'm not on top of a situation,' he confessed to one woman friend, 'I become so nervous and angry I can't even sleep at night.' And while he would stubbornly duck the advice of a two-man panel, for fear of losing prestige, one man was sure of a reasonable hearing. When Italy obtained definitive title to the Dodecanese Islands in 1924, Mussolini's reaction was immediate: he would send a naval squadron to take formal possession. 'But we have held them for ten years,' Guariglia protested. 'If you do that you'll become the laughing-stock of the world.' Though Mussolini scowled darkly, the plan remained a dead letter.

Barone-Russo's tactics were identical. A pastmaster of protocol, the small, eagle-faced aristocrat quickly realized that Mussolini for all his power was still as rough as Romagna's unleavened *piada* bread. At forty he had never owned a morning coat, tails or pumps; as editor of *Il Popolo* his wardrobe consisted of a few ill-pressed ready-made suits. His sole concessions to fashion were his spats and the battered bowler-hat he clung to like a talisman. 'There seem to be only three of us left who wear them' he confided to Rachele, a Laurel and Hardy fan like himself, 'me, Stanlio and Ollio.'

To Barone-Russo's well-bred horror, the Duce one day arrived at Palazzo Chigi wearing a green plaid suit, barred in red like a horse blanket, newly-ordered from a Rome tailor. 'What a beautiful suit for a visit to Scotland, Excellency,' he was quick to enthuse. 'Are you off there now?' Mussolini was as quick to take the point; the plaid was seen no more.

During their brief visit to the British Prime Minister Bonar Law in December 1922 Barone-Russo showed equal presence of mind. As the presidential train steamed into Victoria Station, the diplomat realized that Mussolini was again brandishing the black truncheon-like stick with which he had greeted Curzon at Lausanne. 'On your first official visit to a foreign capital,' Barone-Russo begged, deftly twitching the stick from the Duce's grasp, 'will you allow me to keep this as a souvenir?'

For the most part Mussolini took this grooming good-humouredly. All at sea among jewelled studs and stiff collars, he was sensitive enough to want to shine in an unfamiliar world. In all his life he had never even learned to shave himself; in the early days of their marriage, Rachele had done the job for fifty lire a month. Now he listened attentively while Barone-Russo laid down the law. He must stop wearing spats with a tail-coat. At banquets he must not tuck his napkin into his shirt-front, and he must never water his wine or dunk his bread in it.

It was Lady Sybil Graham, the British Ambassador's wife, who became Mussolini's most valued mentor. As guest of honour at an early Embassy banquet he occupied the traditional place beside his hostess. 'Watch every move she makes,' Barone-Russo counselled the Duce in advance. 'Use the same spoon, the same fork, the same knife as she does.' Then while he and the diplomats sweated, Mussolini did his valiant best through eight interminable courses. A perfect hostess, Lady Sybil picked up each knife and fork so precisely Mussolini could not miss his cue – though at first, seeing bouillon served in cups, a puzzled frown crossed his brow. Then, following her lead, he picked up his spoon, later setting it aside to lift his cup and sip – just as she did.

At the close of the evening, as he kissed her hand, Mussolini smiled broadly and confided: 'I did not know the English drank their soup like beer.'

And there were many such times when he showed himself for what he was: a baffled peasant playing Premier, grappling with an alien world. Money was a dark mystery to him all his life; to see himself and his secretary through a two-week trip, he would trustingly take 100 lire – then worth around £4. Once, when *Il Popolo* had need of a loan to tide it over difficulties, sub-editor Luigi Freddi interviewed the bankers and explained that all would be well if Mussolini signed an IOU. Baffled, the thirty-nine-year-old editor asked him: 'What's an IOU?'

Months later, when the overdraft was repaid, Rachele found her husband beside himself with rage. 'They're robbers,' he shouted, brandishing his bank statement. 'They've robbed me of 30,000 lire.' More versed in the mysteries of finance, Rachele had to explain gently that when banks loaned money it was customary to charge interest.

To Cirillo Tambara, it seemed that the Duce made a herculean attempt to understand. Soon after, on a motoring trip near Lake Como, a wandering friar begged him for alms. Solemnly, not finding a lira in his purse, Mussolini presented him with an IOU.

Superstition ruled his days; he had a pagan's true dread of hunchbacks, cripples, open umbrellas and bearded men. His new red Alfa-Romeo two-seater sported giant green shamrocks on either side of its bonnet. From Padua, Cirillo Tambara had hastily ordered six vest-pocket statues of St Anthony, patron saint of healing – one for each of the Duce's new suits. It was Mussolini's infallible nostrum against ill-health, and he feared to take a step without one.

It wasn't a weakness that could be kept in the family. At Palazzo Chigi, Mussolini's chief usher, the plump rosy-faced Quinto Navarra, had orders to rip all unlucky dates – 13 and 17 – from the desk calendar in advance. No military man could ever enter the Duce's office before noon. And no Palazzo Chigi official ever forgot the day in 1923 when Mussolini read for the first time of the opening of King Tutankh-Amen's tomb and the chain of ill-luck that had pursued its excavators.

Stored in the room below his office was a newly-arrived Egyptian mummy, a recent gift from an admirer. At once, his voice made high by apprehension, Mussolini lunged for the telephone, issuing a stream of near-hysterical orders to ushers and custodians. Though it was already late evening, he demanded action within the hour – refusing even to quit his desk until the ill-fated sarcophagus had been moved to a museum.

His feelings for women were as unbridled. In vain General Emilio de Bono, his new Director-General of Public Security, urged more discretion – for though Rachele and the children remained behind in the Milan apartment, most Romans knew of Mussolini's furtive ascents of the Grand Hotel's service stairway, where Margherita Sarfatti was a weekly visitor. And Margherita was only one among many. Often chauffeur Boratto drove him to discreet addresses all over Rome; at other times women came to his gloomy red-and-black bedroom at Via Rasella, to be hurled bodily on to the floor or the window-seat by the inflamed Duce. All his life, like a stag in the rutting season, he had this constant need to re-assert his virility, and he rarely took time to remove either his trousers or his shoes.

'A man should have a little engine to wind up in his back,' he confided to Boratto. 'That's the only way he could manage to satisfy them all.'

Yet his passion for privacy was almost pathological. No woman ever spent a night at his apartment – 'afraid,' said Margherita Sarfatti, 'that they'd laugh because he wears a nightshirt.' In office days, at *Il Popolo* parties, he had always stood scowling, apart from the crowd, emptying his glass in one decisive gulp. Once, learning that his Milan apartment had been burgled, he moved straight to another, refusing ever to set foot again on territory a stranger had violated.

His voice, low-pitched and confidential when talking man-to-man, took on a harsh imperious timbre – the voice of the Duce, with right finger stabbing magisterially – if another joined the group. Apart from Arnaldo, he had no men friends for his shyness made him almost boorish. Once, when his Via Rasella landlord, Baron Fassini, invited him for a weekend at his seaside villa, Mussolini greeted with blank astonishment Tambara's announcement that dinner was ready and the Baron awaited him.

'Well, who's he waiting for?' he demanded dourly through his bedroom door, 'I'm eating on my own.'

But by 1924, to the mounting dismay of Fascist hard-liners, the Duce, although a lone wolf to the last, was bent on one alliance which they saw as a betrayal of all that the March on Rome had symbolized.

'There is only one way,' he told the astonished Socialist journalist Carlo Silverstri, 'in which to save Italy – by collaboration with all parties, above all, with the Socialists.'

The word passed through the bar of the Chamber like wildfire: trouble was afoot. Hastily the deputies began scrambling from the red morocco-covered sofas, gulping down the heeltaps of their dry white wine. At this first session of the newly-elected Chamber, one sentence was enough to galvanize the men of all parties into action: 'Hurry, there's going to be fireworks – Matteotti's speaking.'

As the latecomers eased through the double swing-doors flanking the President of the Chamber's rostrum, sunlight blazed through the domed glass roof to illumine an astonishing scene. Around the vast horseshoe of crimson leather-padded seats ringing Bernini's seventeenth-century hall, more than five hundred deputies kept up a strident chorus of boos, jeers and whistles. To the left, on a raised dais below the President, the object of their wrath, the Socialist deputy for Rovigo, Giacomo Matteotti, waited tensely for a lull in the riot. To the right, a wall clock and calendar marked a melancholy milestone in parliamentary history: 4 p.m. 30 May, 1924.

For the first time Matteotti's high metallic voice became audible: 'Against the validity of this election, we present this pure and simple objection – that the . . . government, nominally with a majority of over four million . . . did *not* obtain these votes, either in fact or freely.'

At once an angry roar like a mountain storm filled the Chamber. Steadily, rhythmically, the Fascist deputies were banging their desk-flaps, a classic sign of disapprobation. Amid the tumult, some glanced briefly at Premier Benito Mussolini, but as always in such moments of crisis, he gave no outward sign. Motionless, imperturbable, he leaned a face like a death-mask on his hands.

Then, the insistent jangling of President Enrico de Nicola's hand-bell stilled the voices to a discontented rumble, and again Matteotti returned to the attack.

For five years, thirty-nine-year-old Giacomo Matteotti had been the impenitent gadfly of the Fascist Party. The son of wealthy land-owners, yet a convinced Socialist from his teens, he had swiftly taught the Fascists to fear his cold, analytic brain; time and again they had tried to silence his devastating oratory. In Palermo, where the restaurateurs had feared Fascist reprisals if they served him, Matteotti had shrugged and gone hungry. In Ferrara, disdaining a *carabinieri* escort, he had left town besmeared with coal-dust and spittle. Even when kidnapped in his native Rovigo and tortured with a lighted candle up his rectum, Matteotti proved invincible.

Within days the man colleagues nicknamed 'The Tempest' was back at Palazzo Montecitorio, the seat of the Chamber, taking the stairs two at a time en route to the library, the silver pencil that dangled on a chain from his buttonhole poised to annotate more damning facts against Fascism.

And this afternoon, fellow Socialists noted, that pencil had been working overtime on the election results just past. Eight weeks earlier, on 6 April, in the first nation-wide election since the March on Rome, the Fascists had benefited richly from Mussolini's new electoral law, designed to assure them a strong working majority. Whichever party polled a plurality – at least twenty-five per cent of the total vote – gained a bonus of two-thirds of the seats in the Chamber. Now, with votes said to total 4,500,000 against the opposition's 3,000,000, the Fascists claimed sixty-four per cent of the popular vote – and 374 seats in the new Chamber. But, with all the oratory at his command, Matteotti was challenging this verdict.

Out of 100 Unitarian Socialist candidates, he charged, sixty had been debarred by Fascist musclemen from canvassing their own districts. One candidate had been gunned down in his own parlour for daring to run for office at all; the first fifteen voters at one polling station, refusing to vote the Fascist ticket, had been thrashed within an inch of their lives. The destruction of Socialist premises had totalled millions of lire. 'No Italian voter was free to decide according to his own will,' Matteotti's voice rang out. 'The Premier had entrusted the custody of the booths to the Fascist militiamen.'

Pandemonium broke loose. On the Fascist benches, deputies rose to shake papers, briefcases, and above all, fists, at the slim, grey-eyed young deputy. 'You discredit the Chamber,' a Fascist shouted and Matteotti riposted: 'Then you should dissolve the Chamber!' The angry tones of Roberto ('The Slap-Giver') Farinacci were heard for the first time. 'Wind it up or we'll do what we haven't done yet,' he hectored. 'You would only be plying your trade,' was Matteotti's cool reply.

An enraged bull stung by the banderillos, Farinacci bellowed: 'We'll make you change your tune!'

Notes in hand, pale but composed, Matteotti waited resolutely, arms folded, for the tumult to subside. 'We are in power and we mean to stay there,' a Fascist taunted him. Patiently Matteotti told the Chamber: 'I am exposing facts, which should not provoke noise – either the facts are true or you must prove them false.'

Still Mussolini sat silent and immobile. His carefully-laid plans to bring about a merger with the Socialists – even to dissolving his Militia and Grand Council at one bold stroke – were crumbling in ruins. The hard-line Fascists had disavowed his Pact of Pacification in 1921, but Mussolini had never lost sight of this ultimate goal – even though two left-wingers he had chosen for high office, in October 1922, Luigi Einaudi and Luigi Albertini, had refused point blank. To govern effectively, Mussolini knew he had need of the Socialists – but after a speech like Matteotti's, how could he persuade the party's extremists to accept them in the Cabinet? Nor would the Socialists, with fresh evidence of Fascism's reign of terror, prove less intransigent.

The President's hand-bell jangled furiously; in isolated corners of the Chamber Fascists and Socialists were locked in combat on the floor, punching, gouging, choking. 'Honourable colleagues, I deplore what is taking place,' De Nicola reproved them, and as if he feared the bloody momentum of this meeting, he begged Matteotti: 'Conclude, do not provoke disturbances.'

But the granite-willed Matteotti was determined to be heard. 'What kind of way of doing things is this?' he rebuked the President in turn. 'You should defend my right to speak.' When De Nicola bade him speak but speak prudently, Matteotti flashed back: 'I shall speak neither prudently nor imprudently, but according to parliamentary law.'

And speak he did, though such was the mood of the Chamber that the stenographers at the central table were hard put to it to distinguish his words from the babel that threatened to swamp them. What the meticulous Matteotti had estimated as a twenty-five-minute speech took fully ninety minutes to deliver. But for every abuse cited he gave chapter and verse, and his charges held the relentless ring of truth. Socialist printing presses had been destroyed, their electoral publicity burned – but there had been graver abuses yet.

Youngsters of twenty had voted in the names of sixty-year-olds. Registration cards had been seized from people afraid to vote and used ten, even twenty, times by Fascist tools voting under different names. He could prove it, Matteotti affirmed – in many instances the handwriting was identical.

Across the hall, the shouts volleyed back and forth, rising in menace and intensity. 'Wind it up,' snarled railway commissioner Edoardo Torre. 'Must we tolerate his insults?' Rising to his feet, another deputy proclaimed: 'I have been an action squad man, and I intend to quell your spirits!' As if on cue, brawny-armed Fascists rose from their benches, heading for the speaker's dais. Unperturbed, Matteotti concluded: 'For these reasons, we ask a total cancellation of the election.'

As he returned to the Socialist benches, he told fellow deputy Emilio Lussu: 'I've said what I had to say – now I don't care about anything else.' Almost as if shocked at his own temerity, he smiled and told deputy Antonio Priolo: 'I have made my speech – now you can prepare my funeral oration.'

It seemed a timely comment. Those present that day never forgot how Mussolini, his face suffused with rage, strode savagely from the Chamber, across Montecitorio's marble foyer, bound for Palazzo Chigi. He could see no way out of the impasse now; to the end he would be bound to men like Farinacci and Tamburini, the bully-boys who had brought him to power, becoming, like Frankenstein, the victim of his own creation. As he swung into Palazzo Chigi, he bumped into Giovanni Marinelli, the Party's forty-five-year-old Administrative Secretary, a bearded, rancorous man who squinted at life through gold pince-nez.

In the manner of Henry II of England venting his spleen against Archbishop Thomas Becket, Mussolini burst out: 'If you weren't a bunch of cowards, no man would have dared to deliver a speech like that.' It was the kind of bluster that he habitually threw out a dozen times a day – and as quickly forgot.

This time the Duce had cried wolf too often.

Hands clasped behind his head, the man stretched out on the sofa gazed with unseeing eyes at the ceiling. At this moment, 4 p.m. 10 June 1924, his ten-roomed apartment at 40, Via Pisanelli, in a quiet side-street near the Tiber Embankment, was silent and shuttered. His three children. Gian Carlo, six, Gian Matteo, three, and Isabella, one, were enjoying the siesta that millions of Romans called the '*penichella*'. But this afternoon neither Giacomo Matteotti nor his wife, the soft-voiced, blue-eyed Velia, could relax enough to sleep.

'I know,' said Matteotti suddenly, 'that the Fascists must be preparing something. Perhaps I should take the children to the Borghese Gardens.' 'Then don't take your worries too,' Velia counselled him sagely. But after a moment's reflection, Matteotti dismissed the idea: if trouble threatened, the children would be safer inside the flat. And today though the Chamber was closed there was work in the library and at the dingy tumbledown party offices in Piazza di Spagna, where he had worked all the past winter in his topcoat to combat the cold.

It was just one of Giacomo's many aspects that Velia Matteotti loved. The wealthy landowner, whose fight to better the share-croppers' lot had become his life and who freely gave half his deputy's income to a home for orphan girls. The quiet ascetic, who hated strikes, parades and demagoguery in his own party as much as he hated Fascism. The do-it-today man, biting in his criticism of 'armchair Socialists' who wouldn't take to the streets as he did to post bills and sell newsheets. The proud father, who inside the four walls of Via Pisanelli thought only in terms of piggyback rides and wide-open windows to ensure his children fresh air, hasten-ing to the chemist's in a panic if one of them so much as bruised a knee.

A quarter of an hour later Matteotti swung purposefully from the divan and began to dress: white shirt and soft collar, white striped tie, white suède shoes with black socks. As he shrugged into his elegant, grey-patterned jacket, Velia noted with affectionate resig-nation that as usual the pockets were stuffed to bursting with scrap paper for taking notes.

On this sultry afternoon, when the thermometer trembled in the eighties, few others felt so energetic. A hundred yards south of Via Pisanelli company secretary Giovanni Cavanna was relaxed on the terrace of his villa on Via Scialoja, within sight of the sluggish yellow Tiber. Idly he noticed a black six-seater Lancia limousine parked on the corner, pointed towards the embankment. Closer to Matteotti's block, the concierge at 12, Via Mancini, Domenico Villarini, noted it too. On impulse with memories of a recent robbery, he jotted down the licence number: 55 12169.

In his third-floor apartment Giacomo Matteotti was kissing his wife goodbye. Recently, conscious that at times he was being followed, he had often drawn the danger away from home by staying the night with friends. But tonight, he told Velia, it would be like old times: punctually at 8 p.m. he'd be home for dinner and to kiss the children good night. As token of his good intentions he showed her the only cash he had in hand: ten lire. From the landing window, Velia watched as he left the apartment block, striding with his quick elastic step along

Via Mancini to the Tiber Embankment. In the shade of a giant acacia tree, duty *carabiniere* Gavino Lupino watched too, but he had no orders to follow the deputy, merely to guard his house.

At the corner of the street, Matteotti turned, waving goodbye to his wife. He walked towards the waiting Lancia.

The driver of the car, Amerigo Dumini, was just then preparing to call it a day. Thirty years old, a dark St Louis-born hoodlum, he had thrived on violence all his life: in his adopted town of Florence, hundreds gave the widest of berths to the man whose grey, hostile eyes were always alert for insults and whose chilling introduction was 'Dumini – eleven homicides.' Slumped in the car behind him were five recruits from the scum of Fascism: Augusto Malacria, convicted embezzler; Filippo Panzeri; Amleto Poveromo, forty-one-year-old Milan butcher, jailed for armed robbery; Giuseppe Viola, twenty-seven, epileptic, fake bankrupt and wartime deserter; and Albino Volpi, thirty-five, cabinet-maker, jailbird and World War One underwater commando, who night after night had swum naked and painted green across the River Piave, a knife in his teeth, to rip up the bellies of Austrian sentries.

Among the six, only Dumini knew Matteotti's movements well. For days he had dogged the apartment building, ever since his assignment to Paris, as a Fascist undercover agent, had convinced him that Matteotti's Unitarian Socialist Party was master-minding the systematic assassination of Italian Fascists – among them the Paris bureau chief, Nicola Bonservizi. Following his report, Administrative Secretary Giovanni Marinelli had empowered Dumini and his fellow thugs to abduct Matteotti and force a confession from him.

Unknown to Dumini, Marinelli had other reasons for wanting Matteotti's confession. Rumour had it that the Deputy had secured proof that the Sinclair Oil Company of New Jersey was paying out a 150 million lire sweetener to secure Italian oil concessions – a pay-off to be split between Minister of Works Gabriele Carnazza, Minister of Economics, Mario Orso Corbino, Under-Secretary for Home Affairs, Aldo Finzi, Cesare Rossi, Mussolini's Press Secretary, and Filippo Filippelli, editor of *Corriere Italiano*. Proof that Matteotti, the soul of probity, had connived at assassinations would be a powerful deterrent if he tried to make public that accusation. On 30 May, Mussolini's anger with Matteotti had seemed to Marinelli the green light he needed.

But today, as Dumini was later to reveal, had been only a pre-

liminary probe: he had not even known that Matteotti was at home.
At lunchtime they had glutted themselves on expenses at Scarpone's
restaurant outside Porta San Pancrazio – as an afterthought Dumini
realized that not all his band even knew what Matteotti looked like,
let alone where he lived. Soon after 4 p.m. he had taken each of them
singly to point out the apartment block, explaining that Matteotti
normally travelled to the Chamber on the No. 15 tram from Via
Flaminia. Then Giuseppe Viola, who suffered from stomach ulcers,
complained that he had urgent need of a chemist.

A hot wind stirred the plane trees by the Tiber, a bell tolled from
Santa Maria del Popolo, and Dumini gunned the Lancia forward. It
was then that Volpi, beside him, shouted 'Stop!' so suddenly he
thought he must have hit a dog. 'There's Matteotti,' Volpi whooped,
and the rest was spontaneous violence, with hatred sweeping aside all
reason: this was the man who had planned the slaying of the Parisian
Fascists. Beside himself, Dumini rasped: 'Grab the swine!'

Then Volpi, the thick-set killer, was down and running, and
Malacria followed. Momentarily, as he reversed the Lancia back
along the embankment, Dumini's mirror showed only a blur of
grappling forms – but others had a ringside view. Eliseo di Leo, a
young insurance clerk, swimming in the Tiber with friends, blinked
wetly upwards to see a tall man framed at the top of the flight of steps
leading to the river. At this moment two men jumped him, jack-
knifing him with a vicious blow in the stomach. Curiously, as they
vanished from sight, Di Leo decided that three friends were playing a
joke.

Fourteen-year-old Renato Bianchini, on the way to a friend's
house, knew horror when he saw it: four men carrying a screaming,
struggling fifth horizontally, two by the head, two by the feet, with
the Lancia backing up steadily, inexorably, along the gutter. A tall,
moustached man in light gaberdine – Panzeri – stood poised on the
running-board. As the car drew level and a door swung open, all
four made a superhuman effort to fling the writhing deputy bodily into
the back – then a flailing kick from Matteotti's white suède shoe
splintered the window glass. Incensed, the thuggish Volpi sprang
forward pounding with his clenched fists until Poveromo urged,
'Enough, people are coming!'

But they came too late. From his first-floor balcony, company
secretary Giovanni Cavanna had seen the struggle, but at first hung
back. Perhaps it was a police arrest – or a movie company on location?
As Matteotti's cries redoubled he ran downstairs – in time to see

Panzeri leap from the running-board and double down a side-street as the car moved off.

Heading for Ponte Milvio, the city's northernmost bridge, the Lancia streaked like a black bullet up the Tiber Embankment, veering crazily across the tramlines. In the dusty glaring afternoon, the few passers-by stared curiously; the road ahead lay empty, and none could then realize that Dumini's harsh, persistent klaxoning was to drown the piercing screams from the rear. Suddenly an oval red leather disc sailed from a side window: Matteotti's parliamentary identity card, a last vain hope of attracting attention.

Inside the swaying car, men gouged, lunged and pounded in ungovernable fury. Afterwards Amleto Poveromo recalled as little as anyone; in a desperate attempt to overcome his tormentors, Matteotti had flung himself clean on top of him pinning him against the black leather seat-covering. The only man to take little part in the struggle was Giuseppe Viola; his ulcer was paining him and he was crouched back on the strapontin, hugging his stomach at the moment when Matteotti's heel, lashing backwards, caught him in the genitals. Blind with pain, he lurched from his seat, driving downwards with his dagger. Still stifled by Matteotti's weight, Poveromo sensed suddenly that warm blood was soaking his right trouser-leg.

At the wheel, Amerigo Dumini didn't know what was happening. A stranger to Rome, he was driving blindly, and the familiar central streets had long since receded; he was perhaps six miles from Ponte Milvio, and ripening wheatfields and spinneys were gliding past. An urgent pounding on the glass partition brought him to a halt. He descended to open the rear door, then recoiled; a foot away from him Matteotti was hunched forward, vomiting blood. 'Look here, Amerigo,' he recalled Malacria saying, 'he is very bad.' Dumini knew only that he wanted to retch. He did not realize that Matteotti's left carotid artery was severed; he was mesmerized by the car's interior, reeking of blood and sweat and excrement, the dry rattling in Matteotti's throat. 'We must find a fountain,' he stammered, 'he needs water.'

'It won't help,' said Malacria suddenly. 'He's dead.' For a moment there was only the heat and the silence, the crooning of doves in the oak-trees. Dumini was conscious of Volpi beside him. 'So we stuck him like a chicken,' the big man said, 'but he died bravely, eh?'

At midnight, the Galleria Colonna, across the street from Palazzo Chigi, was a place of whispering shadows. As thirty-seven-year-old Arturo Fasciolo made for the lonely halo of neon glowing outside the

Caffè Picarozzi he saw few passers-by and was grateful. As an ex-*Popolo d'Italia* man, now Mussolini's personal private secretary, Fasciolo nowadays cut his social round to a minimum – eating only in the obscurest *trattorie* to duck the crowds of cadgers and favour-seekers who swarmed like flies around the men of Mussolini's inner circle.

It was with mingled distaste and irritation that Fasciolo saw six men he knew well huddled at a corner table: Amerigo Dumini and his companions of the day. To avoid their company he took his milky coffee at the bar – but tonight he suddenly realized their habitual noisy arrogance had deserted them. On every face around the table he saw nothing but bewilderment, despair. Maliciously he teased them, 'Did you kill someone or something?' No one replied. As Fasciolo left the café, all six were staring into space unseeing, like men in shock.

But the secretary's words had broken the spell. Behind him in the Galleria he heard the urgent echo of footfalls. It was Albino Volpi, tugging at his sleeve. 'Look,' were his first words, 'we've killed Matteotti.' As Fasciolo stared aghast, Volpi hastened back inside the café to reappear with a slim leather briefcase. Drawing Fasciolo into the Galleria's darkest corner, he eased from the case two grisly tokens of that day's work: a segment of a car's leather seat-cover, 'crusted with dried blood like parchment', and the passport of Giacomo Matteotti. 'You can take it to Mussolini for us,' Volpi urged. To Fasciolo's angry expostulation, the big man threatened: 'You take it or we'll take it – to show that we've done what we should do.'

In broken sentences, Volpi blurted out the story. After Matteotti had died, he said, they had completely lost their heads. Lowering the blinds of the car they had driven for hours trying to establish a landmark. Once Dumini had turned all of them cold by stopping to ask a *carabiniere* the way. At a critical moment they had run out of petrol. Around 8 p.m., shaken by the realization that they had missed the way and were once again heading for Rome, Volpi had hit upon a thicket 100 yards from the road and decided they must inter Matteotti.

There, in the falling darkness, with only the car tools to aid them – a jack, a file, a monkey wrench – he and Malacria had scooped a hole around eight inches deep by two feet long, a grave so shallow that the body was doubled in two like a book. The location had been somewhere north of Rome – more than that Volpi didn't know.

Fasciolo was horrified, but his loyalty to his chief made one duty plain. To stop the assassins crossing the threshold of Palazzo

Chigi, he accepted the charge of Matteotti's passport. As he trudged home under the stars to his apartment, one thought tormented him above all: How would Mussolini react to this?

But by 8 a.m. on Wednesday, 11 June, Fasciolo found that his closely-hugged secret was already a twice-told story. Some time during that night, hoping to curry favour, Amerigo Dumini had already reported to Giovanni Marinelli – and Marinelli had in turn broken the news to Mussolini. When Fasciolo produced the passport, the Duce seemed angry and on edge, but in no way taken aback. 'Why did you take it?' he threw out irritably. 'Do you too know about this?' Locking the document in his desk, he bade Fasciolo tell no one.

These days, Mussolini was later to avow, were among the darkest in his life. One black-edged date was 13 June when the distraught Velia Matteotti, who had not slept for three days, besought an interview with him. Sweating, trembling visibly, Mussolini received her in an ante-room at Palazzo Montecitorio, along with his Under-Secretary for Home Affairs, Aldo Finzi – soon implicated as the man who had authorized Dumini's missions to France – and Giacomo Acerbo. Despite a nation-wide search, the deputy's whereabouts were still a mystery, but Velia begged that, alive or dead, her husband should be restored to her. To save the face of his regime, Mussolini was forced to lie: 'Signora, if I knew what had happened to your husband, I would give him back to you, dead or alive.'

His words carried no conviction. As Mussolini bade Acerbo escort her downstaris, Velia Matteotti proudly and contemptuously drew her mantle round her: 'Please do not trouble. Matteotti's widow can leave alone.'

Mussolini now saw himself as trapped finally and inexorably in a web of intrigue spun by his own followers. But he set out to discover the truth. Under pressure, Giovanni Marinelli admitted giving Dumini the direct order to seize the deputy – and that, such was his mania for red tape, signed expense-account receipts from each assassin reposed in his office safe. At the close of the session, Fasciolo recalls Marinelli staggering from Mussolini's office 'a finished man, weeping hysterically, his beard and pince-nez bedewed with tears'. Arrested within days, Marinelli still could not comprehend Mussolini's lack of gratitude for his attempt to save him from a Socialist coalition.

Throughout June, while police with tracker-dogs combed the countryside, a tidal wave of arrests swamped the headlines. On 12 June, Amerigo Dumini was seized at a shoeshine stand on Rome's

Central Station; on 17 June, Albino Volpi near the Swiss border; on 24 June, Giuseppe Viola; four days later, in Milan, the last of the assassins, Poveromo. But for his role in despatching Dumini to France, Aldo Finzi was also forced to resign his portfolio. Two men close to Dumini, both implicated in Matteotti's oil-concession exposure – Cesare Rossi, chief of Mussolini's Press Office, and editor Filippo Filippelli, who had lent the hired Lancia – also found themselves behind bars. On 16 June, white-bearded General Emilio de Bono, one of the chiefs of the March on Rome, had resigned as Director of Public Security.

One day later a soft-voiced Republican deputy, Eugenio Chiesa, levelling his pencil like an accusing finger, challenged Mussolini in the Chamber: 'You do not speak because you are an accomplice!' Promptly, Mussolini relinquished his own portfolio as Minister of Home Affairs.

That same evening, the Duce was a star guest at a banquet held for Ras Tafari of Abyssinia in the arras-hung Salon of the Corazzieri in the Palazzo del Quirinale. As he unfolded his napkin, an envelope fluttered to the damask cloth. By the light of blazing chandeliers, Mussolini read the note enclosed: 'You are Matteotti's murderer – prepare for the handcuffs.'

Beside him, King Vittorio Emanuele was scanning a note of his own. He glanced at Ras Tafari, but he had noticed nothing. Then, without comment, he passed the note to Mussolini.

It read: 'Your Majesty, Matteotti's murderer sits next to you – give him up to justice.'

The long silence puzzled Quinto Navarra. It was an hour or more since the usher had heard a sound from the Duce's office. On this warm June evening, the routine call for the evening papers and strong coffee had not come through. Now Navarra was worried. Tiptoeing to the connecting door, he peered cautiously round the jamb.

A second later, profoundly shocked, he closed it and withdrew. It pained him to see any man undergo such profound mental anguish. For what he had witnessed, by the light diffused by the yellow silk lampshade, was Benito Mussolini, kneeling on his office chair, relentlessly, terribly beating his head against its wooden uprights.

The suggestion of complicity in Matteotti's murder had struck the Duce with the directness of a fist in the face. Strangely naive, he could not accept that the moral responsibility for the crime was his –

and doubly so while he remained as Premier. On the phone to Milan, he protested his innocence to his brother Arnaldo, and the younger man rebuked him sharply: 'I've tried more than once to warn you about the people you have around you.' To a woman friend, Mussolini burst out: 'My worst enemies could not have done me as much harm as my friends.'

It seemed to Navarra that Mussolini was a broken man. Unable to face solid food at official banquets, he now gulped down raw eggs in his apartment, then waved away course after course. His suits hung on him like sacks; in less than three weeks he had lost twenty pounds.

In truth, Navarra was one of the few who remained close to him. By 10 a.m. on 27 June, which the Socialists chose as Matteotti's commemoration day, the waiting-rooms and corridors of Palazzo Chigi were as silent as Italy's streets and piazzas – and would remain thus for months to come. On the Tiber Embankment, 1000 Romans stood for ten minutes' silent homage beside a black cross marking the place of Matteotti's abduction, while white-clad school-children, led by nuns, chanted a requiem. Outside Milan Cathedral, the hushed solemnity of 5000 people seemed to blanket the city – as one bystander recalled it, 'the very wings of death passed over every man's soul.' In Venice, the gondolas creaked, unmanned, against the landing-stages; in Turin, people knelt bare-headed in the aisles of halted buses. Only in Cremona did life go on as usual – for the party's big stick Roberto Farinacci had decreed: 'Matteotti has been commemorated enough.'

Not all demonstrations were so passive – and defecting Fascists were in the vanguard. In Milan, hundreds contemptuously tossed their oval, red-white-and-green party badges, nicknamed 'The Bug', down the drains of the Galleria Vittorio Emanuele. In Turin and scores of other cities the Militia refused to mobilize. The Red Flag was borne at half-mast through the suburbs of Catania in Sicily. On Rome's streets, head-and-shoulder poster portraits of Mussolini were overnight adorned with drops of blood that oozed from the Duce's throat.

For Mussolini's myriad enemies, it was a chance in a million – yet to a man they failed to exploit it. On 13 June, 150 opposition deputies – Socialists, Republicans, some Liberals and Popular Party men, with only the Communists sitting tight – filed in silent protest from the Chamber, refusing to resume their seats until Matteotti's abductors were brought to justice. For Liberal leader Giovanni

Amendola and Socialist chief Filippo Turati, the issue was as clear
as noonday: if Mussolini did not resign of his own free will, the King
would step in to right the wrong.

At 8 a.m. on Saturday, 16 August, their hopes were justifiably
high. Three days earlier, a tattered jacket identified as Matteotti's
had been found by patrolling police in a culvert on the northbound
Via Flaminia – and an ambitious young police agent, Ovidio Caratelli,
grew curious. Aided by his father's hunting-dog, Trapani, he began
to comb the nearby tract of underbrush called the Quartarella, fourteen miles from Rome, on the left-hand side of the road heading
north. Suddenly Trapani began scrabbling frantically near the base
of an oak-tree. As the dry earth flew, the agent could clearly recognize
what he saw: a human scapula.

Time and heat and scavengers had done their work, but Rome
dentist Vincenzo Duca made positive identification of the gold crown
he had fitted months back. The cramped mound of death had yielded
up all that remained of Giacomo Matteotti.

Mussolini's enemies made ready. The Fascist regime was poised
on the rim of an abyss called fate – and the King must surely
act.

But to their chagrin, the King stood rooted like a mule on the
constitution. On 24 June, he pointed out, the Senate had given
Mussolini a solid vote of confidence – and in the Chamber, three
former Premiers, Giovanni Giolitti, Vittorio Emanuele Orlando and
Antonio Salandra, prominent Liberals who carried weight, all backed
Mussolini rather than align with the Socialists. And another implacable Socialist adversary, Queen Margherita, the Queen Mother,
had once again made plain her views. So intense was her admiration
for Mussolini that she had made him executor of her will – and
persuaded the King to bestow on him the Collar of Annunciation.
A decoration of ornate gold links, which the House of Savoy granted
only twenty times in six centuries, it now entitled the Duce to address
the King as 'Cousin'.

Now the Queen Mother counselled Mussolini in a personal note:
'Do not be so ridiculous as to think of resignation. I have calmed
the King.'

As always, Queen Margherita had prevailed – and the Militia's
new oath of loyalty, now extended to the King, helped to reassure
him. To the first deputation of Socialists who petitioned for Mussolini's dismissal, he made the symbolic gesture of covering his eyes and
stopping his ears: 'I am blind and deaf – my eyes and ears are the

Chamber and the Senate.' A deputation of war-disabled veterans fared as badly. After listening patiently to their proclamation, the taciturn little King, a master of the calculated non-sequitur, remarked to thin air: 'My daughter shot two quail this morning.'

The rebuff was so patent that as the delegates withdrew in confusion one man, crimson with embarrassment, was stammering: 'I love quail, Your Majesty – they are very good eating, fried with new peas.'

But despite support in high places, the Fascist hard-liners were mistrustful. To Party Secretary Francesco Giunta, it seemed that Mussolini, in the solitude of Palazzo Chigi, was still 'full of a grand passion to return to his Socialist friends'. Hadn't the Duce, three days before Matteotti's abduction, announced to the Chamber: 'The ability and good-will of all must be utilized'? Roberto Farinacci had the same suspicion; to him the sure solution was to wipe out 500 Socialists. To both men, and those of like persuasion, the appointment of the liberally-minded Luigi Federzoni as Minister of Home Affairs, with Dino Grandi as his Under-Secretary, spelt nothing but trouble.

After eighteen months in the wilderness as a Bologna lawyer following his opposition to the March on Rome, Grandi was fully convinced that Mussolini had played no part in Matteotti's murder – and had returned to pledge his loyalty at a time when many were deserting him.

The party's extremists soon saw their worst fears confirmed. On 20 December, after two weeks of backroom conferences with Federzoni and Grandi, Mussolini tossed a casual bombshell into the crowded Chamber of Deputies. The electoral law which had seen the Fascists romp home at the polls in April was to be amended – to pave the way for new elections on a non-proportional basis, akin to the British.

For the party's provincial bosses, it was the writing on the wall: a coalition government meant an end of personal action squads and the rule of the bludgeon. No longer would they rule their districts like private fiefs.

'I have created Fascism, I have reared it and I still hold it in my fist – always!' Mussolini boasted to a Padua congress. Then a handful of determined men set out to prove him wrong.

Towards noon on 31 December, 1924 sixty blackshirted provincial Militia chiefs tramped in grim silence through the frosty streets of Rome. Dwarfed by the towering column of Marcus Aurelius, they passed unchallenged into the deserted courtyard of Palazzo Chigi. As one, they scaled the marble staircase towards Mussolini's first-floor office.

It was a bluff worthy of the Duce himself. For most of the marchers, summoned urgently by wire from all over Italy, this was a routine ceremonial visit to bring New Year greetings to Mussolini – the brainwave of their leader and spokesman, Aldo Tarabella of Udine. Only Tarabella and twelve others knew the true purpose of the mission: to coerce Benito Mussolini once for all into a no-holds-barred dictatorship.

Brushing aside Quinto Navarra thirty-three of these men entered Mussolini's office. Unannounced they strode, not speaking, across the grained hardwood floor. At the far end of the room, against a backdrop of grey tapestries hung with battle-axes, Mussolini, just then in conference with Finance Minister Alberto de Stefani and Militia Chief General Gandolfo, raised his eyebrows in scowling interrogation. By way of introduction, Tarabella passed across the desk a defiant letter from Florence's Tullio Tamburini. In angry silence Mussolini took in its contents: impatient with marking time, Tamburini was that very day launching a swift series of purges against the city's anti-Fascists.

A snarling terrier of a man who weighed a mere six stone, Tarabella lost no time showing his teeth. 'We're tired of slowing down,' he told Mussolini savagely, 'the prisons are full of Fascists – they're putting Fascism on trial and you don't want to take the responsibility for the revolution.' Hemmed in on all sides, Mussolini asked desperately, 'But what do the action squads want? Nowadays we need to normalize things, nothing else.' An angry chorus of jeers greeted his words. Almost as if to himself, Mussolini burst out: 'The body they threw between my feet prevents me from walking.'

'What kind of a revolutionary chief are you,' Tarabella taunted him, 'to be frightened by a corpse? . . . You're bending over backwards to please the opposition – but you only succeed in postponing your own miserable end. You must make up your mind to shoot the chiefs of the opposition.'

Mussolini was furious. 'It is the assassins of Matteotti who should be shot,' he retorted, but Tarabella and the others were implacable: 'First one lot, then the other – just for good measure.' Sensing his weakness, his isolation, they closed in on him. As if to further press home the point, one man drove his dagger into Mussolini's polished rosewood desk, shouting, 'If you want to die, die, but we don't want to die!' 'That you've come here at all is seditious,' said Mussolini feebly, 'punishable by the firing squad.'

Tarabella looked down on him with thinly-veiled contempt. Only a day earlier, Mussolini had told one party boss present, Giovanni Passerone of Casale Monferrato: 'I'm ready to go.' Now Tarabella pointed out with cold logic that when all of them had carried out the March on Rome there had been no question of resignation – 'if we'd failed, the King's Procurator General would have charged us all with sedition.' 'I do not want to be imposed on,' Mussolini repeated petulantly. 'I will *not* be imposed on.' He glared round the circle, striving to simulate the man of iron, reading the same message from every man's eyes: contempt for a wavering leader, determination to go it alone, if need be.

'We're leaving now,' Tarabella told him, adding cruelly, deliberately, 'and we're slamming the door behind us.' Mussolini said nothing. Each man, he noted, dispensed with the courtesy of the Roman salute. In silence he watched a phalanx of shoulders retreating towards the door as purposefully as they had come.

It slammed behind the last man, as Tarabella had promised, clearly audible even above the boom of the time-gun marking noon from the Janiculum Hill. Both echoes fought for mastery, resounding through Palazzo Chigi like a knell.

4. 'If I Advance, Follow Me. . .'

January 1925 – May 1936

'Duce! Duce! Duce! Long live our Duce!'

From a thousand windows, the cries drifted downwards, with bouquets of carnations and dark red roses floating in their wake. But if the wild delirium of the crowds was music to his ears, Benito Mussolini gave no sign of it. Braced on his feet in the back of the scarlet Alfa-Romeo, clad in the grey-green tunic of an Honorary Corporal of the Militia, he gazed with out-thrust jaw at the seething crowds lining colonnaded Via della Indipendenza in Bologna, his hands propped arrogantly on his hips.

At the wheel, the city's party boss, shock-headed Leandro Arpinati, was cruising the Alfa little faster than a man could walk – helping, like a skilled stage director, to wring the utmost drama from these moments.

Six hours earlier, on what was now a routine day of Fascist pageantry, Mussolini had inaugurated Bologna's new Sports Stadium more in the style of a rodeo rider than a Premier – galloping furiously up a ramp on a snow-white horse, to check it inches away from the edge of an unfenced stone podium. Following this, he had made a characteristic whirlwind tour of party headquarters, the Militia barracks and a new gymnasium. Now at 5 p.m. on Sunday, 31 October, 1926, it was growing dark; the warm wind, swirling the dust through the streets, promised nothing but a storm.

The Duce was en route to the central station, and the show was almost over. To Leandro Arpinati, it seemed that the postcard-size stickers which had overnight appeared on Bologna's walls – 'The Duce is arriving but he won't depart' – had been a false alarm after all.

What happened next was always open to doubt. To Benito Mussolini, it seemed that 'a man of medium height' had suddenly broken through the police cordon to present him with a petition. Dino Grandi, now Mussolini's Under-Secretary for Foreign Affairs, riding beside Arpinati, saw instead 'a small man, standing stock-still, his arm outstretched'. For Arpinati, the man himself was a blur in the twilight, but as he rammed the Alfa forward, he alone saw what the stranger held: a military revolver with a lanyard.

Beside Mussolini, the Mayor of Bologna saw nothing at all, then realized with horror that a bullet had punctured his right sleeve – after ripping through the Duce's tunic and his ceremonial sash of the Order of Mauritius. For an eternal second, Mussolini stared un-moved at his assailant. Then the car jerked forward; the man dis-appeared 'in a vortex of hands and upraised daggers'.

Within the hour, a grim-faced Italo Balbo, Commandant-General of the Militia, was reporting to Mussolini at the central station. The would-be assassin, a fifteen-year-old boy named Anteo Zamboni, had died within seconds of the shot – stabbed fourteen times by the berserk crowd. Yet why should young Zamboni, who had put on long trousers for the first time that day and whose only known interest was football, have made an attempt on the Duce's life? Was he the un-witting pawn of the men responsible for the stickers – or had another man fired the shot and escaped scot-free in the confusion? Despite months of patient investigation, the police never knew.

Forty miles away, at Villa Carpena, Forlì, one of Mussolini's summer retreats, it was just another mellow autumn evening. Idling on the porch, the Duce's sons, Vittorio, ten, and Bruno, eight, were watching the cows plod home to their stalls, the moths swooping in the porchlight. Both boys would always recall the headlights of their father's car blazing abruptly through the dusk, and Mussolini, pale and tense, calling as the family came to greet him: 'Look here, under the light, Rachele, a few millimetres more . . .' They recalled, too, that their mother didn't even comment – merely fetched her work-basket after supper to repair both sash and tunic before returning them to the wardrobe.

Rachele had cause to be phlegmatic. Four times in twelve months, assassins had sought to destroy Benito Mussolini – and from these four attempts, with no more than a grazed nose and a torn jacket, he had thus far emerged unscathed. There seemed good reason for even his family to accept the Duce's dictum: 'It is useless for anyone to make an attempt on my life. It has been foretold that I shall not die a violent death.'

In the twenty-two months since the party bosses invaded his Palazzo Chigi office, thousands had found compelling reasons to want Mussolini dead. He had seen the fierce loyalties of his Fascists waning, and his fear proved a powerful spur. On 3 January, 1925, the coercion of the hard-liners was plain, as he assumed full responsibility before the Chamber of Deputies for the entire Matteotti scandal. 'If Fascism has been a criminal association,' he told them defiantly, 'then I am its leader,' and he now assumed a dictator's unfettered powers to deal with dissent. Moderates like Dino Grandi were banished from the Ministry of Home Affairs. The choice of a new Secretary-General – the roughneck Roberto Farinacci – spelt death to all hopes of compromise.

In January 1926, one stroke of Mussolini's pen abolished all political parties save the Fascists. Matteotti's assassins, put on trial in the small country town of Chieti, were awarded token six-year sentences – quashed by a convenient amnesty within two months. Eight new decrees – from the annulling of passports to closing the Civil Service to all but Fascists – swiftly changed Italy into a totalitarian state.

All suspect meeting places, including Masonic lodges, were closed down; sudden searches, arrests without warrants or bail, were the order of the day. Municipal elections became a thing of the past, along with the right to strike and the freedom of the Press. Under the new Mussolini, the Fascist bias now emerged in three-dimensional clarity: a nationalist élite of disciplined military automatons, who saw the needs of the state as paramount.

'Everything for the State, nothing outside the State, nothing above the State,' became their rallying-cry, and it was from the thousands whose rights were transgressed that these stop-at-nothing assassins were drawn.

On the face of it, the first assassin, Tito Zaniboni, onetime Socialist deputy and World War One hero, could hardly have missed. On 4 November, 1925, Italy's Armistice Day, crouched behind the shutters of Room 90 on the fifth floor of the Hotel Dragoni in Rome, the telescopic sights of his Männlicher were already trained on the Palazzo Chigi balcony, fifty yards away, where Mussolini was about to speak. But an informer among the gang of conspirators had succumbed to the lure of blood money. Seized before he ever fired a shot, Zaniboni was sentenced to thirty years in jail.

But where a rifle failed, a revolver might succeed. Thus reasoned the Honourable Violet Gibson, a deranged sixty-two-year-old Irish aristocrat, who thrust from the crowd lining the steps of the Campidoglio on 7 April, 1926, to open fire at point-blank range. By chance, the Duce, who had been opening an International Congress of Surgeons, was just then leering upwards at a pretty girl who had tossed him flowers from a balcony. Missing his brain by half an inch, the bullet ploughed through the bridge of his nose. Hustled back to the surgeons' congress, blood streaming down his shirt-front,

Mussolini rose to the occasion like a showman: 'Gentlemen – I have come to put myself in your professional hands!'

Bowler-hatted, his nose swathed in sticking-plaster, he posed for the photographers, beaming broadly, to announce that no fate more dire than deportation awaited Miss Gibson.

Gino Lucetti placed his faith in hand-grenades – two of them, to be tossed deftly through the side window of Mussolini's Lancia coupé as it slid through Porta Pia, en route to Palazzo Chigi. But at 10 a.m. on 11 September, 1926 – just seven weeks before the attempt at Bologna – Lucetti's luck ran out abruptly. Chauffeur Ercole Boratto, seeing him dart from behind a news-stand, tried first to ram him and then accelerated; unnerved, Lucetti aimed too high and the bomb bounced from the Lancia's roof, fifty yards out of range.

It was with reason that Mussolini now affected the third-person royal: 'The bullets pass – Mussolini remains.' Lucetti, too, was given a thirty-year jail sentence – but soon a new law prescribed the death penalty for those who even attempted Mussolini's life. His person was now as inviolate as the King's own.

On Rome's streets, posters bannered the words that the Duce had pronounced to an ecstatic crowd from his Palazzo Chigi balcony, following the Gibson attempt: 'If I advance, follow me; if I retreat, kill me; if I die, avenge me.'

Month by month the screw tightened. When forty-seven-year-old Arturo Bocchini, Prefect of Genoa, became national chief of police, Mussolini's Italy took on the true colours of a police state. Outwardly a florid connoisseur of lobster suppers and nymphets, Bocchini was a shrewd and ruthless cop – and a budget of £500,000 a year plus a task force of 12,000 special agents weighed further in his favour.

Under Bocchini, no pedestrian ever approached closer than 500 yards to Mussolini's Via Rasella apartment – and on the route from apartment block to office, all streets were closed twice daily. Each yard of railway track on which the Duce travelled was meticulously checked in advance by plain-clothes agents nicknamed 'the bats'. Before he opened a new building, agents splashed murkily through the sewers beneath, alert for time-bombs. When he drove helter-skelter for a swim at Rome's Lido, other agents, doing toilsome duty as hedgers and ditchers, lined every foot of the route.

Threat bred counterthreat on a frightening scale. Each night at ten, phones shrilled in police headquarters all over Italy, as station chiefs compared data on those seized on the streets without the now-mandatory identity cards – often 300 blameless citizens were rounded up in Rome alone. A dreaded network of 680 special agents harnessed thousands of caretakers, waiters and taxi-drivers as undercover men. Known as OVRA (*Organizzazione di Vigilanza e Repressione dell' Antifascismo*, Organisation for the Surveillance and Stamping-out of Anti-Fascism), they bugged telephones, reported on all who received mail from abroad, and even filed reports on the *graffiti* in public lavatories.

For anti-Fascists, classed in the new penal code along with procurers and drug-pushers, it was a bleak prospect. All anti-government parties and papers were now a dead letter. Soon even the jury system was replaced by Special Tribunals, headed by military judges, which denied the right to appeal or call defence witnesses. Those with luck and foresight – perhaps 10,000 in all – escaped, like Mussolini's one-time ally, Pietro Nenni, to France, the United States or England. But on those who stayed, sooner or later, 'La Madama smiled' – the underground code-name for the plight of 10,000 men and women caught by OVRA's spotlight, banished to compulsory residence on the barren Pontine and Lipari islands.

Strangely, it was the roistering Italo Balbo who had doubts as to the outcome of it all. Ferrara's shrewd boss noted that within weeks of his notorious dictatorship speech, Mussolini had collapsed, vomiting blood; for forty days he lay gravely ill with an advanced duodenal ulcer. 'We've forced him to become a dictator,' Balbo conceded, 'but Mussolini just isn't made of the right stuff.'

But to the world's newsmen, Mussolini was a custom-built tyrant, and they did not hesitate to tell him to his face. At Locarno, Switzerland, one month before the first assassination attempt, 200 journalists, covering a five-power boundary commission, vowed solemnly to boycott any press conference the Duce might hold. 'If they've a protest I have a waste-paper basket ready,' he sneered when he heard of it, yet to a man craving adulation the slight of being ignored was too much to bear. Unable to leave well alone, he strode belligerently through the foyer of the Palace Hotel to search out the ringleader, the *Daily Herald*'s George Slocombe.

It was a stinging encounter. Under a battery of curious glances, the Duce marched up to Slocombe to challenge him: 'Well – and how is Communism going?' Ignoring his outstretched hand, Slocombe replied coolly: 'I wouldn't know – because I'm not a Communist.' Out of countenance, Mussolini grated, 'Then perhaps I'm wrong,' turning abruptly on his heel. It was the heaven-sent cue for a diminutive Dutch journalist to pipe up, 'And that often happens to you.'

It was Mussolini's swan-song in free Europe. Thereafter, for twelve years he crossed no other frontiers, rooted firmly on Italian soil where, as a new slogan of the regime proclaimed stridently: 'Mussolini is always right.'

But though the Duce shunned the world, statesmen and savants beat a path to his door. From 1926 on, no man signed more pacts of amity than Foreign Minister Benito Mussolini – eight in four short years. Chief among his admirers was the monocled sixty-three-year-old Austen Chamberlain, British Foreign Secretary, who flattered the Duce and took him yachting to dissuade Italy from supporting France in any line hostile to Britain. And scores of others followed suit: to them Mussolini was the man of action in a world grown weary of words, a man who, by 1929, had granted 60,000 audiences and dealt with nearly two million pleas from ordinary citizens. He was the twentieth-century's new-risen Caesar, who had vanquished Bolshevism and made the trains run to time, and few of the 30,000 well-wishers who sent him Christmas cards each year had opportunity to probe beneath the surface.

His confiding, ingenuous manner, his voice, low-pitched and melodious, made most people take to him on sight. No less a being than Mahatma Gandhi lamented: 'Unfortunately, I am no superman like Mussolini.' The Archbishop of Canterbury saw him as 'the one giant figure in Europe'. Banker Otto Kahn declared: 'The world owes him a debt of gratitude.' 'He was,' avowed Thomas Edison, 'the greatest genius of the modern age.'

Even Winston Churchill, Chancellor of the Exchequer, visiting Mussolini at the beginning of 1927, was impressed after initial misgivings. Entering Palazzo Chigi with his bodyguard, Detective-Inspector Walter Thompson, Churchill was at first flabbergasted when two guards asked him to put out his cigar. To Thompson's astonishment, he meekly complied – but on entering Mussolini's office he noted angrily that the Duce remained seated. Promptly, his face darkening, Churchill pulled out his gold three-cigar case, selected a choice Romeo y Julieta, and took his time lighting it. Then, puffing with happy defiance, he advanced on Mussolini – who now, thoroughly taken aback, rose hastily to pump his hand.

The meeting over, Churchill told newsmen: 'If I were Italian, I am sure I would have been with you from beginning to end in your struggle against the bestial appetites of Leninism.'

Yet there was one admirer whom Mussolini resolutely shunned. About this time a plea reached his desk from Major Giuseppe Renzetti, head of the Italian Chamber of Commerce in Berlin. One Adolf Hitler, the thirty-seven-year-old leader of the National Socialist Party, then 49,000 strong, so profoundly admired the Duce that he sought the honour of a signed photograph.

In letters as large as a noonday headline, Mussolini scrawled across the memorandum: 'Request refused.'

Eighteen-year-old Rosetta Mancini tingled with excitement. Dinner invitations to her uncle's Rome apartment were always the most looked-for treat of the year – a chance for the daughter of Benito Mussolini's younger sister, Edwige, to don the yellow taffeta evening-gown that the Duce so admired and be complimented like a lady of fashion. But on this January night in 1929, she scented an air of something akin to conspiracy at Via Rasella. Dinner over, Mussolini had taken up his Stradivarius and was half-way through a rendering of 'Ramona' when Cesira Carocci, the quiet countrywoman who had replaced Cirillo Tambara as housekeeper, stole in.

Almost whispering, she announced, 'Those gentlemen are here again and want to see you' – and at once, like a guilty schoolboy, Mussolini put his finger to his lips, enjoining silence. 'Wait in my dressing-room,' he bade Rosetta, 'this may be a historic night.'

Now, though her ear was pressed to the connecting door, Rosetta heard nothing but a low rumble of voices – until at last they died away and an outer door slammed shut. But as Mussolini burst back into the dressing-room, Rosetta saw that his face was suddenly radiant.

Agog to share his secret, he pointed a mock-pompous finger like a school teacher. 'Do you know,' he asked, 'what the Roman question consists of?'

Rosetta knew all too well: It was a problem that had divided the nation for almost sixty years. When Italy seized Rome from its papal overlord in 1870, the temporal power of Pope Pius IX was ended. Until 1815, the sovereignty of the Popes had extended over 16,000 square miles, a vast tract of land stretching from the Tyrrhenian to the Adriatic: the Pope himself was as a King. But Pius IX, refusing all compensation or even to recognize the State, became a voluntary 'prisoner' within the Vatican Palace. From then on the 'Roman Question' – the deep schism between papacy and national government – had persisted with every Pope up to the 261st, the stocky seventy-two-year-old Achille Ratti, Pope Pius XI.

Delighted by his niece's pat reply, the Duce laughed aloud. 'Well,' he told her, 'I, Mussolini, am almost certain to succeed where statesmen like Nitti, Crispi and Orlando have failed. Just think – no longer need the Italians be divided between their duty as Catholics and their duty as citizens.'

Though few of his cabinet knew it, Mussolini had been working towards this moment for almost six years. On 19 January, 1923, he had met secretly for the first time with Cardinal Pietro Gasparri, the Vatican's seventy-one-year-old Secretary of State, in a Senator's flat in Via del Gesù – both men reaching the apartment by separate entrances and staircases. To the Presidential Under-Secretary, Giacomo Acerbo, Mussolini confided later: 'Before starting even preliminary conversations, they want to be sure of the stability of our government.' For his part, the Cardinal was impressed by Mussolini's readiness to accord the Pope temporal dominion over a sector of Rome without delay – but thought the Chamber of Deputies unlikely to approve it.

Mussolini saw this as no impediment: the Chamber would have to be changed. Still the Cardinal objected: to change the Chamber without changing the electoral law could only result in the electors returning the same Chamber. 'In that case,' Mussolini retorted, 'we shall just have to change the electoral law.'

But Mussolini had gone further. Over five years he had time and again sought to give the Vatican proof of his sincerity. Encouraged by his devout brother, Arnaldo, he had given orders to restore the crucifix to state schoolrooms and hospitals, whence the Risorgimento had banished it – and brought back compulsory religious instruction. Mass became an integral part of every public function. He had increased the stipends paid to the clergy out of public funds, plucked many priests from their parishes to serve as Militia chaplains, allotted three million lire for the repair of war-damaged churches and exempted neophytes from military service.

For Pius XI, other factors, too, stood high in the Duce's favour. A onetime Apostolic Nuncio to Warsaw, the soft-spoken, bespectacled Pontiff still recalled vividly the stark terror that had prevailed in August 1920 when the Bolsheviks were at the city gates. Though many diplomats fled, he himself had stayed to see the Red Army routed – but his revulsion against Bolshevism had not diminished with the years.

To Pius, Mussolini was the one sure safeguard against a Communist coup – and the moral reforms he had set in train only lent strength to that conviction. Within months of seizing power, the Duce had closed down fifty-three Rome brothels, abolished gambling houses, set up rescue-homes for over five thousand children and closed down 25,000 wine shops – barring the remainder to children under sixteen. At Christmas, 1925, as if to set his own house in order, he and Rachele had re-married in a religious ceremony.

As always, Mussolini's motives were inextricably mixed. To Arnaldo, the one man to whom he could always talk freely, he confessed a nostalgia for the childhood days when their mother had made the sign of the cross on their foreheads before tucking them in at night. An old yellowing prayer book of Rosa's, and her small gold chain bearing a medal of the Madonna which he wore round his neck, were two of his most treasured possessions; it was as if her thoughtful, sensitive nature at times tempered the dark violence of Alessandro. No priest-baiter like the bulk of his hierarchs, he had paid no more than lip-service to the early Fascist manifestos calling for the 'de-Vaticanization' of Italy, the confiscation of all church property. Yet he knew, too, that no regime in Italy could survive indefinitely without the Papacy's tacit approval – and no Premier had ever worked more doggedly than he to secure it.

For the most part, he told the admiring Rosetta, he himself had remained in the wings. Two men above all had thrashed out the twenty successive drafts of the Treaty and Concordat in 150 separate meetings: Professor Francesco Pacelli (brother of the future Pope Pius XII), the consistory's lawyer, and State plenipotentiary Domenico Barone. But earlier that month, following Barone's death, Mussolini himself had taken over negotiations; hence Pacelli's visits – which often lasted from nine each night until 1 a.m.

The Vatican had good reason to be pleased. Under the terms of the Lateran Treaty and Concordat – named after St John in Lateran, the Pope's episcopal church – the Government would pay some £10 million in cash and government bonds as indemnity for the papal states seized by the Risorgimento. Pius's absolute sovereignty over the 110-acre independent Vatican State was confirmed, and so was Roman Catholicism as Italy's official religion. From Mussolini's viewpoint, the Vatican stood pledged to recognize the kingdom of Italy, with Rome as its capital, in perpetuity and to remain outside all temporal disputes – though all bishops must henceforth be approved by the Fascists and swear an oath of loyalty to the state, the king and the government.

'Every cloud,' Mussolini told Rosetta that night, 'will soon be driven away.'

And sooner than even Rosetta had realized. Towards noon on Monday, 11 February, a long cortège of cars hissed through driving rain towards the Lateran Palace, residence of the Bishops of Rome for more than six centuries. In the vast Hall of the Missions, Cardinal Gasparri, after welcoming the frock-coated Mussolini and his ministers, signed the final agreements with a thick gold fountain-pen, then presented it, on the Pope's behalf, to the Duce. Flanked by the smiling Dino Grandi, Mussolini signed in turn.

Outside the rain fell remorselessly, drenching the oddly-contrasted crowd that had gathered before the Palace: seminarists from the local university and black-shirted Militiamen. As Mussolini emerged, the Angelus bell tolled from the Basilica of St John in Lateran; for incongruous moments, the solemn words of the seminarists' *Te Deum* mingled with high-pitched Fascist cries of 'Eja, eja, alalà.'

Next day, Tuesday, a spectacle unfolded that no Roman who witnessed it ever forgot. For the first time since 1870, the tricolour and the yellow-and-white Papal flag flew side by side along the streets. Into the great Basilica of St Peter, a procession marking the seventh anniversary of Pius XI's coronation wound for more than two hours: bearded, brown-clad Capuchins, canons, white-mitred bishops, scarlet-robed cardinals.

Then, as a cry of silver trumpets brought the buzz of *'Ecco il papa,'* a sunbeam slanted through the giant dome to fall athwart Pius himself clothed in his cope of gold, his *sedia gestatoria*, the golden sedan chair, borne by twelve brocade-clad servants, swaying gently towards the Altar of the Confession. Suddenly, unable to restrain themselves, 35,000 people broke into thunderous applause, and Pius, though he had begged for no demonstrations, could no longer hold his emotions in check. The lamps that shone before the tomb of the Apostle showed the tears streaming down his face.

All over Italy that night the people showed their gratitude. From the poorest Sicilian hamlets to the split-level mountain villages above Lake Como, they thronged to the churches for the simple service of thanksgiving. The day they had so long prayed for had dawned at last; the government had made its peace with the Holy Father.

Lit by the golden flames of a myriad candles, millions knelt in prayer for Pius XI, who had 'given back God to Italy, and Italy to

God', and for the man who, in his words, 'Providence has ordained that We should meet': Benito Mussolini.

They sipped dry Martinis – Martinis were all the rage that year – and traded small talk. Outside the Grand Hotel, a March wind blustered through Rome, tossing the white jets of the Esedra Fountain like ostrich feathers; women in mink wraps came grumbling into the cocktail bar, patting into shape the expensive hairstyles by Attilio or Alberto. She did not touch the peanuts, the potato chips and the olives; an actress had to watch her figure. He ate with gusto. He had never worried about his figure, only his hair; it was plastered down with macassar oil and in the office on slack afternoons he kept it in place with a net. He smiled at her mockingly, enjoying her suspense. The pianist rippled into a tune of that day, *'Addio, bella signora'*.

She was Mimy Aylmer, thirty, a star who had known brighter lights and bigger billing. He was Galeazzo Ciano, son of the World War One naval hero who had helped Mussolini climb to power, unsuccessful playwright, sub-editor and hanger-on of Bohemian coteries – now, at twenty-seven, a minor diplomat who had seen service in Rio and Buenos Aires, attached to the newly created Embassy to the Holy See.

Six years before, when her touring company passed through his native Leghorn, they had met and fallen in love. 'You know how sceptical I was,' he had written to her. 'Now I am changed – you have taught me to know love and life.' Another time: 'I am no longer the master of my destiny – only you control that.' She had been his *'Mimy cara'*, his *'Mimina'*; he was her *'Galy'*, her *'Pupi'*. When she came to Rome, they held hands under the table at Babington's Tea Rooms in the Piazza di Spagna, before returning to her flat on Via Veneto. With the clinical half of her mind she had always known him to be 'jealous, complicated, selfish'. Always the talk had been of Galeazzo's projects, Galeazzo's ambitions and future.

Now, out of the blue, in the spring of 1930, five years after a stormy parting, had come this chance meeting at the Grand. It was he who had suggested drinks, and steered the conversation round – deliberately, it seemed – to the recent marriage of the King's son Crown Prince Umberto, with Princess Maria-José of Belgium. Then, smiling maliciously, he told her: 'Soon I'm going to take the great step too.'

She was curious, and angry to find that she was curious. 'Anyone

I know?' she asked, but Galeazzo shook his head teasingly. 'I'll tell you this much,' he volunteered, 'it's a marriage that'll cause a sensation.'

Mimy tried to guess. It could hardly be anyone close to Vatican circles; the priest who had arrived to bless the offices of the new embassy had been outraged to find a card propped on Ciano's desk: 'Get Thee behind me, God.' A link with the Party seemed less likely still. As a student, Ciano had won fame of a sort for his loud-voiced comment: 'Can anyone tell me what these Fascists are? To me they look like a bunch of delinquents.' And once, as they walked in the Borghese Gardens, the Duce had passed in his car, but though the crowds snapped into the Roman salute, Galeazzo had strolled unconcernedly on. 'Don't you salute the chief?' Mimy asked, but the young man only shrugged his shoulders.

'Don't tell me,' she joked now, trying to put a brave face on it, 'that you're marrying a King's daughter?' But still Galeazzo only smiled mysteriously. 'Almost,' was all he would say, 'Almost.'

Flushed and proud in his well-tailored morning suit, the Duce faced his sons, Vittorio and Bruno. 'Boys,' he told them in heartfelt tones, 'resign yourselves to this – when you get married there won't be so much fuss. For me, today's ceremony has been enough.'

Towards 5 p.m. on Wednesday, 23 April, 1930, the youngsters knew how he felt. It was barely six months since the Mussolini family had been reunited in Rome after seven years of separation, when at last, thanks to the kindness of Prince Giovanni Torlonia, they had settled in his high-walled baroque mansion on Via Nomentana, until now often used by the Duce as a summer residence. Then had come the news that their twenty-year-old sister was marrying the diplomat, Galeazzo Ciano, after ten whirlwind weeks of courtship – a bombshell in itself. And finally the sumptuous wedding reception that the normally frugal Duce had given for his daughter had been one to beat the band.

Before sipping champagne and munching oyster patties, 4000 guests stood patiently in line for Mussolini to present Edda and her handsome young husband. Though he had expressly cabled Italy's Prefects to cut down on wedding presents, there had still been a wondrous assortment of gifts on view – a razor in gold and malachite from Pope Pius XI, a gold bracelet inset with precious stones from the King, Far Eastern silk pyjamas from Gabriele d'Annunzio. Overnight a forest of white flowers – gladioli, heliotrope, clove carnations – had filled the forty-roomed house, so many that Rachele later sent four truckloads to Rome's Campo Verano Cemetery.

As Mussolini, knitting his brows, tried vainly to hide his emotion, Rachele, neat in a black satin blouse and plain skirt, delighted bystanders by telling Ciano: 'She's trustworthy, loyal and vivacious – those are her good points. You might as well learn her bad ones too – she can't cook, she can't darn and she can't iron.'

On this soft afternoon of Roman spring, the Duce above all felt a profound relief. Until his family arrived in Rome, his visits home to Milan had been fleeting but Edda had always been the apple of his eye. He had helped to conquer her fear of frogs through handling them and to overcome vertigo by scaling tall trees; as a lively ten-year-old she had been his constant companion in the office of *Il Popolo*. 'To hurt her is like hurting myself,' he confessed once, and Rachele noted that whenever Edda was sentenced to an hour's standing in the corner, Benito promptly set the alarm-clock – more anxious than the youngster that the punishment should end.

Yet in her teens the auburn-haired tomboy, known to her family as 'the crazy filly', showed signs of inheriting more from her father than his jutting jaw and electric stare. At ten Edda had learned from Cirillo Tambara to drive the family car – and would hijack it for a joy-ride if she wasn't watched. Damning her headmistress as an 'old hag', she had run away from boarding-school in Florence. After her youthful crushes on a prize-fighter and a stationmaster, Mussolini had ordered his OVRA agents to check her every move.

Then, in the winter of 1929, a chance visit to the Ciano family box at the opera had brought her face to face with Galeazzo. Typically, her opening gambit had been: 'They say you're very intelligent – is it true?' Admiral Costanzo Ciano had frowned on the ripening friendship, fearing accusations of nepotism, but Mussolini was delighted that his daughter was at last settled. If Romans gossiped unkindly that Edda had made most of the running, what did it matter? 'Galeazzo,' he told one woman friend, 'is a good lad and intelligent. He'll make his way on his own account.'

That evening when Edda and Galeazzo had departed for their honeymoon on Capri, Mussolini, his eyes moist, told Rachele: 'We're getting old – soon enough we shall be grandparents.'

Outside office hours Mussolini, at forty-seven, was for the most part content to live an unpretentious life. It was Rachele who set the key-note. At first sight of the rambling mansion for which Mussolini paid Prince Torlonia a peppercorn rent of one lira per year, she commented drily: "There's plenty to do here – otherwise it'll be like living in a museum.' Unmoved by the thirty-five-acre park, adorned with palm-trees, tennis-courts and servants' lodges, she and her staff of five ran the mansion like any Romagna farmhouse, with Rachele, clad in clogs and sacking apron, feeding her chickens in the backyard. At sundown she sat peacefully on the steps, knitting, with Irma Morelli, the Romagna girl who tended Mussolini's clothes, or cut heaped plates of bread-and-butter for her sons after football – first anxiously patting their shirts to see if they had sweated too much.

Only twice in her life did Rachele ever visit her husband's office; as she explained to friends, 'I'm always busy with something on the stove.' And she paid only two visits to the Palazzo del Quirinale. 'If the Royal family leave me alone,' she told Vittorio once, 'they'll do me a big favour.'

Her willing self-effacement suited Mussolini admirably. 'Rachele's just right for me,' he frankly told his women friends. 'She's a good mother and she doesn't play president's wife.' For his family, which by the time of Edda's wedding included Romano, three, and one-year-old Anna Maria, he felt the deep-rooted loyalty of any Italian father – though he reserved the right to live much of his life like a middle-aged bachelor on the town. But nepotism was anathema to him, and from earliest years he counselled Romano: 'Travel third-class and pay for everything – even cinema seats.' When Vittorio, notoriously weak in mathematics, consistently scored high grades, his father rang the headmaster, raging: 'From now on, mark him according to his deserts – any more of this nonsense and I'll post you to Sardinia!'

On home ground, Rachele could more than hold her own. 'Just run the country,' she told Benito tersely when he poked his finger into any domestic pie, 'and I'll run this household.' Once during their father's absence, Vittorio and Bruno, stuffed with ill-digested Fascist jargon, ventured to criticize the first course at luncheon. 'Spaghetti and meat sauce for sons of the revolution?' they chorused. 'That's a dish for old bourgeoisie.' Impassive, Rachele asked them to repeat it – then let fly to such effect they retreated with cheeks smarting. 'It's all the fault of that imbecile father of yours,' she shouted angrily.

Despite the regime's repressive tenor, the Mussolinis' life at Villa Torlonia was as stable and happy as that of any middle-class household. If Papa, as the children called him, was up at 7 a.m. for a brisk canter round the grounds on his Arab horse, Fru-Fru, one of a stable of twelve presented by admirers, he was rarely back from the office before 1 p.m. – in time to incur the fine Rachele exacted from everyone late for meals. And for the overcharged Mussolini himself, lunch at the big round table in the second-floor dining-room was literally a three-minute affair which he timed with a stop-watch.

'We mustn't waste a minute of any day,' he hoodwinked himself, gulping down clear soup with pasta and wholemeal bread, but the truth was bleaker. Though the ulcer he contracted after Matteotti's abduction had healed, he was now never free from dyspepsia; each mealtime was an unlooked-for penance. Forbidden coffee and wine, he existed on a diet consisting almost wholly of fruit and vegetables. Yet even these caused acute discomfort; ten minutes after eating, he was braced against a chair-back, gasping with pain, knees raised and stomach extended.

But there were livelier moments. Sometimes, striking a note on the glass with his spaghetti-fork, Mussolini and the music-loving Bruno would launch into an operatic duet: '*Questo mar rosso*' from Puccini's *La Bohème*, or '*Secondate aurette amiche*' from Mozart's *Cosi Fan Tutte*. Still an adolescent at heart, he delighted in noisy kickabouts with his sons, jubilant if the football shattered a window-pane – until Rachele levied further fines of thirty lire per head. Wild animals still fascinated him as much as they did the boys, and pets on the household roster included a royal eagle, a falcon, a monkey, two gazelles, two tortoises and Pippo, the ginger Angora cat. For two months father and sons enjoyed a daily gambol with four lion cubs housed on the verandah until Rachele, past patience, packed them off to the zoo.

For family and staff, too, the nightly film-show was a must, though sometimes Mussolini nodded off. But any film with Wallace Beery or Greta Garbo kept him awake beyond his 10 p.m. bedtime, and he came alive on an instant if a Keystone Cops short flickered on to the screen. 'Good, good,' he would mutter, hugging himself ecstatically as the custard pies found their mark, while outside scores of firefly lights glowed among the tree trunks: the cigarettes of police agents, on all-night duty to guard his life, the one overt sign that this was not just another middle-class Roman family.

In most respects his thrift matched Rachele's own. By 1929 he broke the record of Pooh-Bah in *The Mikado*, with six ministerial posts – Home Affairs, Foreign Affairs, War, Navy, Aviation and Corporations – yet didn't always draw even his 40,000 lire as President. Most of what he had then put by – more than 500,000 lire (approximately £5500) in Government Bonds – came from his holdings in *Il Popolo* and from the $1600 a month paid him for a weekly feature by the Hearst Press. Apart from a weakness for bed linen changed thrice weekly, his life was as cost-conscious as on the day when buying Edda's cradle stripped him of his last fifteen lire.

This was Papa – the Mussolini the family knew. At Palazzo Venezia, his office since September 1929, a four-centuries-old yellowstone palace at the foot of the Capitol Hill, usher Quinto Navarra and the staff knew another Mussolini: the Duce. Here, in the second-floor Sala del Mappamondo, named from the ancient map of the universe displayed there, he was a ruler who kept the world at bay – at the far end of a room seventy feet long by thirty-nine feet wide, as remote and empty as an abandoned temple. To one man summoned there, the first impact was of 'two luminous eyes, a day's journey away behind a rosewood desk', for so vast was the room that Duce and staff communicated by means of signals. For example, arms widespread meant, 'Bring a newspaper.' A hand abruptly chopping the air spelt out: 'No more visitors.'

It was a sign he now made all too often – waving away not only supplicants but old and trusted collaborators. Even those who crossed his threshold stood like errant pupils before a headmaster; only visiting dignitaries rated chairs. Military men, even generals in their sixties, hurried across a crimson runner at the double, in the style of Mussolini's old Bersaglieri Regiment; the ex-lance-sergeant would show the top brass who was boss. Smoking was forbidden, and most men stood in foot-shifting silence while the Duce fiddled like a stage electrician with the panel of light switches on his desk; the less important the visitor, the more subdued the lighting. It took Italo Balbo, finding no chair to hand, to perch himself jauntily on the edge of the Duce's desk.

But Mussolini was meting out cavalier treatment to mightier men than generals: power and success were now like a fever in his blood. Two years earlier he had outraged King Vittorio Emanuele III, when his Grand Council demanded the right to approve any successor to the throne – a slight against the anti-Fascist Crown Prince Umberto. 'Rather than suffer this affront,' the King fumed, 'I should prefer to abdicate.' But to his mounting anger, fresh pinpricks followed – snubs he would not forget. By Mussolini's order, the 'Royal March' was now followed after eight bars by the Fascist anthem '*Giovinezza*'. And though newspapers still featured the royal name in normal type, DUCE in capital letters had become obligatory.

Not content to clash with the King, the Duce had crossed swords with Pope Pius XI himself. Only three months after the Lateran Treaty, he stressed the prior right of Fascism to educate Italy's children. 'Book and Musket, the Perfect Fascist,' was his mobilization order to the country's cradles, for even in kindergarten a six-year-old Son of the Wolf, as toddlers were known, was being prepared for the day eight years later when he would don the Fascist black shirt and drill with a musket. 'We have buried the temporal power of the Popes,' Mussolini taunted the Vatican, 'not resuscitated it.' Promptly Pius XI denounced the Duce as the Devil.

The battle was to rage almost three years before a compromise was reached. Determined that his should be the hand to mould the nation's young, the Duce had closed down 5000 Catholic Action clubs, a youth organization akin to the Boy Scouts, and Pius XI could not contain his wrath. He summoned the new Ambassador to the Holy See, Cesare Maria de Vecchi, to his study in the Vatican's main wing. 'Tell Mussolini,' he said peremptorily, 'that his methods disgust me.'

De Vecchi demurred. For an ambassador to say as much 'seemed excessive'.

'Then,' said the angry old pontiff, pushing his white skullcap over his right ear, the sure sign that he had reached boiling-point, 'tell him that he nauseates me – he makes me vomit.'

As always, it was Arnaldo who helped to heal the breach. From the day of Matteotti's abduction, he had worked untiringly to influence Benito – not only over the Lateran Treaty but to rid himself of the thugs and wire-pullers who were battening on the people. It was Arnaldo who had pressed for the dismissal of railway commissioner Edoardo Torre, proved guilty of peculation, and ousted Party Secretary Augusto Turati, flagellant and cocaine addict. Briefed to eliminate the party's 'dead wood', Turati's successor, Giovanni Guiriati, a retired general with a soldierly disdain for politics, expelled or fined fully 120,000 grafters and embezzlers.

And Arnaldo went further. In a scandal that rocked Milan he had toppled city boss Mario Giampaoli, one-time telegraph messenger-boy, who nightly lolled in a box at La Scala with street women decked out from party funds. The probe that followed purged 9000 of Giampaoli's racketeers from the party. Now Arnaldo urged his brother to make his peace with the Pope.

It was almost a dying request. Four days before the foggy Christmas of 1931, the forty-six-year-old Arnaldo, grieving for the death of a favourite son, suffered a fatal heart attack in a Milan taxi. Mussolini was stricken, for in all his life his brother was the one man he had loved and pinned his faith on. As he left the Church of San Marco after the funeral service, he turned sadly to Mario Ferraguti, a family friend.

'Now,' Mussolini conceded, 'I shall have to trust everybody.'

It was as if the Duce, who never ceased to boast of his cunning and animal instinct, reluctantly acknowledged in himself the innocence of the born victim.

But Arnaldo's counsel had borne fruit. In February 1932, on the third anniversary of the Lateran Treaty, Mussolini met Pope Pius XI for the first time – not, as many had feared, in a Fascist's black shirt but in a ceremonial tail-coat of black broadcloth trimmed with gold braid, and a boat-shaped ostrich-plumed hat. When Pius revealed that he had privately prayed for Arnaldo, Mussolini was profoundly moved. Both men agreed that the collaboration of Church and State was vital – and that the Catholic Action clubs, now under control of the Bishops, should remain in being.

To Edda, now in Shanghai, where Ciano had been appointed Consul-General, Mussolini could cable thankfully: 'All quiet on the Vatican front.'

But Pius, like other men who saw a potential for good in the Duce, still worried. It pained him that Mussolini had made public his refusal to kiss the Fisherman's Ring – and that he had only prayed before the tomb of the Prince of the Apostles once lurking photographers had been shooed from the nave. The Pope took advantage of the new-found amity to send a gentle caution through Cesare Maria de Vecchi.

'Tell Signor Mussolini in my name,' Pius said earnestly, 'that this half-deification of himself is unpleasant to me and harms him. He should not set himself up like this, half-way between Heaven and earth . . . get him to consider that there is only one Lord God.'

He ended meaningly: 'Sooner or later the people end by throwing down idols.'

As the embarrassed De Vecchi reported, Mussolini listened intently, half-smiling, half-incredulous. 'And tell me,' he asked finally, 'what do you think?' 'The same as the Pope,' said De Vecchi quietly.

Suddenly Mussolini was grave. 'Go straight to the Pope,' he commanded surprisingly, 'and tell him he is right.'

As De Vecchi left the sombre cavern of an office, he took fresh

heart. If Mussolini heeded the Pope's words, it was still not too late
for the dictator and his regime to alter course.

Then, on Sunday, 24 April, 1932, the Duce fell in love with Claretta
Petacci.

At a discreet fifteen miles an hour, the Belgium Imperia limousine
purred towards the seaside resort of Ostia. It was useless, thought
Claretta Petacci with wry affection, even to suggest that chauffeur
Saverio Coppola increase his speed. A onetime coachman, he handled
the Imperia as if it was a landau – hugging the very crown of the
road at a snail's pace. But luckily the Petaccis – twenty-year-old
Claretta, her mother, Giuseppina, and nine-year-old Myriam –
were in no hurry today. Along with Claretta's fiancé, the handsome
Air Force Lieutenant Riccardo Federici, they were en route to Ostia
for a Sunday afternoon jaunt.

Harsh and imperious, a horn sounded. Just in time, Coppola
swerved to the right. In a blinding cloud of dust a scarlet Alfa-Romeo
two-seater, a blue-bereted figure crouched at its wheel, carved past
them like an arrow. Hot in pursuit came a second car, packed with
armed men. Suddenly, with a cry of recognition, Claretta sprang to
her feet, waving wildly. 'The Duce!' she shouted, transfigured. 'The
Duce!'

Then, to their astonishment, the Olympian Mussolini began a
curious game of tag-on-wheels. Though the Alfa had shot ahead, it
now slowed down, its engine idling. Still in bottom gear, despite
Claretta's pleas, Coppola overtook – in time to see the Duce wave
back his escort. A hundred yards on, his klaxon sounded like a
cavalry charge; again Mussolini overtook, to halt 100 yards beyond.
Choked with dust, cursing madly, the police agents strove to keep the
Duce in sight as both cars joined in the frenzied mechanical romp.
Then, as if tiring of the sport, Mussolini streaked from sight.

For Claretta Petacci, it was a moment out of time. The daughter of
Dr Francesco Petacci, seventeen years a senior Vatican physician,
she had worshipped Mussolini all her life. As a romantic eight-year-
old, she had flung a stone at a workman who heard a donkey bray
and jeered, 'There speaks the Duce.' At ten, she had been soundly
slapped by her grandmother, a staunch Catholic, for cheering the
troops who marched on Rome. Nothing deterred her. At night she
slept with Mussolini's portrait beneath her pillow: at school it was
hidden inside her French dictionary. She sent schoolgirl poems to
Palazzo Venezia, bound in a tricolour ribbon; she memorized his

speeches. She wrote 'Duce' in the sand when she bathed and on the cakes she made in cookery class. Six years earlier, on 28 February, 1926, had come her bitterest disappointment: though she had sent a handwritten invitation well in advance Mussolini had failed to show up at her fourteenth birthday party.

Now Claretta seized her chance. As the Imperia purred on to Ostia's seafront, she saw the scarlet Alfa pulled in to the kerb. Not far off, under the overcast sky, stood Benito Mussolini. At once, despite her fiancé's objections, she decided: 'I'll go and introduce myself. I'll never have another chance like this.'

To Federici, the encounter was as banal as could be. The Duce signalled his police guard to let them through and Claretta introduced herself. Rigidly at attention, the Lieutenant heard Mussolini, whose sharp eyes had taken in their Vatican City numberplate, enquire after Dr Petacci. Emboldened, Claretta spoke of the schoolgirl poems she had sent him. Plainly it meant nothing to Mussolini, though for courtesy's sake he pretended to recall them. But this girl with her curly brown hair framed by a Florentine straw hat, her warm husky voice and deep blue eyes, intrigued him. Suddenly he said, 'You're trembling – are you cold?'

Claretta had to confess it. 'No, Duce, it's the emotion.'

A moment later Federici snapped into a salute and escorted her back to the car. The audience had lasted just five minutes. But time and again, in the days that followed, Claretta with shining eyes, relived those minutes. Both her father, forty-nine-year-old Dr Petacci, and her brother, twenty-two-year-old Marcello, listened tolerantly to her blow-by-blow account – how simple his bearing had been, how magnetic his eyes. Did they really think he had read her poems?

A few afternoons later the phone rang in the Petacci's ten-roomed apartment on Lungotevere Cenci, overlooking the Tiber. Myriam, answering, heard a man, deep-voiced but hesitant, ask for 'Signorina Clara'. A strangled pause, then he added: 'Say it is the gentleman from Ostia.'

'It's for you,' Myriam yelled to her sister. 'He says it's the gentleman from – ' All at once she knew who it was. Within earshot of the mouthpiece, the panic-stricken nine-year-old blurted out: 'Oh God! It's *him!*'

Neither Claretta nor her sister recalled too clearly the details of what followed. But the Duce had read Claretta's poems and wanted to see her. She was to ask both her mother's and fiancé's permission;

her mother was to accompany her as chaperone. At seven that night, clad in a sand-coloured woollen dress with flower-trimmed hat, Claretta for the first time climbed the long flight of stone stairs to the lofty, echoing Sala del Mappamondo. A long way off, immobile behind his desk in the gathering twilight, stood Mussolini.

Just as at their first meeting, his attitude was reserved, respectful. He asked about her tastes – she played the violin and the piano, with Chopin and Beethoven as favourites. She loved sport – riding, ski-ing, tennis – and drove a car. If her father hadn't opposed it, she would have taken her pilot's licence. She dabbled in oil painting. 'Is it true you weren't trembling because of the cold that windy day at Ostia?' he asked suddenly. Almost unwillingly, he admitted he had not slept for three nights, thinking of her. Abruptly he dismissed her: 'It's late – you must go.'

All told, in the next twelve months, Claretta was summoned a dozen times to the Palazzo. Each meeting lasted no more than fifteen minutes. They remained standing, within the stone window embrasures of the fifteenth-century palace, talking of books and music. Not once did Claretta analyse her feelings. It was enough to be with the man she had idolized since childhood.

Millions of Italians then felt as Claretta did. Mussolini had transformed Italy as no man had ever done – or so Party propagandists never tired of telling them. Within the span of ten years he had become a living legend, and to confound the sceptics his achievements were graven across the face of the land: 400 new bridges, including the two-and-a-quarter mile long Ponte della Libertà linking Venice to the mainland, 4000 miles of new roads, with 6000 highway workers to maintain them, giant aqueducts that brought life to arid regions like Apulia.

He was the man who set the twentieth-century pace: travellers by rail from Rome to Syracuse now made it in fifteen hours instead of thirty. From Calabria to the Swiss frontier, 600 telephone exchanges networked the country. He had conquered the oceans with mighty liners like the *Conte Rosso* and the *Roma*; by August 1933 the *Rex* would seize the coveted Atlantic Blue Riband with her four-and-a half day crossing. By July of the same year he was to master the air, when twenty-five planes under Minister of Aviation Italo Balbo, soon promoted Marshal of the Air Force, pioneered the historic Rome-Chicago flight.

He had waged war on crime. 'Five million hard-working Sicilians must no longer be held to ransom by a few hundred criminals,' he declared in his opening salvo in a five-year war against the Mafia, the brotherhood of evil whose rackets embraced everything from smuggling to murder-by-contract. Through the ruthless Prefect of Palermo, Cesare Mori, he struck at the Mafia everywhere from mountain strongholds to stinking back alleys – branding over a million head of cattle to foil rustlers, confiscating 34,000 weapons, arresting 400 key-*mafiosi*, among them Don Vito Cascio Ferro, who for thirty years had masterminded every crime from killing to robbing church alms boxes. Not until murders in Palermo province dropped from an annual 278 to twenty-five could Mori relinquish his post.

The Duce had tamed the land – a 2000-year-old problem as fresh as that day's headlines. South of Rome stretched the waterlogged Pontine Marshes, whose reclamation had baffled both Nero and Julius Caesar, 180,000 acres of desolate primeval swamp. From May to October only the wild fowl thrived there, for the marsh shepherds, fearful of malaria, withdrew their flocks to the mountains. Mussolini saw this as a challenge. He gave Count Valentino Orsolini Cencelli, a stocky one-legged agricultural expert, three years to solve the problem.

Cencelli did. With a task force of 2000 Tuscan labourers – which swelled to 15,000 – he first carved deep channels through the marsh-land, allowing the stagnant water to flow freely. Each day for six months the sea-coast shook with the thunder of 4000 mines, blasting from the soil the tangle of tree-stumps and rotting vegetation in which the mosquitoes thrived. Starting from the soggy heart of the swamp, Cencelli's canals and roads fanned outwards like spokes from a wheel-hub, his labourers operating from prefabricated hutments with mosquito-proof wire-netting windows. By November 1932, one year after he began, the first settlers were moving in to newly-built farmhouses equipped with stock and cattle – one month before the Duce, with true Fascist fanfare, inaugurated the region's first town, Littoria.

Cencelli's triumphal box-score was then 200 miles of canal, 300 miles of new road, and 500 farms. Within two years, 3000 farms and two more townships – Sabaudia and Pontínia – would arise, at a total cost of fifty-nine dead.

'Be proud to live in Mussolini's time,' exhorted the posters in letters as huge as a house, and this is the way Claretta Petacci felt each time she visited Palazzo Venezia. If it was a dream to be at this man's side, she wanted to keep her eyes closed.

No other Italian ruler, the propagandists blared, had ever taken thought of his people from cradle to grave. Who but Mussolini had set up 1700 mountain and seaside summer camps for city children? What other man paid out £1,600,000 to pre-natal clinics each year, or £3,500,000 in family allowances? Who gave the Italians the eight-hour day and codified insurance benefits for the old, the unemployed and the disabled? Only Mussolini who proclaimed on every hoarding that his one ambition was to make the Italians 'strong, prosperous, great and free', had achieved that.

Even the successive death blows he dealt the Italian economy were whooped up by party hacks as the last word in Fascist acumen. Against all his financial advisers' pleas, the man to whom an I O U was a mystery equated the stability of the lira with Italian honour and his own infallibility – pegging it at nineteen lire to the dollar until the public debt rose, by 1939, to an unheard-of 145 billion lire. Avid to control all the country's productive capacity, he founded the Corporate State – twenty-two trade corporations which, like medieval guilds, represented both employers and employees. Now no employer could enlarge or close down his factory, hire or fire labour, without government permission – or pay out any wage not approved by the state. But unions were outlawed, no worker had the right to strike, and wages could be slashed by decree. For both camps, the Corporate State loomed like an unwieldy Egyptian pyramid, piled with the mummies of Fascist bureaucracy.

For eight years from 1925 Mussolini waged his self-styled Battle of the Wheat – aimed at economic self-sufficiency through doubling Italy's wheat production to seven million tons. Fruit, oil and wine production were neglected, and as world prices slumped the wheat could have been imported at half the cost, but the Duce was in his flamboyant podium element – hailing the harvesters as 'Comrades of the Soil', toiling beside them in singlet and sunbonnet to reap two tons of his own, presiding over rallies of farmers in theatres decked with mammoth ears of wheat.

Paying scant heed to over-population, he set out to place the Italian family on a pedestal. From 1927 on, Italy's three million bachelors were singled out for taxes netting over £1 million a year, aimed to stampede them to the altar. Married men with families took preference over all others at employment exchanges – and reaped such benefits as reduced tram fares and gas tariffs. But inevitably the Duce's campaign took on a circus aura – inaugurating Mother and Child Day for the most prolific families, pinning medals on every woman who bore a seventh child. Militia officers had orders to salute expectant mothers on sight, and only narrowly did Mussolini's advisers restrain him from seizing the goods of any husband who died with less than four children.

And swiftly Mussolini the man was being replaced by the ludicrous legend. Press photos showed him in every garb imaginable, in riding-kit, in yachting-rig, in uniform and top boots or bare-chested in the wheatfields, and at every possible activity – driving a sports car, haranguing a crowd, training wild animals, playing his violin. His portrait appeared on women's swimsuits and in baby food advertisements, where the toddler sported a Fascist fez, while entrepreneurs did a brisk trade in perfumed Mussolini soap at two lire per cake. For some his aura had the magic properties of an amulet. Expectant mothers kept his portrait on the bedside table, hoping their new-born would inherit his sterling qualities, or moved, when their time drew near, to a clinic near his native Predappio.

'Halfway between Heaven and earth', as Pius XI had pictured him, he was an object of impious pilgrimage. One ancient journeyed for two months to present him with a barrel of water from the River Piave, site of a World War One battle, borne 350 miles on a wheelbarrow. From Merano, a twelve-year-old walked 450 miles barefoot just to see him. A Turin workman, embraced by Mussolini in a presentation ceremony, vowed never to wash his face again. And at Riccione, on the Adriatic, where his seaside villa was situated, bands of hysterical women plunged into the sea to mob him whenever he took a dip.

But even Mussolini drew the line when a Piedmont schoolmistress wrote imploring him to exercise the medieval *droit de seigneur* on her wedding night. In his stead he sent the *carabinieri*, to issue a stern warning.

Those unable to see him in the flesh venerated Duce relics. At the tenth anniversary of the March on Rome, silent crowds gathered before the blood-stained World War One litter on which, it was said, he had been carried from the battlefield. A mountain inn where he dined put his spaghetti fork in a glass case like an Etruscan vase. One Fascist chief, Cesare Fraccari, who closely resembled him, was flabbergasted to find a *trattoria* chair he had used at lunch snapped up by souvenir-hunters minutes after he vacated it.

Not only the humble and downtrodden fell under Mussolini's spell. Wealthy admirers lavished so many gifts on him – from three freehold villas to stuffed eagles – that once, in genial mood, he joked to Quinto Navarra: 'If I go out of business, I can always open a stall in the Flea Market.' A San Remo horticulturist christened a new black carnation in his honour; a peak of Mont Blanc was re-named Monte Mussolini. At Lausanne, tourist 'musts' took in a wall he had allegedly built and Signora Guelpa, an Italian laundress, who appeared as the new Madame Sans-Géne. 'She may have done Napoleon's washing,' she conceded. '*I* did Mussolini's.'

It would have turned many stronger heads than the Duce's. In the first years of his rule, success had mellowed him, and even impulsively generous gestures were not beyond him. When a Rome fish vendor complained that his market licence had not been renewed, Mussolini drove personally to assure him security of tenure. Another time, pressing a banknote on a vagrant who had solicited no alms, the Duce explained to Italo Balbo: 'When you've been hungry, you understand the glance of another hungry man.' In those years, he could still trade a wisecrack with the crowd. At a mass-meeting in Palermo, when the amplifier broke, one man exhorted: 'Louder!' Promptly Mussolini riposted: 'You'll read it all in the paper tomorrow anyway.' At times his humour was both deadpan and devastating. Once, following a Roman night-club fracas, a young Palazzo Chigi diplomat appeared before Mussolini to justify his conduct.

Was it a fact, the Duce asked, his face thunderous, that he, a member of the Foreign Service, had so far forgotten himself as to knock a jazz-trumpeter cold? The diplomat began to stammer excuses, but Mussolini cut him short: was it true? When the man nodded miserably, the melody-minded Mussolini, leaning forward, solemnly pumped his hand.

But now, fatally, the Duce began to believe his own publicity. If the Mussolini cult had begun spontaneously, he now worked harder than any to fan the flames of adulation. Mass-rallies, 50,000 strong, became the order of the day, while the Duce, hands on hips, ranted at them from the tiny balcony jutting from his Palazzo Venezia office. 'The mob loves strong men,' he would exult as the deafening cheers redoubled, 'The mob is a woman!'

The bedspace he had occupied thirty years ago in the dormitory at Verona Barracks was now sacred soil, marked by a bronze bust. If he appeared on a cinema screen, the whole audience must scramble to its feet. His one-day visit to Turin or Bologna might set the city fathers back £6000 for decorations, banquets and fireworks – and he would travel there in a six-coach train, framed in the window so that no one could miss him.

To be sure, he had built 16,000 public elementary schools but most were Fascist seminaries, where A was for adulation. His portrait loomed on the left of the crucifix in every classroom. For small fry, a dado made up of his eyes ringed the wall three feet above floor level. At morning prayers, pupils intoned solemnly: 'I believe in the supreme Duce, creator of the Blackshirts, and in Jesus Christ, his sole protector.' First-grade pupils wrestled with conundrums like: 'If Mussolini earned fifty-six lire per month as a teacher, how much did he earn per day?' – or learned how Pinocchio was really a disciple of the Duce, who dosed Communists with castor oil.

'The masses must obey,' thundered the Duce, in this year when membership of the Fascist Party became obligatory for all. 'They cannot afford to waste time searching for truth.'

Not only the masses were denied that privilege. In the Chamber of Deputies, rechristened the Chamber of Fasces and Corporations, Mussolini now sat loftily on a raised dais above his colleagues. Almost all his old lieutenants, men who had given him the intimate *'tu'* in March on Rome days, had been kicked upstairs into posts where they had little say in policy. Dino Grandi, who had not shrunk from telling him home truths, was now Ambassador in London; Luigi Federzoni became President of the Senate. Italo Balbo, fired as Minister of Aviation, was sent to govern Libya. Alberto de Stefani, who in 1924 had balanced Italy's budget, was forced into private life. Bologna's Leandro Arpinati, briefly Under-Secretary for Home Affairs, was banished, like any dissident, to the prison island of Lipari.

'Mussolini doesn't want advice any more,' Arpinati told his family bitterly. 'He only wants applause.' Even the Duce himself acknowledged the truth of this. Asked why he had exiled Grandi to London after eight years' fidelity, Mussolini admitted, 'He came to know me too well.'

It was now the cardinal sin. Those close to him now chafed increasingly, for even at Grand Council meetings Mussolini played the tyrant, holding all-night sessions that dragged on until dawn, with each member rising as in a classroom to shout 'Present!' A man who gave a true opinion risked instant dismissal. Once, when an elderly diplomat reported from a Geneva conference on poison gas, the Duce asked curtly which was the deadliest of all gases.

'Incense, Excellency,' was the old man's meaning retort, earning him an instant transfer to the retired list.

Officials who, in Mussolini's parlance, 'resigned' were often the last to hear about it. Typical was the plight of Minister of Education Francesco Ercole, en route to attend the centennial of a noted poet in Catania, Sicily. Boarding a sleeper at Rome's central station, Ercole had barely unpacked his night-things when an eleventh-hour telegram set him to repacking frantically. It read: 'I accept your resignation. Mussolini.'

Few men were thus surprised that by 1933, ten months after meeting with Claretta Petacci, Mussolini believed that he stood head-and-shoulders above any world statesman. In the last week of January he handed a telegram to Agostino Iraci, Chief of Secretariat to the Ministry of Home Affairs. From Berlin, Major Giuseppe Renzetti, now the Italian Consul-General, was reporting on the spectacular rise to power of the Nazi party.

'Tomorrow,' the Duce foretold, 'the new man in Germany will be Adolf Hitler.'

Iraci was circumspect. In November 1923, Mussolini had dismissed the abortive Munich Beer-Hall *putsch* by Hitler and his followers as the work of 'stupid children'. Was it in Italy's interests, he asked the Duce, that Germany become stronger?

Almost incredulously Mussolini stared at him. If the flicker of a doubt crossed his mind in that moment, he as swiftly banished it. His jaw jutted belligerently, his fist pounded the desk.

'The idea of Fascism conquers the world,' he blazed, 'I have already given Hitler many good ideas. Now he will follow me.'

Of all the evenings in the life of Elisabetta Cerruti, wife of the Italian Ambassador to Germany, this one, in the Presidential Palace in Berlin, was perhaps the tensest. All the rigid rules of diplomatic protocol were being waived tonight, but no one had so far explained why. As the most recent arrivals among the ambassadors, she and her husband Vittorio stood last on the protocol list – yet tonight, 7 February, 1933, it was she whom the newly-elected Chancellor, Adolf Hitler, would escort into the annual diplomatic corps dinner.

Beneath the glittering chandeliers of the drawing-room, an august host greeting his 200 guests, stood the President of the Weimar Republic, eighty-six-year-old Field Marshal Paul von Hindenburg, leaning on an ebony cane. Distractedly, Elisabetta Cerruti's eyes roved over the chattering throng, seeking her dinner partner. No man in all Germany was the cynosure of such attention – yet Hitler was nowhere to be seen.

Suddenly, in the farthest corner of the room, Elisabetta Cerruti saw him. He stood alone, pale but calm, his arms folded over the first tuxedo he had ever worn, impassively watching the President.

It was as if, thought Signora Cerruti, he was well content to let Hindenburg enjoy the limelight – knowing full well that the corner in which he stood had become 'one of the cardinal points of the universe'.

Conscious of the electric challenge of the moment, the ambassador's wife still wished that another woman stood in her shoes. As Hitler bent to kiss her hand, she recalled with fear and revulsion the scene only one week earlier, 30 January, the night the Third Reich was born: the vast torchlight procession that wound past the Chancellery, the brutal tramp of jackboots, the animal triumph of the *Horst Wessel Song* bursting from thousands of throats. Then, as the guests followed the thicket of red and black arrows directing them to their seats, she resolutely stifled her dislike. 'Watch Hitler closely,' her husband had briefed her, 'and don't miss a word he says.'

It was no easy task. All through dinner, Hitler's deep-seated rancour against those who had opposed his rise to power broke through in strident anger. Knife and fork clenched in his fists, pale blue eyes blazing, he time and again returned to his theme as to a sore tooth: from now on Germany would be a great nation, whose legitimate aspirations the world must recognize. With mingled horror and fascination, Signora Cerruti saw that he was shaking with rage. His voice had risen to a hysterical scream, 'as harsh as a washer-woman shouting insults'.

Tactfully she thought to check the avalanche by mentioning Benito Mussolini.

The effect was as magical as an invocation. At once Hitler's eyes softened. His voice took on a low, warm timbre. And now the ambassador's wife knew all too well why she sat beside the guest of honour. 'I had too much respect for that great man to disturb him before achieving positive results,' he told her softly, 'but now it is different. I am looking forward to meeting him.'

As if glimpsing a vision, he stared unseeing across the starched white damask and sparkling crystal. 'It will be' predicted Adolf Hitler, 'the happiest day of my life.'

It was a morning made for poets and Venetians. Five thousand feet below the Junkers' starboard wing, the lagoons were a silver filigree against the tender green of the land. Glancing back from the cockpit, personal pilot Hans Baur could see that Chancellor Adolf Hitler was appreciating the solemnity of this moment. Beckoning to Press Chief Otto Dietrich, he was pointing out all the landmarks known only from his favourite art histories: the majestic front of Santa Maria della Salute, like a galleon's prow in full sail on the waters of the Grand Canal, the gleaming bubble-domes of San Marco.

At San Nicolò di Lido airport, Benito Mussolini was in no such receptive mood. On this balmy summer morning, Thursday, 14 June, 1934, he was receiving Hitler for the first time on Italian soil to deliver to him a sharp warning. For months, at Hitler's active instigation, Nazis in Austria had waged an undercover war of terror against the clerical-fascist regime of Chancellor Engelbert Dollfuss. Anxious that Austria should remain an independent buffer state, the Duce harboured no friendly feelings for the man bent on annexing her to Germany: Adolf Hitler, now President, Chancellor, and addressed by right as 'Führer'.

Then, as the Junkers taxied to a halt and Hitler came in sight, Fascist officials gasped. In contrast to Mussolini's black bemedalled uniform, Germany's Führer wore a belted khaki raincoat, grey civilian suit and patent leather shoes. As he descended the gangway, nervously clutching his felt hat, one of the 400 newsmen present heard the Duce's hoarse stage-whisper to his newly-appointed Chief of the Press Bureau, Galeazzo Ciano: '*I don't like him!*'

Aptly, it set the key-note for the whole two-day meeting. Smarting under his disadvantage, the Führer stood as white as a sheet, while Mussolini having welcomed him in German, patted him condescendingly on the shoulder. As the band struck up the *Horst Wessel Song* Hitler, scowling furiously, hissed to German Ambassador Ulrich von Hassell: 'Why didn't you advise me to wear my uniform?'

In truth, Hitler's paean of praise to Elisabetta Cerruti, eighteen months earlier, had been sincerely meant. No other man had pointed out to him the road to power as Mussolini had done, demonstrating how an aspiring leader could shut down parliament and gag the Press, curb the people while he jailed his opponents, and set up an illegal army based on patriotic appeal. Yet now the Duce's barely concealed disdain was almost more than he could bear.

That afternoon, in the richly furnished salon of the palace at Stra, on the mainland, the dictators' first conference proved a total disaster. Inordinately vain of his spotty German, Mussolini would permit no interpreters; the two men debated behind closed doors. Shortly fists pounding on the table and high angry voices became audible, with one word – '*Österreich*' – resounding above the rest.

When they emerged, Hitler tugging angrily at his raincoat belt, both men were flushed, their faces set and angry.

At the Grand Hotel, where Hitler was staying, the newsmen greeted Galeazzo Ciano's communiqué that the two had met in 'an atmosphere of perfect cordiality' with ribald mirth.

As Hitler had begun to perceive, Mussolini had many things on his mind. Apart from his concern for Austria's independence, he had a genuine liking for the diminutive forty-one-year-old Dollfuss, with his boyish smile and timid, low-pitched voice. In August 1933, he and his lovely wife, Alwine, had been the Duce's guests at the family villa at Riccione; both men had relaxed in a leisurely round of boating, swimming and motor jaunts. 'I'll let it be known in Berlin that Austria is to be left alone,' Mussolini vowed, and he had donated two million schillings to aid Dollfuss's counter-propaganda.

But as recently as March, when Dollfuss again sought support in Rome, Mussolini had confided to his son Vittorio, 'The saucepan's boiling under poor Dollfuss and it's Hitler who's stoking the fire.'

A personal problem gnawed Mussolini, too, on this June afternoon. Within days, Claretta Petacci was to marry her lieutenant in Rome: already she and the Duce had made their farewells. 'Well, then, *piccola*, you're going away,' had been his parting words. 'I shan't see you any more. Be happy.'

He did not regret that their relationship had remained platonic, for he respected her youth and sincerity. But he had to admit he would miss her fervent, unquestioning hero-worship, the sense of eternal youth that she had given him.

Irritably, his thoughts returned to Hitler. He had not yet forgiven him his summary rejection of advice the Duce, as elder statesman, had offered, through Ambassador Vittorio Cerruti, in the spring of 1933. 'The anti-semitic question,' he had warned, 'could turn Germany's enemies, including her Christian ones, against Hitler.' At first the Führer had answered calmly enough, but suddenly, like a man possessed, he shouted: 'Allow me to observe that Mussolini understands nothing about the Jewish problem! The name Hitler will be glorified everywhere as the man who wiped the Jewish plague off the face of the earth.'

But when Baron Konstantin von Neurath, Germany's Foreign Minister, secretly urged the Duce to condemn Hitler's stand publicly, he made no move. He would not advertise to the world at large that any man had ignored his advice.

But the knowledge had rankled – and for the next thirty-six hours he took exquisite pains to make his guest feel small. At the Friday morning parade in Hitler's honour, the Führer stood fuming on the reviewing stand for more than half-an-hour with no sign of the Duce. Then, as Mussolini arrived and the band struck up, Hitler's eyes widened – and with reason. Past the saluting base shambled file after file of Fascist Militiamen, out of step, unshaven, their uniforms unpressed and shabby with age. Though the Führer only half-suspected it, Mussolini had ordered that the troops should parade in just such dishevelled array – the most blatant way he could devise of showing his contempt.

Mussolini had by no means finished. While Hitler watched in silence from a window, he held a wildly-cheering crowd on Piazza San Marco spellbound with his vision of Italy's great future – as an afterthought gesturing in Hitler's direction, to signal spattered applause. Following a woeful lunch at the Lido Golf Club – a disapproving chef had slipped salt in Hitler's coffee – the two dictators paced the greens out of earshot, wrangling for two long hours. Protocol decreed that Mussolini should take the Führer on a motor-boat trip of the canals – but not that he should stifle his yawns when Hitler, quoting from *Mein Kampf*, belittled all Mediterranean peoples as tainted by Negro blood.

Halfway through that evening's reception for the Führer, Mussolini unceremoniously walked out. Until the morning farewells at the Lido Airport, he saw his duty as done. The Chancellor would return to Germany in no two minds as to Mussolini's opinion of him – and know that so far as Austria was concerned he was in grim earnest.

'He's a garrulous monk,' he told one party official contemptuously, 'and he'll be taught a lesson.' To General Pietro Badoglio, Chief of Army General Staff, he was more caustic still: 'He's a barbarian . . . a gramophone with just seven records.'

It was Galeazzo Ciano who decided that Hitler should receive this message in clear. He had always fancied himself as a policy-maker, and since his new-found promotion the Duce's son-in-law was reaping the fruits of his intimacy. An opinion that Mussolini reserved for his chosen circle could, Ciano thought, given the right official leak, wing its way to Berlin.

Sipping tomato juice – that year's most fashionable drink – in the Hotel Danieli's bar, his high-pitched voice let drop the first of many calculated indiscretions to the eager newsmen.

'Hitler's obsessed with the idea of a preventive war in Europe,' he told them. 'But do you know how the Duce described him? He calls him the new-style Genghis Khan.'

On the crisp damask cloth before Vittorio Mussolini the remains of a leisurely lunch were scattered like a still-life – the curling ring of an orange, a creamy Bel Paese cheese, his last cup of strong black coffee. Through the drawn shutters of the Villa Mussolini at Riccione filtered the sights and sounds of a drowsy Adriatic afternoon – dappled sunlight from the beach, the rustle of the sea, a warm wind stirring the palm trees. Draining his coffee, the Duce's nineteen-year-old son made ready for the beach.

The car came up the carriage-sweep so fast his first intimation was flung gravel, spattering the window like spindrift. Dabbing at his lips with a napkin, Vittorio ran for the door. His parents were away on a country drive and not due back until nightfall; the last person he expected to see in the hall was Rachele. Beyond, he caught a glimpse of his father's broad shoulders retreating to his study. White-faced, knuckles pressed to her mouth, Rachele told him: 'This morning they killed Dollfuss.'

Vittorio was appalled – and not only by the tragedy itself. Only eleven days earlier, on 18 July, 1934, Dollfuss's wife, Alwine, with their two children, Rudolf, four and Evi, six, had arrived at the villa that Mussolini had rented for them not far up the coast. All morning they had been playing on the beach with Romano and Anna Maria. Tomorrow the little Chancellor himself had been due to arrive on holiday. Now Benito Mussolini must find some way to break the news.

Closeted in his study, the Duce was seeking up-to-the-minute facts. The first alarm had come from Eugenio Morreale, the Vienna bureau chief of *Il Popolo d'Italia*. Soon after 1 p.m. hearing a broadcast announcement that Dollfuss was no longer Chancellor and that the Nazis held the radio station, Morreale had quit his lunch to bolt to the Italian Legation. He was convinced that the little man was already dead. Still painfully fresh in Morreale's mind was his talk with Dollfuss one day earlier, when the Chancellor hesitantly sought his opinion on the gift he was taking to Mussolini – an eighteenth-century guide to Vienna, printed in Italian.

'The family are there now,' Dollfuss had told him, 'and the little one is speaking Italian already. This morning when they called, he said, "*Papa, come stai?*"'

Though Legation officials were dubious, a call went through

to Fulvio Suvich, Under-Secretary of State for Foreign Affairs in Rome. It seemed likely then that Dollfuss was the Nazis' prisoner. Unable at first to contact the Duce, Suvich called General Federico Baistrocchi, Under-Secretary for War. Without mincing words, he told him; 'There are tragic events in Vienna. I'm sure when we reach Mussolini he will give only one order: "Mobilize!" '

His face dark with anger, Mussolini paced his study. He had few illusions as to what had happened, fewer still concerning Adolf Hitler. Only fifteen days after their first meeting in Venice, the Führer, in a bloody weekend known as 'The Night of the Long Knives', had liquidated scores of the Storm Troops who had supported him. Shocked, the Duce told Rachele: 'He is more pitiless than Attila. He didn't hesitate to kill comrades who helped bring him to power. It's as if I had ordered the killing of Grandi and Bottai . . .'

At four that afternoon a storm broke over the Adriatic. Hissing white curtains of rain blotted out the sea. Still Mussolini stayed at the phone, pressing Rome for fresh bulletins. It was dark before he knew the worst: Dollfuss was dying. At 1 p.m. Nazis dressed in Austrian Army uniforms had broken into the Federal Chancellery in Vienna, trapping the Chancellor as he tried to flee. As he stood at bay in the great hall where the Congress of Vienna had made peace in 1815 after the Napoleonic Wars, nine men battered down the doors and shot him at close range in the throat.

Dollfuss died slowly. For more than three hours he lay slumped on a sofa in a nearby salon, refused all medical aid by his killers, as the blood drained out of him. As he grew weaker, he whispered to the faithful attendants at his side: 'Children, you are so good to me . . . I only wanted peace. God forgive the others.'

Mussolini acted fast. Along the Bavarian border, he knew, was encamped an Austrian Legion of thousands, ready, with Hitler's full approval, to occupy Austria at a chosen moment. On the line to General Baistrocchi in Rome, he now confirmed Suvich's standby warning. Four divisions – almost forty thousand men – were to move at once for the Brenner Pass dividing Italy from Germany. That night, at posts all along the border, German troops could hear the rumble of tanks, the tramp of marching feet, as Italian troops took up battle stations.

'Now let them come,' the Duce threatened blackly. 'We'll show these gentlemen they cannot trifle with Italy.'

It was enough. By midnight Hitler had climbed down. The official German news agency's despatch rejoicing in Dollfuss's downfall was withdrawn; a new version spoke of the murder as a purely Austrian affair. The *putsch* had been premature, and with Mussolini solidly proclaiming Austrian independence, along with France and Britain, the Führer must bide his time.

Now the Duce faced the worst task of all: somehow the news must be broken to Alwine Dollfuss. For a moment he hesitated whether to leave it until morning, then Rachele stiffened his resolution. In driving rain, his wife silent at his side, Mussolini drove for the Dollfusses' villa.

That night, the ever-confident Duce found himself at a loss. Weary after a long day of sun, Frau Dollfuss had retired early but she donned a robe and hastened downstairs. Rachele, too, was non-plussed, for she spoke no common language. As her husband, in hesitant German, broke the news that the Chancellor had been 'seriously injured', she did the only thing a wife and mother could do at such a time. She gripped the other woman's hand tight.

Somehow, the Duce's halting broken phrases, the pressure of Rachele's fingers, showed Alwine Dollfuss the true dimensions of the nightmare that lay ahead. Soon she was weeping softly, and as Rachele's arms came about her the grief broke in her like a wave.

White lightning split the sky above Riccione, the women clung to one another, and Mussolini stood silently apart – 'feeling,' he told Suvich later, 'so helpless and alone'.

The whole family was silent – Rachele, Vittorio, Bruno, Romano and Anna Maria. As if hypnotized, their eyes were fastened on Benito Mussolini, at the head of the long dining table. Solemnly, rhyth-mically, his fork was enmeshing the long yellow ribbons of tagliatelle. It was 11 p.m., long past the younger children's bedtime, but on such a night as this all household routine had gone by the board.

As if he sensed their eyes upon him, the Duce looked up. With the forkful of tagliatelle half-way to his lips, he paused. He spoke matter-of-factly, but for all his life Vittorio was to remember his words.

'And now,' he said, 'I think we've seen the end of peace in Europe. Fine speeches won't mean anything any more, you'll see. We shall need fine guns.'

For an afternoon's loafing outside his beach chalet at Castel Porziano, near Rome, his outfit would have passed muster – white linen trousers, jacket with patched elbows, open-neck shirt, disreputable sneakers worn without socks. But to see Benito Mussolini thus attired in the solemn confines of Palazzo Venezia made Mario Pansa's heart sink. It was 1 p.m. on Monday, 24 June, 1935 – barely fifteen minutes before the official luncheon at Rome's Excelsior Hotel.

Pansa, a young diplomat from the Ministry of Foreign Affairs, protested weakly: 'But we shall be late for the lunch, Your Excellency. You can't possibly change in five minutes.'

For answer, Mussolini laughed harshly. 'What!' he exclaimed. 'Do you think I'd change for that fellow? The idea never occurred to me.' Then defiantly jamming an old tweed cap on his head, he ordered curtly, 'Let's go.'

His mind troubled, Pansa followed. He knew too well what Mussolini had in mind, and he would have given a year's salary to dodge this luncheon. Just as the Duce, one year earlier, had set out to humiliate Adolf Hitler in Venice, his guns were now trained on Robert Anthony Eden, Britain's elegant thirty-eight-year-old Minister without Portfolio for League of Nations Affairs.

Like every Foreign Ministry official, Pansa knew of the bad blood between the two. It had been plain enough in the icy interchange of the past two hours. Using the same tactics as with Hitler, the Duce's opening move had been to keep Eden waiting almost an hour before their first meeting. 'I'm fed up with these damned English who claim that all the world should bow before them,' he announced. And as the first conference broke up and Eden departed, Mussolini's reactions were summed up in one withering sentence: 'I never saw a better-dressed fool.'

Then, despite the imminent luncheon, he changed, following his unvarying custom, into lounging gear for the beach.

At the British Embassy, Eden's reaction was even terser: 'He is not a gentleman.'

On the face of it, the British diplomat's mission was routine: an exchange of views on the current Anglo-German naval agreement. But Mussolini had not been deceived for an instant. Through Italian secret service agents who made a nightly study of documents inside the British Embassy, he knew full well the reason for Eden's visit: an eleventh-hour attempt to halt him from waging war on the last independent kingdom in Africa, Abyssinia.

From the Duce's standpoint, his reasons were good and sufficient. At one and the same time he sought to gain a fertile foothold in Africa, challenge the power of the League of Nations, wipe out the shame of the Battle of Adowa, thirty-nine years earlier when Abyssinian troops had massacred 8000 Italians, and to solve his growing unemployment problems. As far back as January, his new Finance Minister, the tall, smiling Count Paolo Thaon di Revel, had overnight placed Italy on a war footing – slashing imports, forcing holders of foreign securities to convert them into government bonds, limiting stock dividends to six per cent, prohibiting all export of Italian currency.

Already Mussolini had warned the British he would brook no opposition. As emissary he had employed for the first and only time his twenty-five-year-old daughter Edda, just then on a visit to London. 'If they oppose our policy,' he had emphasized, 'there'll be war.' At dinners and parties, Edda had not scrupled to make this as plain as could be. 'Father means to have it all,' she told the Foreign Office's Sir Robert Vansittart. Even Eden himself had few illusions about the task that lay before him. At one reception on the eve of his departure, Edda hailed him cheekily across the drawing-room: 'What are you going to do in Rome, Mr Eden? Don't you know that my father doesn't like you?'

Now as his car inched through the press of lunchtime traffic along the Via del Tritone, en route to the Excelsior, Mussolini burst out: 'That frozen tailor's dummy! I may be a blacksmith's son, but I do know how to hold my own.'

Pansa knew why Mussolini's anger was unappeasable. To him, Eden's visit was one more example of traditional British perfidy. Two months previously, in the tree-lined resort of Stresa, on Lake Maggiore, British, French and Italian statesmen had gathered round a green baize table with one primary aim: to censure Germany's creation of a national-service army and air force in direct defiance of the Treaty of Versailles. In fact the subject of Abyssinia was not on the agenda – but in a December 1934 flare-up between Abyssinia and Italian troops at Walwal, 100 miles inside Abyssinian territory, thirty two Italians had died. Promptly, in the style of his Corfu exploit, Mussolini had demanded £20,000 indemnity, an apology and a salute to the Italian flag. To any sophisticated statesman, the next moves were plain.

Some weeks before Stresa, Mussolini put out feelers. To the Italian Ambassador in London, Dino Grandi, went a cable posing two urgent questions: were the British ready to give Italy the green light in Abyssinia? And how firmly would they support the Duce in guaranteeing Austria's independence under Dollfuss's successor, Kurt von Schuschnigg?

Over pre-lunch sherries at a Londonderry House luncheon party, Grandi had broached these points with the Prime Minister, Ramsay MacDonald. 'England,' MacDonald replied cautiously, 'is a lady. A lady's taste is for vigorous action by the male, but she likes things done discreetly – not in public. Be tactful and we shall have no objection.'

As Mussolini saw it, the events of Stresa bore this out. Although the Foreign Secretary, Sir John Simon, brought Abyssinian experts from the Foreign Office, they kept discreetly silent. At one open-air restaurant, newsvendors moved among the tables hawking that day's *Corriere della Sera*, its black banner headlines reading 'ITALIAN TROOPS PASS THROUGH SUEZ CANAL!' More than 200,000 men, 50,000 pack-horses and 10,000 trucks were already on the move.

But British delegates, chatting happily with Italians, made no demur. To Mussolini, it seemed that he had received the unmistakable go-ahead.

Yet on Austria he won no support. In vain he protested: 'I can't always be the one to march to the Brenner Pass.' Ramsay MacDonald, presiding, opined that Austria was a ripe fruit, ready to fall into Germany's lap. France's Pierre Laval saw it as primarily of interest to Italy. When the Allied Premiers, at the conference's end, pledged themselves to maintain peace in Europe, the Duce seized one last chance to underline the fine print.

Pen poised for signature, he glanced meaningly along the green baize table, twice repeating the words, 'In Europe.' Again, for fear that he would leave the League, not a voice was raised.

It was thus with a smarting sense of grievance that Mussolini strode, two months later, into the Excelsior's green-and-gold banqueting room. From the corner of his eye, Pansa noted his unholy look of satisfaction as the cocktail chatter faltered and died. Immaculate, despite the heat, in cutaway and striped trousers, Eden did not even raise a well-bred eyebrow at the sight of his host's garb – but the other guests proved less impervious. Even Sir Eric Drummond (later Lord Perth), the British Ambassador, wore a look of comical dismay.

As the guests in strained silence took their seats at the long table, the Duce, tugging at his chair, turned ostentatiously to the left, presenting his back to the hapless Eden. Plainly his words were too precious to waste on the man from London.

In truth both he and Eden had reached a total impasse. From Dino Grandi, the Duce was cynically aware of what had prompted

Britain's embarrassed *volte-face*: within forty-eight hours, publication of a peace ballot taken months earlier by Lord Cecil's powerful League of Nations Union revealed that more than ten million Britons had voted in favour of economic sanctions against an aggressor state. Obviously, Premier Stanley Baldwin's government, elected only sixteen days earlier, could not ignore the forceful opinion of half the electorate. The result was Eden's helter-skelter arrival with a compromise designed both to appease the Duce and keep Italy within the League: a portion of the Ogaden desert, bordering Italian Somaliland, and cession of the British port of Zeila, on the Gulf of Aden, whose sole landward access was by camel track.

Contemptuously, Mussolini, who already ruled 100,000 square miles of the Sahara, had spat out: 'I am not a collector of deserts.'

Calling for maps, he had shown Eden what he wanted from Abyssinia: the townships of Adowa and Aksum in the north, a tract of territory connecting Italian-held Eritrea and Somaliland, the total disbandment of the Abyssinian Army. 'If I go to war,' he warned Eden, 'the name of Abyssinia will be wiped off the map.'

Eden was dubious: he thought it unlikely that Haile Selassie, Emperor of Abyssinia, could ever accede to such demands. Again he warned Mussolini to draw back. 'It is too late,' Mussolini told him irritably. 'I must go on.'

The lunch over, Mussolini retired to a corner of the room to chat with a minor functionary. Still he had given no sign that Eden even existed. Sir Eric Drummond, approaching Mario Pansa, made a last desperate attempt. It was truly unfortunate that Eden's known ability as a classical scholar had provoked a newspaper gibe: 'Mr Eden may read Homer in the original, but he can't understand Mussolini, even in translation.' It was vital that the two should be seen talking amicably, to eradicate any impression of ill-will.

Mussolini listened in cold silence as Pansa relayed the message. Then, shoulders straining against his patched jacket, hands thrust deep in the pockets of his stained trousers, he answered cuttingly: 'The distance between us is exactly equal. If he wishes to speak to me, it's his business to come over here.'

Pansa gave up. Plainly there was nothing more to say.

All through the night, hour after hour, the trucks had hurtled by. Along the Viale Benito Mussolini, the main street of Asmara, Eritrea, the window shutters rattled convulsively, as if a sand-storm was blowing up. The drivers, grimy and begoggled, swathed mouths and noses in damp handkerchiefs against the brown talcum-like dust; beyond the town, their headlights dark, they took the twisting roads more cautiously. Already in the pre-dawn darkness the highways were alive with marching troops. Scattered to either side of the road were the great encampments that spelt out the magnitude of this enterprise; thousands of mules tethered in picket lines, artillery parks, whippet tanks so small they could pass beneath a man's outstretched arm.

To veterans in this endless defile, the chalked legend 'Rome to Addis Ababa' recalled a day thirteen years earlier when they had marched on the Eternal City. It was 4.45 a.m. on 3 October, 1935.

In a cramped stone hut on the brow of the Coatit Mountain, eight miles from the Abyssinian frontier, war correspondents watched curiously as sixty-nine-year-old General Emilio de Bono, spry and goat-bearded, conferred with his staff. It was light enough now to see the maps spread out on the table, yet on the Asmara plain, half a mile below, not a spark of light showed, though thousands were on the move. Thirty miles to the left of the plateau, 35,000 men of the First Army Corps, under General Santini, were poised for Adigrat – a fifteen-hour forced march through gorges 9000 feet high, terrain so hostile that troops would finally stand in for the mules of the mountain artillery. Below De Bono, the second column – 40,000 Askari troops under General Pirzio Biroli – had as objective Entiscio. Thirty miles to the right General Maravigna's Second Army Corps would head for Adowa.

It was 4.50 a.m. Slowly to the east the horizon paled, saffron deepening to rose. For the first time the chocolate-brown saw-tooth silhouette of the Danakil Mountains was visible. Hard-faced and sombre in their grey-green uniforms, the staff officers stared ahead, chain-smoking, conversing in low tones. A few took hasty swigs of cognac. Apart from the subdued clicking of telegraph instruments, a bird's uncertain song, silence was absolute.

For three years General De Bono had awaited this moment. In the autumn of 1932, the General, swiftly restored to favour after the Matteotti scandal to become Minister of Colonies, had sensed Mussolini's covetous eyes cast on Abyssinia. 'If there is going to be a war down there and you think me worthy,' he ventured, 'would you give me the honour of leading it?' To De Bono's joy the Duce had agreed. Could it be that at sixty-six, he was too old? 'No,' Mussolini had answered, 'because no time must be lost.'

De Bono lost no time at all. Early in 1933 he summoned to Rome

Lieutenant-Colonel Vittorio Ruggero, Military Attaché to the Italian Legation in Addis Ababa. Briefed by De Bono, the Colonel returned to the Abyssinian capital with loaded chests of the national currency, heavy silver Maria Theresa thalers. As chief of the new-founded political bureau, his assignment from then on was to set up consulates all over the interior – their sole purpose to buy up Haile Selassie's malcontent chieftains.

Ten months back, though still officially Minister for Colonies, De Bono had arrived in the Eritrean port of Massawa as High Commissioner for East Africa. From the outset, the true purpose of his mission was blanketed in secrecy. Though the region lacked everything of vital military importance – water, food, communications, roads – to import Italian labour would arouse suspicion. At first it was native construction gangs who went to work, sinking hundreds of wells, rounding up cattle to provide meat on the hoof, carving the seventy-seven-mile-long road from Port Massawa to the frontier town of Asmara.

On 30 December, 1934, Mussolini personally assumed command of a war so secret only five copies of the Order of Battle were ever printed. His plan, he explained to De Bono, was to strike the following autumn, as soon as Africa's rainy season was past. To steal a march on the British, who might yet close the Suez Canal, he briefed the old General to lay in three years' supplies. The least of his problems would be men. 'You asked for three divisions by the end of October,' Mussolini wrote. 'I intend to send you ten; I repeat, *ten*.'

To De Bono, onetime commander of the Blackshirt Militia, the Duce's reasons were plain. To blazon that this war was the will of the people, five of these divisions would be Blackshirts, for above all Mussolini envisaged the conflict to come as a rockribbed Fascist triumph.

Both De Bono and General Rodolfo Graziani, the ramrod-stiff, six-foot-two joint commander, had urged Mussolini not to alert the enemy with any formal declaration of war. The go-ahead would be a personal telegram from the Duce worded: 'Your report received.' On 29 September, Mussolini himself had chosen dawn on 3 October as H-Hour.

To the war correspondents, now arranging their typewriters on the sandbagged parapets of Coatit Mountain, it was an uncanny experience. As the minutes ticked away, a mighty war-machine was about to grind into action, waiting an appointed minute to invade the last independent kingdom in Africa. At 4.55 a.m. they hammered out the first six-word bulletin which would set the presses spinning; in scores of countries, the world would awaken to read of the opening shots in one more war. Their messages were identical: 'Italians commenced invasion Abyssinia 5 a.m.'

Five a.m. H-Hour. The world seemed made of glaring rock and prickly sweat; even in the shade the temperature was soaring to 115°. Heliographs were blinking from the mountain tops. Signallers hurried to carpet the ground with red and white strips of cloth spread in strange patterns – pre-arranged pointers for the Caproni bombers about to strafe the city of Adowa, forty miles distant. Trains of tank-trucks and donkeys bearing big canvas water sacks were on the move; long serpent-like columns of men, mules and trucks were pouring across the ford of the Belesa river. By nightfall the three columns would have seized 2000 square miles of Abyssinian territory.

Slowly, De Bono and his Chief of Staff paced the plateau. Between them no word had been spoken to mark the momentous act: Abyssinia at 4.59 a.m. uninvaded, and Abyssinia at 5.01 a.m., violated territory. Through field-glasses they watched grey-green figures wading the wide, shallow Belesa river, singing, their rifles held high above their heads.

Faintly the words drifted back to observers on the lower slopes. It was the anthem of the March on Rome, the Fascist hymn, '*Giovinezza*'.

The night was warm for May, yet he was shivering. Beneath the grey-green uniform jacket, the black Fascist shirt was drenched with sweat. There was never any moment before facing a crowd when Benito Mussolini did not quake like an actor awaiting a first-night curtain: wavering between timidity and arrogance, he needed the whipped-up hysteria of the crowd before he could strut and preen in the style that had become his hallmark. And tonight at Palazzo Venezia, shortly before 10.30 p.m. on 9 May, 1936, he had sufficient cause to tremble. He was announcing the birth of the Second Roman Empire.

Four days earlier, on 5 May, 20,000 men under General Pietro Badoglio, who had swiftly replaced the cautious De Bono as campaign commander, had ridden in triumph through the eucalyptus groves fringing the Abyssinian capital of Addis Ababa. Emperor Haile Selassie had fled in a British warship, his dominions in chaos; rival chieftains were warring with one another. At a cost of only 1600 dead, the Duce's war was over.

Right. During the Swiss
exile 1922-4, Mussolini was
bricklayer, errand-boy, above
all, agitator
Below. His eighth (1915)
arrest in Rome's Piazza
Barberini for militarist
propaganda

Early Mussolinian poses, martial and magniloquent: *Left*. Near the Isonzo river, December 1916, as a corporal in the Bersaglieri Regiment. *Right*. Outside St Mark's, Venice, with obligatory pigeons, following wounding and demobilization

Above. Family portrait, post 1917. Editor Mussolini (now wedded to spats) with Rachele and their daughter Edda in a photographer's studio. *Below.* The Premier: in frock-coat and riding-breeches, Mussolini posed in his Hotel Savoia suite for the sculptor Caprino within 24 hours of seizing power

The Mussolini Myth

At Rome's Zoo, with his lion cub 'Italia'

At Cogne, ready to descend a coal mine

Clearing a hurdle with Fru-Fru

Ski-ing at Terminillo

Mobbed by fans at Riccione, on the Adriatic

At the controls of his private plane

Waging the Battle of the Wheat

Motor-cycling at a Fascist rally

Among the cannon-fodder of
the Duce's wars

From the Palazzo Venezia, Mussolini pro-
claims: 'Book and Musket, the Perfect Fascist'

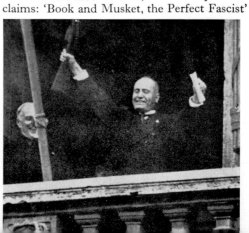

Above. Among early Fascist chie
were four who combined to topp
him in the 1943 Grand Council
Giuseppe Bottai (extreme left),
Dino Grandi (third left),
Giacomo Acerbo (fifth from left
at rear) and Cesare Maria De V
(behind Mussolini to left)
Left. In June 1924, the abductic
and brutal murder of Socialist
Giacomo Matteotti (centre) cam
close to finishing Mussolini

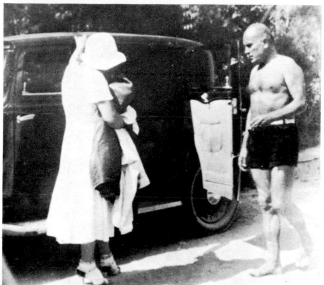

Top. Rome's 40-roomed Villa Torlonia which Mussolini rented for one lira a year
Middle. Mussolini enjoyed trips to the beach at Ostia with Rachele
Left. From the Villa Torlonia, Mussolini gave his daughter Edda in marriage to the ambitious, amoral Galeazzo Ciano

Above. Mussolini, Ciano and Dollfuss
at Ostia in 1934
Left. He meets Hitler for the first
time in Venice in June 1934, and
warns him, 'Hands off Austria!'

Like forty-five million other Italians, the Romans had waited seven months for this moment. Now on a still blue night, fragrant with orange blossom, it had arrived. All over the city, sirens and church bells vied with the braying of klaxons; in an irresistible tide the crowds surged towards Piazza Venezia. Soon the wide square before the palace was impassable, but still they came – crowding the 100-yards-wide marble steps of the Unknown Warrior's Tomb, lining the wide Via del' Impero, packing the Corso Umberto, the Via del Plebiscito. More than 400,000 people, massed in murmuring suspense, as the swallows wheeled and flickered and a honey-coloured moon hung above the broken outline of the Colosseum.

That crowd, and millions like them, Mussolini knew, had been behind him all along. From the moment that fifty League of Nations countries – with only Austria and Hungary abstaining – voted to boycott the war with anti-Italian sanctions, the people had closed their ranks. As almost all Italians saw it, the nations who for years had snubbed and humiliated Italy, who had cheated her at Versailles, now denied her a place in the African sun.

Everywhere the response was electric. Poverty-stricken peasants walked 300 miles to enlist. Political exiles from the time of Matteotti came home to back the regime. Intellectuals like the philosopher Benedetto Croce and ex-Liberal Premier Vittorio Emanuele Orlando, publicly offered their 'patriotic support' to the fatherland.

It was the same at all levels. Restaurant owners, opting for two meatless days a week, dug up World War One austerity recipes – or created new ones like 'Sanctions Soup'. Jazz, foreign perfumes, even foreign words, were boycotted – the Piazza di Spagna became the Piazza General De Bono and the Eden Bar ignominiously closed down. Toyshops flaunted mimic battles between Italian and Abyssinian lead soldiers. Housewives, following the lead of Queen Elena, filed in thousands to cast £16 million worth of gold wedding-rings into open-air crucibles, and brides, hastening straight from the altar to party headquarters, traded in their shining rings for token steel bands.

From the gifts that admirers had lavished on him, Mussolini himself donated over five thousand pounds of solid gold, although café wags had it that the Duce's true sacrifice was known only to his intimates. For the duration, he had given up women.

Now at 10.33 p.m. on this night the Duce's animal instinct told him that the moment was ripe to meet his people. With a curt gesture he motioned his aides to fall back. Mounting a six-inch rostrum, he passed through the glass doors on to the narrow ledge of his now-famous balcony. At once a spotlight swivelled to trap him in its glare, framed against a backdrop of crimson tapestries and wavering candles, tinting his face the colour of old parchment. There was a cry of silver trumpets and with an ear-splitting roar a salute of twenty-one guns erupted on the Roman night.

Booming through amplifiers, his voice, rich and vibrant, rang out in high-flown Fascist oratory: ' . . . Blackshirts of the revolution, Italian men and women, at home and throughout the world, hear me . . . Italy has at last her Empire . . . a Fascist Empire.'

Under the soft evening light, a vast mosaic of pink faces gazed upwards, enthralled. The title of Emperor of Abyssinia, he told them, had been that day assumed by King Vittorio Emanuele, and would descend to his successors. And this Empire the Italian people had created with its blood.

Few aside from Mussolini and his generals knew that in the battle just past, the elements, not the Abyssinians, had been the enemy. Advancing on a forty-five-mile front, 30,000 engineers had somehow contrived to build thirteen new bridges and 300 miles of new roads. Weighed down by 50 lb. packs, their boots slashed by rocks or eaten by termites, infantrymen slogged along mule tracks and stream beds in a temperature of 140° – though tank crews, stifling at 170°, had it worse. The troops who marched on Azbi prospected terrain where no white man had ever set foot; for more than a week, the men who took Neghelli were down to two pints of water a day. Yet thanks to stream-lined prophylaxis, only 600 men had been fatally stricken by tropical diseases.

The Emperor's troops had been the least of it. Against the Italians' 400 aircraft, the bearded Haile Selassie could match thirteen – of which only eight, all of them unarmed, ever left the ground. Of his 250,000 troops, only one-fifth had modern weapons. Against the ruthless Badoglio – who had not scrupled to spray the flanks of his advance with mustard gas, crippling thousands of tribesmen – the Abyssinians never stood a chance.

But on the night of 9 May, Mussolini spelt out none of this to his devoted people. He spoke only of glory. As he reached the climax of his speech, his voice soared into a peroration that held millions all over Italy spellbound. 'Raise up your banners, stretch forth your arms,' he exhorted them, 'lift up your hearts and sing to the Empire which appears in being after fifteen centuries on the fateful hills of Rome.'

Then, in the style he had made his own, he appealed to each one of his listeners directly: 'Will you be worthy of this Empire?' A roar of voices like a hurricane carried the answer back to him: '*Si, si, si!*'

In that moment, the city went wild. Thousands took up the cry, 'Duce, Duce, Duce,' a wild, mindless chant, swelling finally into a barrage of sound in which the words were no longer distinguishable. Across the piazza, the august Governor of Rome, Prince Piero Colonna, fought his way to a traffic cop's rostrum, seized the man's white baton, then conducted the crowd like a cheer-leader. And other reactions, though more private, were as deeply felt. In a modest Topolino car parked in a side-street, Rachele Mussolini, no wife to push herself forward, listened to a portable radio and felt a lump in her throat: both Vittorio and Bruno, her sons, as well as Galeazzo Ciano, her son-in-law, had served as aviators in this war. At the Villa Ada, his private residence, two miles from the city, King Vittorio Emanuele felt his knees trembling so uncontrollably he had to sit down. In this moment of becoming a full-scale Emperor, the pusillanimous little King had momentarily forgiven Mussolini every pinprick, every slight.

For the real triumph was the Duce's. In nine months he had decisively worsted every enemy. He had beaten Anthony Eden, who had urged the League of Nations to extend its timid sanctions beyond arms and money to the oil that was vital to Italy's campaign. But the League, fearful of Mussolini's withdrawal from Geneva, had held back. He had defeated Adolf Hitler, whose undercover agents had supplied the Abyssinians with 16,000 rifles and 600 machine-guns, in the hope that a weakened Italy could take no stand on Austria's future. In six weeks' time, when the League shame-facedly withdrew all sanctions, he would snap his fingers at the fifty nations that had imposed them. He had become, in the words of John Gunther, 'the most formidable combination of turncoat, ruffian and man of genius in modern history'.

Now, his face set and expressionless, he stared out over the sea of faces, his hands planted on the stone balustrade, immobile, in the glare of the floodlight. It was close to midnight, for the crowd, refusing to relinquish their idol, had recalled him forty-two times to the balcony.

Among the ranks of top brass clustered to his rear stood forty-seven-year-old Achille Starace, four years Party secretary, a humour-less yes-man who even made use of a mechanical device to strengthen his handshake. Beside him, one hierarch, noting Starace's rapt expression, commented softly, 'He's like a god.' And Starace, in cold earnest, with no sense of bathos, replied: 'He *is* a god.'

Signora Giuseppina Petacci felt the stairs would never end. Always she had felt overawed by the medieval aura of Palazzo Venezia, whence Popes and Kings had sent forth their edicts. The heavy oaken cross-beams, sunlight slanting through stone-mullioned windows, the black-coated footmen with their red and silver facings, had always strengthened that impression. Today, summoned to the presence of the man who had just declared the empire, she felt a terrible trepidation.

It was three years since Claretta's plump, talkative mother had even seen Mussolini. Following her marriage in June 1931, Claretta too had lost touch with the Duce for almost a year – time enough for both her and Lieutenant Federici to repent bitterly and at leisure. Stormy quarrels, often in public places, were followed by tearful but brief reconciliations. Following Federici's service in East Africa, Claretta had agreed to give the marriage one more chance, but again the result was disastrous. Applying for a legal separation, she returned to the family apartment.

Three visits to Palazzo Venezia had followed – each one as courtly and remote from Mussolini's habitual tactics with women as in the past. Then out of the blue had come this summons for Mama Petacci to visit him.

At the far end of the Sala del Mappamondo, where the marble flooring shone dully in the gloom, Mussolini awaited her. Attired in the black uniform of the Militia's Commander-in-Chief, he stood at first as still as a statue. Suddenly, with jerky marionette's steps, he marched to greet her – so brusquely that the old lady's heart skipped a beat.

Then she saw that Mussolini was as white as a sheet. This 'godlike' being trembled before her like a young clerk beseeching his boss for a rise.

'Signora,' the Duce gulped out, 'have I your permission to love Clara?'

5. 'I'll Stick to Him, Rain or Shine'

May 1936 – June 1940

As the stutter of the drums sounded, muffled yet insistent, across the Königsplatz in Munich, Albrecht von Kessel glanced upwards. Six yards to his rear, the powermongers of the Nazi Party stood rigidly at attention on the podium, resplendent in their snuff-brown, gold-braided uniforms: Führer Adolf Hitler, Deputy Führer Rudolf Hess, Minister of Labour Robert Ley, the club-footed Propaganda Minister, Josef Goebbels. But on this mellow autumn afternoon, von Kessel, a thirty-four-year-old diplomat of the Chief of Protocol's staff, had no eyes for the party's top brass. His gaze was fixed on Benito Mussolini.

Up to now, von Kessel was satisfied. At 3 p.m. on 25 September, 1937, the Duce's first visit to Germany was only seven hours old – yet to date it had gone as badly as von Kessel had hoped. Mentally, he ticked off the disasters on his fingers. The ceremonial drive from the Hauptbahnhof to Hitler's five-room apartment on Prinzregentenplatz – a misfire from first to last. Barely a soul had cheered the man who three years earlier had dared speed troops to the Austrian border. The one-hour parley between the two dictators – worse still. Friendship with Japan, contempt for Britain and France were safe topics – but that sullen silence along the streets had irked Mussolini. Just as in Venice, he bit off his words, barely courteous.

To von Kessel's delight, the official luncheon was equally a fiasco. His mood growing blacker, Mussolini uttered barely a dozen sentences. Hitler, ignoring his buttered vegetables, chewed instead at his finger-nails. His hands clenched and unclenched convulsively. For von Kessel, as for other officials of the Auswärtiges Amt, the Foreign Ministry, the prospect of an Italo-German alliance after centuries of mistrust and enmity was suicidal. Yet ten months earlier, in November 1936, Mussolini, angered both by the League's sanctions and by their impotence to halt Hitler, had spoken for the first time of a line 'lying like an axis' between Rome and Berlin. Above all, von Kessel hoped to see that axis remain a figment of Fascist speech.

Then, as he later recalled, von Kessel 'witnessed a tragedy – the birth of the Axis then and there.' Across the stone flags of the Königsplatz tramped file after file of brown-shirted storm-troopers and black-shirted S S, 2000 men, goose-stepping ten abreast to the crash of the drumbeat in bloodless assembly-line precision, voices defiantly proclaiming '*Deutschland über Alles*'. 'With their blond curls,' von Kessel was to recall, 'they looked as strong as oxen – and Mussolini's whole face was radiant as he watched them.'

In truth, the Duce, self-avowed pastmaster of bluff, was reacting just as Hitler had hoped he would. All his life a weak man who worshipped strength, he now saw the once-despised Hitler as the personification of muscle and might, the man who could make the world tremble as eleven-year-old Benito Mussolini had once dreamed that he might do.

Since that apocalyptic night on the balcony of Palazzo Venezia, Mussolini had been destined for this moment. Daily, his speeches grew more bellicose – 'the olive branch of peace springs from a forest of eight million bayonets', he snarled at one Bologna rally. As a dictator who decreed that all able-bodied Italians began military training at six, he had scant patience with Austria's pacifist-minded Chancellor Kurt von Schuschnigg, who even refused to attend his summer manoeuvres. In a brutally candid interview with the *New York Herald Tribune*'s John Whitaker, Mussolini explained: 'Next fall I am going to invite Hitler to . . . make Austria German. In 1934, I could have beaten his army . . today I cannot.'

But what, the journalist asked, of Italy's future if by 1940 no combination of world powers could stand against Germany? 'In that moment,' Mussolini cried, brandishing his clenched fist, 'Italy will be the ally of Germany.'

Thus Hitler's formal invitation to visit the Third Reich aroused all Mussolini's gnawing inferiority. 'We must appear more Prussian than the Prussians,' he fussed, and at once set three tailors to work designing a brand-new gala uniform for receptions, a high-necked black tunic studded with gold buttons. To dispassionate observers, it seemed that the Duce, who now sported eleven medal-ribbons and six different hats, often changing his uniform five times a day, was already fast moving in that direction.

All through his whirlwind four-day trip Mussolini was enthralled by a display of naked power. At Mecklenburg, he revelled in the autumn manoeuvres, as thrilled by light tanks mounting only machine-guns as he was by the low-level air attacks of the new Luftwaffe, with Junkers 52 transport planes standing in as bombers. He marvelled at the German Fleet's mock-attack on Swinemünde and at the fiery inferno of the Krupp steel factory at Essen.

The trivial held Mussolini as rapt as the fundamental. As his ten-coach armoured train neared Spandau-West station, over seven miles from Berlin's city centre, he sprang from his seat like a school-boy. As if from nowhere, Hitler's train had drawn alongside on an adjacent track. For fifteen minutes the coaches ran side by side, exactly level – a masterpiece of driving which the engine drivers had rehearsed for days – until suddenly, as Heerstrasse approached, the Germans crept ahead. Their train reached the terminus platform seconds before the Italians – in time for Hitler to walk the few brief paces and shake the beaming Mussolini's hand.

A simpleton for statistics, he took every Nazi shadow for substance. Following one inspection, the Duce summoned his entourage to his private coach to impart some hush-hush intelligence: according to Dr Josef Goebbels, in the event of war, Germany's reserve supplies included over sixty million tins of corned beef. Patiently Count Leonardo Vitetti of the Foreign Office broke it to him: this equalled Germany's population, and worked out at one tin per citizen.

For his part, Hitler viewed the fragile truce more cynically. To be sure, apart from his secret arms-sales to the Abyssinians, his muzzled Press had given the Duce's war wholehearted support – for Mussolini's flouting of the League of Nations had helped Germany's cause. On 3 March, 1936, Hitler's troops, defying the Treaty of Versailles, had marched into the demilitarized Rhineland. And following Italy's rift with Great Britain, she was now in the market for six million tons of German coal each year – as against 9000 tons from Britain.

Yet at heart Hitler still distrusted Italy profoundly. 'In an un-reliable world,' he told one official, 'there is only one thing that can be relied on – the unreliability of Italy and Mussolini.' His Minister for War and Commander-in-Chief of the German Armed Forces, Field Marshal Werner von Blomberg, was more blistering still. As an observer at Italy's 1937 summer manoeuvres, he had been flabbergasted to see forty men defending every pill-box – and to learn that the shortage of trained non-coms made this imperative. Pressed by German journalists as to the likely victor of a future war, Blomberg replied: 'Whichever country doesn't have Italy as an ally.'

It was ironic that the one Fascist official Hitler truly hated had done most to goad the Duce into toeing the Axis line: his son-in-law, thirty-four-year-old Galeazzo Ciano, nicknamed 'The Ducellino', who one year earlier, to the horror of seasoned diplomats, had become Mussolini's Minister of Foreign Affairs.

'We all felt humiliated that Italy had to deal with the world through a boy like that,' Dino Grandi was to recall, and with reason. Even Mussolini's sternest critics knew that nepotism was alien to his nature, and that only his love for Edda could have prompted such a blunder. But though it had taken Ciano only six years to rise from Vice-Consul to Minister, he had settled into his sumptuous Palazzo Chigi office less than six days before, placing a new accent on foreign affairs – the '*tono Fascista*', the Fascist tone.

To Chigi men, Abyssinia had been an incident – but Ciano saw it as the birth of a new era. From now on, the keynote of his policy was a savage disregard for custom, with diplomatic meetings staged like head-on military encounters. Playing on Mussolini's hostility to the western powers, Ciano won him over, against his better judgment, into aping Hitler's support of the Nationalists in the Spanish Civil War. In Germany he himself had sealed the pact committing 70,000 Fascists to Spain. Within two months of his ill-starred trip to Germany, the Duce, following Hitler's lead, would quit the League of Nations.

More than any other man Ciano reduced Italian diplomacy to a new low. At Palazzo Chigi, officials found that any memo more than a page long was tossed aside: the new Minister spent more time in his private bathroom, straightening his pearl-grey bow-tie or checking his flabby 180 pounds on the scales. Most of his schemes were dreamed up at Rome's fashionable Acquasanta Golf Club, where sycophants hung on every word of his biting, malicious prattle, for he was rarely found at home; though Ciano loved his children, Fabrizio, six, and Raimonda, four, he and Edda had early agreed to live their own lives. For Edda, life was now a round of smart couturiers, dry Martinis and all-night gambling parties; for her husband, the beach at Ostia, surrounded by a bevy of movie starlets.

But Ciano had little time for those outside his circle. 'You won't find any foreign diplomats at *my* parties,' he bragged to one Italian ambassador, and often the wives, at least, were grateful. Soon reports reached Hitler that at diplomatic receptions, Ciano unabashedly pinched German wives like any tramcar Lothario – and this, along with his pomaded hair, his habit of cabling Consul-General Giuseppe Renzetti 'Fix women' before ever he took a trip to

Germany, early led the Führer to dub him *'Der abscheuliche Knabe'* (That disgusting boy).

Yet all through Mussolini's September tour of Germany, Ciano was like a shadow at his side – braced at attention, mechanically parroting: 'At your orders, Duce,' loudest in his condemnation of the democracies. On the night of 28 September, it was symbolic that he stood closest to the Duce as, perched on a podium in Berlin's Maifeld, he set the seal on Italy's fate.

'When Fascism has a friend,' he told the million Germans gathered in drenching rain to hear him, 'it marches with that friend right to the end,' and though few could hear his halting German above the hissing downpour, he saw through the twilight a million arms raised in the Roman salute. Drenched to the skin but jubilant, he hastened to call Claretta Petacci in Rome from his private apartment in the President's Palace. 'It was a triumph,' he told her. 'I want to feel you near me at this moment.'

Both the Duce and Galeazzo Ciano knew the price of that triumph: the rape of Austria. They had learned as much from one German who never hesitated to lay it on the line: Reichsmarschall Hermann Göring, Commander-in-Chief of the Luftwaffe. At Karinhall, Göring's vast estate forty miles from Berlin, Mussolini and his aides watched patiently while the corpulent Reichsmarschall gambolled with his pet lion cubs, put his electric train-set in motion and demonstrated a patent massage machine.

Suddenly, without a word, he unrolled before them a vast map of Europe. Its import shocked even the cynical Mussolini. Already, as with Germany, the 32,000 square miles of Austria were coloured blood-red. Raising his eyebrows, the Duce commented: 'That's a little previous, isn't it?'

Göring stared at him, his blue eyes guileless. His face puckered in amusement like a mischievous urchin's. 'Well – ' he shrugged – 'it represents what the position will be one day – and I'm too poor a man to go on buying myself new maps all the time.'

The Colosseum was burning. Greedily the flames clawed towards the evening sky; the Tiber's dark waters trembled with the ruddy glow. From more than four hundred churches sounded the sad tolling of the Angelus. On any one of Rome's seven hills a watcher that night saw the city slip back eighteen centuries, when the fires for which men blamed the Emperor Nero raged from street to street.

At that moment – 8 p.m. on 3 May, 1938 – the true culprit was relaxed in the back seat of his black Lancia, grinning as hugely as a stage director after a triumphant first night. Ahead of Benito Mussolini clip-clopped a six-horse state carriage, flanked by mounted escorts in gleaming cuirasses and horsetail-plumed helmets, carrying King Vittorio Emanuele and his guest of honour, Adolf Hitler, to the Palazzo del Quirinale. Behind him streamed car-loads of Fascist dignitaries and Hitler's 500-strong retinue.

It was small wonder the Duce was proud. As far back as November he had begun, like a born impresario, planning for Hitler's return visit – and in those months more than a hundred telegrams on pinpoints of protocol had passed between the capitals. But tonight the results were Wagnerian enough to impress even the Führer. The 'burning' Colosseum – amphorae of flaring magnesium lit by red bulbs – was just one facet of a £1,000,000 display, from the brand-new façade of Ostiense railway station, used for barely ten minutes, opening on to the newly-christened 'Piazza Adolf Hitler', to the 100 miles of electric wiring that lit Bernini's rippling fountains. Along the three-mile route from station to Quirinale, 100,000 soldiers, packed eight deep, cordoned the pavements, beneath jet-black swastikas and golden fasces bannering from housefronts painted '*Viva il Führer.*'

The police of both countries had been busy, too. Ahead of Hitler, on his first-ever visit to Rome, had gone 500 bi-lingual security agents of the *Sicherheitsdienst* (SS Security Service), disguised as tourists, working in cells of three. And for good measure, Italy's OVRA had placed 6000 citizens whose loyalties were suspect in preventive custody – among them a workman who hailed a gang of roadmenders: 'Easy to see the Germans are coming – you're digging trenches.'

At the Palazzo del Quirinale, where Hitler was to stay, Nazi officials, impressed by the drilled formations of students wheeling to form a swastika, showered the euphoric Duce with compliments.

Soon after, despite the evening's crowded schedule, Mussolini found time to call Giorgio Pini, editor of *Il Popolo d'Italia*, 400 miles away in Milan. So incoherent with excitement the journalist could barely hear him, the Duce burst out: 'Pini, do you know what Goebbels just asked? He asked who were the young officers lining the route – he couldn't believe it was the Party youth movement. He called it "a perfect spectacle"!'

For Mussolini, bent on proving himself 'more Prussian than the Prussians', no higher praise was possible.

On that night and in the week that followed the Duce was too

blind with vainglory to realize that subtle undercurrents were stirring
– undercurrents of hatred which five years later were to sweep him
and his regime away like flotsam on a riptide. That night he knew
only that Hitler, who now revered him as 'the last Roman', stood
forever in his debt.

Seven weeks before, on Sunday, 13 March, one of the shortest
diplomatic messages on record had been routed from the Hotel
Weinzinger at Linz, Hitler's Austrian home town, to Palazzo
Venezia, Rome. It read: '*Mussolini dieses werde Ich Ihnen nie vergessen.*
(Mussolini, I'll never forget this.) Hitler.' And to his emissary,
Prince Philip of Hesse, who two days earlier had been closeted with
the Duce, Hitler had vowed emotionally, 'Whenever Mussolini
should be in need, or in danger, he can be sure that I'll stick to
him, rain or shine – and if the whole world were to rise against
him . . .'

To rate this pledge of undying loyalty, the Duce had done only
what Hitler expected of him over the invasion of Austria – precisely
nothing. At the eleventh hour, following non-committal discussions
on Austria's future, the Duce had proved 'unavailable' on the telephone to Chancellor Kurt von Schuschnigg. No Italian divisions had
been rushed to the Brenner Pass on the damp March night when
German troops tramped into Austria to add seven million subjects to
Hitler's Third Reich.

'I congratulate you on the way you have solved the Austrian
problem. I had already warned Schuschnigg,' had been Mussolini's
oblique intimation that he would stand on the sidelines.

Despite this, within one hour of setting foot in Rome, Hitler
was seething. No man whom Mussolini had created a Corporal
of Honour of the Fascist Militia, he told his aides angrily, should
have been forced to ride in an antediluvian horse-drawn carriage
with the man he spitefully christened 'King Nutcracker'. ('In fifty
years' time, Führer,' Mussolini consoled him, 'there's hope that the
Court will discover the internal combustion engine.') As the Duce's
guest, he would have been content to stay at the Grand Hotel along
with Goebbels and Hess – but not, as the King's guest, at the Quirinale. 'In this dirty old museum,' he told SS chief Heinrich Himmler
balefully, 'you smell the true air of the catacombs.'

His fury was nothing beside the King's. Already the misanthropic
monarch had made plain to Mussolini how bitterly he disapproved
of the growing ties between Italy and Germany. 'These Germans are
like priests and women,' he grumbled. 'Give them a finger and they

want the whole arm.' Irked that Hitler had seated himself first in his state coach, he was angrier still at entertaining an ex-corporal to a state banquet – a man who against all court etiquette insisted on his personal photographer, Heinrich Hoffman, having a place of honour.

Over dinner, to his chagrin, Hitler launched into a strident lecture. 'Mussolini is not only my friend, but my master, my chief,' he asserted. 'He has awakened dreams in my spirit and in the spirits of millions of Germans.' He could have probed no sorer point. Five weeks earlier, the King, 'white with fury, his jaw quivering', as Mussolini later recalled, had been enraged to find the Duce was bulldozing through a law creating two First Marshals of the Empire – placing himself on the same level as the King. For days Vittorio Emanuele had refused to sign the decree – then, typically, had given in. 'At any other time but one of crisis, I would have abdicated,' he spluttered, 'I would tear off this Marshal's braid.'

Now, grunting tersely at Hitler's extravagant praise, he bent so ferociously to his favourite dish, potato dumplings with butter, that few other guests even tasted it. The moment the royal fork was laid aside, footmen, following etiquette, whipped away their plates.

The Royal Family felt as strongly. Crown Prince Umberto had been angry enough at having to quit his private apartment – no other suite had been thought good enough for the Führer. But to make matters worse, the head of the German Chancellery's Ceremonial had ordered an elaborate brocade bedspread, embroidered with a German eagle, to be made at Umberto's expense. 'Burn the damned thing,' the Crown Prince ordered passionately, following Hitler's departure, 'I never want to see it again.'

The stately Queen Elena, descending the main staircase, was shocked to see Hitler's black-uniformed SS bodyguard lurking behind pillars, hands clamped on their holsters. 'Policemen in my house?' she demanded in outraged accents. 'See that they leave *immediately!*' Nor did Josef Goebbels endear himself to the King. Baring his teeth in a contemptuous grin as he crossed the Throne Room, he commented: 'Keep that gold and velvet object, but put the Duce on it – the other chap's too small.'

In all these encounters there were danger signs the Duce failed to read.

Instead, Mussolini saw only the pomp and fantasy of a six-day programme designed to surpass everything he had been shown in Germany . . . the manoeuvres at Centocelle, when 50,000 Italian troops lifted their rifles to fire a volley echoing as a single shot . . . the breathtaking naval review in the sunlit bay of Naples, when Hitler, standing with the King on the admiral's bridge of the *Cavour*, watched ninety black submarines, moving in nine parallel lines of ten, cross the bows of the flagship. Abruptly, in seventy-five seconds, they vanished from sight – to surface within five minutes, still in perfect formation, all their deck-guns blazing. Then, as darkness thickened, the hills and waterfront of Naples blazed into life under an £85,000 display of lights – a huge sky-sign, 'HEIL HITLER', vying with the angry red glow of Vesuvius.

But the prize Hitler sought above all – a firm alliance with Italy – eluded him. 'A treaty with Mussolini is due,' he told Hans-Georg von Mackensen, his new Ambassador in Rome. 'He can have a free hand in the Mediterranean and we in the north-east.' But though Hitler raised the point with the Duce three times in six days, Mussolini was evasive. And despite his pro-German leanings, Galeazzo Ciano adroitly sidestepped all approaches by Hitler's new Foreign Minister, the arrogant, vengeful, forty-five-year-old Joachim von Ribbentrop. The Axis friendship, Ciano smiled, made any alliance superfluous.

Hitler's irritation grew. The comic-opera brilliance of the naval review did not fool him for an instant: his observers had reported that three-quarters of Mussolini's fleet was obsolete and that due to a shortage of trained officers almost all the submarines were commanded by yeomen. Yet display followed futile display . . . an entire town built of cardboard at Furbara airfield, erupting with a roar as Italian bombers carried out a low-level attack . . . Italian infantry advancing behind a barrage of live shells . . . more than £200,000 squandered in one morning solely to impress him. Even Hitler's cherished trips to the Pantheon had to be sneaked in at dawn, before yet another display of non-existent military might.

Amid the blaze of light and colour, one small island of buildings remained obstinately dark: the tiny Papal State across the Tiber. Angered that all his efforts to obtain guarantees for his Church in Austria had failed, Pope Pius XI had refused even to remain in the same city as the arch foe of Catholicism. 'The air of Rome has become unbreathable,' he stated publicly. Retreating to the papal summer residence at Castel Gandolfo, seventeen miles from Rome, he closed down the Vatican Museum, which Hitler had planned to visit, and barred the Vatican City to the entire German party.

'Sad things are happening,' he told a general audience on the day of the Holy Cross, one day after Hitler's arrival, 'among [them] . . .

the fact that it has not been considered . . . untimely to hoist in Rome the emblem of a cross that is not the Cross of Christ.'

If Mussolini saw this as a danger sign he shrugged it off.

Hitler, like many an unwelcome guest, was quick to sense the hostility. All Rome hummed with the rumour – diligently spread by the King – that at 1 a.m. on his first night at the Quirinale, Hitler had roused the entire household, vowing he could never sleep until a woman had turned down his bed before his eyes. Only when a chambermaid had been recruited from a nearby hotel would he retire to rest. Following a gala performance of *Aïda* in the San Carlo Opera House in Naples, fragrant with thousands of white roses, the Chief of Protocol, Vicco von Bülow-Schwante, had allowed Hitler too little time to change out of tails. As the King, in full dress uniform, watched maliciously, the Führer was forced to inspect his guard of honour in an ill-fitting frock-coat and a silk hat that almost enveloped his ears.

'Do you realize what you've done?' Hitler stormed at the hapless Bülow. 'You've forced me to cross Naples dressed like the President of the French Council!'

The sullen apathy of the crowds galled Hitler too. At Florence, his four-hour tour of the Uffizi Picture Gallery was marred by the realization that the cheers rending the air were a polite fiction: crowd-effects from an Italian movie were being relayed from open windows by scores of amplifiers. And once, when Mussolini, perturbed by the chilly unease, urged some onlookers to cheer, the crowd instead broke into a storm of 'Duce! Duce!' 'Not me! *Him!*' Mussolini exploded, but at last, grinning, he was forced to give up.

To State Secretary Baron Ernst von Weizsäcker, Hitler confided with a sigh: 'You don't know how happy I am to be going back to Germany.'

As clearly as any diplomat, one woman sensed the trouble that lay ahead. At 10 p.m. on Friday, 6 May, along with her fifteen-year-old sister Myriam, Claretta Petacci was one of an audience of 60,000 seated beneath the flood-lit umbrella pines of Piazza di Siena, in the heart of the Borghese Gardens. Fifteen yards to her left, his eyes fixed on the grassy arena, sat the man she loved, Benito Mussolini. Ahead of him, in the front row of seats, Adolf Hitler, plainly irritated by his host, the King, fidgeted and chewed his nails.

As 800 picturesquely-garbed couples spun and pirouetted in their regional dances, the lighted arena was a swirl of colour: the crude sheepskins of Sardinian shepherds in striking contrast with the

violet corsages of the women from the Apennine Mountains, the
scarlet bell-shaped skirts of Calabria.

The symbolism was lost on the Führer. Twice screwing round in
his chair, he pantomimed mute interrogation. Each time, caught fast
in the vice of protocol, Mussolini shrugged apologetically, shaking
his head. Without the King's permission, he could not approach
the ceremonial chairs of the front row.

Abruptly Hitler lost patience. Ignoring the King, he craned
backwards. He beckoned peremptorily, as if to a slow-witted servant.
Claretta watched the Duce, irresolute, half-rise to his feet.

Thoughtfully, to the fifteen-year-old beside her, she murmured:
'You know, I don't like that – I don't like that at all.'

Benito Mussolini listened intently, but all the house was sleeping.
Primrose-yellow light flooded his bedroom as dawn broke over the
Adriatic. Then, towelling robe over his swimming trunks, he stole
quietly down the stairs of the nine-roomed family villa at Riccione,
through the door giving access to the beach.

At discreet intervals, weary plainclothes agents ducked from
behind breakwaters, but the Duce motioned them back. Soon his
stocky figure, walking with a rolling gait that recalled a sailor's, was
a distant speck along the tan-coloured sand.

Claretta was waiting where she always did – in the lee of the
fishermen's boats drawn up along the shore. She wore the white
swimsuit, the white straw hat trimmed with blue ribbon, that was his
favourite costume. This morning, as at every summer dawn in
Riccione, the two would first pace the shoreline, talking. Then with
a run and a splash Mussolini was away, cleaving the water with a
powerful claw stroke, Claretta following in his wake. A hundred
yards back, a spaced and implacable line of agents kept rubberneckers
clear of the beach.

By late afternoon, when the Duce took his 'official' swim, and
women of all ages and classes plunged into the sea – often fully
clothed – to mob him, Claretta would be seven miles away down the
coast at Rimini. In a rowing-boat, the patient Myriam at the oars,
she would be heading steadily for a point 1000 yards off shore. When
the Duce, tiring of the fan-worship, boarded a motor-launch and
set out for the open sea, this was the rendezvous he sought. Here they
talked again and swam from the launch until the sun went down.

Afterwards, looking back to that summer of 1938, it was the
dawn meetings Claretta recalled most keenly. Once, throwing off

his robe, Mussolini stood bare-chested in the early light, declaiming to the waves: 'I love this girl, I adore her! Let the sea know it, I'm not ashamed to say it. I adore her – she is my youth, my spring, the most beautiful thing in all my life.' And still he bellowed, while Claretta stood, half-frightened, half-enraptured: 'I swear it in front of the sea, in front of this sun rising before me . . .'

At times she stayed for hours, sipping mineral water, on the private beach of Rimini's Grand Hotel where her family spent the summer, waiting for his call. Occasionally they managed an evening drive along the dusty Romagna roads, the scenes of his boyhood, then at 8 p.m. returned for family dinner: the Duce to Villa Mussolini, Claretta to the Grand Hotel. Often enough her day ended with family friction. Signora Petacci was thrilled by her daughter's distinguished protector, but her husband, distrait and taciturn, was frostily disapproving – until Claretta's genuine happiness won his grudging assent.

For the twenty-six-year-old Claretta, incurably in love with a man of fifty-five – so age-conscious he now forbade the newspapers to signal his birthday – it was a life as painfully circumscribed as an invalid's. Yet she had accepted it uncomplainingly from the day of the first Palazzo Venezia visit following her mother's summons, when Mussolini, keeping her hands in his, quoted a sonnet from Petrarch:

> *Blest be the day, the month, the hour, the year,*
> *In which my eyes looked into hers . . .*

From then on, their life together was ruled by the seasons. In summer, the dawn and sunset meetings at Riccione – or in the beach chalet at Castel Porziano, near Rome, a gift to Mussolini from the King. They ate picnic lunches, then played with a medicine ball, before the Duce studied that day's newspapers. To rule out gossip from the police agents, Myriam always made one of the party and she was present, too, at the ski-ing sessions at Terminillo, the new winter resort north of Rome. Often the Duce came a cropper a dozen times in one session, attempting a right hand Christiania turn, yet he would flounder on for seven hours non-stop.

Normally Claretta's life was bounded by an apartment's four walls – the three-room Cybo suite on the top-floor of Palazzo Venezia, reached only by a lift. Each day from 3 p.m. she whiled away the hours in the Zodiac Room – named for its sky-blue ceiling, spangled with gold stars – waiting for Mussolini to slip away and join her. She asked nothing more of life than this: to read poetry with him, play a violin duet, listen to a new Chopin record or hear him expound his grandiose plans for Italy.

Each day she resorted to small ruses to recall her presence to him. There was the coloured wooden ornament reposing on his desk in the Sala del Mappamondo, a rustic dwelling with a heart, inscribed 'A Cottage and your Heart'. There was her vase of flowers, placed before his mother's portrait – roses, violets, peach-blossom. And the letters she wrote him twice daily, on notepaper crested with a white eagle and a black dove, bearing printed mottoes: 'I am you and you are me' – or 'I can't live with you or without you.'

On many days, caught up by affairs of state, or momentarily wearying of her company, 'Ben' left her to live without him. Then Claretta read, sipped the tea brought at 4 p.m. by the sympathetic Quinto Navarra, tried on one of the fifteen brightly-coloured silk dressing-gowns trimmed with velvet collars that the Duce had given her, or experimented with a new perfume – Lanvin's *Arpège* and *Rumeur* were favourites. Or she paced the room, listening for his footfall, imprinting every detail of the apartment on her mind: the Turkish divan covered with yellow brocade, the imperial writing desk, the radiogram, with its albums of records. Knowing how he hated tobacco, she forbore from smoking. At 8 p.m. she went down in the lift, took the wheel of her Lancia-Aprilia and drove sadly home.

But home, any time after 1936, was a kind of prison too. At first it was her parents' apartment; later, from December 1938, a glittering ten-roomed show house, Camilluccia, perched on top of Monte Mario and overlooking all Rome. It was the house her mother had always craved, with picture windows and a reception hall as wide as a swimming-pool, but for Claretta, the change of locale made little difference.

All morning in her airy first-floor bedroom, dominated by a life-size photo of Mussolini playing the violin, she awaited his impulsive calls to Rome 35820 – and these were many. Fiercely jealous, he rang so often that Palazzo Venezia wits pictured Claretta going from room to room with a telephone head-set – a joke that had substance. Her rose-pink telephone with its ultra-long flex stood on a dumb waiter, enabling her to wheel it freely all over the upper storey. The family lawyer still avows: 'I wouldn't ask my worst enemy to live a life like that.'

She sought no larger stake in the Duce's life – or even lavish gifts. Apart from providing her wardrobe of dressing-gowns, to woo her with presents, or even offer financial support, never once crossed the frugal Mussolini's mind. She knew that he profoundly respected Rachele, the mother of his children – but no wife, after twenty-eight years, could give her man the blind adulation of a young girl. When his seven-year-old daughter, Anna Maria, was stricken with polio, Claretta shared Mussolini's agony; even the arrogant Duce confessed that he had prayed to God to spare her. Rome's foreign correspondents, overcoming their innate hostility, presented him with a life-size doll to speed the child's recovery – and Claretta knew how Mussolini's stern exterior had cracked. Tears trickling down his cheeks, he hugged the doll to him, utterly speechless, before turning to Press Minister Dino Alfieri.

'I can't reply to this speech,' he whispered strainedly, turning away. 'You must say something.'

But Claretta was jealous of all other women, and with reason. Typically, in any such affair, the Duce lived by his own double standard – 'recognizing,' as Myriam said later, 'Claretta's right to be jealous, his own right to pursue any opportunity that came his way.' As always there were many, and honey-tongued friends did not scruple to keep Claretta abreast of the box-score.

The Duce had broken with Margherita Sarfatti, but a few favourites, like the blonde Angela Curti-Cucciati, whom he had known since 1920, were still on the scene, along with some newcomers – Cornelia Tanzi, a gossipy brunette, and Magda Fontanges, a French journalist who related how the Duce's first act of courtship was to tweak off her black silk scarf and pretend to strangle her.

Finding Palazzo Venezia banned to her, Mlle Fontanges became convinced that the French Ambassador, Count Paul de Chambrun, was privy to the plot. Waylaying him at the Gare du Nord on his next visit to Paris, she drew a pistol from her bag and shot him ignominiously in the buttocks.

'I've got more horns than a basketful of snails,' Claretta exclaimed wrathfully to one woman friend. 'He has these women seven at a time.'

Then some spontaneous incident, like the morning he declaimed his love to the sea, would convince her all over again that he needed her. One such occasion was when Mussolini's long-time factotum, Camillo Ridolfi, who was both fencing-master and riding-master, organized a private shoot in the woods at Castel Porziano. Both Claretta and Myriam recalled other shooting parties that had followed this pattern: though the Duce let fly with both barrels his shots almost always went wide of the driven birds.

'Excellency, we are here to hit them,' Ridolfi would reprove him, but Mussolini would only shrug, grinning: 'It makes work for the gunsmiths.'

He would never, Claretta knew, have shed his iron-man aura to confess that he aimed deliberately wide, unwarrantably distressed if he brought down a pheasant or a dove. 'They're too beautiful, too beautiful,' she had heard him mutter.

But at one shoot, the results were almost fatal. All of them were standing inside the chalet that day, laughing and talking – Mussolini unaware that Ridolfi had loaded his gun for him in advance. Teasingly he sighted on Claretta. Though she implored him to stop, he continued to menace her playfully. Suddenly, she clamped her hand over the barrel, forcing it downwards. At that moment, to the Duce's horror, the gun went off. The bullet ploughed into the floor, inches from Claretta's foot.

Hurling the gun aside, Mussolini took her in his arms. Oblivious of both Myriam and Ridolfi, he repeated over and over, 'I might have killed you, *piccola* – I might have killed you.' It was just like a man, thought the teen-age Myriam dispassionately, to be so distraught that Claretta had to master her own shock to comfort Mussolini.

'I've got a tough skin,' Claretta reassured him. 'Fate didn't mean me to die like that.' Smiling through tears, she told him: 'After all, you know I'll be ready to die for you.'

Without ceremony, Marshal Italo Balbo, Governor of Libya, ex-Minister of Aviation and former intimate of Benito Mussolini, rammed his boot against the restaurant's revolving door. Into the hushed and opulent silence of the Ristorante Italia, Ferrara's most exclusive luncheon place, his guest passed first. The door spun to admit Balbo, his blue eyes flashing defiance. Deliberately, in full view of waiters and diners, he linked a comradely arm in his companion's. An embarrassed unease, punctuated by a subdued buzz of approval, swept through the room.

In years past, the sight of the man taking his seat opposite Balbo would have been occasion for a task-force of waiters, headed by the maitre d'hôtel, to bow him to his table. Today, though, the restaurant staff were playing it by ear. As of 14 July, 1938, two months after Hitler's visit to Rome, Balbo's guest, the handsome, saturnine Renzo Ravenna, Mayor of Ferrara, was a man apart. One among 57,000 Italian Jews, he stood proscribed by the new anti-semitic Aryan Manifesto which Mussolini, in slavish emulation of Hitler, had just then promulgated.

As Italo Balbo noisily set waiters scurrying, the diners exchanged meaning glances. Plainly, there was truth in the rumours that had filtered from Rome to Ferrara: rumours which had it that many of Mussolini's old-time collaborators – among them General De Bono, Giacomo Acerbo, Luigi Federzoni, and Cesare Maria De Vecchi – had joined with Balbo to oppose the Duce's latest proof of uneasy vassalage. Not only had the Marshal flown 650 miles from Tripoli to Rome to make his protest. Moving on to his hometown, Ferrara, he had paid a token call on every prominent Jew – then invited Mayor Ravenna, the community's leader, to break bread with him.

Incredibly, until now, no man had extended a warmer welcome to fugitive Jews than Benito Mussolini. And he had done more than send that sober warning to Hitler in the first days of his rise to power. Jews harried from Poland, Hungary, above all from Germany, found places in Italian universities for half fees, even gratis. Condemning Hitler's measures as 'stupid, barbarous and unworthy of a European nation', Mussolini was to go on record: 'There are two things a politician should never attack – women's fashions and men's religious beliefs.'

Now, overnight, he had given himself the lie, hardening his heart like Pharaoh against the children of Israel. From this moment, no Jew could marry an Italian, or hold a position on the bench, in the Army or in a government school. The schools were closed to foreign-born Jews, nor could they establish residence in Italy. A Jew could not open a new shop, nor own a store with more than a hundred employees.

Thanks to the native goodwill of Italians – even, ironically, of Mussolini – the laws would prove more menacing than meaningful. Over 3500 families were at once exempt, through special services to Fascism or long-standing party loyalty. US Ambassador William Phillips's plea on behalf of 3000 refugees already in Italy was not made in vain. Some Jews, like physicist Bruno Pontecorvo (who later defected to Russia), were forced to leave, but many more – among them Dr Giorgio del Vecchi, Rector of Rome University – found succour, through Pope Pius XI, within the Vatican City.

But the Duce's banal biological propaganda on the need to 'purify' the Italian race deceived nobody. Millions saw it for what it was – blatant lip-service to Adolf Hitler – and many were as quick to speak their minds. The old King warned him petulantly: 'President, the Jewish race is like a beehive – don't put your hand inside it.' And once again Pope Pius XI, who now despaired of Mussolini, proved as implacable as he had done when Hitler first crossed the Brenner. 'Spiritually we are all Jews,' he took pains to declare to a group of pilgrims, and on the page-proof of an article attacking Fascism in the Vatican newspaper *L'Osservatore Romano*, he wrote like an approving school-master, 'Ten out of ten.'

'You should be ashamed to go to school under Hitler,' was Pius's personal message to Mussolini, who was now more determined than ever to justify his policy. 'He who hesitates is lost!' Mussolini proclaimed in a rabble-rousing speech to Genoa Fascists, words for which the Pope found an immediate and chilling rejoinder. 'He who strikes at the Pope dies!' he thundered from his summer residence at Castel Gandolfo.

None was more outspokenly contemptuous than Italo Balbo. For two years now his barbed sarcasm had riled the Duce more and more – 'Would it disturb the Founder of the Empire too much if I had a word with him?' he would ask, peering round Mussolini's office door. On this anti-semitic law, his scorn was so manifest as to reduce Mussolini to apoplectic fury. 'You seem,' Balbo lisped maliciously 'to be ready to black Germany's boots.'

Shaking with anger after one such encounter, the Duce ground out: 'I won't guarantee the future of that man.'

There were many issues on which the Duce and his collaborators were now at daggers drawn. Within weeks of his return from Berlin, Mussolini had angered both the King and the Army by making compulsory the '*Passo Romano*' (the Roman step), a thinly disguised version of Germany's goosestep. Though the sycophantic Galeazzo Ciano applauded it, Emilio de Bono, promoted Marshal following the Abyssinian campaign, spoke for the entire Army when he protested: 'The soldiers' average height is 5 feet 5 inches . . . you will have a parade of stiff-necked dwarfs.'

'It is a step that the sedentary, the pot-bellied and the half-witted will never be able to master,' Mussolini announced in public defiance of the King. 'For this reason we like it.'

Abetted by Party Secretary Achille Starace, the Duce now contrived to raise the Fascist regime to the very pinnacle of preposterousness. Along with the Roman step came the abolition of the handshake, replaced by the barked greeting 'Salute the Duce', akin to 'Heil Hitler'. At party rallies, middle-aged Fascists floundered after the exhibitionist Starace to bounce on a trampoline or leap through hoops of fire. All Party members were now forbidden to drink tea, wear silk hats, visit night-clubs, or use motor-cars when cycles were handy. Plainly Mussolini was out to transform the practical, volatile Italians into a nation of grim-visaged automatons.

For many March on Rome veterans, Mussolini's vanishing sense of proportion was now disquieting. His eyes were so intent on the trees, he rarely even saw the wood – ruling that troops must march six abreast if more than a hundred were on parade, with the band striking up a new tune for every thousand men. He spent hours personally auditioning for a drum major who could throw his baton the highest.

'Two things are essential to govern Italians,' he told usher Quinto Navarra, 'policemen and music in the piazza.' But Navarra, who had served four ministers, could recall no Premier who had insisted on choosing the band's music himself – or on deciding the exact day when traffic cops donned their summer whites.

In the driving-mirror of the Duce's car, chauffeur Ercole Boratto beheld the same view. The Mussolini he had known once took a swift glance at the water-logged Pontine Marches, then left the rest to the experts. Hitler's would-be disciple sat crouched with a small black note-book on his knees, scribbling down details of every pothole for the Minister of Public Works – or ducked from the car to present a prize to any roadmender working in the rain. Often brief trips gave birth to incredible ideas he had forgotten by next morning. Once, seizing the telephone, he instructed an astonished surveyor: 'The course of the Tiber winds too much – prepare a plan to straighten it.'

Even his wife could no longer reason with him. For six years now the frugal Rachele had been using her savings to restore a crumbling forty-roomed mansion, Rocca delle Caminate, commanding the Romagna plain, a gift from the people of Forlì. Work had stopped and started, started and stopped, as her budget permitted, but she never lost faith that Benito would retire here while he was still at the peak. 'Let's finish now,' she urged him. 'We've been too lucky – let's go to Rocca.'

But Mussolini had no intention of quitting the fray. A man who felt habitually threatened, he was relaxed only when life's hostilities were out in the open – and he had come to believe himself as omnipotent as Hitler. 'The Italians can do without the Vatican,' he blustered once. 'One sign from me would be enough to unleash all the anti-clericalism of the people . . .' His head shaven to recall Caesar, he saw himself as above the Pope. 'If people go to church now,' he boasted, 'it is only because they know the Duce requires it.'

And still he failed to heed danger signs that were plain to others.

Twice a week, on Mondays and Thursdays, attired in bowler hat, black jacket and striped trousers, he waited on the King at his private residence, Villa Ada, taking decrees for the monarch's signature. For sixteen years this had been the rule, and Mussolini was now so certain of his ascendancy he no longer put a curb on his tongue.

Comfortably ensconced on a sofa beside the King, he confided: 'There are 20,000 spineless people in Italy who are moved by the fate of the Jews.'

When the opportunity now arose to administer a right royal snub, the King never hesitated to seize it. 'Yes, Duce,' he replied coldly. 'I am one of them.'

Some were more prescient. At Leghorn's exclusive Circolo del Mare, Galeazzo Ciano threw a party one gala night that summer. It was a perfect setting. Fireworks ripped and spat between the pine trees, red, white and green, the colours of the tricolour, lighting the fluttering pennants; showers of golden sparks drifted like fireflies on the warm wind from the Tyrrhenian Sea.

All those present agreed that Galeazzo was in top form. His imitations of Hitler, von Ribbentrop, even of Achille Starace, sent screams of high-pitched laughter above the tearing sound of rockets. No one could deny that Galeazzo had done well for himself – his sumptuous flat on Via Secchi in the newly-fashionable Roman suburb of Parioli, the country place his father had built for him, inland from the sea at Ponte a Moriano, were proof of that. If he had benefited hugely from the regime, who could expect him to take its excesses too seriously?

Suddenly the laughter died. Standing on the long lit terrace to face his laughing guests, Ciano had backed against a wall – and as instantly recoiled. 'Let's move inside,' he urged them unexpectedly, 'I can't touch a wall without a shiver going down my spine.'

In the whirling golden light of a Catherine wheel, Ciano had gone white. There was a polite murmur of surprise. He elected to pass it off as a joke. 'Every time I go near a wall,' he explained uneasily, 'I always feel there's a firing squad ready to take aim.'

A thunderclap of laughter exploded from the terrace, soaring with the rockets over the green swell of the sea. Everyone felt it was Galeazzo's best witticism in years.

Abruptly at 8.30 p.m. on 29 September the glass double doors of the salon on the first floor of the Führerbau on Königsplatz swung

open. On this momentous autumn night in 1938 the delegates at
the historic Munich Conference were adjourning for dinner. Along
with his colleagues, journalist Asvero Gravelli of Rome's *Il Mattino*
pressed forward, eager for any crisp new crumb of information.

For more than six hours Gravelli and the others had watched,
through the sound-proof doors, a silent pantomime that was deciding
the destiny of Europe. They had seen the German Foreign Ministry's
interpreter Paul Schmidt heatedly demanding that his translations
be heard without interruption, like a schoolmaster trying to keep
an unruly class in order. They had watched Adolf Hitler, his face
black as thunder, fidgeting on a sofa, legs crossed defiantly, unfolding
his arms only to glance at the watch in his hand like a baleful timekeeper. The British Prime Minister Neville Chamberlain no longer
lived up to his recent boast that he was 'tough and wiry'; he had
yawned repeatedly all through. Premier Edouard Daladier of France
also seemed dispirited, often adjourning to an ante-room for a tot
of his favourite Pernod.

Only Benito Mussolini, pacing the room hands in pockets, seemed
bored and remote from the strife, as if he knew too well that the
outcome was already decided.

Now, as Mussolini made to leave, Gravelli, long in the inner
councils of the Fascist Party, hastened forward. As he helped him
struggle into his topcoat he asked eagerly: 'How did it go, Duce?'
With the magnanimous air of a man who has done posterity some
small favour, Mussolini replied: 'Well, not too badly – I'm sure I
have saved Europe.'

A few paces away, the Duce's chauffeur nodded fervently. Ten
hours earlier, arriving with Mussolini's entourage at Munich's
Hauptbahnhof, he had noticed a strange phenomenon: this morning
Hitler's SS bodyguard were all wearing grey-green, not the black
uniforms that Boratto recalled from the past. And when the chauffeur
buttonholed a non-com known to him, the reply had been discon-
certing: 'But this is war, old friend. We're ready to march, and no
conference in the world can stop us!'

At 6 p.m. on 28 September, when Mussolini, along with Galeazzo
Ciano and his entourage, left Rome's Central Station for the border
town of Kufstein, silence hung over the city like a curtain. It seemed
that nothing could now avert an armed showdown in Europe. As a
pretext for seizing and destroying the Republic of Czechoslovakia,
a creation of the World War One peace treaties that he so detested,
Adolf Hitler had fomented a revolt among the three and a quarter

million Sudeten Germans who lived as a minority within its borders – an uprising which the Government had only checked by declaring martial law.

Already, following the rape of Austria, the Führer's armies surrounded the Czechs on three sides – and Hitler had resolved to 'wipe Czechoslovakia off the map'. On 14 September, urged by Daladier whose treaty obligations were to defend Czechoslovakia in the event of attack, Neville Chamberlain had made his first-ever flight to Berchtesgaden, Hitler's mountain retreat at Obersalzburg, to seek a peaceful solution.

Even then, Galeazzo Ciano noted, the Duce saw in embryo the shape of things to come. 'There will be no war,' he prophesied, 'but this is the liquidation of English prestige.'

On that same evening, while Chamberlain sat stiffly in Hitler's private sitting-room at Berchtesgaden, Mussolini, on the line to editor Giorgio Pini in Milan, had blocked out a crucial leading article for next day's *Il Popolo d'Italia*. Though the Duce held no brief for Czechoslovakia, Italy's resources, following Abyssinia and the Spanish Civil War, were at rock-bottom. As Mussolini saw it, war was out of the question – but there were ways in which harsh words and sabre-rattling might still yield Hitler all he wanted without a fight.

Overtly an 'Open Letter to Lord Runciman', Chamberlain's mediator in the Sudeten question, the Duce was in truth spelling out to the Führer just how to achieve 'one more simple modification of the map of Europe' – a nation-wide plebiscite designed to carve Czechoslovakia into zones. 'You . . . have simply to propose a plebiscite,' Mussolini counselled Runciman, 'not only for the Sudetens but for all the nationalities which demand one. Will [Czechoslovakia] refuse? Then you could let them know that England will think seven times seven before entering war to preserve . . . a "sausage state". If London lets the world know that she will not move, nobody will move. The game just isn't worth the candle . . .'

Shrewdly he struck Germany's key-note: 'If Hitler wanted to annex three and a half million Czechs, Europe would rightly be moved – and to act. But if Hitler were offered [them] he would kindly but firmly refuse such a present. The Führer is troubled about three and a half million Germans, and only about them . . .'

As events now turned out, Mussolini was right. Despite their ostensible resistance, Britain and France were ready to go to any lengths to avoid war – as ready to let Hitler call the tune as Mussolini himself. Already, at Berchtesgaden, Chamberlain had agreed in

principle to the secession of the Sudeten region. What followed at
Munich was only the shabby proof of Mussolini's prophecy.

Many delegates had never before seen the dictators side by side,
and one factor struck them above all. Despite his patent irritation
over eleventh hour trivialities, Hitler seemed entirely in Mussolini's
hands. Even during their worst disagreements, recalled André
François-Poncet, France's shrewd and courtly Ambassador to Germany, a bust of the Duce had always been a showpiece in Hitler's
study. Now his admiration was plain for all to see. Never once did
Hitler take his eyes from Mussolini's face. If the Duce nodded or
shook his head, Hitler followed suit.

Though few knew the inside details, Mussolini had just given
the Führer a firm reminder as to who was the master and who the
pupil.

In truth, the Duce's 15 September *Il Popolo* article had plunged
Hitler into a blacker, uglier mood. He was spoiling for a jack-booted
march into Prague, and the Duce's talk of pro-Nazi plebiscites struck
a discordant note. Yet by 27 September Hitler was hesitating.

France was mobilizing – and within six days sixty-five divisions
would face a mere dozen of Germany's across the frontier. On
28 September, the British Fleet would mobilize too. Romania and
Jugoslavia – in accord with Mussolini's ambassadors in Bucharest
and Belgrade – had warned Hungary that they would move if she
attacked Czechoslovakia.

What followed was an uneasy blend of farce and tragedy. At 10.30
that night Hitler, sensing that he was outmanoeuvred, urgently wired
Chamberlain in London suggesting one final talk. Now, as the British
Premier eagerly accepted, it was Mussolini's turn to lose control.
'That old fool Chamberlain is going to spoil everything,' he ranted to
Galeazzo Ciano. 'Hitler is going to spoil everything. They think they
can do without me!'

Though Mussolini had no intention either of betraying Hitler or
of fighting for Czechoslovakia, he was not going to lose face in the
eyes of the world. It was his last belated attempt to show Hitler that
the Third Reich must consult its Axis partner.

At noon on 28 September – two hours before Hitler's ultimatum
to the Czechs expired – Mussolini's envoy, Bernardo Attolico, erupted
into the Reichskänzlei. Flushed and hatless, the stooping, scholarly
Italian Ambassador had no sooner received the Duce's instructions
than he leapt into a taxi, not even waiting for the official car. As
Hitler left his office along with interpreter Paul Schmidt, Attolico,

peering through his thick-lensed spectacles, shouted unceremoniously: 'I have an urgent message to you from the Duce, Führer.'

Expertly Schmidt translated its text: through Lord Perth, its Ambassador in Rome, the British government announced that it would accept Mussolini's mediation in the Sudeten question. The Duce thought it wise to go along with this British proposal – but begged Hitler to refrain from mobilization. After a split-second, Hitler replied: 'Tell the Duce I accept.'

Mussolini now worked hard to establish his ascendancy. Four times within three hours on that critical Wednesday afternoon, Attolico returned to Hitler with further suggestions from the Duce – proposals which by 12.45 p.m. on 29 September, had resulted in the four-power conference assembling at Munich's Führerbau. The Duce's last act before leaving Rome had been to press a 2000 lire (£20) bonus on the switchboard operator who secured twenty priority calls, assuring him of his finest hour.

For the next thirteen hours, Mussolini held all the diplomatic aces. At the border town of Kufstein, where he joined Hitler's train, he was monosyllabic and unsmiling – 'as magisterial as a Buddha', recalled Filippo Anfuso, one of Ciano's aides. To Hitler's defiant greeting: 'I have finished the Siegfried Line, Duce,' he made no answer at all. The proposals on which the two now reached final agreement were embodied in a draft memo from three men – Hermann Göring, Baron Konstantin von Neurath, and State Secretary Ernst von Weizsäcker – but it was, Mussolini knew, the identical solution he had plumped for fourteen days back in the columns of *Il Popolo*.

That afternoon, as legal advisers, secretaries and adjutants packed the conference room, swelling the tense crowd gathered round the nations' premiers, Mussolini played other trump cards. The one man with halting proficiency in German, English and French, he moved expertly from delegate to delegate – clarifying an obscure clause, identifying a map reference, revelling in his role as master-mediator.

Nor did his conscience once prick him over Munich's most shameful aspect: the total absence of Eduard Beneš, President of Czechoslovakia, whom Hitler had expressly refused to admit. In the agreement that yielded up to Germany 11,000 square miles of Czech territory – including seventy per cent of its heavy industries, eighty-six per cent of its chemicals and all its fortifications – no single Czech representative had any voice at all.

Unusually, at dinner that night in Hitler's private apartment, Mussolini ate and drank with a relish to rival Göring's. Chuckling, he confided a secret to the disgruntled Hitler: if the British had only called his bluff at the time of Abyssinia, extending their sanctions to oil, his campaign would have lasted exactly one week.

Soon after 1 a.m. on 30 September, when the four powers signed the Munich Agreement – and found the inkstand dry – the Duce's strangely naive conviction that he had 'saved Europe' and preserved the rump state of Czechoslovakia from invasion was absolute in his mind. The wild cheers from the tense crowds lining Munich's streets even at 2 a.m. blinded him to the fact that he had mistakenly boarded Chamberlain's car, flying the Union Jack.

Yet twenty-four hours later the cheers struck a harsh note in his ears. Once more he was the man of the hour who had saved Europe from war; the King had even journeyed to Florence to greet him. But now he heard Italian cheers on Italian soil and saw Italian peasants kneel in prayer beside the railway lines, and the knowledge galled him – how could the imperial people he was striving to mould greet news of peace with such acclaim? Along the Via Nazionale leading from the Central Station to Palazzo Venezia, he rode in silence, his teeth gritted, beneath floral arches of laurel leaves.

At 6.30 p.m. on 1 October, he again faced the crowds from his Palazzo Venezia balcony – but this time his mood of disenchantment was there for all to see.

'I have brought you peace,' he flung at them disdainfully, like a man tossing a scrap to a dog, and his lip curled, looking out over the vast mass of upraised tearful faces. 'Isn't peace,' he asked them with ineffable contempt, 'what you wanted?'

Soon it would be dawn. Along the upper loggia of the Courtyard of San Damaso, the heart of the Vatican City, a faint blue light crept by inches, tinting Raphael's swirling frescoes. This morning, Friday, 10 February, 1939, Pope Pius XI would not see the dawn. It was 5.20 a.m., more than an hour before his normal rising, and he was dying.

The next day was the tenth anniversary of the Lateran Treaty which he had spent seven years negotiating, in the hope of settling the Roman Question and much more besides. But somehow eighty-two-year-old Achille Ratti, who had chosen 'Pius' as the name of peace, had found keeping the peace with the Fascists almost beyond him. Though he had suffered three heart attacks the past November, he had refused to rest. In his third floor apartment, the Supreme Pontiff of the Holy Roman Church, the Vicar of Christ on Earth, had received his cardinals propped in a chair, emphasizing 'The Pope must be Pope and not stay in bed.'

In the courtyard the cardinals in their purple robes were alighting from black Fiat limousines. The halberd-bearing Swiss Guard stood immobile in the dawn. Upstairs, Pius was in a coma, sinking fast. Much earlier, standing near the bedside, his physician had heard him sigh: 'We have so much to do.'

He had uttered no other word at 5.31 a.m. when his breathing stopped and the bright lights came on in the shuttered room.

A white veil covered his face, and the low chanting of the Penitential Psalms and the Office for the Dead filled the death chamber. The Cardinal Camerlengo, sixty-two-year-old Eugenio Pacelli, Vatican Secretary of State, knelt apart on a violet pillow. Within twenty days, on his 63rd birthday, blue-white smoke furling from the chimney of the Sistine Chapel would proclaim that the Conclave of Cardinals had made its choice, and across St Peter's Square, twenty loudspeakers would chant the name of the ascetic Eugenio Pacelli as Pope Pius XII.

But all this lay in the future, and this morning there were solemn rites as yet unperformed. Now the servants bared Pius's face, and Pacelli, approaching with two other Cardinals, struck the Pope's broad placid forehead three times with a silver hammer.

Three times, in the age-old ritual, they called him by name: 'Ratti – are you alive or dead?' Then, out of the silence, Pacelli said: 'The Pope is in truth dead,' and all those in the brightly-lit room fell to their knees.

The largest of all St Peter's bells, the eleven-ton *Campanone*, boomed across the city. In Trastevere the pious, fun-loving, labouring-class quarter south of Vatican City, the women heard, then drew their grief about them like a cloak, and knelt before the flickering candles of the wayside shrines. In the narrow streets across the Tiber the iron shutters were clattering up on the bars, the fruit and vegetable stalls were opening, and on the pavements people were crying.

The harsh jangling of a telephone shrilled through the silent rooms of Villa Torlonia. In the library, Benito Mussolini, already up, reached absently for the receiver. Curiously, the Duce's son Bruno, leafing through a book, wondered who would call at such an hour.

'*Finalmente se n'è andato!*' he heard his father burst out, '*Quel vecchio ostinato è morto.*'

Mussolini was smiling, but with savage exultation and his voice was as harsh as a death-rattle: 'He's gone at last! That obstinate old man is dead.'

For Galeazzo Ciano, the words jolting from the receiver of his bedside telephone held a painful and immediate intensity. There was no doubt that Benito Mussolini, on the line from Rome, was an angry man. 'Go ahead without any hesitation,' he was rasping, 'and reach some military agreement. Whatever happens, don't delay.'

What frightened Ciano was the Duce's erratic timing. In the luxury Hotel de la Ville, Milan, the clock on Ciano's night-table showed midnight – no hour for Mussolini to be reaching a decision that would turn Europe upside down. Attired in his favourite mauve silk pyjamas, Ciano was making ready for bed, yawning pleasurably as he reviewed the banquet held that evening at the Hotel Continental in honour of Joachim von Ribbentrop.

For once he had found his arrogant grey-eyed German colleague 'pleasantly calm' – and the whole evening indeed had followed that same tranquil pattern. Consommé, trout from Lake Como, beef in aspic, strawberries; polite speeches and heel-clickings; brimming glasses of Spumante raised in toasts. But talk of a military alliance – that had been the very farthest thing from Galeazzo Ciano's mind.

And the last thing, he could have sworn, to have preoccupied Benito Mussolini. Sixteen days earlier, on 20 April, both the Duce and Ciano had been aghast to hear from Ambassador Bernardo Attolico of 'imminent' German action against Poland. For this conference with Ribbentrop, Ciano had arrived in Milan with Mussolini's written instructions to make one thing plain: it would be fully three years before Italy was ready for war. To Ciano's relief, Ribbentrop agreed: even five years would be in accord with Hitler's schedule.

Now, as angrily as if Ciano's counsel had been all to the contrary, Mussolini had performed an inexplicable diplomatic *volte-face*. Ciano was to seek out Ribbentrop and at once conclude a military alliance.

Pacing the thick-pile carpeting of his suite, Ciano pondered the riddle. Had the Duce so soon forgotten his humiliation of 15 March, when Hitler, totally disregarding the pledge made at Munich, had sent his troops pouring over the borders of Czechoslovakia? Mussolini had even, Ciano recalled, shrunk from giving this news to the Press. 'The Italians would laugh at me,' he complained bitterly. 'Every time Hitler occupies a country he sends me a message.'

Ciano also knew a bitterer truth that no one had dared reveal:

so preoccupied was Hitler with his 'total solution' for Czechoslovakia that to inform the Duce never even crossed his mind. By sheer chance, the Italian Consul-General, Giuseppe Renzetti, had wind of the coup over dinner at Hermann Göring's – and vehemently insisted with his host that Mussolini must be told.

'Even the stones would cry out against a German alliance,' Mussolini had agreed then.

Typically, it was Ciano who had proposed a way to save his master's face before the people: the unprovoked invasion of the rocky mountain kingdom of Albania. In the small hours of Good Friday, 1939, four Italian columns seized the tiny domain with scarcely a shot being fired, thus ensuring Italy food supplies across the Adriatic in the event of war. Any initial doubts the Duce had nourished were stilled once he knew the King opposed it.

'Why grab four rocks?' the King had grumbled, advancing every possible obstacle. Maliciously, as his parting shot, he told the Duce: 'I hear that in certain German circles you are now known as "The Gauleiter of Italy".'

'If Hitler had had to deal with a nincompoop of a King, he would never have been able to take Austria and Czechoslovakia,' Mussolini fumed, setting his seal on the Albanian venture once and for all. 'One manifesto,' he declared later, in white-hot passion, 'would be enough to liquidate the monarchy.'

As usual, the cynical young minister had no doubt that he had interpreted his chief's instructions correctly. That very afternoon, when leaving his hotel for the conference with von Ribbentrop, he had let fall one of his famous calculated indiscretions for the waiting newsmen: 'One thing's certain, we don't intend to get our bellies ripped up over Poland.'

Now, nine hours later, the Duce was instructing him to convene a press conference and announce an imminent military alliance to the world.

The idea of a binding military pact wasn't new – but even Ciano, who had done his utmost to bring the dictators closer together, had never quite gone this far. Germany, set squarely in the heart of Europe, was a brutal reality Italy could not ignore – but beyond a policy of collaboration Ciano would not go. All through Hitler's Italian tour he had furthered Mussolini's delaying tactics by every means in his power. Recently Ambassador Attolico, a dedicated pacifist who abhorred Hitler, had proposed the alliance again – on the grounds that a treaty would inevitably impose conditions on

Germany. But Ciano's Director of General Affairs, Count Leonardo Vitetti, argued: 'A treaty will establish a moral link – and that we don't want.'

Yet Mussolini saw no such risk. 'Now,' he was to emphasize to Ciano, 'Germany cannot take decisions that don't coincide with our interests.' And above and beyond this reason, the old virus of inferiority was once more working in his blood. In America, commentators had reported that Milan was receiving the German Foreign Minister coldly – proof positive of the Duce's waning prestige.

To the House of Commons, following the Albanian invasion, Winston Churchill had declared: 'I am still not convinced that Italy has made up her mind – particularly the Italian nation – to be involved in a mortal struggle between Great Britain and France.'

For the Duce, the need to reassert to the world that he and Italy were as one overrode all other factors.

Ciano was as yet ignorant of the Duce's reasoning. He would still be in ignorance when he first broached this question with Ribbentrop the next day, and even on 22 May, in Berlin, when the signing of the 'Pact of Steel' became a monstrous and inescapable fact.

Only three months later, pacing beside von Ribbentrop on a sunlit terrace in the diamond-clear air of the Austrian Alps, would Ciano comprehend all the reasons that had brought about this midnight call and set Italy on the road to ruin.

Then von Ribbentrop, his ice-grey eyes glaring fixedly at Ciano, would tell him, 'We want war!'

'He's not only an idiot,' Ciano exploded. 'He's a great stubborn ignoramus. He wasn't even able to reply to the reasons which I gave him, following your instructions.'

Never in his life had Galeazzo Ciano – now, since the recent death of his father, a full-fledged Count – been more acutely aware of disaster. His cramped surroundings only heightened his mood of savage irritation. On this breathless August afternoon, the smell of varnish filling the telephone booth at Rome's Littorio Airport came close to stifling him; the air quivered with the sound of Caproni engines waking to life. And Ciano's right hand was so blue and swollen he could barely hold the receiver – he had banged too hard on the conference table, trying to convince von Ribbentrop and Adolf Hitler that Italy was in no position to fight.

Now, such was his vexation, he could have thumped the walls of the booth. The Duce seemed so slow in comprehending.

'But,' he was saying, 'there's a communication here from the German news agency speaking of 100 per cent agreement on every point.'

'It's false,' Ciano told him despairingly, 'false.'

Ciano knew that this, like every other call under the Fascist regime, was being monitored by telephone-tappers of the Ministry of Home Affairs. On the open line he must speak cautiously, giving Mussolini, at Riccione, only the salient details he needed to know. What he must impress on the dictator, above all, was that his two-day conference with the Germans had in every respect gone fatally wrong: that the suspicions he had harboured of Hitler's double game had been damnably accurate.

'But what do you mean?' Mussolini kept asking perplexedly. 'What about this story the Press are running?'

Despite himself, Ciano laughed bitterly. No news agency in the world – let alone Hitler's Deutsches Nachrichten Büro – would have dared run the inside story of those two days of angry argument. First at Schloss Fuschl, Ribbentrop's summer residence twelves miles from Salzburg, there had been the disastrous pre-luncheon meeting which made plain that it was now Poland's turn to be absorbed – using as pretext almost 400,000 Germans within the Free City of Danzig.

'We're at the point of blows,' Ciano murmured darkly to his diplomatic entourage as the conference broke for lunch.

The frigid von Ribbentrop's attempt to enliven his guests with a discourse on shooting snipe was a dismal failure. As if the words stood out on a lighted screen, Ciano's mind turned time and again to the fatal Article III of the 'Pact of Steel', which he had signed in the Reichskänzlei:

'If one of the Contracting Parties becomes involved with military complications with another Power, the other Contracting Party will immediately step to its side as an ally, and will support it with all its military might . . .'

With incredible naivety, Mussolini had never pressed for a built-in clause that both parties would observe the three-year time lapse discussed by Ribbentrop and Ciano in Milan – 'Hitler would never lie to me,' he comforted himself. Only on 30 May – eight days after the signing of the pact – had the Duce sent a belated aide-memoire, stressing that Italy would need at least three years for military and economic preparation.

On the afternoon of 11 August, pacing the terrace of Schloss Fuschl, Ciano had asked Ribbentrop point-blank: did Germany want Danzig or the whole Polish Corridor? Ribbentrop's answer went through him like a dagger: 'Not that any more. We want war!'

In vain Ciano had argued that the conflict was bound to involve England and France. Ribbentrop's sneering answer was to propose a bet – which he never paid – that the Allies would remain neutral: an Italian painting, if Ciano was wrong, against a suit of old armour. That night, four men – Ciano, Ambassador Attolico, Count Leonardo Vitetti and Count Massimo Magistrati, Italy's Chargé d'Affaires in Berlin – met secretly in Ciano's bathroom at Salzburg's Oester-reichischer Hof Hotel. To foil bugging devices they talked against the sound of running water. On one thing Ciano was determined: that no German news bulletin should link Italy with Germany's prepara-tions. Yet even in this, Ciano learned, on arriving at Littorio Airport, Hitler had contrived the supreme double-cross.

'It's the usual lies,' he reassured the Duce from the phone booth. So far he had made no mention of Hitler, and Mussolini asked cautiously: 'And the other one? What about the other one?'

Ciano gave him such crumbs of comfort as he could. 'Generally speaking he recognized our good reasons,' he replied. 'He assured me he won't ask for our help.'

It was true – yet the meeting with Hitler at his Berchtesgaden retreat had been stormier than the encounter with Ribbentrop. At lunch, Ciano had gone out of his way to be as unpleasant as he could be. He poked fun at Hitler's flower arrangements and took pains to criticize the salad dressing. At tea-time he listened incredulously to Hitler's bitter complaints of Germans persecuted by Poles – 'it seemed as if the man believed his own atrocity stories.' Then, with all the eloquence he could command, Ciano repeated that Italy could not follow Germany into any such adventure. At length, rising from the tea-table, Hitler uttered a single plaintive word: *'Warum?'*

'Why?' Ciano echoed. 'Because the British and French will fight.'

Then, as Ciano was later to relate, the storm broke. Passionately Hitler dismissed any such possibility as fiction. To Ciano it was made crystal-clear that Italy's place in the alliance was as a stopgap. Negotiations for a German-Soviet economic pact were virtually concluded: Poland would be liquidated within weeks. Italy's aid would not be needed.

Now, striving to make Mussolini realize the enormity of what was happening, Ciano told him: 'He's a man possessed – he's using the Corridor as an excuse, but his intention is to clean up the whole apartment. Maybe with The Bear.'

'But that's criminal,' protested Mussolini weakly.

Ciano was relentless. 'Perhaps it's not going too far to say that appetite grows with eating. Maybe he'll want a summer holiday near San Giusto.' He guessed that the Duce would interpret his Adriatic allusion correctly: the invasion of Jugoslavia.

'And that,' grunted Mussolini, more hopefully than he felt, 'may give him indigestion.'

All that was left to do now was wait – and pray. He had awakened a full hour before his normal time, 6.30 a.m. He knew at once what day it was, 1 September, 1939, and all that this signified. Rising from the simple brass bedstead, he crossed the parquet flooring with haste. A white, tapering, perfectly manicured finger depressed the bell push – marked with the twin emblems of the tiara and the crossed keys – the arms of the Papal See.

His manservant, Giovanni Stefanori, was startled. Rarely did Eugenio Pacelli, Pope Pius XII, summon him to his second-floor private apartment at Castel Gandolfo until he had shaved with his American electric razor and dressed himself. But today was no ordinary day. Behind his gold-rimmed spectacles, the Pope's eyes were troubled.

'Nothing from Cardinal Orsenigo?'

'Nothing, Santità.'

The manservant withdrew. From Cardinal Cesare Orsenigo, Papal Nuncio in Berlin, would come, he knew, the word that Pius XII so anxiously awaited: Hitler's final move in the battle of nerves over Poland.

Now the tall, ascetic Pontiff crossed the room to his desk. From the windows the landscape of the Roman campagna that he loved stretched fifteen clear miles to the city: the yellow stubble fields, the orchards circled by trim box hedges, the olive groves. Two thousand years back Virgil had described such a panorama – as remote from the naked horror of war as any scene on earth.

From this desk, twenty-four hours earlier, the Pope had launched a last desperate appeal to five countries – Germany, Poland, England, France and Italy. Germany and Poland, he pleaded, should preserve a fifteen-day truce pending an international conference held by the five governments – with observers from Belgium, Swizerland, Holland, the United States and the Vatican sitting in. Its purpose was fundamental: a revision of the Versailles Treaty, followed by a non-aggression pact to secure the peace of Europe for all time.

'Nothing is lost with peace,' Pius had warned the world one week earlier. 'All may be lost with war.' With these words, with this last appeal, he had done everything that one man could humanly do.

To a lesser man it would have seemed ironic that he had chosen as his coat-of-arms a dove of peace hovering above a storm-tossed sea. But every fibre of Pius's being was dedicated to preserving peace in Europe and in Italy: after nine years as Cardinal-Secretary of State, he would carry on Pius XI's unflinching hostility to Nazism. And although the Fascists had frowned on the nomination of the handsome Neapolitan, Cardinal Luigi Maglione, as Pacelli's successor because, as former Papal Nuncio to Paris, he was feared as a Francophile, Pius had stood fast.

No more than Pius XI would he subordinate the Church's interest to the lay power. On 11 March, he had announced Maglione's appointment.

Now it was Maglione's voice, on the line from Vatican City, that brought Pius the news he dreaded to hear. Cardinal Orsenigo had reported from Berlin: at 5.45 a.m. the first Panzer divisions had shattered the border, and all over Poland death was falling from the sky.

In this moment, St Matthew's account of the nailing of Christ to His Cross sprang as a painful parable to Pius's mind: 'There was darkness over the face of the earth.'

From his bedroom Pius passed to his private chapel. Giovanni Stefanori watched him go blindly across the cool green marble floor, like a man in shock. He groped towards the polished chestnut-wood fald-stool.

Broken sobs racked his body. The tears streamed down his cheeks.

All that autumn, Romans trudging early to work across Piazza Venezia saw the lights already burning in the windows of the Sala del Mappamondo. It was their one outward sign that Benito Mussolini was still unchallenged dictator of Italy. He no longer harangued them from the famous balcony. Instead a cryptic message appeared in shops and on factory bulletin boards: 'The Pilot must not be disturbed when navigation is difficult . . . the day that I appear on the balcony it will be to announce supreme resolutions.'

To many it seemed that one of the last slogans Mussolini had coined before Europe caught fire now had a hollow ring. 'Better to live one day as a lion than 100 years as a sheep,' he had exhorted the people – yet on 26 August, in a few brief hours, his spur-of-the-moment decision had ranked him with the sheep.

In fact, the true decision had lain with Galeazzo Ciano. At 10 a.m. on that day, the young Count entered the ante-room of the Sala del Mappamondo to find the Duce's military chiefs glumly awaiting an audience – General Francesco Pricolo of the Air Force, Minister for War Production General Carlo Favagrossa, the Navy's Admiral Domenico Cavagnari. Adhering strictly to the letter of the Pact of Steel, the Duce had warned Hitler that Italy could intervene only if Germany furnished her with arms and raw materials – and had summoned his service chiefs to provide their estimates.

Now the wily Ciano urged each man: 'Whatever figure your department gave you – double it!'

It was a masterly evasive tactic. Soon after noon, Ciano telephoned Ambassador Attolico in Berlin with a list that 'would choke a bull – if a bull could read.' To wage war for no more than twelve months, Italy would need seven million tons of oil, six million tons of coal, two million tons of steel and one million tons of timber – to say nothing of copper, rubber, raw materials and 150 ack-ack batteries to protect her industrial cities. Attolico now went one better. Von Ribbentrop asked when this material was needed, and the Ambassador had a brainwave. 'Why, at once,' he replied guilelessly, 'before hostilities begin.'

Faced with a demand for almost seventeen million tons of material – it would have taken 17,000 freight wagons a whole year to ferry it – Hitler was forced to let his partner out. Unable to meet the Duce's demands, he asked him to concentrate instead on military demonstrations and Axis propaganda.

Yet now Mussolini writhed in the grip of humiliation. He had shown weakness – 'unworthy of a man of historic stature'. And though he deplored the war, repeatedly offering to mediate in the hope of repeating his triumph at Munich, any man who spoke against Germany incurred his bitter wrath – as Dino Grandi was the first to discover.

As Mussolini's new Minister of Justice, brusquely recalled from London at Hitler's request, Grandi was on fire with grievances. For the eighteen months of his ambassadorship he had clashed repeatedly with Ribbentrop, and now he saw his career sacrificed to his enemy's whim. At a Cabinet meeting on September 1, Grandi declared roundly that Italy's declaration of non-belligerence was not enough. Not only should Italy announce her neutrality but she

should formally denounce the Pact of Steel – publishing to the world
the full details of Germany's betrayal.

Angrily the Duce cut him short, closing the meeting. Later that
day a personal message from Mussolini reached Grandi through
Ciano. 'Mussolini didn't welcome your intervention this morning,'
Ciano told him frankly. 'You're to remember that you are now
Minister of Justice – completely outside all foreign policy.'

Daily, almost hourly, Mussolini grappled with the problems
caused by his own distorted ego. His first instinct had been to side
with Hitler whatever the cost; to Ciano's horror, Hitler's troops had
not yet crossed the Polish frontier when a draft telegram from Mussolini, announcing that Italy would march with Germany, arrived on
his desk at Palazzo Chigi. 'Finished!' was Ciano's one bitter comment
as he passed it to Count Leonardo Vitetti.

His subordinate thought that all was not yet lost. 'Let's go to lunch,'
he suggested, 'After all, it's got to be coded first.'

Following a leisurely lunch, both men returned to Ciano's office.
Just as Vitetti had guessed, Mussolini had twice called from Palazzo
Venezia. What had happened to his cable to the Führer? It was at
present in the coding office, Ciano assured him. 'Then don't
send it,' Mussolini ordered, sheepishly.

Within weeks – on the flimsy excuse that he had misemployed
a militiaman to exercise his dogs – the Duce had fired his rabidly
pro-German Party Secretary, Achille Starace.

Such was the climate of Italy at the outset of World War Two.

And while the Roman-in-the-street saw nothing of the Duce,
the diplomats and heads of legations saw little more. Unable to
formulate any hard-and-fast policy, Mussolini stayed behind closed
doors. The Pope's envoy, anxious to sound out the Duce's true
intentions, was summarily told to see the Foreign Minister. And to
the disconsolate André François-Poncet, now French Ambassador
in Rome, it seemed that he might well have stayed put in Berlin.
Not once during that autumn did the Duce receive him – angered,
perhaps, by the Frenchman's description of the Führer as 'the natural
son of Joan of Arc and Charlie Chaplin'.

Autumn slipped into winter; the maple leaves drifted to cover the
gravelled walks of the Borghese Gardens. And still the lights burned
early and late in the Sala del Mappamondo, but the glass doors leading
to the balcony stayed resolutely shut.

The pine needles were a soft dun-coloured carpet, hushing their footfalls. Dense woods surrounded the clearing in which they walked, bare of life save for five small wooden cabins, littered with fishing tackle: fly boxes, split-cane rods, red tying silk, No 2 lines. Near at hand, a mountain torrent boiled white over tumbled rocks. Stark simplicity was the keynote of life at Sant' Anna di Valdieri, King Vittorio Emanuele's summer fishing camp, hidden in the mountains sixty miles from Turin.

Attired in a linen suit, sports shirt and soft brown hat, the King looked every inch what he most wished to be – a country gentleman divorced from politics. From Sant' Anna, at the season's close, he would move on to San Rossore, his model farm near Pisa – as far away from the tumult engulfing Europe as he could conceivably place himself.

Those seeking to involve him more directly found him as unavailable as the Duce. When his daughter-in-law, Crown Princess Maria-José, invited her mother, Queen Elizabeth of Belgium, to stay at the Quirinale, the King scented a trap. 'I have a bad case of whooping cough and it's likely to last three months,' he told the Queen firmly over the telephone, 'so it's better that we shouldn't meet.' The American Ambassador, William Phillips, who journeyed to Sant' Anna, fared no better. Faced with President Roosevelt's plea that he should use his influence to avert war, the King, as in the time of Matteotti, took refuge in the constitution. He could do no more than refer the message to his government.

Would the King soon return to Rome, the Ambassador wondered? Impossible, the monarch explained, he had caught only 700 trout and his annual average was 1000. He could not think of breaking camp until he had evened the score.

None the less, with the concern for his own security that typified all his actions, the King saw the need for a man on the spot in Rome to watch his interests. Such a man now kept pace beside him: the suave, bearded Minister of Justice, forty-four-year-old Dino Grandi.

Soon after the declaration of the Empire, the King had confided in an equerry: 'I go with Mussolini because, whether he's right or not, he's lucky.' But with each turn of the Axis screw, the King wondered afresh. That August, watching the ragtail manoeuvres of a motorized division near Turin, it was to Grandi that the King had turned and remarked spitefully: 'And with curates and notaries like these, Mussolini plans to make war?'

Now the little King was appealing to Grandi as the patriot he knew him to be – a man bitterly opposed to the Axis, long soured by the excesses of Fascism. There were difficult times ahead, he prophesied, and he looked to an hour, when he, as King, might be obliged to put the constitution to work again. Now he begged Grandi, both as patriot and monarchist, not to leave him alone.

Grandi temporized. Had it not been for the King's insistence he would have refused the post of Minister of Justice, returning to his legal practice. He thought there would be many times when he and Mussolini would clash on principles of law.

The King's cold pale eyes never left his face. 'Mussolini,' he told Grandi, 'is like my camels at San Rossore. Their palates are so thick they eat prickly pear and don't notice the thorns. Modify the decrees – Mussolini won't even notice.'

Almost whispering, he added: 'Don't give a thought but to save what remains of the constitution. I need you, and very soon I will send for you.'

Deeply moved, Grandi came suddenly to attention, putting himself at the King's disposal. 'That one,' the King reminded him with sly malice, and Grandi knew well enough of whom he spoke, 'thinks he has destroyed the constitution. No – he has only corroded it.'

The only sound in the room was the dry scratching of Galeazzo Ciano's pen. Outside Palazzo Chigi, piled snow was reduced to black icy slush on the pavements of the Corso and passers-by were few. On this night of New Year's Day, 1940, most Romans were snug at home with their families.

Soon Ciano would be on his way – to whose party he hadn't yet decided, for the engraved invitation cards on his office mantelshelf were many. Nor was it yet a certainty in whose arms he would seek consolation that night. Since he and Edda had gone their separate ways, the opportunities had been numerous, though the favourite of the moment would soon enough join the ranks of discarded beauties, 'Galeazzo's widows'. But tonight, as every night before leaving the office, there was one duty to perform. In the amber glow of his desk lamp, Ciano was making up his diary.

For three years now, Ciano had set himself this nightly task – faithfully charting the double-dealing, the twists and turns of Fascist and Nazi foreign policy. Recorded, too, in the blue and red leather-bound volumes kept in the workroom safe adjoining his main office was the unvarnished story of Mussolini's infatuation with the Axis – abetted, until those traumatic August days at Salzburg, by Ciano himself.

Above all, the diary was a key to the enigma that was Benito Mussolini – the decisions he had reached, the decisions he had still to formulate. In the last months, though, the fine lines had become blurred. No man could now predict with certainty what Mussolini would do. As Ciano leafed back through recent entries, Mussolini's changes of heart more faithfully resembled a psychograph than the reasonings of a politician.

On 4 September, 1939, one day after the outbreak of war, Ciano had written, 'At times the Duce seems attracted to the idea of neutrality . . . to gather economic and military strength . . . but immediately afterwards he abandons this idea. The idea of joining the Germans attracts him.'

25 *September:* 'The Duce is more than ever convinced that Hitler will rue the day he brought the Russians into the heart of Europe.'

9 *December:* 'Fundamentally he is still in favour of Germany.'

26 *December:* 'He is more and more distrustful of the Germans. For the first time he desires German defeat.'

And no man shared this desire more fervently than Ciano himself. 'Tell His Holiness,' he had begged Monsignor Francesco Borgongini Duca, Apostolic Nuncio for Italy, 'that since Salzburg I have done nothing but strive for peace.' But by now Ciano knew Mussolini too well to criticize the Axis directly: at once the Duce would veer to the other extreme. Often the Count contented himself with childish retaliations for Salzburg – such as assuring the new British Ambassador, Sir Percy Loraine, that Italy would never fight against Britain and France.

Through the grapevine the news had reached Berlin almost as soon as it reached London – adding one more grudge to the tally kept by the implacable Joachim von Ribbentrop.

But most often, in keeping with his nature, Ciano was cynically fatalistic. 'It's like throwing a stone at a lion eating a man,' he said to André François-Poncet at the time of Danzig. 'The man would be eaten just the same.' 'You forget,' the French Ambassador reminded him, shocked, 'that Danzig is Europe's symbol of liberty.'

Tonight, Ciano again felt fatalistic. On New Year's Day, 1940, what lay ahead for Italy? His entry was ominously brief: the pendulum had swung full circle.

1 *January:* 'A keen pro-German feeling is reawakening in the Duce . . .'

On the surface Marshal Italo Balbo and Marshal Pietro Badoglio had little in common. At heart Balbo was still the impulsive soldier of fortune who had helped organize the March on Rome. Well aware that for five years he had governed Libya as penance for his plain-speaking, he still told Mussolini the truth as he saw it – often, when memos went unanswered, flying in from Tripoli to do just that. Embittered by his 'exile' and the knowledge that newspapers could mention him only once a month, Balbo governed well by fits and starts. At times, seized by the demon of restlessness which had made him Italy's most energetic Minister of Aviation, he threw himself into the work of colonizing Libya, down to such details as furnishing a box of matches for every new settler's kitchen.

Then, as reaction, black apathy set in. Night after night, Balbo's legendary dinner-parties kept his servants up until the small hours; golden lanterns blazed from the palm trees surrounding his palace, an invisible orchestra played, and red-cloaked Spahis stood immobile against a backdrop of white marble. Aided by brimming champagne glasses, beautiful women and choice cigars, Balbo forgot his loneliness in feudal splendour.

Sixty-eight-year-old Marshal Pietro Badoglio lived each hour according to plan. A shrewd campaigner, the victor of Addis Ababa had a fetish for method; even on desert campaigns he would cut short a briefing half an hour after noon because it was lunch time, play bridge each evening, then retire at 10 p.m. His card-index brain never forgot an injury – 'I strangle my enemies little by little with a velvet glove,' he liked to say. A taciturn chain-smoker, his ice-blue eyes missed nothing to his advantage: following the Abyssinian war he had intrigued for lands, a dukedom and extra allowance until his annual income topped two million lire a year. His ducal motto was: 'I swoop like a falcon.'

Yet on 26 May, 1940, both Badoglio and Balbo found common cause. They stood before Benito Mussolini in the Sala del Mappamondo and both were bereft of speech, stunned by what they had heard. As soon as the Duce had summoned them from the waiting-room they had guessed the matter to be important; hands on hips, he stood behind his writing-desk, staring at them for minutes on end. Even the phlegmatic Badoglio found sudden difficulty in breathing. Abruptly Mussolini broke silence.

'I wish to tell you that yesterday I sent a messenger to Hitler,' he told them, 'with my written declaration that I don't intend to stand idly by with my hands in my pockets. After 5 June, I am ready to declare war on England.'

Irked by their appalled silence, Mussolini opened his eyes wide, awaiting comment. At last Badoglio found words.

'Your Excellency,' he blurted out, 'you know perfectly well that we are absolutely unprepared – you have received complete reports every week.' Desperately he strove to recapitulate the gist of those reports: fully twenty Army divisions had only seventy per cent of their equipment, another twenty had no more than fifty per cent.

'We haven't even sufficient shirts for the army,' Badoglio hammered out. 'How is it possible to declare war? It is suicide.'

It was small wonder that Badoglio was horrified. No man knew these facts better than Benito Mussolini: Italy could wage no war worth the name. For months, experts from every service department had compiled dossiers and marshalled statistics to make this plain. To every report, one factor was common: even combat by World War One standards would tax Italian troops and supplies beyond endurance.

As far back as February, Minister of Currency and Exchange Raffaello Riccardi had warned a conference of service chiefs that the country's annual imports totalled twenty-five million tons of food – none of which might be available in the event of war. 'The keys of the Mediterranean,' Riccardi opined, 'are in the hands of the English Admiralty.' Though Mussolini at once closed down the meeting, he could not close his ears to other warning voices. The Air Force had fuel for just forty sorties. The Army had barely enough material to equip seven divisions.

It was the same in every potential theatre. From Tripolitania, Marshal de Bono reported on weapons better suited to a war surplus dump: rusting water-cooled machine-guns, obsolete World War One artillery, tanks so frail that trucks were needed to transport them into battle. From Libya, Balbo had already sent word of cannon dating from Garibaldi's time, mounted precariously on garbage trucks.

No man had summed up the position more succinctly than General Carlo Favagrossa, Mussolini's Minister for War Production. If industrial plants worked non-stop shifts, Favagrossa thought, Italy could conceivably enter the war nine years from now – in 1949. Failing this, he would set the date at 1959.

For Mussolini, obsessed with dreams of the country's destiny, any such decision was unthinkable. It meant admitting not only Italy's inferiority, but his own besides. 'We should be like Switzerland multiplied by ten,' was his appalled conclusion.

For months he had been under almost constant pressure – to stay neutral, to intervene decisively. The taciturn US Under-Secretary of State, Sumner Welles, arrived on February 26 to urge the neutrality of a man who 'looked fifteen years older than his actual age of fifty-six . . . ponderous and static', a man who moved like an elephant, his temples snow-white, his face flabby. Twelve days later, as Mussolini debated the wisdom of Welles's proposed meeting with President Roosevelt in the Azores, Joachim von Ribbentrop arrived in Rome to press the need for an urgent meeting with the Führer.

'The minute hand,' Mussolini told Welles, 'is pointing to one minute before midnight.'

Then on 18 March, 1940, the Duce met Hitler for the fourth time amid head-high snowdrifts at the Brenner Pass, 300 yards from the German frontier. To interpreter Paul Schmidt, sitting in on the conference in Mussolini's private coach, it was evident that the two dictators no longer met on equal terms. His Polish victory an accomplished fact, Hitler bragged of troop strengths, casualty figures and reserves, while Mussolini only 'goggled in wonder like a child with a new toy'.

'I'll need snow as far as Etna if I'm ever to turn the Italians into a race of warriors,' the disgruntled Duce confided in Standarten-führer (SS Colonel) Eugen Dollmann, Himmler's representative in Rome.

Schmidt noted, too, that Hitler made no mention of the sneak attacks on Norway and Denmark, timed for three weeks later on 9 April – a fact which even the interpreter had learned from Foreign Office sources. Hitler's faith in the Duce was absolute, but he had conceived a bitter distrust of the Royal Family and the Italian General Staff – 'that aristocratic Mafia'. From now on, Mussolini, as junior partner, would learn no more than the Führer chose to tell him.

And the hour, too, would be of Hitler's choosing. Soon after 4 a.m. on 10 May the strident summons of a telephone awoke Mussolini at Villa Torlonia. It was Galeazzo Ciano, warning that within the hour Ambassador Hans-Georg von Mackensen would be calling with a personal message from Hitler. Only then did the Duce learn that promptly, at 5.35 a.m., German troops were pouring into Belgium and Holland.

Now determined to intervene within weeks, Mussolini could only reflect bitterly on the assurances he had given his old mentor of the 'twenties, the Marchese Paulucci di Calboli, formerly Giacomo Barone-Russo, recently appointed Ambassador in Brussels. 'Should we go as tourists or take our furniture?' Paulucci had asked sceptically at the time. Confidently the Duce had replied: 'Set up an embassy – the Germans will never attack Belgium.'

For the space of days – before his fateful pronouncement to Badoglio – Mussolini had been a man tugged by the winds. Twice he sent barbed messages through Dino Alfieri, the Holy See's new Ambassador, to Pius XII himself: the Church's constant sermons in praise of peace were a thorn in the Duce's flesh. But Pius was secure in the knowledge of duty done. 'We do not fear,' the Pope replied serenely, 'even to go to a concentration camp.'

Yet Dino Grandi never forgot the visit he paid to Palazzo Venezia on 17 May, only nine days before Mussolini summoned Badoglio. He found Mussolini immobile before a beflagged wall-map of France, studying troop dispositions. 'Come here,' the Duce instructed him, his pointer stabbing at the Seine where the German advance had that day halted. Now he told Grandi that though the Germans believed they had defeated France, they would never reach Paris.

'There will be a new Battle of the Marne,' Mussolini predicted, 'the hated Boche will break their heads for a second time and all Europe will be liberated from them.'

Mindful of his autumn meeting with the King at Sant' Anna, Grandi felt profound relief. No man so confident of Germany's downfall could be contemplating an eleventh hour intervention on her side.

Within days, Mussolini saw his optimism had been groundless. Almost overnight, the Germans threatened to overwhelm France. For the first time in modern history, a German threat to Italy loomed not from the north or the east, but ultimately from the west.

An intervention on the Allied side? 'Even if Italy were to change her attitude and go over bag and baggage to the Anglo-French side she would not avoid an immediate war with Germany,' Mussolini had argued in a top-secret memorandum of 31 March, 'a war which Italy would have to carry *alone*.' As an alternative, his Brenner Pass meeting with Hitler recalled to his mind the dictum of Niccolò Machiavelli: two ways exist to defend oneself against an enemy, to kill him or to embrace him.

When reports reached him that the war scare had brought land-office business to furriers and jewellers in the north, a hedge against inflation, the Duce commented tersely: 'The Milanese should know it's better to negotiate than have the Germans in Milan.'

But on 26 May, to the stunned Badoglio and Balbo, he would admit to no fears of Hitler. 'You are not calm enough to judge the situation, Marshal,' he told Badoglio patronizingly. 'I can tell you everything will be over by September, and that I need only a few thousand dead to sit at the conference table as a belligerent.'

But at Palazzo Chigi, others besides Ciano saw how one warning word from the Germans set him scuttling to placate them. On 27 May, the day following the Duce's meeting with Badoglio, one official, Count Luca Pietromarchi, received a stinging reprimand from Palazzo Venezia. Until now, Pietromarchi was congratulating himself that patient months of negotiation were bearing fruit. That very day, as the Master of the Rolls, Sir Wilfred Greene, announced in London the British were about to relax their contraband controls against Italy in the Mediterranean. The news, relayed to Berlin, had brought a sharp rebuke from Hermann Göring, through the German Embassy.

'You're to cancel every agreement you've made with the British and the French,' Pietromarchi was told. 'The Duce says that he's not a brigand, doing business with a gun in one hand and a Bible in the other.'

From this moment on, Mussolini saw life as in a splintered mirror – on the one hand, the reality he was shrewd enough to perceive; on the other, the distorted image that he urged himself was the truth.

There was no lack of sycophants to persuade him that all was well. Even Badoglio, following his token protest, stayed on as Chief of the Supreme General Staff – loath to resign and give up emoluments of two million lire a year. To put up a show of martial might, General Ubaldo Soddu, Under-Secretary for War, raised the Army's on-paper strength from forty to seventy-three divisions, stripping every existing division of one regiment to swell the total. At reviews, Soddu knew, Mussolini never spotted that some of the artillery was fourteenth-century cannon made of brass – or realized that the armoured cars were loaned by the police, painted khaki for that day's parade.

To men who spoke the blunt truth, like General Giacomo Carboni, the slim, handsome Chief of Military Intelligence, Mussolini gave a grudging hearing – then sought out men who told him what he needed to hear. On a four-day visit to Germany in January, Carboni shrewdly assessed much of Hitler's vaunted strength as bluff: food and raw materials were lacking, rolling stock was obsolete, he found the Army High Command pessimistic. Contemptuously Mussolini rejected his verdict as 'the report of a man who dislikes Germans'. Then, to prove Carboni wrong, he sent a colonel from the Italian Youth Organization to check his findings. Exactly four days later the docile officer reported on a survey of 200 perfectly equipped front-line divisions.

At 6 p.m. on Monday, 10 June, for the first time in nine months, the glass doors swung open and the Duce, who twelve days earlier had appointed himself Supreme Commander of the Armed Forces, sprang nimbly on to the Palazzo Venezia balcony. Within fifteen minutes, his voice strangely high-pitched, chopping off his words as with a knife, he told a well-drilled crowd mustered by the new Party Secretary, Ettore Muti, the fate that awaited Italy.

'One man alone,' in Winston Churchill's words, had 'ranged the Italian people in deathly struggle against the British Empire, and deprived Italy of the sympathy and intimacy of the United States.' He had consulted neither his Cabinet of Ministers nor even the Grand Council, knowing that the old guard from the March on Rome – Balbo, De Bono, De Vecchi, Grandi, Giuseppe Bottai – were as bitterly opposed to the Axis as was Ciano. Only the disgraced Achille Starace was the lone voice declaring: 'For me, war is like eating a plate of maccheroni.' Most Italians felt a true sense of horror as the Duce's voice crackled out on amplifiers all over Italy; in Genoa and Turin, the crowds stood in sullen silence, without a cheer, without a handclap. And in Milan's cathedral square, just as in Matteotti's time, men were seen crying that day, under the clear and windy sky.

'The hour destined by fate is sounding for us,' Mussolini trumpeted. 'The hour of irrevocable decision has come. A declaration of war has been handed to the ambassadors of Great Britain and France.'

At last, saluting the Führer as chief of the great allied Germany, he closed with a shout: 'Italian people, rush to arms and show your tenacity, your courage, your valour!'

As the crowds dispersed glumly, Fascist Party hacks were posting up notices announcing that from this night Italy would be blacked-out for the duration, and workmen, mounting tall ladders, began painting the street lamps blue.

One hour earlier, in the Villa Camilluccia, the Petacci residence on Monte Mario, Myriam had answered the telephone to hear

Mussolini on the line. His voice was low-pitched, somehow unreal, and the girl, bewildered, asked what was the trouble.

'In one hour's time,' Mussolini told her, 'I shall declare war. I'm forced to declare it.' Like most other Italians then, Myriam thought of this as a token *coup-de-grâce* against France, not a move that could involve a war of blood with England. 'But it will be short, Duce?' she asked. 'No,' he disillusioned her quietly, 'it will be long – not less than five years.'

Mussolini's last words made Myriam's blood run cold, as she fore-saw for the first time what lay ahead for all of them. 'Hitler's tree,' the Duce said, 'reaches as high as the sky, but it grows only towards ruin.'

The Abyssinian War

Top. Engineers carved 300 miles of new roads.

Middle. Despite bitter battles like Neghelli, Italy's true enemy was hostile terrain.

Left. Among 400 crack pilots were the Duce's sons Vittorio and Bruno (left and right) and Galeazzo Ciano (centre)

Left. At Bologna, Mussolini boasts of 'eight million Italian bayonets'
Below. Reviewing Fascist Militia at Genoa

Above. From September 1937
Mussolini was irrevocably
wedded to the Axis
Left. Hitler listens attentively
to Mussolini's views

Above. Excesses of the regime included the compulsory Bersaglieri trot at army manoeuvres. *Below*. New excesses included rallies where Party Secretary Starace leaped through fiery hoops

6. 'Enough, Stop It! We're on Your Side!'

10 June, 1940 – 24 July, 1943

'How can he do such a thing?' Adolf Hitler raged. 'This is downright madness.'

Joachim von Ribbentrop exchanged glances with Field-Marshal Wilhelm Keitel, joint-chief of Hitler's Supreme Command. Neither man could find words. 'Downright madness' seemed an understatement. On this bleak morning of 28 October, 1940, the blind folly of their ally Benito Mussolini posed a direr threat to the Axis cause than any Allied counter-thrust.

Promptly at 9 a.m. the Führer's armoured nine-coach train jolted into Bologna's central station. From the railway station telegraph office, Hitler, en route to Florence, had learned to his fury that he was two hours too late to halt Mussolini in his reckless invasion of Greece.

To Paul Schmidt, Hitler's ever-present interpreter, it had all seemed to happen with bewildering suddenness. Already, as his train neared the German border, the Führer's mood had been black enough. At Hendaye, on the Franco-Spanish frontier, nine hours of pleading with General Francisco Franco either to enter the war or to admit the German Army on to Spanish soil had met with point-blank refusal. 'I would rather have three or four teeth yanked out than go through such an interview again,' Hitler had vowed. Then, on the homeward journey, within hours of Berlin, had come catastrophic news from the German Embassy in Rome of the Duce's intentions.

As the train at once swung southward Schmidt felt the tension travelling like an electric current from coach to coach. A well-worn cliché from detective fiction sprang to his mind: 'The police hastened to the scene of the crime.' That night at dinner, Ribbentrop summed up the position succinctly. 'The Italians will never get anywhere against the Greeks in autumn rains and winter snows,' he told the assembled company. 'The Führer intends at all costs to hold up his crazy scheme.'

In truth, Mussolini's tactics had been baffling Hitler for more than four months. The Duce, he supposed, had declared war on 10 June to tie in with some top-secret strike against Corsica or Tunis – yet for eleven days thereafter Mussolini made no move at all. No objectives were allotted to either the Navy or the Air Force, for as Mussolini told Badoglio positively: 'I don't intend trying anything new.' Only at dawn on 21 June, the day after France had requested an armistice with Germany, did Italian troops pour across the French border from Mont Blanc to the sea – with strict orders never to fire first.

But for the soldiers, clad only in thin summer uniforms, it was not French bullets but the paralysing rigours of the French Alps that took their toll. For Mussolini, the shameful cost of this brief two-day campaign was 800 dead and 3200 in hospital.

Now Hitler learned that his fruitless all-night journey had been in vain. Pounding his fists on the polished table in a paroxysm of rage, he still couldn't credit it – even though a clear warning that Mussolini was taking this decisive step had come three days earlier from the German Foreign Office. Yet as recently as 4 October, when the two dictators had once again met on the Brenner Pass, Mussolini had uttered no word.

'If he wanted to pick a fight with poor little Greece,' Hitler asked Keitel rhetorically, 'why didn't he attack in Malta or Crete? It would at least make some sense in the context of war with Britain in the Mediterranean.'

Neither man could plumb the Duce's complex psychology to divine the real reason: the Italian's life-long persecution-phobia. At the Brenner meeting, Hitler had made no mention that within three days he was sending troops to occupy Romania. Until now, Mussolini had been content to heed Hitler's mid-August warning against any action in the Balkans – but the knowledge of Hitler's Romanian coup reduced him to trembling fury.

'Hitler always faces me with a *fait accompli*!' he exploded to Ciano on 12 October. 'This time I am going to pay him back in his own coin. He will find out in the papers that I have occupied Greece. In this way the equilibrium will be re-established.'

Although Mussolini sought to trump up valid strategic reasons – Greek ports were needed to attack British convoys to Egypt – it was this childish impulse to even the score that overrode all other factors.

Other men than Hitler were quick to perceive it as criminal folly – foremost among them Marshal Pietro Badoglio. As the Chief of the Supreme General Staff pointed out, Italy had only four combat divisions available against the Greeks' fifteen: fully twenty divisions would be needed to ensure success. Unimpressed by the Duce's argument that advance work done by the Italian Fifth Column would more than offset this, Badoglio protested hotly. But once again his protests at first stopped short of resignation – though the shoddy planning of the campaign, mocked-up in less than a fortnight, bore all the hallmarks of the ex-lance-sergeant Benito Mussolini.

When Badoglio objected that the terms of the alliance made it imperative to inform the Germans, Mussolini retorted angrily: 'Did they tell us about Norway? Did they tell us about the western front? They behaved as if we didn't exist.'

'I am no longer an Italian if the troops find difficulty in fighting the Greeks,' declared the Duce, who saw it as no more than a lightning two-week campaign. Warned that Greece had 250,000 men under arms, he listened instead to those who assured him that only 30,000 Greeks would fight. Incredibly, six weeks earlier, after Hitler had halted his Balkan plans, Mussolini had begun to demobilize his army – and 300,000 men had already been sent home.

Yet no shadow of doubt crossed the Duce's face as he paced the platform at Florence on 28 October, awaiting Hitler's arrival. The timing of his own *fait accompli* had been perfection. Not until 22 October, had he written to Hitler – predating his letter 19 October – outlining his proposed action but leaving the exact date obscure. Now Hitler's trip to confer with Franco had delayed delivery still further. It was supreme irony that the date appointed by Hitler to meet in Florence had been the very date Mussolini had chosen for his invasion.

As always, faced with the challenges of history, the Duce took refuge in inessentials. As the Führer's train, shrouded in steam, slid along the platform, Mussolini gave the sign to the sixty-strong *carabinieri* band as if he himself were the bandmaster – then abruptly whirled on his heel gesticulating furiously. Forgetful of just who they were welcoming, the band had swung into the Italian Royal March.

Then, once the band switched hastily to the German national anthem, he recovered himself. Hitler's face, smiling strainedly, appeared at his compartment window, and Mussolini strode down the ceremonial red carpet to greet his discomfited ally. In the high-flown style of a Fascist war bulletin, he hailed him: 'Führer, we are on the march! Victorious Italian troops crossed the Greco-Albanian border at dawn today!'

Already, as the two dictators clasped hands, then retired for preliminary talks to a newly-decorated waiting-room, the shortcomings of Benito Mussolini as an ally were becoming plain to the Führer. His first words to the Duce, he told Keitel later, were: 'The whole outcome will be a military catastrophe.' But neither man could foresee that with this one foolhardy gesture Benito Mussolini had doomed both the Third Reich and his own Fascist regime.

Within weeks, the Duce's ill-equipped troops were in headlong retreat, surrounded at the ports of Durazzo and Valona, their backs to the sea. To rescue them and to maintain German supremacy in the Balkans, Hitler had to divert 680,000 troops to strike at Greece through the puppet states of Romania and Bulgaria. But the hardy Jugoslavs rejected the vassal's role in which a Tripartite Pact had cast them and Hitler, angered by their defiance, sought to crush them. To achieve this in April 1941 called for a ruinous change of priorities. 'Operation Barbarossa', Hitler's treacherous attempt to bring his Russian partner to her knees, had to be delayed four weeks, until 22 June – time enough to bog down the German armies in the subzero nightmare of a Russian winter.

Nor did the Führer's efforts to redeem his ally's criminal folly save the 20,000 Italians who died on Greek battlefields, the 40,000 wounded, the 26,000 taken prisoner, the 18,000 crippled with frost-bite.

Within weeks, the thousands of Italians who secretly tuned in each night to Radio London would hear their leader's crass vanity perpetuated in the popular peacetime tune, 'Long live the Tower of Pisa', newly supplied with mocking and macabre lines:

> *Oh, what a surprise for the Duce, the Duce,*
> *He can't put it over the Greeks,*
> *Oh, what a surprise for the Duce, they do say,*
> *He's had no spaghetti for weeks . . .*

Gently yet persistently, Rachele Mussolini tugged at her husband's shoulder. To the Duce's wife, 3 a.m. on Sunday was a brutal hour to rouse any human being, but the terrifying summons of the telephone in the night had brooked no refusal – any more than the excited Prince Otto von Bismarck, Minister Plenipotentiary, calling from the German Embassy in Rome. Benito grunted, stirred, then came instantly awake, his black eyes squinting against the harsh light of the bed lamp.

Rachele watched him re-orient to his surroundings, his bedroom in the Villa Mussolini at Riccione, then broke the news. The Germans had insisted that he must be wakened and informed without delay: Hitler had declared war on Russia.

For one moment, before anger mastered him, Mussolini stared at his wife blankly. Then, matter-of-factly, without even a tremor of emotion, he spelt out the writing on the wall: 'My dear Rachele, that means we've lost the war.'

As he struggled into a dressing-gown and hastened to the telephone, his wife was not surprised. It was as if, on 22 June, 1941, Benito was struggling to cushion his mind against shock by a bland acceptance of every blow that fate could deal him. He was oblivious now of the smallest details of household routine. Often, Rachele noticed, he missed shaving for two days at a stretch. At Villa Torlonia he came so late to lunch that he paid more fines to her piggybank than any other member of the family. Each night he seemed dazed and beaten. Yielding his favourite seat without a struggle to Pippo, the ginger cat, he would sink on to any chair handy.

All Italy besides Rachele knew his reasons. Twelve months after the Duce's declaration of war, the news from every battle front was of blow after crushing blow. The Greek débâcle had swiftly led in December to Marshal Badoglio's resignation – and from Libya, too, came smarting humiliations. Outgunned and outmarched, 150,000 men under Marshal Rodolfo Graziani, who had succeeded Italo Balbo in Libya when Balbo's plane was mistaken for a British bomber and he was shot down and killed, held out only fifty-seven days before crumbling under General Richard O'Connor's Western Desert Force, 36,000 strong. Vainly awaiting 1000 tanks that never arrived, Graziani's sole comment before his headlong retreat was a telegram invoking the patron saint of artillery: 'Santa Barbara, protect us.'

For the second time, a shamefaced Duce found himself indebted to Adolf Hitler. Where Graziani's men had failed, the tireless determined General Erwin Rommel, placed in overall command of Italo-German forces in North Africa, succeeded within twelve days – recapturing Libya, besieging the vital Mediterranean port of Tobruk and striking for the Egyptian border.

There was news from the Mediterranean and the Aegean too, and all of it was bad. Lacking both radar and effective air support, the Italian Navy was time and again caught napping by Admiral Andrew Cunningham's Mediterranean Fleet – not only in punishing battles like Cape Spada but in the sneak moonlight attack of November 1940 on the naval base at Taranto, when Swordfish torpedo bombers swooped 170 miles from the carrier *Illustrious* to sink the dreadnought *Cavour* and cripple the battleships *Littorio* and *Duilio*. Four months later, on 29 March, 1941, in a dead-of-night naval encounter south-west of Cape Matapan, few guns except the British ever opened fire in a three-minute battle which cost 3000 Italian sailors their lives.

Only then, faced with the harsh evidence that aircraft carriers, which he had for years vetoed, could alone assure the Navy air support, did Mussolini order the conversion of the transatlantic liners *Roma* and *Augustus* – too late for either carrier ever to enter active service.

Though Rachele didn't suspect it, Mussolini also nursed a deep personal sorrow. In July, 1940 Claretta had broken the news that she was expecting his child – but six weeks later, on 18 August, she collapsed in agony. Hastening to Villa Camilluccia, Mussolini was horrified to find that the doctors had operated for an extra-uterine pregnancy and that her life was in danger. 'Please save her for me,' he begged Professor Petacci. But the doctor had known it would be no easy task. By 4 p.m. on 1 September he and Professor Noccioli, the Rome gynaecologist, were battling to save Claretta's life. For three hours Mussolini sat 'as immobile as a block of marble' in an adjoining room, waiting to know the worst. 'God, don't let her die, don't let me lose her,' he prayed, for the second time in his life, in a silent monotone.

At last the doctors emerged to break the news: Claretta had survived, though the crisis point had not yet passed. But the surgery had precluded all hope that she could bear another child. Mussolini could only embrace them fervently, mumbling his thanks.

Then, for the first time in years, Mussolini ceased to take Claretta for granted. He was at Villa Camilluccia at all hours, feeling her pulse, stroking her forehead. If conferences kept him at Palazzio Venezia, he scribbled her notes from his desk. But most often, chauffeur Ercole Boratto recalled, he drove Mussolini to her parents' villa two, even three times a day – sometimes at 2 a.m., with medicine collected from an all-night pharmacy.

But at dawn on 22 June, 1941, Mussolini's term of trial was only just beginning. Month after month the disasters rocked him like body-blows – from every theatre of war and in his personal life. Around 11 a.m. on 7 August, 1941, he told Claretta later, he was stepping into the lift at Palazzo Venezia when an official hastened up.

'There's been a crash at Pisa, Duce,' he announced. 'Your son Bruno is wounded and his condition is critical.'

Already both the Duce's sons were serving as Air Force Captains with No 274 Squadron at Pisa, while Edda had forgone her dry Martinis and all-night card-parties to work as a Red Cross sister in Albania. But Bruno was the Duce's favourite son, with whom he had so often sung operatic duets, and his habitual scowling aloofness deserted him. Closing his eyes and steadying himself against the lift cage, he asked simply, 'Is he dead?' With the confirmation, said the official later, it was 'as if something switched off inside Mussolini for ever'.

Within hours, at San Giusto airport, Pisa, Mussolini learned the stark details from Vittorio. The engine of the P108 bomber Bruno was testing had failed 300 feet above the ground. Trying for a pancake landing, his son had side-slipped and crashed fatally, though two of the crew were saved. His last words, Vittorio reported, had been: 'Papa – the field.'

From this time on, no man dared predict Mussolini's mood with safety. At times he seemed outwardly serene, as when he told General Francesco Pricolo, Under Secretary for Air: 'You see me in front of you calm, because that's how I have to show myself, but inside I feel torn with grief.' Yet when Colonel Gori Castellani, Bruno's commanding officer, called to offer his condolences, Mussolini suddenly sprang from his office chair like a cornered tiger.

'I know what you are here for,' he snarled at the astonished Colonel. 'I know that you and everyone are pleased that I have had this loss. I don't want to hear anything from you. You can get out!'

His decisions, too, were fatally warped – even though Italian lives were at stake. 'He had no sense of judgment left,' Pricolo recalls. 'He listened to any suggestions put forward.' But none aside from Mussolini had suggested offering Hitler four Italian divisions – three infantry, one cavalry – to serve beside the Germans in Russia, plus ninety planes lacking an anti-freeze system.

Outfitted with the same summer uniforms and cardboard shoes that had served them in the French campaign, these troops were to die cursing their Duce in temperatures 36° below zero. But Mussolini's ego was mortally wounded that Rommel's men had redressed the balance in Libya, and Badoglio's successor, the tubby self-seeking General Ugo Cavallero, was too weak to oppose him.

To flaunt his unity with the Wehrmacht, Mussolini reviewed his Russian Expeditionary Force at Verona accompanied by only one man – General Enno von Rintelen, the tall, aquiline German Military Attaché in Rome. As the Duce took the salute, bolt upright in his car, the German in the back seat struggled with conflicting emotions – pity for the marching men in their threadbare uniforms, the slap of their broken shoes on the stone flags drowned only by the drumbeat, and amazement that any man as intelligent as Mussolini could so delude himself.

As the last contingent, to a fanfare of brass, wheeled towards the waiting troop-trains in Verona station, the Duce turned to von Rintelen, his eyes misty. 'There,' he told the speechless General, 'go the finest troops in the world.'

Ten months later, when the fate of the Third Reich had been sealed forever in the snows of Stalingrad, Mussolini was to offer Hitler another six divisions.

Yet one hint of a reverse from any battlefront and he was swift to place the blame on the War Department, his Generals, or even on the 'finest troops in the world' – on any man except himself. Once Edda was moved to write frankly from Russia, where she was now serving: 'It's going badly here, dear Benito.' By return came her father's reply: 'If Michelangelo had had only butter to work with, he wouldn't have been able to produce those eternal statues.'

As often in the past, Mussolini found comfort only in Claretta's uncritical hero-worship. And apart from a brief trip to Budapest in February 1942 for the annulment of her marriage, she was now entirely at his beck and call. The war had put an end to their ski-ing trips and horseback rides; her life was more than ever bounded by the four walls of the Palazzo Venezia suite. At night, she slept by the telephone, awaiting his call.

'There's a big piece of news,' he told her mysteriously on the evening of 27 June, 1942, temporizing until she begged him not to keep her on tenterhooks. At last, his ego satisfied, he relented, announcing dramatically, 'I'm leaving for Africa.'

Claretta was appalled. Begging him to think of the danger, she urged him to consider his life as sacred. In turn, Mussolini stressed his responsibility – he had to 'galvanize the troops'. Then, too, he admitted, he was keen to be present at the victory; the triumphant moment when Rommel's Afrika Korps – now poised before El Alamein, sixty-five miles from the Nile – entered Cairo and Alexandria. At Derna, on the Libyan coast, a white charger awaited Mussolini's triumphant entry, clad in the snow-white uniform of Marshal of the Empire, into Alexandria. The famous 'Sword of Islam' that Balbo, as Governor of Libya, had once presented to him, was a part of his baggage; his own appointed Governor of Egypt would travel with his suite.

'You *are* the guiding spirit of everything,' Claretta encouraged him. 'But you must realize how anxious I shall be.' Now Mussolini in turn assured her. If all went well, he would be back in ten days.

But it was three weeks before Claretta heard his voice again – the voice of a sick, disillusioned man who sees everything he touches turn to dross. The 'Sword of Islam' had remained in its scabbard; the white horse of victory stayed tethered in its stall. As Commander-in-Chief of the Armed Forces, Mussolini had inspected troops and prisoner-of-war camps but he got no further to the war than Bardia, 500 miles from the front line. Hamstrung by inadequate reinforcements, the fruits of Hitler's blind obsession with Russia, Rommel had not advanced – and, furious with Mussolini's impatient messages, had refused to spend time journeying to Bardia.

Acute intestinal trouble, following his abortive African trip, stripped fifty pounds from Mussolini's chunky frame. Often it was from his sick bed at Villa Torlonia, his physician, Dr Arnaldo Pozzi, in attendance, that the Commander-in-Chief and Marshal of the Empire read of that winter's savage toll of reverses – Lieutenant-General Bernard Montgomery's pile-driving thrust at El Alamein, the Anglo-American landings in Morocco and Algeria.

'What is he, after all?' one specialist called in commented cynically. 'Just a failed journalist with ulcers.'

At times Rachele was alarmed to see him roll on the floor clutching his stomach and writhing in agony – though Mussolini was still shrewd enough for self-diagnosis. 'I'm suffering from an attack of convoys,' he told one official wryly, and with reason. By January 1943, losses in the Mediterranean had risen to one-third of all the men and supplies transported.

His sense of humour, once his saving grace, had long vanished. For years, vain of his white tapering fingers, he had sent twice a week for the manicurist at Attilio's smart hairdressing boutique to tend his nails at Palazzo Venezia. Egged on by the Duce, she would relate the latest anti-Fascist stories – and often Mussolini choked with laughter. Soon after his involvement in Russia, when he enquired as usual for new stories about the regime, she asked him innocently: had he heard the one about the Milanese anti-Fascists who came all the way to Rome to assassinate him? Mussolini glowered and shook his head. They got only as far as Piazza Venezia, the manicurist explained, then gave up the project. They found they had to join a queue.

Abruptly the Duce snatched his hand from the buffer, dismissing her. Weeks passed into months, but she was never again summoned to Palazzo Venezia.

Incredibly, even now, Mussolini rejected with pride and pain that such coffee-bar anecdotes could reflect the way the people felt. Yet for a long time the signs had been there to see – as far back as 11 December, 1941, when the Duce, following the Japanese attack on Pearl Harbour, joined Hitler in declaring war on the United States. Sensing the crowd's sullen apathy, he had pruned his speech to a bare five minutes – for he had ranted so often now from Palazzo Venezia's balcony that cynical Romans nicknamed him 'Juliet'. If he appeared on a newsreel screen, erect on his horse at a march past, the cinema stayed ominously silent. And soon after El Alamein, the people showed their true fears – with a run on the banks so grave that the Banca d'Italia had to print forty billion lire worth of bank-notes to honour the withdrawals.

Yet still Mussolini believed he embodied the people's will – and that as such they cherished him. One longtime colleague, Giovacchino Forzano, who tried to disillusion him, never forgot the tempest of anger he aroused.

'The love of the people for their leader,' Forzano told him, 'lasts just as long as things are going smoothly.' And he added: 'If the King sent four *carabinieri* to Palazzo Venezia, nobody would lift a finger to help you.'

Never had he seen Mussolini react with such ungovernable violence. The Duce sprang from his chair. His fist came down with agonizing force on the polished surface of his desk. High-pitched words poured from him in a torrent.

'I'm sure of the love and fidelity of the Italians,' he screamed, 'sure of it, I tell you, sure of it, sure of it . . .'

Still the fist hammered, the voice raged, until spittle flecked the corners of his lips: his black eyes blazed insanely. Forzano stood frozen, shocked.

Only one man, it seemed, would never cease to doubt that he spoke with the tongue of forty million Italians: Benito Mussolini himself.

Neatly set out in double-spaced typescript, the memorandum was at first glance like a hundred others issuing from Palazzo Vidoni, the Army High Command's Headquarters, in that spring of 1943. It was detailed and precise covering three sheets of paper. Only three features singled this memorandum out from any other: it bore neither Army crest, addressee nor signature.

Even so, reflected General Giuseppe Castellano, the implacable fifty-year-old Assistant to the Chief of General Staff, discovery of the document which Ciano, his host, now read so avidly, could set him in the space of days against a wall in Forte Boccea, facing a firing squad. The charge: conspiracy to topple the Fascist regime, and most particularly its leader, Benito Mussolini.

Now, seated in his host's elegant office on Via Flaminia, Castellano could see this blueprint for a *coup d'état* with painful clarity in his mind's eye. Point One was something both Castellano and his chief, General Vittorio Ambrosio, the stiff, taciturn Piedmontese who in February 1943 succeeded Cavellero as the Army's Chief of Staff, had discussed many times. That was to arrest Mussolini during a military exercise at the Nettuno Artillery Range, thirty-eight miles from Rome. Point Two was a plan less feasible – to seize the Duce at Palazzo Venezia itself. Both Ambrosio and Castellano were determined to avoid civil war and each time Castellano's ADC took the Duce the daily war bulletin, he reported the palace strongly guarded by loyal Fascists.

This left only Point Three – to imprison the Duce at the moment he left the Quirinale following his twice-weekly audience with the King.

'With this,' Castellano told his host, who now laid aside the memo, 'I have put myself completely in your hands.'

For answer, Galeazzo Ciano, newly-appointed Ambassador to the Holy See, shrugged his elegant shoulders, arranging his pomaded hair. 'Your secret is safe with me,' he assured the General. Broadly he hinted that some of the Fascist chiefs, too, were groping for a like solution – thus far with no results.

Castellano had a shrewd inkling who those chiefs might be. On 5 February, 1943, Mussolini had announced one more 'changing-of-the-guard' – the Cabinet reshuffles by which he could bow to popular discontent without ever admitting that the mistakes had been his own. Prominent among the men replaced, although all retained their seats on the Fascist Grand Council, were Minister of Justice Dino Grandi, Minister of Education Giuseppe Bottai, and Ciano. It was after Ciano, against Mussolini's wishes, had opted for the Holy See – 'the position may open many possibilities,' he noted in his diary – that Castellano paid the first of many tentative calls on the Count.

Now on this March morning, with the damning memorandum spread openly between them, Castellano had put his cards on the table. He and General Ambrosio had but one aim: to cut loose from the Axis alliance and negotiate a separate peace with the Allies.

Castellano wasn't truly surprised by Ciano's cool acceptance of a plot against his own father-in-law. The General's peace plans brought him in daily contact with many Palazzo Chigi officials – senior diplomats like Count Leonardo Vitetti and Count Luca Pietromarchi – and even as Foreign Minister, Ciano had talked openly of Italy's need to pull out of the war. Recklessly he had even told Gaetano Polverelli, Minister for Popular Culture and a Duce man to the last: 'Mussolini's the obstacle – if he agrees to step down we can transact on an equitable basis with Churchill and Roosevelt.' To others he had argued: 'One day we'll have the courage to say to Mussolini one word that nobody's uttered since Matteotti's time – Enough!'

Even before the stewards at Acquasanta Golf Club, Ciano contemptuously referred to Mussolini as 'Old Soft-in-the-Head'. Once fulsome in his praise of the Duce, his rancour now knew no bounds. With Edda he was visiting his native Leghorn on the night of the first Allied bombardment. At the first wail of the siren, a look of ill-humoured protest crossed Ciano's face. 'And that bungling father of yours doesn't want to believe we'll lose this war,' he sneered, then stamped off to the bomb-shelter, leaving Edda hurt and angry.

Himself no Fascist, General Castellano was well aware that Ciano's overwhelming ambition was to fill Mussolini's shoes. But he was willing to cultivate any source that might foster peace – and who better than this new Ambassador, the key to channels leading even to Pope Pius XII himself?

Only in one respect, the General told Ciano frankly, did he and his chief differ. The correct, ramrod-stiff Ambrosio insisted that Mussolini himself was the man to disengage from Germany – though Castellano maintained stoutly that the Duce would never have the courage. In vain, Ambrosio had tried even insults to goad Mussolini into action. 'You are alone, you no longer have a single Fascist behind you,' Ambrosio shouted to him once. But still Mussolini made no move to contact Hitler and bring Italy out of the war.

During his weekly visits to the Quirinale, Ambrosio fared no better. Though he urged the need for the King's intervention, the little King stood as if turned to stone, listening intently, saying nothing. Only the frequent visits of Pietro, Duke of Acquarone, an immaculate, wall-eyed cavalry officer who served as Comptroller of the King's Household, gave the generals fresh heart. The King saw the justice of their proposals, Acquarone, a wily Genoese, assured them, but he was still seeking 'a constitutional solution'.

The plan for arrest, Acquarone told Ambrosio, was 'premature'.

On this March morning, Galeazzo Ciano emphatically disagreed. 'I think it's a marvellous idea,' he told Castellano enthusiastically. 'Bring troops down to Rome, as well, to stop any armed Fascist reaction. But above all take no chances. Arrest Mussolini!'

In his office at Palazzo Wedekind, shadowed by the Column of Marcus Aurelius, Carlo Scorza shook his head slowly. Study them whichever way you might, the reports on the desk of the newly-appointed Fascist Party secretary added up to one thing. The people were angry, and the people had just won a notable victory over Fascism.

In three humiliating years of war, three men had occupied the party secretary's leather-padded swivel chair at Palazzo Wedekind. This morning, Saturday, 17 April, 1943, forty-six-year-old Carlo Scorza made a fourth – a human dynamo, appointed by Benito Mussolini in one more desperate attempt to stay the rot.

And despite his inmost feelings, Scorza was just then preparing to go through the motions. Within weeks, the blond, blue-eyed Tuscan Fascist, who had led the Lucca contingent in the March on Rome and had once shaved his head in slavish imitation of the Duce, would fire four senior Party officials and twenty provincial secretaries. 'If we must die,' he would rally the party in an interminable three-hour speech, 'let us swear to die in style.' Yet the reports now before him told him that all was lost.

Six weeks earlier, a shock-wave of Communist-inspired strikes had detonated through all Northern Italy. Embittered by months of night-long Allied bombing, rising food-costs and frozen wages, workers in vital war plants like Caproni, Fiat and Westinghouse had downed tools. At Milan's Pirelli tyre plant, soldiers sent in as strike-breakers had thrown aside their arms to embrace the workers as brothers. Worst of all, one star conciliator, Tullio Cianetti, of the Fascist Grand Council, had been showered with stones and hounded from the plant.

On 3 April, after one month's industrial chaos, Mussolini had conceded defeat, promising substantial wage increases and bonuses. To a realist like Scorza the outcome was plain.

'I myself feel,' he told the aide who had laid the reports before him, 'that I've been called to the bedside of a dying man.'

Wasn't he exaggerating? asked his stooge hopefully.

'You're right,' Carlo Scorza agreed, his voice as always calm and paternal, 'I *am* exaggerating. I should have said a dead man.'

Along the corridors of the Palazzo del Quirinale, a rippling scale from a Bechstein piano wavered on the still May afternoon. Then the notes, as abruptly as they had sounded, died away. But the footmen on duty, sweltering in their scarlet swallow-tailcoats, had tuned in to the message. Crown Princess Maria-José was free to receive anyone among the random visitors who so often sought her out.

The blue-eyed, thirty-six-year-old Belgian princess, with her tip-tilted nose and cheeky smile, was popular with the palace servants. As the devoted mother of four cherished youngsters, Maria Pia, eight, Vittorio Emanuele, six, Maria Gabriella, three, and Maria Beatrice, three months – she had early won their sympathy, so plainly estranged both from her husband, the handsome Crown Prince Umberto, and her father-in-law, King Vittorio Emanuele, who had not once received her in two years. The staff responded warmly to her need for human contacts – and the piano-scale signal was part of a friendly conspiracy.

Not one among them suspected that Maria-José was the polarizing force of an anti-Fascist resistance network, located there in the very heart of the Quirinale – or that in the four rooms on the mezzanine floor that she styled her 'bachelor-girl' apartment, the Crown Princess received emissaries from the underground political parties that were mushrooming all over Rome, and even from the Vatican City.

Three years earlier, on 10 May, 1940, the day that the German panzers had lanced into her native Belgium, Maria-José had declared her own private war on Benito Mussolini, whom she disdainfully nicknamed '*Provolone*' (Big Cheese). On that day of desperation, she told her bosom friend, the talkative, outspoken Marchesa Giuliana Benzoni, 'If they declare war, I'll go outside the Quirinale and shout "Long live peace" through the streets.'

Giuliana counselled prudence: there were surer ways of striking at Mussolini than proclaiming her hatred from the housetops. Now, more than three years later, on 26 May, 1943, it was the Marchesa Giuliana that Maria-José awaited – with news of the most unlikely political pact that even Fascism had spawned.

For these two women, it had been no easy task. When the hour was ripe, the one man who could take decisive action was the King – yet the King had always distrusted his forthright, intelligent daughter-in-law. Despite her tireless war-work as Inspector-General of the Red Cross, he detested her unconventional habits – taking bicycle trips without her lady-in-waiting, dropping incognito into open-air *osterie* to eat bread and salami with tram drivers. Bitterly resented, too, was the tribute paid her by more than one admirer: 'Maria-José is the only man in the House of Savoy.'

Divided from the King by a stone wall of prejudice, Maria-José had hit upon a medieval story-book device to keep him abreast of the many parallel plots brewing against Mussolini. Day by day she fed titbits of news to the one man in the Royal Household who cherished a hopeless and unrequited passion for her: the dandified Pietro, Duke of Acquarone, whose financial wizardry in paring the Royal expenses had won him the King's undying trust.

And in three years there had been much for Acquarone to report. Kicking off her shoes and sprawling on her divan in a characteristic posture, Maria José lit one of the black, pencil-slim cheroots the King so hated and reviewed all that she and Giuliana had done to date.

There had been the politicians, many of them refugees within the Vatican City, whose trust they had sought and won – men like sixty-nine-year-old Ivanoe Bonomi, former Premier of Italy, and such Christian Democrats as Alcide de Gasperi (later his party's first Premier). Each day two envoys reported to Maria-José on the hopes that these men cherished for a new Italy: Professor Ferdinando Arena, physician to the House of Savoy, and Dr Carlo Antoni, the Princess's tutor in constitutional law. Assured that these politicians would be willing to serve under the King in a new government, following the overthrow of Fascism, the Marchesa Giuliana next brought Guido Gonella, the cherubic, bespectacled, diplomatic correspondent of the official Vatican newspaper *L'Osservatore Romano*, to Maria-José's bachelor-girl apartment.

During a score of meetings Gonella had forged one more vital link in the chain – and soon the Marchesa Giuliana was an almost daily visitor to the Vatican City office of Monsignor Giovanni Battista Montini (now Pope Paul VI), Deputy Secretary of State for Pope Pius XII.

Infected by Maria-José's burning enthusiasm to rid Italy of Fascism, it wasn't always easy for the Marchesa to abide by Vatican protocol. Mostly, as she rattled on with new contacts, new plans, Montini sat gravely in profile, chin on hand, as silent as an image. Once, past patience, forgetting to address him as 'Your Eminence', the Marchesa burst out: 'My son, if you don't speak soon I'll go mad.' Hands spread wide, his eyes upraised to Heaven, the future Pontiff replied tactfully: 'Mother, the good Lord didn't give me your mental agility. Before I decide and speak, *I* need to think.'

But it was Monsignor Montini, after meeting with Maria-José, who had filtered the names of the loyal politicians to Harold Tittmann, Roosevelt's Chargé d'Affaires at the Vatican, and Sir Francis d'Arcy Godolphin Osborne, British Minister to the Holy See. The crucial question was, would such men be acceptable to Washington and London, should Italy disengage from the war?

Like General Castellano, Maria-José cast her net widely. In August 1942, on her own initiative, she had met secretly in a wooded glade near Cogne, in Piedmont, with one man who truly hated Mussolini – Marshal Pietro Badoglio. The Marshal declared himself more than ready to command the Army when the time came. 'If Germany wins,' he declared, 'we'll never be rid of Fascism.'

But shrewdly the Princess had recognized that any successful *coup d'état* needed more than the tacit support of Pope Pius XII and the King. The wave of strikes that had so troubled Party Secretary Scorza made this plain. Like it or not, the conspirators had need of the Communists – and it was news of their decision that Maria-José awaited from the Marchesa Giuliana Benzoni.

Through the tutor Carlo Antoni, the Marchesa had made contact with Concetto Marchesi, a dapper, moon-faced Professor of Latin at Padua University, one of the Communists' most powerful underground men. Would Marchesi, she asked point-blank, relay a message to Italy's Number One Communist, who for eighteen years of Russian exile had represented Italy in the Comintern – fifty-year-old Palmiro Togliatti?

And now, promptly at 4 p.m. on 26 May, the Marchesa bubbled into the room, chattering excitedly – an expressionless, forty-eight-year-old spinster whose inconsequential society manner hid the heart of a lioness. From Moscow, Togliatti had replied to Professor Marchesi's request with a ringing affirmative. The Communists would 'loyally collaborate' with King Vittorio Emanuele in any forthcoming coup against Mussolini.

They asked, Giuliana explained, only one service in return: one minister without portfolio in any newly-formed government. As proof of their goodwill they would, at a given signal, bring every factory in Italy to a standstill.

Marchesi, said Giuliana, had added one rider of his own that made her blood run cold. 'Four hundred thousand heads,' the Communist had prophesied, 'will have to roll in Italy.'

In the living-room of his luxurious villa on Rome's Via Bruxelles, Marshal Pietro Badoglio, as restless as a caged animal, paced the polished parquet. Nine months had now elapsed since that first clandestine meeting with Crown Princess Maria-José, yet still no summons came from the Quirinale. Now Badoglio was beside himself. He did not realize that the Crown Princess had summoned him on her own initiative. Still smarting that he had been forced to resign following the Greek débâcle, Badoglio felt that a chance to get even with Benito Mussolini had been dangled before him by the King, then as capriciously withdrawn.

Although Mussolini had reluctantly allowed Badoglio's petition to be exempted from income tax following the Abyssinian War – instructing Finance Minister Count Paolo Thaon di Revel to collect it, then reimburse it – the Marshal had hated Mussolini since the days of the March on Rome. And since Greece his grudge had thrived.

'Give me the go-ahead,' he had told his sons repeatedly. 'I'll put 150 men to the wall and that's done.' Now, as time went by, he was growing rebellious. 'If the King doesn't make up his mind to carry out the *coup d'état*,' he snorted, 'I'll do it myself in agreement with Crown Prince Umberto.'

Abruptly the Marshal halted his pacing. A servant had announced Dr Ferdinando Arena. Both the Royal Household and Badoglio shared the same physician, and to Badoglio this could only betoken the summons he awaited.

'Have you a message?' Badoglio queried, eyes shining, as he hastened forward to seize Arena's hands. 'Are you sent by the King?'

'Why no, Marshal,' the bewildered physician had to confess, 'I just came to check your blood pressure.'

Claretta Petacci started. Without warning her taxi had braked on the very threshold of Palazzo Venezia, at the side entrance in Via degli Astalli which she had used every afternoon for seven years now. Unceremoniously, the plainclothes agent who had waved it to a halt thrust his head through the window.

'You cannot enter, Signora,' he told her drily.

Claretta was flabbergasted. 'Can't enter?' she echoed. 'Why not? What is all this?' But the man only replied stolidly: 'Turn back! Those are the Duce's orders. I can't say more than that.'

Her thoughts in a whirl, Claretta at once urged the driver to take her to Quinto Navarra's house close by, alongside the church of San Marco. The Duce's usher, long her good friend, would surely know what was amiss. But Navarra, pained and confused, could offer no explanation. Though he had heard of Mussolini's order, he had no idea why it had been given. Stricken with grief and humiliation, Claretta could only return to Villa Camilluccia.

In vain the twenty-year-old Myriam urged her sister: 'Drop him and forget all about him! Don't go running after him again, after what he's done to you! He doesn't deserve it!' It was advice Claretta was incapable of following. That same evening she wrote to Mussolini begging for an explanation – then, next day, two more letters. When no answers came, she picked up the telephone. But though Extension 51 at Palazzo Venezia stayed obstinately silent, Claretta persisted. If Mussolini had found another woman, let him have the courage to tell her – but what, above all, was going on in the Duce's restless, tortured brain?

It was a question many others besides Claretta asked themselves in these sultry days of May 1943. To most, it seemed that Mussolini's conduct had now lost all semblance of logic – as if, conscious that his grandiose plans had brought Italy to the verge of ruin, he now sought to hasten the inevitable end.

At last, after five days' silence, it was he who telephoned Claretta. His voice hard and distant, he would vouchsafe no more than this: 'I had decided not to see you again. I had my reasons.' Yet Claretta sensed he was relenting, and pleaded: 'Even a man who is sentenced to death gets an explanation.' Only when she returned to Palazzo Venezia did she realize, with a sinking heart, that Mussolini had no rational explanation to give.

As she entered the Zodiac Room, she exclaimed sharply. Suddenly it was a stranger's room – the radiogram, the books, the vase of flowers, had all disappeared. 'I had them all taken away when I decided not to see you again,' Mussolini told her, as if this explained everything.'

'And my photograph?'

'I tore it up,' he told her in the same tone, 'when I was feeling angry.'

In truth, harried by innumerable problems, Mussolini had tried frantically to deal with the only one capable of solution: Claretta herself. Her daily presence at Palazzo Venezia was common gossip in every Roman salon, and incredibly, only Rachele, who never moved outside her close-knit Romagnol circle, was still unaware of the liaison. Flailing at terrors, the Duce's personal reaction to all such problems was to run and hide. On 13 May, when all Axis forces in Africa surrendered, he at once retreated to Rocca delle Caminate, his summer place near Forlì, where he spent days clipping out newspaper articles, underlining sentences with red and blue crayon.

For the men close to Mussolini, his mental chaos was spotlit in sundry ways. To usher Quinto Navarra, it was his slovenliness – once his desk had been a model of neatness, yet now it spilled over like a junk-stall with half-opened books, Fascist badges and medals, sheaves of wheat bound in tricolour ribbon. To General Antonio Sorice, Under-Secretary for War, it was his fatal delay over decisions. Formerly an indefatigable do-it-today man, the Duce now dallied two weeks or more – always to no avail. Once, when Sorice pressed him to decide on two long-delayed memos, Mussolini obliged within the hour. Though each outlined a scheme radically opposed to the other, Sorice found the Duce had approved both.

The tragedy for Italy was that Mussolini dared not admit disaster. That summer a group of Milanese industrialists called at Palazzo Venezia for an economic conference. As they left, one man, raising his arm in the Roman salute, declared hopefully 'Vinceremo!' (We shall win). To his astonishment, Mussolini shouted furiously, 'We don't need to win! We have won already! We have! Morally we have won!'

Yet von Rintelen, the German Military Attaché, found him defeatist to a fault. Years before World War Two, Fascist propaganda had proclaimed the island of Pantelleria, south-west of Italy, an impregnable fortress – Mussolini's 'anti-Malta', honeycombed with underground hangars, housing squadrons of planes, forty batteries and a garrison of 12,000 men. Early in June, under non-stop air attack, Admiral Gino Pavesi, its commander, twice refused to surrender.

Then, late on the morning of 11 June, von Rintelen arrived at Palazzo Venezia to find Mussolini on the phone. From Pantelleria, Pavesi was reporting an acute shortage of water. To the German's astonishment, Mussolini instructed the Admiral: 'Radio Malta that because of lack of water you give up all further resistance.'

Von Rintelen could scarcely credit it. For months Mussolini had insisted that Pantelleria would be defended to the last man – yet now the Allies had captured it without even setting foot on it. And Mussolini himself, barely conversant with the facts, had ordered its surrender.

To many it seemed that Giuseppe Bottai's acid verdict on the Duce nine months back could well stand as his epitaph: 'A self-taught man who had a bad teacher and was a worse pupil.'

What embittered him was the knowledge that most Italians had lost the will to fight. Daily his doctor dosed him with Bellafolina and Alucol, relaxants to ease his stomach cramps, but each time fresh evidence of front-line apathy reached him his pains redoubled. One report told of a fortress on the Jugoslav frontier lacking grease to lubricate its guns. When a captain protested, his colonel replied: 'Don't you know we've got to lose this war to free ourselves from Fascism?' From Tobruk came the story of a bomber squadron which had indented for spare parts – and received from base 150 pounds of old newspapers.

'Whenever I try to find the culprits,' Mussolini raged to one woman friend, 'I come up against a blank and impenetrable wall!' To a longtime colleague he confessed that he was fast finding the Italians ungovernable.

'Every man is trying to cash in on the business for his family,' he admitted. 'How can I ever hope to pay a high enough salary to stamp out graft?'

One Fascist official, Giovanni Balella, never forgot a committee meeting over which the Duce presided in June 1943. On this hot oppressive afternoon, a dozen delegates were listening in silence as Minister for Agriculture Carlo Pareschi explained why that summer's harvest had fallen short of expectations. Suddenly Mussolini held up a lordly hand. 'Do you know what the birds do?' he asked them in a conspiratorial whisper.

Mystified, vaguely uneasy, each man shook his head. 'Days ago,' Mussolini confided, 'I was out in the country – and I saw what the birds do. They alight on the wheat stems so that their weight bends them over and they can't be seen. Then they eat the grain.'

Suddenly, with almost manic intensity, he ordered: 'Kill the birds – kill them all!'

Minutes later, in strained silence, the meeting broke up. Until they were safely away from the Duce's office, no man said a word.

'But he's going crazy,' Balella, the President of the Confederation of

Industrialists said softly, summing up all their feelings. 'Just plain crazy.'

From the villa's formal green gardens the harsh cry of a peacock grated on the ears of the men sitting in uneasy conference round the ground-floor billiard-room. It was as harsh, thought Dino Alfieri, the polished, impassive Ambassador to Berlin, as the voice of their host, rising and falling in monologue. For almost an hour now, since 11 a.m., ten of them had been pinioned here like captives in the seventeenth-century Villa Gaggia, fifteen miles from the Veneto town of Feltre, while Adolf Hitler, a table placed conveniently within range of his fist, told Benito Mussolini exactly how World War Two would be waged from now on.

'If we could safeguard all the regions containing raw materials of military importance,' Hitler ploughed on, 'the war could be carried on indefinitely. This is a question of willpower. If we are to save the nations from ruin we must shrink from no hardship.'

Already more than one man found his attention wandering. The wide french windows of the room framed a scene of pastoral beauty; against the green lawns, the peacocks and golden pheasants made vivid splashes of colour and deer cropped the parkland sloping down from the Alps. Giuseppe Bastianini, Under-Secretary for Foreign Affairs, wondered if Mussolini was even taking in a word the Führer uttered. At 8.30 that morning, arriving in his private plane at Treviso airport, he had looked both sick and finished, his sunglasses as dark as a blind man's against his pale face. Dr Pozzi, who had flown with him, noted that as always in crises he was fretful over inessentials. At Riccione airport he exploded because trumpeters played his fanfare out of tune. En route to the field Pozzi narrowly restrained him from leaping from the car – to berate some passing peasants who hadn't given the Roman salute.

Now he sat shifting uneasily in his deep leather armchair, sighing heavily, pressing his left hand behind his back in the region of his stomach ulcer – but his face was so devoid of expression he might have heard nothing.

To Mussolini's anger, it was Hitler himself who had convened this conference on Italian soil on 19 July – the thirteenth between the dictators – giving him only a scant twenty-four hours' notice. Though no reason for the meeting had been given and no common agenda drawn up, the Duce had none the less agreed – but had promptly left Rome for Riccione before either Bastianini or General Ambrosio could consult with him on common policy.

Now, as if willing him to speak, the Italian delegation never took their eyes from Mussolini's face. The hour of crisis had struck, and all of them knew it. Nine days earlier, at 1 p.m. on 10 July, War Bulletin No 1141, had announced the worst news yet: in the night just past, 160,000 Allied troops had stormed ashore in Sicily. Plainly only two courses now lay open to the Duce: to demand from Hitler weapons, tanks and aircraft to help repel the invaders or to announce firmly that Italy could no longer sustain this war.

True to his vow, General Ambrosio had struck the first blow. On the train journey from Treviso airport to Feltre that morning he had taxed Field Marshal Wilhelm Keitel bluntly: what plans did Germany have to provide motorized divisions to repel the invasion? How many tanks, Ambrosio demanded icily, how much fuel, how many aircraft, would be forthcoming? But Keitel was evasive. Few German reinforcements, he thought, would be available for two months yet. 'The two leaders will discuss all these matters, you know,' he brushed off Ambrosio.

As Keitel well knew, the plan drawn up the night before at Berchtesgaden provided a very different answer from the one Ambrosio sought. As Hitler envisaged it, a German command, under the Duce's nominal authority, would from now on oversee the entire Mediterranean front – with Germany assuming total military control over Italian armies and the Air Force.

'All power to the Duce is the motto of the day,' was Keitel's clipped greeting to General von Rintelen as the military attaché met his plane that morning. Astonished, von Rintelen replied, 'But he *has* all power already. He's just no longer able to keep his hands on the reins.'

Only now did von Rintelen realize that Hitler had convened this hasty conference in a perfunctory attempt to save Mussolini's face – proclaiming the Duce's authority at the identical moment that he took over his armies.

It did not deceive the Italians. Angrily Dino Alfieri watched the German generals 'nodding like marionettes' as Hitler's harangue grew shriller. 'There are bourgeois people in Germany who think it's time to end the war,' he was saying, 'and to leave conquest in the East to future generations. Wrong again! Germany will not have – not in 300 years – another man like me.'

Why doesn't Mussolini speak? thought Giuseppe Bastianini in

black despair. Now is his chance to explain that Italy no longer has resources. Doesn't he realize it's his last chance?

Abruptly Hitler switched to another tack. 'Take tank production,' he invited them. 'If the war had not broken out, Germany would have continued to mass-produce the Mark I, II and III tanks. But today we have learned from our war experience that these tanks are absolutely useless . . .'

Irritated, Hitler broke off. Timidly, bearing a sheet of paper, Nicolò de Cesare, Mussolini's private secretary, had entered the room. Hastening to the Duce's side, he whispered urgently. On the table beside him Hitler's stubby fingers beat a small tattoo of displeasure.

For the first time that morning Mussolini spoke. His voice shaking with emotion, he blurted out in halting German:

'Führer . . . gentlemen . . . at this moment the enemy is carrying out a heavy air attack on Rome.'

At one minute past 11 a.m. Clara Ambrosini took a last look at herself in the full-length mirror. Then, regretfully, the long white wedding dress shimmered to the bedroom floor – discarded along with the white veil, the bouquet of orange blossom. With a secret glow of content she reminded herself that she was now Signora di Pasquale – soon to depart on honeymoon with her husband of two hours, Lance-Sergeant Alfredo di Pasquale of the Italian Air Force.

Already the six hired landaus, drawn by gleaming chestnuts, were drawn up outside her mother's house at 42 Via degli Equi in Rome's clamorous labouring-class eastern district of San Lorenzo. In the living-room Alfredo and her mother, along with a score of guests in their feast-day best, were sipping coffee and exclaiming over the wedding presents, killing time while Clara, a dark, petite twenty-five-year-old, changed into her travelling costume.

Carefully adjusting a pair of diamond earrings, Clara recalled that she and Alfredo had spent months planning this day. First, the wedding at the Church of the Immaculate Conception, then the carriage-ride to the reception at the Ristorante Tor Carbone on the ancient Appian Way. And two whole weeks of honeymoon at Florence and Assisi were to follow – days they would remember all their lives.

Few Romans saw this July Monday, 1134 days since war began, as such a red-letter day. The hope uppermost in everybody's mind was to see an end to a conflict irretrievably lost. This morning the thermometer showed 86°F in the shade, and in San Lorenzo, as elsewhere, the women planned to finish their marketing early. Already, in long vociferous lines, they were queuing everywhere along the sun-drenched pavements – for scarce olive oil at 100 lire per litre, for potatoes at ten lire per kilogram and spaghetti at double that price. Few without black market contacts ever saw coffee, wine or eggs in these days, and in San Lorenzo most pet-lovers kept a close watch on their cats – a wartime delicacy, they already fetched £1 apiece.

At 11.05 a.m. hundreds of pairs of eyes turned upwards to the sky – from market-stalls, from tenement balconies, from cool dark doorways. The ominous sound of explosions had sounded to the north. At that moment the high shrill note of the air-raid siren wavered and cried on the stifling air.

No man reacted quicker than thirty-one-year-old Alfredo di Pasquale. Clara would always remember with pride that her husband, a veteran of Benghazi, sensed immediately that danger threatened. Gently, methodically, he was already relieving Clara's elderly relatives of their cups, coaxing them, 'Let's leave the coffee for later – better head towards the shelter.'

A few others had premonitions. Across the street Angela Fioravanti, a forceful blue-eyed seamstress of thirty-eight, recalled an appalling dream: one month back she had seen 'all Rome buried like a cemetery'. Urgently tugging her six-year-old twins Alberto and Jolanda away from their puppet-theatre and urging her husband Menotti to follow, she hastened from her second-floor apartment to the porter's lodge below. But to most the Vatican City across the Tiber was the reassuring symbol of Rome's immunity. In the San Lorenzo freightyards hard by, engine-driver Gaetano Ianni was just reassuring a nervy comrade. 'Virgilio, relax, you should know better – Rome just doesn't get bombed.'

Neither Ianni nor any of the district's 50,000 inhabitants had reflected that almost all southbound rail traffic bearing arms and reinforcements to Sicily passed through Rome – most particularly through the great 375-acre marshalling yards of Tiburtina and San Lorenzo that hemmed the area in. At this very moment, twenty miles north at Monterosi, 500 American bombers droned steadily for their appointed rendezvous: 20,000 feet over San Lorenzo.

The realization was slow to come. In his office west of the marshalling yards, Rodolfo Coltellini, the coal merchant, was riffling through a pile of lire bills when an employee begged him: 'Come outside,

Signor Rodolfo, and see how the planes shine!' From San Lorenzo's Franciscan convent, less than a mile away, the tall bearded Brother Nicola da Mondovì saw the first bombs falling to catch the rays of the sun 'like golden tears'. For one long moment, all over San Lorenzo, thousands stood staring, watching the spectacle in silent disbelief. Then the bombs struck home.

A whistling ear-splitting inferno engulfed the narrow streets of San Lorenzo. More than a thousand tons of bombs rained down on the marshalling yards. Whole buildings disintegrated. Yellow pinpoints of light seared through the smoke like deadly rockets as an ammunition train caught fire. Yards of shining track, locomotives, trees, steel girders and switchgear spewed skywards – to loop in the wires of the tram-cars or land on the shattered roofs of tenements. Rodolfo Coltellini watched 3000 square yards of his piled fuel take fire like a blast furnace, burning with a light so bright he could not watch it. Down the five storeys of the Pantanella Spaghetti Factory streamed a molten cascade of red-hot flour. But inevitably some bombs fell wide of their targets, and everywhere there were scenes of apocalyptic horror. Racing for the shelter, Angela Fioravanti saw the terrified carriage horses of the wedding procession rearing and screaming between the shafts in the moment before bombs blew them and the coachmen apart. Through the black billowing smoke, whirling spirals of birds – swallows, pigeons, sparrows – swooped in mindless terror.

Clara di Pasquale was petrified. In the street the landaus were smashed to matchwood; from the carnage of flesh she could barely distinguish man from horse. The tenement opposite had collapsed in yellow choking clouds of plaster-dust, barely missing Alfredo; minutes earlier he had darted clear after vainly trying to drag people from the ruins. Now his new dark suit was as white as a painter's overalls. All of them stumbled through acrid smoke to the courtyard of the Trattoria Ramponcini – scattering to cannon into fresh arrivals with each thunderous explosion.

Suddenly Clara was laughing hysterically. The scurrying figures lunging and recoiling seemed all at once like a Mack Sennett comedy – and her father, Francesco, calmest of all, kept up a non-stop commentary like a radio reporter: 'They're coming round again . . . they're levelling out . . . No 26 has just exploded!'

Some had survived by a miracle. Hospital nurse Rosa Benigni, squeezed under an infirmary sofa, owed her life to her four-year-old daughter Anna Maria. That morning the child had proved so irritating – pelting passers-by from the loggia – that Rosa, in slapping her, had knocked her against a wall and drawn blood. Contrite, she had rushed her to the infirmary for treatment at the very moment a bomb destroyed her tenement building and 120 lives.

On the 10.30 a.m. suburban train from Guidonia to Rome, tele-communications expert Nicola Giordano had forgone the privilege of his reduced-rate ticket and travelled third class. Ahead, the coaches were jammed with swimmers bound for the Tivoli baths, and Giordano, en route to the office, wanted to keep his white linen suit immaculate. At Prenestina, the last stop before Rome, bombs wiped out the first two coaches – and Giordano, diving headlong from the carriage window, was screened from the flying fragments of bomb-casing by the slag-heap of dust that engulfed him.

At such a time every man, woman and child felt the need for prayer. Much later, when a workman dragged Giordano clear, his eyes and mouth packed with coal-dust, he gasped out to his rescuer: 'If we live through this, we'll have to erect a shrine to the Madonna right here.' Linda Lauretani, a young archivist who took refuge with fifty others in a shelter beneath a Fascist branch headquarters, remembers that 'most were invoking St Anthony'. At the Campo Ver-ano Cemetery whose southernmost tip was an island in the heart of the freightyards, many had sought out family tombs as the safest place to pray, calling on long-departed relatives 'to help us from up there'.

But at 1 p.m. the bombers were still coming, glinting silver against the vivid blue of the sky, and slowly the mood was changing. From passive acceptance and prayer, the people of San Lorenzo, sweating and grimy, shaken by rage and by grief, were approaching breaking-point.

In the courtyard of the Trattoria Ramponcini, Clara di Pasquale remembered, Vittorio, the waiter, was the first man among 50,000 to voice what all of them felt. Suddenly he grabbed a white cloth from a table. Racing to the centre of the courtyard, he waved it wildly aloft like a flag of truce.

Above the awesome din of the oncoming planes, Clara heard him shout: 'Let's all go to Piazza Venezia and wave this! Let's scream, "Enough, stop it! We're on your side! We're good people, good! We see things like you!" '

Not a muscle moved in Adolf Hitler's face. He stared ahead, not looking at Mussolini, a tight, prim smile on his lips – a man enduring, with fortitude, a trivial and unseemly display of Latin temperament. Mussolini, agitated, was demanding a detailed report, and Secretary de Cesare was explaining that all lines to Rome were jammed.

'Insist on getting through!' the Duce instructed angrily.

De Cesare withdrew. For a long moment the two dictators gazed at each other, immobile. Suddenly, as if he stood before a crowd in a vast stadium, Hitler announced: 'Germany needed fifty years to rise again. Rome did not rise again. This is history speaking!'

His voice calmer, he again resumed: "Today, tank production, as I said, is good . . .'

The three men were standing like the members of a tribunal, willing him to stop, when Mussolini passed the open door. For a moment before joining them the Duce hovered uneasily in the doorway. 'I am most upset to be away from the capital at a time like this,' he said. 'I shouldn't like the Romans to think . . .'

Dino Alfieri held on to his temper with difficulty. All morning, until the news of the raid, Mussolini had let Hitler ride roughshod over him. Now his sole concern was that the Romans might think he had run away.

At 1 p.m. when Hitler's Chief of Protocol announced the luncheon interval, Alfieri had at once buttonholed Bastianini. 'We just can't go on like this,' the Ambassador exploded. Bastianini, a hatchet-faced veteran of the March on Rome, agreed. A messenger was sent hastening to the washroom to fetch General Ambrosio. 'Mussolini ought at least to have interrupted Hitler,' were Ambrosio's first outraged words as he joined them.

Ambrosio had reason to be angry. For fully another hour, following De Cesare's first entry, Mussolini had again sat silent while Hitler in a shrill diatribe had flayed the Italian defenders of Sicily, from general to private, as incompetent cowards. If 400 aircraft had been lost on the ground, he shouted, then the airfield organization was bad. Men who deserted army batteries while a single round of ammunition remained should be shot on the spot. 'What has happened in Sicily,' he bellowed, 'must not be allowed to happen again!'

Now, incensed that he had not spoken one word in defence of his own troops, the three faced Mussolini resolutely. 'No one in Rome will think you have run away,' Alfieri reassured him, 'but the Romans, all Italians, are expecting this conference to produce decisive results. What the Führer said was harsh, negative and unjust. It's up to you, Duce, to seize the initiative and counter-attack.'

Never, Alfieri stressed, would Mussolini have a better opportunity to clarify the situation. How much longer was Italy to remain a bastion of the Reich? He offered General Ambrosio his cue: it was said the Army could not offer effective resistance for more than another month.

'I confirm that statement,' Ambrosio put in heavily, 'and the Duce knows that I have made it.'

Then, Alfieri plunged on, if the situation was so tragic, it must be faced. Better that a separate peace should be made while the State was still in being. General Ambrosio was blunter still. The Duce had just fifteen days, he told him sharply, to pull Italy out of the war.

Abruptly Mussolini gestured to them to sit down. His voice, Alfieri noted, still trembled with emotion. This problem, he told the three, had long tormented him, but was it so simple? 'One fine day,' he conceded, 'we broadcast a message to the enemy. But what would be the result?' Answering his own question, he pointed out that Italy would be forced to capitulate. 'Are we prepared to wipe out twenty years of Fascism at one stroke?' he asked them.

He wound up. 'It's so easy to talk about a separate peace. But what would be Hitler's attitude? Can you believe that he would allow us to retain liberty of action?'

Moments later, the anxious De Cesare again appeared. The Führer was impatiently awaiting Mussolini in his private dining-room.

As the Duce rose wearily to comply, Alfieri spoke the last word for all three. 'Only you can find a solution!' he told him. 'Only you can find a way out. But you must see to it that Italy is spared fresh disasters.'

Across the wastelands of dust-shrouded rubble, the word spread like news of a rescue party. Pope Pius XII had arrived – *Il Papa* himself! Already, before the all-clear sounded at 2 p.m. he had sent Monsignor Giovanni Montini to make a round of the collection-boxes in St Peter's – the total was 60,000 lire. Then, for the first time since June 1940, Pius's black Mercedes, flying the yellow-and-white Vatican flag, had slid through the Portone di Bronzo into Mussolini's Rome – and beleaguered San Lorenzo.

Almost without being told, the people knew his focal point: the Church of San Lorenzo Without-the-Walls. The fine romanesque structure, with its thirteenth-century campanile, was the fifth of the Papal basilicas. This afternoon it seemed to symbolize all that had

befallen the district in three hours of stark terror: only a few of its
pillars still rose sheer to the sky. Over mounds of stone and tiny
glinting shards of glass Pius picked his way with difficulty, a pale,
aquiline man with gold-rimmed spectacles.

On the steps of the Basilica he paused, looking out over San
Lorenzo. The smell of burning wood, plaster and rubber caught at
his stomach. Those close at hand saw that he was weeping, and with
reason. Over seven hundred dead – by some counts, 1200 – lay
along the shattered buildings, and more than 1200 wounded. In
the afternoon heat-glare dishevelled women clawed among the
smoking ruins, alongside men who grappled painfully with grief.
Stretchers passed, bearing the dead and wounded, and everywhere
priests knelt to give absolution to the dying. As the Pope recited the
De Profundis – 'Out of the depths, O Lord, have I cried unto Thee' –
and blessed the vast crowd pressing about him, many knelt to kiss
the hem of his robe. Some would always recall that the white linen
was blotched with the blood of the dying.

As the crowd drew closer the cries of '*Viva Il Papa*' grew in intensity, then redoubled. Many, too, added the cry '*Viva la pace*' (Long
live peace) and the words which swelled slowly to a chant had a
strangely menacing undertone that spelt trouble for the Fascist
regime and Benito Mussolini.

At that moment King Vittorio Emanuele III arrived in San
Lorenzo.

Despite his peaked cap and the grey-green uniform of Marshal
of the Empire, few people recognized him at a glance. At seventy-six,
the King looked even older – as wrinkled as a turkey, his moustaches
snow-white, his jaw trembling uncontrollably. In three years of war,
'Little Sword' had become almost a stranger to his people. On his
country estates he lived the life of a recluse, his frugality now amoun-
ting almost to mania – scribbling memos on torn-up scraps of newspaper to save stationery, searching the gravelled drive for nails that
might puncture the royal tyres. Only Queen Elena, his aides noted,
was still capable of evoking tenderness – on country walks the King
still plucked small nosegays of wild flowers to carry back for 'La
Mamma'.

All morning the King had stood at the ivy-framed window of
Villa Ada, listening to the distant thunder of explosions, opening
and clenching his left hand. Events were driving him towards the
decision he shrank from making. Two weeks earlier, returning to
Rome, he had once more met General Ambrosio. Plainly, all Ambro-

sio's counsel and the secret intelligence of Maria-José, relayed by the Duke of Acquarone, had borne fruit. For the first time, the King's aide, General Paolo Puntoni, noted, he had spoken of replacing Mussolini with a military dictatorship headed by Badoglio. But the invasion of Sicily gave the King fresh heart. If the Duce visited the front and was killed or captured there, he need never take the decision at all.

Supposing the Duce, on this day at Feltre, should surprise them all by severing from Hitler? Yet supposing again that he didn't, but sensed that a conspiracy was brewing against him and combined with Hitler to dethrone the King? That afternoon, as he left Villa Ada to view the damage, the King still had no answer. But now, to his undying mortification, the people of San Lorenzo gave it to him.

It was Angela Fioravanti who spotted him first. Half an hour after the raid had passed, the seamstress was beside herself; with an ear-splitting roar, her whole apartment building had fallen in. With her bare hands she had prised the twins and Maria, aged thirteen, free, but Elda, eleven, and her husband, Menotti, were still walled to their necks in plaster dust. Stumbling into the street for help, she saw the King only three yards away, alighting from his black limousine – 'his arms wide open, his jaws hanging, his eyes goggling with disbelief'.

Suddenly a terrible mindless rage consumed Angela Fioravanti. Screaming like a fury, her white dress plastered with blood, she ran blindly towards him. 'Look at him!' she challenged the crowds. 'He's come to look at the massacre, to look at the view.' She flung at him the deathless insult of the Roman street-folk. '*Va a mori' ammazzato!*' (Go and get yourself killed!) She struggled wildly, kicking out as one of the King's aides tried to cover her mouth. 'You got us into this war, along with the Germans,' she screamed. 'What have our children got to do with this dirty war?'

Others, emboldened, took up the cry, and as the King's aides, following the Pope's example, tried to distribute money, some crumpled the bank notes and flung them in the rubble. 'We don't want your dirty money,' one cried, 'we want peace.'

As the car moved off, the King sat white and trembling, not speaking. He, Vittorio Emanuele III, had been subjected to a barrage of abuse like a street-vendor. His thousand-year-old dynasty stood in peril – brought to this point by Mussolini. Suddenly his gloved right fist came with a smack into the palm of his left.

'The regime can't go on,' he whispered, 'not after this. At all costs we must change.'

It was past 9 p.m. on 20 July when the Duce pushed aside his papers, snapping off the desk lamp. Now the vast Sala del Mappamondo was lit only by a ruddy glow, transmuting the iron-barred windows to stained glass. Twenty-four hours after his return from Feltre, the fires of San Lorenzo were still a potent reminder of the mounting humiliations.

Within the past twenty-four hours they had been many. The luncheon with Hitler at Feltre had only resolved itself into one more painful harangue. The Führer devoured rice in Béchamel sauce with relish, talking all the time with his mouth full; the Duce scarcely took a bite. Hitler had spoken darkly of a new Reprisals Air Fleet that would raze London to the ground within weeks, of new-style submarine warfare. But the 2000 aircraft that Mussolini had requested from Germany had been refused outright – the Russian front took priority.

The two dictators had not parted until 5 p.m. but Mussolini could remember little more. The air raid had disturbed him too profoundly. To interpreter Paul Schmidt in Berlin had gone a tantamount admission that the thread of the day's talks had entirely escaped him. Before commenting on Hitler's proposals – which amounted to totalitarian military reorganization of southern Italy by the Italian Seventh Army, under German control – Mussolini must study the verbatim report.

This very day, 20 June, General Ambrosio had forced from him one more painful admission: the question of Italy's withdrawal from the war had never once been broached. Instead, the Duce promised, he would draft a letter to Hitler, asking to be released from the alliance. Ambrosio, who had tried in vain to resign, dismissed the subterfuge. 'It will end in Hitler's waste-paper basket,' he said with biting contempt. 'A disengagement could only have been achieved verbally – and at Feltre.'

For Ambrosio and his deputy, General Giuseppe Castellano, Mussolini's chicken-hearted refusal to face up to his fellow dictator spelt out one word: Action.

At 10 p.m. the Duce's last caller was announced: thirty-four-year-old Yvon de Begnac, his biographer, whose eight-volume study had been appearing with Mussolini's blessing for close on seven years. Tonight, De Begnac noticed, his subject's face was 'clay-coloured, unshaven'. In six weeks he had lost fifty pounds in weight: his uniform hung on him like a sack.

Now he riffled through the draft chapter laid before him, plainly too tired to take it in. 'This work of yours,' he mused, 'has lasted ten years. You were a boy when you came here the first time.'

De Begnac said nothing. Almost as if to himself Mussolini murmured: 'It's a life that's over already – but the struggle will go on.'

As the express jolted painfully over the ruptured tracks, the acrid smell was like a gas-attack in Dino Grandi's nostrils. Rome was burning. At dawn on 21 July it struck the Fascist chief that his mission to the city from his native Bologna had become perhaps the most urgent of his life.

And this morning Grandi was a determined man. Almost four years had now passed since that meeting with the King in the pine-woods at Sant' Anna di Valdieri – years in which, powerless to act, he had watched Italy's heritage crumbling. Now, in July 1943, Italy lay naked to its enemies: only seven infantry divisions, lacking armoured cars, stood ready to defend the entire peninsula. Only three of the Navy's six battleships were fit for combat – with sixteen cruisers and destroyers, most of them obsolete, scattered from Taranto to La Spezia. Since November, the Air Force had lost 2190 planes – while no more than seventy fighters were in shape to battle for the sky over Sicily.

Manpower was a pitiful problem. The flower of almost ten divisions had perished in the Russian snows. The Greek campaign had written off more than 100,000 men. Somaliland, Eritrea, Abyssinia, all were lost – and with them, over 250,000 prisoners.

Although the Cabinet reshuffle of February 1943 had robbed him of his post as Minister of Justice, Grandi had remained President of the Chamber of Fasces and Corporations, and in this role he had contrived to see the King twice each week. Now, with the Allies in Sicily, the time for talking was past. Somehow he must goad the King to act.

An ardent monarchist, Grandi had still come to despise his King. As a Major in the Alpine Regiment, he had served in the six-month Greek campaign, along with other Fascist leaders – among them the cold, ambitious Giuseppe Bottai, former Minister of Education. Both men had agreed that the need to get Italy out of the war as fast as could be was paramount – and out of their weekly meetings at the Officers' Club in Tirania, Albania, had emerged the draft

resolution which Grandi had presented to the King as long ago as
May 1941.

With stark simplicity it offered two dramatic solutions. Either
Mussolini must agree to reinstate the Chamber and the Grand Council as working entities, reviving all constitutional liberties – or restore
to the King both command of the armed forces and the 'supreme
initiative of decision as head of the state'.

To Grandi's disgust, the King who in 1939 had begged him
to remain loyal to the Crown now told him, smiling thinly: 'Dear
Grandi, you can trust me not to show this to your chief. The time
will come – but it has not come yet.'

Now, two years later, boarding a taxi at Rome's central station,
Grandi had reached breaking-point. In his breast-pocket was a
letter to the King, calling on him roundly to give back to Italy 'liberty,
unity and independence' – a letter he planned to deliver personally
before the day was out.

Headed for his Rome apartment on the fourth floor of Palazzo
Montecitorio, the seat of the Chamber, Grandi was unaware of a
chain of events he had already set in motion. Eight days earlier,
Party Secretary Carlo Scorza had invited thirteen Fascist chiefs to
attend regional meetings all over Italy, spurring the people to resist.
Grandi had refused point-blank. Soon other chiefs, too, began to
drag their feet. 'A few days ago,' Giuseppe Bottai objected to Scorza,
'Mussolini said the enemy would never place his foot on Italian soil.
People have good memories . . .'

Then, three days before the Duce met Hitler at Feltre, a group of
scheduled speakers – among them Bottai, Marshal Emilio de Bono,
Cesare Maria de Vecchi and Cremona's blustering Roberto Farinacci
– called on Mussolini at Palazzo Venezia, along with Scorza. As the
Party Secretary later recalled, it was he who first ventured to observe
that it was four years since the Grand Council had met.

This 28-strong body, consisting of eight leading members of the
Cabinet, the leaders of the Chamber and the Senate, the presidents
of Fascist corporations and a few others appointed by Mussolini,
had long since lost both sting and status. For years the Duce had
ridden roughshod over its members, not even bothering to convene
them when he declared war – but their powers were there if they
dared to use them.

If Mussolini saw any such danger, he brushed it aside. 'You want
the Grand Council,' he told the malcontents irritably before dismissing them. 'You shall have the Grand Council! But since the

Duce works, since the Duce has many engagements ahead of him, it will take place when he has the time.'

Dino Grandi knew nothing of this. Now as he opened the door of the Montecitorio apartment, a bulky envelope caught his eye, lying on the polished mahogany hall table.

It was a typed summons from Carlo Scorza. For Grandi it was a bombshell. Yielding to pressure, the Duce had convened the Grand Council to meet four days hence at Palazzo Venezia at 5 p.m. on Saturday, 24 July.

All at once the idea swept over him. Why go now to 'that coward of a King'? He would only say that the time was not ripe.

'This is our chance,' Dino Grandi said aloud. '*This* is our chance.'

7. 'It's the Crumbling of the Whole Damned Thing'

24–5 July, 1943

Quinto Navarra checked the room again, but everything was in order – lined-up for the forthcoming Grand Council as meticulously as for a Fascist field-day. Twenty-eight ebony pen-rests and jotting pads, arranged on the polished horseshoe of tables, flanking the eight-inch dais draped in crimson plush. Twenty-eight crystal ink-wells, glistening under the heavy wheel-shaped wrought-iron lamp that lit the Sala del Pappagallo (Hall of the Parrot) on the second floor of Palazzo Venezia. Six desk lamps placed at discreet intervals, casting an amber glow on gold-framed masters by Veronese against a backdrop of walls lined in royal-blue velvet.

It was 4.45 p.m. on Saturday, 24 July, 1943, five days after Mussolini's degrading encounter with Hitler at Feltre.

Already Navarra could hear tyres grating in the gravelled courtyard below: the first delegates were arriving. As they picked their way among the clipped oleander bushes and the statues of Cupid, the usher could plainly hear their exclamations of surprise. For the first time in memory, the Duce's own bodyguard was not on duty. Most were on heavy rescue work in the ruins of San Lorenzo; this evening only a corps of special police were standing guard. And for the first time in 180 meetings the Fascist pennant was not flying; it remained in its red leather case at Party headquarters. As Carlo Scorza had told General Enzo Galbiati, Commandant of the Militia, that very morning: 'The Duce wants to keep this meeting as quiet as possible.'

Many now arriving in their black Saharan battledress and tight leather boots were newcomers – men who had been elevated in the four years since the last council. Luciano Gottardi, President of the Industrial Workers' Confederation, was bustling from delegate to delegate, introducing himself: 'Gottardi – the pleasure's mine.' Carlo Pareschi, forty-five, two years Minister of Agriculture, found himself mounting the stairs along with portly, bespectacled Alfredo de Marsico, the new Minister of Justice. Respectfully he asked: 'What does one do at a Grand Council, sir? How do things go?'

De Marsico was non-committal. As a lawyer, he had spent long hours pondering the legality of the resolution before the Council with his predecessor, Dino Grandi, and had an inkling of what might lie in store. The scrupulous De Marsico had even dismissed his car and chauffeur as of this moment, convinced that by the time the meeting ended he would no longer be Minister of Justice.

A few felt entirely confident. Roberto Farinacci, swaggering into the conference hall, was sure that fate, which for twenty years had kept him in the wilderness as party boss of Cremona, was at last about to redress the balance. Stepping into his car outside the Grand Hotel, Farinacci, convinced that change was imminent, had told the manageress: 'Tomorrow *I* shall be ruling Italy.'

But most delegates had an uneasy sense of impending trouble. Giovanni Balella, head of the Confederation of Fascist Industrialists, had been warned in a phone call from Giuseppe Bottai: 'There'll be some trouble tonight – better stay at home, pretend to be ill.' But Balella demurred: if decisions were needed at his first Grand Council meeting he was coming. Even Galeazzo Ciano, outwardly gay, jesting that 17.00 hours was an unlucky number, seemed tense to those who knew him best – and friends had noted that as he changed into uniform earlier, the irreligious Ciano had crossed himself before the Madonna.

Together with a dozen other members this night, Ciano was fully in the picture. At 5 p.m. on 21 July the Ambassador to the Holy See had been summoned to Bottai's house on Via Mangili to meet for the first time in months with Dino Grandi. At first, Grandi had protested bitterly. Unaware of Ciano's four-month parleys with General Castellano, he viewed him merely as 'a despicable youngster' – and moreover the affair involved Ciano's father-in-law. But Bottai had urged that they needed every man they could get, and one glance at the five typewritten sheets that composed Grandi's Order of the Day was enough for Ciano. 'If my father was alive, he would have been with you,' he told Grandi. 'Why do you forbid me to do what I'd do in his name?'

That night, at supper with friends, Ciano, raising a brimming champagne glass, had offered a toast: 'Here's to the Old Man's downfall.'

Dino Grandi, now arriving, had been a busy man these past three days. His first move had been to prepare three dozen copies of his draft resolution, based on his 1941 memorandum to the King, for scrutiny by Grand Council members. Then he sent his friend, Annio

Bignardi, Secretary of the Agricultural Workers' Confederation, to collect opinions – and, if possible, signatures. Bignardi's first contact was Marshal de Bono. 'Well, I must sign it,' the old man sighed, reaching for his pen. 'This is the best way for the country. But someone is going to come to a sticky end.'

The Marshal was not the only man to have misgivings. The prudent Party Secretary, Carlo Scorza, took one glance at the document Grandi had left with him, then at once hastened with it to Mussolini. As the Duce was later to record, he found the motion 'vile and inadmissible' – yet he still agreed to receive Dino Grandi, on 22 July. Unwilling that the motion should be regarded as a secret conspiracy, Grandi had sought an audience with Mussolini, hoping to persuade him to go voluntarily to the King and withdraw from public life. In Grandi's view, the way would then lie open for the King to approach the Allies, at the same time declaring war on Germany.

As Grandi recalled it, the ninety-minute meeting was surprisingly tranquil. The Duce listened quietly, almost patiently, before saying: 'You would be right if the war was really lost – but it isn't. The Germans are preparing a secret weapon which will completely reverse the balance.' Mussolini later claimed that Grandi said nothing of what was to come, but he knew well enough what was in the wind, thanks to Scorza.

Now the delegates were clustered in uneasy knots on the great hall's tessellated floor, whispering excitedly, exchanging covert glances. Every man in the secret was wondering if Grandi would dare present his motion formally – and just how Mussolini would contrive to override it, as he had overridden objections in the past.

A late arrival on the scene was General Enzo Galbiati. The stalwart Commandant of the Militia was a worried man. A soldier who did things by the book, Galbiati was not given to deep analysis, but tonight all the omens seemed wrong. The Duce's specific instructions that no militia were to be on duty, the absence of the Party flag – all were disturbing factors. Now, as he entered the Hall of the Parrot, he scented conspiracy as a countryman smells rain. Grandi was showing some papers to four others – Bottai, the lion-maned Alberto de Stefani, former Finance Minister, and two veterans of the Feltre Conference, Foreign Secretary Bastianini and Ambassador Alfieri.

He had taken only three steps when Grandi hailed him: 'Galbiati, would you sign this?'

Galbiati was puzzled. 'Sign what? What's all this about?'

There was no time to answer. From Carlo Scorza, at the hall's far end, came a thunderous cry of 'Salute the Duce'. Through the door of the ante-room strode first Quinto Navarra, carrying the Duce's zip-fastened briefcase, followed by Mussolini himself – black-shirted, clad in the grey-green uniform of Honorary Corporal of the Militia. Every man present took his seat, mechanically echoing Scorza's cry, and twenty-eight arms were raised in the Roman salute.

Now, as Scorza called the roll of names, each man answered after his fashion – the old hands bored and indifferent, the tyros, feeling the drama of the situation, leaping to their feet with a cry of '*Presente!*' Gaetano Polverelli, Minister of Popular Culture, always remembered the aching silence which followed that roll-call, as if a shadow was cast upon the room.

At the head of the horseshoe, on the Duce's right, Dino Grandi drew a deep breath. Better than any man present tonight he knew the score. Among the Council's members, he and his followers had found time to sound out only fourteen. Twelve had been in agreement – but so far only ten had appended their signatures to the Order of the Day lying before him.

Thus Grandi had thought it well to be fully prepared. Earlier that day he had been to confession – but he had taken time, too, to visit his country cottage at Frascati, outside Rome, along with an old friend, General Agostini. On rough ground away from the house, the General had put him through a strange refresher-course for a man bent on a sober round-table conference: how to jerk the pin from a live grenade.

The grey-painted Breda grenade, a relic of his service in Albania, was hard against his thigh as he sat down. If it came to the crunch and Benito Mussolini called in the Militia to seize him, they would never take him alive. Dino Grandi, Count of Mordano, was going to blow himself sky-high.

It was as if a plague had struck the city. Along Corso Umberto, the streets were empty, menacing. The heat was an inescapable presence; even at 7 p.m. the temperature was still in the nineties. In the bone-dry fountains, only the four side-spouts trickled water, and the asphalt gave back the day's relentless sun. South of Rome, the campagna stretched for miles, sere and brown; there was a heat-haze on the Alban Hills that night, and people remembered the smell of new-mown hay, fragrant on the stifling air.

Myriam Petacci was chafing. Only her abiding affection for Claretta would have brought her into the city centre on this sultry night to loiter in a deserted side-street near Palazzo Venezia like a teen-ager on her first date. But tonight Claretta was at Villa Camilluccia, unwell, and she had desperately needed someone to carry a message to Mussolini.

Now Myriam's date was with Quinto Navarra, to whom Claretta had phoned in advance, and already Navarra was five minutes late.

In her mind's eye, Myriam could still see Claretta seated at her writing-desk, frantically scribbling the message to Mussolini. How often in the past months she had warned him that scores of his enemies had daggers poised to plunge home, and how often he had pooh-poohed it! Marshal Badoglio, he had scoffed, was just an old brass-hat who liked playing bowls, though Claretta warned him vehemently: 'He'd like to play bowls with your head.' Now, through contacts in Roman society, she had word of a more ominous plot.

'Only three or four of them are on your side,' she had written. 'The others are all against you. If it comes to a vote they'll have you out.' Shrewdly she had counselled, 'If you let them get out of Palazzo Venezia, it's all over. You can trust Galbiati. Order him to arrest the others and you're safe!'

Suddenly Myriam was aware of Quinto Navarra hastening towards her. She had a sudden painful presentiment. The plump, normally rosy-faced usher, was pale. His hands trembled so uncontrollably he could scarcely grasp the envelope she held out.

'How are things going?' the girl asked but the question seemed a formality. 'Bad – very bad!' was all that he could choke out. Stuffing the envelope in his pocket, he hastened away. Myriam watched him go, mortally worried.

Navarra was sixty-five and overweight, but something was happening inside Palazzo Venezia to make him run like a man in fear of his life.

He stared at them contemptuously down the long table – his Ministers, his hirelings, his March on Rome men. On his immediate right, as befitted veterans of that march – though seated on a lower level – Marshal de Bono and the pompous Cesare Maria de Vecchi. To his immediate left, the egg-bald Carlo Scorza. And scattered down the two Ls of the table, twenty-five other men, whom he had made or tamed according to his whim – the suave, bearded Grandi; the squinting, rancorous Giovanni Marinelli who had ordered Matteotti's death, now, at sixty-six, as deaf as a post, his hand cupped perpetually to his ear; Bottai, the sarcastic intellectual; the bull-voiced Luigi

Federzoni; Farinacci, the roughneck; his own son-in-law, the cocky, amoral Ciano.

For months well-wishers, sycophants and police agents had warned him of an impending conspiracy by these men – warnings he had brushed aside. Only two days earlier, Chief of Police Renzo Chierici, after presenting him with a chapter-and-verse dossier on the meetings of Grandi, Bottai and Federzoni, had returned to tell his colleagues hopelessly: 'He just won't believe it.' Even in his own home the Duce was no longer immune. 'Have all of them arrested!' had been Rachele's parting words, echoing Claretta's, as he left Villa Torlonia for the meeting. To his son Vittorio, Mussolini joked resignedly: 'According to your mother, I'm surrounded by traitors, spies, saboteurs and weaklings.'

Central to all the Duce's thinking were the words with which he had dismissed Chierici: 'These people exist because *I* exist – they live in reflected glory. I've just to make one speech, you see, and they'll fall into line.'

Now, for close on two hours, this speech justifying his conduct of the war had been in progress – delivered in a near-monotone, head bent over his papers under the harsh light of the desk lamp. He had never, he told them, desired command of the Armed Forces – that initiative belonged to Badoglio. After his illness in October 1942 he had even thought of giving up but he had not done so – what commander could have 'abandoned the ship in midstream'? Painstakingly, as if every news-item were fresh as paint, he thumbed through the long catalogue of disasters: Alamein . . . Rommel's 'blunders' in Africa . . . Pantelleria . . . now Sicily. Could Germany have helped more? He thought not. Emphatically, as if this made everything right, he began to recite statistics: the tonnage of all the raw materials imported from Germany since 1940.

The party bosses stared back incredulously. All at once they were like men visiting an invalid's bedside, innocent of the true gravity of the complaint; until a sudden uncontrollable spasm of pain told them the sickness was mortal. Bemused, Grandi's lieutenant, Annio Bignardi, heard Mussolini airily dismiss Pantelleria with: 'It might have been the Stalingrad of the Mediterranean – but only Stalin and the Mikado can give orders to resist to the last man.' Even Gaetano Polverelli, the Duce's devoted follower, found his statistics confusing. Just what did it prove that in thirty-one months the factories had turned out 5000 heavy guns as against 3700 in the same period of World War One?

Now, all down the table men were muttering uneasily, not daring to meet one another's eyes. Try as they might, they could make no sense of the disquieting rigmarole. At one moment hard facts emerged: the Army had only two efficient divisions left, the Air Force was down to 200 planes, the Navy could no longer venture into the open sea. Then, without warning, Mussolini switched to El Alamein.

'I predicted the date of the attack,' he told the incredulous delegates, '23 October, 1942 – and why? The British quite deliberately tried to mar the solemnity of the twentieth anniversary of the March on Rome.'

Now some were more in the dark than ever. On Grandi's right, Giacomo Acerbo, the Duce's first Presidential Under-Secretary, wrinkled his brow perplexedly. He knew nothing of Grandi's resolution and could make neither head nor tail of Mussolini's monologue. Suddenly Grandi slid him the Order of the Day. To the startled Acerbo, 100 words stood out as diamond-clear:

'The Grand Council declares that to achieve this unity [of the Italian people] it is necessary to restore immediately all functions belonging to the State, ascribing to the Crown, the Grand Council, the Government, Parliament and the Corporations, the tasks and responsibilities laid down for them by our State and constitutional laws . . . invites the Head of the Government to pray His Majesty the King . . . that for the honour and safety of the country he now assume effective command of the armed forces on land, on sea, and in the air, in accordance with Article 5 of the Statutes of the Kingdom and therewith the supreme initiative of decision . . .'

'But that means – ?' whispered Acerbo, aghast. Grandi only nodded. 'What about the King?' Acerbo asked. 'I don't know,' Grandi said, 'but that man must go. Do you agree?' Without a word Acerbo signed the resolution, then passed it back.

Eleven signatures, Grandi thought. Seventeen men to go.

As if he scented the defection, Mussolini now turned to Grandi's motion. Suddenly he had all their attention. Grandi's motion, he told them severely, called upon the Crown. It was an appeal not so much to the Government as to the King. In such a case the King had only two choices: to ask Mussolini to continue in office or to liquidate Fascism. Playing on every man's fear for his job, he warned them: 'Gentlemen, beware! Grandi's motion may place the very existence of the regime in jeopardy.'

Tensely, Grandi awaited his moment. But first Marshal de Bono, as senior man, launched into a quavering defence of the Army in

Sicily. 'Give me a hand, Cesare,' he muttered pathetically as he sat down, and De Vecchi followed suit. With pitiless logic, Alberto de' Stefani told the Duce: 'From your own report I have deduced, and all the others along with me, I think, that the war is lost.' Half-way down the table, on Grandi's right, Farinacci blustered to his feet. Avowedly pro-German, he blamed the mounting toll of disasters on Italy's generals. He demanded that Ambrosio, as Chief of the General Staff, should be called to justify himself before the Council.

It was, Grandi thought, now or never. He rose to his feet. His first words were calculated to hearten all those who were wavering: a man could tell Mussolini the unvarnished truth and live to talk about it. 'I am not speaking to the Duce, who already heard from me the day before yesterday everything that I am now going to tell you. I am speaking to you . . .' And with a gesture he turned away from Mussolini, confronting his colleagues.

Covertly he watched their faces as he read the resolution: to many it was completely new. Then, his voice cold and modulated, he plunged on. It was the dictatorship, he charged, and not the army's weakness, that was responsible for Italy's plight. 'The Italian people,' he said, 'were betrayed by Mussolini on the day when he first began to Germanize Italy. That is the man who drove us into Hitler's arms. He dragged us into a war that is against the honour, interests and feelings of the Italian people.'

The great hall was as still as a death chamber. On the dais Mussolini sat inert, slumped in his chair to the left, away from Grandi, his hands shielding his eyes from the harsh light of the desk lamp. Carlo Scorza watched his right knee moving rhythmically like a pulse – a sure sign his ulcer was paining him. Every man present could feel his acute discomfort and their own besides. Blue velvet curtains shut out the night air and there were no electric fans; the air was stale and scarcely breathable. General Enzo Galbiati, fuming at Grandi's attack, was none the less conscious that his black shirt was drenched with sweat. For Giovanni Balella, Grand Council Night would always mean leather boots so tight they cut his instep. Suddenly, with a stifled cry, Carlo Pareschi fainted. Those nearest helped him to an ante-room. Others, held by Grandi's words, didn't even spare him a glance.

Grandi was facing Mussolini now, his finger levelled like a pointer. It was as if the two men stood isolated, facing one another over twenty years, as Grandi delivered a coroner's report on Fascism. 'You believe you have the devotion of the people,' he told the Duce with biting contempt, 'but you lost it the day you tied Italy to Germany. You have suffocated the personality of everyone under the mantle of a historically immoral dictatorship. Let me tell you, Italy was lost the very day you put the gold braid of a marshal on your cap.' With mingled compassion and anger, Grandi shouted: 'Take off those ridiculous ornaments, plumes and feathers! Be again the Mussolini of the barricades – our Mussolini!'

'The people are with me,' the Duce retorted angrily for the first time.

Grandi struck to wound. In World War One, he said deliberately, more than six hundred thousand Italian mothers who lost their sons at least knew they had died for King and country. 'In this war,' he challenged, every word a dagger thrust, 'we have already 100,000 dead – and 100,000 mothers who cry "Mussolini has assassinated my son!"'

'It is not true!' shouted Mussolini, goaded. 'That man is lying!' But Grandi, resuming his seat after one hour on his feet, flung back words that Mussolini had uttered as far back as 1924, when he still sought union with the Socialists: 'Let all factions perish, even Fascism, so long as the nation can be saved!'

Now tempers were at flash point. Bottai followed – at first sarcastic and drawling, in the manner the Duce so hated, but soon red in the face, pounding at the mahogany table. 'Your report has been a sorry blow to our last illusions and hopes,' he told Mussolini. Dumbly, the Duce's supporters awaited rebuttals that did not come. Ciano next – quiet, logical, charting each of of Hitler's treacheries following the Pact of Steel. 'We have been not so much the betrayers as the betrayed,' he summed up. Mussolini stared with icy loathing at his son-in-law. 'I know where the traitor is,' he said, his words loaded with menace. Now Farinacci, strident and hectoring. Defending the principles of dictatorship, he still proposed a resolution of his own: the full implementation of the Feltre decision that the Germans must take over the Italian High Command.

Only Giovanni Marinelli still sat, hand cupped to his ear, not seeming to catch a word.

To General Galbiati, things had gone far enough. Plainly Mussolini was reaching the end of his tether. Across the table he signalled to Scorza, and the Party Secretary, taking his point, scribbled a note and passed it to Mussolini. 'Because of the hour,' Mussolini announced, 'some comrades propose the meeting should be postponed until tomorrow.'

But Grandi would have none of it. Sensing a trap, he sprang to his feet. 'No, no,' he argued. 'In the past you've often kept us here till dawn discussing less urgent things. We don't leave tonight until we've discussed and voted on my Order of the Day.'

'Very well,' said Mussolini, gesturing wearily, 'let us continue.'

He heard out Federzoni and then Bignardi, both supporting Grandi, then abruptly, ordering a fifteen-minute adjournment, retired to his study.

Two blocks away, in Piazza Colonna, the clock on Fascist Party Headquarters showed midnight.

In the small salon adjoining the Hall of the Parrot, they gulped down the last glasses of orange squash. It was 12.25 a.m. and the Grand Council was reassembling. Annio Bignardi could scarcely believe his eyes. Seven hours earlier Grandi's motion had had just ten supporters, yet this brief refreshment interval had produced 'an absolute rain of signatures'. Even newcomers like Carlo Pareschi, now recovered from his fainting fit, no longer had any doubts. Two days earlier, when Bignardi first approached him, the Agricultural Minister had told him frankly: 'Political questions aren't of interest to a technical Minister – I certainly shan't sign.'

Now Pareschi, a former protégé of Balbo's, made immediately for the Order of the Day lying on Grandi's blotter. Appalled by Mussolini's rambling irrelevancies, he told Bignardi: 'You can say I'm signing for Balbo.'

The last man to add his signature was Ambassador Dino Alfieri. The interval had no sooner begun than the Duce had summoned him peremptorily to the Sala del Mappamondo. In the dim light of a reading-lamp, sipping a cup of sweetened milk, he asked Alfieri vaguely: 'What's happening in Germany?' Once more Alfieri urged the views that he and General Ambrosio had advanced at Feltre: the Duce must make one last attempt to persuade Hitler to see reason. 'Is this the voice of the Italian Ambassador to Berlin?' was Mussolini's cold reply as he dismissed him.

Past patience, Alfieri left the study, giving place to Scorza – and ran full tilt into Grandi. Without further ado, Alfieri added his signature – the twenty-first and last.

No man felt the threat of danger more than General Galbiati. All through the interval the Militia Commandant hastened from ante-room to ante-room, seeking the adjutant who accompanied him to Palazzo Venezia. The man had simply vanished from sight; only later did Galbiati learn the special police had cordoned off the entire building. He saw only the palace ushers, collars limp with heat, eyes scared, and a few Council members who markedly gave him the cold shoulder. To a passing official, summing up the prevailing mood, Galbiati growled: 'They're all shitting themselves here.'

Now, as they once more took their places at the table, Grandi and all his supporters wondered: how would Mussolini fight back? Marshal de Bono, for one, was convinced he had spent the interval phoning for the Militia. One thing was certain: he would use all his cunning, all his skills as an actor, to retain his ascendancy.

Speaking slowly, dully, Mussolini began on a note of pathos. 'It seems there are people here who would like to be rid of me,' he acknowledged. Accepting full responsibility for the war, he spoke of his work over twenty years, confessing for the first time that he was sixty – 'and might even in such circumstances contemplate ending this wonderful adventure.'

Many now felt a momentary true compassion. To Luigi Federzoni, the Duce was 'like a great old actor, fluffing his lines for the first time in memory'. Annio Bignardi felt both sad and bitter: it was as if a family had gathered together 'to discuss the failure of a father who could no longer support them'. Former Under-Secretary of Home Affairs, Guido Buffarini-Guidi, of the Duce's faction, thought incongruously of Caesar receiving the conspirators' daggers 'as if they were wounding another man'.

But little by little, malice coloured Mussolini's words. Swivelling his blue Florentine-leather crayon from face to face, like a schoolteacher's pointer, he posed the question: if there was a rift between the Party and the Italian people, mightn't it be because many Party bosses had enriched themselves at the public expense? At once compassion veered to irritation. If the Duce could name names and cases, why hadn't he done so long ago? His next sentence was like a child propounding a riddle: 'I have in my head a key which will resolve the war situation. But I will not say what it is.'

Slowly, Grandi saw, Mussolini was gaining confidence. 'But I will not go!' he told them. 'The King as well as the people are on my side.' The diabolical bluff took Grandi's breath away. The Duce knew well enough that at this stage Grandi could not compromise the monarchy. No one had intervened, and Mussolini pressed home his advantage. 'When I tell the King about this meeting tomorrow, he will say, "Some of your men have left you, but I, the King, will be with you." '

They were wavering, Grandi thought. And the Duce was quick to perceive it. 'I never had a friend,' he told them, playing once more on their fears, 'but the King is with me. I wonder what will happen tomorrow to those who have opposed me tonight?'

He smiled at them strangely down the long table knowing no man could find an answer. For a moment Grandi saw a flash of the old Duce and glanced, disturbed, at his colleagues. On every face he read only blank resignation.

'The Duce is blackmailing us,' he cried. 'He is forcing us to choose between our old fidelity to his person and our devotion to Italy. Gentlemen, we cannot hesitate a moment. It is Italy.'

Carlo Scorza was on his feet. Following Mussolini's instructions during the recess, he proposed a third resolution. As draconian as Farinacci's, it called not only for a complete overhaul of the Army General Staff but for full powers, even martial law, to be granted to the Fascist Party.

Now President of the Senate Giacomo Suardo, an advanced alcoholic, rose shakily. Tearful and trembling, he withdrew the signature Grandi had coaxed from him in the interval. Gaetano Polverelli, a recent convert, was another apostate. 'I was born a Mussolinian,' he declared shrilly, 'and I'll die a Mussolinian.'

Grandi was back to nineteen signatures – and how many more would renege once the chips were down? We have lost, he thought bitterly.

A few suggested a compromise. Why not, suggested Ciano, withdraw all the motions? Then the Committee could draft a new resolution acceptable to the Duce? Again Grandi sprang to his feet. He refused to withdraw – every line must stand as written. And with that he thrust the motion at the dictator.

Mussolini glanced through it, Alfieri recalled later, 'with studied indifference'. If the number of signatures surprised him, nothing showed in his face.

Suddenly, harshly, he announced: 'The debate has been long and exhausting. Three motions have been tabled. Grandi's takes precedence over the others, so I'll put it to the vote. Scorza, call the names!'

Elbows propped on the table, he leaned forward, eyes boring into them, as if willing their support.

It was 2.40 a.m. Now, to the consternation of all those present, Scorza broke precedent. Though seniority ruled Marshal de Bono voted first, the Party Secretary flung down a psychological trump card for Mussolini. Calling his own name, he replied with a firm, 'No!' It was De Bono's turn then. 'Yes,' he replied clearly, but his old voice seemed to die in the absolute silence of the hall.

The voting continued – Scorza scribbling 'Yes' or 'No' beside each man's name as they replied. Suardo abstained altogether. Farinacci voted for his own motion. Both Gottardi and Pareschi, the doubtful newcomers, voted 'Yes' – clearly encouraged by Mussolini's seeming acquiescence. Suddenly Scorza called Ciano's name. Mussolini's eyes, half-closed, sought those of his son-in-law. The two men, Alfieri recalled, 'exchanged a long penetrating look'. And Ciano held the Duce's gaze with perfect tranquillity as he answered 'Yes'. Slowly it dawned on Grandi that the incredible was happening. They were winning.

What was in Mussolini's mind at this moment? Grandi still wondered. The grenade hard against his thigh recalled his fears of ten hours back: the Duce would arrest them all if they dared see this through. Did he even want the vote to go against him, hoping to present Hitler with a *fait-accompli* putting Italy out of the war? In truth, the Duce – like Grandi himself – knew nothing of the parallel conspiracies of General Ambrosio and Crown Princess Maria-José. Galling as it might be, this was still, to Mussolini, no more than a rank-and-file revolt of his own puppets.

Scorza was counting the votes now. The silence seemed interminable. But at last he announced: 'There are nineteen Ayes, eight Noes and one abstention.'

Mussolini half rose. 'Then,' he said, shuffling up his papers, 'Grandi's motion has been carried, so the others lapse. The meeting is closed.' He stared with naked hatred at the man who had masterminded it all. 'You have provoked the crisis of the regime,' he recalled saying later, though Grandi himself recalled starker words: 'You have killed Fascism.'

Incredibly, as he rose from his seat, Scorza again raised the ritual cry 'Salute the Duce!' Even Alfieri found himself mechanically echoing beneath his breath, 'We salute him.' At once Mussolini gestured like a man brushing something obnoxious aside. 'No, no,' he told them savagely. 'I free you from that!'

In the silence following his departure came the querulous tones of the stone-deaf Marinelli: 'What did he say? What's happening? Was Grandi's motion approved?'

Claretta Petacci was wide awake when the phone shrilled. It was almost 4 a.m. Mussolini, still in his study, was calling from Palazzo Venezia. As on every night for seven years the call was being monitored by Ugo Guspini, Operator G 21 of OVRA's wire-tapping service from his tiny office in the Ministry of Home Affairs. At first, he recalled later, the Duce was cryptic, withdrawn, and Claretta complained: 'You're frightening me.'

'There isn't much to be frightened of,' Mussolini said dully. 'We've come to the epilogue – the biggest turning-point in history.' For a moment the spools of Guspini's recording machine revolved in silence. Then almost as if to himself, Mussolini added: 'The star is dark.'

'Don't torment me,' Claretta begged him. But despite his weariness, the Duce still sought to convey a fearful urgency. 'It's all over,' he told her, 'and you must try and take refuge. Don't think about me – hurry!'

Claretta tried to find some words of comfort: 'It must be just an idea of yours,' she consoled him.

The Duce's voice came tonelessly. 'Unfortunately it's not like that at all.'

Afterwards, it was the waiting that all of them remembered. As the minutes ticked away on this breathless oven-hot Sunday, 25 July, the chief participants in the drama found each hour an eternity, wondering what cards fate would deal them before the day was out.

By 9 a.m. Marshal Pietro Badoglio, beside the telephone in his villa, was gasping like a landed fish. He wore his grey-green Marshal's uniform, just as General Ambrosio and the Duke of Acquarone had instructed when they called on him an hour earlier: the *coup d'état* would take place that very day. The Grand Council's action had precipitated everything; the King, fearing a Militia counter-coup, would no longer await the usual Monday audience to dismiss Mussolini. Meanwhile Badoglio must remain in readiness, but after three years in mufti his uniform was so tight he could scarcely breathe. Ordering some Veuve Clicquot, one of 5000 bottles in his cellar, to be put on ice, he sat sweating and fearful, awaiting the royal summons.

At this same hour, General Enzo Galbiati was in his ground-floor office at Militia Headquarters, on Piazza Romania. Morosely he leafed through the report he had worked on through the small hours, from the moment the Grand Council broke up. Now he awaited a call from the Duce, but if word didn't come, he would go personally to Palazzo Venezia to present his memorandum. It called for the immediate detention of all who had voted for Grandi in the night just past, plus a plea to absent himself on urgent duty. To co-ordinate more closely the security services of Fascist Italy and the

Third Reich, Galbiati planned to call, within twenty-four hours, on Heinrich Himmler in Berlin.

Fearful of just such a move, Galeazzo Ciano restlessly paced his elegant second-floor apartment at 9 Via Angelo Secchi. This morning the Count was alone, expecting no callers except the expressionless men with the broad-brimmed hats which were the badge of the OVRA agent. Between 9 a.m. and noon, he made two phone calls. The first was to Edda, in the countryside at Ponte a oriano with the children, urging her to return to Rome. 'Why the urgency?' Edda asked languidly. 'Have they landed?' In reply, Ciano snapped: *'Abbiamo mosso un macigno, adesso c'è la valanga!'* (We moved a stone – now we've got a landslide.)

Next he called his old friend, Count Leonardo Vitetti of the Foreign Ministry, who like Ciano was privy to Ambrosio's plan. 'Keep away from here,' he warned. 'I may be arrested any minute – but don't worry, I'll be free once they get Mussolini.'

Dino Grandi, unlike Ciano, knew nothing of the Army's plan. One hour after the Grand Council's meeting, Grandi had met the wily, immaculate Duke of Acquarone for the first time in the house of a mutual friend. This two-hour meeting, Grandi realized later, resulted in Acquarone's 8 a.m. call on Badoglio. 'Tell the King we have put into his hands the constitutional means for action as head of the state,' Grandi urged. 'The Army must be reorganized to fight the Germans. Every hour of delay brings the Germans nearer.'

It had been noon when a call reached Grandi's flat at Palazzo Montecitorio. The Duce, his Chief of Secretariat told him, wanted to see him immediately, but he had been purposely vague, as ordered. Grandi rang Acquarone for instructions: should he obey Mussolini's summons? 'The King,' Acquarone told him, 'says you are not to go. *Le jeu est fait.*'

Now, relaxed in a sports-shirt over a tall drink, Grandi too was waiting and wondering what the King's game might be, just how soon they could expect a German reaction.

At Villa Wolkonsky, the German Embassy, in the city's eastern zone, it was just another leisurely Sunday. The Duty Officer, twenty-nine-year-old Gerhard Gumpert, bored and sweating in the annexe building, was thinking not of Mussolini but wistfully of the beach at Ostia. Gumpert, like every other Embassy official, knew of the Grand Council's meeting, but to him, as to Ambassador Hans Georg von Mackensen, this was a matter of internal politics – nothing to affect the course of the war.

Nor did it strike von Mackensen as strange that Marshal Badoglio had several times that morning tried to contact him. Busy with despatches and telegrams, he had given the switchboard instructions that he was out.

Gumpert found one incident disquieting. Around 2.30 p.m., Mackensen had called him to the main building to despatch an urgent telex message to Ribbentrop at his weekend retreat, Schloss Fuschl. As he took in the contents, Gumpert had started, almost exclaiming aloud. The ambassador, he knew, was an austere nineteenth-century Prussian, who took no soundings outside his own immediate circle – the warnings of his police attaché, Herbert Kappler, that trouble was imminent invariably went unheeded. Yet now, replying to von Ribbentrop's request for a situation report on Italy, the ambassador was making the most unenviable kind of diplomatic history. It was to earn him, within twelve days, a permanent recall to Berlin.

'The Duce's position,' ran his draft telegram, 'has never been stronger.'

Towards 4.45 p.m. Benito Mussolini felt this same sense of security. Those close to him sensed he was sloughing off his initial anger with something of his old resilience. To be sure, he had irritably dismissed Dr Arnaldo Pozzi, when the physician visited Villa Torlonia at 10 a.m. and found him still in bed in his nightshirt. 'Let it go for today,' he told Pozzi, refusing his customary injection of sodium benzoate, 'I've hardly slept a wink, I'm too agitated.' But at Palazzo Venezia, as the morning wore on, he felt surer of himself. The important thing was to hear the King reaffirm his implicit faith. At 12.15 Mussolini's secretary, Nicolò de Cesare, walking neatly into the royal trap, phoned to request an audience for this same day.

Now, with De Cesare beside him, Mussolini was relaxed in the back of his black Asturia as chauffeur Ercole Boratto steered through the silent airless streets towards Villa Ada.

Earlier that afternoon, while touring the ruins of San Lorenzo, he had assured General Galbiati: 'The King's always been solidly behind me.' And to Galbiati's chagrin he refused to sanction any mass arrest of Grand Council dissidents. Standing rock-steady on the constitution, he explained that before dismissing Ministers and Under-Secretaries he needed the King's agreement – Grandi and Ciano in particular both had, like himself, the Collar of the Annunciation and could address the King as 'Cousin'.

Already one man, Minister of Corporations Tullio Cianetti, had hastened to Palazzo Venezia to withdraw his vote – convinced, he explained later, that it was 'wrong to diminish Mussolini's political prestige when defeat was imminent'. Others, the Duce was confident, would follow suit. As he told Galbiati contemptuously, 'These faint-hearts don't realize that if the man who raised them up wasn't here, they'd be in the gutter with the mob.' And to Under-Secretary for Home Affairs Umberto Albini, a Grandi supporter, he had made his views brutally clear: 'Your vote and the vote of your friends hasn't the slightest importance. The Grand Council is merely called to give its opinion. I've looked up the rules and the King will confirm I've a right to ignore the vote.'

Folded neatly in the briefcase De Cesare now held was the Duce's pat solution for the entire military imbroglio – yet another reshuffle of the armed forces, with seven newcomers slated to replace the existing chiefs. Only the heat of the previous night's discussion had checked him from announcing the appointments on the spot. Then, too, he had conceived a subtle plan to bring the war to an end. This morning he had begged the Japanese Ambassador, Baron Hidaka, to contact President Hideki Tojo immediately. Tojo must put pressure on Hitler to end the Russian war and begin peace negotiations.

It had all taken hours of thought and planning. It was 3.30 p.m. before he hurried home to Villa Torlonia for a hasty bowl of soup. To his irritation, Rachele was astounded he had sought an audience at Villa Ada. 'You must not go!' she insisted. 'The King is the King – if it suits him he'll throw you overboard.' 'The King,' Mussolini returned drily, 'is my best friend – perhaps the only friend I have at the moment.' But to appease her, he promised he would almost certainly arrest the Grand Council's 'traitors', if the King granted him power.

Momentarily he was puzzled to learn that three times since noon the Quirinale had rung to insist that for that afternoon's audience he must wear mufti, not uniform. Then he shrugged it off. Since the March on Rome, during 2000 audiences with the King, he had almost always worn tails. But the King's command must be obeyed.

At 4.55 p.m., as the Asturia approached Villa Ada's high wooden gates, he was clad in a sober blue serge suit with the inevitable high-crowned bowler, carrying pearl-grey gloves in his left hand. Now, slowing down, chauffeur Boratto gave the usual signal to the gate-keeper: two sharp blasts on the horn.

Behind, the Duce's two-car bodyguard of police agents braked sharply. As always, following etiquette, they would remain parked outside the gates.

A quarter of a mile away, on the north side of the villa, screened from view by thick boxwood hedges, Paolo Vigneri, a *carabinieri* captain, heard the horn and tensed silently. It was the signal he had awaited for seventy-five minutes now. His fifty-strong force of *carabinieri* heard too, and exchanged troubled glances. At 3.30 p.m. when they had left Rome's Pastrengo Barracks, every man thought their quarry was Anglo-American parachutists. Now, hidden in Villa Ada's grounds, along with three armed plainclothes agents, their canvas-topped truck, and a white-painted Red Cross ambulance, they knew what they had to do.

Vigneri, dark and dapper, had briefed them only ten minutes back. Until 2 p.m. he himself knew nothing of the task ahead. Then, wondering just which cardinal sin they had committed, he and his colleague, Captain Raffaele Avversa, had been summoned to the office of General Angelo Cerica, newly-appointed Commander-in-Chief. The General was tense and chain-smoking, as well he might be. It had been 12.25 p.m. when he in turn received his orders from General Ambrosio and the Duke of Acquarone – orders which spurred him to cancel Sunday leave at every barracks in the city, pending his official inspection.

'In a few hours,' Cerica had told the stunned Vigneri, 'following the orders of His Majesty Vittorio Emanuele III, you must arrest Mussolini at Villa Ada.'

Bustling into the ground-floor salon in the wake of his 'Cousin' the King, Benito Mussolini fairly radiated confidence. It would all go as smoothly as it had done 2000 times before. What was more, the King, today wearing a Marshal's grey-green uniform, trousers seamed with a thick red stripe, had approached the main door to greet him, along with his aide, smiling and extending his hand – something that had never happened in twenty years. As the doors closed behind them, leaving De Cesare with the A D C, Mussolini led off assuredly: 'You'll have heard, Your Majesty, about last night's childish prank...'

The King cut in immediately. 'Not a childish prank at all!' he exclaimed sharply. Mussolini noted, perplexed, that the King had not invited him to sit down. He stood staring, while the King, his words 'a jerky painful mumble', began pacing the room in agitation, his hands behind his back. 'It's not necessary,' the King said, as

Mussolini tried to produce his papers, 'I know everything – ' He stopped short, and again the Duce tried to speak. 'Your Majesty, the vote of the Grand Council is of no value whatsoever . . .'

The King interrupted him. He much regretted, he stammered, that he could not share the Duce's opinion. The Grand Council was a State organ which Mussolini had himself created – approved by both the Chamber of Deputies and the Senate. At the time, he had warned the Duce, it might prove a two-edged sword – but clearly its every decision was of vital import to the State.

'My dear Duce,' the King went on hurriedly, nervously, 'things are not working out in Italy any longer. The Army's morale is low, the soldiers don't want to fight any more.' He stood rooted to the red Turkey carpet, gnawing his nails. 'The Alpine Brigade,' he said, 'are singing a song that they will no longer fight for you.' Incongruously, in Piedmontese dialect, he chanted a snatch from it: 'Down with Mussolini, who murdered the Alpini.'

Behind the half-closed door of the ante-room, the King's military aide, General Paolo Puntoni, listened intently. Fearing trouble, the King had told him to stay close at hand – but now, as always, Puntoni saw, the King's problem was to make the Duce face facts. Only three days ago he had tried to convince Mussolini that he was the sole obstacle to peace – an interview that had made the little King shake with anger. 'Either he didn't understand or he didn't want to,' he told Puntoni. 'I might have been talking to the wind.'

Now twenty years of silent struggle between the two was ending, and the King could no longer control his deep-seated rancour. 'As for those ragamuffins Farinacci and Buffarini,' Puntoni heard him snap, 'when no one knew whether I would sign the decree putting you in charge of the armed forces, they said, "He'll sign it or we'll kick his backside." ' Still Mussolini said nothing.

'The result of the Grand Council's vote is tremendous,' the King explained patiently. 'Nineteen votes cast for Grandi's resolution! Don't have any illusions. Don't think that vote doesn't express the way the country feels towards you. Today you are the most hated man in Italy. You cannot count on a single friend except me.'

Mussolini strove to grapple with the logical outcome of all this. 'But if Your Majesty is right,' he said with difficulty, 'I should present my resignation.'

'And I have to tell you,' the King answered, snapping home the trap, 'that I unconditionally accept it.'

Suddenly, the King recalled later, Mussolini staggered violently, 'like a man hit by a .305 cannon shell'. 'So this is the end . . .' he whispered painfully, sinking unbidden to a chaise-longue.

In the driving-seat of the Duce's Asturia, chauffeur Ercole Boratto was just then yawning through the Sunday paper. Abruptly Giuseppe Morazzini, police chief for the royal household, thrust his head through the driver's window. 'Hurry, Ercole,' he told Boratto, 'you're wanted on the phone. I'll come with you – I've a call to make too.'

Boratto glanced at his watch. 5.10 p.m. – useful to know, if Rachele was calling from Villa Torlonia to ask when the Duce would return. Time and again in the past he had hurried like this to the telephone-box in the porter's lodge, fifty paces from Villa Ada's gateway. Morazzini followed. But now, to the chauffeur's horror, he had no sooner entered the box than Morazzini and two strangers jumped him from behind. Strong arms pinioned him, wrenching away his gun. The police chief's voice was sibilant in his ear: 'Listen carefully! There is no Duce any more. Badoglio is the new Head of Government . . .'

Inside the King's salon, Mussolini had just heard the same incredible news. 'I have come to the conclusion,' the King was saying, 'that the only person who can control the present situation is Marshal Badoglio. Badoglio is the man of the moment. He will form a government of officers and carry on the war. He enjoys the full confidence of the Army and the Police.'

'And the Police,' Mussolini repeated stupidly, staring dully into space.

North of the villa, Captain Vigneri was just then boarding the ambulance, together with Captain Avversa, the three plainclothes agents and three non-coms skilled in unarmed combat. The fifty *carabinieri* remained lined up out of sight. Now Vigneri rapped sharply on the glass partition. Silently, free-wheeling on the sloping drive, the ambulance slid through the sunlit garden to the east side of Villa Ada – seven yards from the porticoed front entrance. Carefully the driver backed up until the rear doors faced the steps.

There was no sound at all, Vigneri recalls, except for the bees drowsy in the lavender-beds, the faint clatter of china from the royal kitchens.

At the head of the steps, footman Vittorio Piccoli stood rigidly at attention – a motionless automaton in black jacket and blue red-striped trousers, the House of Savoy's livery. All the time Vigneri kept his eyes on the footman's face. Piccoli's swift reaction when the moment came would determine if this coup could be brought off without a bloody intervention from Mussolini's bodyguard.

In truth, as Vigneri knew, the King had hotly contested an arrest on the royal estate. 'Never as long as I have breath in my body,' he told the Duke of Acquarone that afternoon, 'shall I give an order like that.' But an arrest on the narrow Via Salaria outside the Villa, Acquarone argued, with the Duce's bodyguard standing by, would provoke a bloody battle – even a fascist counter-coup and civil war. The sure solution – though against all known canons of hospitality – was to seize the Duce while he was still the King's guest and spirit him away in the ambulance to a *carabinieri* barracks.

Typically, as General Puntoni later recalled it, the King had said neither yes nor no – merely spread his palms wide in a hopeless gesture. Quick to take this for assent, the wily Acquarone had authorized the arrest in the King's name.

In the salon, the King was binding the wounds. 'I am sorry, I am sorry,' Puntoni heard him repeating, 'but the solution could not be otherwise.' Afterwards, Mussolini recalled with anger that the King took both his hands like a trusted friend, assuring him: 'Have no fear whatsoever for your personal safety. I shall give orders for your protection.'

Mussolini claimed, too, that he warned the King: 'The crisis will be regarded as a victory for Churchill and Stalin.' But General Puntoni heard no word from the stricken Duce as the King piloted him towards the door. Glancing at his watch, he noted that it was 5.20 p.m. Once his interests demanded it, the King had taken twenty minutes to put an end to twenty years of Fascism.

On the gravelled driveway, Vigneri saw Piccoli, the footman, nod curtly. Next instant the flunkey had slipped from sight. Neither the King nor his aide could be seen as the captain crossed the drive in swift purposeful strides, cutting in on Mussolini as he came heavily down the steps, followed by De Cesare. Unobtrusively, Avversa circled in to cover the secretary. Momentarily the armed agents dropped from sight, crouching behind Mussolini's car.

'Duce,' Vigneri said, snapping to attention, 'by order of His Majesty the King we beg you to follow us, to protect you from possible mob violence.' Mussolini stared uncomprehendingly. 'But there's no need,' he said wearily, turning towards the Asturia. 'Duce,' Vigneri insisted, 'I have an order to carry out.' He stepped nimbly in front of Mussolini, blocking his path. 'You must come in my car,' he told him, shepherding him towards the ambulance.

As the rear door was flung open, Mussolini recoiled. After two hours under the sun, the interior was like a furnace, reeking of tardisinfectant. Gently but inexorably, his hand beneath the Duce's left elbow, Vigneri propelled him in, and De Cesare followed. Agents and non-coms came doubling to join them. 'Not these people, too?' Mussolini protested, but Vigneri only spread his hands resignedly. 'Get aboard, boys,' he told them, 'and make it fast.'

From the head of the steps, Piccoli, the footman, watched them go. One last ludicrous cameo of the Duce's downfall would remain for ever in his mind: Mussolini, both hands raised to his head, securing his bowler hat, as the agents clambered awkwardly aboard, their side-arms clanking, before the steel doors banged shut and the ambulance jerked forward.

Lieutenant-Colonel Santo Linfozzi felt at peace with the world. It was like any July Sunday evening at Rome's Podgora *Carabinieri* Barracks, where Linfozzi was commandant: the parade-ground dotted with groups of proud relatives armed with meagre food parcels and magazines for their menfolk, the sun dipping beyond the palm trees, shadows barring the mustard-coloured stone.

Drawing deeply on a cigarette, the Colonel wondered when General Angelo Cerica would arrive. Like every other commandant this Sunday, he had stayed put since the noonday message,. awaiting the Commander-in-Chief's inspection.

Suddenly Colonel Linfozzi gasped. An ambulance had whirled through the barracks' high iron gates, braking hard near the doorway in which he stood. From the rear, two *carabinieri* officers descended, then eight civilians whom he didn't recognize. Abruptly he let fall his cigarette 'as if it had been a wasp', and braced to attention. Not General Cerica, but the head of the government himself had arrived from out of the blue.

'Duce,' said Linfozzi fatuously, approaching the group, 'what an honour!'

Mussolini just stared at him. 'Colonel, sir,' said Vigneri drily, returning the salute, 'the Duce is our guest. Please open the Officers' Club so that he can accommodate himself.'

Nimbly the Colonel led the way. At the outer door Vigneri drew him aside, watching Linfozzi's jaw drop comically as he learned the true position. Once again Vigneri took over escort duty – along a corridor to a small lounge with Empire-style furniture, overlooking a trim garden. Still, as Mussolini made no sign, De Cesare approached the Captain. 'What happens if the Duce wants to leave?' he asked.

Vigneri was impassive. 'He can't leave.'

'And if he wants to telephone?' De Cesare persisted, gesturing at the instrument on a side-table. Vigneri shook his head. 'He can't telephone.'

'Then how,' asked De Cesare acidly, 'would you define all this?'

'Excellency, I am just carrying out orders,' Vigneri said woodenly. 'It's not up to me to give definitions.'

Both men fell silent at the entry of one of Linfozzi's staff officers. Not sparing a glance for the frozen tableau – Mussolini nervously fingering his upper lip, De Cesare seething with anger, the inscrutable Vigneri – he advanced on the telephone.

Then, with three decisive strokes of the penknife in his hand, he sawed deliberately through the wire.

It was around 7.30 p.m. when Private Nicolò Monaci boarded the tramcar. The minute he paid his fare he knew there was something wrong. It was so obvious, the cold silence that descended as he passed along the coach – everyone eyeing his Militia uniform, then shifting away as if he was a leper.

Up to now Monaci had been feeling good. For the first time since the San Lorenzo raid, the twenty-nine-year-old private, one of the Duce's 800-strong bodyguard, had had a day off from heavy rescue work. All through the sultry afternoon he had strolled through the fairground near Piazza Argentina, trying his hand at the shooting-galleries, with a side-trip to the Chamber of Horrors. Yet now he was positively glad when the tram halted at the Trastevere stop, the nearest to the 'M' Division Barracks, where he was quartered. Suddenly these Romans seemed downright unfriendly.

Monaci had taken only one step through the barrack gates when he knew why. From the pell-mell confusion of scurrying soldiers, he spotted one man from his own company. 'Mussolini's fallen,' his mate yelled. 'Have you any civilian clothes? It's time we weren't here!'

Although three hours were to pass before any official announcement, somehow the news of Mussolini's downfall was spreading through Rome along an invisible grapevine.

Some got the news in code. Leopoldo Piccardi, a Liberal in the underground movement, answered the phone to hear the Marchesa Giuliana Benzoni, Maria-José's irrepressible friend, announce: 'The King put The Big Cheese in the cupboard.' Enzo Storoni, the Crown's lawyer, rang his father-in-law with a formal invitation: 'Come over tonight for coffee and cigars.' At first the old man exploded wrathfully, then the implication hit him. Twenty years back he had forsworn tobacco, vowing never to take so much as a puff until the Fascist regime had toppled.

A few heard with shame. In the dining-room at Villa Ada, Queen Elena took her husband bitterly to task. 'You cannot treat guests like that,' she rebuked him. 'The rules of royal hospitality have been violated. He could have been arrested anywhere, not at our house.' White with anger, the King wiped his lips with his napkin, then withdrew from the table. Crown Princess Maria-José felt the same shame. After all her months of groundwork with Acquarone, the King, just as she might have guessed, had resorted to shabby subterfuge. At dinner in a friend's apartment, she beat her head against a wall-mirror, crying: 'It's not done like this – it's *not* done like this.'

For others, the fall of Mussolini came as a formal declaration. Vexed beyond endurance by Badoglio's repeated attempts to contact him, Ambassador von Mackensen sent his First Secretary, Ulrich Doertenbach, to the Marshal's villa to see just what it was he wanted. Now, beside the Embassy's swimming-pool, Doertenbach, pale-faced, was reporting to the submerged Ambassador: Badoglio wished to announce Mussolini's resignation and his own appointment as Premier.

Water draining from his vast torso, the stupefied von Mackensen came bolt upright in the pool, spluttering: '*Der Badoglio ist ein Schwein.*'

In Prince Otto von Bismarck's apartment it was the white-gloved butler, serving coffee and liqueurs, who broke the news: 'I regret to announce that His Majesty has deposed Mussolini.' Pouting prettily, his wife, Princess Anne Marie, commented: 'How ungrateful of him to do that to the dear Duce!' The Assistant Military Attaché, Friedrich Karl von Plehwe, had it from his cook, Maria. Dancing into the room in a frenzy of joy, she sang out: 'Now they'll kill the stinker.'

At Villa Torlonia, Rachele Mussolini, worried that Benito had not yet returned, was hearing the full story of the Grand Council session from one of his few loyal supporters – the fat, unctuous Guido Buffarini-Guidi. Suddenly the phone rang, and a frightened voice whispered up the wire: 'They've just arrested the Duce!' Almost at once, refusing to identify himself, the man hung up.

Rachele became so distraught with worry that at last Irma Morelli, Mussolini's Romagna chambermaid, burst out that the Duce had not always merited such devotion. For seven years he had been keeping a mistress called Claretta Petacci.

For Rachele, living a life as secluded as Claretta's own, the news was a mortal blow. She knew, to her distress, that Benito had many such fleeting affairs – but a liaison of seven years' standing was plainly serious. 'Why did you keep all this to yourself?' she upbraided Irma. 'Why do you only tell me at a time like this?'

Claretta, too, was frantic. That afternoon she had waited more than an hour in the Zodiac Room, sipping tea and chatting with Quinto Navarra – the Duce, the usher thought, was due any moment now. Navarra hadn't at first grasped the implications when a despatch rider brought word that Mussolini had gone to Villa Ada – but Claretta had. 'I told him not to go and see that man,' she almost screamed, leaping to her feet. 'He won't listen to me.' Abruptly, she hastened back to Villa Camilluccia for another interminable night's vigil by the telephone.

Both Claretta and Rachele were now convinced that only one man could both find the Duce and restore him to power: the staunchly loyal Commandant of the Militia, General Enzo Galbiati.

In his ground-floor office on Piazza Romania, Galbiati had no such faith. By 7 p.m. he had been waiting two hours for Mussolini's call, but no news of any kind had reached him. The General telephoned Palazzo Venezia, but the switchboard didn't answer. A despatch rider sent to Villa Ada reported that the Duce's Asturia had left half-an-hour ago. In truth it had, with Marshal Badoglio, following an audience with the King, sitting snugly in the back seat, but Galbiati did not know this.

Galbiati grappled with the problem. At least ten motor-cycle patrols were out searching for the Duce, but Sunday was always a slack day at Militia Headquarters – almost everyone was on weekend leave. Tonight there were fewer than fifty people in the building, including civilian employees and clerks.

About 7.30 p.m. General Giuseppe Conticelli, the Deputy Chief of Staff burst into his office. At the Ministry of Home Affairs, Under-Secretary Umberto Albini had told him of Mussolini's resignation. Another officer brought the rumour that the Duce had departed straight for his Romagna retreat, Rocca delle Caminate, by special train. On the line to Villa Torlonia, Galbiati talked long and earnestly with Buffarini-Guidi, who had stayed on to comfort Rachele. Buffarini suspected that the Duce had been kidnapped, but could offer no proof, aside from that alarming call to Rachele.

Each ring of the telephone brought more confusion, more uncertainty. His office was filled with wrangling members of staff, and Galbiati was having to shout into the mouthpiece to make himself heard. From outlying regions of the city came reports of militiamen being assaulted, their black shirts torn from their backs. Next Galbiati tried raising Militia Commands at Bologna and Settevene. Each time the reply was the same: the lines were dead.

By 8 p.m. on this confused unhappy night, Galbiati was in despair. Some officers loudly urged a show of force – but against whom wasn't clear. And recently, for reasons which now became all too plain, General Ambrosio had transferred many militia units like the 'M' Division to the Army command. The nearest troops were twenty-two miles away on a training course with unfamiliar German weapons. And if the Duce *had* resigned of his own free will, what action was there to be taken?

Galbiati could not then know that the orders to General Cerica's *carabinieri* that morning had included other targets than Mussolini's person. Already they were moving in to occupy Radio Italia headquarters with its outlying stations, post offices, telephone exchanges and the Ministry for Home Affairs.

At 8.30 p.m. Major Giuseppe Marinelli, his adjutant, gave a sudden exclamation. Across Piazza Romania, in the thickening dusk, he reported three tanks of the Ariete Division with 75 cm guns just forty yards away. Galbiati was busy with a phone call. 'In which direction are the guns pointing?' he asked.

Marinelli, motionless at the window, answered quietly, 'Straight at us.'

Some Romans had waited a lifetime for this night. By 10.45 p.m. on this moonlit Sunday, they knew it had arrived. From the commandeered radio station on Via Asiago, the incisive tones of the newscaster speaking for Marshal Pietro Badoglio rasped through thousands of radio sets: 'Italians! By order of His Majesty the King and Emperor, I have assumed the military government of the country with full powers. The war continues. Italy . . . will keep her given word . . .'

Across the seven hills of Rome, the news leaped from street to street like a firestorm. The city which had seen the triumphs of Caesar and Domitian now witnessed an explosion of emotion that none could ever forget. Those who had heard the broadcast telephoned frantically to relatives and friends who might have missed it –

or yelled wildly from open tenement windows. Just as they were, they tumbled downstairs on to the pavements – in nightgowns or pyjamas, some in slippers, some barefoot. Dishevelled and panting, they embraced one another, laughing and weeping.

It was a night to do all the things one had never dared in twenty years to do. In the backroom of the Caffè Aragno on Corso Umberto, where writers gathered, one saw a colleague seize a bar-room chair and shatter it to matchwood over the head of a Militia officer drinking at the next table – 'just like in the movies.' Soon scores of them were invading the offices of *Il Messaggero*, Rome's leading daily, on Via del Tritone – some to bring out a special 'freedom' edition, others to smash pictures, typewriters, anything that was breakable. From the nearby Hotel Majestic a throng of admirers bore a popular actress clad in yellow silk pyjamas shoulder high through the streets. Screams of '*Evviva il Re*' and '*Evviva il Papa*' rent the night. On Via Veneto, a leather-lunged demonstrator told everyone within earshot: 'I can shout "Bloody Mussolini" and no one arrests me!' A bystander responded cynically: 'Try shouting "Bloody Badoglio" and see what happens.'

Outside the gates of Villa Torlonia swarmed a frenzied horde of half-dressed Romans, led by a man playing a trombone – causing the terrified Rachele Mussolini to take refuge in an outhouse. But in fact no one in the crowd gave the Duce's wife a thought; they had three years of hunger to appease. Their goal, until *carabinieri* drove them off, were Rachele's pigs and chickens.

It was a night to flout authority – all and any authority. Some rushed to hail trams – then scrambled aboard, like disobedient children, through the door marked 'Exit'. Others tore up their ration books, scattering them like confetti; no one took seriously Badoglio's face-saver that the war would go on. Armed with the strangest weapons – hunting-guns, even lances – they rampaged into Fascist branch offices, piling desks, chairs and portraits of Mussolini on to yellow crackling bonfires. Across the façade of Palazzo Venezia 'Long live Matteotti' appeared as if by magic, daubed in white paint. On tall ladders outside scores of buildings stone-cutters went to work, chipping away the hated 'fasces' that had for so long spelt servitude.

For many, it was still an uneasy freedom. Along the Corso, a wag raised the alarm: 'Look out – the Duce's coming!' And for a moment everyone scattered. But what came instead was a bronze bust of him, hurtling over a balcony – to be quickly harnessed with cords and dragged towards Piazza Colonna, the head rumbling like a cannon ball over the asphalt, followed by screaming crowds.

On Via Nazionale the posters of the Teatro Eliseo's latest show stood out clearly in the leaping light of bonfires: *Goodbye To All This*.

For many in Rome – unaware that nine months of German occupation were to follow – this was truly the night the war ended. At an ack-ack battery on the Anzio road, an Army private celebrated the Duce's downfall with two whole litres of cognac – then dropped dead from alcoholic poisoning. Near the Campo dei Fiori, a mother struck a warmer note with a gesture all women could acknowledge this night. Holding aloft her newly-born baby, she explained to everyone around: 'I want him to breathe fresh air.'

To a few, the sudden change of Government was literally the razor-edge between life and death. In Regina Coeli Prison, the great grim pile on the Tiber's north bank, Ottavio Galeazzo, a nineteen-year-old medical student, heard the key grate in the door of the punishment cell and prepared for the worst. For almost a year, he had been incarcerated here, condemned for an anti-Fascist conspir-acy,which could merit a sentence of death. Now he saw that the warder, unbelievably, was smiling – and that the Fascist party badge, the 'bug', had gone from his lapels.

'You've heard, eh?' were the words which told the young student he would not die. 'It isn't Mussolini any more, it's Badoglio.' Then, hastily, as a million others were just then doing, the man made it plain where he stood. '*I* was never Fascist, you know,' he announced.

Overnight, it seemed, there were no more Fascists. Black shirts were suddenly as rare as frost in August. The northbound Via Nomentana was a gleaming golden carpet of Fascist badges. On the Tiber's yellow waters, hundreds of discarded uniforms now drifted, black and bloated, towards the sea. In all Italy, only one man – Manlio Morgagni, President of the Stefani News Agency – thought Mussolini worth the supreme sacrifice. 'My life was yours,' he scribbled in a last note to the Duce, after locking himself in his bedroom. 'I die with your name on my lips.' Then he blew out his brains.

But for millions it was a champagne time of rejoicing. In Bologna Communists bore King Vittorio Emanuele's portrait in a wildly-cheering procession to the foot of the Garibaldi statue – then crowned it with the Red Flag. In Milan factory workers declared a one-day strike by way of celebration; at the Alfa-Romeo Plant, the Duce's obligatory portrait was captioned 'Butcher's Meat at Bargain Prices.' On the Naples waterfront the market-women launched into a wild tarantella in the moonlight.

Not far away, at *carabinieri* headquarters, one man caught up on history in the same offbeat way that many Italians learned the news on the 25 July. Bone-tired after a day's duty, twenty-four-year-old Ezio Berti of the Political Squad trudged into the canteen to witness an unprecedented sight. Watched by three incurious colleagues, an officer in full-dress uniform was pitching tomatoes at the portraits of the King and the Duce on the wall.

As the gooey pulp trickled down the glass, Berti felt neither shock nor surprise nor indignation at the irreverence. He reacted like fifty million other hungry, disillusioned, war-weary Italians: 'Two tomatoes are a day's ration!'

For Fabrizio, eleven, Raimonda, nine, and Marzio, five, it was time to say good-night – but on 25 July Edda Ciano had a different kind of bedtime story to tell her children. All that day, ever since Galeazzo's phone-call to the ivy-clad two-storey family mansion at Ponte a Moriano, near Lucca, she had been postponing this moment. But now the children had to know.

To the Duce's headstrong, auburn-haired daughter, the news of the Grand Council had come as no surprise. Clear-sightedly she had recognized that sooner or later 'the twenty cockeyed years', as she irreverently styled her father's regime, would have an end. Only recently she had predicted at an all-night bridge party: 'In two years' time we shall all be hanged in front of Palazzo Venezia.' It was time that the children, too, faced something of this black reality.

Now, at 9 p.m., she called them to the drawing-room. Tonight, with Galeazzo away, the house seemed forlorn. The smell of stale cigar-smoke hung in the silent billiard-room like a shroud. Outside, moonlight silvered the cherry orchards sloping to the village, and an owl hooted in the full-leafed chestnut trees.

Edda watched the children's eyes grow wider as they heard of the events in Rome. It was Fabrizio who asked for all of them: 'What do you suppose is going to happen to us? Shall we all be killed?'

A determinedly modern mother, who had always insisted the children use her Christian name, Edda Ciano did not shrink from the facts. She did not see death as imminent, but they must be ready for anything. At the best, Galeazzo would lose both his job and his fortune. But the greater likelihood was prison or exile.

The children's eyes grew rounder still and in that moment Edda felt the urgent need 'to give them a role to live up to'. 'Our country is in mortal danger,' she told them. 'Nothing matters any more as long as our country lives. And people like us must be ready to take the rough with the smooth when it comes, and put a brave face on it.'

It was what Mussolini's daughter really believed. 'We are all doomed,' she recalled thinking later. 'Rats in a trap – but there can be beauty even in the death of a mouse.' Suddenly, springing up, she wound the handle of the gramophone. 'Let's have music,' she rallied them. 'It's our last night. Let's make a night of it.'

Slowly the record revolved. The children clustered silently, huddled close to her feet. Through the wide open windows the rich strong notes of Tschaikovsky's *Capriccio Italiano* stole out on the summer night, across the gravelled carriage-sweep, among the moonlit trees.

On the terrace of the villa code-named 'The White House', the American who had struck the first mortal blow against Mussolini's regime was finishing breakfast. All the omens on this glorious Monday morning at La Marsa, Tunisia, seemed propitious. Across the Bay of Tunis, the blunt contours of Cap Bon trembled in the heat-haze – and the porridge, baked beans and hot coffee had tasted all the better for the news he had just received. Shortly before 8 a.m. on 26 July the news of the Duce's downfall had reached the Allied Commander-in-Chief, North Africa, General Dwight D. Eisenhower.

A soldier who hated war, Eisenhower had good reason to rejoice. From his La Marsa villa, he was this morning scheduled to attend a three-hour senior commanders' conference at Amilcar, the Advance Command Post of Allied Forces Headquarters. The terms of reference: the forthcoming assault on the mainland of Italy. Now Eisenhower saw the way clear for the Italians 'to withdraw from the war quickly and honourably'.

To the two men sharing his table, Eisenhower excitedly outlined his beliefs. The new Badoglio regime would be almost certainly anti-Nazi. Its policies could affect not only the seventeen-day-old Sicilian campaign, but the rest of the war in Europe. As Eisenhower saw it, even the 110,000 Italians thus far taken prisoner in Sicily might be rapidly repatriated – provided they would work to overthrow the Fascists and Germans still on Italian soil. Now he urged a bridging link: a message should be broadcast to the King's government, urging them to send a peace emissary.

His companions, both civilians, shook dubious heads. As diplomats, both Robert Murphy, Franklin Delano Roosevelt's representative in North Africa, and Harold Macmillan, the urbane spokesman for Winston Churchill, were of one accord. Allied Forces Head-quarters lacked all authority to initiate political manoeuvres. Before broadcasting any such message, Eisenhower must seek permission from the Combined Chiefs of Staff in London and Washington.

'In the old days before rapid communications,' Eisenhower sighed, 'generals were free to do what they thought best.'

Both men responded instinctively to Eisenhower's human warmth – but neither shared his innate conviction that the end was in sight. Macmillan, who had heard of Mussolini's fall at midnight from the BBC Overseas News, even thought better of waking General Harold Alexander, British commander of the Fifteenth Army Group. In Alexander's mess, war talk was shop, frowned on as bad manners. Murphy, too, felt his optimism diminished by the prospect of a bitter battle on Italian soil.

As Eisenhower's planners were swift to point out, lack of landing-craft and air cover ruled out any assault on the mainland before 7 September. Even this would be a hazardous and daunting holding operation, a limited five-division thrust, with thousands of troops reserved for the long-awaited invasion of Northern France. Mean-while, two-thirds of the Italian Army were scattered outside the kingdom – and who knew how quickly the Germans would build up their strength?

'The Italians may want peace,' Macmillan summed up bluntly, 'their problem is how to get it.'

For this very reason, Eisenhower urged, time was of the essence. Macmillan must at once draft telegrams to London and Washington outlining a suggested declaration to the Italian people, plus ten simple conditions should Badoglio sue for an armistice. Untimely delay could mean civil war in Italy between Fascists and anti-Fascists – or battles between Italians and Germans. Every effort must be made to persuade the Italians that the unconditional surrender policy of the 1943 Casablanca Conference – which Eisenhower privately styled 'very difficult and silly' – would not mean peace with dishonour.

As staunch an optimist as he was a leader, Eisenhower's face was radiant as he dwelt on Mussolini's fall. 'Bob,' he exhorted them, 'Harold – believe me! It's the crumbling of the whole damned thing.'

8. 'Preserve the Blood of the Duce'

25 July–12 September, 1943

It was hardly a dinner to grace a Field-Marshal's table: clear soup, salami and gherkins, a brimming glass of beer. But then, thought Standartenführer Eugen Dollmann sadly, as orderly officers in white woollen gloves served the meagre rations, Field-Marshal Albert Kesselring, Wehrmacht Commander-in-Chief, Southern Command, cared so little for food that a simple field-kitchen meal was almost always enough. Often the fastidious Dollman, Himmler's personal representative in Italy, viewed an evening summons to Kesselring's Frascati headquarters, fifteen miles from Rome, as the signal to take an earlier, choicer dinner in the city.

And tonight, plainly, dinner had been little more than an excuse for an informal get-together. The salami finished, Kesselring at once pushed back his chair, departing to the lounge for coffee together with his Chief of Staff, Major-General Siegfried Westphal, and their guest of honour, General Kurt Student, jovial, crop-headed commander of the 11th Air Corps, veteran of Rotterdam and Crete. In the bleak dining-room of the nineteenth-century villa, Dollman found himself alone with two men – Obersturmbannführer Herbert Kappler, the Embassy's cool blue-eyed police attaché, and Otto Skorzeny, the towering (6 ft. 4 ins.) Austrian who had arrived with Student. Strangely, on this stifling night of Tuesday, 27 July, Skorzeny wore a Luftwaffe Captain's fur-lined flying jacket.

'In the name of the Führer,' Dollmann recalls Skorzeny beginning, 'I must ask you to promise that what follows will be treated as top secret.'

Both Dollmann and Kappler felt a quickening of interest. Rare in 1943 were the junior officers summoned to Hitler's presence. Rarer still were those to whom he gave his time. But the day before, Skorzeny had been called for a special reason. The blond burly giant, with cheeks sabre-scarred from a student duel over a ballet-dancer, had been handpicked by Adolf Hitler to find Benito Mussolini.

Towards 9 p.m. on 26 July, at the Führer's HQ in the sombre

pine forests at Rastenburg, East Prussia, the thirty-five-year-old Skorzeny, a Haupsturm führer in the Waffen S S, had stood before Hitler for the first time in his life. For the past three months he had been chief of VIs, the top secret training school of Department VI of the Central State Security Division. High politics, changes of government in Italy, were not even remotely his concern. From his headquarters on Berker Strasse in the Berlin suburb of Schmangendorf, Skorzeny's job was to train potential agents for the field – in every skill from self-defence to sabotage.

Now, Skorzeny told Dollmann and Kappler, he had himself become an agent in the field. 'Mussolini, my friend and loyal comrade in arms,' Hitler had told him emotionally, 'was betrayed yesterday by his King and arrested by his own countrymen. I cannot and will not leave Italy's greatest son in the lurch. I will keep faith with my old ally and dear friend – he must be rescued promptly or he will be handed over to the Allies.'

But this was only one leg of the mission that had brought Student and Skorzeny hotfoot from the Führer's headquarters with no more personal baggage than a toothbrush and the clothes they wore. Already, despite Badoglio's assurance that 'the war would continue', Hitler was convinced of Italy's defection. On 25 July only eight fully efficient German divisions had been stationed on Italian soil – but by dawn on 26 July three more divisions, their soldiers' helmets daubed 'Long live Mussolini', were swarming across the Brenner, the Tarvis and the Little St Bernard Passes. Hitler's counter-coup, code-named 'Operation Alaric', and involving the mass-disarming of the Italian forces by Student's parachutists, might soon be a grim reality.

'Have the Field-Marshal and Mackensen been informed?' Dollmann asked Skorzeny.

Grimly Skorzeny shook his head. Neither the Army Commander nor the Ambassador, Hitler had stressed, must know anything of his mission. 'They have a completely mistaken view of the situation,' the Führer grumbled, 'and would tackle the job in the wrong way.' Apart from the three now present, only two men in all Italy would know of Skorzeny's mission – Student, and Obersturmführer Karl Radl, Skorzeny's deputy.

Already reinforcements were on the way. Within forty-eight hours, 10,000 paratroopers of Student's corps would land at Rome's Pratica di Mare airfield. Skorzeny, too, had been busy. From the Führer's headquarters a non-stop barrage of teletype messages and phone calls had bombarded the harassed Karl Radl in Berlin. Alerted by the code-phrase, 'The macaroni's burning,' Radl had a shrewd idea of the unit's destination – but only by playing the ultimate ace of the *Führerbefehl*, Hitler's personal order, had he managed to round up the material his chief had demanded in nine hours flat.

In addition to twenty picked instructors from the school, all Italian-speaking, Skorzeny had called for tropical uniforms, civilian suits, weapons and silencers, laughing-gas, tear-gas, smoke-screen apparatus and thirty kilograms of plastic explosive – plus, for good measure, a stock of forged British pound notes and two complete outfits for Jesuit priests. By 7 a.m. on 27 July, one hour before Student and Skorzeny left for Rome, Radl and his men, their bizarre property-list complete, were clambering aboard JU 52 transport planes at Berlin's Staaken Airport.

Kappler, calm, courteous, now charted the pitfalls ahead. Until Ferbuary 1943 there had been no German Secret Service in Italy. Hitler had forbidden all intelligence work against his friend and ally, the Duce. Only then had the Chief of Department VI, Walter Schellenberg, disregarding the Führer's orders, sent Obersturmbannführer Wilhelm Höttl, a twenty-eight-year-old Austrian history professor, to work with Kappler in Rome. The two had even risked installing a secret radio station with a direct link to Berlin in Kappler's Via Tasso office – something even von Mackensen didn't know. For five months they had warned their chiefs of Italy's imminent collapse – and week by week had seen their warnings brushed aside.

Now, Kappler cautioned, his contacts were improving daily, but his personal staff numbered only four. With years of leeway to make up, finding Mussolini might prove an insuperable task.

For answer, Skorzeny reiterated Hitler's words: the Duce must be found before the Allies seized him. This was the first stage. If he was in some fortress prison, the second was to devise a plan to storm it. 'We must do everything in our power,' he wound up, 'to carry out the order.'

As the meeting broke up, Kappler maintained a discreet silence. Vividly he recalled the hard-hitting verbal report he had delivered in Berlin as recently as May to two men who found his words profoundly disturbing – the florid, hard-drinking, Dr Ernst Kaltenbrunner, Chief of the SD, his immediate boss, and Baron Adolf von Steengracht, Under-Secretary of State for Foreign Affairs.

'Fascism,' Kappler had told them then, 'is like a vast beautiful palace with a breathtaking façade – but, gentlemen, it's riddled with termites! One little tap from a hammer and it will crumble into dust.'

Three months later, his prophecy confirmed, Kappler had his own private conception of what to do with Benito Mussolini. Find and free him by all means, give him a castle on the Rhine, a golden cage surrounded by sycophants – but never again restore him to power.

If the aim of Skorzeny's mission was to set the Duce back in the saddle, Herbert Kappler had resolved that no one on earth would ever find Mussolini.

As they ambled along the dockside, nobody gave the sailors a second glance. In this last week of August 1943 naval ratings of the German *Kriegsmarine* had become a commonplace in the sleepy naval base of La Maddalena Island, off the northernmost tip of Sardinia. Arguing spiritedly as they toted a bundle of dirty shirts wrapped in a straw mat, they were plainly bound for the laundress's cottage on the outskirts of the port, high on a hill above Villa Weber.

The slighter of the two, fair-haired and cheerful, had been a familiar sight around Maddalena for almost two weeks – already known as orderly and interpreter to Captain Hunäus, the gouty old German Harbour Commandant. He was notorious, too, in every dockside tavern, as a man who took his liquor strong and often, who would propose bets on anything at the drop of a hat. The burly giant beside him was a stranger – probably a rating from the E-boat flotilla anchored in Anzio Harbour, 170 miles away on the mainland.

Only the twenty picked agents of Department VI, now quartered at Rome's Pratica di Mare airfield with Student's paratroopers, would have recognized these sailors as Obersturmführer Robert Warger, ex-Tyrolean mountaineer and until recently a fanatic teetotaller, now being soundly tongue-lashed by his chief, Otto Skorzeny. 'Why didn't you report there was more than one telephone line leading into the Villa?' Skorzeny was demanding furiously. 'One oversight like that could ruin our whole operation.'

If Skorzeny was in the blackest of moods, he had reasons. An additional telephone line for which he hadn't bargained was typical of the problems that beset him. He and his men had now been engaged on this wild-goose chase in search of Mussolini for twenty-nine frustrating days. Time and again they had come within inches of putting their fingers on him – only to find the wily Italians had once more spirited him away. Not until 10 August had this most promising lead developed. From La Maddalena, Captain Hunäus reported the garrison had abruptly been strengthened. Further, local telephone workers had orders from the admiral commanding the base to install a direct line between his own office and Villa Weber, independent of the central switchboard. Rumour had it the Duce had arrived at the weatherworn villa as early as 3.30 p.m. on 7 August, off the destroyer *Pantera*, and was now guarded by 150 *carabinieri*.

Now, if all went well, 6 a.m. on 28 August – twenty-four hours ahead – was H-Hour on D-Day. By then, the flotilla of six E-boats anchored at Anzio would have entered La Maddalena on an official visit and be lying up under a breakwater. One day earlier, a flotilla of minesweepers and M-boats would collect volunteers from the Corsican SS Brigade under Karl Radl and anchor at the mole of Palau across the bay. Ostensibly both flotillas would leave harbour at dawn on a naval exercise – then, at a given signal, while the E-boats gave covering fire, commandos from the minesweepers and the M-boats would storm ashore to seize Villa Weber.

The plan, which Hitler had personally approved, called for split-second timing – and luck. The Italian ack-ack batteries on the hills around the harbour would have to be kept in check by German batteries on the opposite side. The port's military barracks housed 200 naval cadets in training – so this flank, too, must be secured. The moment Mussolini was aboard an E-boat, a special commando must lower one of the booms, allowing for a speedy getaway.

There was no doubting the Duce's presence in Villa Weber. At first the teetotal Warger had resisted strenuously Skorzeny's order to break his pledge in lieu of duty – but as Karl Radl put it: 'Whoever saw a teetotal sailor?' Armed with wine and cognac, the two had lured him inside their Frascati billet to enforce obedience. 'My dear friend,' they had coaxed him as he gagged over the first tot, 'it's not as bad as you think.' And their coaching had paid off. Two days after arriving at La Maddalena, Warger, in his cups, had proposed a bet to a bibulous fruiterer: a bottle of cognac that the Duce was dead.

Delighted to find a pushover, the man had led Warger to a house nearby and pointed wordlessly. There on a narrow terrace of Villa Weber's east wing, barely three feet wide, the young commando had seen Benito Mussolini, bolt upright on a wooden chair, staring at the sea.

But many tactical problems still loomed over this operation. Hiding beneath a minesweeper's awning as it cruised the harbour, Skorzeny had taken photos of the villa – but from several hundred yards' distance. Today, as he and Warger passed its gates, apparently deep in argument, and Skorzeny spotted that additional telephone wire, parties of *carabinieri* were patrolling outside and a machine-gun post was set up – but high walls shut off all further view. What mattered most was a view of the ground floor. Now Warger's trip to the laundress's cottage with a pile of the Captain's shirts would furnish the cover they sought.

As Warger tipped the soiled linen on the woman's kitchen table, Skorzeny asked urgently for the toilet. 'It's this dysentery I've had,' he moaned, grimacing with pain. 'I feel as if my insides were ruined.' But the woman apologized, shamefaced, that her house was too humble, and Warger expertly picked up his cue. 'There's a rockslide fifty yards up the road,' he told his companion. 'I'll wait for you here.'

Crouched among the piled rocks, his trousers lowered for realism, Skorzeny peered down at Villa Weber. Bougainvillea made vivid splashes of colour against the siena-coloured stone, and the walls bristled with terracotta lions and eagles. At this moment Mussolini must be taking his siesta, but at least twenty guards strolled unconcernedly on the broad terrace. For a moment Skorzeny was puzzled. Wasn't the Duce allowed to sit on his own terrace?

Even now he couldn't believe he was so close to him. For over three weeks he had followed his movements – though always too late – as intimately as if he had shared his prisons. At first the reports that trickled into Kappler's third-floor office on Via Tasso had been bewildering in their variety. Eight-hour coffee and cigarette sessions had been followed by tray-meals as Skorzeny, Radl, Kappler and Dollmann wrestled to sift fact from fantasy. Mussolini had committed suicide, ran one report. The Duce was in a northern clinic, mortally sick after a stroke, announced a second. He was in Spain as General Franco's honoured guest – or disguised as a humble Blackshirt on the Sicilian front.

Pressured by Student, even Field-Marshal Kesselring tried his hand at sleuthing. To mark Mussolini's sixtieth birthday – 29 July – Hitler had sent him a complete set of Nietzsche's works bound in blue morocco leather. 'You must personally see to it,' Student urged Kesselring, 'that the Duce gets them.' Kesselring approached both the King and Badoglio – to learn only that 'Mussolini was well and under the King's personal protection.' In due time, Badoglio promised, he would pass on the Führer's gift.

On 4 August, an informer in the *carabinieri* gave Kappler the first tentative lead. Mussolini had stayed only one hour at Podgora Barracks. From there the ambulance had whisked him to a converted waiting-room adjoining the commanding officer's flat at Legnano

Carabinieri Barracks, a mile away. Then, in a Rome restaurant, Karl Radl ran up against a talkative grocer who supplied customers on the coast near Gaeta, eighty-five miles south. The man had heard from a German sergeant, courting a local housemaid, that 'a very high ranking prisoner' had been sent to the prison island of Ponza, twenty miles off the coast.

Within hours, the astonished sergeant had been hustled to the mainland, brought before General Student, then flown to Hitler's secret hide-out, the *Wolfsschanze* (Wolf's Lair). To the Führer the sergeant had blurted out the scene that he had witnessed: around midnight on 27 July, when an air raid emptied Gaeta's streets, a six-car convoy had drawn up on the deserted wharf. Guarded by police agents, the Duce had stepped from a closed car to embark on the corvette *Persefone*.

At the same time, sources close to Rachele, now under house arrest at Rocca delle Caminate, confirmed that two trunkloads of clothes for Mussolini had been entrusted to a lobster fisherman plying between Ponza and the mainland.

But Hitler, after calling for maps, thought it likelier that his ally was on the neighbouring island of Ventotene – almost inaccessible when the sirocco blew from the African coast. 'Nothing good,' the Führer raged to Student, 'ever comes out of those damned Italians.'

Daily, the blue folder marked '*Geheime Reichssache*' (State Security Documents) housed in Kappler's office safe, grew bulkier. From Heinrich Himmler in Berlin came one report they greeted with howls of derision: the Duce had left Ponza and was aboard the battleship *Italia*, almost three hundred miles away in La Spezia. Skorzeny and all of them knew that the desperate 'Heini', as they called him, had even recruited top astrologers to predict the Duce's whereabouts, fêting them with champagne and Russian salmon. 'File it and forget it,' was Kappler's decision – as with reports that Mussolini was simultaneously on Caprera, east of Sardinia, and in a convent hospital at Santa Maria. Then came Hunäus's report from La Maddalena – and now Otto Skorzeny was within striking distance.

Hastening back down the hillside to rejoin Warger, he found him chatting with a *carabiniere* of the guard. Amiably, sharing out the grapes he bought from the laundress, Skorzeny launched into a paean of praise for all things Italian – the fruit, the sunshine, the girls, the wine. It was such a pity, Warger put in artlessly, about the Duce – the German radio had that morning announced he had died of fever. Bored, the *carabiniere* dismissed the news as false. 'I know it for a fact,' Skorzeny cut in. 'I had all the details of his illness from a doctor friend of mine.'

'No, no, Signor,' the *carabiniere* reiterated, 'it's impossible. I was a member of the Duce's escort this morning – I saw him with my own eyes. We led him to the white rescue plane with the red cross and I saw it take him away.'

As if whirled by an invisible wire, Skorzeny spun round. It was true. The enamelled bay lay at their feet, glinting under the sun. But the Red Cross rescue plane he had seen at anchor off the coast for eight days now had gone – and with it, all hopes of the dawn rescue of Benito Mussolini.

Almost five hundred miles north of La Maddalena two men paced lazily beside the wind-ruffled surface of Lake Starnberg, fifteen miles from Munich. 'Do be honest with me,' Galeazzo Ciano begged his companion suddenly. 'I promise not to take offence. What am I – your prisoner or your guest?'

Obersturmbannführer Wilhelm Höttl debated how to dodge the question. But it wasn't easy. Ciano had put it to him, always with the same gently mocking smile, for days now – ever since he had installed the Cianos and their children in the lakeside Villa Starnberg. The problem was that the dark curly-haired Austrian didn't know. Was he the Cianos' jailer, their interrogator, or just a genial host? On 31 August, after four days in residence, Höttl was still waiting patiently for Heinrich Himmler to enlighten him.

Around 9 a.m. on 27 August, as the Ciano family scrambled aboard their unpressurized JU 52 transport at Rome's Ciampino airfield, Höttl had known precisely where he stood. On Hitler's direct orders, he was the family's conducting officer – with strict instructions to 'preserve the blood of the Duce in the veins of his grandchildren'. Although the Badoglio Government had placed Galeazzo Ciano under house arrest, this had proved no bar to resourceful agents like Höttl, Kappler and Eugen Dollmann. At 8.15 a.m. Edda and the children, who had walking-out privileges, left the family apartment at Via Angelo Secchi – their pretext a boating trip on the Tiber. Twenty yards from the door on the next street corner, Höttl's driver picked them up. Minutes later Ciano, wearing green-tinted glasses, also crossed the threshold – to spring aboard the slow-moving sports car, its passenger door flung open, that idled near the kerb.

In fact, Höttl's instructions had said nothing about Ciano, but Edda had been loyally adamant. Either Galeazzo, the father of her children, came too, or the passage from Rome to Munich – thence, she hoped, to Spain and the Argentine – was off.

It had been a nightmare five-hour flight – Höttl was still shuddering at the memory. At 18,000 feet over the Alps the children, huddled on boxes in their linen shorts, had been literally blue with cold. To ward off the chill, Höttl had doled out two whole bottles of cognac provided by Skorzeny. Yet the paralysing cold, he noted, made little impression on Ciano or his wife. Almost before take-off the young Count was pulling gold cigarette-cases, bracelets and rings from his pockets, while Edda, upending her daughter's white lacquered shoulder-bag, began a brisk inventory of snuff-boxes, tie-pins and jewels.

At Riem Airport in Munich Höttl breathed a sigh of relief: his conducting officer's mission was over. But now a shock awaited him. Barely had he reached Villa Starnberg, where a cook and chamber-maid were in attendance, than a written order from Himmler was handed to him. Höttl was to stay on and await instructions.

For the first time Ciano had put the question to him point-blank: were they to consider themselves prisoners or guests?

Even then, Höttl had wondered. Himmler had given no specific orders to treat the Cianos as prisoners. Plainly Mussolini's daughter, whom Hitler esteemed enough to rescue from Badoglio, was free to travel anywhere, but since the Führer didn't yet know her husband was with her, Höttl's instinct was to keep quiet about him. It had been no easy task. Ciano's blithe disregard of elementary security was an ever-present nightmare. Armed with ration permits which State Security Chief Ernst Kaltenbrunner wheedled from the Ministry of Economics, Höttl took the family to shop at Schober, Munich's leading furrier. Suddenly, while Edda debated the merits of Persian lamb or squirrel, Ciano vanished from sight.

Sweating moments of panic followed – until Höttl ran him to earth in a changing-room, trying to date one of the models.

'Despite the blackest days, there's always a bond of understanding between us,' was the way Edda explained this ultra-modern marriage. But the SS man cautioned Ciano sharply: 'For God's sake, keep your coat-collar turned up and wear dark glasses – you're not even sup-posed to be in Germany.'

That same evening, after Ciano, disgusted with the cook's pasta, donned an apron to prepare dinner himself and then retired to bed, Höttl learned, for the first time, of the famous Ciano diaries.

It was during one of the lazy, relaxed, after-dinner conversations that he and Edda had night after night, with neither side pulling their punches on the disasters the Axis had brought about. 'For years,' Edda told him, 'we've kept a very explicit diary of everything that's happened – all the blunders. We can prove these things before history.' At once Höttl froze. If what the Countess said was true, Ciano's diaries must contain evidence that Höttl and his chief, Ernst Kaltenbrunner had long sought: irrevocable proof of the criminal folly of Joachim von Ribbentrop.

For Höttl and Kaltenbrunner the war could take only one direction from now on: northwards, out of Italy and over the Alps. Both Italy and the Axis alliance had become a dead letter, a burdensome millstone round the neck of the Third Reich. Mussolini could be safely left for the Allies – who would surely find him as much of an encumbrance as the Germans had done. But so long as Ribbentrop ruled the Foreign Ministry, no such move seemed feasible. Now Höttl saw a likely way to discredit him forever in the Führer's eyes – with Ciano's diaries furnishing chapter and verse.

At first, when he broached the subject, Ciano was wary. 'I don't think we should trouble the Colonel with our private affairs, dear,' he reproved Edda sharply. But as Höttl pressed for more details the astute Count saw the chance of a bargain. In return for services rendered, the diaries would be deposited, as down payment, in a Swiss bank. What Ciano sought in return were passports for himself and his family to the Argentine, via Spain.

Now, as Ciano and Höttl paced the lakeside, the SS man was worried. Thus far all was well. Kaltenbrunner had approved the deal; the passports were ready. But against all his advice, Edda had insisted on making the journey to see her father's old friend and ally at Rastenburg. Hitler knew well enough now that Ciano was on Lake Starnberg, for the Munich Gestapo had spotted him in a city barber's saloon and reported his presence. Plainly embarrassed, Hitler was biding his time until General Student located the Duce. But Höttl feared that Edda's untimely visit would bring the whole tender issue out into the open.

If Ciano was his prisoner he was still none the wiser. Nor did Höttl realize that he had unwittingly involved Mussolini in the most painful dilemma of his life.

She had forgotten that 1 September was her birthday, but Adolf Hitler had remembered. He was like that, Edda Ciano thought, a man who would never forget a woman's birthday, or a grudge. The two fan-shaped bouquets of blood-red roses lay before her on the polished walnut table of Hitler's Pullman saloon – parked now in the private siding, code-named 'Görlitz', a three-minute drive through the forests from the *Führersperrkreis*, the high-fenced personal compound that held Hitler's map-room and living quarters.

Unusually for him, Hitler was monosyllabic. Vittorio Mussolini, who had flown to Germany as far back as 28 July to seek help in tracing his father, said nothing either. The angry conversation now in full spate was monopolized by Edda and Joachim von Ribbentrop.

A few minutes earlier, meeting his sister outside the train for the first time in two months, Vittorio had been horrified. 'You must be out of your senses to come here!' he greeted her. 'You couldn't have made a worse choice.' Four weeks in Germany in the company of many old-guard Fascists who had fled Italy after 25 July, men like Guido Buffarini-Guidi and Roberto Farinacci, had taught Vittorio that no man was so hated and despised as Galeazzo Ciano.

Now, to his consternation, he heard his sister speak as confidently of the forthcoming trip to Spain as if Hitler himself was the travel agent. It was possible that she and Ciano would then separate, she confided, but the Count's principal wish was to write his memoirs. As a matter of business, she proposed that if the Führer could change six million lire into pesetas, the Third Reich could pocket the difference in the exchange rate.

Ribbentrop chose to misunderstand. Was Ciano dissatisfied with his quarters? 'The Count's accommodation is of the best and entirely in accordance with his position,' he stated coldly, 'Why go to Spain? In Germany he can be assured of security, and await our certain and inevitable victory.'

Shrewdly, Ribbentrop had more than an inkling of the material Ciano's memoirs would contain. It was vital, he urged Hitler, that the Count never set foot outside German-controlled territory. Unaware of Kaltenbrunner's hatred, he had even confessed to the SD Chief that Ciano, once abroad, might start 'a fearful stink' (*eine Schweinerei*) against him. Josef Goebbels, too, had supported Ribbentrop. 'The dirty scoundrel will start writing against us before he's been gone a month,' he warned.

Vittorio, yearning for a cigarette in Hitler's tobacco-free sanctum, saw that Edda was at snapping-point. They must, she insisted violently, be allowed passage to Spain. Hitler said nothing. But Ribbentrop brusquely shook his head. 'Out of the question,' he replied.

'But we're virtually prisoners,' Edda shouted at Hitler. 'What's the matter with you all? The war is already lost, don't you realize, unless you negotiate a peace with Russia?' Suddenly, Hitler's cheek muscles began to jump alarmingly, seized by an uncontrollable tic. 'Is it ever possible to mix fire and water?' he demanded harshly. 'No, never! We shall fight on the steppes of Russia, in the cities of Russia, to the last rifle shot, even to the last man, against Communism!'

As he rose, terminating the interview, Vittorio glanced covertly at his watch. Fifteen minutes – yet it had seemed to take a full hour.

Outside, the forest was pitch-black, warm and resin-scented, despite the fresh Baltic air. Sentries seemed to lurk behind every tree trunk. Wordlessly, Edda and Vittorio fumbled for cigarettes. They knew the truth now. Ciano was trapped.

The whisky was Johnnie Walker Black Label, swigged from enamel mugs. To the unwary Italian General, who had never before tasted it, it scorched the throat like liquid fire. The handshake was as lusty and forthright as Kansas itself. At 5.15 p.m. on Friday, 3 September, General Giuseppe Castellano had just signed, on behalf of Marshal Pietro Badoglio, the armistice putting Italy out of the war. And suddenly, as he toasted his new-found allies in precious Scotch, General Eisenhower himself was warmly pumping his hand.

Eisenhower had good reason to feel elated. To him this war was a 'great crusade' to free Europe once and for all from the cruel bondage of the Axis. Now, in this dusty tent, lit only by an electric bulb shielded by an inverted rations tin, sited in an olive grove at Cassibile, near Syracuse, he had witnessed one chapter of that crusade come to a triumphant end. Dapper in his blue civilian suit, Castellano had sat down at an ordinary barracks table covered with a felt cloth to sign the typed twelve-point memorandum that he now knew almost by heart. Facing him across the table, General Walter Bedell Smith, Eisenhower's brilliant Chief of Staff, put on heavy horn-rimmed spectacles to scrawl his own signature.

Within weeks, as a direct result of those signatures, the entire Italian Navy and Air Force, plus 45,000 combat volunteers would pass from the Axis to the Allies. On 13 October, Badoglio, too, would declare war on Germany.

All through the tortuous negotiations that had led up to this moment – three cloak-and-dagger weeks, in which Castellano, masquerading as 'Commander Raimondi' had shuttled from Rome

to Lisbon and back again, conferring with Allied envoys – one factor
had troubled Eisenhower. Both Bedell Smith, who had represented
him in Lisbon, and Brigadier Kenneth Strong, his British Chief of
Intelligence, had spelt out the conditions of surrender to the Italians
as crisply as Eisenhower himself had done. For Italy, no co-belliger-
ent status was remotely feasible unless Badoglio accepted whatever
surrender conditions the Allies imposed.

But acting on express instructions from Churchill and Roosevelt,
Eisenhower had to enforce two sets of conditions on the Italians – not
only the 'short term' armistice, which Castellano had just signed, but
a second 'long term' armistice, whose forty-four punitive clauses were
only now to be revealed. Designed to place Italy's political, economic
and financial affairs indefinitely under Allied control, the politicians
had feared that Badoglio would withhold his support – vital to a
successful assault on the mainland – if he knew what lay in store. With
a soldierly disdain for politics, Eisenhower had condemned it as 'a
crooked deal'. It was the reason that had brought the warm-hearted
Commander-in-Chief to Cassibile on this autumn afternoon. Unwilling to set his seal on the document himself, he was still anxious
to shake hands with an Italian who was 'trying to come out of this
thing manfully'.

Now, anxious to avoid the drama's last act, Eisenhower ducked
impulsively through the tent's V-shaped opening. Suddenly,
reaching up, he plucked a twig from the gnarled olive tree overhang-
ing the entrance. Solemnly, one by one, others followed suit. Once
more, after twenty centuries, the olive branch was again a symbol of
peace.

In the twilit tent, Bedell Smith silently handed Castellano the
bulky folder of peace terms drawn up by the State Department and
the Foreign Office. The General had guessed that more was to come.
Clause 12 of the 'short term' armistice had laid down: 'Other conditions of a political, economic and financial nature with which Italy
will be bound to comply will be transmitted at a later date.' But he
had expected nothing like this. Now, as he studied the terms of this
harsh peace, he was, Robert Murphy saw, 'visibly shaken'.

Among the welter of clauses, it was Clause 29 that leapt from the
printed page: 'Benito Mussolini . . . will forthwith be apprehended
and surrendered into the hands of the United Nations . . .'

Beneath his feet, the corvette *Baionetta* (642 tons) lit only by a dim
blue riding light, lay gently at anchor on the swell, two miles off the

Adriatic coast at Ortona. Before him, he devoutly hoped, lay refuge in some safe corner of Italy where the German writ did not yet run – he had pleaded that they flee to Tunisia or Sicily, but the King had forbidden it. Behind him, his country lay in chaos – its generals lacking precise orders, its capital city undefended, its army disintegrating hourly as the soldiers, deserted by their officers, scrambled aboard trains and lorries to make tracks for their homes.

But Marshal Pietro Badoglio, Duke of Addis Ababa, was snug and safe, clad prudently in a grey civilian suit and soft hat. At midnight on 9 September, following a headlong nineteen-hour flight from Rome, the last man to whom he gave a thought was Benito Mussolini. So precipitate had been his departure that, even now, no written orders existed to decree the Duce's fate.

At 6.30 p.m. on 8 September, Badoglio had been horrified by Eisenhower's radio announcement from Algiers that the armistice was now in being – timed, as agreed, six hours before 169,000 Allied troops spilled ashore at Salerno, thirty-three miles south of Naples. More frightening still was Eisenhower's peremptory signal that Badoglio fulfil his part of the bargain with a broadcast of his own. Though Badoglio, quaking, had been forced to comply, it was plain now that the date he had guessed at – 12 September – had been woefully wrong. Before committing his army to battle, he had sought firm assurances of a fifteen-division landing as far north as Leghorn and Ancona – assurances which had not been forthcoming. For Badoglio and the King, there was only one answer: to flee, leaving Rome to its fate.

It was as sorry a chapter as any in Italian history. As early as 5.10 a.m. on 9 September, a seven-car cortège slid away from the side entrance of Palazzo Vidoni, the Ministry of War. In the lead was the King's open 'Berlina' Fiat 2800, its mudguards bearing the blue ribbons and five gold stars of the House of Savoy. Clad in a long military raincoat that came to his ankles, the King, riding with Queen Elena and two ADCs, sat silently clutching a cheap fibre attaché-case. To the rear came other staff cars carrying Badoglio, the Duke of Acquarone, and a score of general staff officers. Among them was Crown Prince Umberto, relieved that his wife, Crown Princess Maria-José had escaped into Switzerland with their children, yet glowering and resentful, protesting repeatedly that the flight was 'shameful'.

In fact, Umberto, like every other soldier under the King's command, had no option but to obey orders – but what disgusted him and every man in the column was Badoglio's naked terror. Soon after they set off, Badoglio's car broke down, and the Marshal scrambled aboard Umberto's Alfa-Romeo 2500. In the sharp dawn he was shivering with cold; at once, Umberto peeled off his General's dress overcoat. Long after, the Prince would recall with disdain that as the Marshal put it on he was slyly rolling up the sleeves, hiding the badge of rank. 'The Germans will have the heads off all of us,' he repeated, drawing his finger across his neck like a knife-blade.

Though Badoglio didn't know it, the risk was minimal. In the chaos that followed the armistice announcement and the Allied land-ing, few German patrols even spared them a glance – and Field-Marshal Kesselring, anxious to avoid any SS coup, had deliberately issued no orders to apprehend the King or his staff officers. But all that day, convinced the Germans were hot on their heels, the party's plans veered like a compass needle. At Crecchio, 150 miles from Rome, Umberto at last hit upon a temporary headquarters – the castle of his old friends, the Duke and Duchess of Bovino. From Pescara, fourteen miles away, Acquarone, sent ahead by the King to recon-noitre, reported over a hundred planes standing by at the airport.

But closer inspection showed that none had been serviced, and at 6 p.m. the King made a firm decision. Since Admiral Raffaele de Courten, his Chief of the Navy, reported the corvette *Baionetta* was thirty miles off Pescara, the party would board her at Ortona, thirteen miles down the coast, at midnight. Meanwhile, the Royal party stayed on at Bovino castle – where the Duchess later reported that her VIP guests had consumed twenty-eight chickens through lunch and dinner.

All except Badoglio. That afternoon, when the King returned to the castle, the Marshal stayed on at the airport bar – chain-smoking, gulping cup after cup of coffee. By 8 p.m. De Courten, who had remained to keep radio contact, reported the *Baionetta* off Pescara. It was the chance the Marshal awaited. By midnight – the appointed hour of the rendezvous at Ortona – Badoglio had already been three hours aboard the corvette, gladly missing a chicken dinner in favour of a prior claim to safety.

On the dockside, conditions were chaotic. By now more than seventy cars, their headlamps dark, were packed on the slippery cobbles. Fully 250 people – staff officers, drivers, batmen, of whom no more than a quarter stood a chance of boarding the corvette –

were milling and cursing in the darkness, hastily discarding uniforms, even pigskin suitcases. Only two four-ton fishing boats at first stood by to act as ferries and above the steady putter of their engines came the hoarse cries of the townsfolk, alerted by the noise, 'Go on, leave us, but go fast – and don't bring more disgrace.'

By 12.40 a.m. the King was chafing. Still no word had come from Badoglio. 'Do you think he's betrayed us?' he asked one of his party harshly. Finally, past patience, he ordered the royal family to embark on the six-ton *Littorio*. To the King's chagrin, as the fishing-boat neared the blacked-out corvette, Badoglio's voice sounded officiously from the poop: 'Not more than thirty men aboard this ship.'

All that night the *Baionetta* ploughed southwards down the Adriatic. The King and Queen slept, huddled in deckchairs. Dawn brought the cruiser *Scipione* as escort – and disturbing news from the ship's radio. From Rome to Milan, unit after unit was surrendering as 'Operation Alaric' became reality and the Germans moved in and took over. 'It's all invented,' Badoglio, now in good heart, jocularly assured anyone who would listen to him. 'I'm a stubborn Piedmontese – I'll have the King back in Rome inside a fortnight.'

Towards 4 p.m. on 10 September, the *Baionetta* neared Brindisi, 250 miles south of Ortona, on Italy's heel. Tensely, the King's party lined the rails. De Courten signalled the port's commander, Admiral Rubartelli, asking to be met – cautiously making no mention of his cargo of fifty-seven VIPs.

As the Admiral's launch bobbed into view and Rubartelli scrambled aboard, he was flabbergasted to find himself facing the King of Italy. Vittorio Emanuele greeted him tersely: 'Are there any Germans in Brindisi?'

'No, Your Majesty.'

'British then?'

'No, Your Majesty.'

'All right, then – let's go,' said the King called 'Little Sword'.

Herbert Kappler was a sorely frustrated man. Now that 'Alaric' was accomplished fact, with the Italian troops disarmed, the King and his Ministers in headlong flight, and most of the Grand Council on the run, Kappler was giving of his brilliant best, convinced that Hitler would never restore Mussolini to power. And at 3 p.m. on 11 September, steering his Volkswagen through Rome's near-deserted streets, he was almost sure he knew where the Duce was. But 'almost' was not good enough for the meticulous General Kurt

Student. The lives of 120 of Student's men would hinge on Kappler's intricate eleventh hour calculations.

Beside him, in the passenger seat, Karl Radl, Skorzeny's dumpy, amiable Number Two, echoed his thoughts. 'Student won't risk an action unless we're positive,' Radl rubbed it in.

In silence, both men chewed over the data. It had been Student himself who had given them this latest tantalizing lead – the first to seriously engage their attention since Skorzeny's bitter disappointment at La Maddalena. To trace that mysterious Red Cross rescue plane, the General had called on the service of a JU 52 seaplane squadron, based on Lake Bracciano, thirty-two miles north of Rome. Over lunchtime coffee, before Student had even broached the reason for his visit, the commander had airily dropped a bombshell. Around mid-morning on 27 August, under cover of an air-raid alarm, a rescue plane had touched down in one of the lakeside pens. From it had stepped Mussolini – to be hustled into an ambulance which sped towards Rome.

Once more, like some story-book genie, the Duce had vanished in a magic spiral of dust.

Then Kappler had a stroke of fabulous luck. A keen colour-photographer, he often took early morning drives on the old Appian Way, both to increase his stock of slides and to meet an informer from the Ministry of Home Affairs. Around 1 September, his man handed him a radio message routed to the Ministry by a senior agent. It read: 'Security precautions round Gran Sasso d'Italia have been completed.'

Kappler and Skorzeny called for maps. Seventy miles east of Lake Bracciano, the sharp cruel spur of Monte Corno of Gran Sasso jutted 9000 feet above the sunlit plains – snow-crowned and terrible, the highest peak in all the Italian Apennines. At its foot lay a plateau, 6500 feet high, running twelve miles south-west, known as Campo Imperatore, a longtime favourite with ski-ers. Sole access to the resort's one hotel was by funicular which ran 3000 sheer feet from the village of Assergi.

Events now moved quickly. Around Assergi, Kappler's agents reported many *carabinieri* moving into billets. Checkpoints had been set up on all roads leading to the village. Angry locals claimed that the staff at Hotel Campo Imperatore had been fired without notice – to make room for the Duce. Kappler sent men foraging for hotel prospectuses and tourist maps at every Rome travel agency. Curiously, all such literature had vanished from their counters.

Now Student tried a tack of his own. To Leutnant Leo Krutoff of the 11th Air Corps' medical staff went a priority briefing: to find a convalescent home for urgent malaria cases. 'There's a hotel on Gran Sasso,' Student told him. 'Whatever the circumstances, you must inspect it yourself. Don't let them turn you back.' When he hinted that 'a person of high standing' was being kept there, Krutoff had more than an inkling of the job ahead.

At the funicular's Assergi Valley Station, Krutoff found the *carabinieri* cold-eyed, unfriendly. Requests to board the cable-car were met with a curt: 'Impossible!' Pulling his rank and expounding his mission, the medical officer insisted on direct contact with the officer in charge at Campo Imperatore. The non-com cranked an old-fashioned wall phone, haggling at length with a voice 3000 feet above them in the mountains. Abruptly, replacing the receiver, he told Krutoff: '*Signor tenente*, if you don't leave at once I'll have to arrest you.'

Hearing this, Student nodded thoughtfully, smiling, before dismissing Krutoff. There could be no doubting the Duce was a prisoner in that mountain fortress – but how long before they once more spirited him away? All plans for a daring rescue operation were now laid. But could he be finally sure enough to give the green light?

As the Volkswagen cruised into Piazza del Viminale this same question was bedevilling the minds of Radl and Kappler. It was just then, Karl Radl always remembered, that both men spotted a group of uniformed officers outside the Ministry of Home Affairs. In their midst was a middle-aged man with a toothbrush moustache, wearing civilian clothes. 'That's General Soleti of the *carabinieri*,' Kappler told him, and at once Radl ribbed him, 'Well, why don't you ask *him* where Mussolini is?' On impulse, Kappler agreed to the bluff. He cut the Volkswagen's engine. Descending, the Germans strode across to Soleti. Without preliminaries, Kappler taxed him: 'Where is Mussolini?'

'I don't know,' Soleti replied. The smile on Kappler's lips did not touch his ice-blue eyes. 'You're a liar,' he said evenly, holding Soleti's gaze. There was a small shocked pause.

'Well,' the General admitted lamely, after a moment, 'I know where he was *yesterday* – because I sent provisions up to the Hotel Imperatore.'

Without a word, Kappler turned on his heel. The thought crossed Radl's mind almost the moment they were out of earshot. 'I'll take that General to the Gran Sasso,' he vowed, 'but this time in uniform.'

It was late when Leutnant Elimar Meyer-Wehner stole into the briefing-room. At 11 a.m. on Sunday, 12 September, almost five hours after the scheduled time, the first HE 126 towing-planes ordered from Marseilles were finally touching down at Pratica di Mare. Now, having checked his own glider in position, the young pilot was hurrying to catch the last of General Student's briefing at Traffic Control. As he silently took his place, Wehner, catching the General's first words, gasped with astonishment '. . . Then I must once again point out that we must risk this operation on the basis of very defective data. The latest information about the Gran Sasso is already some days old . . .'

The briefing-room was absolutely hushed now. Thirty-six men – towing pilots, glider pilots, military commanders – were listening in tense silence. With increasing bewilderment, Wehner heard Student continue: 'Whether Mussolini is still there is rather uncertain . . .' But how, he wondered, did Mussolini get into this? All along Wehner had thought his outfit, the 1st Airborne Wing, was going to fight the Americans at Salerno.

A few whispered queries, and the newcomer was quickly in the picture. Suddenly he knew he was up to his neck in one of the war's riskiest exploits. At 12.30 p.m., twelve HE 126s would be airborne from Pratica with a dozen frail DFS 230 gliders in tow. Each of these light fabric and steel-tubing structures would carry, with their pilot, ten armed men, either paratroopers or Skorzeny's SS men. One hour later, at 3600 feet above Gran Sasso, the towing-planes would cast off their cargo. Then 108 men – including Wehner himself – would be alone to face the deadly mountains and whatever fire Mussolini's captors might bring to bear.

Student's voice still, high-pitched and paternal: 'Keep your nerve – this operation will be executed as a peacetime manoeuvre. The surprise will be so great that probably no shot will be fired by the Italians. You have only to concentrate where you land and keep to your landing-places . . .'

Immobile before the wall-map, the General watched the crews exchange glances. A glider pilot who had crashed as far back as 1920, Student knew just how they felt. Yet he faced a dreadful dilemma. A ground-based thrust against the valley station was out from the start – all too soon the *carabinieri* could immobilize the funicular. And aerial reconnaissance proved a drop was out of the question; air currents would swirl most of the parachutists into the terrible fissures below Monte Corno. That limited it to gliders, but even now his technical experts forecast eighty per cent casualties. The craft, delayed by technical snags in southern France, should have been on tow fully six hours earlier before the peril of thermals – currents of warm air rising to meet the icy air of the upper reaches – could heel a DFS clean over like a suddenly-tilted tray.

Now Student's Intelligence Officer, Hauptmann Gerhard Langguth, took over the briefing. Due to Hitler's espionage veto, no aerial reconnaissance pictures of Gran Sasso had existed until 8 September, the day of the armistice. Then Langguth and Skorzeny in a Heinkel 111 had carried out two hasty over-flights. But the angle had been bad on the first; too high, at 4000 feet, on the second – worse still, a murderous Allied bombing of Kesselring's Frascati headquarters had knocked out the photographic laboratory. From a makeshift lab, experts had prepared the smudgy 8in × 8in prints the pilots now saw.

Craning closer, glider pilot Wehner saw little cause for comfort. Towards the left-hand corner, a dark smudge – most certainly the hotel, for a white concrete terrace rimmed its southern face, ending in the funicular. The rest was a lunar landscape, its contours flattened unnaturally, scarred by the white seams of torrents that ran in crazy patternless directions. Only one oblong patch, to the west, suggested a stretch of tarmac, the one likely landing spot.

Methodically, Otto Skorzeny checked off details with Leutnant Otto von Berlepsch, commanding the operation's seventy-five paratroopers. As the one man, apart from Skorzeny and Radl, who had ever glimpsed the target, Langguth would travel in the navigator's cockpit of the first towing-plane. Gliders 1 and 2 would be manned by Berlepsch's paratroopers; gliders 3 and 4 by SS men dressed as Luftwaffe officers, under Skorzeny and Radl. The task of these men was to storm and occupy the hotel and disarm the *carabinieri*. At the same time paratroopers approaching from Assergi, under Major Otto-Harald Mors, would seize the valley station. If the Duce was found, Student had made Skorzeny responsible for his personal safety.

No man must fire a shot unless alerted by a red Very light – but if the plan went awry, the remaining paratroopers were to pin down the Italians with mortars and machine-guns. At a given moment, General Ferdinando Soleti – already known to the *carabinieri* and booked to travel in Skorzeny's glider – could effectively intervene.

And this morning, it seemed to Karl Radl, pacing beside Soleti outside the briefing-room, that the General, happily labouring under a delusion, was the calmest man present. He had readily agreed to drive to Pratica to see Student – indignant that German paratroopers had disarmed his *carabinieri*. Placating him with vague promises that the arms would be restored, Student told him: 'Before discussing this, we are going to liberate Mussolini. I presume you'll be glad to see him and shake his hand?'

Soleti agreed so readily that the impossible now struck Radl. The General thought they were going by car.

Suddenly the air-raid sirens wailed. The ack-ack roared into life. At 12.30 p.m., take-off time, wave after wave of RAF bombers hit the airfield. Hugging the ground, Radl found Skorzeny beside him. Straining his lungs, he yelled out the password that the SS had chosen as their own for this operation: 'Take it easy!' Skorzeny grinned back in reply. But precious time had passed before the all-clear warbled, and now some gliders had suffered minor damage. Student ordered half-an-hour's delay.

In a bumpy sheep-pasture at Castel Gandolfo, thirty miles from the airfield, Hauptmann Heinrich Gerlach was just then glancing at his watch. As Student's personal pilot, the slim thirty-year-old Gerlach had been allotted a vital role in Mussolini's rescue. At 12.30 p.m. when the towing-planes left Pratica, Gerlach was to take off from this makeshift airstrip in a tiny Fieseler-Storch spotter plane, arriving over the target at the identical moment as the paratroopers.

Except for a helicopter, the Fieseler was the one plane that could land in a confined space and take off with a minimal runway – and Gerlach had good reason to be sure he was on time. If all went well, his passenger on the return flight would be Benito Mussolini.

Soon after 12.30 p.m. he was clambering into the Storch's cockpit. In one hour's time, with luck, he would be over Gran Sasso. Away at Pratica, all telephone contact with the sheep-pasture had been cut off by the earlier Frascati raid – and there was now no way to tell Gerlach that the rescue had been postponed by half an hour.

As petulant as a thwarted child, Mussolini swept the solitaire cards from the green baize table. Rumpled, unshaven, his black eyes enormous in his sallow face, he rounded furiously on sheep-breeder Alfonso Nisi. 'You and your damned false prophecies,' he exclaimed shrilly. 'You're trying to make a fool of me.'

In Room 201, the Duce's low-ceilinged one-room apartment at Hotel Campo Imperatore, the old farmer regarded him sorrowfully.

Four days earlier, tending his flocks at their summer pasturage nearby, he had met Mussolini for the first time, when Lieutenant Alberto Faiola, commander of the seventy-strong security guard, had suggested he might at times keep the Duce company. Nisi had agreed, though finding him irritable and dejected by turns – until the Duce, hearing of his skill, had begged him to read his future in the cards.

To pacify him – for Mussolini had refused to touch his lunch – Nisi had laid out the cards and spelt out the banal message he read into them: 'You are due to be rescued in rather romantic circumstances.' But the Duce's instant reaction was this puerile outburst of rage.

In truth, the man Nisi saw before him, in his creased shiny blue suit and scuffed shoes, was a man who no longer believed in rescue. He was a broken peasant cursing the fates, acknowledging his own rueful destiny. In the night just past, following a radio announcement that Badoglio planned to hand him over to the Allies, he had made a pathetically amateurish attempt to gash his left wrist with a razor blade – at once summoning Faiola, who treated the superficial scratch with iodine. He was a far cry from the prisoner who, at Legnano Barracks, had perplexedly asked a *carabiniere*: 'Why doesn't the band play "*Giovinezza*" any more?' Gone was the wounded pride of the captive on Ponza, whose face puckered resentfully when a nun told a band of saluting schoolchildren: 'We don't do that any more, boys.' This was a man who no longer believed in rescue.

Heinrich Gerlach found it hard to believe, too. At this very moment, his Storch was hovering at over nine thousand feet, lonely as a bird, on the far side of the mountain – using the cold stark spur of Monte Corno as a screen between himself and the hotel's guards. But already this grim game of hide-and-seek had lasted half-an-hour and Gerlach's fuel was perilously low. A Storch's flying time was three-and-a-half hours – too little to cruise in circles awaiting gliders that didn't come.

Suddenly, as he slid round the peak, using the updraughts of the crosswinds to save petrol, Gerlach saw them. Two gliders! My God, he thought, only two – did they bomb the others? Can eighteen paratroopers pull it off? If they could, Gerlach decided, then he would be with them.

Otto Skorzeny felt mortally afraid. It was all going terribly wrong. For some reason he couldn't fathom, minutes after the flight began, the first towing-plane, Langguth's, had made a left-hand circuit over Tivoli, then vanished from sight. In fact, fearful of thermals, Langguth had given a hand signal to gain altitude, and now with the second towing-plane in his wake, was flying to the rear. But all Skorzeny knew was that his was now the lead glider. Ahead the Henschel had let go the fifty-foot wire tow-rope; the glider jerked sickeningly downwards. Straddled on the crossbars, each clinging to the other, Skorzeny's men heard no sound at all but the crying of the wind in their ears.

In the cockpit ahead of Skorzeny, pilot Meyer-Wehner checked aerial photo and map. The black spot was taking shape – a white, squat, horseshoe-shaped building. They were diagonally over it at 450 feet; tiny ant-men were spilling from its main doors. In that moment Wehner and all the pilots saw the 'oblong stretch of tarmac' for the cheat and the snare that it was. Their cherished landing-ground was the main ski-run.

The ground was racing to meet them now, scrub, parched grass and boulders, nearer by the second at fifty miles an hour, and Wehner made the split-second decision. He jerked the glider sharply upwards, jolting the crew painfully against their seats, and in that instant the brake flaps went out. In a grinding, rending landfall, 2000 pounds of men and glider struck the ground, the barbed wire that wrapped its skids to shorten the sliding distance snapping like twine as the deadly rocks bit into it. Swaying and shuddering, splintering like matchboard, it wrenched to a halt, sunlight flooding in to blind them, barely twenty yards from the hotel's terrace.

Inside the building, Inspector-General Giuseppe Gueli reached a swift decision. A written order from the Chief of Staff to the *carabinieri* in Rome had specified only one course to follow in event of a rescue attempt: Mussolini was to be gunned down. But Badoglio's flight had made all of them jumpy and already, as the Germans took over, police headquarters in Rome were counselling 'extreme prudence'. Stark naked in his third-floor room, enjoying a siesta as the gliders skidded to a halt, Gueli leapt from his bed just as Lieutenant Faiola crashed in. 'What do we do?' Faiola asked, and Gueli ordered: 'Give up without hesitation.' Both men hung frantically from the window, shouting 'Don't shoot! Don't shoot!' as the rescuers streaked for the hotel. In the vanguard came General Soleti, as white as a sheet after the most terrifying flight of his life, screaming the same instructions. At his second-floor window, Mussolini's bald head was plainly visible as he called: 'Do not shed blood!'

Pandemonium reigned. All over the plateau the gliders were

smashing to a halt; the roar of the towing-planes' engines rolled like thunder from the mountains. Boots shattered on the hotel's steel-treaded stairs; guard-dogs yelped hysterically in the cellars below. Obersturmführer Karl Menzel, heaving from his glider, was so stirred by the sound of battle and his first-ever glimpse of Mussolini than he let loose with a stentorian 'Heil, Duce!' Then a searing pain shot up his right leg. Toppling unwarily into a ditch, he had broken his ankle.

Otto Skorzeny, followed by his tough non-com, Otto Schwerdt, rushed for the main building. At the same moment both men glimpsed through an open door a soldier hunched over a transmitter. One swipe from Schwerdt's boot sent the stool flying from under him: the butt of Skorzeny's P.38 machine-pistol, all its owner's 206 pounds behind it, smashed downwards on the terminals. No warning could reach the outside world now. But the radio-room gave no entry to the main hotel. A non-com offered a back and Skorzeny scaled the nine-foot terrace. Panting, sweating men clambered after him. Up to now, not a shot had been fired.

Racing anti-clockwise along the terrace, Skorzeny reached the main entrance. A surge of *carabinieri* in grey-green blocked his path, fighting to get out. Again he clubbed with his machine-pistol, beating his way against a tide of men. Schwerdt followed, shouting *'Mani in alto!'* (Hands up.)

Ahead, to the right, was a staircase. Taking the stairs three at a time, Skorzeny pounded up it, Schwerdt still behind him. His would be the honour of liberating Mussolini now – nothing could stop him. On the second floor, obeying instinct, he flung open the door of Room 201. One quick glance took in the scene: a small hallway with a hatstand and wardrobe, a yellow-tiled bathroom annex, double-bed, leather easy-chair, a photo of Bruno Mussolini framed in black. In the centre of the room, three men, staring at him dumbfounded – Gueli, Faiola and Mussolini. Yes, it *was* Mussolini – as a tourist, Skorzeny had seen him in 1934 on Palazzo Venezia's balcony. Yet it was hard to recognize 'this old, broken prisoner' as the unchallenged Duce of Fascism.

With a fine instinct for an entrance line, Skorzeny introduced himself: 'Duce, the Führer sent me! You are free!' Fervently Mussolini embraced and kissed him, exclaiming: 'I knew my friend Adolf Hitler would not leave me in the lurch.'

Just four minutes earlier, Skorzeny calculated, his glider had hit the ground.

Now a strange lull fell upon the plateau as men realized for the first time what they had accomplished. Only Glider No 8 had been badly smashed up with casualties. Herded into the main dining-room, the *carabinieri* had been disarmed without resistance. A white bedspread flung from a window signified surrender; on another bedspread, stretched out as marker on the plateau, Gerlach brought the Storch gingerly in to land. Upstairs a *carabiniere* handed Skorzeny a goblet of red wine, announcing chivalrously: 'To the victor!'

In Assergi's Valley Station, the phone shrilled and Major Mors leapt to answer it. It was Otto von Berlepsch, announcing 'Mission fulfilled. The Duce's alive.' Mors could scarcely take it in. They had triumphed – and the clock on the wall showed only 2.17 p.m.

Deputizing for Skorzeny, Karl Radl found himself alone with Mussolini. A few moments' small talk, then Radl sensed a rekindling of the old Mussolinian bombast.

'And what are my Romans doing?' he asked pompously.

Radl was brutally frank. 'Looting, Duce.'

Mussolini made a gesture of irritation. 'I don't mean the looters. I mean the true Fascists.'

'We didn't find any, Duce,' Radl told him. Suddenly, he noted, Mussolini looked 'old and sad'.

It was time to go. And now, at 3 p.m., the Duce needed all the cool courage he could muster. The paratroops and SS men were leaving too, but by an easier route – four at a time down the funicular, with an Italian soldier as hostage on each trip, until the last men down destroyed the switchgear. But for a prize as great as Benito Mussolini, a road journey through 100 miles of unknown territory was too risky. Gerlach's Storch offered the only way out – and as a pilot with 17,000 flying hours, Mussolini knew just what dangers were involved.

A moment earlier, from the valley, had come alarming news. As arranged, a second Storch had left the sheep pasture at the same time as Gerlach, landing near the funicular. But now its pilot radioed that he had damaged a wheel. There was no way to take Otto Skorzeny, Mussolini's conducting officer, to Pratica di Mare, from where he was to fly on with the Duce in a Heinkel to Aspern airfield, Vienna.

Suddenly, to Gerlach's horror, Skorzeny came to a decision. He too, he argued, must fly with the Duce. Gerlach refused categorically. The Storch was a two-seater. How could it accommodate pilot, passenger and the fifteen-stone Skorzeny? The giant Austrian fought him tooth and nail. 'You're going alone by air,' he urged. 'How much flying time have you got? Suppose something happens on the way and you're killed. If so, he's alone in a desert. And if he's lost and I fail in my duty to the Führer, I have to put a pistol to my head.'

Gerlach was distraught with worry. As *carabinieri* and paratroopers, chatting and joking, posed for a war correspondent's camera, he once more paced out the primitive 200-yard downhill runway they had cleared for him – by moving away the larger boulders. Above him Monte Corno soared sheer to the autumn sky. No take-off was possible in that direction. Instead, Gerlach must take off with the perilous north-east wind behind him – the engine at full throttle, brakes on, until the moment of taxi-ing forward. With luck, the Storch would be airborne by the time the runway petered out – on the lip of the ravine.

But with Skorzeny aboard, they didn't stand a chance. Striding angrily back, Gerlach told him as much.

Still Skorzeny argued. Hitler would never forgive such an end to the venture. Whatever befell the Duce, he must share it. He persisted for so long that finally Gerlach snapped: 'Well, for God's sake come – but if something happens on take-off, it's *my* responsibility.'

Thankfully Skorzeny clambered aboard, his vast frame bent double, crouched behind the passenger seat. Clad in a shabby blue topcoat and soft brown hat, Mussolini followed. The Storch's engines were roaring now, drowning out the mingled cries of '*Evviva*' and '*Heil!*' 'Hold tight to the struts!' Gerlach warned his passengers. As the plane jerked forward the paratroopers gave it the Roman salute.

Standing guard over the Duce's suitcases, which he was personally escorting to Rocca delle Caminate, Karl Radl watched them go – juddering away down the slope at 100 mph. Abruptly, like a puppet with its strings cut, he collapsed on Mussolini's luggage. Five yards from the edge, Gerlach had put his flaps down, trying to bring the Storch up, yanking with all his force on the stick. Suddenly, with an unholy jar, the right wheel struck a rock. The left wing canted downwards. Next instant the Storch bounced crookedly off the edge of the ravine, plummeting towards the valley like a lift out of control.

Skorzeny cried out sharply. Mussolini said nothing. But now the determined Gerlach pushed the stick forward, increasing the Storch's speed, waiting for the slipstream to raise the wings level until suddenly, at maximum speed, he could pull the plane from the dive. Now, flying all the time against the wind, they swooped at 100 feet

over farms and vineyards translucent with golden grapes, heading for
Rome. Suddenly, to Skorzeny's astonishment, Mussolini began a
non-stop running commentary like an excursion pilot: 'That's
L'Aquila – I addressed a huge crowd there twenty years ago . . .'
Towards 5.30 p.m. they touched down at Pratica di Mare in a risky,
rocketing, two-point landing, the oil feed leaking, a starboard strut
crumpled beyond recognition.

Pumping Gerlach's hand, Mussolini said in German, a language
he would now have urgent reasons to perfect: 'Thank you for my life.'

If the car hadn't broken down, she might never have heard the
speech. In the recreation room, a radio was blaring all the old marches
of Fascist times, but there had been no mention of a speech.

It was 9.30 p.m. on 18 September. In the tall hangar of an airfield
near Bergamo, north-east of Milan, German mechanics were fixing
the Petaccis' car. Thirty-six days earlier the Badoglio government
had flung four of them – the Professor, plump anxious Mama,
Claretta and Myriam – into a stinking cell nine feet square in Novara
Jail. But once the Germans took control in Italy, Claretta's brother,
thirty-three-year-old Marcello, now a naval lieutenant, had secured
their release. They had been en route to Marcello's home at Merano,
in the Adige Valley, when the car had broken down and their German
escort brought them to the airfield.

Myriam never caught what it was the announcer had said. It was
the voice which followed that held her spellbound – drained – lifeless,
a dead man's voice. 'Blackshirts,' it said suddenly. 'Men and women
of Italy. After a long silence you hear my voice once again, which
I am sure you recognize . . .'

With a strangled cry Claretta bolted from the hangar. Following her
to the recreation room, Myriam saw that she had fallen on her
knees before the radio – her arms encircling it as if it had been a
child. Only the gist of the speech came home to her: from Radio
Munich, Mussolini was calling on all Italians to unite again under
his leadership in a Republican Fascist Party. Then the radio, the
walls of the room, rocked before Claretta's eyes.

Myriam's arms were there to catch her as she fainted.

9. 'You Must Drink the Cup of Bitterness . . .'

12 September, 1943–23 January, 1944

Three days before Mussolini's momentous broadcast, the talks which made it inevitable had already been concluded. Soon after 2 p.m. on Tuesday, 14 September, after travelling with Otto Skorzeny via Vienna and Munich (where Rachele and the children brought from Rocca delle Caminate by a SS unit awaited him), the Duce had been closeted with Hitler in his private quarters in the *Führer-sperrkreis* at Rastenburg.

On the surface, the reunion of the two ageing dictators on the Rastenburg airstrip had been as cordial as could be. General Karl Wolff, newly-appointed Commander of the SS and police in Italy, never forgot 'the beam transfiguring the Duce's sunken ravaged face' as he came down from the Heinkel, the tears streaming from his eyes. 'Führer, how can I thank you for all you have done?' Wolff heard him exclaim. 'From now on I shall do everything in my power to remedy my mistakes.' Hitler, too, seemed deeply moved, stepping impulsively forward to grasp Mussolini's hands.

Like old friends, too, they retired to Hitler's private sitting-room, a bright, airy, chalet-type retreat furnished in blond woodwork with pastel curtains. A low round table, flanked by easy chairs, was set before a crackling fire – the kind of deep comfortable chairs that seem made for old friends to chat in.

Weary, depressed, racked by acute pain that he feared was stomach cancer, Mussolini was in no shape to discuss the Italian situation. Above all, he prayed for rest and retreat. But soon enough, as he was to tell his family and collaborators, Hitler was offering him no respite. For the best of strategic reasons, the Führer had need of Italy; not only was her northern industrial potential unimpaired, but her disbanded army was a rich source of slave labour. Then, too, her natural defences – Monte Cassino, north-west of Naples, the so-called 'Gothic Line', stretching from Pisa to Rimini, unbroken until September 1944 – offered Germany precious time in the battle for Europe: time to contest the Po Valley before an ultimate withdrawal

to the Alps. But just as in Hungary and elsewhere, a puppet state
had need of a puppet ruler: Benito Mussolini.

Reproaches in plenty were heaped on his head – Badoglio's
capitulation had gravely damaged the German war effort. In Germany, too, there had been moral repercussions. There were even
flashes of irony. 'What is this Fascism,' Hitler asked, 'that it melts
like snow under the sun?' Mussolini listened in silence, hoping that
soon it would end.

Then, with uncharacteristic brevity, Hitler came sharply to the
point. 'We cannot lose a single day,' he said energetically. 'It is
essential that by tomorrow evening you make a radio announcement
that the monarchy is abolished and that an Italian Fascist State with
powers centred upon you has taken its place. In this way you will
guarantee the full validity of the German-Italian alliance.'

Mussolini gestured feebly. He would need, he said, a few days
in which to reflect. Hitler's voice, rising sharply, cut his short. '*I* have
already reflected – and enough. You'll proclaim yourself Duce once
again. Then you will be, just as I am, both Head of State and of
the Government. And its constitution must be provided for within
one week.'

The ruthless Hitler now stipulated other conditions. Most of the
'traitors of the Grand Council' had managed to flee from Italy. Dino
Grandi and his family had escaped to Lisbon on false passports
provided by the King; Alberto de Stefani, an old friend of Chiang
Kai-Shek, was hiding in the Chinese Embassy to the Vatican;
Umberto Albini had also taken refuge in the Vatican. Giuseppe
Bottai had vanished – later he was to enrol under an assumed name
in the Foreign Legion. But one of the first acts of the new government
must be to put the finger on all who could still be reached – Count
Galeazzo Ciano, 'a traitor four times over', above all.

'If I had been in your place, probably nothing would have pre-
vented me from dealing with him with my own hands,' Hitler told
his appalled junior partner. 'But I am returning him to you because
it is preferable that the death sentence should be carried out in Italy.'

Mussolini protested vigorously. At Munich's Government
Guest House, he had met Ciano again at Edda's express request – an
interview as embarrassing as any Otto Skorzeny had ever witnessed.
'I won't stay to see him,' Rachele had shouted violently. 'I'll spit in
his face if he comes near me.' And, followed by her daughter, she
stormed from the room. Mussolini had stayed – to hear out in icy
silence his son-in-law's voluble explanation that he had only acted

as a patriot. Yet Hitler's demand that Ciano forfeit his life, the Führer told Josef Goebbels later, was more than Mussolini could stomach.

'This is the husband of my daughter, whom I adore, this is the father of my grandchildren,' was the Duce's shocked reaction. Then, Hitler replied implacably, Ciano deserved punishment all the more – 'not only because he betrayed his country, but also his family.' Almost pityingly he added: 'Duce, you are too good – you can never be a dictator.'

Now that the situation was outside his control, Mussolini characteristically sought to evade responsibility. He no longer, he told Hitler, had any personal ambitions. Fascism was beyond all mortal aid. He could not assume responsibility for unleashing a civil war. Yet all through he had the impression Hitler was barely listening. 'I must be very clear,' the Führer said. 'If the Western allies had been able to exploit it, the Italian betrayal might have brought about an instant collapse of Germany. My intention was at once to give a terrible example of punishment in order to intimidate our other allies.'

On that note of suspense, he abruptly broke off the talks. Yet Mussolini had a presentiment of what was to come. That night Vittorio, who shared his father's frugal dinner in his private chalet, recalled how the Duce sank despondently into the deep armchair he affected to despise. 'Are we supposed to stand at the window,' he asked suddenly 'and watch while they burn down the house?'

At 11 a.m. on 15 September he returned to the Führer's Tea House. There, in harsh spare syllables, Hitler spelt out the fate that awaited Northern Italy if Mussolini withheld his consent. Harking back to the Reprisals Air Fleet he had mentioned over luncheon at Feltre, he defined them as 'devilish arms', designed for the destruction of London. Clenching his right hand slowly into a fist, he all at once snapped wide his fingers to symbolize this reign of terror. 'It is up to you,' he challenged Mussolini, 'to decide whether these weapons . . . are to be used on London, or tried out first on Milan, Genoa or Turin.'

Never once, the Duce maintained, did Hitler allow him any other choice. It was a punitive plan in embryo – due to be carried out the very hour Mussolini disappointed his longtime friend. 'Northern Italy will envy the fate of Poland if you do not agree to honour the alliance,' Hitler wound up. 'In such an event, naturally Ciano will not be handed over to you – he will be hanged here in Germany.'

Was Hitler bluffing? Mussolini could not know. He was in any case too tired and disillusioned to view the situation clearly. Nor did he even know that if Student's rescue plan had failed, two other Fascists had been on the short list as Gauleiters of Northern Italy: former Minister of Agriculture Giuseppe Tassinari, dismissed by Hitler after half-an-hour as a 'typical professor and theorist', and Roberto Farinacci. But Farinacci's venomous personal attack on his old chief so angered Hitler that he sprang to his feet shouting: 'I forbid you to speak like that of Mussolini!' To his undying mortification, Cremona's party boss was hustled like a schoolboy from Hitler's presence.

Now, after forty-three days as Badoglio's prisoner, Mussolini had returned to fill the uneasy role of puppet governor that Hitler had all along kept open for him. Some time before noon on 15 September, he told Hitler: 'I'll take in hand the direction of Italian affairs in that part of the country which has not yet been invaded.'

Within days, in one more attempt to bolster his crippled self-esteem, he was consoling himself that in the republican government he had 'created a shield for the protection of Italy'.

More shrewdly, Josef Goebbels noted that Hitler was at last beginning to write off the Duce politically. Long after midnight, the Führer and the gnome-like Goebbels paced the concrete-roofed map room, debating Mussolini's present sphere of usefulness. Goebbels could see that Hitler was strangely regretful – how could he ever have re-armed the Reich or annexed Austria without the Duce? Yet despite all services rendered, the time had come for the parting of the ways.

Towards 4 a.m. Hitler, in one cogent sentence, summed up the stark reality overshadowing the 600 days that Mussolini had still to reign. 'The Duce,' he told the approving Goebbels, 'has no great political future.'

Mentore Ruffilli rotated the desk calendar. A kaleidoscope of days passed before him – then 25 July gave place to 23 September. Eight weeks and five days since the young houseman had gone about his duties at Rocca delle Caminate – yet here was the Duce once again regarding him, his eyes 'like pinpoints', a rare glass of Spumante in his hand. 'Well, young man,' Ruffilli recalls his jaunty enquiry, 'how's it going?' Then abruptly, as his eye caught the glint of binoculars through the window-pane, his expression changed. On the terrace outside, black-garbed SS guards were scanning the sky, alert for any aerial counter-coup the Allies might stage.

'So high,' Mussolini muttered disgustedly, 'and now so low.'

His stable world had shifted irremediably, and he knew it. Five days earlier, installed with his family at Schloss Hirschberg, near Weilheim in Southern Bavaria, he had picked up the one Category 'A' military telephone Hitler ever allowed him to resume contact with his diplomats – and heard them rebuff him almost to a man. From Madrid, his old mentor, the Marchese Paulucci di Calboli, who had lectured him on the niceties of wearing spats and drinking soup: 'I don't consider myself free from my oath to the Crown.' Renato Bova-Scoppa, from Bucharest: 'Mussolini? Impossible, he's a prisoner – I can't hear very well at this end.' In Berne, Massimo Magistrati: 'The war's finished, lost. Frankly, Switzerland will want no representative of yours here.'

Now, on this mellow autumn day, leaving Rachele and the children at Weilheim, he had flown back to his native Romagna, clad in a borrowed black shirt, with no more than 15,000 lire in his wallet. Facing him now was the bitter truth that he must embrace any collaborators who sought him out – after the Germans had first screened them for suitability. In the days of his power, fully 2400 correspondents had claimed some blood-relationship with him: now the flood of begging letters had halted like a dammed torrent. After 25 July, Badoglio had imprisoned 850 Fascist bigwigs in Rome's Forte Boccea – yet out of forty names the Duce had picked to form his government, only three had accepted. A city-wide recruiting campaign to flesh out a new Militia produced fifteen lonely volunteers.

Even his Minister of Defence and Chief of the General Staff, the neurotic, white-haired Marshal Rodolfo Graziani, had been brutally thrust upon him by Hitler. 'He does not enjoy my confidence,' the Führer admitted, 'because his true feelings are anti-German. But no other general can claim his prestige and popularity. The acceptance of Graziani is an indispensable condition of my renouncing any reprisals plan.'

Like many of Mussolini's new cabinet, Graziani had personal reasons for accepting: his life-long hatred for Pietro Badoglio. So insanely jealous of Badoglio that he once sent his horse to represent him in a parade he couldn't attend, Graziani was again ready to rob the Marshal of his share of the limelight. Others saw fat pickings from the new regime, like Guido Buffarini-Guidi, the beringed, unwashed

Tuscan, Mussolini's reluctant choice as Minister of Home Affairs. Some had old scores to settle: Alessandro Pavolini, the squat, moustached, gutter Robespierre who was now Party Secretary, nourished a life-long envy of the playboy whose protégé he had been, Galeazzo Ciano.

But as the new ministers arrived at La Rocca on 27 September for their first Council and an inaugural luncheon – pasta served on cracked blue china – few echoed Pavolini's exultant cry: 'It's worth risking everything to live this hour.' It was a last-ditch stand, and all of them knew it. To prepare La Rocca for the Duce's return, Buffarini and his strongarm men had wrested everything – cars, food, even scrubbing-brushes – at pistol-point from the hostile Romagnols.

'My ship set sail with the survivors of a shipwreck,' Mussolini was to sum up sourly. 'They were not all the crème de la crème.'

If he dreamed of a triumphant return to Palazzo Venezia, he was swiftly disillusioned. Von Mackensen's successor, Rudolf Rahn, a shrewd, beetle-browed diplomat, had urged that the Duce should never again set foot in Rome. Not only, he told Hitler, was it impossible to guarantee Mussolini's safety. For Kesselring to maintain law and order with the Duce in the capital would pose a grave problem.

Rahn had won the day. Though no one bothered to tell Mussolini for eight days after his first Council, the Germans had picked the rambling Villa Feltrinelli, on the western shore of Lake Garda, 500 miles from Rome, as his new residence – with offices at Villa Orsoline, a few hundred yards along the lake. Nearby, the town of Salò gave its name to the puppet 'Salò Republic' – which many Italians called 'the republic of Cain'.

The fear that the Germans would tie his hands with silken ropes was strong in Mussolini before ever he set foot beside Lake Garda. On 27 September, when his Ministers had departed, he sat down at his desk to write a long pleading letter to Adolf Hitler. 'The Republican Government . . . has only one desire, one single wish,' he wrote, 'and that is that Italy takes its place again as quickly as possible in the field. But in order to achieve this supreme aim, it is necessary that the German military authorities limit their activities to the military field only. For the rest, they should let the Italian civil authorities function . . .

'Should this not be realized, Italian and world public opinion would judge the Government incapable of governing, and the Government itself would fall into discredit again, and, even worse, into ridicule . . .'

On the very morning that Mussolini addressed this appeal to Hitler, lawyer Renato Sansone was trudging wearily from Naples's Public Tribunal towards his home in the Vomero, a hillside suburb three miles west. Halfway there – for all public transport had ceased – Sansone saw that ahead of him black-clad S S men had cordoned off Piazza Dante. At once swerving into a side street, he ran for his life, pounding over the cobbles.

Panting east and then north, Sansone at last reached the silent Via San Giuseppe dei Nudi. Only a few women, cowled and expressionless, stood watching from their doorways. But as he hastened on, one called to him: 'Where are you going, sir? To Via Salvator Rosa? The Germans are taking the men there, too.'

With this she hustled him almost bodily into her low-roofed dwelling, smuggling him behind a massive teak wardrobe. Huddled there in dry-mouthed silence, the lawyer realized suddenly that inside the wardrobe another man was concealed. And beneath the ample iron bedstead he espied the boots of two more. The woman, meanwhile, was keeping watch at the door.

For a long time – was it half-an-hour? an hour? – everything was quiet. Then, far away up the street, a woman cried: 'You can come out – the bastards have gone.' As Sansone emerged along with his companions, he saw to his astonishment, fifty other men of all ages and sizes duck blinking into the sunlight from doors along the street, then fearfully take to their heels.

All over the sprawling sun-drenched seaport, almost 200,000 men were entering on their twentieth day in hiding. Some were roosting like bats in gloomy caves and grottoes, in church crypts and in the cold stone channels of the sewers. Others were hidden on the top floors of abandoned buildings, alerted for a sudden getaway over the roof-tops. The luckiest ones had comfortable beds at the city's Hospital Cardarelli – where the chief intern thoughtfully arranged appendectomies for any fleeing the Germans.

That the fugitives had multiplied ever since the armistice was due to two men – Gauleiter Fritz Sauckel, Hitler's slave labour boss for occupied Europe, who was preparing to ship 600,000 Italian prisoners to Germany, and Colonel Scholl, Naples's spruce, smiling garrison commander. Five days earlier, on 22 September, his chilling black-lettered proclamation had loomed on walls and bulletin boards all over the city: 'Only 150 people have so far responded to the decree concerning obligatory work service. According to official figures more than thirty thousand should have reported. From tomorrow, military patrols have orders to round up all citizens failing to report . . .'

And quite suddenly, on this fateful Monday, the 600,000 voluble sun-tanned citizens of Naples realized they had been pushed beyond the point of passive endurance. Already 22,000 Neapolitans had died in 105 air raids. Gone, too, were forty per cent of all the city's pre-war buildings. Now, what the Allies had started, the Germans seemed determined to finish. On 16 September, Scholl had ordered the clearing of a zone 300 yards from the waterfront – and the evacuation of 35,000 families. Then, the tragic exodus complete, his soldiers began a ruthless systematic destruction of the city's industrial potential until the mighty harbour was a nightmare of gutted tenements, grotesquely buckled girders and broken, sagging cranes.

They had no water, no gas, no telephones, no lighting – and the bread ration had been cut to one ounce a day. But they had the wrathful courage of a threatened people, and only twenty miles away was General Mark Clark's 5th Army.

Around 10.30 a.m. they struck. Not all of them at first, for only a handful realized that another vital landmark stood in danger. The word came from Maddalena Cerasuolo, the dark twenty-three-year-old cobbler's daughter as she burst into her father's living-room-cum-workroom at 23, Vico della Neve. 'Do something!' she panted. 'They're going to mine the Ponte della Sanità.'

Her father was horrified. Only fifty yards from the house, the great northbound viaduct, seventy-three yards long by twenty-four wide, was the vital artery linking the city to the Rome highway. Plainly the Germans, fearing an Allied thrust from the north, planned to demolish it. But below the viaduct and flanking it to east and west were scores of the cramped slum dwellings that made up the city's northern quarter Now Carlo Cerasuolo decided violently: 'No, that they'll never do! It would mean losing all our houses, too.'

With three of her father's comrades, Maddalena raced for the bridge. Nearest to them, on its southern approach, two German soldiers were ramming a manhole in the right-hand corner with dynamite – too busy to notice the little band as they stole down the stone stairway on the left, leading to the piers. There, all four piled into the lift cage and rode eighty feet in aching silence, back to bridge level. Now they were behind the unsuspecting Germans at the moment they set the fuse. At once, one partisan opened fire. Simultaneously, shots raked the southern approaches: prone behind the statue of King Umberto I, Maddalena's father was taking aim. One German dropped dead in his tracks. The second ducked and ran towards the truck parked 100 yards away, beyond the northern approach. In that instant, Dino del Prete, a brave twenty-three-year-old infantry lieutenant, ran towards the boxes of dynamite, tugged at the smouldering fuse and hurled it into infinity.

The bridge was saved – but now the Neapolitans prepared to contest every yard of their tawdry, cherished city.

By early morning of 28 September the barricades were going up on every littered street. To the east, machine-gun barricades covered the Piazza Nazionale, denying the Germans all access to their main vehicle depot at Poggioreale. To the north, old men, women and children laboured on a mammoth 300-yard barricade made up of thirty stalled trams, manhandled into position, reinforced with iron bars planted like anti-tank poles and 20lb blocks of tufa rock. Then as groaning lines of German trucks moved out to round up the labour force, the long-concealed men, squinting against the intense sunlight, came out from their dark burrows and fought.

Now the Germans saw Naples for what it was – a deadly trap, ready to close on every man, every motor-cycle, every truck. Rifle-shots cracked and whined from dark alleyways that never saw the light of the sun. Machine-guns hammered from behind washing lines – the 'national flag' of Naples – strung like ships' pennants between the stinking tenements. From behind the barricades of brass bedsteads, school benches, paving stones and gaily painted ice-cream carts, grenades came whistling to send trucks skidding out of control. Over everything hung the reek of cordite, plaster-dust, sour wine and putrefying garbage.

It was no blueprint insurrection, planned long in advance by strategists. No man could then know that 'The Four Days of Naples', the Italians' first spontaneous rejection of the rebirth of the Axis, would pave the way for a nation-wide Resistance movement. Rather it was the cry of an old man manning a barricade at northern Capodimonte on 29 September which set the improvised key-note: 'Today's St Michael's Day – the day he drove the Devil out of Paradise. So now let's drive the Germans out of Naples!'

But for months, in hopeful anticipation, a thousand houses had hidden more lethal contraband than fugitives – arms and ammunition smuggled from the barracks of the *carabinieri* or from the Finance

Guards, who controlled excise. At Ponte della Sanità, butcher Ferdinando Castellano took pot shots at the Germans with the revolver he had all along kept hidden behind a huge calf's head in his shop. Railway inspector Giovanni Abbate had smuggled grenades into his first-floor apartment using the wicker basket his wife lowered from the window when street-vendors came round. Giuseppe Sanges, in charge of the city's vending machines, had stocked up on cartridges in the leather satchel he used to collect the takings.

Most resourceful of all was Federico Zvab, a burly Trieste-born Communist, for more than a year a patient in the Ospedale degli Incurabili, the city's main hospital. From barracks all over the city, hidden under juicy layers of grapes and oranges, fruit vendors' carts had brought Zvab a choice store of fifty revolvers, 300 hand-grenades and three stripped-down machine guns. The grenades and guns had been stored in the lockers of the hospital's mortuary. The machine-guns Zvab had reassembled himself – working in the cell of an unsuspecting nun, to which he had obtained a key. Now these arms were rushed by hand to whatever hard-pressed outpost might need them.

Those without weapons made frantic shifts to get them. In a friend's house near the Parco Cis, Alfredo Parente, the scholarly librarian of the Institute of Italian History, worked with seven others to make primitive Molotov cocktails from empty wine bottles and plundered barrels of petrol. Insurance agent Giulio Schettini did get a musket finally, from the armoury at the juvenile reformatory – but only after a prissy official had insisted on a signed receipt. A fireman carrying out a daring reconnaissance of the German-held Villa Floridiana saw the sentries in conference a little way off and the machine-gun guarding the gateway unmanned. Lunging forward, he seized it, then backed away, covering his own retreat.

Neither age nor sex – nor even infirmity – was a barrier in this desperate bid for freedom. On the terrace of the Filippine nuns' convent, commanding the northbound Via Santa Teresa, Maddalena Cerasuolo fought alongside the men to repel whole truckloads of Germans – stylish with high boots and a bandolier, her shoulder bruised blue by the recoil of a .91 rifle she had only now learned how to fire. Captain Stefano Fadda, wounded at El Alamein, still hadn't cast aside his crutches, but at the head of a yelling band of citizens he stomped into the Prefecture, doled out the arms he found there and set up strongpoints along the westbound Via Chiaia. From his first-floor apartment in Vomero, Professor Antonino Tarsia in Curia watched the Germans pulling out from the Liceo Sannazzaro across the way, the high school from which the Fascists had compulsorily retired him twenty years ago. Promptly the seventy-year-old Professor, natty in his light grey suit with straw hat, brown-and-white shoes and malacca cane, walked unhurriedly to his old classroom to set up the partisans' first command post.

Soon, though the teacher's desk was piled with sheeted corpses, armed patriots were flooding in for orders and to help set up a soup kitchen, guided by the 100 neatly-typed manifestos the Professor had thoughtfully tacked on the plane-trees in nearby avenues.

Although fewer than 1600 people were officially listed as combatants, thousands more risked their lives behind the scenes – to carry ammunition, tend the wounded or to strike at the Germans somehow. Foremost in the mind of twenty-eight-year-old Don Matteo Lisa, the slim, bespectacled, assistant priest at the Church of Santissimo Sacramento, was the thought that he must not kill yet must find some way to fight. At 2 p.m. on the second day of the rising, Don Matteo's chance came.

Up the steep incline of the Via Salvator Rosa, where the church stood, groaned a twenty-strong convoy of German trucks heading for Vomero. From the flat roof of his narrow six-storey house, Don Matteo watched them come, framed against the blue backdrop of the Bay of Naples, the frowning cone of Vesuvius to the left. Already he and two altar boys had perfected their plan of campaign. As the leading truck drew level, Don Matteo shouted, 'Now!' Tugging mightily at a heavy stone urn of geraniums, all three toppled it over the ledge.

Like a deadly thunderbolt, the urn hurtled straight for the driving cabin, ripping through the metal roof like a bullet puncturing paper. As the truck spun out of control, slowing to a halt, Don Matteo and his teenagers followed up. A veritable hail of urns, bricks and roof-tiles burst about the angry Germans as they tumbled from their trucks. At last, after two hours' fruitless attempt to rush the building, they withdrew.

The *scugnizzi* fought as courageously as any – the tough little dead-end kids of the old port, with their dangling cigarettes, wise and cynical beyond their years. Fourteen-year-old Enzo Bruno battled all through with a musket lacking even a butt; though it earned him the lifelong nickname 'Mezzo Fucile' (Half-a-Gun), nothing was better suited to his puny frame. And to the fury of Maddalena Cerasuolo, she was dogged everywhere by her eleven-year-old cousin, Gennaro Capuozzo, persistent in his piping demands that he too should be armed like a man. 'You stay home and knit,' he had told his mother masterfully, before he set out. Even as early as the Ponte della Sanità, butcher Castellano recalls, Gennaro had tussled with a colonel for a tripod machine-gun, bursting into tears when it was wrested from him. 'I need arms like the others,' the little boy blubbered. 'I want to fight too.'

By 3 p.m. on 29 September, Gennaro had won his point. Weirdly garbed in a sailor's outsize blouse and a *carabiniere's* helmet, with a musket bigger than himself, he was prone beside Maddalena on the terrace of the Filippine convent. It was the cruellest fate that a quarter of an hour later six Tiger tanks, advancing from the north, skirted the tram-car barricade below the convent as Gennaro broke cover – to hurl a Molotov cocktail as the tank gunners opened up.

Then the battle raged so intensely all over the city that hardly any survivor could give a coherent account of the next eight hours. Not until 5 a.m. on 30 September, was there a lull, enabling Maddalena and her father to carry Gennaro's body to the cobbler's workroom at Vico della Neve – the first flashpoint of the rising. And shortly, alerted by the strange grapevine of the slums, his mother arrived to claim her dead. 'What did I tell you?' she burst out in mindless grief and anger, and it was Gennaro to whom she spoke. 'You thought you were so smart. Look at you now!'

But at this same hour one man's audacious bluff had already turned the tide and brought an end to the slaughter. For twenty-six hours, rebels under Captain Enzo Stimolo, a one-armed veteran of Albania, had penned a force of more than sixty Germans in the stands of the Campo Sportivo – the football stadium north-east of the city. Yet the odds were suicidal. At first, Stimolo mustered no more than sixteen men, many of them teenagers. The Germans, they knew, held forty-seven Italian hostages – and could fight back, if need be, with a four-gun anti-aircraft battery.

Stimolo's daring answer was to string out his men all along the stadium's perimeter, briefing them to fire at will, meanwhile rallying a 'ghost army' with cries of '150 men to the left – 150 men to the right.' Since the reinforcements for which the Germans signalled. by flares never arrived, his psychological warfare paid off. By 2 p.m. on the 29th, when the German commander sought a parley under a flag of truce, Stimolo, backed now by ninety men rushed to him by Professor Tarsia, could assure him, poker-faced, that 3000 Neapolitans had Campo Sportivo surrounded.

At dusk, inside Parker's Hotel, the German headquarters, Stimolo's envoys were presenting the harassed Colonel Scholl with terms he was more than willing to accept – an exchange of prisoners and a safe-conduct from the hornet's nest that had been Naples.

The dawn of 1 October revealed to the Neapolitans the full extent of their triumph. Under a white flag of truce, choking files of German cars and trucks had moved northwards towards the River Volturno and Rome. Preceding them to the city's periphery was a jeep draped with both flag and tricolour, Captain Stimolo in front. Promptly at 9.30 a.m. the tank treads of the King's Dragoon Guards, the vanguard of the Allied 5th Army, were shattering over the cobbles of the Piazza Garibaldi, three miles south.

In their wake came an armoured car bearing the man who was soon to award the whole city a gold medal for its collective valour – General Mark Clark. To the tall New Yorker, one factor stood out eerily on this sullen overcast morning: everywhere eyes peered from behind closed shutters, yet barely a soul was on the streets. He felt that he was 'riding through ghostly streets in a city of ghosts'. And in a sense he was. Not far from the football stadium, in the Cimitero Vecchio, the Neapolitans were burying their dead. In plain wooden packing-cases, most of the 562 men, women and children who had died for their city were laid to rest.

Autumn light glinted from the upended glass bottles gummed with typed slips of paper that marked each grave – a light not yet grown as bright as a beacon but as clear and shining as a free soul.

At first they were few – perhaps 80,000 – fleeing the labour round-ups, fired by the solemn achievement of the Four Days of Naples. But within eighteen months their numbers swelled to a formidable 200,000 – the partisans of Italy – and the Allies, recognizing their potential, parachuted them 6500 tons of supplies.

Names like 'Hannibal', 'Lionheart', 'Storm' and 'Jaguar' masked their true identities – bearded, desperate men with a code all their own, many serving in the new Garibaldi Brigades that Italy's No 2 Communist, shock-haired forty-three-year-old Luigi Longo, seasoned by twenty years' resistance, had gone north to organize in Milan. Their slang was their own, too: 'a handkerchief' was a Fascist prisoner, and to give a prisoner 'a passport to Switzerland' was to despatch him some dark night with a knife thrust or a hail of bullets.

From makeshift headquarters – bakeries, cemeteries, cattle barns – they launched countless thousands of sorties against the military convoys and troop trains of Mussolini's Salò Republic. But through two long winters their greatest enemy was privation. Often they were holed up for months in the mountains, wearing only the thin summer clothes in which they had fled to freedom, their broken shoes patched with dusters, feet poulticed with axle grease to ward off frostbite. One cigar shared puff by puff between fifteen men was commonplace, and for long weeks their arid diet would be maize porridge and chestnuts.

Their true pot of gold was the farmhouse family who at dead of night would take down the last salami, and yield up still warm bed sheets to the numbed and shivering strangers.

Marshal Rodolfo Graziani was their most strident recruiting agent: the compulsory draft on which he insisted, against all advice, produced, in the words of one Fascist dissident 'an army held together by the constant threat of the firing squad'. Party Secretary Alessandro Pavolini helped too, for his new-formed Black Brigades, designed to harass the partisans, drove thousands into the rebel camp. In the factories and on the farms, the forces that would shape a new Italy were at last stirring, and the password was whispered from village to village: 'The way to the mountains is the way to glory.'

The air was thick and stifling. In the first-floor study at Villa Orsoline two porcelain stoves kept the temperature in the eighties day and night. Yet this morning, 18 December, as fog rolled in over Lake Garda, Mussolini shivered with more than his habitual cold. The showdown he had so long dreaded was taking place here and now. Facing him across the desk, his daughter Edda was passionately demanding her husband's right to live.

Outside the study, Vittorio Mussolini heard his sister's voice raised in defiance and shook his head. He had begged Edda to postpone this confrontation but in vain. Thin, pale, his cheeks sunken, his eyes red-rimmed, Mussolini in his shabby greasy Honorary Corporal's uniform seemed in no shape to sustain such an onslaught. But Edda had proved implacable – and now her voice, harsh with anger, carried clearly even through the closed door.

'You're crazy, all of you,' she shouted at her father. 'The war is lost. It's useless to have illusions – the Germans will resist a few months, no more. And under these conditions Galeazzo is condemned!'

Vittorio could not hear his father's mumbled reply, but he knew with what trepidation the Duce had awaited the meeting. Vividly,

Mussolini had recalled the day of Bruno's funeral three years earlier – when the iron-willed Edda, determined not to cry, had bitten her lip until the blood trickled down her chin. 'My daughter could prove a fearful adversary,' he confided to one of his Cabinet.

For eight weeks now, Mussolini's personal demons had allowed him no respite – since the day when Galeazzo Ciano, arrested at Verona airport on his return to Italy, had become Prisoner 11902 in the city's sixteenth-century jail. Held in adjacent cells were the only five Grand Council members whom the Fascist police had located: seventy-eight-year-old Marshal de Bono, the stone-deaf Giovanni Marinelli, Tullio Cianetti, whose vote for Grandi had been withdrawn within hours, and those two tyros who had sided with the majority, Luciano Gottardi and Carlo Pareschi.

Yet on 14 November, the Fascist Party Congress debating the new government's eighteen-point manifesto for eight hours in the smoke-filled confines of the Castelvecchio in Verona had called unanimously for their deaths. The city's Federal Police Chief, Major Nicola Furlotti, had crystallized the angry clamour of 200 delegates: 'The traitors will pay, and as soon as possible!'

After twenty stormy years the wheel had spun full circle, and Mussolini knew it. On 8 January, 1944, when the six prisoners faced a Special Tribunal in the courtroom at Castelvecchio, the Duce would be as much under pressure from the Party's hard-liners as ever he had been on the day when the Militia chiefs stormed into his Palazzo Chigi office to force the dictatorship upon him.

She had long guessed, Edda told her father contemptuously, the way things would go. At the very outset of the Salò Republic, when Mussolini was still interviewing his Ministers at La Rocca, she had asked Alessandro Pavolini point-blank about the new regime's attitude towards Ciano. Without even deigning to reply, the Party Secretary had left the room. Promptly Edda took the first steps to safeguard her hostages to fortune by sending Vittorio to Germany to bring the Ciano children on to Italian soil.

Then, in a letter of icy formality she had upbraided Mussolini: 'Duce, my husband has been in a prison cell for two months and is denied the relief of the two hours' exercise extended to . . . even the worst criminals . . . I have had my first meeting with him, but in the presence of a representative of the Reich, another of the Fascist Party, also the prison commandant . . . at a distance of three yards . . . here is a wife, Duce, who claims that the rights sacred to every prisoner may be granted to her own husband.'

Feebly, Mussolini now strove to justify his actions. He could not ride roughshod over the law to intervene for his own son-in-law. He himself had forgiven Ciano, even suggesting to the perplexed Ambassador Rahn that Ciano might be an ideal Foreign Minister for Salò. But scores of others, he knew, would neither forget nor forgive. Hitler, Ribbentrop, Pavolini, were all waiting to see if he had strength to stand aloof from Galeazzo's trial. Here was the desperate dilemma of a man so weak he dared not show compassion.

Even Rachele was wrathfully opposed to clemency. 'The Duce,' she had shouted at Ciano when they met at Schloss Hirschberg, 'is not a piece of furniture to put in the attic when you're tired of it.' From early November, when she returned to Lake Garda with Romano and Anna Maria, she had never ceased to urge that Ciano must stand trial. Mussolini was too resigned to argue. The presence of Claretta Petacci, who had moved with her family and an SS bodyguard to nearby Villa Fiordaliso, was already causing stormy scenes when he returned from the office.

Outside the door, Vittorio heard the meeting reach its unparalleled climax. Edda knew she had lost. Now in a blind rage, she turned on the father who had adored her, seeking only to wound. 'And it's because of people like you that my husband is being sacrificed,' she reviled him. 'If you were kneeling before me dying of thirst I'd take the last glass of water in the world and empty it before your eyes.'

The door burst open then. As Edda emerged, Vittorio saw that she was distraught and trembling, but her eyes were on fire with a wild determination. 'We'll see,' she said with awful finality. 'We'll see.'

North of Milan, the cold was bitter. By noon on 7 January snow was drifting from the Alps, a white noiseless cloud blanketing farms and fields, but it brought no added warmth. At nightfall, the thermometer showed twelve degrees below freezing, and still falling. Fifty miles from the city, nothing moved on the Brescia-Verona highway.

Half-running, half-stumbling through this white and silent world, the woman's footfalls were muffled. At intervals she looked back desperately, scanning the darkness, hoping against hope for the muffled glow of headlamps. Already, one lift from a lone motorist had saved her precious hours, though the car had gone only as far as Brescia. Yet she had been lucky; her identity remained a secret.

Never once had the driver suspected that his passenger was Edda Ciano, the Duce's daughter, who had just thirty minutes left to rendezvous with Galeazzo at Kilometre 10 after his escape from Verona Jail.

Since that last soul-shattering quarrel with her father, Edda had borne little resemblance to the impulsive dictator's daughter of the past. For the past three weeks she had been a frightened, desperate woman, calling on her last reserves of strength to save her husband's life.

Six days before she saw the Duce, on 12 December, Edda had taken the first decisive step – smuggling her children to safety over the Swiss border with the help of a family friend. Her plan then had been to follow them within days, after retrieving Ciano's diaries from their hiding-place in Rome. Surely the threat of publication would frighten her father into calling off the trial?

Then, at Verona Jail, on 27 December, as she made a last vain attempt to see Galeazzo, fate had taken a hand. A petite twenty-two-year-old blonde who had free access to the prison – and to Ciano's cell – introduced herself as Frau Hildegard Beetz, personal assistant to Obersturmbannführer Wilhelm Höttl.

Ever since the days beside Lake Starnberg, Höttl had never lost hope that he could use Ciano's diaries to topple Joachim von Ribbentrop. For this reason he had sent Frau Beetz to Verona to keep daily contact with the Count. Now, on her chief's behalf, Hildegard Beetz outlined a deal that called for Edda's co-operation: the diaries in exchange for a planned jailbreak staged by German agents.

Hildegard Beetz had already discussed the plan with General Wilhelm Harster, Verona's bland, monocled SD chief – and Harster, in turn, had met Dr Ernst Kaltenbrunner in Innsbruck. Both men had agreed to the setting-up of 'Operation Count' – an eleventh hour plan to free Ciano without Hitler's knowledge – subject to one condition. First, Edda must furnish sample volumes to be studied by Kaltenbrunner and Himmler.

From this moment on, Edda had lived a life of tension that far outdid any madcap escapade of 'the twenty cock-eyed years'. Strapped tightly beneath her bosom on this freezing January night, so that she ran doubled like a hunchback, were eight volumes of Ciano's diaries, stripped of their covers, which she had retained as a final bargaining counter in case of treachery.

She could never have achieved it without the Marchese Emilio Pucci, a gallant World War Two aviator and Edda's constant companion. It was Pucci who had journeyed to Rome with Hildegard Beetz and two SD agents to collect Ciano's documents from their hiding-place under the parquet flooring of a retainer's apartment. Pucci, too, had conceived the plan of secreting the diaries beneath his top coat in case Höttl tried a double-cross – at first handing over only six volumes of conference transcripts. But back in Verona, General Harster had raised no objections. He ordered that the volumes should be photostated, part-translated, and flown to Berlin for Kaltenbrunner's approval. On 6 January, the SD Chief had cabled back: 'Operation Count' was on.

Suddenly, peering back along the road, Edda saw a solitary cyclist battling the curtain of snow. At first the man stared appalled at this turbaned apparition emerging from the night – but he readily agreed to give her a lift on his handlebars. Bleakly Edda gazed ahead, her face wet with snow. The wind from the Bergamo Alps cut like a scythe. One thought obsessed her above all: the rendezvous was at 9 p.m. She would be one hour late.

The coup was timed for the stroke of 8.30 p.m. At that hour, claiming there was an Italian plot to free Ciano, Harster would send troops to occupy the jail. Among them would be two special agents sent from Holland, men trained in the deadly art of silent killing if the Fascist guards put up a fight. No man would be left alive to confute Kaltenbrunner's report to Hitler: Ciano had escaped with Italian help. By 9 p.m., the Count, the agents and Hildegard Beetz would be at the milestone marking Kilometre 10, waiting for Edda to arrive with money and jewels for her husband. Ahead of him lay a hazardous flight: from the first German-controlled airfield – probably Innsbruck – to Budapest, and from there to the Transylvanian estate of Count Festetic, a contact of Kaltenbrunner's.

Once confirmation came that Ciano had reached Turkey along an existing SS escape route, Edda was to hand the remaining diaries to Frau Beetz.

But at 8 p.m. on this icy night the Duce's daughter had seen everything go wrong. Once Emilio Pucci had brought the diaries from Rome, she had hidden them for safekeeping with family friends at Varese, near Lake Como. Late that afternoon, after again collecting them, she had set off in Pucci's car for Verona. Then, close to Brescia, disaster struck: a rear tyre blew. Leaving Pucci to guard the remaining documents, Edda struggled on alone.

At last, peering through darkness, she saw the squat white pillar of Kilometre 10. Gasping her thanks, she dismounted from the cycle, hobbling through piled snow. Would the rest of the plan work, she wondered? The silence was absolute, and there was no sign of Galeazzo.

Tensely, she huddled against a plane tree, the cold invading all her body like an anaesthetic. Suddenly a headlamp's faint pencil silvered the trunks ahead. She stumbled to meet it. At last Galeazzo was coming! Then, abruptly, she took fright. Höttl had tricked her. Ciano would never be freed. Instead they were going to arrest her and take the diaries. Her heart pounding, she crouched immobile in the ditch. The car passed, fighting for traction on the black ice. At last she straightened up.

On this freezing night of her calvary, she lost all count of time. Once she was startled almost into hysterics by the sudden ghostly appearance of a workman on a bicycle. 'What a pity I've a wife,' the man sang out. 'There's a house near here with a good fire.' Once, in another life, Edda remembered, she had been proud of her sense of humour. 'It would be nice,' she chaffed him in turn, 'but it's not possible.'

What seemed like a lifetime later she heard a truck grinding through the dawn from the direction of Brescia. Stepping forward like any hitch-hiker, the Duce's daughter thumbed a ride. On the outskirts of Verona the clocks showed 5 a.m.

In four hours and fifteen minutes, Galeazzo would be on trial for his life.

The slow tolling of a handbell echoed through the raftered fourteenth-century hall. As the nine black-robed judges filed into the courtroom of Castelvecchio, public and accused struggled to their feet from the hard wooden benches. Solemnly, a scarlet-clad usher intoned the opening ritual: the Verona Trial was in session.

It was 9.15 a.m. on Saturday, 8 January, 1944 – a day of paralysing cold. Ice fringed the River Adige below the castle walls; snow lay thick on the ivy-mantled battlements. As impassive as waxworks on their dais, the judges shivered in topcoats beneath their robes. To their right, in the well of the court, the six accused were huddled painfully like survivors on an ice-floe – Galeazzo Ciano in a raincoat buttoned to the neck, old Marshal de Bono almost enveloped in a thick woollen scarf.

Yet many men shivered with something more than cold. It was a trial as formal as a masque and all who took part in it knew. Even the setting seemed designed for tragedy: on black velvet curtains lining the room the Fasces stood out as white as skulls – in macabre contrast to the scarlet cloth draping the judges' table. And almost every man who sat at it had fought to avoid this duty. To Judge Renzo Montagna it was all along 'an act of revenge, not justice'. Judge Franz Pagliani, a surgeon, had protested to Party Secretary Pavolini: 'A doctor's job is to save life, not condemn men to death.'

Inside Verona Jail, few of the accused had any more faith in the outcome. So great was the fear prevailing, it had been hard even to brief defence attorneys – Ciano was without counsel to the end. Only Marshal de Bono, blissfully certain of an acquittal, had sent word to a cousin: 'It's only a matter of three days – be sure to have a good dinner when I return.' The others shared the bitterness of Ciano, in Cell 27, when he wrote to Edda on 6 January: 'While you still live in the blissful illusion that I'll be free in a few hours and that we will all be together again, for me the agony is beginning.'

Earlier that evening – twenty-four hours before Edda's vigil at Kilometre 10 – Hildegard Beetz had brought Ciano the disastrous news that 'Operation Count' was off. Alerted by Ribbentrop and Goebbels that a plot was afoot, Hitler had called in Himmler and Kaltenbrunner, forced an admission from them, then berated them soundly. On the line to General Harster in Verona, the Führer had bellowed: 'If Ciano escapes, you'll pay with your head.'

When Kaltenbrunner protested that Hitler was virtually condemning Ciano to death, the Führer only laughed harshly. 'My dear Kaltenbrunner,' he retorted, 'Mussolini will never permit the father of his beloved grandchildren to be put to death. It's all just a bit of Italian bluff.'

In fact, Hitler was wrong. Two months earlier, in the medieval Palazzo Scaligero housing the Prefecture in Verona, two old-guard Fascists had already passed sentence of death on the six gentlemen of Verona – Pietro Cosmin, a lean, pencil-moustached, ex-naval officer stricken with lung cancer, and Major Nicola Furlotti, the bespectacled, whisper-voiced commandant of the Federal Police. From the day Cosmin had created himself Prefect at gunpoint, with Furlotti as his staunch follower, both men had been resolved on one thing. Mussolini notwithstanding, if Ciano was acquitted, he would die at Furlotti's hands in the prison van taking him from Castelvecchio to Verona Jail.

Coughing violently into his black silk handkerchief, the chain-smoking Cosmin told Furlotti: 'The whole Fascist regime can topple if an example isn't made.'

Hitler's Visit in 1938

The swastika flew for the first time on Italian streets

King Vittorio Emanuele III, beside Queen Elena, opts for old-style salute

At the Casino Borghese an awed Führer and puzzled Duce survey a Canova statue

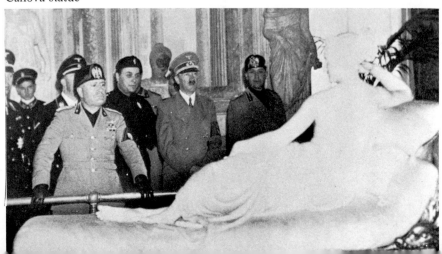

Rachele Mussolini – for
eleven years unaware
of her husband's love
for Claretta Petacci

Claretta Petacci at
Rimini

Top left. Marshal Pietro Badoglio, seen here with Abyssinian chieftain's robes.
Top right. The Belgian Crown Princess Maria-José, Inspector General of the
Italian Red Cross. *Above*. With his SS liberator, Otto Skorzeny, Mussolini
prepares to leave his Gran Sasso prison

The Execution of Count Ciano

Verona, Forte San Procolo, 11 January 1944. The condemned men of the Grand Council. From left to right De Bono, Pareschi, Gottardi, Ciano (facing squad) and Marinelli, with Major Furlotti standing by

The 30-strong firing squad takes aim

Prison Chaplain Don Giuseppe Chiot administers extreme unction to Ciano

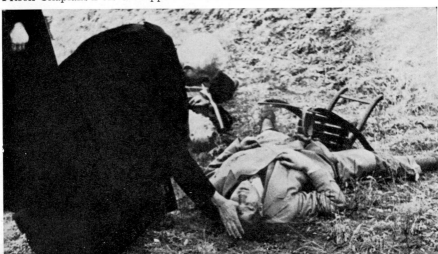

The Duce of Salò

Right. Family group on Lake
Garda
Middle. Inspecting trainees in
Germany

Below. Mussolini revived in a fighting speech at Milan's Teatro Lirico to pledge
the ultimate defence of the Po Valley 'with our nails and with our teeth'. To his
right, Presidential Under-Secretary Francesco Baraccu and the blood-crazed Party
Secretary Alessandro Pavolini

Caught up in the race to stop the Allies seizing Mussolini were General Raffaele Cadorna, Resistance military commander

Marshal Rodolfo Graziani, (*left*) with Federal Secretary Vincenzo Costa

Count Pier Luigi
Bellini delle Stelle
('Pedro'), his partisan
captor

Walter Audisio
('Colonel Valerio'), his
Communist executioner

Milan, Piazzale Loreto, 29 April 1945: for Mussolini and Claretta Petacci, the grim and inevitable ending

Furlotti had taken his point. Now, before Andrea Fortunato, the venomous one-armed Sicilian Public Prosecutor, rose to open the trial, the police chief took him aside. 'You'll manage all right, eh?' he whispered. 'The fact that these men are important won't affect you?'

Vehemently Fortunato shook his head. Between Furlotti and Cosmin, across the courtroom, there passed a silent, significant nod.

All through this freezing overcast Saturday, Furlotti chafed impatiently as the trial droned on. What a waste of oratory, when all were plainly traitors to Fascism! Each man claimed that he had not sought to dethrone Mussolini – yet to Furlotti their words in their own defence only made the treason plainer. 'If you did not look favourably upon the meeting of the Grand Council,' the Prosecutor put it to Ciano, 'how is it that you did not take the trouble to mention it to the Duce?'

'As I was no longer Foreign Minister,' came Ciano's lame reply, 'I had not the opportunity to approach Mussolini readily.'

'Why did you go to the session knowing of a plot?' De Bono was asked. 'I should like *not* to have gone,' the old Marshal told the court frankly. 'I expected the session to be long – and I suffer from drowsiness.'

Pareschi next: 'It was hard for me to understand anything.' Cianetti: 'I began to realize that a plot was hidden there . . . I immediately withdrew my vote.' Gottardi: 'I believed Grandi's initiative aimed at strengthening our fighting capacity.' Last, Marinelli: 'I was ten yards away . . . I could grasp only a small part of the discussion because of deafness.'

On Sunday morning, as the speeches for the accused began, Cosmin grew restive. One advocate, Riccardo Marrosu, spoke so persuasively of De Bono's years of service that the Prefect at once strode towards the defence attorney's table to the left of the court. 'An inspired speech, wasn't it?' one man hailed him incautiously. His eyes fixed balefully on Marrosu's face, Cosmin replied: 'Defence lawyers would do better to walk with their eyes down. If it's needed, there's lead for them too.'

But not until 10 a.m. on 10 January did the real fear of 'a French Revolution tribunal' come upon them all. Following a ninety-minute speech by Tommaso Fortini, defending Cianetti, a frightened secretary approached Gottardi's lawyer, Advocate Perani: 'Tell the other lawyers, when the President reads the sentence, for God's sake keep your heads down.'

Baffled, Perani and a colleague approached the rear of the court. Until now the benches had stood empty – yet suddenly they were packed out with black-shirted strangers. Every entrance, every stairway, was guarded by Fascists, machine-pistols at the ready; every door was blocked. 'Don't take this badly, lawyer,' one man sneered, 'we've nothing against you – but if those over there are found not guilty, we're here to finish the job. So just remember to duck.'

At a snail's pace the small wooden box moved up and down the baize-covered table. In a small chill ante-room at the rear of Castelvecchio, the judges were voting. Now there was absolute silence save for the dry rattle of small balls dropping into the box as each man's fate was decided – white balls for innocent, black for guilty.

Judge Renzo Montagna felt near to vomiting. A stalwart forty-nine-year-old Militia general and March on Rome veteran, he believed passionately that the guilty men of the Grand Council night had escaped scot-free and that these six were scapegoats. More and more he was convinced that the whole trial had been rigged from the start. Long before the voting began, he had argued forcefully in favour of Marshal de Bono – citing his age, his World War One record, pleading for a distinction between the categories of accused. For answer, Judge Enrico Vezzalini, who had daily conferred in secret with Cosmin, snarled: 'Only one distinction is possible – to shoot the first lot in the back, the second lot in the stomach.'

Montagna had pleaded with Judge Giovanni Riggio to support him – and Riggio, a voluble Sicilian, had wavered. Again Vezzalini had cut in: 'You're betraying Fascism and the revolution.' At once Riggio, shamefaced, climbed down: 'As an action-squad man, it's my duty to vote for capital punishment.' Bitterly Montagna acknowledged the truth: the regime was fighting for its life, and clemency was at a premium.

As a surgeon, Franz Pagliani spoke up for Marinelli: a man so deaf could barely have grasped the implications. But the majority rejected it. To prove deafness would call for a physical examination, and the trial *must* be hurried. What of Gottardi and Pareschi, perhaps bemused by such a great occasion? Judge Otello Gaddi, a diehard Militia chief, boomed: 'If I, a simple lieutenant-colonel, can understand, they could have understood.'

To Judge Montagna, it seemed the argument would rage forever until at last the voting began; but despite his plea for De Bono, the rattle of the little balls told the story: four in favour – five against.

Only Tullio Cianetti, who had withdrawn his signature from Grandi's motion, scraped through: five in favour, four against.

On Marinelli, only Judge Pagliani, the surgeon, stuck to his guns, making one in favour, eight against.

They voted on Galeazzo Ciano last.

Nine black balls.

A ragged veil of smoke lay like fog over the field. From the elm trees bordering Forte San Procolo, the rooks took angry flight; their harsh cries, the echoing *spang* of rifle-fire, drowned the whimpers of the five men strapped to slatted bar-room chairs, writhing helplessly in the snow. As the smoke from Pietro Cosmin's cigarette mingled with the drifting acrid cordite, a German officer beside him turned away in tears. 'I can't understand you Italians,' he burst out uncontrollably. 'Your hearts are too warm or else too cruel.'

Cosmin had no such qualms. Only one thought had obsessed him in the night just past: that the last-minute appeals for mercy which the condemned men had signed, as was their right, should never reach Benito Mussolini's hands. It was lucky that determined Fascists who felt as he did had backed him all the way: Party Secretary Pavolini and the bullying, bandy-legged police chief, Tullio Tamburini. At first Pavolini had tried to coerce Piero Pisenti, the able, scrupulous Minister of Justice, into rejecting the appeals, but Pisenti was inflexible. 'Leave them with me,' he told Pavolini, 'I will take them straight to the Duce.' Angrily Pavolini refused. 'We cannot subject him to that pain.'

Not until 3 a.m. on 11 January did someone in Cosmin's smoke-filled office suggest that Colonel Italo Vianini, as Fifth Zone Inspector of the National Republican Guard, had authority to reject the petitions outright. But the Colonel, roused from bed, had resisted stubbornly. It had taken five hours' bullying by Cosmin, Tamburini and Public Prosecutor Fortunato before Vianini, on direct orders from General Renato Ricci, his boss, had given in.

But at 9.20 a.m., when Major Furlotti's right arm rose and fell in signal, the firing squad had already been lined up for four hours at Forte San Procolo. Signature or no, this was the ending Cosmin had always foreseen.

It was a bloody and awful end. Of the thirty-strong firing squad, aiming twelve yards from their targets, not one had ever made part of an execution. 'It's here you must aim,' Furlotti had told the six crack marksmen, touching each man's temple, but these had been their only instructions.

Now it was Dr Renato Carretto, the prison doctor, who walked among the dying, begging for an end to the butchery. Pareschi had fallen to the left, after shouting 'Long live Italy!' but of the six who took aim, only two had hit him; he needed one *coup-de-grâce*. Marshal de Bono had echoed that cry, but, like Gottardi, he was already dead. Marinelli had been carried to his chair fighting and weeping, crying out for a woman called 'Giulia', and he was still alive. The doctor beckoned and Furlotti approached, his 7.65 Beretta automatic cocked. It took two *coups-de-grâce* in the nape.

Lastly Ciano. He had not called out but at the last he had somehow wrenched his head round to face his executioners and the fire had spun him backwards, the chair a dead weight above him.

Horrified, the doctor realized he was still alive. 'One,' he told Furlotti, and the Major pulled the trigger, but still Ciano lived. 'Again,' Dr Carretto said, and Furlotti put the Beretta's muzzle against Ciano's right temple, against the hair smeared with blood and snow and Macassar oil. 'Two,' the doctor said, then Ciano went into the last great struggle, and died.

Noiselessly, the priest entered the dictator's study. He found that he was not afraid yet sensed that the man who did not raise his eyes from his desk knew fear. He sought to play Duce, with abrupt questions and jutting jaw, but for all that he was 'a man overcome by family sentiment and longing'. A man who knew that Don Giuseppe Chiot, the aquiline, white-haired chaplain to Verona Jail, who twelve days earlier had shared with the accused their last night on earth, could tell him what he needed to know.

'How did this tragedy go?' asked Mussolini bluntly. 'As you wanted it to,' the priest threw back at him.

Now the Duce's eyes leapt to meet his. 'What do you mean – I?' 'Those you called to the Grand Council dared to give you advice,' Don Giuseppe told him stonily, 'and you condemned them to death.' Mussolini bounded to his feet. 'You ignore the fact that there were judges at this trial,' he defended himself. But the priest brushed the objection aside: 'No one would have dared to sentence them without your consent.'

Quietly, without fear, Don Giuseppe took the dictator to task. He had confused the betrayal of Fascism with the betrayal of Italy. 'The Italian people separated the two things a long time ago,' he warned him, 'I can tell you that this is everyone's opinion.' Mussolini's head was between his hands now; he was no longer Duce. 'How did they pass the last night?' he begged, wetting his lips.

All of them, the priest recalled, had been very close to God. Inside the jail, though gates clashed and footfalls echoed all night long, an uncanny calm prevailed. The cell doors stayed open, and all of them gathered in De Bono's cell to talk their last night away . . . Plato's dialogue on the Immortality of the Soul . . . the Last Supper . . . Christ in the Garden of Gethsemane.

Huddled in a circle round a glowing stove, men gave voice to strange, almost mystical thoughts. Carlo Pareschi had asked one last boon – that his green christening shawl should be laid on his body. De Bono mused on a soldier's career: sixty years ago, as a green second-lieutenant, he first saw service in Castelvecchio, where a court had now condemned him for high treason. 'Do we see the Madonna as soon as we die?' he asked Don Giuseppe simply.

Ciano had remained bitter almost to the last. 'I'll never give Hitler and Mussolini that satisfaction,' he raged when each man was invited to sign the appeal for mercy. Only when Tullio Cianetti urged that he would prejudice his comrades' chances did Ciano sign with the rest.

'You have got to know it all,' Don Giuseppe insisted. 'Your son-in-law cursed you because you had not granted the pardon.' It was De Bono who had changed his mind, placing his hands squarely on Ciano's shoulders, recalling that they were all about to appear before God's tribunal. 'You are right,' Ciano said then, 'we are all caught up in the same storm. I die without rancour – tell those close to me.' Trembling, Mussolini interrupted: 'He said, "Tell those close to me"?' 'Yes,' Don Giuseppe assured him, 'that meant *you*, too.'

For one long moment Mussolini stared at the priest. Then the grief broke in him like a haemorrhage and he fell forward, weeping convulsively.

The thought jumped into Chiot's mind: That appeal was never sent. He never saw it, yet he won't admit it. He's afraid to show how men like Cosmin have him in their power.

Claretta Petacci, too, knew how Mussolini had awaited the petitions all that night, phoning her almost hourly – convinced they would come, too eaten up with false pride to insist on precise information.

'Offer your sufferings to God,' Chiot urged him now. 'You must drink the cup of bitterness to the dregs.' Mussolini, wet-eyed, grasped his hands, trying to smile. 'They forgave me, isn't that so?' he begged, and kept tight hold of the priest's hand. Then after a moment the old sick inferiority triumphed once again, even over deep compassion. 'Don't tell the others what you have seen here,' he pleaded.

Chiot looked at the man whom Adolf Hitler had four months back appointed Gauleiter of North Italy. He seems a child, he thought, just as the condemned of Verona seemed in those last hours.

10. 'They Call Me Benito Quisling...'

23 January, 1944–18 April, 1945

Mussolini's private secretary, Giovanni Dolfin, smiled covertly. The unabashed indignation of the top brass clustered in Villa Orsoline's waiting-room was a sight for the gods. Barely four days had elapsed since Don Giuseppe's visit, yet here was another priest summoned by the Duce – and walking in, to take precedence over the fuming ministers and generals. Even the Minister of Popular Culture, Fernando Mezzasoma, who accompanied him, promptly withdrew, leaving them alone.

The two were not strangers. As far back as 1920, Giusto Pancino, the son of Milan's stationmaster, had eked out his pocket-money helping at the news-stand on Foro Bonaparte and had sold *Il Popolo*'s hustling editor his daily papers. Before taking holy orders, Pancino had been a constant playmate of Edda, as they romped through games of cops-and-robbers in the gardens of the Castello Sforzesco. Twenty years later, in 1941, when they met again at Dhermi Military Hospital in Albania where Edda was nursing, it was natural that she should present the young chaplain to the Duce on his visit to the front.

Now, yielding to the advice of mutual friends, Mussolini had two vital charges for Don Giusto Pancino: to find Edda, who had fled to Switzerland with the help of the Marchese Pucci two days before the Verona executions, and to bring about a reconciliation.

'Duce,' Edda had written at Pucci's prompting, before crossing the border, 'I have waited until today for you to show me the slightest feeling of humanity and justice. But if Galeazzo is not in Switzerland within three days . . . everything I know and have the proof of at hand will be used quite mercilessly . . .'

It was just this fear, Pancino suggested, that had led General Harster's men to scour all northern Italy for Edda. But to his astonishment, Mussolini had not known of the search. The knowledge enraged him as nothing else could have done. 'Who touches my daughter touches my person!' he shouted, his chest heaving.

No easy task faced the tall, brown-eyed, bespectacled priest. His first step was to hasten to Rome, seeking from Monsignor Domenico Tardini, the Vatican's Deputy Secretary of State, an introduction to the Papal Nuncio in Berne. But back at Lake Garda on 5 February, a jarring shock awaited him.

A weary fornicator, sickened of the flesh, Mussolini had long pondered the Romagnol proverb: 'When you are young, give your body to the Devil; when you are old, give your bones to God.' Now, at their second meeting, he declared himself a convinced Catholic who wished to die in that faith as serenely as Ciano had done. Already a problem had begun to gnaw Pancino's mind. If Mussolini offered to confess himself, what should he, an obscure thirty-six-year-old country priest, do?

As the weeks passed, Don Giusto's problems mounted. At first it was so hard to enter Switzerland that he was forced to return to Rome and seek Pope Pius XII's intervention. Not until 4 March did he reach Berne – and three more weeks dragged by before he located Edda in a clinic at Ingenbohl.

It was a heart-rending meeting. The priest found 'a shattered woman' on the verge of a breakdown, who clung to Ciano's diaries day and night for fear SS agents tried to snatch them. At the first mention of her father she froze into herself. 'Tell him there are only two solutions that will rehabilitate him in my eyes,' she flung at Pancino, 'to run away or to kill himself.'

Three days later Mussolini heard those words with horror and desolation. For ninety minutes he plied Don Giusto with pitiful questions. Yet, to the fury of the top brass, ever-present in the Duce's waiting-room, the priest was summoned back by Mussolini next day.

Now, as Don Giusto had half hoped, half feared, the dictator came straight to the point. In a trenchant speech to the House of Commons, Winston Churchill had avowed that Mussolini again appeared on the front page of history after staining his hands with Ciano's blood. 'Father Pancino, you know that it is not true,' the Duce pleaded, 'but how many others do? Now Churchill's statement will mean that I take my place in history as the murderer of my son-in-law.'

He paused, struggling for words. Suddenly he blurted out: 'Listen, Father, I feel very deeply the desire to put my soul at peace . . . I beg you to try and reconcile my soul with God.'

Pancino felt a vortex of emotions. He had never thought Mussolini an evil man – but sooner or later any priest must contend with that fatal inferiority complex. 'Essentially he was good-hearted,' Pancino declared later, 'but he was timid – he dared not admit his humanity.'

Even now he was confessing shamefacedly, 'When my mother was alive, I used to pray – but what would they say now if they saw Mussolini entering a church?' But the priest had to face the challenge. Mussolini wanted *him* as his spiritual father.

Deeply perplexed, he returned to Switzerland – to hand Edda a last unavailing appeal from her father and to help her secure Ciano's diaries in a strong-box at Berne's Credit Suisse. Already the Germans, through General Harster, had vainly offered him 100 million lire to steal them. On 18 April and again on 28 April he talked long and earnestly with Mussolini, begging him to reconsider. 'I'm the wrong person to be your spiritual father,' he urged, but Mussolini would have none of it. And now Don Giusto reflected humbly: If I'm near to him, even supposing I'm nothing, perhaps I *can* help.

Then on 1 July came a bolt from the blue. In theory a priest can absolve anyone in the world, but Pancino could not administer the sacrament to Mussolini outside the territory of his jurisdiction without special Papal permission. This he had already sought through the Nuncio. Now, on this sunlit July Saturday, in the Nuncio's Palace overlooking Berne's tree-lined Thunstrasse, the jovial Monsignor Filippo Bernardini handed him a personal message from His Holiness Pope Pius XII. It read: 'Most certainly you have the power to hear Mussolini's confession and to absolve him for all that has happened.'

Pancino was thunderstruck. Yet now, returning to Lake Garda, he found Mussolini evasive, uncertain. Soon enough the priest divined what was troubling the Duce – his seven-year-old love-hate relationship with Adolf Hitler and the Third Reich.

For Mussolini, who had so admired their power, now groaned beneath its weight. First the Germans had picked his living quarters, then they had detailed thirty SS men to guard him day and night. Over two square kilometres, 700 flak troopers manned a cat's-cradle of checkpoints. Even Claretta had been installed on Garda thanks to the SS General Karl Wolff – who, to her indignant fury, ordered her to report on the Duce. But Wolff's eyes and ears were everywhere. All Mussolini's calls – even those to Claretta – were monitored and tapped. Beyond the German road-blocks of 'Zone C', the Duce's writ no longer ran, for to seal him off effectively his ministries were dotted as far afield as Padua and Cremona.

Even his doctor, by Hitler's orders, was now German: Hauptmann Georg Zacharias, who treated his duodenal ulcer and partially blocked bile duct with vitamin injections and hormones, cutting his milk consumption to nil. Despite his frustrations the Duce responded, until his stocky frame turned the scales at 162 lb.

Yet with only two inter-city telephone lines allotted him, he wielded less power than the Mayor of Salò, and he knew it. 'They call me Benito Quisling,' he confessed sourly to the journalist Carlo Silvestri, 'and they're quite right. What real authority do I have?'

And the price of his humiliation was mounting steeply: from December 1943 the Republic was to pay the Reich ten billion lire per month 'protection money'.

Sometimes he reacted with sarcasm and bitterness. 'If it wasn't blasphemous,' he told one caller, 'I'd shout "God rot Hitler and that polecat Rahn" at the pitch of my lungs.' At times self-pity overwhelmed him. Once, after freeing a swallow that was trapped in his room, he choked out, tears in his eyes: 'If only I could have flown with it . . .'

Often he was consumed with blind rage. Graziani's call-up of the 1924/5 class netted 65,000 men, four complete divisions – yet most after training in Germany, were sent home again for lack of equipment. It was clear that after 25 July Kesselring had little faith in them, and the slight struck Mussolini like a body-blow. 'Why aren't the Germans using them?' he ranted to Secretary Dolfin, the veins standing out on his temples like whipcord, 'They don't want my Republic to have an army!'

On Sunday, 4 June, came the most painful news of all: 500 miles south, heralded by the password 'Elefante', the first US armoured cars had nosed through Rome's Porta Maggiore, and in the age-old tradition of victors, General Mark Clark mounted the steps of the Campidoglio. The Duce at once ordered three days' public mourning for the city he would never see again.

But most often he contracted out of everything, shuffling aside his papers in favour of a book; in the 600 days of Salò, he held only seventeen cabinet meetings. Sometimes, Dolfin noted, he spent hours annotating a copy of Socrates; once, when Ambassador Rahn dropped in, the Duce, like a guilty schoolboy, tried vainly to hide Plato's *Republic*. At his own insistence, he drew only a civil servant's salary of 12,500 lire per month – yet to Rachele's vexation he was forever checking that the rations in the larder didn't exceed the family's quota.

His old liberator, Otto Skorzeny, paid a fleeting visit to the lakeside villa, then returned to Germany full of foreboding. 'He's not a dictator any more,' he reported to the shocked Karl Radl, his Number Two, 'he's a philosopher.'

Then, soon after 20 July, Don Giusto called on the Duce to find him strangely elated. It needed no probing to find out why. On 20 July, at Rastenburg, he had visited Hitler's HQ, just three hours after Count von Stauffenberg's ill-fated bomb plot. The Führer had shaken hands with his left hand, shown Mussolini his singed uniform and the smoking ruins of the map room, then in a kind of apocalyptic rage had vowed destruction on all his enemies. At the tea-table Mussolini had sat in embarrassed silence, crumbling chocolate cake in his fingers, listening to one more monologue. Yet strangely, once Hitler had overcome his tantrum, he postponed the phone call ordering the liquidation of 5000 people to send for Mussolini's greatcoat in case he took cold. Mussolini had been pompous. 'In such a moment of history, dear Dollmann,' he told Himmler's aide, 'a Duce does not catch cold'.

But as he finished his recital, the priest saw that he could restrain himself no longer. With the realization that others too could endure the humiliation of 25 July, Mussolini was hugging himself with glee. 'Even to him,' he was chortling. 'It can happen even to *him*.'

The damp Baltic air seemed to split apart. Deep in the pine forests of Rügen Island, off Germany's north-east coast, the steel-and-concrete bunker shook convulsively. Despite the glare-glasses that he wore, twenty-seven-year-old Luigi Romersa felt something brighter than a thousand suns sear across his eyeballs. Outside, milky-white smoke boiled and bubbled as if the very earth was erupting. At 11.45 a.m. on 12 October, 1944, Romersa found ashamedly that he was wet through with sweat.

Dazedly the young war correspondent thought back over the week just past – the seven most apocalyptic days of his life. On 10 September, the eager Romersa, veteran reporter of the Tunisian campaign and for two years a Mussolini favourite, had thought it honour enough to be summoned to Lake Garda and handed a unique assignment: a see-for-yourself German tour of Hitler's much-vaunted secret weapons. Yet at the end of September, as he set off for Berlin, he had not dreamed that the two top-level introductions to Hitler and Goebbels reposing in his brief-case were passports to a nightmare.

To be sure, the sight of Hitler in his bunker at Rastenburg had shocked him profoundly. Ever since the bomb plot, Doctor Theo Morell, the quack in whom Hitler had put his faith, had been dosing him with strychnine and morphine injections, liable to damage the brain tissue; shaking and palsied, Hitler was a pitiable sight. Yet the light of veneration that came into his eyes once Mussolini was mentioned was unmistakable. The launching sites at Peenemünde, the Central Works near Nordhausen, deep in the Harz Mountains, where 10,000 slave labourers were at work assembling 6000 long-range rockets – as an envoy of the Duce, Romersa was free to see everything. 'What we have,' the Führer said softly, 'is formidable.'

Formidable, thought Romersa now, had been an understatement. The slim, savage warheads of the A 4 long-range rockets, already strafing London, had been impressive enough. But it had taken six unbelieving days to realize the full and deadly potential of Hitler's armoury. At Peenemünde he had witnessed trials of the Me 163 rocket-fighter – and had heard that 1000 would soon leave the assembly lines. He had seen blueprints of the '*Wasserfall*', an anti-aircraft guided missile which could soar to 50,000 feet, and had watched the Me 262 jet-fighter scream into action. The vertical take-off of the Bachemnatter fighter, the Boersig submarine, geared to reach and attack New York undetected – these, too, had left him open-mouthed.

Yet to Romersa, all these fearsome weapons paled before the mysterious 'disintegration-bomb' whose test, a mile and a half distant, he had just witnessed on Rügen Island – most probably, since Hitler's scientists never perfected the atom bomb, a forty-ton sixty-five-foot-long missile with an atom-splitting warhead.

It was 5 p.m. before a phone shrilled, signalling that Romersa and his three Army officer escorts could safely leave the bunker. Before departing, they donned white sterilized overalls and plastic diver-style helmets. Soldiers in the same garb led the way. Ahead, Romersa recalls, the earth seemed 'as if shaken to pieces', seamed with giant fissures. It was as if a searching fire had swept the forest; for almost a mile the trees were blackened stumps. At intervals, brick shelters he had noted earlier were now powdery drifting rubble.

His foot jarred against something. Bending, Romersa saw that it was a goat – now a stinking carbonized shell, the head 'smashed as with a hammer'. And all around dying goats cried out pitifully 'like the cries of men'.

Yet despite these horrors, Romersa thought, his report of all he had witnessed must surely put fresh heart into Mussolini. If the

Germans moved fast enough, victory was theirs – and on ticking seconds of borrowed time the Salò Republic would live on.

Obersturmführer Franz Spögler gulped frantically at his breakfast coffee. The cup was still rocking in its saucer as he hared for the main entrance of the Hotel Garda and Suisse. Within minutes, he was gunning his Volkswagen along the lakeside, heading for Villa Fiordaliso. The voice of Claretta Petacci, coming sharply over the line minutes earlier, had suggested that at ten o'clock on the rainy overcast morning of 24 October, she was expecting nothing but trouble.

The blue-eyed, twenty-nine-year-old SS officer, appointed bodyguard to the Petaccis by General Karl Wolff, admired Claretta deeply. Despite his periodic reports on her movements to Heinrich Himmler, a warm brother-and-sister relationship had sprung up between the two. Even protecting the family, Spögler had found, was less of a problem than feeding them; the Petaccis were living on savings, yet the frugal Duce was appalled even by Claretta's modest request, using Spögler as envoy, for a loan of 3000 lire. Often, to keep the ice-box filled, Spögler and Claretta were driven to poach in Lake Garda, running a seventy-yard cable from villa to waterside to electrocute whole creels of fish.

Now, as Villa Fiordaliso showed ahead, Spögler saw the cause of Claretta's alarm. Outside the high iron gates loomed Rachele Mussolini, formidable in a checked suit, a trench-coat over her arm, together with Minister for Home Affairs Guido Buffarini-Guidi and a truckload of fifty policemen. Outraged that her rival had dared take up permanent residence on the lake, Rachele, after fuming for months, had decided on a showdown.

Spögler thought fast. Somehow he must keep Rachele and Buffarini at bay until he had consulted both Claretta and the Duce. 'I must insist on speaking with that lady,' Rachele greeted him peremptorily, but the German played for time. Unlocking the gate, he first pretended to ring the door-bell. Then, hastily excusing himself, he slipped to the rear of the house. Upstairs, he found Claretta in her linenfold bed overlooking the lake. A hasty conference, then Spögler returned to Rachele.

'Either there's nobody at home,' he told her, 'or I can't make them hear.' Rachele would have none of it. 'I know perfectly well the lady is at home,' she shouted.

Then, Spögler proposed, he would return to his hotel and tele-

phone – but first he must insist they wait outside the gate and
send the policeman away. Simmering with fury, Rachele finally
agreed.

Piling into the Volkswagen, Spögler raced to the Hotel Garda.
On the phone to Mussolini he hastily outlined the situation, hearing
the Duce's gasp at the other end of the line. But at last he decided
grandly, 'I have nothing against a meeting of the two – if Rachele
can just see her, she'll realize she's a lady.' He cautioned Spögler
'But if either of them raises her voice, you will put an end to the
conversation.'

Spögler felt no such optimism. Back at Villa Fiordaliso, he found
the enraged Rachele trying to scale the nine-foot-high iron gate.
Buffarini, tugging frantically at her skirt, was imploring her 'Excellency, come down.' Under cover of the fracas, Spögler slipped in, to
find Mussolini had already phoned Claretta, persuading her to agree
to the meeting. Now, as the young German hovered uneasily on the
first-floor landing, Claretta dressed herself to kill – an eye-catching
dress of fur and pale blue velvet, with matching jewels. As he offered
his arm to escort her downstairs, Spögler thought uneasily: That's
just a shade provocative.

Nor was he wrong. In the Red Room, on the ground floor, Rachele
was plumped on the sofa, with Buffarini staring from the window.
Both seemed ill at ease among the walls lined with crimson brocade,
the gilt coffered ceiling, the miniature wall-fountains. Addressing
the room at large, Rachele set the key-note: 'What elegance! The
kept woman is really elegant! This is how a woman dresses when
she's kept by the head of a nation – and look at me, I'm married to
him.'

It was the worst of all beginnings. At the words 'kept woman'
Claretta reacted violently. Not only kept, Rachele insisted, but the
most hated woman in Italy. Everyone knew that she and Mussolini
were planning to escape by submarine from La Spezia. She was a
liar, Claretta fired back, and Rachele rose wrathfully. 'She's mad,
dangerous! Get her out of here,' Claretta shouted as Spögler lunged
between them, then fainted dead away. As the German hastened for
cognac, Rachele, unimpressed, commented: 'I know these faints – I
know them! Nobody dies for such a trifle.'

Recovering, Claretta went straight to the phone and rang Mussolini. In a white heat she demanded: 'Do you know what she called
me? She called me a whore!' 'What?' came the Duce's strangled
voice. 'Give me Spögler.' Then, when the German came on the line,

'Spögler, try to keep this conversation within reasonable bounds.'
'Duce,' Spögler told him, meaning every word of it, 'the situation is
very painful to me.'

Doggedly Rachele returned to the attack. For her sake and for the
sake of Italy, she demanded that Claretta put an end to the relationship. The younger woman fought back: the Duce needed her, she
was his spiritual support. He needed nothing, Rachele countered,
but to be left in peace. But it was the Duce, Claretta cried, who
would not leave *her* in peace. His letters proved it. 'Show me!'
challenged Rachele.

Claretta returned to the phone – and to the sweating Mussolini.
She asked formal permission to read Rachele some extracts from his
letters. 'Is it really necessary?' stammered the badgered Duce.
'Indispensable,' Claretta told him. 'Well, all right – but don't let
the situation become worse,' said Mussolini, on pins.

Claretta departed in triumph. In the Red Room, Rachele sat
gnawed with worry. All morning she had felt a strange unease.
Not only was this girl's presence the talk of the lake but suddenly
disaster seemed to threaten. From August on, the Germans' execution
of fifteen partisans in Piazzale Loreto in Milan had prompted a wave
of threatening anonymous letters; overnight, the tiny square had
become a symbol of partisan vengeance. Only that morning Rachele
had received one such missive which troubled her profoundly. It
read: 'We'll take *you* to Piazzale Loreto.'

And now, when Claretta reappeared with the hated letters bound
up in pink ribbon, it was the last straw. As the girl began to read,
phrases like 'I need your words,' and 'Today I missed you,' stung
like acid. 'Is that really his writing?' asked Rachele, nonchalantly
edging nearer – then tore them from her grasp. 'Stop her!' Claretta
shouted, and again Spögler leapt in. 'Your Excellency,' he insisted,
'those letters must not leave this house.' Incensed, Rachele drew her
nails down his left hand as they grappled, a wound so deep that the
polished cicatrice still survives. To the fat and tremulous Buffarini,
she yelled: 'Aren't you Minister for Home Affairs? Well, use your
authority!'

Though Buffarini did his best, Spögler was adamant. In the confusion Claretta had again rung Mussolini, who once more called
for the German. 'This is terrible, Spögler, stop them, stop them!'
came his anguished tones.

To the German the whole affair now hovered uneasily between
tragedy and a Borghese Gardens puppet show.

But at length Rachele saw that it was useless. Spögler was bleeding badly, but he had regained the letters and had no intention of giving them up. Bitterly, after more than two hours, the Duce's wife acknowledged defeat.

But at last, still tormented by that sinister anonymous message she once more lost control. Storming through the front door, she shouted over her shoulder, out of rage and frustration, yet scarcely knowing why: 'You'll end badly, Signora! They'll take you to Piazzale Loreto!'

Along the foggy streets of Milan the voice rose and fell, vibrant, hypnotic. Even in the raw cold people stopped despite themselves, listening spellbound – crowding to the doors of bars and cafés, sitting bolt upright in hospital beds. For over a year the sceptical, war-weary Milanese had secretly believed that Mussolini, unseen, unheard, was truly dead. Now, after fourteen months of silence, came this old-style fighting speech.

At 11 a.m. on Saturday, 16 December, 1944, before an audience in Milan's 2000-seater Teatro Lirico, he gave a bravura display of silver-tongued oratory, relayed by loudspeakers all over the city. Awed by Luigi Romersa's report, he spoke defiantly of the secret weapons which would pave the way to ultimate victory – confident that within weeks he would return to Palazzo Venezia. 'We will defend the valley of the Po with our nails and our teeth,' he declared, in the week that the Fifteenth Army Group, commanded now by General Mark Clark, dug in along the high Apennines, preparing for their spring offensive.

That morning as he left the theatre, one man recalled the city as 'like an ocean rising'. Women broke ranks to thrust bouquets upon him, tearing off his epaulettes, imprinting his hands with lipsticked kisses. And next day, in the triumphal procession through the city to the Castello Sforzesco, 40,000 people cheered hysterically. Once more he addressed the crowds from the top of a tank, reviewing a massed march past of Salò Republic troops – the dreaded Black Brigades, Prince Valerio Borghese's 10th Torpedo Boat Flotilla. 'Even passionate anti-Fascists,' one eye-witness marvelled, 'were cheering like crazy men.'

Despite all Prefect Mario Bassi's entreaties, the Duce insisted on travelling in an open car moving at walking pace. 'Otherwise they'll say I hid myself in a tank,' he grumbled.

Behind him, Vincenzo Costa, Milan's beetle-browed Federal

Secretary, breathed a sigh of relief. Pale and proud, like an elocution coach with a prize prodigy, he had stood behind Mussolini all through his Lirico speech – typed in enormous capitals to save the Duce's wearing spectacles in public – and everything had gone better than he expected. After months of argument he had at last persuaded Mussolini to come to Milan and show himself. Now only one thing remained: to convince the Duce of the daring plan that he, with Party Secretary Pavolini and others, had been working on in secret over the past three months.

It had begun soon after the abortive bomb plot against Hitler. Then the German Consul-General in Milan, Gustav von Halem, had arranged a secret meeting with Costa. In the event of the Germans evacuating North Italy, he explained, they could offer a secure passage for 10,000 Fascists and their families to a forest twenty-five miles from Munich. Costa must provide an urgent list of eligible families, stating ages, kinships, the value of goods they were leaving behind. But, von Halem stressed, nothing must be said to Mussolini. Against all logic, he was still obsessed about resisting on the Po.

A loyal old-guard Fascist, Costa did not like it. What was to stop the Germans using the Fascists as a bargaining counter with the Allies? On 6 August, 1944, he had gone covertly to Lake Garda to tell Mussolini everything – and be as summarily dismissed. The Duce did not believe any such transfer would take place – Hitler had undertaken to resist on the Po. And he, Mussolini, could look after his Fascists without the Führer's help.

But Costa had persisted – just as Mussolini had now for some weeks suspected. That afternoon he acknowledged the cheers of 30,000 people on the balcony of the Fascist Federation in Piazza San Sepolcro, where Fascism had been born twenty-five years ago. Abruptly re-entering Costa's office, he asked: 'What are you preparing in Val Tellina?'

Now Costa laid his cards on the table. Despite Mussolini's initial rebuff, he had gone into a huddle with Colonel Ferdinando Gimelli, the Black Brigades' Chief of Staff. Pavolini sat in on many of their meetings, as did Vice-Secretary Pino Romualdi. One plan appealed to them above all others: in the event of a German surrender, the Fascists would retreat simultaneously to a mountain redoubt, with Mussolini at their head, free to make such decisions as he saw fit, without German pressure. To surrender? To retreat to Germany? To move into Switzerland? Or put up a few weeks' token resistance?

The decision would be Mussolini's, and his alone, when the time came.

Costa's choice of redoubt was the forty-four-mile-long Val Tellina, eighty-five miles north of Milan, and his reasons were persuasive. Fortifications from World War One still ringed the valley. There were electricity generating stations and TB hospitals where the wounded could be lodged. It offered direct access to Germany through the 9000-foot Stelvio Pass, and to Switzerland through the Bernina Pass to St Moritz. Already, on his own initiative, Costa had despatched 170 artillerymen, 200 riflemen and four .145 cannons to Val Tellina.

Mussolini listened in silence while Costa presented his *fait-accompli*. 'I didn't know you were a strategist,' he commented sarcastically then. But Costa could see that he was intrigued. As wholeheartedly as he had seized on Luigi Romersa's report he now sought reasons to disbelieve it. 'And even if we didn't have any more land than my hand,' he said loudly, 'we would win just the same.' Then, in an undertone: 'At any rate we must believe this – if not we could no longer even breathe.'

Seeing him waver, Costa drove his point home. 'If we have to die,' he told him, 'we want to be hanged on the Italian flagstaff. If we're to live, we want to live with you, near the Italian flag . . .'

Mussolini stared at him, seeing nothing but glory. Now, if need be, Fascism might still achieve peace with honour, free from the German yoke that bound 'Benito Quisling'. He nodded his approval. 'I like this programme very much.'

Crouched above the uncertain flames, Allen Dulles energetically plied the bellows. The wood sputtered, then caught. Towards 10 p.m. on 8 March, 1945, the courtly former diplomat, head of America's top-secret Office of Strategic Services in Switzerland, was as absorbed as he had ever been. Kneeling before the library fireplace of a rented ground-floor apartment on the Genferstrasse in Zürich, he sought to coax a pine-log fire into a merry blaze.

As the flickering light wavered on the rows of morocco-bound books, Dulles momentarily relaxed. If a big conference was on the agenda, he set tremendous store by holding it round a wood fire – it had the subtle effect of making the participants feel at ease, shedding their inhibitions. And if you yourself needed time to answer, a fire helped in the by-play of lighting a pipe. Tonight, the bespectacled Dulles was especially anxious that everyone should be at ease. After tortuous months of negotiation, he at last glimpsed the end of the war in Italy.

Hastily he checked his watch: five minutes to go. Once more he ran through the handwritten document before him, which his guest-to-be had sent via an intermediary earlier that day – one of the most astonishing documents Dulles had ever seen in his career as an intelligence agent. As he said later, it was more the kind of *curriculum vitae* a man prepares when applying for a job with a company – though in a sense his visitor was.

KARL WOLFF

SS Obergruppenführer and General of the Military SS, Highest SS and Police Leader and Military Plenipotentiary of the German Armed Forces in Italy.

Information about the above person can be given by:

1. The former Deputy of the Führer, Rudolf Hess, at present in Canada.
2. The present Pope: Visit in May, 1944 . . . he stands by to intercede, if desired, at any time.

There were pages more of it, together with letters of reference from prominent churchmen supporting claims that Wolff had saved precious paintings from the Uffizi, had stopped general strikes without bloodshed, helped Field-Marshal Kesselring avert the destruction of Rome, and protected the partisans from German labour round-ups. As Dulles summed up to his aide, Gerd von Gaevernitz, 'He wants to show us just who'll vouch for him in case we have any wrong ideas.'

And promptly at 10 p.m. when Wolff entered the library with Professor Max Husmann, the stocky, cigar-smoking Swiss headmaster who had helped put Dulles in contact with both Italian industrialists and German top brass, the General, significantly, wore a grey civilian suit. To Dulles, he repeated what he had already stressed to Husmann on the train journey from the Italian border town of Chiasso to Zürich. 'Neither Hitler nor Himmler,' he emphasized, 'know anything of this trip.'

Pouring Scotch, Dulles proposed that Husmann should first summarize the facts that had emerged on the five-hour train journey. Meanwhile he studied his man – a distinguished forty-five-year-old with slightly receding blond hair, whose sharp green eyes never quite met his interlocutor's.

'He concedes,' Husmann wound up, 'that the war for Germany is irrevocably lost.'

Covertly Dulles watched the stiff-necked Wolff relax little by little, lulled by warmth and Scotch. He invited him: 'Suppose you state your own position fully and frankly.' Wolff came directly to the point. 'Until last year,' he told them, 'I had complete faith in Hitler. But I realize the war is lost and that to continue it is a crime against the German people. Now *I* control the SS forces in Italy – I am willing to place myself and my entire organization at the disposal of the Allies to terminate hostilities.'

Although Dulles and his thirty-strong staff had begun undercover operations from Berne's American Legation as long ago as November 1942, it was not until late 1944 that Milan industrialists had begun to make peace feelers, conveyed through the Cardinal Archbishop, Ildefonso Schuster, to Monsignor Bernardini, Berne's Papal Nuncio. The tenor of every approach had been: if the Germans withdraw from Northern Italy without destroying vital industrial plants the Church might act as middlemen to keep the growing army of partisans in check. A month ago, an envoy from Ambassador Rahn, the mastermind behind the plot, had visited Switzerland to spell out the message all over again.

As an earnest of his intentions, Wolff had already released Resistance Chief Ferruccio Parri, a saintly white-haired World War One hero who had fought the Fascists for twenty years, and Dulles was now hiding him in a Zürich clinic. In the event of a retreat, Wolff now assured them, he had given orders to carry out only token sabotage of industry.

But, Wolff emphasized, the SS in themselves were not enough. He had to win over the commanders of the German Armed Forces. Already he had talked with his old friend Kesselring and thought he might be persuaded. If Dulles could assure negotiations at the level of Field-Marshal Harold Alexander, now Supreme Commander, Kesselring or a deputy might visit Switzerland to parley a surrender.

A self-confessed eternal optimist, Dulles christened this bold plan to remove 800,000 pawns from the board at one stroke 'Operation Sunrise'.

But now an hour had ticked by and Dulles felt that for tonight they had gone as far as they could. Much now depended on Kesselring's attitude. But one last question was mandatory: was Mussolini a party to these plans?

For almost the first time Wolff looked him squarely in the eye.

'Mussolini knows nothing,' he told the American, 'and he will know nothing. This much is certain – we can't trust Mussolini.'

His face suffused with rage, Benito Mussolini crashed his fist down on the desk of his Villa Orsoline office. Furiously he rounded on the Foreign Ministry's Chief of Secretariat, Count Alberto Mellini Ponce de Leon. 'Either they're irresponsible or else in bad faith,' he exploded, 'maybe both! But these assurances in general terms are useless! What I want to know is, what plans they've got to stop all the Po Valley crumbling like a ripe pear. But no, these gentlemen are too presumptuous to tell me what they've got in their haughty heads!'

Mellini stood silent, feeling for Mussolini. This was indeed the last straw. Early on the morning of 18 April, he was reporting to Mussolini on a recent meeting with Rahn and Wolff, and, incredibly, both had seemed euphoric with optimism. Yet two days earlier US troops had taken Nuremberg, and Marshal Giorgi Zhukov's Russian armies had crossed the Oder. In Italy, General Mark Clark's 15th Army Group was forging ahead; the British 8th Army was closing on Argenta, and General Anders's Poles were hammering the crack German 1st Parachute Division at Bologna. But Rahn spoke of good news from Germany and Wolff had recently avowed that the Italian front would hold, too. Hence Mussolini's blind fury in the face of such groundless optimism.

Over the past weeks the Duce's anger against the Germans had reached boiling-point – most especially at a 14 April conference, when their disbelief in the Val Tellina plan had been all too plain. Only Alessandro Pavolini had raved about the thousands of loyal Blackshirts who were yearning to come – recalling the 50,000 of Thermopylae. But every German face, Mellini noted, had been 'stony, sceptical'.

Mussolini, of course, could not know that virtually every German present – General Baron von Vietinghoff, Kesselring's successor as Commander-in-Chief, Southern Command, General Wolff, Rahn – were parties to the deal with Allen Dulles to avert just such a massacre as Pavolini propounded.

But the Germans were not the only delegates who had been sceptical. To Marshal Rodolfo Graziani, the whole Val Tellina project smacked of Party politics, something career officers would do well to avoid; unlike Fascist Party officials, they would qualify as legitimate prisoners of war. Even a preliminary study made by his experts had proved it impracticable. The buildings Federal Secretary Costa had reported existed right enough, but they lacked central heating. Moreover, the area teemed with Communists who had threatened to blow up the generating stations if the Fascists moved in. The 2000 labourers promised by the Todt Organization had never showed up on site.

To Mussolini's chagrin, even one of his ablest commanders, the outspoken Prince Valerio Borghese commanding the 10th Torpedo Boat Flotilla, was wholly unhelpful. How, Borghese demanded, could 20,000 men be moved to Val Tellina with neither trucks nor petrol? Bluntly he told Mussolini: 'Any time Mark Clark wants to roll up the peninsula like a carpet he can do it – and any time the partisans want to come and take you prisoner they can do that too.'

For Borghese was privy to the vital secret unknown to Graziani and the others. He knew that General Wolff was negotiating with Dulles. On 13 April, one day before the Val Tellina meeting at Villa Orsoline, the SS Chief had visited his headquarters near Brescia and confided: 'I must tell you we're trying to get out. Will you fire against us?' Borghese's tough anti-partisan force, 50,000-strong, was the one unit the Germans truly feared. The Italian temporized. Before deciding, he wanted a firm undertaking that no industrial plant would be blown up as the Germans withdrew – an undertaking Wolff was swift to obtain from Admiral Karl Doenitz, the Naval Commander-in-Chief. But in turn Borghese had given a pledge of his own: nothing must be revealed to Mussolini. Inevitably, Wolff stressed, Claretta or Rachele would learn of it, and the secret would be out.

Unaware of these last-ditch manoeuvres, Mussolini remained obsessed by his historic last stand. To go down in glory in Val Tellina would preserve his legend for all time; time and again he harked back to his great days as mediator, only seven years back at Munich, when his presence had been a world force.

Brushing aside all ideas of personal salvation, he summarily rejected every hare-brained scheme to transport him to safety . . . Tullio Tamburini's plan for a twelve-man submarine, costing three billion lire, which after 100 days underwater would carry Mussolini to Ibù island, east of Borneo . . . General Harster's concept of a giant airliner to spirit the Duce, Jules Verne style, to South America . . . Ambassador Rahn's offer of a private plane to Eire.

A month ago he had seen Don Giusto for the last time. All told, they had met twenty times, and the priest had never ceased to urge another kind of salvation. But Mussolini, gently but firmly sought to dismiss him: 'Father, let's say goodbye now, because I know I'm going to be killed.' Don Giusto made one last herculean effort. He could hear the Duce's confession even there, in the study at Garda. Still Mussolini hung back. 'We'll talk it over later,' he promised without conviction. 'There's still time.'

Pancino was pressing. If the Duce felt death was imminent, time was running out. Even now, false pride held Mussolini back from confession, from communication. He kept hold of Pancino's hand for a long time as the priest spoke to him, smiling gently. At last it was time to play the trump card. 'Ciano confessed,' the priest reminded him. 'He put himself straight.'

Mussolini was still smiling, but he did not reply. There was rejection in his eyes when Don Giusto at last turned away.

About the fate of his old friend Adolf Hitler, the Duce had no illusions. Three months earlier, in the second week of January, he had received General Renzo Montagna, who, following the Verona Trial, had become his Chief of Police in October 1944. Mussolini was on the phone, speaking in German, when Montagna entered. A moment later he hung up. 'That,' he told the police chief, 'was the Führer. He's leaving his headquarters to go to Berlin and take over the last defences. He's hoping for some miracle to be able to repel the Russians.'

Then, to Montagna's astonishment, Mussolini looked him squarely in the eyes and predicted slowly: 'Hitler will die in Berlin and nobody will find his body. Within ten – or maybe 100 – years, the Germans, who love creating myths, will say that the Führer went to heaven in the heart of the flames and they'll make him a national hero. If something similar happened to me . . .'

He stopped then. Montagna was always to remember afterwards that Mussolini could never bring himself to finish that sentence.

On this same morning, while Mussolini raged at Count Mellini, Claretta Petacci, a few miles away in the Villa Mirabella, was determined that the Duce should suffer no such fate. In mid-November, following her bitter showdown with Rachele, Claretta had moved, on Spögler's advice, to this small villa within a park to work out a private plan. This morning, in the big first-floor salon, she was deep in it as ever, thumbing through a pile of snapshots.

To a layman's eye they would have seemed scarcely worth the

snapping – close-ups of a crude peasant hut set in a clearing among a thick grove of firs. There were other photos too, showing ice-capped mountain peaks, the kind a keen amateur mountaineer might take on summer vacation. But to Claretta, they represented the ultimate salvation of Mussolini both from Fascist intrigues and from General Mark Clark's advancing army – a refuge 9000 feet up in the Dolomites where she and the Duce could hide out, if need be for years.

For months, together with Spögler, Claretta had debated this plan, and it was the German who had hit on the solution – a hut, kept by an old couple, in a pine-forest that he owned up on the Jöcherhof peak above the Ritter saddle – two hours' steady mountain trek above the cut-off village of Lengmoos, where Spögler, in peacetime, kept a guest-house. Twice he had taken Claretta there by sled and they had talked to the old peasants, explaining that although two people might live there for years, no questions must be asked. Once they had agreed, Claretta had persuaded Spögler to broach the subject to Mussolini in her presence.

To her heartfelt relief, Mussolini didn't at once explode or pooh-pooh it, as he had done with the other plans set before him. Instead he had listened attentively, just saying, 'I see, I see.' Then, finally, 'Well, Comrade Spögler, what does this place look like?'

Spurred on by Claretta, Spögler had asked a friend to take snaps on the spot, using the excuse that city-bred Italians wouldn't believe such godforsaken places existed. It was pictures of this desolate hut that Mussolini himself had pored over some weeks ago – 'a place,' as Spögler said, 'where the foxes say good-night to each other'. When Claretta was out of earshot he phrased it more saltily: 'Duce, it's the ass-end of the world.'

Up to now they had talked it over with Mussolini fully twenty-five times. To Claretta's despair, he blew hot and cold according to how Pavolini and Costa had been working on him. One day the plan would be on, the next off. 'The flower of Fascist youth is gathering in the Val Tellina,' he told Spögler after the abortive 'Thermopylae Conference'. 'They need me there as a symbol.' He had qualms, too, as to whether he shouldn't let General Wolff in on the plan, but Spögler had dissuaded him.

As SS telephone-tapper-in-chief, Spögler had made investigations when Wolff had hived off two lines in the local exchange without informing him, and he now knew – though Claretta didn't – just why Wolff was making all those calls to Switzerland.

Claretta got out the map and pored over it. Already she and Spögler had worked out every detail of the route: from Garda to Brescia, thence to Mendola and Bolzano, and on through the Val Sarentino. Some of the journey would be hard sledding, undertaken on foot and at night – but Spögler was faking transit permits so that German road-blocks wouldn't trouble them, and he himself would be there as escort.

Meanwhile, after an inner struggle, Claretta defied superstition and made ready to pack. Until late afternoon at least she must keep her fingers crossed. But if Mussolini held to what he had agreed with both her and Spögler only twenty-four hours ago, that very night, at 8 p.m., the three of them would move north to the Jöcherhof.

Rachele Mussolini beat time appreciatively. It was 5 p.m. on 18 April in the drawing-room of Villa Feltrinelli, and eighteen-year-old Romano at the piano had just rippled into 'The Blue Danube'. Suddenly, realizing that his father had entered wearing a topcoat, he struggled to rise from the piano stool but Mussolini restrained him. 'No, no, don't get up,' he reassured him, 'go on playing.' Then, grinning, he teased the jazz-loving Romano, 'Since when have you liked waltzes?', caressing the hair of Anna Maria, sixteen, who had never fully recovered from polio. 'Courage, Anna Maria,' he rallied her as always, 'we must dance that last waltz soon.'

Romano loved his father, who had always been ready for a game of table-tennis or skittles, who had nicknamed him 'Pythagoras' because he was so bad at math, and only occasionally flew into a rage, as once when Romano left his guitar on the stairs and Mussolini put his foot through it. But neither he nor Rachele looked on this entry of Mussolini's as any kind of farewell. The Duce said only that he was off to Milan for a conference, and that soon he would be back.

But his family, like Claretta Petacci, had reckoned without his deep-seated rancour against the Germans. 'At Salò I'll never know anything,' he had fumed to Count Mellini that morning. 'Every contact I make is supervised by them. I cannot govern Italy from this damned hole!' And he stormed on. All along, in a dizzying reversion to his pre-Fascist days, he had sought to proclaim the Salò Republic as a Socialist State, working with his Minister of Corporations, Angelo Tarchi, to nationalize every branch of industry. But on Lake Garda all his efforts to achieve full rapport with Italian workers had been blocked not only by the Germans but by the

Communists and Milan's industrialists. Yet now, at last, he was decided. On 20 April, in Milan, he would announce total socialization – one more gambit to go down in glory.

By noon, in Milan's Prefecture, Prefect Mario Bassi who for months had been urging Mussolini to take a stand against the Germans was rubbing his hands with glee. From Lake Garda a secretary had just then phoned through a code message: 'The parcel has been despatched.' Bassi understood the import, for he had fixed the code with Mussolini himself. Unmindful of his promise to Claretta, in direct defiance of General Wolff, whom he had promised to stay put, Mussolini was leaving for Milan.

At 5.50 p.m., as his column moved off, Rachele and the children noted that his usual S S escort was in attendance. Even in Wolff's absence, a twelve-strong bodyguard under Kriminalinspektor Otto Kisnatt and Untersturmführer Fritz Birzer dogged him everywhere, Rachele could not know that fifteen days ago Kisnatt had received an order from Berlin that was chilling in its implications – an order he would comply with whatever the cost. It read: 'If Mussolini tries to reach Switzerland, restrain him, if need be by force of arms.'

Though Adolf Hitler was fifty feet below ground in his Berlin bunker and would never emerge from it again, Karl-Heinz – as the German escort codenamed Mussolini – was as much his prisoner now as ever he had been.

11. 'We Have to Write the Word *Finito*'
18–28 April, 1945

In the first-floor three-room suite he had taken over in the Palazzo Monforte, the Prefecture of Milan, Mussolini was alone. His eyes red-rimmed, he stared unseeing at the painted ceiling with its Romulus and Remus motif, the thick pile carpet embroidered with the fasces, the gilt-and-mahogany furniture.

Now, at noon on Tuesday, 24 April, six days after leaving Lake Garda, he saw nothing ahead but the bitter end of everything for which he had striven.

At first his plans had gone with a swing. After deciding to disband his ministries, he had begun by paying advance salaries to all employees . . . made arrangements for a mass address on 21 April, anniversary of the birth of Rome . . . with a Cathedral ceremony for the Fascist dead to follow . . . then a muster of 300,000 Fascists at Castello Sforzesco, prior to a retreat to Val Tellina. There he planned to hold out for six months, with printing presses and a radio transmitter to chart every milestone of his historic last stand. Envoys had even been sent to Ravenna to disinter Dante's bones, a precious cultural symbol.

The one thing that momentarily disconcerted him was Claretta's tearful arrival in Milan, escorted by Franz Spögler, on 19 April. But he accepted that she was anxious to bid farewell to her family who, with Ambassador Rahn's help, were flying to Spain within days.

Then, on 21 April, the bitter reverses began. On the very day he had planned to proclaim Socialism to the Milanese, the Allies entered Bologna. Now, in the Prefecture, the tension was so great that the warring factions on Val Tellina almost came to blows before his eyes – and even he could no longer blind himself to the issue. Swollen with pride, Alessandro Pavolini was crowing about the orders he had sent to the Black Brigades in the provinces of Emilia, Liguria, and Veneto, instructing them to head for the Po Valley and Lake Como, thence to Val Tellina. 'In the next few days,' he bragged, 'we'll have up to fifty thousand men in the Como region'. Abruptly Marshal Graziani lost control. 'It's a shameful thing to lie like this until the end,' he yelled, stabbing his Marshal's baton at Pavolini, 'you know very well it's absurd to think of a resistance in Val Tellina – even so, you go on betraying the Duce!' Advancing with menace, Pavolini grated: 'Marshal, my respect for your person is one thing – to put up with insults is something else again.' Scarlet in the face, Graziani bellowed back: 'Bologna has fallen! What lies ahead of us is a military rout!'

Calmly, as if someone else's fate was involved, Mussolini intervened. 'Then another 8 September?' 'Much worse,' said Graziani darkly. Cheeks flaming, Pavolini asked permission to leave, then slammed from the room.

And two days later, the situation was still more desperate. On 23 April, the Party's vice-secretary, Pino Romualdi, sent by Mussolini to prospect the front, returned dusty and sweat-stained to tell the stark truth. 'It's disastrous,' was all he could at first choke out, 'there's nothing left.' 'But the Germans are defending the Po,' Mussolini persisted stolidly. 'The Germans are defending nothing, Duce!' Romualdi almost shouted. More patiently he explained: the Germans on the Po had just one plane left and no heavy artillery. By the 27th they would have fallen back on Milan. 'You should order an immediate retreat to Val Tellina,' urged Romualdi, 'the German Command doesn't exist any more.'

'They say they're throwing flowers to the Allies in Bologna,' Mussolini said, aghast. 'That can't be true?'

Romualdi was dour. 'Unfortunately it is. The people are very ready to greet anyone who brings tranquillity.' Mussolini, he noted, was too mortified to reply. But when he spoke of the need for renewed resistance, even Federal Secretary Costa was dubious. 'Once you said a man could even serve the country by guarding a drum of benzine,' he grumbled, 'but now that drum is empty.'

On one issue Mussolini was firm. Despite the pleas of his old-guard fanatics, he would not turn Milan into another Stalingrad. Time and again he emphasized: 'Milan mustn't be destroyed. There'll be blood anyway, there'll be a holocaust, but I didn't agree to form this government for myself. It was the one hard road to stop the Germans oppressing our people.' Of this he had convinced himself, his niche in history already decided.

Now, determined on Val Tellina, Mussolini made one more hasty change of plans. On the phone to Rachele, he explained that Mantua had fallen, blocking his way back to Lake Garda. She and the children should head for the Villa Reale, the old royal residence at Monza, seven miles north of Milan; from there an escort would bring them to Lake Como. Following this, there had been another vital plan to put into effect. Over the weekend he had worked with Carlo Silvestri, a Socialist newsman convinced of Mussolini's good faith, on a four-point programme which outlined the transfer of power to the partisans of North Italy – all save the Communists – following the withdrawal of the Germans and Fascists.

It had taken the partisans just thirty-six hours to reject it out of hand.

This was the bleak news that Silvestri had brought him at noon on 24 April – and now his ever-present shadow, the heavily-built forty-eight-year-old Kriminalinspektor Otto Kisnatt, again entered the room, this time without even knocking. On the Sunday, when he tried to pin down the date of Mussolini's return, the Duce had been evasive – but now Kisnatt was out for the truth. He didn't like the signs he saw about the streets and in the courtyard of the Prefecture. Cars packed with Fascist families and suitcases were flooding into Milan. Day by day, the Fascist troops were melting away. Faced with Kisnatt's implacable front, Mussolini had to admit it: 'I shall never go back to Garda.'

Kisnatt stood by the book. 'I know that wherever the German Embassy is, the German authorities wish you always to be in the vicinity.' And he pointed out: the Embassy had now moved from Fasano, Lake Garda, to Merano on the Austrian border. It was imperative that the Duce should transfer there too. To his puzzlement, Mussolini produced a map, spread it on the sofa and indicated the strangest route – due north and then east, via Como, Menaggio, Sondrio. 'We'll reach the German Embassy that way,' he decided. It didn't then dawn on Kisnatt that the itinerary passed just north of Val Tellina. Instead he argued, 'That's a very dangerous way – the partisans control it.'

But the route, Mussolini pointed out, also lay close to the Swiss border. 'If the situation became critical, I could take refuge there.'

Kisnatt was steely. 'I repeat: the German authorities insist that you should never, for any reason, enter Switzerland. In any case, the Swiss would not grant you asylum.'

Idly, Mussolini picked up the morning paper. From the bunker on the Wilhelmstrasse Hitler had issued one last insane rallying call to the Duce: 'The battle for life or death against the forces of Bolshevism and Jewry has reached its final stage . . . the course of the war in this historic moment will decide the fate of Europe for centuries to come.' Hypnotized, Mussolini read on, as if listening for the last time to the harsh voice he had heard so often – at the Brenner, at Feltre, at Rastenburg – rising and falling in monologue.

Then in a low dead voice he said: 'So nothing in Switzerland either.'

In the old dust-smelling library of the Salesian oratory at 12, Via Copernico, behind Milan's Central Station, one man was striving to avert the bloodbath that Mussolini so feared. Outside in the cloisters, silent black-cassocked figures guarded every approach to the locked and shuttered room. Facing his fellows of the Committee of National Liberation, the Christian Democrat delegate, fifty-one-year-old Achille Marazza, was reporting on a vital meeting that had taken place twenty-four hours earlier at the moment when Mussolini had seen his world falling apart. It was 8 a.m. on Wednesday, 25 April.

To the gentle, slightly-built Marazza, that meeting had been as strange as the meeting-place itself – the city pawnshop in a narrow side-street behind the luxurious Continental Hotel. Under the grimy domed glass roof old women were pawning gold medallions and redeeming shabby furs, while Marazza and a smartly-dressed Milanese industrialist, Gian-Riccardo Cella, talked in low tones of an issue that was political dynamite: the surrender of Benito Mussolini.

A devout Catholic, Marazza had used his contacts with the Archbishop's Palace to secure hide-outs for his fellow-resistants – even the Communists – in monasteries and convents all over the city. Now, following the resistants' summary rejection of Mussolini's transfer-of-power plan, the Duce was making one last appeal to avoid bloodshed following his departure from the city. As his envoy, he had hit upon the wealthy Cella, who had bought the printing plant and premises of *Il Popolo d'Italia*, knowing that he, too, had close contact with the Church. Mussolini, Cella explained, wanted the Archbishop to arrange a private meeting with General Raffaele Cadorna, military commander of the Volunteer Freedom Corps, the Liberation Committee's fighting arm.

At first Marazza had misunderstood. The meeting, he suggested, could be held in the Archbishop's Palace, for this was neutral ground – but Mussolini should surrender to the Committee itself, not to the military chief. Then he could be taken under the Archbishop's protection until the time came for him to face an appointed tribunal. But – he had to emphasize it – the surrender terms would be unconditional.

Cella balked. He did not think he could tell Mussolini that. He felt the dictator had no intention of surrendering. He merely stressed that Mussolini was worried about the fate of those Fascist families who would not make part of the Val Tellina column. Still Marazza urged a meeting at the Palace. It was the one sure way to avoid bloodshed in the streets.

Now, facing the committee, Marazza was putting all the force he could muster into his argument. He knew it would be no easy task. For months there had been a no-holds-barred struggle among the committee members. Of the men assembled, only the Liberal representative, Giustino Arpesani, shared Marazza's moderate views. The Action Party's deputy chief, Leo Valiani, standing in for Ferruccio Parri who was still in Switzerland with Dulles, was ranged with the others of the left-wing – Sandro Pertini, the hotspur who represented the Socialists, and Emilio Sereni, Milan's No 2 Communist under Luigi Longo. They too were staunch patriots, but their terms were stark and uncompromising. They favoured no negotiations with the Fascists, no trials – only 'surrender or die'.

But to Marazza's relief, the objections, as he outlined his case, were few. 'All right,' Sereni said finally after much general discussion, 'we accept, as Communists, but it's nothing binding.' And he stipulated: no one from the committee would parley with Mussolini. If he wanted to surrender at the Archbishop's Palace, that was a military matter. General Cadorna would be sent to accept it.

Promptly Marazza excused himself, together with Arpesani. His first step now was to fix an urgent rendezvous with the Cardinal's negotiator, Don Giuseppe Bicchierai. If Milan was to be spared civil war, with Mussolini as the flashpoint, there was no time to lose.

Marazza only half-suspected it, but the men he left behind in the oratory felt the same. At 9 p.m. on 24 April, all three had tuned in to the BBC on their secret radios to hear the news they had long awaited: the first of General Mark Clark's units, the 10th Mountain Division, had crossed the River Po. Soon the Allies would reach Milan.

For Emilio Sereni, the chubby Neapolitan Communist, the day held special significance. This very morning his chief, Luigi Longo, had woken him in his flat. 'Well,' was Longo's blunt greeting, 'shall we dive in?'

Sereni knew exactly what his chief meant. The day of the armed rising, which the Allies had done their painstaking best to prevent, had dawned. Twelve days earlier, on 13 April, General Mark Clark in Florence had broadcast an urgent warning to the partisans: 'The time for your concerted action has not yet come – do not squander your strength. Do not be tempted to precipitate action.'

Simultaneously, from San Leocco, south of Naples, Allied Forces Headquarters had instructed twenty-five OSS teams poised for action in the woods and the mountains: 'It is the desire of the Allies to take Mussolini alive. These HQ will be notified if he is taken and he will be held in security pending the arrival of Allied troops.'

Of this last message, the three men in the oratory as yet knew nothing – but the Communists' instructions had been made plain within hours of Clark's broadcast. From Rome, the Communist chief Palmiro Togliatti, who had returned from Moscow under Allied auspices, cabled Longo: 'Don't obey General Mark Clark! It is in our vital interests that . . . the population . . . should destroy the Nazi-Fascists before the Allies arrive . . . Choose your own moment for insurrection . . .'

To ensure the Communists maintained their hold on the people, the implications were plain. The armed insurrection must go ahead, heedless of the Allied warning. Already Luigi Longo's orders had gone out: 'No passes, no golden bridges for those retreating – only a war of extermination.' And, as patriots, the other left-wingers, too, saw the need to prove they no longer depended on the Allies but were their equals and collaborators. Argued Sandro Pertini: 'We're not their servants. To kill Mussolini would be to assert our independence.'

Both Sereni and the others knew the programme. At 2 p.m. the workers would seize the factories. Fascists who had not surrendered within four hours would be shot on sight. Every man who had marched on Rome would face a popular tribunal – which, in the case of the Duce and his big-wigs, would award only the death penalty.

Such was the Communist decision, and the others had little choice but to follow. In the north, the Communists controlled fifty per cent of all arms, funds and transport. More than 100,000 workers now held the Party card. After long years in Spain, Vichy France and Mussolini's penal camps, their leaders were battle-hardened, torture-hardened, and they saw no reason why Mussolini should be spared to face an Allied trial, bringing black disgrace to Italy.

On this, at least, all the left-wingers were agreed. That morning in the oratory Leo Valiani summed up the feelings of them all: 'It's gone on for twenty years – let's end it. We have to write the word *finito* one way or the other.'

For all three men, and their absent chiefs, Longo and Parri, that word could be written only in letters of blood.

From the window of her parents' apartment overlooking Milan's Largo San Babila, Claretta Petacci stared out over the scattered morning traffic. The man behind her stood in silence, patiently awaiting her command. Abruptly she reached a decision. 'If you could get me a Woman's Auxiliary Force uniform,' she told Asvero Gravelli, one of the few Party officials who didn't view her relationship with the Duce with deep distrust, 'I'd be truly grateful.'

In six days Claretta's determination had hardened. Three days earlier, when her parents and Myriam departed for Spain in a camouflaged plane furnished by Ambassador Rahn, her younger sister had made one last attempt to change her mind, 'If you come with us,' she pleaded, 'you'll at least spare *him* that worry. Then when everything's finished you can come back.' Claretta just stared at her, trying to hide her desolation. 'And you believe I could come back?' she challenged Myriam. 'You believe I could look him in the face after having abandoned him in danger?' She shook her head decidedly. 'It's not possible. Too many people are turning their backs on him for that.'

As the family entered the lift, Claretta's face was briefly framed in the frosted glass window. She was trying to smile, and for an instant Myriam had the eerie impression of the last close-up in a movie, before 'The End' flashes on the screen. Then the lift cage slid towards street-level.

But if the end was imminent, Claretta was still making every effort to save something from the wreck. On 23 April she had sent a letter to friends at the Villa Mirabella, listing extra clothes that she needed. The stay in Milan was proving longer than she had expected and she wanted 'Ben' to see her at her best. She had asked them to send both the red and green nightdresses and the black one with hand-painted flowers. She wanted the black velvet dressing-gown with the fur collar, the pink lace summer one with bunches of flowers, her white silk lounging-pyjamas and all her cosmetics, stockings and medicines. To Franz Spögler, to whom she entrusted the letter, she confided her fear that Pavolini's Val Tellina fantasy would prevail over their Jöcherhof sanctuary. 'We'll just have to pack him into a car and take him,' Claretta said despairingly.

But now, after thirty-six hours, Spögler hadn't returned and fear had assailed her. Supposing Mussolini left suddenly for Val Tellina?

All her fine clothes would be useless then. She needed a grey-green Auxiliary Force uniform by this afternoon, she told Gravelli. The Fascist promised he'd do his best.

'Please, Asvero,' Claretta urged; then added, almost as if it was a commonplace: 'I'm going to die with him.'

Don Giuseppe Bicchierai leaned forward to slip the doorcatch and Achille Marazza slid from the car's passenger seat on to the pavement. A brief wave of the hand, then Marazza was lost to view in the web of side-streets behind Milan's Central Station. Hastily, the sturdy forty-eight-year-old priest let in the clutch of his Fiat 1100, heading southwards across the city for the Archbishop's Palace in the lee of the Cathedral.

After two years as Cardinal Schuster's liaison man with the Resistance, Don Bicchierai had developed an uncanny nose for trouble. And already, by noon of this momentous Wednesday, the mood of the city had subtly changed. Many shops had pulled down their shutters; the streets wore a sullen, deserted air. Outside most public buildings the guards had blatantly discarded their uniforms, donning civilian suits. To one man, it was as if the whole city was involved 'in a vast closing-down sale': typewriters, radios, even telephones, had been ripped from public buildings.

On the first floor of the sixteenth-century Palace, Cardinal Schuster, Archbishop of Milan, was at his frugal lunch, together with his secretaries, Monsignor Guglielmo Galli and Don Ecclesio Terraneo. As Bicchierai entered, he saw a scene which he had witnessed literally scores of times in the past. Clad in his scarlet silk soutane and red buckle shoes, the frail, blue-eyed Cardinal sat at a table as bare as a Benedictine monastery's, the order from which he sprang. Vegetable soup with a little cooked *pasta* were all the Cardinal took at this main meal of the day, and as always his priests were worried. Both of them loved Schuster deeply, an Archbishop who would serve them Mass with his own hands, a privilege to which only Pope Pius XII was entitled, and who never used his bell to summon them but came courteously to his study door.

As always, they were chiding him, 'You should have eaten more, Your Eminence,' and as always he replied, 'It's enough for me, my mother was just the same.'

Knowing the Cardinal's hatred of verbiage, Bicchierai reported tersely. Following Marazza's phone call, he had picked him up outside the station and driven at random through the streets, urging the need for a peaceful solution. Marazza, he knew, was fully convinced, and would come to the Palace that afternoon if need be. Arpesani, too, would lend support if something positive was afoot. And to both men, General Cadorna had confirmed: 'If Mussolini wants to meet me, I am at your disposal.'

Schuster's calm, reedy voice issued precise orders. Cella, the industrialist, must contact one of Cadorna's aides, so that word could be sent to both the General and the dictator that the Archbishop awaited them. It seemed unlikely that the left-wingers would put in an appearance. But if Mussolini and the Fascists could be persuaded to come to terms, the rising which could bring only untold suffering to the hungry city might never take place.

That the Cardinal had done his utmost to avoid a second Stalingrad, his staff knew well. As far back as 13 February, in a letter to Mussolini, he had pleaded with him not to create his last defences in the city. 'Please save Milan' he begged, 'from a gesture which I know is not yours, but which is foolish and desperate.'

Now it seemed that his unsparing efforts might be fruitful. Lunch over, he sent Monsignor Galli to the room beyond his reception chamber, overlooking Piazza del Duomo, the square lying beneath the Cathedral's fretted Gothic spires. A simple guest-room furnished with only a bed and fald-stool, it was normally used by visiting bishops, but on an inspiration Schuster had that morning asked the grey-robed nuns of the Order of Maria Bambina to have it made up for an unexpected guest. Now he wanted Galli to check that everything was ready.

Tonight, if all went well, he was expecting no prelate to share his frugal board but the Duce of Fascism and First Marshal of the Empire, Benito Mussolini – assured of sanctuary until the Allies came to collect him.

Plump little Monsignor Galli bustled back into the Cardinal's study. 'Everything is in order, Your Eminence,' he announced. Then he realized that Schuster had not heard him, any more than Don Bicchierai or Terraneo. Their ears strained, they were listening to a far-off crying that came nearer, then nearer, until the high-pitched blasting of sirens seemed to vibrate within the very walls of the old stone Palace. And outside, on the Piazza Fontana, and swiftly along the 153 miles of track within the city, the trams were heading for their depots.

The Milan uprising had begun.

He stood to face his judges against an unlikely backdrop – Cardinal Schuster's audience chamber, its walls lined with crimson damask, its semi-circle of eight armchairs facing a divan upholstered in rose-pink plush. Now that the trams had stopped, no sound penetrated the lace-curtained windows from the cathedral square beyond. As they advanced to meet him across the waxed nutwood parquet, he had the uncertain ingratiating air of a man unused to asking favours.

As a last resort, Benito Mussolini was meeting the resistants face to face. On the mantelshelf a green-black marble clock showed 6 p.m.

It had been almost three hours since Mussolini had arrived, telling almost none of his hierarchs save for his Minister of the Interior, Paolo Zerbino, his Under-Secretary, Francesco Barracu, and the Prefect, Mario Bassi – all three now mingling uneasily with the resistants entering the audience chamber. Marshal Graziani, too, had been summoned by despatch-rider at the last minute. But Party Secretary Alessandro Pavolini, who had no belief in a peaceful transfer, had been told nothing of the mission.

The one man Mussolini had been unable to evade was Kisnatt's SS deputy, Untersturmführer Fritz Birzer. Convinced that the Duce was boarding his Alfa-Romeo to make good his escape, the stocky Birzer, holder of an SS Silver Medal for athletics, sprinted after the accelerating car and, jerking open the rear off-side door, landed heavily on Mussolini's lap.

Once at the Archbishop's Palace, the Duce had waited so long it seemed the resistants would never come. And although the Cardinal had been hospitable in true Benedictine tradition, pressing on him a glass of *rosolio* liqueur and a biscuit, the conversation lagged. He had been badly served by his hierarchs, Schuster told the Duce, mincing no words, yet he must be considered mainly responsible for all that had happened. Clearly the Cardinal had no faith that the Duce could recruit even 3000 men to follow him to Val Tellina. 'More like 300, Mussolini,' was his own sceptical estimate.

At first the resistance leaders entering the room were wary, hostile. By now, Birzer's SS men were packing the cobbled courtyard, their machine-guns set up in the cloisters beneath the crumbling statue of San Ambrogio, Milan's patron saint. Uneasily the patriots scented a trap – then realized Mussolini's men were fearful too. In the ante-room the industrialist Gian-Riccardo Cella buttonholed Cadorna, urging a peaceful solution; angrily, the tall hawk-faced General flashed back: 'Go to the devil.' The Liberals' Filippo Jacini who lingered in an ante-room was accosted by Under-Secretary Barracu. To his surprise, the Fascist whispered, 'Let's all get together in a block against the Germans.' 'It's a little late for that now,' Jacini responded coldly.

Achille Marazza, arriving with Cadorna, noted that it was just as he had thought: the one left-winger present was Riccardo Lombardi, of the Action Party, Prefect-delegate of Milan. But his instructions from his chief, Valiani, had been clear-cut: 'Mussolini's in no position to dictate terms. You'll talk nothing but pure surrender – and for one hour only.'

The last man to slip into the meeting was Giustino Arpesani. As Schuster made formal introductions, the Liberal, glancing at Mussolini, whispered to Cadorna, 'Do we have to shake hands with him?' 'Well, I did,' the General confessed. Dubiously Arpesani followed suit.

Now the little Cardinal offered to withdraw – but when the Duce urged him to stay he readily complied. He had a real fear of violence in this room. He remained on the sofa, at Mussolini's right hand. The others faced them in a semi-circle, rigid, intransigent – Cadorna, Arpesani, Marazza, Lombardi, Graziani, Zerbino, Barracu, Prefect Bassi.

His face now closed and hard, Mussolini opened the meeting. 'Well,' he demanded curtly, 'what are your proposals?' for all the world as if he was a schoolmaster back in Gualtieri, demanding an explanation from errant pupils. All eyes turned to Marazza, silently appointing him spokesman. 'My instructions,' he answered carefully, 'are very precise and limited. I have to ask for and accept nothing but unconditional surrender.'

The Duce started as if he had been struck. His chest swelled visibly and his hand clasped the sofa arm like a claw. 'I have not come for this!' he almost shouted. Indignantly he spelt out his conditions: safeguards for Fascist families, Fascist troops to be treated as prisoners of war under The Hague Convention, accredited diplomats to receive the protection of international law. He went on so long that finally Lombardi chipped in: 'These are details. I think we have authority to negotiate them.'

General Cadorna was less certain. No Allied guarantees for prisoners of war, he said emphatically, mindful of the savage reprisals of Pavolini's Black Brigades, could be stretched to cover war criminals. A heavy silence descended on the Fascists. Marshal Graziani jumped from his chair. 'We can't sign any agreement without telling the Germans first,' he protested to Mussolini, 'to be faithful to our Allies is a point of honour.' Nettled, Marazza flung at him: 'If it comes to honour, we don't need lessons from you.'

After a moment, holding his temper in check, Marazza went on: 'It seems the Germans haven't the same yardstick . . .' In the stunned silence that followed he exploded his bombshell: in the ante-room, just prior to the meeting, Don Giuseppe Bicchierai had revealed to him and Cadorna that General Wolff's negotiated surrender was almost accomplished fact. Pink with embarrassment, the Cardinal had to call in Don Bicchierai to confirm it.

Quietly the young priest recited from memory details of the conversation he had held only yesterday with Colonel Walter Rauff, Wolff's envoy in Milan. The Germans, he wound up, had even offered to disarm Fascist units before the Allies arrived.

Mussolini was electrified.

'For once,' he stormed, 'we can say Germany has stabbed Italy in the back. They have always treated us like slaves.' Twice, in insensate fury, he repeated: 'And at the end they betrayed *me*!' Vainly Schuster tried to calm him, pointing out that the surrender was not yet signed, but Mussolini would not be mollified. 'To begin negotiations behind my back is already treachery!' he burst out.

The resistance leaders watched him with unholy fascination. Small incongruities stood out in their minds. To Giustino Arpesani, it was the Duce's tragi-comic pompousness, his unshaven chin, his dirty boots, that he would always remember. For Lombardi, it was the stain of milk on his uniform lapel; he felt a genuine revulsion at sitting in the same room. Soon men would fight and die in the streets because of Mussolini. Cadorna felt at first 'the pity of any human for a man toppled from a pedestal' – then his resolution hardened. This was a man who had sacrificed everything to his own ambition, and the face of Italy was trampled by invaders.

Now the Cardinal saw that events were moving beyond his control, Mussolini's rancour could no longer be contained. Paramount in his mind was a determination to seek out the Germans and confront them with their treason. Schuster begged him to hold back; he had given the Church's pledge of secrecy. Graziani, his face like a death mask, said nothing. Now Marazza urged Mussolini that there was no time to lose. Already partisans were liberating towns all over Lombardy. 'Let's have done with the bloodshed,' Mussolini agreed readily. But still he made no move.

Suddenly he leaped to his feet. 'I have decided,' he announced harshly. 'I will go to the Germans and settle accounts.' But the resistance leaders demanded a time limit and Mussolini agreed: 'In one hour I will be back to reach an agreement.' The shadow of a sceptical smile hovered on Marazza's face. Then, after the lightest brushing of fingers with the partisans, the Duce strode from the room – his entourage hurrying after him down the long dadoed marble corridor, through the Hall of the Saints, the Hall of the Cardinals, lined with the paintings of long-dead Princes of the Church in their scarlet robes.

Schuster all the time was stumbling to keep pace with him, urging him to stay on in the accommodation that had been prepared, but Mussolini wasn't listening. At the last Schuster managed to pluck Graziani by the sleeve, 'I beg you to prevent Mussolini doing anything impulsive,' he pleaded, and the Marshal promised to do his best.

Among the resistance workers clustered at the head of the stairs was a secret agent who watched Mussolini coming, 'his face buff-coloured like an envelope'. For 600 days he had been working against the Salò Republic in the north, but now, in the presence of the fabled Duce, he forgot whose side he was on. Automatically his hand shot up in a Roman salute. Never would he forget the look of revulsion which crossed Mussolini's face.

'This one,' he heard the Duce grind out, 'is crazy.' Then he was gone, clattering two at a time down the stone stairs towards the courtyard.

Gian-Riccardo Cella was distraught. It had all promised so well and now it was going terribly wrong. All through the ride back from the Archbishop's Palace, Mussolini was trembling uncontrollably like a man in shock – and as the car swung in through the Prefecture's gates, he seemed beside himself. To Cella's horror, he suddenly brandished a small gold-plated Beretta revolver. 'Yes, I was armed,' he yelled 'and I wanted to kill them all. There shan't be another 25th of July!'

Others saw him coming and were riveted in their tracks. From an upper window recess, Federal Secretary Vincenzo Costa, who didn't even know where Mussolini had been, watched him accost Untersturmführer Birzer, his face livid. 'Your General Wolff has betrayed us!' he spat out, 'He has signed the surrender.' Amazed, Birzer's hand went up to his mouth. 'General Wolff? Betrayed?' he echoed stupidly. On the first-floor landing, General Renzo Montagna saw

Mussolini taking the stairs two at a time, shouting, 'They're criminals, assassins – you just can't treat with them.'

By 7.30 p.m. chaos had descended on the Prefecture. The scene
in Mussolini's high-ceilinged first-floor office more resembled a
confrontation than a consultation. Everyone, Montagna recalled,
was 'shouting at the tops of their voices, offering proposals and
counter-proposals'. 'Give your orders,' the Duce told Pavolini
tiredly, and for the first time the Party Secretary, sickened by this
half-hearted treating with the partisans, seemed to rebel. He raged
'Duce, *what* orders? You've just spoken of leaving for Como.' At once
Costa chipped in, 'What kind of business is this? Ten hours ago it
was Val Tellina.'

Close to Mussolini, a blinded war veteran was weeping. 'Don't
leave ... I've given my eyes for Fascism ... I'm ready to give my life.'
Journalist Carlo Silvestri also had his say above the shouting: 'Don't
give your enemies that satisfaction.' Patiently, like a well-trained
butler, Colonel Vito Casalinovo, Mussolini's ADC, kept urging
him to put on his coat.

The news that Graziani now brought to the conference only
heightened the confusion. The Allies had crossed the Adige – and
the advance guard of Mark Clark's forces might reach Milan within
the hour. Vittorio Mussolini saw a sudden gleam of light. Then,
he urged his father, why move at all? Why not stay here in the Prefecture, which could be held against the partisans until the Americans
came? 'And be put in a pillory in the Tower of London,' Mussolini
raged back, 'or in a cage like a wild animal in Madison Square
Garden? Never!'

To Vittorio, the shock of Wolff's betrayal, the inflexibility of the
resistants, the fear of Allied ridicule were the three factors combining
to unbalance his father in this crucial hour. A three-time loser, his
old inferiority complex now decreed that a last great stand was
mandatory to redress the balance.

Across the city, in the Archbishop's Palace, things were no better.
In the ante-chamber the Resistance leaders waited in small uneasy
groups, fidgeting, glancing at their watches – impatient for some
word of Mussolini's 'within-the-hour' decision. Suddenly a furious
commotion was heard in the corridor. Across the waxed parquet,
like avenging angels, stormed Leo Valiani and Emilio Sereni. Uneasy
at Lombardi's long absence, the thought had crossed their minds
that Marazza and Arpesani, determined to honour the Armistice
clause and hand Mussolini over to the Allies, had talked their man

into acquiescence. Behind them came the Socialist Sandro Pertini, who had only now heard that a meeting had taken place. In a white heat he had driven on the horn all the way to the Palace, determined there should be no negotiations.

'You should never have allowed yourselves to parley with him,' Pertini shouted at General Cadorna. 'Summary justice is what we want.' Marazza objected spiritedly. 'If Mussolini surrenders to us, we must keep our word,' he reminded Pertini.

At this moment the Cardinal emerged from his audience chamber. Impervious to the shouting, he warned every man of the grave consequences if they tried to take Mussolini by force. 'It may lead to civil war,' he charged them. 'The wheel's spinning,' Pertini retorted, 'and neither you nor I can stop it now.' Schuster was adamant: 'You must promise your Archbishop there will be no armed insurrection.' The furious Emilio Sereni, the Communist, shouted: 'In the first place, you're not my Archbishop, and *yes*! there *will* be an armed insurrection.'

To Sereni and the others, it still seemed on the cards that Mussolini would return to the Palace and surrender, placing himself under the Cardinal's protection until the Allies took him. Purple in the face, one man shook his fist under the Archbishop's nose, vowing, 'You'll pay for this!' Swiftly Don Giuseppe Bicchierai stepped in, interposing a muscular shoulder between Schuster and the furious left-wingers.

Back at the Prefecture, the argument raged as hotly. To Vincenzo Costa, the Val Tellina pioneer, the idea was fast occurring: if need be, they would seize Mussolini and take him to the mountains by force, so that Fascism 'could die in beauty'. Zerbino and Barracu, still hoping for a peaceful transfer, were trying noisily to dissuade him. Minister of Corporations Angelo Tarchi was urging Mussolini to stay in Milan, as was Minister of Justice Piero Pisenti. The Ministers could retire to Castello Sforzesco and await the Allies until Graziani had surrendered the Army. But again Mussolini underwent a mercurial change of mind. All would head for Lake Como, thirty miles north, and perhaps continue negotiations with Schuster from there.

To the very end Mussolini was sitting on the fence, reaching no hard and fast decision. In Como, according to how the wind blew, four roads still lay open: to keep contact with Schuster; to head for Val Tellina, if Pavolini could muster enough troops for a token stand; to try for Switzerland; to follow the Germans on to Merano.

And now it was Graziani who threw his weight into the balance, his right arm coming up in a military sweep to consult his watch. Clearly he had not forgotten the partisans' one-hour ultimatum. 'As it's almost 8 p.m. Duce,' he cut in briskly, 'I suggest we continue this discussion in Como.'

Galvanized, Mussolini strode to the window. *'Sofort alles fertig machen,'* he yelled peremptorily to the waiting SS men. Minutes later, Prince Valerio Borghese, smiling cynically, watched him bustling swiftly through the courtyard, bending from car to car. To both Pavolini and Vincenzo Costa he gave his firm pledge: an 8 a.m. rendezvous at Como's Prefecture on Thursday, 26 April. Overnight they must scour the city's barracks, rounding up every man available for Val Tellina. All over the courtyard the cry went up: 'To Como . . . to Como.' Still, like a lament, came the voice of the blind veteran: 'Duce, don't leave . . . Duce, don't leave.'

All round him, unheeding, the hierarchs were piling into their cars. Mussolini sat clumsily in the back of his open Alfa, holding a machine-pistol he didn't know how to use that a soldier had pressed on him. Some were jaunty, some were apprehensive, but whatever the mood, all were in a hurry. Now, standing apart, Prince Borghese watched an astounding spectacle. Although the courtyard had but one exit, more than thirty cars and trucks had manoeuvred into line as swiftly as if skilled garage mechanics were at the wheel. Within minutes they had gone – seeking not only the Duce but his SS escort – and Borghese was left alone, a solitary figure in the vast courtyard.

It was just then, Minister of Justice Piero Pisenti would always recall, that telephones began to shrill all over the empty palace, reverberating along the deserted corridors – urgent calls from Prefects and Federals in the last bastions of Fascism, seeking the Duce's instructions.

In the Prefect's office, Mario Bassi lifted the phone to hear Don Giuseppe Bicchierai calling from the Archbishop's Palace. The resistants were growing impatient for Mussolini's decision. Bassi was terse: 'The Duce has left – he has nothing further to say.'

In the shadowed ante-chamber of the priest's office the resistants stood grouped like pressmen awaiting a hand-out. Now, as Don Bicchierai told them the news, a slow smile crossed the face of Leo Valiani. He was looking, one man present noted, 'as calm as an apostle'. Of all the resistance chiefs, he was perhaps the first to realize the full significance of Mussolini's flight.

Now the ultimatum had expired. The Duce had put himself
beyond the law.

It was the dark of the night. A few minutes earlier, in the Milan
office of Colonel Alfredo Malgeri, Commandant of the Lombardy
Finance Guards, the phone had rung. Whispering up the line, Malgeri recognized the voice of Major Egidio Liberti, one of Cadorna's
staff officers: 'This is Collino. We must operate tonight. Within half
an hour you'll receive the written order.' He ended: '*In bocca al
lupo.*' Translated, this meant 'In the wolf's mouth,' or 'Good luck.'

Now the fifty-three-year-old Colonel scanned the order from
Leo Valiani which had been rushed to him by messenger. 'The
Finance Guards have orders to capture the Prefecture of Milan
tonight . . .' Behind sandbagged windows, in barracks catscradled
with barbed wire, Malgeri checked over H-Hour details with his
officers. To seize the Prefecture, one of a chain of strongpoints, 400
of Malgeri's excise officers had to cross a city teeming with 12,000
Fascists and Germans, setting up nine road-blocks in order to isolate
the building. 'It's suicide,' a major muttered, and Malgeri hadn't
the heart to contradict him.

At 4 a.m. they set off: 400 men in grey-green, yellow flames
adorning their lapels, tramping grimly through the pre-dawn chill.
Every street, each fog-choked alley, was a potential ambush; no man
broke the complete silence that reigned. Not far from Corso Monforte, site of the Prefecture, a machine-gun hammered; kneeling,
Malgeri's men hit back with rifle fire. Then the miraculous happened. The firing died, and they realized they had reached the
Prefecture unscathed.

'Come on, boys,' cried the gallant little Colonel, and without
hesitation they stormed through the courtyard where only nine hours
back Mussolini had given his followers the watchword: 'To Como!'
But in the cellar Malgeri's men now found only five quaking civilian
employees. The rout was on.

Swiftly, the rising took shape. Street after street came alive with
hurtling truck-loads of partisans, red flags fluttering defiance – some
men even attired in carnival outfits as devils and Red Indians. And
no man who saw it ever forgot the headless torso, a Chianti flask
jammed obscenely into the windpipe, lolling on the pavement near
La Scala – forerunner of the many who would die this day.

Now, as dawn paled in the sky, thousands of men checked their
watches and did what they had to do. All over the city they struck,

swiftly, noiselessly – at barracks, police stations, telegraph offices. In the dining-room of the Hotel Principe e Savoia, breakfasting German diplomats stared open-mouthed. As if on cue, the white-jacketed waiters serving coffee and rolls had backed against the walls. Hands went up as one to tweak away their black ties, as if by magic substituting red neckerchiefs. Then a bearded partisan burst in, gun levelled. 'Stay where you are,' he told the petrified Germans. 'Put your hands behind your necks.'

Simultaneously, a small convoy of jeeps and trucks was converging on the radio station at Porta Ticinese. Fifteen men in civilian suits dismounted silently, armed with Thompsons and Berettas, and shouldered their way through the glass swing doors. Prudently, the Fascist night staff offered no resistance. Partisan chief Corrado Bonfantini, commander of the thousands-strong Matteotti Brigade, doubled up the stairs to the fourth floor, then as the air-raid siren screamed over the city, signal that all key-points were taken, seized the microphone. As far south as Taranto, 600 miles away, as far north as Switzerland, millions of Italians, with an absurd leaping of the heart, heard his impassioned cry: 'This is Corrado speaking and saluting from liberated Milan all the people of Italy, free at last . . .'

Then, tears streaming down his face, he set down the mike.

Benito Mussolini heard that news in stony silence. It was the repeat broadcast at 1 p.m. rasping through the dining-room of the Golf Hotel at Grandola, 1000 feet above the grey waters of Lake Como. Along with ten party chiefs and Claretta Petacci, who had followed him from Milan without even awaiting Spögler's return, the Duce was waiting for lunch to be served. Even now, seventeen hours after leaving the city, his plans were as fluid as ever.

At midnight, from the Prefect's flat at Como, he had written Rachele the last letter she would ever receive from him. 'I have come to the last chapter in my life, the last page in my book,' he scrawled in blue crayon, signing his name in red. 'I ask your forgiveness for all the harm I have unwittingly done you. But you know you are the only woman I have ever truly loved.' Now, though Rachele was less than a mile away, billeted in a villa with the Blackshirt escort that had brought her from Monza, he urged her not to delay an instant. Somehow, she, Romano and Anna Maria must try and seek refuge in Switzerland. He and his column must head for Val Tellina.

Despite his dreams of destiny, the Duce was none too certain. All that night in the Prefecture the arguments had raged back and forth, as if in continuation of the débâcle in Milan. At one point

Mussolini was determined to head for the Brenner with all speed, to join Hitler. At another, he veered towards Switzerland and precious time was spent phoning the US Consulate in Lugano. At first Allen Dulles's OSS agent, Don Jones, had held out hope that Mussolini and two Ministers could cross the border up to 1 a.m., but the Swiss refused to extend the time limit.

As Dulles was later to explain, this was his own decision. Until now, the Swiss had turned a tactfully blind eye to an OSS mission operating on neutral soil. The Duce's presence, as General Wolff made ready to sign the surrender, might produce grave international complications.

Suddenly, his nerves cracking, Mussolini had screamed: 'Enough, silence! We've got to reach a decision.'

But after all the wrangling he found it impossible to sleep. Towards 3 a.m. someone suggested moving a few miles north to the Federal Secretary's villa at Menaggio, where the Duce could rest until Pavolini's troops came to escort him to Val Tellina. Then, fearful of being abandoned, the party chiefs had tried to panic after him down the stairs. Only Marshal Graziani, angrily drawing his gun, had halted the stampede. 'If anyone dares to move a step, I'll fire!' he yelled at his hastily retreating colleagues.

At Menaggio, following a cup of milky coffee and a half-hour's catnap, Mussolini's heart was still set on Val Tellina – yet there was one vital drawback. No word had so far come from Pavolini. An officer suggested a move to Grandola's Golf Hotel, off the lakeside road, to wait until the situation clarified.

Now, hearing Bonfantini's broadcast in the little dining-room, they were silent, wondering. Had Pavolini ever left Milan? No man liked to voice his innermost thoughts. The servants were bringing in cooked pasta, boiled meat, coarse bread for the twelve men who now sat down to table, Mussolini at their head. 'Milan is freed from Fascism,' the radio kept intoning, until an official switched it off.

A heavy silence fell. At last, staring intently down the table, Mussolini said, 'Let me at least look at the faces of the faithful of the last hour.' Again there was an aching silence, then the sudden scraping of knives and forks as they ate hastily, without appetite, to cover their embarrassment.

In the dining-room of the Hotel Barchetta at Como, Marshal Graziani and his staff officers lunched with gusto off trout and mayonnaise. Towards them across the parquet, in a towering rage, strode Federal Secretary Vincenzo Costa with Commandant Franco Colombo of the Black Brigades.

To the grimy Costa, the whole scene stank of treason. Graziani had seen the Duce as far as Menaggio, then, significantly, had headed back for Como – towards the advancing Allies. Outside, his green Alfa-Romeo 2500 cabriolet with its silver and ivory steering wheel was parked in readiness – his black Shumbashi chauffeur standing by, just as in the days when the Marshal had been Viceroy of Abyssinia.

At eight that morning, Costa exploded to Graziani, he and Pavolini had brought 3000 men north from Milan to keep the appointed rendezvous. They had found both the Duce and Graziani gone. At once panic began to spread through the ranks. If Mussolini, their rallying-point, had escaped to Switzerland, as was rumoured, what chance was there for mere soldiers? Pavolini had decided that these men must be reassured – and fast.

Costa had gone post-haste to Menaggio, only to be told that Mussolini was resting and couldn't be disturbed. 'You'll get your orders by noon,' Under-Secretary Barracu had told him firmly. Perplexed, Costa had reported back to Pavolini but Pavolini wasn't satisfied. He himself must confer with the Duce. Now, after hours of waiting, there was no word from him. What action, Costa demanded savagely, did Graziani propose to stop the rot? The front was crumbling, men were deserting hourly.

Graziani, immaculate, reeking of expensive cologne, stared disdainfully at the sweating Fascists. 'Well, what do you want?' was all he said. 'We want to know how we're going to die,' Colombo told him insolently. 'We do have that right.'

Graziani was evasive: 'It may be the Duce will decide to go to Val Tellina – it may not. At present he's awaiting an important communication.'

Both Costa and Colombo saw that it was hopeless. They guessed now that Graziani was only awaiting the right moment to surrender. Earlier, at Como's Prefecture, he had been overheard announcing: 'I'm a man of honour, not a puppet! I'll go to the front and when the Americans are ten yards away from me, I'll turn myself in as their prisoner.'

'If Mussolini ends badly,' Colombo threw over his shoulder as they trudged away, 'the responsibility is yours. All of us here are going to die like rats.'

His nerves screaming with protest, Kriminalinspektor Otto Kisnatt uncoiled from the wire springs of the truckle-bed. It was 2 a.m. on 27 April. Although he had settled for an early night in the empty Blackshirt barracks at Menaggio, retiring at 9 p.m., this was the third time Mussolini had sent a messenger to disturb him in the last five hours.

Busy collecting documents at Lake Garda on the day that Mussolini left Milan, Kisnatt had spent the last forty-eight hours in frantic pursuit of him – hoping against hope that Untersturmführer Birzer, at least, had managed to keep pace. But when Kisnatt at last caught up with him at Grandola's Golf Hotel, the Duce's open-armed welcome stifled even his angry words. At length he had talked Mussolini and his party into returning to Menaggio's Fascist barracks. Then, a pistol beneath his pillow, he sought to catch up on sleep.

The first time the Duce had awoken him had been at 10 p.m. Hearing that partisans were streaming down from the mountains, he had sent Pavolini, who had recently arrived, back to Como for ten armoured cars and all available forces. Could ten armoured cars sustain a siege? he wanted to know. 'With ten armoured cars,' Kisnatt soothed him, retiring to bed, 'we can do anything.'

It was midnight when Mussolini summoned him again. He was still in the Commandant's office, awake and studying maps. No sooner did the German enter than he began to shout: 'What do you think of this? There is no trace of Pavolini and the armoured cars! Nobody knows where I can find the Party secretary.' Abject self-pity engulfed him. 'It seems my tragic destiny that in all important moments of my life I find myself alone.'

Wearily, Kisnatt reassured him. Later on, they would send out scouts.

Now, at 2 a.m., he struggled cursing from the bed to answer his third summons. He found Mussolini so red in the face Kisnatt thought he would have a seizure – and with him Pavolini, pale and agitated. 'Yes,' Mussolini said harshly, enunciating every word, 'here is Pavolini, and where are the ten armoured cars? He has brought only two, and old ones at that – it's shameful!'

'And how many men?' Kisnatt asked him.

'Well, tell him,' the Duce railed, as Pavolini hesitated.

Pavolini had to confess it. 'Twelve.'

At that moment Kisnatt saw the Army of Salò fall apart. Only a dozen middle-aged old-guard Fascists had been prepared to follow Pavolini up the lakeside. Their faith shaken by Mussolini's disappearance, fearful of the partisans in the mountains, the rest were staying put in Como – hundreds of them donning the red neckerchiefs of the resistance. At long last the Val Tellina dream was shown for what it was: a Fascist fantasy, as bombastic and empty of meaning as a Palazzo Venezia speech.

Now Mussolini was left with just one decision: to honour the Axis Pact until the bitter end. He told Kisnatt: 'We leave at 5 a.m. Let's hope we can reach the German Embassy at Merano before nightfall.'

Eleven miles north of Menaggio, on the lakeside road, the shutters of a stone house on the main street of Musso village creaked open. Peering from the window, Captain Davide Barbieri, the local partisan commander, saw that the fog was lifting from the lake, though a fine rain fell steadily. Suddenly, above the steady splashing of the rain on the flagstones, he heard the groan of an engine. Over his shoulder, to the partisans grouped behind him, he said: 'That'll be Mussolini all right.'

No man uttered a word. The time was 6.50 a.m.

As he saw the armoured car that headed the convoy, with the fine 20mm machine-gun in its turret and two smaller guns at its sides, Barbieri motioned his men to stay quiet. The convoy was almost two-thirds of a mile long, forty vehicles in all. Lightly armed as his men were, they were in no shape to tackle an armoured car or the trucks that followed. Silently Barbieri led his men out into the rainy garden, beneath the steep fir-clad mountains where his farm was sited. Now, as the Ministers' cars began filing through the narrow street, Barbieri swung his rifle skywards. A volley split the damp morning – a signal to others who lay in wait.

Racing up the hillside, level with the lakeside road, Barbieri's men heard the brittle crack of rifle fire ahead. At once the armoured car's machine-gun chattered into life. Stumbling through bracken and hazel saplings, Barbieri and his men flung themselves prone on primrose-carpeted grass, aiming at the rolling tyres 100 yards below. Slowly the column had ground to a halt. Ahead of them they had seen the road-block.

During the night an agent had brought Barbieri news that this German convoy was forming up at Menaggio, strengthened now by 200 retreating Luftwaffe flak personnel under Leutnant Hans Fallmeyer. Mussolini was said to be one of the passengers. Promptly Barbieri had arranged a barricade of chestnut trunks and rocks on the lakeside road, a mile distant from Musso – at the bend, where the road hugged the cliff by the Scalini marble quarry, before dropping steeply to the village of Dongo.

From their Volkswagen Kubelwagen behind the armoured car where Mussolini rode with Pavolini and other chiefs, Birzer and Kisnatt, guns drawn, tumbled to the road. Ahead they saw that the right rear tyre of the armoured car had been pierced by a three-edged partisan nail. Thirty yards ahead loomed the barricade. To their left, the rocky bank rose sheer to the mountains. To the right, it dropped steeply to the lake. It was a perfect spot for an ambush. Then, above the low stone wall that spanned the lakeside, a white handkerchief fluttered on a sten-gun barrel. The partisans were coming to parley.

At the head of the partisans' three-man committee, Count Pier Luigi Bellini delle Stelle, known as 'Pedro', held his breath. At twenty-five, the lean, black-bearded Florentine nobleman, a detachment commander of the mountain-based 52nd Garibaldi Brigade, was about to pull off the biggest bluff in his ten months as a partisan.

As the one German whose Italian was fluent, Leutnant Fallmeyer came forward as spokesman. The column was en route to Merano, he explained, and had no wish to pick a quarrel with Italians. Bellini shook his head. His orders were to stop all armed columns and let no man through.

When Fallmeyer objected, the young commander was adamant.

'You are covered by my mortars and machine-guns,' he told Fallmeyer, his expressive brown eyes boring into the German. 'I could wipe you all out in fifteen minutes.'

As Fallmeyer went on arguing, Bellini saw his Political Commissar, Urbano 'Bill' Lazzaro, beckon him urgently. Squatting on the low stone wall, sharing a cigarette, the young Count listened while Lazzaro imparted chilling information, joined now by Michele Moretti, the flint-eyed Communist plumber, who was Brigade Vice-Commissar. While Bellini parleyed with the German, Lazzaro had made a quick sortie down the column. What he saw appalled him. Every truck had a heavy machine-gun, mortars, sub-machine pistols, even light anti-aircraft batteries.

'If it comes to a fight,' Lazzaro stressed, 'they can wipe *us* out.'

And now Bellini was shaken by his own temerity. Though Fallmeyer couldn't know it, his 'army' consisted of eight men he had brought down from the mountains in a search for precious tobacco. Each man was armed like Bellini himself – with a Beretta, sten and three grenades. Although three heavy machine-guns raided from a barracks covered the road from above, many of the dozen-odd locals Bellini had recruited the day before had no weapons training at all. At best, the Count could muster a fighting force of just on fifty men.

But he had one surefire ace in the hole: with the war as good as over, was Fallmeyer likely to want to start a fight?

From the moment when, half an hour ago, he had heard the convoy was en route, Bellini had made preparations for this elaborate bluff. Despatch-riders had been sent to warn all garrisons, road-blocks and patrols northwards along the lake. As many men as possible, Bellini ordered, must be sent down from the mountains with heavy weapons and mortars. Machine-guns were to be set up at conspicuous intervals behind the stone walls. In Dongo village, men were already at work mining the next bridge north with gelig-nite.

Everything depended now on how fast they could work – for if the Germans persisted, Bellini was determined to blow the bridge.

His mind racing, the Count returned to Fallmeyer. How many Italians did he have with him? he wanted to know. Impassive, Fallmeyer wrote off Benito Mussolini and all his Ministers. 'A few civilians – who are no concern of mine. My concern is only with my men.'

Bellini hit upon his second gigantic bluff. To allow Fallmeyer through, he explained, he must have clearance from his division. If the German accompanied him to state his case he might get leave to proceed. There was a heated argument under the drizzling rain, but Fallmeyer finally agreed.

Bellini doubled towards Lazzaro. A despatch-rider must go ahead, warning every checkpoint to have all available men out there on the road. 'Send the others into the hills,' he instructed, 'but see that they keep in sight – make them wear something red. Whatever happens, the Germans *must* think they're armed.'

Fritz Birzer heaved a sigh of relief. Five hours had elapsed since Fallmeyer had departed with Bellini and in the meantime there had been no word at all. Now towards 1 p.m. he saw two cars carrying the German, Bellini and their partisan escort, grinding back up the road from Dongo. All down the long column there was a stir of expectation.

Within minutes the shaken Fallmeyer was reporting to Kisnatt and Birzer. The situation was desperate. All the way to divisional headquarters at Chiavenna, nineteen miles north, his binoculars had picked out red neckerchiefs, armed men crouching among the rocks, while the cars jolted over mined bridges. The bluff had worked so triumphantly that Fallmeyer was only too ready to do what Bellini had hoped – dissociate his own men from those of the Fascists. They were the one remaining force, Fallmeyer reasoned, that had anything to gain from a fight.

The Italians in the column must stay put, he told Kisnatt. On this the partisans were adamant. But if the Germans moved on to Dongo and submitted to a search, with both sides pledged not to use arms, they would be guaranteed transit towards Germany.

'We can't advance and we can't turn back,' Fallmeyer urged. 'They've blown the bridges behind us. If you can't accept these conditions, I'll have to separate my men and act alone.'

Morosely, Kisnatt and Birzer chewed it over. Both men sensed that whatever they did would be wrong. Mussolini was still their responsibility, but it was insane to spill one drop of blood over a cause already lost. After ten minutes' muttered argument, they accepted Fallmeyer's conditions. 'If 200 men aren't enough to join battle,' Birzer summed up, 'thirty are even less so.'

But both men had their own private plans for Mussolini. They were about to broach them when the armoured car's rear door opened and the Duce called. Among the dozen fugitives huddled inside, Birzer noted Claretta Petacci wearing a man's blue overalls and crash helmet. At once Mussolini hailed them: 'Here is a lady whose destiny is very important to me. Can you take her under your protection?'

The Germans dodged the issue. Soon, Kisnatt stressed to Mussolini, the convoy would move on. His one chance of safety now was to board a German truck disguised as a German soldier. As yet, neither man revealed that his following was to be left behind.

The Duce clung desperately to his image. 'But when I meet the Führer and tell him I've been forced to use this trick,' he expostu lated, 'I shall feel ashamed.' 'But any resistance would be useless,' Kisnatt implored, and Birzer supported him. 'This is the one hope you've got of passing the road-block,' he told the Duce.

Grumbling that he would 'think about it', Mussolini made to close the door, and Kisnatt saw red. 'Duce, there is no time to think,' he bellowed. 'Make up your mind now because we're leaving.' Suddenly Claretta began to scream, 'Duce, save yourself!' – so shrilly that Colonel Vito Casalinovo, Mussolini's ADC, told her sharply to be quiet. Fuming, Mussolini slammed shut the door – but within seconds a German soldier wrenched it open, flinging in a Luftwaffe sergeant's topcoat and a German helmet.

'I'm leaving,' the dictator told Pavolini bitterly as he struggled into them, 'because now I trust the Germans more than the Italians.' Crimson with shame, Pavolini hung his head.

Minutes later Mussolini emerged – his helmet back to front, the topcoat so long it brushed his feet. Patiently Kisnatt and Birzer set the helmet to rights, fitting him out with dark glasses and pressing a P.38 machine-pistol into his hand. But now Mussolini began to protest that his Ministers must come too. That, Birzer told him stonily, was impossible. 'Then at least my friend,' the Duce pleaded, pointing to Claretta in tears on the running-board. 'That too is impossible, Duce,' said Birzer finally. 'You must go it alone.' Tamely, screened from view by the Germans, Mussolini clambered aboard the convoy's fourth truck. Punctiliously, Kisnatt noted the licence plate: WH 529 507.

Promptly at 3.10 p.m. the German trucks moved off, followed by screams of execration from the abandoned Ministers. 'Hide, Duce,' Birzer had whispered. 'Don't look out.' Five minutes later the vanguard of the convoy groaned on to the wharf of Dongo harbour, where 'Bill' Lazzaro had his cordon drawn up. Only Leutnant Fallmeyer, as agreed with Bellini, descended, accompanying the partisans as they moved from truck to truck. On a house-front opposite truck No 4 a familiar Mussolini slogan loomed large: 'Only God can bend the Fascist will – men and things never.'

Through a slit in the canvas of the leading truck, Birzer watched with dread and fascination. His own check was completed but still he worried for Mussolini. There's no hope, he tormented himself, that they won't recognize those magnetic eyes. Should he have given the order to fire? Yet could he, in the end, have justified starting the war all over again for Mussolini? He watched them pass the second truck, the third, then abruptly the shouting began.

In the second truck 'Bill' Lazzaro was busy checking German documents. Both he and Bellini had heard from Captain Barbieri the rumour that Mussolini was in the convoy, but to both men this was story-book stuff – neither had believed it. Suddenly Lazzaro, too, heard the high-pitched shouting: someone was calling his name. Dropping from the tailboard, he saw Giuseppe Negri, the Dongo clogmaker's son, haring towards him.

A one-time naval gunner on the ship that had taken Mussolini from Ponza to La Maddalena, Negri had once seen the Duce face to face – nor had he forgotten.

'Bill,' Lazzaro heard his frantic whisper now, 'we've got the Big Bastard!'

In the cypress-flanked Villa Strozzi, Florence, not far from the yellow waters of the Arno, twenty-four-year-old Major Max Corvo checked the wording of the signal once again. But there was no possibility that the partisan High Command in Milan could misinterpret his request. Under the terms of Clause 29 of the 'Long Armistice', Major Corvo was demanding the person of Benito Mussolini.

As Chief Operations Officer of America's Office of Strategic Services, the dapper, moustached Corvo had wanted Mussolini for longer even than the 600 days he had reigned over his puppet state. As long ago as 26 July, 1943, Franklin Delano Roosevelt had set the search in motion, with a memo to Winston Churchill suggesting that in the event of a separate peace with Italy, 'the Head Devil should be surrendered.' Churchill had agreed: the one problem, as the Prime Minister saw it, was what fate should befall him, a question to be agreed, when the time was ripe, with the Soviet authorities. 'Some may prefer prompt execution without trial except for identification,' Churchill wrote, 'others may prefer that [he] be kept in confinement till the end of the war in Europe ... Personally, I am fairly indifferent ... provided that no solid military advantages are sacrificed for the sake of immediate vengeance.'

Yet until now Corvo's quest had spelt frustration all the way. Using much the same sleuthing tactics as Otto Skorzeny, his Rome agents had also pinpointed the Duce on Ponza and La Maddalena – but as Allied Commander-in-Chief, General Eisenhower had vetoed the propositions as too risky. Both islands lay outside the maximum security zone of the US Navy's Palermo-based PTB that would have carried Corvo's twelve-man teams to their target.

A few days earlier, Eisenhower's successor, Field-Marshal Harold Alexander, had vetoed Corvo's third plan: a daring parachute drop which would have plummeted the Major and thirty picked OSS agents on to San Siro racetrack, three miles north-west of Milan, to seize the Duce and his top hierarchs and spirit them to safety.

Yet at 6 p.m. on 27 April, Corvo saw it as more than ever vital to lay hands on Mussolini. He did not yet know that the Duce had been seized at Dongo – or even that he had ever left Milan. His agents had all along believed that, following the meeting two days earlier, the dictator would seek sanctuary with Cardinal Schuster. But with no certainty that the war was about to end, Mussolini, at best, might furnish vital information on Hitler's future plans. At the least, a captive Duce could no longer prove a rallying-point for fast-diminishing Fascist forces.

Now, undaunted by Alexander's veto, Corvo had come up with a fourth plan: a C-47 transport plane which would touch down at Bresso Airport, a grass emergency strip five miles outside Milan. The field had neither flarepath, control tower, nor runways – which called for a daylight landing by a skilled pilot. But it was the one sure way to get Mussolini to Alexander's Headquarters at Caserta, near Naples, under maximum security conditions.

Once again Corvo checked the wording of the message:

TO GC AND CLNAI STOP PLEASE INFORM EXACT SITUATION MUSSOLINI STOP IF YOU ARE READY TO GIVE HIM TO US WE WILL SEND A PLANE TO COLLECT HIM STOP AGH

Corvo did not think this fourth attempt would fail, and for one good reason. Within hours of the partisans receiving this message, long before the plane ever landed, his Lugano agent 'Mim', known to the OSS as Captain Emilio Daddario, would arrive in Milan to secure Mussolini for the Allies.

'Calm down, Signora,' Count Bellini delle Stelle implored, 'please calm down. No harm will come to Mussolini, unless attempts are made to rescue him.' In a small high-windowed room on the ground floor of Dongo Town Hall he was trying vainly to stem the torrent of words that flowed from the distraught Claretta Petacci. Soon after her detention, together with the other Italians in the convoy, Claretta had discarded her overalls. Now the harsh light from a naked electric bulb showed her as immaculate as always – a tobacco-brown corduroy suit, worn with a white blouse, a mink coat flung carelessly over the chair-back.

'Rescue him?' she echoed Bellini. 'If you only knew what I have seen these last few days. They all ran away. All they thought of was saving their own miserable skins. Traitors, the lot of them!'

It was three hours since 'Bill' Lazzaro had boarded the truck to challenge the Duce, and Bellini, ironically, had begun to feel that of all his prisoners Mussolini was the least troublesome. It was strange how dully he had accepted defeat when Lazzaro tapped him on the shoulder and shouted, 'Cavalier Benito Mussolini!' 'I shall not do anything,' he had assured them all in a weird trance-like voice as he descended from the truck. And inside the Town Hall he had sat like a man in shock, asking for nothing more than a glass of water – a man with neither regret for the past nor curiosity for the future.

Bellini had no intention of harming him or letting him be harmed, but he feared a Fascist countercoup. Nor did he trust the trigger-happy newcomers who were hourly swelling the partisan ranks, many of them lured by rumours of the Salò Republic's reserve funds that had travelled with the convoy – several billion lire worth of gold bars and foreign currency that allegedly found its way into Communist Party coffers. By 7 p.m. Bellini had personally trans-ferred the Duce to a cell in the Finance Guards' Barracks at Ger-masino, four miles from Dongo, 2000 feet up in the fog-shrouded mountains.

Once in the barracks, Mussolini had sheepishly begged the Count to send his regards to 'the lady held in the Town Hall', revealing her as Signora Petacci. Now, for the first time, Bellini recognized her – this notorious kept woman whom he despised as much as the fifty other prisoners he held both here and at Germasino. Among them were Alessandro Pavolini and Claretta's brother, Marcello, masquerading as the Spanish Consul.

Yet Claretta's initial reaction puzzled him. For a self-seeking courtesan, it seemed too violent, too genuine – though he found her over-emphatic delivery artificial. 'How long will he be in your hands?' she kept pressing him. But Bellini didn't know. A local *carabinieri* sergeant had telephoned word of Mussolini's capture to Milan, but he was still awaiting instructions. 'You ought to hand him over to the Allies,' Claretta objected.

Bellini would have none of it. He was responsible only to his government and the Allies had nothing to do with it. 'On the con-trary,' he told her, 'I shall do what I can to see that he doesn't fall into their clutches.'

In a sudden spasm of grief Claretta reached out to him. 'How can I make you believe that I was with him all those years simply because I loved him?' she cried out, as if divining his thoughts. 'The only time I lived was when I was with him . . . you must believe me!' Hunched up on the hard cane-bottomed chair, she buried her tear-stained face in her hands.

Bellini moved restlessly across the room. The sight of a woman crying distressed him profoundly. Now he begged her not to look upon him as an enemy; he would do all he could to see she suffered as little as possible. 'I would never have thought that an enemy could be so kind and good,' Claretta replied tearfully, 'it encourages me to ask you a great favour. Could you grant it?'

Bellini drew up a chair to face her, lighting a cigarette. But though he listened attentively, the woman took her time. Speaking in a low, monotonous voice, she rambled on about the years with Mussolini and their first meeting. It went on so long that Bellini prompted her: 'Tell me what it is, and I promise I will do anything I can to help you.'

Claretta leant forward, willing it, grasping his hand. 'Put me with him!' she begged. 'Let us be together. What harm is there in it? Don't say it can't be done.'

But Bellini, withdrawing his fingers, gently demurred. If anything happened to Mussolini she too might be in danger. At once Claretta rounded on him. 'I realize now,' she accused him, 'you're going to shoot him!' Bellini denied it hotly: 'Nothing of the sort!'

Then, to his astonishment, Claretta uncovered her face, slowly drying her eyes with her fingers. 'Promise me,' she asked, 'that if Mussolini is shot I can be near him until the last, and that I shall be shot with him.' She urged him: 'My life will be nothing once he is dead. That is all I am asking: to die with him.'

The young partisan had rarely been so profoundly moved. So this is what a woman's love can mean, he thought, and felt ashamed for having despised her.

'I will think it over and discuss it with my friends,' he said, and it was all he could do to keep his voice steady.

Around 9.30 p.m. in the old *Il Popolo d'Italia* premises on Piazza Cavour, Milan, the presses were ready to roll. At the compositor's stone, Leo Valiani was checking galley-proofs. To the new editor of the Action Party's freedom-sheet, *Italia Libera*, it was sweet satisfaction that the presses which had churned out more than nine thousand issues of Mussolini's brazen-tongued journal should be about to announce the triumph of the people.

An overalled compositor hailed him: Valiani was wanted on the phone. It was the Communists, Longo and Sereni, calling, he thought, from the Partisan Command Headquarters. Somewhere in the background the Socialist, Sandro Pertini, was urging, 'We mustn't give him up.'

'Federico,' Sereni said, using Valiani's battle-name, 'listen to this – the Allies have asked for Mussolini.' His voice trembling with indignation, he read over the text of the message Major Corvo had pondered earlier that evening back in Florence.

'What do we do now?' Sereni asked.

'Aldo,' said Valiani gently, before replacing the receiver, 'we don't do anything at all.'

Three blocks north of La Scala, on the first floor of Palazzo Cusani, the newly-requisitioned offices of the partisan command, General Raffaele Cadorna was still at his desk. It was long past midnight, but the fifty-six-year-old General was snowed under with worries. As military commander of the resistance, Cadorna was still uncertain whether in these last hours two German divisions were moving west across the city – a route which might result in unparalleled bloodshed. Suddenly Cadorna looked up. Two shadows had darkened the pebbled glass of his office door.

The General knew both the men who entered. The first was one to make his presence felt: the tanned, clean-shaven Walter Audisio, thirty-six-year-old Communist liaison officer, known as 'Colonel Valerio'. As a veteran of the Spanish Civil War's International Brigade and a penal settlement victim, Audisio wore his Colonel's stars with a swagger, gesticulating imperiously as he laid down the Party line. By contrast, his companion, forty-six-year-old Aldo Lampredi, a studious-seeming, bespectacled ex-carpenter, would have passed unnoticed in a crowd. Yet Lampredi, another Spanish War veteran, now Vice-Commandant General of the Garibaldi Brigades, was one of the most implacable of all Communist resistants.

'An order from the Committee, General,' Audisio told him. 'We are to go north and execute Mussolini.'

Cadorna thought at once: That came from the insurrectional committee, the five-man panel of left-wingers behind the rising, and almost certainly the Communists had proposed it. Yet he recalled that the Central Committee of National Liberation had basically approved the execution of leading Fascists. 'Do you have any written order?' he asked. Both men shook their heads.

'The Americans are in the vicinity of Como,' Lampredi told him. 'As soon as they know of the capture, they'll apply to take Mussolini over, so there isn't much time.'

Cadorna knew the truth of this – and he too had no wish for the Allies to take Mussolini. Although he swore later that Major Corvo's telegram never reached his desk, he had earlier on his own initiative asked Italo Pietra, Commander of the Outer Po Pavese Division, to go north as escort. But Pietra had resisted. On such a night of chaos, his 1000 disciplined partisans were needed to police the city.

Chain-smoking pungent 'Oriental' cigarettes, Audisio quietly and persistently stood his ground. Ever since 6 p.m., he told Cadorna, he had been urging Colonel Alfredo Malgeri, Commander of the Finance Guards, to make this trip. He had met him, even bombarded him with phone calls, but the little Colonel was unyielding. Even if Mussolini was being held in the Finance Guards Barracks at Germasino, Malgeri argued, he was still a prisoner of the partisans. Why should they yield him up to a total stranger? Nor did he like the tone in which Audisio had hinted: 'Anything will be justified to prevent him escaping.' Malgeri was still temporizing at 11.20 p.m. when Audisio himself had been picked by Luigi Longo.

As if he took Cadorna's silence for assent, Lampredi began listing their requirements. They would need passes into the zone, since neither he nor Audisio were known on Lake Como . . . a dozen of Pietra's men to make up a firing-squad . . . transport.

Cadorna was still wrestling with the decision. He had to decide at once, as a soldier should – and at midnight, with Milan's problems assuming priority, he couldn't take time to check with every member of the Committee of Liberation that they confirmed this death sentence. Moreover, the General knew full well that the Communists held all the aces.

In his eight months as military commander, Cadorna had clashed so often with Luigi Longo that he had already threatened to resign and serve as a humble partisan in the field. Only Allied intervention had persuaded him to change his mind. Yet the Communists were so certain of their power that at one recent meeting where Cadorna had presided they had even jeered at his attempts to call Longo to order. 'What do you want to preside over?' one man demanded pityingly. 'You're not presiding over anything.'

Suddenly the General lost patience. Now 1 a.m. was past, the fate of thousands of Milanese was still in the balance, and these Communists were arguing over what to him was 'a very small thing'. He made a sudden angry gesture. '*Ma si*,' he burst out. '*Fatelo fuori.*' (Finish him off.)

The eyes and mouth were three black slits in a huge white ball of lint. Count Bellini delle Stelle thought of the movie of H. G. Wells's *Invisible Man*, seen long ago as a teenager in his native Florence.

Yet the effect was masterly. His head wound in a tight cocoon of bandages to resemble a wounded partisan en route to hospital, no one could now have recognized the man shivering in a *carabiniere* greatcoat, a military cape wrapped round his shoulders, as Benito Mussolini.

It was now almost 2 a.m. on Saturday, 28 April. In the cramped stone cell of the Finance Guards' Barracks at Germasino, Bellini was bidding farewell to Mussolini's partisan captors of the last hours. Too many people, he explained, now knew where Mussolini was hidden. They were moving him to a safer place, in yet another disguise that Mussolini had accepted without protest. Outside, in the rain-swept darkness, a Fiat 1500 was ticking over.

The order to move Mussolini from Germasino had reached Bellini around 11.30 p.m. It had come from General Cadorna's Town Commander in Como, Colonel Baron Giovanni Sardagna. On orders from Cadorna's Chief of Staff, Mussolini was to be taken from Germasino to Blevio, a village four miles north of Como on the eastern side of the lake. Disguised as a 'wounded English officer', he was to be hidden in a villa owned by a wealthy industrialist friend of Sardagna's pending a transfer to Milan.

Around 1 a.m. Sardagna received another call from Cadorna's headquarters: 'the Blevio operation' was suspended. Instead, some refuge must be found for the Duce in Moltrasio, just north of Como. But in the pitch dark, with many phone wires north of Como now cut, there had as yet been no way for Sardagna to reach Bellini and countermand this order.

As the Fiat dipped at top speed down the sluicing mountain road, Bellini broke the good news to Mussolini. He had consulted with Brigade Vice-Commissar Michele Moretti, 'Bill' Lazzaro and Luigi Canali, Lombardy Regional Inspector. All three had agreed that Claretta's plea to join the Duce should be respected. At first, clearing his throat, fiddling with his bandages, the dictator seemed both startled and embarrassed. As they neared Dongo, Bellini ordered the driver: 'Pull into the right by the bridge and stop at once. There should be another car waiting.'

Now the dimmed glow of headlamps picked out another Fiat, and Moretti splashing towards them in the darkness. Behind him came Claretta, followed by Canali and two more partisans. To Bellini, the reunion of Mussolini and Claretta on this rain-drenched night was absurdly formal.

'Good evening, Excellency.'

'Good evening, Signora. Why are you here?'

'Because I wanted to be.'

It was an oddly stilted conversation, as devoid of drama as two near-strangers meeting in a crowded street.

For the dog-tired Bellini, the hours that followed stretched his nerves to snapping-point. Shivering and soaked to the skin, he saw nothing in view but another sleepless night. Ahead, the lead car with Moretti, Canali and Claretta, threw back a steady deluge of yellow-brown water. One hundred yards to the rear came Bellini's car, Mussolini slumped in the back between the Count and a woman partisan. Time and again they were checked by road-blocks, and Bellini could see Canali, in the light of storm lanterns, explaining the urgency of getting the wounded man through.

Five miles north of Como, in the lakeside town of Moltrasio, everything went abruptly wrong. Across the lake the sky beyond the mountains was spangled with rockets. They heard the woodpecker chatter of machine-guns. Hastily Canali knocked up a bar kept by a fellow resistant, who confirmed the worst. Major-General Vernon E. Prichard's 1st US Armoured Division, nearing the outskirts of Como, was mopping up pockets of Fascist resistance.

Huddled in the doorway, Bellini conferred with the others. It was Canali who suggested an alternative – a tiny farmhouse not far distant where the two could be hidden. Calm, seemingly resigned, Mussolini only asked if there was much farther to go. For the next forty-five minutes, until the lead car splashed to a halt, he dozed huddled up in blankets. Then Canali trudged back to them. 'Everyone out, please,' he ordered, 'the rest of the way is on foot.'

The rain was still sheeting down. Slowly, through a world of blackness, hemmed in by low stone walls, they toiled upwards. Cloud-cloaked mountains loomed above. As Claretta slipped on the wet pebbles, both the Duce and Bellini offered their arms. Suddenly Bellini was struck by the incongruousness of it all – partisans ahead and to the rear . . . Mussolini's bandaged head, stark-white against the night . . . Claretta in mink and high-heeled shoes, sliding and stumbling . . . Bellini himself in a threadbare green jacket, his black beard dishevelled, clanking with weapons. Fifteen minutes of this nightmare progress brought them to the foothills hamlet of Giulino di Mezzegra.

It was 3 a.m. In the dripping darkness Canali's knocking boomed like thunder – but smallholder Giacomo de Maria, a resistant himself, opened up almost at once. Though he and his wife Lia had no idea who their guests were, they readily agreed to give them shelter.

Scalding hot *ersatz* coffee came quickly from the kitchen range. All of them drank gratefully – except Mussolini. He sat close to Claretta, drawn back from the fire, staring at the red embers. She sat silent, her chin in her hands. Meanwhile Lia de Maria hastened to the second-floor bedroom to awaken her sons, sending them to spend the rest of the night with relatives nearby. Then, once she had remade the bed, Bellini and the others mounted to check security arrangements.

It was a cold little peasant chamber, as poor as the room in which Mussolini had been born sixty-two years earlier. Light from an enamel shade showed a big farmhouse bed set square on a red-brick floor under white-washed rafters. There was a steel mirror, an enamel wash-bowl and pitcher, a cane chair, but that was all. From window to ground, Bellini calculated, was a good fifteen-foot drop.

'Treat them well,' Canali told the De Marias as they clumped downstairs. 'They are good people.' Two young partisans were left behind to stand guard, and Bellini promised that he would be back early that afternoon. After explaining to Lia that the gentleman liked two pillows, Claretta asked him shyly: 'The room is ready. Shall we go up?' But Mussolini was still staring at the fire as the partisans trudged off down the mountainside.

Bellini found it in his mind to wonder what would become of them. He did not know that this was the first night the two of them had ever spent together.

Radioman Giuseppe Cirillo thought it the most astonishing signal he had ever transmitted. As chief radio operator for the Partisan High Command, he had in the past six months sent something like seven hundred signals to his OSS counterparts in Florence and Siena – but this was one he'd never forget.

When the courier delivered it to the third-floor flat at 27, Via Moscova, Cirillo's first reaction had been to call Command HQ and demand confirmation. As he later recalled events, it was Socialist Gian-Battista Stucchi, Pertini's deputy, who came on the line – though Stucchi has no distinct recollection. But whoever it was brushed aside Cirillo's doubts. The message now lying before him – pencilled and not, as usual, typewritten – could be coded and sent.

In the evening just past Cirillo had received not one but two signals from Major Max Corvo. Each time he had judged them important enough to don his old weatherproof, hurrying the four blocks to Palazzo Cusani to hand them over personally – the first to the Command's secretary, Alberto Cosattini. Meanwhile, at Via Moscova, Cirillo's operator was decoding Corvo's second message. This one was a terse command:

TO CVL AND CLNAI STOP PLANE WHICH WILL COME TO COL-
LECT MUSSOLINI WILL LAND 6 P.M. TOMORROW AIRPORT
BRESSO STOP PREPARE SIGNALS FOR LANDING AGH

Again Cirillo had delivered the message himself – this time to the Action Party's Fermo Solari. But as the hours dragged by, the courier had brought no replies to the Via Moscova apartment. Plainly the partisan command found it hard to hit on a foolproof way to put the Americans off the scent.

Now, following a stroke of individual genius – by whom, Cirillo never knew – they had achieved it. Hastily Cirillo blocked out the code. Then, as his operator lifted the battered 6olb Mark 3 radio set on to the kitchen table, he poured himself a glass of milk. He watched the man adjusting his head-set before his fingers stabbed at the keys. The message read:

CVL TO AGH SORRY COULD NOT DELIVER MUSSOLINI WHO
JUDGED BY POPULAR TRIBUNAL WAS EXECUTED SAME PLACE
WHERE FIFTEEN PATRIOTS PREVIOUSLY EXECUTED BY
NAZI-FASCISTS.

The time was 3 a.m. on 28 April – four hours and ten minutes before Walter Audisio and his party had even set out for Dongo.

Captain Emilio Daddario was a confused and angry man at 4 a.m. on Saturday, 28 April. So much had happened in the past twelve hours that his search for Mussolini had temporarily dropped from sight. Now, from the unlikely venue of a German command post, the young OSS agent from Lugano's US Consulate, was desperately trying to raise General Cadorna.

At 8 p.m. on Wednesday, 25 April – the very time when Mussolini was leaving Milan's Prefecture – Daddario's orders from Allen Dulles had been explicit. As the Chief of the OSS mission saw it, Daddario and a twelve-man team of Italian agents had more chance of finding and isolating the Duce than the entire US Army. The one thing Dulles feared – and had expressly warned against – was any shoot-up between GIs and partisans for Mussolini's person. As he crossed the Italian border at Ponte Chiasso, his brief-case crammed with his uniform and two American flags, Daddario, a dark, taciturn law-graduate, knew that his whole assignment was as delicate as skirting a minefield.

By 5 p.m. on the Friday, his entire team had crossed the border, jumping the wire at pre-selected rendezvous. Now a five-car convoy of agents and resistance workers, they reached Cernobbio, three miles from Como, to find wild confusion. Inside General Wolff's former headquarters, the Germans and Lieutenant Vittorio Bonetti, another OSS agent, were besieged by local partisans. As Daddario's tan-coloured Alfa-Romeo Spider cruised into view, flying the American flag, Bonetti darted out to greet him with hair-raising news. He had just accepted the surrender of Wolff's overnight guest, Marshal Rodolfo Graziani.

To calm down both Germans and partisans had taken precious time. And in Como Daddario had found an identical situation, first parleying with the Germans before accepting their surrender and arranging a security cordon to await the 1st US Armoured Division. It was midnight before the column hit the Milan road, crawling at less than twenty miles an hour through driving rain.

Then, at 2 a.m. in Milan's blacked-out city centre, all hell had broken loose. A few blocks from the Cathedral, their headlamps probing the darkness, the convoy was caught in the savage cross-fire of three machine-guns. A deadly barrage burst about them, ripping the US and Italian flags to shreds. In the lead car, Graziani's Alfa, Daddario, the Marshal and the black chauffeur hugged the floor as Bonetti at the wheel gunned the accelerator, and the car screamed from Via Dante into Piazza Cordusio. Again fire raked them and Bonetti cut the headlamps. Momentarily blinded, they found themselves within sight of the looming pile of La Scala, backed up against the Hotel Regina.

From all five cars the agents piled out and hit the dirt. Now Daddario could hear guttural voices; eyes were peering at them through an observation slit, beyond a door screened with barbed wire. He realized they were one yard away from the Hotel Regina, Headquarters of Milan's SS. 'Achtung, achtung,' Bonetti shouted, 'we are Americans.' Soldiers doubled to drag away the barricades and Daddario and his party passed in.

Inside, the downstairs lounge was like a Bacchanalia. Drunken Germans lolled everywhere, slumped among the champagne bottles littering the floor. A man and woman lay stark naked on a black velvet settee. As Bonetti marvelled, Daddario 'with as much dignity as if he were Eisenhower', ordered: 'Take me to Colonel Rauff.'

Upstairs, in the office of Wolff's deputy, Daddario was now thinking fast. As the first American to hit Milan, the twenty-six-year-old
agent was acutely aware of the responsibility resting upon him. The
city was a hot-bed of German strongpoints, all of them cut off from
Rauff – who had not heard from General Wolff in days. To avert a
massacre in the city he must first try and persuade the Germans to
sit tight until General Willis D. Crittenberger's IV Corps arrived to
take surrenders. Above all, he must find General Cadorna, urge him
to keep the partisans in check and hand over Graziani. Then would
come the mission of a lifetime: running down Benito Mussolini.

Now Rauff barked an order. An SS officer helped Bonetti place a
call to Cadorna's headquarters.

'Lieutenant Bonetti, United States Mission,' the young officer
led off proudly. 'I am speaking from the Hotel Regina.' But mention
of the notorious SS strong-point proved too much for Cadorna's
staff officer. 'You bloody fool!' he screamed, slamming down the
receiver. 'This is no time for jokes!'

Now it was Daddario's turn to fume. It was 4 a.m., time was
running out, and he must reach the partisans. 'Call them again,'
he ordered, 'and this time let *me* talk to Cadorna.'

In the small panelled antechamber adjoining General Cadorna's
office, Colonel Vittorio Palombo, the genial Chief of Staff, was
listening intently. Through the glass connecting door the wavering
figures of Cadorna and Captain Daddario were like images blurred
in water. More distinctly, he could hear Daddario's voice speaking
fluent and angry Italian. 'We were shot at repeatedly and this kind
of thing's got to stop,' Palombo heard him say, 'people around here
are acting a lot fiercer than they ought to be.'

There followed Cadorna's deep explosive laugh as the General
tried to soothe his guest's ruffled feelings. 'My dear fellow,' he said,
'things are very ugly all over. Even I, the military commander,
was shot at the other day near La Scala.' A few minutes later Palombo
heard Daddario ask, 'What is the latest information on Mussolini?'
And Cadorna's voice was rock-steady as he replied, 'To date we have
no information whatsoever.'

How long, Palombo wondered, could each side sustain this
elaborate double-bluff? If Daddario knew the partisans held Mussolini, he was giving nothing away. He had not even once announced
that the Duce's person was among his primary objectives. But tonight
Cadorna and the duty staff held all the aces. From his frequent

trips into Switzerland, one man on the premises knew both Daddario and Allen Dulles intimately – fifty-four-year-old Ferruccio Parri, the professorial white-haired Chief of the Action Party.

One glimpse of the American entering Palazzo Cusani and he hastened to tell Cadorna: 'Daddario's after Mussolini. If you have him, see that somebody else gets there first.' He added: 'Daddario is a good friend, we've done many missions together, but in this matter – *niente!*'

It was enough. Already, in a schoolhouse on the Viale Romania, fourteen men of Italo Pietra's partisan division, dead to the world on piled straw, were being shaken awake in the harsh light of a storm lantern. Their grim assignment: to form a firing squad under Colonel Valerio.

Now Palombo hastened down the corridor to the secretary's office. Already a typist was at work on the pass that the Chief of Staff had drafted. By sheer good fortune, the ambush that had forced Daddario to take refuge in the Hotel Regina had given Palombo a precious inspiration. All unwitting, the man who sought Mussolini for the Allies was going to help the partisans get there first.

Daddario, Palombo knew, had signed many passes helping resistants to cross the Swiss border. A whole batch was now awaiting his signature to enable liaison officers to negotiate local surrenders. But in the midst of the pile Palombo was inserting one which the typist now handed him:

'Colonel Valerio', (otherwise known as Magnoli, Giovanbattista di Cesare) is an Italian officer belonging to the General Command of the Volunteers' Freedom Corps. The National Liberation Committee for North Italy has sent him on a mission in Como and its province and he must therefore be allowed to circulate freely with his armed escort.

E. Q. Daddario, Captain.

Now Palombo heard the unmistakable sounds of a conference breaking up. Hastening back along the corridor, he buttonholed the young American just as he left the General's office. 'He never even knew what he was signing,' he reported later. 'He was all upside down over Graziani.'

In a sense Palombo was right. Lacking all information on Mussolini, Daddario had swiftly decided that Graziani and the powderkeg city of Milan must take first priority. He must stay put and stabilize things until American troops arrived. Already it had been agreed that Graziani should be considered an American prisoner, transferred from the Hotel Regina to the Hotel Milano, with the American flag flying from the balcony. As Daddario saw it, it was priority to keep the Marshal alive and away from the Communists. If the war in Germany was going on, Graziani, no less than Mussolini, might provide vital knowledge for the next military and political phase.

Around Palazzo Cusani, the secret was closely guarded. Minutes after Mussolini's departure, Cadorna was conferring with his Town Major, General Emilio Faldella, when the door opened and Audisio swaggered in. The Communist, Faldella recalled later, was carrying a rifle at the trail, a tricolour scarf at his throat, and shrugging into a brown leather raincoat. 'Well,' he announced, 'I'm off.' 'All right,' Cadorna replied, 'let's do things properly.'

'What's all that?' Faldella asked. 'Where's he going?' Cadorna was calm. 'They've caught Mussolini and he's going to collect him.' He wasn't more specific.

It never occurred to Faldella that Mussolini would not be taken alive. On his own initiative, back in his office, he uncradled the phone and called the governor of San Vittore Prison: twenty cells were to be put aside to receive the Duce and his bigwigs.

Dry-mouthed, Count Bellini delle Stelle rose slowly from behind the massive eighteenth-century walnut desk. As his hand went to the top of his revolver-holster and unfastened it, his face was sombre. In a few minutes he might be involved in a gun duel for the custody of Benito Mussolini.

The phone message relayed to him in his new headquarters at Dongo Town Hall spelt nothing but trouble. The Partisan Command at Menaggio, eleven miles south, had just phoned a breathless warning: a black Lancia-Aprilia, registration RM 001, had just crashed like an armoured car through a barricade of stones and tree-trunks, ignoring all orders to halt. Hard behind was a heavy yellow-painted removal truck packed with armed men.

Bellini guessed who they were: a Fascist assault force en route to rescue Mussolini. At this hour he had pitifully few men available to ward off an attack – most were on the road-blocks or guarding the scores of prisoners. Suddenly a runner doubled in. The truckload of armed men had arrived in the square. Their officer was demanding the local CO.

Bellini played for time. The officer, he sent word, was welcome to find him in his office. Hastily he called 'Bill' Lazzaro at Domaso and broke the news. 'Collect as many men as you can and get on over,' he urged. 'I'll need support.' The runner's hasty re-entry strengthened his fear. On hearing the message, the officer below had flown into a towering rage, threatening to arrest everyone if Bellini did not come down. The typical old-guard Fascist tactics, Bellini thought. I'll have to go down and stall.

He descended the stairs. In the portal of the Town Hall he stopped dead. The whole square seemed deserted. The rain had stopped; beyond the lake the peaks of Val Tellina gleamed white and beautiful in the sun. Yet the shutters of the houses were down, not a citizen was in sight. Now he saw why. Twenty yards away, a line of fifteen men, silent, watchful, stretched from wall to wall across the piazza, cutting off all access. Their uniforms were new, too new for partisans; their sub-machine-guns oiled and shining, cocked in readiness.

To Bellini, their presence was brooding, evil, 'like a threat hanging over everything', and until their leader stepped arrogantly forward, no man spoke a word.

12. 'God, What an Ignoble End...'

28-9 April, 1945

Below his blue partisan's beret, Walter Audisio's eyes were narrowed, intolerant. 'Colonel Valerio of the Volunteer Freedom Corps,' he announced peremptorily. 'I want to speak to you privately on a matter of great importance.' The voice grated too, Bellini thought, a hectoring Fascist voice. Yet, alone, he knew he could handle him. As the Colonel's men trooped after him towards the Town Hall, Bellini had a brainwave. Wouldn't the men, he asked them, like to eat? Now he took heart. Cheering like boys let loose from school, they stampeded for the cook-house.

The odds are even now, Bellini told himself. Fingers brushing his revolver-holster, he gestured to Audisio to precede him up the Town Hall steps. If it came to a showdown, he could handle this swaggering Fascist until 'Bill' and the others arrived.

As they mounted the stairs, Walter Audisio was almost beside himself with rage. Despite his attempts to send Colonel Malgeri on this mission, Luigi Longo had chosen him – yet from the moment he and Aldo Lampredi had left Milan at 7.10 a.m., everything had gone wrong. The firing squad had been late and the truck provided was not big enough for its macabre purpose – he'd had to requisition a removal van in Como. And in Como, too, resistance chief Oscar Sforni and his staff, irked by Audisio's bullying manner, had refused to accept his credentials. As convinced as Bellini that he was a Fascist, they would give him no help. Already Sforni had decided to bring Mussolini to Como and consign him to the fast-approaching 1st Armoured Division.

In a burst of passion, Audisio had drawn his gun, ordering Sforni from his own office, then phoned Longo in Milan. 'They're all against me here,' he raged. 'I swear they're in league with the Americans.' His voice dry and implacable, Longo offered him just two alternatives: 'Either you shoot Mussolini or we shoot you.'

Enraged, Audisio now found that while he was phoning, Lampredi had sped on to Dongo as if his presence counted for nothing. And when he made to follow suit, Sforni and an aide insisted on coming too.

Sullenly Audisio gave in – but when a naval officer joined the group, sent by the Rome Government to negotiate Mussolini's surrender, the Communist moved fast. At the first garage where they took on petrol he jammed a gun in the officer's ribs. 'You aren't concerned in this,' he told him thickly, 'get down!'

All the way to Dongo his truck had driven on the horn, crashing every road-block – only to find one more partisan commander doubting his credentials. As they reached Bellini's office Audisio, livid, slapped them down on the desk. But now Colonel Palombo's plan stifled all Bellini's doubts. One glance at Daddario's signature and he acknowledged the worst: like it or not, Audisio was in command. Then Aldo Lampredi appeared, a silent withdrawn man in a white raincoat, along with Michele Moretti, who vouched for him. This was indeed the Vice-Commandant-General of the Garibaldi Brigades, the most powerful Communist in the North after Longo.

It was the cruellest fate that Sforni and his aide had left too hurriedly to remember their own credentials. Now, denounced by Audisio as Fascists, they found themselves hustled by the firing squad into the same bolthole where Claretta Petacci had been held. As Bellini put himself under the Colonel's orders, the enraged drumming of their fists drifted up from the ground floor.

'We're going to shoot every bigwig,' Audisio told him brusquely, 'those are my orders: shoot the lot of them.'

Bellini was dumbfounded. For a moment the words stuck in his throat, then he protested violently. To shoot men without trial was as bad as anything the Fascists ever did. Overruling him, Audisio shouted violently for a nominal roll of prisoners. Then, disregarding Bellini's stammered protests, he began to mark it up with black crosses. Benito Mussolini – death. Claretta Petacci – death.

'You'll shoot a woman?' Bellini burst out, appalled. Audisio was indifferent. 'She's been behind his policies all these years,' he stated flatly. 'She was nothing but his mistress,' Bellini snapped. 'To condemn her for that . . .' 'I don't condemn anyone,' Audisio corrected him, 'the judgments have been pronounced by others . . .'

At this stage the Count knew nothing of Clause 29 of the 'Long Armistice'. Nor did he realize that no man on the insurrectional committee, not even Luigi Longo, knew that Claretta was held along with Mussolini. Still he groped for a compromise. It would be best, he suggested, if Audisio stayed put while he, Bellini, fetched the remaining prisoners from Germasino. Moretti could fetch Mussolini and Claretta. All the captives would be delivered to Audisio here at

Dongo. After that Bellini and his men refused to accept any responsibility or co-operate further.

Uneasy at Audisio's frantic haste, Bellini didn't know that at 3.59 p.m. the advanced units of 1st Armoured Division in Como were signalling IV Corps: 'The Big Shot will be turned over to us this afternoon.' His one instinct was to play for time. At least, he consoled himself, Audisio didn't know where Mussolini was hidden – and would not be told.

As he set off fast for Germasino, one item had escaped him. Michele Moretti, the Brigade's Vice-Commissar, was his companion-in-arms – but first and foremost a fanatic Communist. And the night before Moretti had been one of the party who took Mussolini and Claretta to the farmhouse.

Parked outside the Town Hall was a black Fiat 1100, driven by twenty-five-year-old Giovanbattista Geninazza, one-time jeweller's chauffeur, sent by the partisans of his village to stand by as a reserve driver. At 3.15 p.m., while Bellini was en route to Germasino, Moretti was indeed carrying out the young Count's instructions. As Geninazza's Fiat, which he had commandeered, pulled away across the square, Moretti was in the back seat on his way to fetch Mussolini and Claretta.

But beside him was Aldo Lampredi, and in the front seat beside the driver, his body swinging tensely with every curve of the road, muttering, 'Get on with it, get on with it,' was Walter Audisio.

The Fiat toiled round the hairpin bend into the cobbled main square. It stopped by the arch, near the stone wash-trough, where three old women were pounding clothes. Doors slammed as all four men descended. It was 3.50 p.m.

Now, purposefully, without exchanging a word, Lampredi and Moretti set off up the flagged main street. They walked level, their footsteps scraping. Eyes watched them from behind closed shutters. For a moment Geninazza was left alone with Audisio, restlessly chain-smoking his pungent 'Oriental' cigarettes. Suddenly, as if it was a reflex action, he fired a single burst from his machine-pistol into the air. The sound boomeranged from the mountains and the small stone cottages. Then he too was gone, walking fast along the street.

Nearby Signora Rosa Barbanti, a refugee from bombed Turin, was walking her dogs. Now she approached to ask Geninazza curiously: 'What's going on?' 'I don't know,' the driver told her, 'I don't know what I'm here for.' It was true, and besides, he wasn't anxious to talk. Before leaving Dongo he had been told: 'Watch out – very soon you'll see people and things of great importance. Better forget them quickly if you value your head.'

Intrigued, Signora Barbanti still lingered. Towards 4 p.m. she saw five people heading back down the street. In the lead was a man in a brown raincoat who shouted at her, 'Out, get out of here.' As she hastened away, she noted from the corner of her eye that the party included 'an old man and a woman'.

As he entered the bedroom, Audisio claimed later, he greeted Mussolini: 'I've come to liberate you.' He wanted to lull the Duce's suspicions, and, Mussolini, moved, replied, 'I'll give you an empire.' But the level-headed Aldo Lampredi heard no such theatrical interchange. 'Mussolini,' he still affirms, 'knew perfectly well his time had come.' As one of the Party's directorate, Lampredi was here to see that Luigi Longo's orders were carried out to the letter – 'No stage effects, no historical sentences, just execution.'

From the cottage window, Lia de Maria watched the party go, Claretta carrying her personal belongings bundled in a scarf. All day Lia had been wondering what time they would be fetched, though they were no trouble, she thought, such nice people. Towards noon she had served them a meal, which they ate off a packing-case draped with a red cloth at the foot of the bed, their blankets serving as foot-warmers – the woman took milk and maize porridge, the man mortadella, bread and salami. Lia was a little hurt that neither had touched her home-made cheese – yet she couldn't help but warm to them. When she took them their food and later, when she was hoeing in the fields, she saw the man leaning from the window, showing the woman the peaks of Val Tellina.

It struck her how much like Mussolini he was and she said as much to the young partisans on guard outside the bedroom door. Both had laughed and replied, 'Yes, he does look like Mussolini – but of course, he isn't.'

As she climbed the stairs to re-make the bed she saw the two youngsters hurrying after the vanishing party. For the first time a suspicion crossed her mind. In the little brick-floored chamber, she saw that the darned pillows were stained with tears and mascara.

But as the Fiat pulled away from the main square, Claretta was no longer crying. She sat in the back seat, holding tight to Mussolini's hand, and both of them, to Geninazza, seemed 'strangely tranquil'. Coasting downhill, the car was now moving as decorously as a hearse, for Lampredi walked unhurriedly ahead of it. Moretti, too, had gone ahead, doubling down a field-path. Only Audisio, crouched on the right mudguard, facing backwards, his machine-pistol pointing into the car, seemed painfully tense. 'Go on, go on,' he muttered constantly.

Five hundred yards beyond the hairpin bend Audisio ordered a halt. The driver saw they were approaching the spot that the Communist had stared at on the way up – the high iron gateway of Villa Belmonte, five yards farther on, with its cobbled entrance, the stone walls topped by thick clipped privet hedges. It was a peaceful backwater, shaded by a giant copper beech, screened from the village above by the hairpin bend. As Geninazza cut the engine, Audisio vaulted from the mudguard, crossing the road to rattle vainly at the locked gate of the orchard opposite the villa. Returning, he ordered Mussolini and Claretta, 'Get out.' Keeping them covered, he motioned them towards the villa's left-hand gatepost.

Fifteen yards away, downhill towards the lake, Moretti watched tensely. On the curve, fifty yards back, the two young partisans blocked anyone coming from the village. Between them and the boot of the car, eight yards from Audisio and the others, stood Lampredi. There was no escape.

Inside Villa Belmonte, Giuseppina Cordazzo, the thirty-three-year-old housemaid, wondered what was going on. Earlier she had seen a car full of men in blue berets, flying the red flag, grind past. Now, cleaning a second-floor room, drinking in the perfume of rain-fresh wistaria, she heard the car returning and abruptly stop. At once she ran to the house-guest who was reading in a deckchair in the garden, complaining, 'There's a car trying to come into our garage.' To their horror, both women now saw a man staring at them through the gate. 'Get inside or we'll kill you!' he shouted harshly.

Frightened, Giuseppina bolted to find her mistress. 'There's something very ugly happening outside our front gate,' she burst out. Now all three women ran to the villa's top floor to look down. Dimly they saw a woman trying to embrace a man and two men facing them.

Geninazza never caught what it was that Audisio said. For the Communist, it was a formal death sentence: 'By order of the High Command of the Volunteer Freedom Corps, I have been charged to render justice to the Italian people.' But to the driver only three yards away it was just a gabble of words – drowned by Claretta's sudden scream, as she realized, quicker than Mussolini, that this was truly the end. 'You can't kill us like that! You can't do that!' she cried out. 'Move aside or we'll kill you first!' Audisio rasped back at her.

Now, the sweat pouring down his face, he squeezed three times on the trigger of the machine-pistol. But the gun had jammed. Cursing, he tore his revolver from the holster; the trigger clicked drily, but that was all. Backing, covering them with the jammed weapon, he shouted to Moretti: 'Give me your gun!'

From fifteen yards away Moretti hurried to hand him the weapon which would go down in Communist history – a long-barrelled French machine-pistol, 7.65 D-Mas model, 1938, serial No F.20830, bearing a tricolour ribbon.

Sick to his stomach, Geninazza saw Mussolini unbutton his grey-green jacket – as if for the first time in his life he had risen above fear. 'Shoot me in the chest,' he told the Communist distinctly. But Claretta tried to seize the gun barrel, and as Audisio fired, it was she who fell first, shot through the heart, a sprig of flowering creeper in her hand. Then, at three paces, Audisio fired two bursts – nine shots – at Mussolini. Four struck the dictator in the descending aorta; others lodged in the thigh, the collar-bone, the neck, the thyroid gland, the right arm.

Inside Villa Belmonte, the three women were racing panic-stricken down the stairs. Those two staccato bursts had reached their ears – then a terrible silence. In the hallway, they huddled together, shaking, speechless. Faintly, thunder rumbled from the mountains.

From the burnished brass taps hot water gushed into the marble basin. In his suite at the Hotel Gallia, Milan, Colonel Charles Poletti, newly-arrived Military Governor of Lombardy, bent grate-fully forward to sluice his face and arms. Now the American could look back with equanimity on one of the most awful nights he could ever remember.

With his deputy, the British Colonel Arthur Hancock, Poletti had driven all through the night from Florence in the belief that the Americans had liberated Milan. For much of the way an escort of excited partisans had ridden shotgun on his Alfa-Romeo's mud-guards. Only at 9.30 a.m. on this spring Sunday, 29 April, did Poletti realize that Mark Clark's Deputy Chief Civil Affairs Officer had been too optimistic. Arriving in Milan twenty-four hours ahead of their commanding general, Willis D. Crittenberger, Poletti and Hancock found instead that the partisans held the city.

Poletti was still at the basin when his driver darted in. 'Hey, Colonel,' he gasped out, 'Mussolini's in town!' Poletti's heart sank. 'Oh, not after all we've been through tonight,' was his first weary reaction. 'Where?' Hastily the corporal consulted with the chamber-maid, who had broken the news – 'in a place called Piazzale Loreto.' Poletti steeled himself for further action. He decided: 'Let's get down there.' When Hancock objected that he would like to finish shaving, Poletti admonished him, 'Don't be such a British sonofabitch! We're not in town with Mussolini every day.'

Unaware that Mussolini had even been caught, Poletti fully expected they were about to witness the Duce's last harangue to the people.

It was an unforgettable morning. As the car with its partisan escort swung away from the hotel, the whole mountain mass of Monte Rosa, ninety miles away on the Swiss frontier, stood out like a cardboard cut-out. Under a high and watery sun women Fascists, their heads shaven, the hammer-and-sickle painted in scarlet on their foreheads, were being paraded through the streets. Then, as the car nosed through a black sea of humanity into Piazzale Loreto, an incredible sight met Poletti's eyes. In his first-ever glimpse of Benito Mussolini, the American saw the Duce upside down – literally being hoisted by his boots to the girders of a bombed-out filling-station. Beside him hung Claretta Petacci, her skirt lashed into place with a partisan's belt, and the corpses of thirteen other Fascist notables – among them Alessandro Pavolini and Claretta's brother, Marcello, whom Walter Audisio's firing squad had executed in Dongo's main square following Mussolini's death. In the yellow removal truck, commandeered in Como, they had been driven to Milan and dumped under cover of darkness – the grim retribution the Communists had all along planned for the fifteen patriots exe-cuted here by the Germans in August, 1944.

At first the crowds had been no more than curious – circling the bodies as they sprawled on the pavement as if at a macabre lying-in-state. Someone had placed a sceptre in Mussolini's hand and his head lay propped on Claretta's white blouse. Newsmen stood by registering quick clinical impressions. Stan Swinton of *Stars and Stripes* noted Claretta's neat ringlets, a glimpse of baby-blue under-wear. Milton Bracker of the *New York Times* watched photographers tilt the Duce's face towards the sun, supporting his jaw with a rifle-butt.

The United Press reporter, James Roper, trying to get things in perspective, sought enlightenment from a partisan. If Mussolini was Italy's most-hated son, why in the world put him together with his mistress for one last night in a house with a lakeside view? For answer, the man spread wide his hands: 'We're all Italians, after all.'

Abruptly a jungle savagery set in. A man darted in to aim a savage kick at Mussolini's head – to the *New York Times* man the sound was 'a hideous crunch'. People began to dance and caper round the corpses; to the *Baltimore Sun's* correspondent, Howard Norton, their mood was 'black, ugly, undisciplined'. One woman fired five shots into Mussolini's prostrate body – one for each of the sons she had lost in the Duce's war. Another ripped off his shirt, fired it and tried to thrust it in his face. Others moved in to commit the supreme indignity on a man once mobbed by hysterical women whenever he took a bathe; spreading their skirts, they urinated upon his upturned face.

To one partisan commander it was suddenly like 'a savage circus'. His chief, Italo Pietra, set ten men to fire in the air, striving to keep the crowd at bay – but it was hopeless. Hacking, cursing, swaying, the people were trampling the corpses, blind with the hatred of years. Even 300 *carabinierei* couldn't restrain them; hastily they retreated, uniforms ripped to shreds. Next the Fire Brigade struggled to the scene, but even their white hissing jets could not extinguish that hatred.

At the Archbishop's Palace, it was the first time his secretaries had ever heard Cardinal Schuster raise his voice. 'Get Cadorna!' he shouted when news that the bodies had been strung up reached him. On the phone to Prefect Riccardo Lombardi, he threatened: 'Either you take those corpses down or I'll come down there myself.'

To Colonel Poletti's astonishment, one victim was still to come. Into the square drove a truck-load of partisans, hemming in a lone prisoner – the long-disgraced Party Secretary, Achille Starace. Then and there, after giving a last Roman salute to his Duce, he too fell riddled with machine-gun bullets. To himself, Poletti muttered decisively, 'This has got to stop.'

Yet as Starace's body was hoisted to join the others, Poletti sensed a sudden calm falling. The screams of execration ceased and now there was only silence and awe – 'as if it was God's will and this was the end.'

'Imagine,' a woman murmured, staring up at Claretta. 'All that and not even a run in her stockings.'

As Poletti struggled back to the car, the bells of Milan were pealing.

And still the bells rang out: the deep-toned Cathedral bells; the wild sweet chimes of Santa Giovanna alla Creta; the doleful cadence of San Babila; the solemn tolling of San Ambrogio. The Duce is dead, was their burden, rejoice, victory is ours, freedom is ours, the Duce is dead. They carried the news through Milan and all Italy; they carried the news to the world.

Adolf Hitler heard the fate of his old ally that afternoon in the Führerbunker at Berlin, soon after he had married Eva Braun. Those round him felt that he did not really take it in at all. The Russian tanks were only half a mile away and he had learned that Heinrich Himmler, whom he had trusted as *der treue Heinrich*, was negotiating with the Western Allies. That night he said goodbye to everyone in the bunker, preparing for his own macabre end.

Winston Churchill was at Chequers when the news reached him. Elated at the fall of the tyrant, he rushed in to his dinner guests, crying 'The bloody beast is dead.' But when he read of Claretta, and of Audisio's 'treacherous and cowardly action', his chivalrous soul was stirred. In whitehot passion, he cabled Field-Marshal Alexander: 'Was Mussolini's mistress on the list of war criminals? Had he authority from anybody to shoot this woman? The cleansing hand of British military power should make enquiries on these points.'

General Dwight D. Eisenhower was in the red-brick schoolhouse at Rheims that was the Supreme Headquarters of Allied Expeditionary Forces. To his Chief of Staff, General Walter Bedell Smith, he burst out: 'God, what an ignoble end! You give people a little power and it seems like they can never be decent human beings again.'

Almost two hundred miles away, in his own headquarters at Florence, the man who had pursued Mussolini to the bitter end felt much the same. Shocked and disturbed, General Mark Clark still reflected that perhaps it had been for the best. 'Even his own people had at last come to hate him.'

Most Italian resistance chiefs felt the same. At first, hearing of Piazzale Loreto, General Cadorna raged: *'Finiamola con questo sconcio!'* (Let's put an end to this stinking business.) Then, as he awaited the first American troops at the entrance to the autostrada, a group of women hailed him: 'You killed him too quickly – better to have taken him round Italy and spat upon him.' Then the General began to feel that this, after all, was the vengeance the people had demanded.

Leo Valiani hastened in to his flat near the Central Station, alerted by the shrilling of the telephone. It was a sub-editor from *Italia Libera*, telling him: 'We'll have to get out a special edition. Mussolini is hanging in Piazzale Loreto.' One of Mussolini's four judges felt one emotion above all: that the people now execrating the fallen in the piazza were not the resistants who had struck four days ago but the Fascists who a few weeks ago had fawned on him.

Walter Audisio was off duty too, but not sleeping. He lay on a truckle bed in his quarters at Palazzo Cusani, struck down by a raging fever of 103°. One man who looked in as the bells pealed saw him wide awake, staring at the ceiling, 'his cheeks still stained with fear'.

For those who still clung to Mussolini's credo, it was the blackest day in all their lives. A lifetime ago, sixteen-year-old Giovanni Ruzzini had marched on Rome, his black shirt still damp with dye. Now Captain Ruzzini of the Salò Republic's Army shivered on the edge of a hospital bed in Corso Porta Romana, machine-gun bullets from a partisan ambush embedded in his leg, hearing the mob baying past the window en route to Piazzale Loreto. Out of deep despair he told his room mate: 'I don't know, but it seems to me that everything is lost. Perhaps I was wrong, but I still believe in him.'

Federal Secretary Vincenzo Costa was in Cell 36 of Como's San Donino prison, together with twenty others whose Val Tellina dreams had come to dust. It was night. The iron bolt of the cell slid back and a warder ushered in the Duce's nephew, Vito. In a voice so low they could scarcely hear, he told them the news. There sprang to Costa's mind the old cry of the action squads when one of their number had perished, and like a parade-ground sergeant he shouted: 'Benito Mussolini!' A score of voices answered for the Duce: '*Presente!*' Unrepentant, they chanted the songs of the March on Rome, looking back to a world that was young.

Rachele Mussolini was in the woman's wing of that same prison. The partisans had caught her and separated her from the children and it was this, above all, which troubled her. In the chaos only one woman had recognized her, and she had begged her to keep silent. The others were too busy telling the stories of their own arrests. Outside in the courtyard a voice was intoning a list of names; there was a stutter of machine-gun fire, then the rumble of cart-wheels. The revolution was ending as it had begun, in blood. The women screamed and clung to the iron window bars, but Rachele was calm, wondering only when she would be reunited with Romano and Anna Maria.

The headlines had told her of Benito's death, but she had reached a point where grief could no longer help. Only tomorrow would she recall her strange prophecy to Claretta: 'They'll take you to Piazzale Loreto.'

Close at hand a woman noted her uncanny calm and couldn't fathom it. 'You're not crying?' she asked Rachele. 'You haven't lost anyone, then?'

Side by side, the two American Army officers climbed the great marble staircase of the Prefecture, their footfalls muffled by the long black and red stair carpet. It was 2 p.m. Colonel Charles Poletti and Major Max Corvo were making their first post-liberation contact with the Partisan Command.

Earlier, in these first-floor offices, there had been bitter dissension over the insurrectional committee's action. Liberal Giustino Arpesani complained furiously that until this morning even the news of Mussolini's capture had been kept from him. 'My name has been put to proclamations that I have never seen at all,' he charged furiously. Achille Marazza felt the same. Despite his role in things, Sandro Pertini also recoiled from the obscenity of Piazzale Loreto. Almost speechless with horror, he croaked to Emilio Sereni: 'Have you seen? The insurrection is dishonoured.' Vainly Sereni tried to reconcile him with the Communist Party's line: 'History is made that way – some people must not only die, but die in shame.'

Ferruccio Parri of the Action Party couldn't keep silent – not over Claretta, not over a display like 'a Mexican butcher's shop'. No sooner had he and Poletti exchanged greetings than he confided his fears: 'It's ugly and unfitting – it will injure the partisan movement for years to come.'

'It's done now,' Poletti tried to console him. 'Emotions run pretty high in war. But I did come to counsel you to take those bodies down and to stop stringing others up. Those are my orders.'

Parri agreed. 'Very well – but where shall we take Mussolini? The mob may tear him to pieces.'

Poletti considered. It seemed 'almost a part of history' to be pondering the last decision that would ever be made concerning Benito Mussolini. 'In America,' he told Parri, 'we have something called a morgue. Don't you have a morgue?'

'We have a poor man's morgue.'

'Then, fine,' Poletti decided. 'Take him there. Have him guarded by the partisans and let nothing more happen to him, because it's over now. Let no more harm come to that man – no more harm at all.'

Appendix A

'The Same Fanatics Who . . . Burned Joan of Arc'

(Job 54, Frames 026797–026802; 027659–779, U S National Archives. Translated from the Italian by Maria Teresa Williams)

Despite his many English admirers, Benito Mussolini spent only eight days in England – at the London Reparations Conference of December 1922. To him, the English always remained a mystery – a nation whom he believed ate five meals a day and donned dinner-jackets to take five o'clock tea. But from 1932 to 1939 a shrewd interpreter of the London scene endeavoured to bring Mussolini closer to the reality – Count Dino Grandi, Ambassador to the Court of St James's, who laboured also to keep Anglo-Italian relations on an even keel throughout the storms of the Abyssinian and Spanish Civil Wars.

Here Grandi reports to Mussolini and Foreign Minister Ciano on the foibles of the mysterious English as he saw them:

Italian Embassy,
4 Grosvenor Square, W I
18 August, 1933

Dear President,

Following my information about the press, I'm sending an article, 'France and Fascism', published in today's *Morning Post*. It is inspired by your recent article 'Sunset and Twilight of Democracy' – your previous article, 'After London', of the 24 July, plus the abovementioned, have caused a great sensation, and have provoked some leaders like that of Huddleston in the *Daily Mail*, the *Sunday Times*'s: 'Fascism with a difference', 'Defining of an Epoch' in the *Evening News*, 'The Meaning of Fascism' in the *Morning Post*.

I have already cabled that never have the British people shown such interest in new ideas and Fascist movements in various parts of the world as in these days. The newspapers were quick to catch the new mood, judging by the headlines.

You will also find a brief report of recent publications on the setting-up of a Bird Sanctuary in the park of a Villa near Padua. I stress this because it illustrates the strange psychology of this country, and therefore the elements which it is important to keep in mind in relation to what I call the 'organization of sympathy' that a nation creates for its advantage in the world.

The Chancellor of the Exchequer, Neville Chamberlain, the day before the Budget in the Commons, wrote a letter to *The Times* to urge the London County Council to protect some poor little birds (wagtails) that flock in St James's Park beneath the windows of the Treasury.

I can assure you that the British are more interested in the fate of these birds than in the Budget. Apropos of this, I draw your attention to a book by Paul Morand about London, which no doubt you will know (I have never yet mentioned a book without your saying that you knew it already). Morand is an ex-French diplomat, perhaps the only one who has understood England, and he says: 'This curious and mysterious race has aspects which are incomprehensible to us Europeans.' Last night at the première of an historical film (incidentally co-produced by an Italian, Toeplitz) called *The Private Life of Henry VIII*, the censor cut out the cock-fight but left untouched two macabre sequences depicting the executions of Anne Boleyn and Catherine Howard, with the sharpening of the axe, women screaming, and the final scene of the beheading. It seems that this country needs to compensate with its love for animals for its inborn cruelty to man.

I enclose finally an article (already mentioned) in *The Times*, about the traffic in Rome, which you may have already read. The English without exception, speak of Rome, Your Rome, as an enchanted Paradise. But often they say: 'What a pity . . . the noise.' I invariably reply: 'Wait a bit. Mussolini will soon settle even that.'

With Devotion,
Grandi

6 November, 1936

Dear Galeazzo,

While you were on the phone the day before yesterday, Ribbentrop was here. He arrived in London a few days ago and contacted me straight away, which on the surface at least was intended as a gesture of deliberate cordiality and camaraderie. He has been here twice already. To his show of cordiality I, of course, have made an adequate response. It is right that the British should have the impression that the representatives of the two great Fascist countries are working together. I told Ribbentrop that my four years of experience in London were at his disposal, and he seemed grateful. Unless you instruct me otherwise, I'll give Ribbentrop plenty of rope: I think it necessary to keep an eye on him.

Ribbentrop's arrival three months after the official announcement, the German Embassy having been without a representative for six months, has been very noisy. He was preceded by several cars, a crowd of reporters and Press attachés who have immediately begun 'beating the drum', and by his son, a boy of fourteen, whom he has enrolled at Westminster School. This has led to all the British papers publishing pictures of this boy dressed in the 'clownish' uniform of Eton, with far-from-sympathetic comments on the Nazi Ambassador: 'The Nazi Ambassador is having his son educated English-style . . . when young Ribbentrop goes back to Germany he will have forgotten how to give the Nazi salute . . . '

This, in my opinion, has been Ribbentrop's first big mistake; he has shown his ignorance of the fact that the British respect only those people who don't accept them as superior.

The second mistake was to give an interview as soon as he arrived at Victoria Station. He told reporters that he had come to London to strengthen the ties of friendship between Britain and Germany, but it wasn't easy (first blunder), that it would take a long time (second blunder), but that in the end a common ground of understanding would be reached because both countries had a common enemy: Communism (third blunder). This interview has let all hell loose, for two days the papers have printed nothing else. In the cuttings I'm sending (not only from left-wing papers), you'll see that the kindest words for Ribbentrop are: 'Impudent – gaffeur – faux-pas – false start – Ambassadors who can't keep their mouths shut shouldn't be Ambassadors.' As a diplomatic start, Ribbentrop has behaved like the proverbial Teutonic elephant walking over china plates.

Neurath[1] was right when he told you that it was easier to sell champagne to the British than to engage in politics with them.

But there is more to Ribbentrop's action; in spite of Vansittart[2] and a few anti-German die-hards in the Cabinet, the majority of the British people, and even the Cabinet itself, wish an accord with Germany, to dispel the threat of another war. Ribbentrop is only the spearhead of a vast and more complex situation. It will depend chiefly on how Hitler reacts to the British overtures, which are more and more towards an understanding. The problem of Anglo-German relations is especially important to us because it has a direct bearing on Anglo-Italian relations. You, dear Galeazzo, have seen this perfectly in your historic meetings with Hitler and Neurath. Just as in 1935 British policy destroyed the *entente* which the Duce had established with Laval, so in 1937 British policy shows signs of wanting to divide Germany from Italy.

Your recent journey to Berlin has been an international event which the British have followed with anxiety. The close German-Italian alliance which has crowned the Duce's diplomatic year, Year XV, worries England . . . if Italy and Germany pursue this strict alliance, Britain will be compelled to come to terms with Rome and Berlin at the same time . . . this is

1. Freiherr Konstantin von Neurath, German Minister for Foreign Affairs, 1932–8
2. Sir Robert (later Lord) Vansittart, Permanent Under-Secretary of State for Foreign Affairs, 1930–8

the key to our policy which you have so effectively illustrated to the Führer.

The British Liberals, Labourites, etc, especially the latter, are a con-glomeration of fanatics, necessarily anti-Fascist, who represent what I call the 'historical beast' of England. They are the same fanatics who six centuries ago burned Joan of Arc and four centuries ago beheaded Mary Stuart and later Charles I. Not for nothing was Mary Stuart's executioner an ancestor of the Cecil family, of which Lord Cecil is the last notorious descendant. A year ago the 'beast' almost got the upper hand. But it did not succeed in dragging the British people into a crusade against Italy, although it managed to drag the Baldwin Government . . .

Anti-Fascist fanaticism has made them (the Labour Party) accept the Conservatives' rearmament programme not as a necessity of defence but as a means of defence against the Fascist threat . . .

The more Italy and Germany show their unity, the more England will be compelled to negotiate with the two great Fascist peoples . . . The [treaty] documents signed by you and Hitler must be considered, in effect, as a new lever that the Duce has put under this 'old and creaking Europe'.

Yours,
Grandi

Appendix B

'Love-Letters of a Dictator'

(Job 53, Frames 026456–026491, US National
Archives, Washington. Translated from the Italian
by Maria Teresa Williams and Maria Teresa Vasta)

*Between 1932 and 1945, some 300 letters passed between Benito Mussolini
and Claretta Petacci – almost all of which have survived for posterity in
Washington's National Archives. Of the selection printed here, most were
written by Mussolini in the early autumn of 1940, during Claretta's convalescence following an emergency operation for an extra-uterine pregnancy.
All were written from Palazzo Venezia; almost all are undated:*

My little one,
Just a few words, otherwise I'll be late visiting you. You must get well
soon. I want it, my love; our love – love with a capital letter, because it is a
true great love – wants it.
From the 8th to 15th (you must) convalesce. Sunday the 25th, at Palazzo
Venezia.
Your Ben embraces you.

My dear little one,
Imagine you are climbing the 'Holy Steps' of recovery. You have
already climbed twenty steps and in this week, which promises to be full
of sun, you will climb another twenty. Then you will get up and the
climbing will be quicker – In a few minutes I'll go to your room, which is
how you left it and it is waiting for you. Everything is waiting there: the
books, the music, the violin, the dressing-gowns. Ben, too, is waiting,
so happy with his role as nurse. Tell me that this is speeding up your recovery. Today I will ring. Ben embraces you, with the tender feelings
you know.

My dear little one,
I'm coming to you with just one wish: to help you in regaining your
former health. I'll help you in any case, with what you desire and like.

So that one day I may see you in your room, which looks empty without you.

Your Ben, who loves you.

My little convalescent,

Your bulletin fills me with joy: with this letter and my afternoon visit you will leap many steps. Be patient, you don't lack the courage, for a few more days. Then there will be the convalescence, during which everything will seem as new to you, never before seen, surprising. The only thing not new or surprising will be Ben and his love for you.

My darling sick girl, now recovered,

I want these words of mine to make up to you for Phoebus, who today, lazy one that he is, has deserted us. Today I will call on you with the infallible 'magnetism', which will make you climb several steps. I can tell from your voice that you are feeling better. Patience and courage; you do have them. Your love embraces you.

My dear little one,

Forgive me if last night I was a bit harsh. Sometimes I don't even notice it. It is the way I live that regrettably makes me so. This sheet of paper is the forerunner of the great magnetism that I will bring today. Days like today will ensure the 'climb' to recovery takes less time. I will be at your side with the soul that you know and which belongs to you. I beg you to use your courage for your recovery and your love which will make Ben happy.

My dear little one,

As I write the sun has swept away the sirocco clouds and is flooding my desk. Similarly I wish that my tenderness would envelop your soul and coax your will-power towards recovery. It is only a question of will-power, now. I have already marked the stages: from the 15th to the 22nd in bed, from 22nd to 29th up and then at Palazzo Venezia. The memory of these anxious and painful days is already fading. Tomorrow everything will look better, and you will feel on top of the world. I beseech you to obey me, just this once. Your Ben embraces you as ever.

My dear little one,

At last the news I was awaiting with anxiety: the sudden pain is receding, you are altogether better and this week will be the turning-point. Dear, today I will visit you, maybe late, but I will come. Next week you'll be back in your room, which I visit now and then, full of melancholy. I embrace you, Ben.

My dear little one,

What a glorious sun, and what sadness to know you are in bed after the grey night. I'm so happy that I brought you so much magnetism. I will bring a lot today as well. I'm sending the Nestrovit, four vitamins in one which I myself take. It is an exceptional tonic which comes in liquid or tablet form. Take it immediately, in the prescribed doses. Don't take solid or semi-solid food today, only sugared water, camomile, coffee. It is a month today since you took to your bed: it is time to recover. I'm sending my embraces and all my deep tenderness. Ben.

My love,

I think, in my ignorance, that what is happening is a sign of recovery. Henceforth the problem is one of morale. You must be calm, and you can be calm. I'm beginning to get very detached from everything and everybody, to wit, the world, especially since you have been ill. Since then I have always been thinking of your recovery. I do not know if these letters have helped, somehow. I hope so. The nature of my work doesn't allow me much lyrical fancy, but my tenderness and my love for you fill up my soul. Rise, walk, get better. But you must pay attention to what the doctors say: they know more than we do. Do not get sad little whims, now that the end is in sight, helped by your willing nurse, Ben, who embraces you.

My little but great love,

Your voice tells me that you are getting better, that the way of recovery lies open before you and you are leaping the stages. I'm travelling beside you and I'm sustaining you in your task.

Take notice that next week you must be ready to return to your room which is waiting for you, in every single detail. Get up, walk. I want it, your youth wants it and, above all, my love wants it, the love of your Ben.

My dear little convalescent,

You have given me the bulletin I wanted: 'a long restful sleep'. Now you must get up and stimulate your will-power. The will to recover resolutely is getting you half-way there already. Some more leaps and you will be there. Your room is waiting, exactly as you left it. Don't delay too long. Make use of these magnificent days and the love of your Ben.

My dear little one,

I did not really expect a first bulletin of 'tearlets' because of the coffee. I hope they gave it to you in spoonfuls. Today you could get up at about 11 a.m., for a while. The weather is radiant, my love for you equally so. By the time you read these words your eyes will be dry, I hope; if I could be near you I would dry them with my caresses.

Dear little one,

A month has gone by since you submitted bravely to the surgeon's knife. We have had our ups and downs during these interminable days, but now full life is coming back to your body and your soul. This splendid weather has helped and maybe my love has helped a little. As soon as you have received this, get ready to get up and ask to be taken outside in the open air. You will experience a great and reviving emotion. Life is truly beautiful, even when there isn't full sunshine and a deep blue sky. It is worthwhile to fill it with a great love, such as mine for you. From Monday 30th I will be waiting for you here. Everything is waiting for you here, including, of course, Ben.

Dear love,

Today is the beginning of the second month of your illness: the one of your recovery. I will help you again and forever with my love; you must help yourself with will-power. Put together, these elements become an Axis and Victory will be in sight. Enough of suffering, life must go on and will go on with its daily needs such as walking, especially in this September. Soon you will be up and about and this fills me with joy, Ben embraces you as before, as ever.

On 2 October, 1940, two days before meeting with Hitler at the Brenner Pass, Mussolini penned this note to Claretta. Ten days later, furious that the Führer had occupied Romania without consulting him, the Duce decided on his ill-starred invasion of Greece:

My dear beloved little one,

While I'm about to leave, I address you a prayer and a wish that comes from the bottom of my heart: you must get better. Better still: you must speed up your recovery, shortening the term of convalescence.

Even from afar I will be near you and will do my best to let you hear my voice, that one time you liked. I see from the calendar that today is the feast of the Guardian Angels. May they add their protection to that which comes from my love. Please be here, when I come back. Ben embraces you.

August, 1941 – the month in which Mussolini lost his favourite son, Bruno – was also the month in which he and Hitler visited the Ukraine. A few days before his departure on 27 August, he wrote to Claretta:

Dear,

In spite of the sun and the sea, these ill-fated days of August 1941 are sad and long. I have been thinking of you a lot and I will be thinking of you on this journey which I undertake without great enthusiasm.

It will be an absence of five or six days. Be calm and get well. My mind is almost empty but in my heart you are always present as before, as to-morrow, as always. Your Ben embraces you for ever.

Often Claretta was bitterly – and justifiably – jealous of the Duce, to the extent of having him followed when he visited other women. In this letter – possibly also written in August, 1941 – Mussolini replies to one such accusation:

Dear little one,

Your services work very well. It is a fact that Sunday 24th I went to the home of R. and if for four months you had not been so informed, it means that your informers are honest, because I had not been in that house or in other places for the past four months. You have a tendency to dramatize the event: I'm grateful to you. I can assure you that it is hardly worth the bother, apart from my humiliation. There is only one thing for you to worry about: to get better and get back to your task of little 'mascotte', more necessary than ever now. Your room in awaiting you, becomes sad. Come back soon, Monday for example, it will be a great joy for your loving Ben.

Here Mussolini, in chastened mood, endeavours to bring about a reconciliation following a lovers' quarrel:

Clara,

All that has happened between 13.45 and 14.10 is so far from my mind that I can hardly recollect it. I telephoned you during a break from work, at about 17 hours, I came to your room to look for you. I feel so humiliated that I don't dare to meet you. I'm waiting for your word. Tomorrow I will go – we will go – to the sea. The 17th is not a day, or a number, that is propitious, but I do not believe in superstitions. We both need a little sea. I would like to end this letter with the words that you know, but I'm afraid you might reject them. Come what may, I am and will be your Ben.

In a rarely-dated letter – 3 February, 1938 – Claretta in turn is begging Benito's forgiveness:

My love,

Forgive me. My heart is full of anxiety. You rang me up and I was not there, I could not hear you, maybe you were calling me to you . . . and I was going crazy with desire for you . . . I feel like crying . . .

I had to go with my mother to visit Grandmother who had had a heart attack and was in danger. I left soon after 5 p.m. I reached home when you had just rung for the second time, and then I dashed in, in the hope of seeing you and apologizing. Oh, forgive me; don't be cross, it wasn't my fault. I am always waiting and this is my joy, the reason of living. I love you, and your voice is my only blessing; to see, to talk to you, my immense happiness . . .

Tell me that you are not upset; how can I say what I feel, I can only apologize most humbly. I don't know what to say: I adore you and beg you to forgive me. My dear, the pain is choking me, I wish I could run to you, you are so close to me, I wish I could look in your eyes and see if they are as sweet as ever . . .

Accept, please, my apologies with the offering of my love, infinite and devout, while I tremble at the thought of having displeased you.

Claretta herself noted the date on this letter – 20 May, 1942. Distraught with worry as his armies crumbled, the Duce, returning from an inspection of Sardinian coastal defences, was pleading for a temporary suspension of their relationship:

Clara,

The sacrifice I have asked of your love, of your sensitivity and submissiveness might be and is enormous, but, I repeat, it is necessary, to clarify everything and so that persons, things, events, can be seen in a calm way.

I repeat that one day – soon, I think – you will be thankful for this, and will be happy about the eclipse of a habit that was dear to you and to me. I beseech you to not read in what is happening anything different from what my heart told you. Please rest and get better. My nerves and yours need peace and quiet.

When the horizon is free from clouds, we will see an unextinguishable flame and these letters will keep it alive.

From Meina, on Lake Maggiore, where she and her family fled after 25 July, 1943, Claretta poured out her heart in a letter to Mussolini, uncertain even as to whether he was dead or alive:

My beloved Ben,

I have no ink and the village is far away. I cannot wait to tell you a sudden thought which has come to me, violently, last night, and made my blood race, leaving me breathless. You might say that there is nothing, apart from this tragedy which has upset the world and the very existence of things and will upset the universe. What anguish, my God! And here is my thought, violent and sudden. Is it possible to die twice morally, spiritually? I'm afraid – I will explain it, Ben. I died last Sunday, the tragic Sunday of your downfall, your incredible, unlikely downfall, the day of the treason, the day in which the most horrible stain has clouded the sun of Italy, which will never shine on the shame, the selling out by Judas. I have died for what happened to you as Head, as Duce, as Supreme Human Being, master of the destiny of Italy. I have fallen with you in your tragic crash, in the moment when all our dreams, hopes, the dedication of your entire life, was spent in raising up the Italian people . . .

Because I was in your heart, as ever, as when I collected your photos as an adolescent, or learned your words, mastering your diabolical political adroitness, so I was with you in these last grey years of world torment and your daily torment, while we tried to forget our problems in the problem of the bloody war, I continued to share your pains and your struggle, participating with my sensitiveness and awareness. And in that tragic moment I felt what went on in your heart, all your suffering, the disgust, the nausea, the detachment from filthy humanity. All that you thought, I thought, hour by hour, minute by minute; I have been near you and I am near you and I will always feel near you. This loving you, beyond events, this belonging to you even today when you are alone, abandoned by everybody and deathly sad, gives me the strength to go on living, living for you, continuing to give you my youth, my love, the sole reason for my existence. Tonight one of your sentences has recurred over and over again: 'It has gone, the image has vanished with time, I don't recollect her face – her voice, her eyes, gone for ever.' Thus more than once you talked about the women in your life. It is also true that you said: 'No woman has ever had the place that you have in my heart, and if I look back I have loved only you.'

It is true and I don't want to become a mere portrait in the gallery of your past loves, my love is too alive, violent. But tell me, tell me I cannot lose all with time. No, love conquers time, dominates it, and rises above it, fulfils it and makes it worthy of life. Ben, forgive my thoughts: it is like a series of photos, one superimposed on the other, in a game of light and shadow, barely distinguishable. Then all is confusion, everything revolves and I'm happy for a while. But when my mind comes back to earth, there is only one thought: I have left you for a moment, and then I cry because I feel helpless. You understand me.

Think how absurd I can be, my Ben. Sometimes I'm very jealous and turn against all the women that crossed your life, all the women who have partaken of what I thought was only mine. I think of all the wounds you inflicted on my heart, of which I still feel the pain. How you made me cry, and how you could have made me happy: I won't forget those bitter hours. I have forgotten a lot but some things have left a deep scar. It was not fair to make me cry, the span of our love was so short . . . I would like to go back and stop you from doing this to me again. And now what happened to all that? . . . of all that you crudely defined as . . . lavatory? . . . It seems impossible, but even filth makes one suffer, and how much have I suffered. I remember how you laughed at my outburst, how amused you were to see me lose my temper.

Why cannot I be near you, Ben; why don't they let me? I would sleep on the floor . . . I would wait on you in the most humble chores, anything to be near you . . . to share your torment, to offer my immense devout love . . . Ben, my love, let me come to you, let me kneel at your feet, look at you, hear your beautiful voice, warm, unique, (nobody in the world has your voice, your eyes, your hands). Ben, call to me, I'm your little slave, take my life, but please do not suffer, do not feel too alone, I'm near you with all my heart.

This morning a youth who came to mend a pipe in the house was singing 'Battalions, Battalions of death, Battalions of life'. He sang with gusto, devotion, and gave me a timid and at the same time shrewd look. I cried and he cried, too. And so many have cried and are crying, in the silence of their houses, with their memories. Ben, the miserable treason of the Judases will be revenged, and, above all, those who try to erase the work of a man of genius like you will be punished. Many were not worthy of being near you, but Italy is great, and I pray to S. Rita, to whom you too were devoted. Ben, my beloved, send me a sign, help me not to die; without you, everything is lost, everything is without light, without hope. Please send a word, my love. I cannot go on any longer.

All his life tormented by self-doubt and a gnawing sense of inferiority, Mussolini heard from Claretta the words he needed to bolster his wavering ego. In this second letter from Lake Maggiore – which it is doubtful he ever received – Claretta, as she had done for seven years, sought to reinforce his vision of himself as the man whose name would be 'written in the sky of the Fatherland':

My beloved, my poor great love . . .

What are you doing? what is it happening to us all? . . . This nightmare is never ending: is it a cruel reality? It doesn't matter if they know that I'm writing to you, let them know that I'm not repudiating you, and I don't repudiate the love I had for you and will have for you. If to love is a crime, I am guilty. In the terrible hours, while the barbarians were sacking my father's study – thirty-five years of work dedicated to the healing of bodies and souls while they stormed the villa shouting that all your immense work was destroyed – I felt like crying, I felt like dying. Only one person helped us [the Petaccis' chauffeur] and to him we owe our lives. I have now arrived at Meina, at Mimi's, and it is due to him that I can communicate with you. You have understood without me mentioning his name; be comforted by the thought that good people still exist. Now I'm here, I don't know for how long. We have no means, no strength; we are stupefied by grief, crushed by reality. If I could be near you, be of some use to you . . . What cruel fate weighs down our love . . . Here I am desperate, dry-eyed . . . tormented by your humiliation, your sorrow, and I cannot kneel in front of you and tell you of my love, of my devotion, or give you comfort . . . Although you did what you did . . . You killed all that loved you, all that had faith in you . . . you left many in desperation, and now they cannot believe that it is all over, that a Man, Great like you, Unique, Divine Creature, is crushed by fate. They do not believe it, and it cannot be believed.

Twenty-three years of work, toil, fight: twenty-three years of sacrifices, renunciation, turmoils, bitterness; twenty-three years of immense building, the Navy, the Air Force, all due to your immense will-power. You have moulded men and things, you have served this bloodless multitude like a labourer, in an attempt to infuse it with the lymph of your generous and honest peasant blood. Why have you been so good? Why have you not spilled the blood that would have saved humanity? I cannot keep silent. I cannot, in this tragic moment, but give voice to my anguish. I dissolve into tears. How I envy your wife . . . She can still hear your words, listen to your voice . . . look in your eyes, share your infinite grief . . .

The thought that I might not see you any more . . . I'd rather die . . . tell me that it isn't true, that I will see you and that this hope is what keeps you alive . . . What will they do with you? What have you done . . . Go, please, go beyond . . . Go where there is no sun, you'll find peace . . . You might let me know if there is somebody who can still be trusted . . . I don't know if Ridolfi is still alive . . . or if Albino is still with you. But you must give me your news . . . I beg you: the years of intimate and spiritual life, spent in the sweetness of our love – which cannot be confused with vile insinuations, will conquer time and events. I'm with you as yesterday, as today, with all my heart . . .

How can they erase, or obliterate your name, which is carved in the stone of history? Whatever happens, you will be the creature elected by God, the Genius that every few centuries carves his name on grey and uniform humanity.

You are what you are, and what you have done will remain with you, around you, after you. Your name will live through the centuries: your light, your work will shine immense and magnificent. It is no use: whatever might be said you are the Genius and if the little men, the timorous, the envious, want to destroy your work, your name will still be written in the sky of the Fatherland, and in the sun of truthfulness.

If I could talk to you, I could tell you many things: I would tell you that if you have been guilty, it has been that you have been too good, too generous, too much of a Caesar. Snakes should be stamped on before they have a chance to bite: but it is no use now, and you know my thoughts. The only reality is the daily one which is killing us. I'm heavy with this burden and depressed, for never before have I realized what you mean to me, what you are and will be for me. I don't know if you have time to remember me, I don't know if you want to remember me, all the same, I am by your side and I live with my memories. I'm indeed guilty of loving you.

Dear, let me know about yourself as soon as possible, no matter how, tell me that you have the strength to survive the pain, the tragedy. Tell me that you feel me near you, that you are ready to take my little hand in your tired ones, as where we walked together, as when I helped you in the grey hours, as you helped me with my troubles. I cannot live without you, without your voice, without your warm words, without your lively mind, your imagination, your unique phrases. How can I live without gazing in your eyes? What will happen to me, what will become of us? Ben, please, believe me if I tell you that I cannot replace you in my heart with others.

It is not possible, after loving you, to love, to live with others. I'm smouldering like a dying fire, in anguish, without comfort . . . I have not the strength to go on living . . . if you are not with me, nothing matters . . . Tell me that it is not over . . . What anguish, you know how much I'm suffering . . . Tell me, at least, that my words bring you comfort, tell me that you feel my little heart near you, that my tears are reaching you, that I'm helping you in this bitter hour. Take heart, Ben. Be strong for History . . .

Appendix C

'Hitler . . . Is Very Sensitive'

(Job 170, Frames 050253–276, US National Archives, Washington. Translated from the Italian by Maria Teresa Williams)

For almost twenty years, Major Giuseppe Renzetti reported on the German scene to Benito Mussolini – as Consul-General in Leipzig (1927–9); as founder and chairman of the Italo-German Chamber of Commerce in Berlin (1929–35); as Consul-General at Berlin (1937–41). A convinced supporter of National Socialism up to 1937, Renzetti was on intimate terms with Hitler, Göring and Goebbels, and during these razor-edged years of the Nazis' rise to power occupied a ringside seat from first to last.

Here, between 1931 and 1933, he briefs the Duce on the aspirations of Adolf Hitler:

> Undated; probably soon after
> 10 October, 1931, Hitler's first
> meeting with President Hindenburg.

Hitler was very pleased with his meeting with Hindenburg who had listened to him with great understanding and had promised that in case the Brüning Cabinet[1] did not get the necessary majority, he would call on the National Socialists to form a government. In his talks with Hitler, the President has reaffirmed his determination to keep strictly on constitutional grounds.

Following this meeting Hitler's position was now 'legal'. Therefore Hitler has told me that he could visit His Excellency officially and begged me to convey his wish to the Duce.

Hitler had mentioned this intention a few months before: I told him that I had not thought it advisable to pass it on, in view of the difficulties that might arise from the visit. Hitler had added that the leaders of the Socialist Party had visited Paris and London, while he wanted to visit Rome first, because of the sympathy he had for Italy, because of his admiration for the Duce, and to emphasize his determination for closer Italo-German relations, to be complemented by Anglo-German ones. What shall I reply?

1. Heinrich Brüning: former head of Catholic Centre Party; Reich Chancellor from 1930; forced to resign by Hindenburg, 30 May, 1932

Berlin, 20 November, 1931

I have informed Hitler about the Duce's opinion on the risk that National Socialism would run if it tied itself hand and foot to the Centre Party, to form a coalition Government. Hitler had asked me to reassure His Excellency that he will keep his advice in mind and would not enter into negotiations, unless he was sure of being in a dominant position. Neither would he pursue accords with the various *Länder* until the central question was solved.

The negotiations with the representatives of the various groups are proceeding well; even the 'Economic Party', which until a few weeks ago supported Brüning, is now on Hitler's side. However a change of government isn't on the cards yet. The strife between the Nazis and other right-wing groups goes on. In an effort to smoothe things out I propose to invite to my house the representatives of the groups in question on Friday, 27th. I would like to bring about the merger of the German-Nationalist Party with the National Socialist Party and make the 'Steel Helmets' the Militia of Hitler's party. I am well aware of the difficult task but I hope to succeed.

Hitler is very happy to be able to come to Rome and present his regards to the Duce. He could leave 11 December in the evening and reach Rome the following afternoon. He would be accompanied by myself, Göring, Secretary Hess and a member of the Party. His stay in Rome would be brief, in view of the internal German situation. After Hitler's visit others would follow, from members of Parliament, SA leaders, Youth Organization leaders, etc. I have proposed to Hitler exchange visits of party groups chosen from among the most outstanding members of the Party, not only to study Fascism's achievement but also to foster friendship between National Socialists and Fascists.

Hitler has told me how sorry he was to hear of the founding, in Munich, of an Italo-German Association under the patronage of the Consul General; the head of this Association was Herr Zentz, who was a notorious Freemason and an enemy of National Socialism. His party, Hitler said, was the best Italian-German Association. I replied that this type of association was useful in some fields and no political intentions were involved.

And speaking of these associations, in view of the German situation it is my advice not to interfere; in any case Munich exercises only a limited influence on German life and it is a myth to think that the city is an important centre. Munich is the capital of Bavaria but it is also a city like many others in Germany. Hitler has founded his party there but the main Headquarters is going to be moved to Berlin very soon; Hitler in fact conducts all his negotiations in the capital.

In my humble opinion, we must only acknowledge the formation of the Italian-German associations, without taking part in them. This type of Association reflects the local mood and we must not antagonize the various groups, by taking sides. The Berlin Association was not well accepted by the right wing, so much so that another one is being formed. It is wise to keep away from both at the moment. Our authorities should follow this line: until now, anyway, such associations have had no influence whatsoever and have attracted only minor personalities.

The German ambience is far from easy or simple and there is a need to get well acquainted first, in order not to be used by interested parties.

Berlin, 12 January, 1932

I have talked with Hitler today about the planned journey to Rome. He told me that he was well aware of the obstacles facing the realization of the visit and wasn't therefore pressing the matter. He asked me to keep in mind that in the present situation he did not know when he could leave Germany. I repeated that the Duce was thinking of Germany and was trying to help, having a deep knowledge of the German situation.

To please them [the National-Socialists] I would suggest the possibility of inviting Göring to Rome. It goes without saying that his journey would be private and motivated by health reasons (Göring has a broken rib after a fall in Sweden; he needs a rest because he is overworked and also because he is still grieving after the loss of his beloved wife). The journey would be above suspicion and the National Socialists would be happy. I haven't mentioned this to anybody.

Rome, 9 June, 1932 Pro-memoria

His Excellency, the Head of Government, has told me that he will receive Hitler from 15 July and has asked me to arrange details with his private secretary.

Rome, 12 June, 1932

The 9th inst. I had the honour of expressing to His Excellency, the Head of Government, Hitler's fervent wish to visit Rome. Hitler wished to present his regards to the Duce of Fascism and Prime Minister, as he intended to strengthen his ties of friendship. He wanted to start his visits to foreign powers with Italy; he also thought that this visit would influence the German people towards his party.

Hitler would like to make the visit between 1 and 15 July. By that day he wishes to be back in Germany to fight the elections for the new Reichstag. I have added that, in my opinion, with his visit, Hitler was binding himself morally to Italy. On the other hand the visit would have repercussion on the Leader of the Brown Shirts, who was a sentimentalist at heart, because the visit had taken place before attaining power.

His Excellency the Head of Government has given preliminary approval to the visit. Hitler would travel as a civilian and stay two or three days. He would visit His Excellency, and the Secretary of the Party, whose guest he would be. If convenient, he could inspect the Militia. The visit would be official, not to give way to suspicions from enemies.

His Excellency has asked me to make arrangements for the visit with Chiavolini, his private secretary. In respect of those requests I have summarized as above.

I have said nothing to Hitler and others, of course, while I await instructions from Chiavolini, instructions which will be followed to the letter. The instructions concern:

  a) the time of visit
  b) the day Hitler would be informed
  c) programme of visit (gatherings, events, security)

I have not made any promise to Hitler, although it is clear that Hitler is very keen to come. He is well aware of international repercussions, but at the same time he doesn't think they are of much consequence as his Party was virtually in power. He has said that even without the visit, his policy towards Italy wouldn't alter. From our point of view, if the visit doesn't take place it would result in a loss of influence on Hitler, in case we should want to use him.

Berlin, 21 June, 1932

I have conveyed to Hitler the points outlined by His Excellency. Hitler has listened with ill-concealed delight, glad and proud of the Duce's interest and sympathy towards him. Hitler, as I have often said, worships Mussolini.

The Leader of the Brown Shirts has read about the attempts against the Duce's life; he has reminded me of what he told me a year ago when there was a rumour that Mussolini might visit Germany. The Duce will be able to come to Germany only when we are in power. There won't be any danger to his life and the people will be able to show their admiration.

Speaking of Austria, Hitler has told me that he could not count on that nation; the political men there were talking of an *Anschluss* only to get money. France was paying and things went on as ever.

He wasn't worried about the Bavarian threats or about the activities of Prince Rupprecht. (Hitler hates the Hapsburgs and the Wittelsbachs.) The Prince was touring the Catholic areas and a few days before he had been entertained to a banquet by the Catholic industrialists of the Rhine region at Düsseldorf. The two SA will be enough to settle the separatists, Hitler said.

Hitler then asked me for news about the journey to Italy. I replied that the Duce was glad to see him but was wondering if it was advisable to come before 31 July. The internal German situation – I pointed out to

Hitler – required his presence in Germany and it was also advisable not to upset the negotiations taking place in Lausanne.

Hitler, very reluctantly (he had already planned the journey: one day in Florence, two in Rome, one or two in Naples, travelling to Verona or Milan from Munich by plane and then by car), has agreed to my suggestion (he is indeed dying to meet the Duce) . . . I don't know if I have acted with excessive prudence, but I have prejudiced nothing, leaving Hitler, who is very touchy, with the conviction that the realization of the journey doesn't rest with us.

Hitler is isolating himself more and more from the present Cabinet; it is easy to detect that he is following the suggestions I have offered him in the past. He has described the present leaders as 'weaklings' who could be manoeuvred at will. 'I will reach my target sooner than might be believed,' he said, when he saw me.

S. Benedetto del Tronto
[an Adriatic seaside resort
where Renzetti was on leave]
To Achille Starace, Secretary,   15 June, 1932
National Fascist Party, Rome

Excellency,

I have received orders from Gr. Uff. Chiavolini to contact Your Excellency personally regarding the visit that the Head of German National Socialism is going to make shortly and about which I have already conferred verbally with Your Excellency.

Hitler would like to come to Italy between 1 and 15 July next, for only three or four days, to be back in Germany to fight the election campaign. Hitler would be accompanied by his deputy, Göring, who last year had the honour to be presented to the Duce, by Secretary Hess, and some other members of the Party (once back in Germany I will send the list and qualifications of people coming and the itinerary of Hitler's journey plus any special requests of the guests).

The group would be guests of the Party. A special security service could be in force from the moment they cross the frontier and the people in charge could keep in strict contact with me.

Hitler is a vegetarian, and doesn't drink wine; he is very fond of music and if it is not too hot will wish to visit some monuments and Museums in Rome. He is very sensitive and any warm welcome to him will make a lasting impression. He speaks only German.

This is what I have to say about the visit; I also think it is advisable that I should communicate the details of the journey to Hitler only a few days in advance to avoid overmuch publicity. The journey in my opinion should take place at the end of the Lausanne conference.

I will be here till tomorrow night, if I don't hear anything to the contrary; the 16th, I will depart for Berlin. If Your Excellency has nothing against it, my instructions could be given by telephone, avoiding, of course, any mention of Hitler.

With devotion,
Renzetti.

Berlin, 23 January, 1933

In the last few days negotiations have taken place between the various groups of the right to form a National Front. The German-Nationals, breaking their silence, have declared war on von Schleicher,[2] and the Steel Helmets have approached them and the Nazis with a view to taking part in the growing front.

In right-wing political circles there is a conviction that this time an accord will be reached and there is hope that, faced with this, Hindenburg would drop Schleicher, and call the men of the front to power.

Much store is set by the mediation of von Papen,[3] who has great influence in the Presidential entourage.

The new Cabinet, according to the intentions of the 'conspirators' would be:

Chancellor – Hitler
Vice-Chancellor and Foreign Affairs – von Papen
Economic Affairs – Hugenberg[4]
Labour – Franz Seldte[5]
Home Affairs – A member of the Party
Finance – Von Krosig, the present holder
War – General Beremberg, Commander of the group of Divisions in
    East Prussia (non-political)
Presidency and Home Affairs in Prussia – A member of the Party.

The merger of the national groups would have the composition which I have mentioned in the past (the meeting of the 1st instant at my home has put in contact the very people who are now merging).

Hitler is very confident, and convinced that his intransigence was right. The Strasser affair[6] is virtually concluded; in this matter, when Strasser made his dissident declarations, I told Hitler, who was in a black mood,

---

2. Kurt von Schleicher, Hitler's dominant opponent. Reich Chancellor from 1 December, 1932; dismissed by Hindenburg, January 1933, in favour of Hitler. Murdered by the SS in the Night of the Long Knives, 30 June, 1934
3. Franz von Papen, short-lived Reich Chancellor from June–December 1932
4. Alfred Hugenberg, head of right-wing Nationalist Party. Joined Hitler as Minister of Food and Agriculture; dismissed, June 1933
5. Leader of right-wing veterans' private army, the Stahlhelm (Steel Helmets)
6. Gregor Strasser, leader of the National Socialist Movement during Hitler's

that he should not give way. I told him that no matter how painful it was to part company with an old comrade, he should make an example of this case: a revolutionary movement could have but one Leader and one ideal, as in a religious movement.

I do not know how much my words have influenced Hitler; one thing is certain, a few minutes later he broached the same ideas before the parliamentary group and repeated them in my presence to H. E. Balbo.

I have many times told Strasser to make it up with Hitler and I told Göring of the need to seek a reconciliation; unfortunately Strasser, although he stayed in the Party, had let himself be influenced by von Schleicher and had virtually destroyed himself. In some circles it is said that the Chancellor is seeking a formula to dispense with the dissidents.

The crisis of the Brown Shirts Party, barring other complications, is practically solved; it is of no consequence whether Strasser is in the Party or not, as he hasn't any special position. Another problem, however, is going to face Hitler, when he tries to dismiss Colonel Röhm,[7] Chief of General Staff of the Militia, accused of homosexuality. Up to now Hitler has been reluctant to do anything about it, but if there is an accord between Nazis and Steel Helmets he will be compelled to act. Röhm is a splendid organizer and a faithful friend, but he cannot stay in command without damaging the good name of the Militia.

I have urged the various Nazis, as in the past, to be careful and not to precipitate events; if it was difficult to gain power it is even more difficult to remain in power, a false move would mean the end of the entire movement. Before gaining power they had to be sure of having men capable of command.

I have talked about that with Hitler and Göring many times in the past; I hope they will know how to act and that, once having gained power, they will be capable of holding on for scores of years, confounding those who groundlessly prophesy that Hitler won't last above three months.

Berlin, 31 January, 1933
Further to my communication of the 23rd instant I report as follows:
The fall of Schleicher was given for certain as the evening of the 26th; nobody, not even the right wing, had expected events to move so rapidly. In fact, in some right-wing circles, the nomination of Hitler was still considered doubtful and it was thought that Schleicher would hold on for a few more weeks.

(1924) term in jail; employed both Heinrich Himmler and Joseph Goebbels as private secretaries. Another victim of the Night of the Long Knives.
7. Ernest Röhm, chief organiser of the SA, the strong-arm squads that brought Hitler to power and chief victim of the June 1934 purge

The sudden collapse of the Chancellor was due to his many mistakes and to the isolation in which he had found himself, coupled with his ineptitude.

While I will send details of what happened as soon as possible, I can inform you that only on Sunday 29th was agreement reached between the various groups, although at the last minute the accord seemed to be in danger, because of Hugenberg's excessive demands. It was in an effort to stifle further manoeuvring that Hindenburg appointed Hitler Chancellor and had the ministers sworn in straight away.

In the night between Sunday and Monday rumours were afoot of the threatened military putsch to depose Hindenburg. Nobody knows how well-founded such rumours were. I have told the Nazis, with whom I have spent days and nights, that the threat sounded ridiculous. In any case true or not, I am sure that the friends of Schleicher will be dismissed.

Schleicher is completely discredited. I have always mistrusted him and his ambition (his wife is also very ambitious, a dangerous factor in any case, and even more in Germany, where the women want to meddle in politics).

Schleicher, in my opinion, and I told him so more than once, had a great opportunity to help the Nazis and build up a National Front; he hasn't been able to exploit the situation and has indulged in setting men and groups against each other. A master of manoeuvring and intrigue, a true follower of Brüning, without the latter's adaptability, he has behaved like a 'dilettante' and lost his political and military standing. In the last few days it looks as if he has lost his head as well.

The weak link of the new government is Hugenberg. Apart from the fact that I doubt his capacity to deal with the economic situation, there is the hidden dissent between German-Nationalists and National Socialists. I have told my friends that they must either get rid of Hugenberg without provoking a crisis, or make him toe the line. I have urged them to have a general election as soon as possible (Hitler, during the great march past of last night, told me that he agreed entirely with the suggestion). Seldte, Göring, Schacht[8] and many others have thanked me warmly for what I have done to bring about a merger of the national forces. The Harzburg front was born in my house, the accord with the Steel Helmets was due mainly to me, and the meetings in Rome last November; and lastly the meeting in my house of the 1st instant has had great influence on the events and so on. I am glad that such efforts have been recognized and praised as Fascist and Italian.

I cannot forecast much at present, but I can say that Hitler and the other Nazi leaders with whom I have conferred (Hitler wanted me near him during the march past but I have avoided being seen) are convinced that a

8. Dr Hjalmar Horace Greeley Schacht, President (until 1930) of the Reichsbank, financial wizard who stood in as marriage-broker in the unholy alliance between Hitler and Germany's leading magnates

failure this time would mean the end of the movement and the beginning of chaos in Germany. All the initiatives taken in this period (and I have suggested plenty) will have the aim of strengthening the Nazi position and preventing reaction as in the past; they will also have the task of putting men of trust in key posts, of reorganizing the police and inflicting severe blows against the left.

I would like to confer personally with His Excellency about the situation. If it is acceptable, I could be in Rome during the second half of the month.

Berlin, 31 January, 1933

Hitler has called me today to the Chancellery to make the following declaration: 'As Chancellor, I wish to tell you, so that you may refer it to His Excellency, that in my position I will pursue with all my might the same policy of friendship toward Italy that I have always invoked. Minister Neurath shares my view in the matter; there are, however, great difficulties in the Ministry itself. It is impossible to do everything at once. You know that I haven't yet got all the cadres capable of replacing the incumbents in the Foreign Ministry. My men lack experience, but I hope to be able, gradually, to have only faithful men around me. I would like to have a meeting with Mussolini and in the meanwhile I beg you to convey my regards and admiration. Now I can go where I like; ultimately I could go to Rome by plane, if necessary in a private capacity. I owe my position to Fascism; if it is true that the two movements differ, it is also true that Mussolini has created the *Weltanschauung* that unites the two ideologies; without such realization I might not have reached my position. If it is true that ideologies and systems are not for export, it is also true that ideas expand like the rays of the sun and the waves of the sea.'

I replied:

'I will convey to His Excellency what you have had the graciousness to tell me. His Excellency, who as you know has followed your movement and your work with the utmost sympathy, will be glad of your success and will also be glad to receive the declaration that you asked me to convey. I am well aware of the difficulties that you have to overcome, but I am sure, as I have been sure in the past, of your true destiny, that you will conquer them.

'Italian policy is simple: its aim, to reach a Four Power agreement in Europe. To obtain it we need Italy, Germany and Great Britain in accord, to compel France either to be isolated or to take part in the group. The accord, however, is not feasible should one of the nations enter into a separate agreement with France.

'Italy and Germany could sign a cultural-ideological accord as well as a political and economic one. The two Nations look forward, or better, will look forward from now on, to the realization in Europe of a new doctrine, a new political theory. It is therefore necessary that the two nations understand each other even in this field, to be able to bind together ideal ties, to be able to work together for the advance of the new revolutionary idea, which must extend to the whole of Europe.'

Hitler listened very attentively to what I said; he nodded in agreement many times and then begged me to keep in close contact with him, with the same friendship of the past years.

Acknowledgments

The information for this book came mostly from those whose lives were bound up with Mussolini's own – from those who fought him tooth-and-nail, those who followed him blindly, those who were merely swept up by the riptide of history. All told, over 530 people contributed to this book. Over a period of three years, beginning in 1967, they submitted patiently to lengthy in-depth interviews, often supplementing them with written accounts. They furnished private diaries, contemporary letters, rare photographs and newspaper clippings, and personal documentation.

These memories were dovetailed into a jigsaw compiled from American, Italian and German archives. Conference transcripts, war diaries, intelligence and secret reports, interrogation summaries and unpublished despatches from the Duce's diplomats, were obtained, to be cross-checked with and supplemented by leading military and political figures of the period. The result – one-quarter of a ton of research material – filled 272 bulky files, containing such diverse items as the current value of Mussolini's autograph on the New York collector's market (£33 as against Hitler's £41) and the life-long wish of Emperor Haile Selassie to open a branch of Harrod's in Addis Ababa.

The entire project owes everything to Lila and De Witt Wallace of *The Reader's Digest*, who placed at my disposal the unparalleled research resources of their organization, and who underwrote almost all the costs. I would like to record my gratitude, too, to Hobart Lewis, President and Executive Editor of the *Digest*, and to Harry H. Harper, Jr, Vice-President, for their encouragement and patience over the long years of research; to the *Digest*'s Maurice T. Ragsdale and Kenneth Wilson, who held my hand from the beginning; to Fulton J. Oursler, Jr, whose counsel and warm support were always a guiding light; to Walter Hunt, Patricia W. Tarnawsky and John Wulp for valuable discussion and analysis. But so many *Digest* men and women in the United States and Europe provided such vital contacts and gems of research, or undertook key interviews, that I feel it only fair to name them in alphabetical order by bureau. *Madrid:* Victor Olmos. *Milan:* Guido Artom, Carlo Rossi Fantonetti, Giampiero Negretti, Emma Pizzoni. *Montreal:* Lois K. Parkhill. *New York:* Gertrude Arundel, Heather Chapman, Christian Scott-Hansen. *Paris:* Yvonne Fourcade, Francis Schell. *Rome:* Ugo Apollonio, Luigi Fiocca. *Stuttgart:* Arno Alexy, Brigitte Berg, Annelies Gekeler. *Washington:* Kenneth

Gilmore, Virginia Lawton, Julia Morgan. The secretaries, too, displayed unflagging zeal and perseverance, notably Titti Campanelli (Rome), who cheerfully bore the brunt of my impossible demands, Iris Laing (Paris) and Lorenza Lasorte (Milan). Administration-wise, the whole project owed much to Dr Brandolino Brandolini d'Adda (Milan), Frau Anne Mörike (Stuttgart), and, above all, to John D. Panitza, European Editor, for his supreme co-ordination of my research needs.

Next I must thank the US Department of Defence for permission to research in the historical archives. In particular, at the National Archives and Records Service, I want to acknowledge the help of Dr Robert Krauskopf, Director of Modern Military Records Division, and his associates: Lois C. Aldridge, Richard Bauer, Thomas E. Hohmann, Dora L. Howard, Hildred F. Livingstone, John E. Taylor and Robert Wolfe, all of whom gave time to me and my *Digest* collaborators during our months-long examination of the records. Others, most especially Joseph A. Avery and Charles D. Phillips III of the Washington National Records Centre, Suitland, Maryland, were equally helpful, along with countless officials of the Adjutant General Department of the Army, Office of the Chief of Military History, the Magazine and Book Division, Office of the Secretary of Defence and the Historical Office, Department of State. Their concerted efforts made possible the clearing and investigation of miles of microfilm and the discovery of thousands of Italian documents.

For the meticulous translation of these and several thousand other sources, I am forever indebted to Marisa Beck, Michael Langley, working from Milan with a team of eight translators, backed by their indefatigable secretary, Catherine Stuart-Hunter, and, above all, Maria Teresa Williams, who spent almost eighteen months painstakingly checking hitherto classified microfilm. Invaluable, too, in the long task of examining and synthesizing bales of material were Elizabeth S. Cohen, Sandra Knott, Anthony Paul, Nadia Radowitz, Angelica Guyon de St Prix, and Ornella Wenkert, who also undertook many interviews in Rome and Naples.

I owe especial debts of gratitude to all those whose involvement with the project became almost personal – and who not only gave freely of their time for interviews but took pains to check my perspectives, suggest new leads and provide supplementary memos. At Indio, the late President Dwight D. Eisenhower provided an invaluable background briefing; General Mark Wayne Clark clarified many points and proved a matchless host in Charleston, SC. General Maxwell D. Taylor spared me hard-won time at the height of the *Pueblo* affair, and in Washington and New York the late Allen Dulles and Robert Murphy were equally generous. I am grateful, too, to Colonel Charles Poletti and Major Max Corvo for casting much fresh light on the dark days of April 1945 in Milan; to Burton Benjamin of CBS for a valuable private screening, and to Barrett McGurn of Rome's US Embassy. In Germany, former Ambassador Rudolf Rahn, General Enno von Rintelen, General Kurt Student and General Siegfried

Westphal furnished me and my associates with many intriguing sidelights on the last five years of Mussolini's life. My thanks, too, to Otto Skorzeny in Madrid, and Franz Spögler in Bolzano, for generously submitting to some of the longest interviews in the history of documentary research.

Inevitably, the main burden of my quest was borne by the Italians who lived out their lives under Mussolini – some of them eminent historians and authors who helped solve many controversial points. Among these, I have first and foremost to thank Professor Gianfranco Bianchi, Professor Franco Catalano and, most especially, Professor Renzo de Felice, for his invaluable loan of books that had proved untraceable – and others to whose kindness I am indebted for the long-term use of their libraries include Dr Paolo Monelli, Count Pio Luigi Teodorani and Countess Rosina Teodorani.

I found this same willingness all over Italy. At the outset, Professor Filippo Donini, Cultural Attaché, Italian Embassy, London, provided many key introductions – which in turn led to others. The Marchesa Giuliana Benzoni generously furnished many contacts concerning 25 July; Senator Augusto de Marsanich and Senator Alessandro Lessona helped locate scores of March on Rome survivors; Count Alberto Mellini Ponce de Leon proved the key to Salò Republic veterans; Professor Mario Missiroli opened doors for me everywhere. Senator Mario Palermo, Nanni Loy and Paolo Ricci were all crucial forces in tracing the men and women of the Naples Rising. But in this respect my eternal debt is to Dr Piero Parini and his wife, Signora Melpo, who not only arranged scores of introductions but both in Milan and at Le Grazie provided the kind of hospitality that is hardest to repay.

There were many others whose aid was precious. Former Ambassador Giustino Arpesani, Count Pier Luigi Bellini delle Stelle, General Raffaele Cadorna, Commandant Giuseppe Cirillo, General Emilio Faldella, Aldo Lampredi, Riccardo Lombardi, Luigi Longo, Senator Ferruccio Parri, Sandro Pertini, Oscar Sforni and Leo Valiani – all contributed vital chapters to the story of the Resistance. In the diplomatic field, Count Dino Grandi, though plagued by illness, gave unstintedly of his time, and I had matchless co-operation, too, from the late Baron Raffaele Guariglia, the late Count Massimo Magistrati, Count Luca Pietromarchi, and Count Leonardo Vitetti. Rear-Admiral Giuseppe Fioravanzo and Admiral Angelo Jachino were my willing experts on naval matters; General Enzo Galbiati and General Renzo Montagna unravelled the mysteries of the Militia. Monsignor Giuseppe Bicchierai and Don Giusto Pancino were key witnesses to Mussolini's last days. These men, too, proved determinant witnesses, liberally prodigal of time: General Giacomo Carboni; Count Valentino Orsolini Cencelli, for his revealing tour of the Pontine Marshes; Vincenzo Costa; Nino d'Aroma; the late General Giorgio Manes; Eugenio Morreale.

I owe a particularly personal debt to the families of those no longer living. On all the occasions that I met them, Donna Rachele Mussolini and her sons Romano and Vittorio answered my questions about Benito Mussolini frankly and fully, without ever attempting to influence my ultimate portraiture. I am similarly grateful to the Marchesa Myriam Petacci and to Isabella and Gian Matteo Matteotti for their co-operation in what must sometimes have been painful moments.

Finally, those who worked closest to me throughout rate a mention all their own. Donatella Ortona, who conducted seventy-five interviews throughout the length and breadth of Italy, made an invaluable contribution to the end-product. In London, Joan St George Saunders and her research team never failed to come up with eleventh hour answers that were needed – and in the early stages Robin McKown, too, weighed in with vital information from New York. Carlo Trotini and J. W. C. Garner solved almost all my considerable photographic problems. Signora Maria Vasta Dazzi functioned all through as a redoubtable one-woman clippings agency. Both Graham Watson and John Cushman, my agents in London and New York, solved my many queries with their habitual monumental calm. As always, Jill Beck's supervision of the final draft was a miracle of precision.

A special paragraph embodies a special tribute to Maria Teresa Vasta. For three-and-a-half years, she made Benito Mussolini's rise and fall her life – a life of relentless seven-day weeks that involved not only pioneer research and translation but typing, re-typing, filing, collating, telephoning, plus the entire arrangement of each day's schedule. Standing in as interpreter at 276 interviews, she swiftly became the infallible Mussolini expert upon whom all the rest of us – not least the author – came to depend. Without her, it often seemed, there would have been no book at all.

Lastly, to my wife, who carried out much of the research in the United States, Great Britain and France, typed and re-typed successive drafts from handwriting grown well-nigh cabalistic, and, above all, kept the home together during long years of research, goes, as ever, my deepest gratitude.

Bibliography

Printed Sources

Abbati, A. H. *Italy and the Abyssinian War*. London: General Press, 1936.
Acerbo, Giacomo. *Fascism in the First Year of Government*. Rome: Giorgio Berlutti, 1923.
Acerbo, Giacomo. *Fra due plotoni di esecuzione*. Bologna: Cappelli, 1969.
Adami, Eugenio. *La lingua di Mussolini*. Modena: Società Tipografica Modenese, 1939.
Aglion, Raoul. *War in the Desert*. New York: H. Holt, 1941.
Alatri, Paolo. *Le origini del fascismo*. Rome: Editori Riuniti, 1956.
Alatri, Paolo. *L'antifascismo italiano* (2 vols). Rome: Editori Riuniti, 1956.
Albrecht-Carrié, René. *Italy from Napoleon to Mussolini*. New York: Columbia University Press, 1960.
Alessi, Rino. *Calda era la terra*. Bologna: Cappelli, 1958.
Alessio, Giulio. *La crisi dello stato parlamentare e l'avvento del fascismo*. Padua: CEDAM, 1946.
Alfieri, Dino. *Dictators Face to Face* (transl by David Moore). London: Elek Books, 1954.
Alfieri, Dino and Freddi, Luigi. *Mostra della rivoluzione fascista*. Rome: PNF, 1933.
Allason, Barbara. *Memorie di un antifascista*. Milan: Avanti!, 1961.
Allen, H. Warner. *Italy from End to End*. London: Methuen, 1927.
Alvaro, Corrado. *Quasi una vita: giornale di uno scrittore*. Milan: Bompiani, 1951.
Alvesi, Fabrizio. *La ribellione degli Italiani*. Rome: Fratelli Bocca, 1956.
Ame, Gen Cesare. *Guerra segreta in Italia, 1940–43*. Rome: Gherardo Casini, 1954.
Amicucci, Ermanno. *I 600 giorni di Mussolini*. Rome: Faro, 1948.
Anche l'Italia ha vinto. Rome: Mercurio, 1945.
Andrew, Roland G. *Through Fascist Italy*. London: George Harrap, 1935.
Anelli, Marco. *L'Etiopia*. Chieti: Bonnani, 1935.
Anfuso, Filippo. *Du Palais de Venise au Lac de Garde*. Paris: Calmann-Lévy, 1949.
Ardemagni, Mirko. *Supremazia di Mussolini*. Milan: Treves, 1936.
Argenton, Mario and Piasenti, Paride. *L'Italia dal Fascismo alla Costituzione Repubblicana*. Rome: 'Fondazione del Corpo Volontari della liberta' 1966.
Armellini, Gen Quirino. *Con Badgolio in Etiopia*. Milan: Mondadori, 1937.
Armellini, Gen Quirino. *La crisi dell'esercito*. Rome: Priscilla, 1945.
Armellini, Gen Quirino. *Diario di Guerra*. Milan: Garzanti, 1946.
Artieri, Giovanni (ed.). *Le Quattro Giornate*. Naples: Alberto Marotta, 1963.
Artieri, Giovanni. *Tre ritratti politici e quattro attentati*. Rome: Atlante, 1953.
Artieri, Giovanni. *Il tempo della Regina*. Rome: Sestante, 1950.
Ascoli, Max and Feiler, Arthur. *Fascism: who benefits?* London: Allen & Unwin, 1939.
Asfa Yilma, Princess. *Haile Selassie*. London: Sampson Low, 1936.
Augenti, G. P., Mastino, G. and Carnelutti, F. *Il dramma di Graziani*. Bologna: Cesare Zuffi, 1950.
Aversa, Nino. *Napoli sotto il terrore tedesco*. Naples: 'Le Quattro Giornate', 1943.
Avetta, Ida. *Mussolini e la folla*. Mantua: Paladino, nd.
Bac, Ferdinand. *Promenades dans l'Italie Nouvelle*. Paris: Hachette, 1933.
Badoglio, Marshal Pietro. *The war in Abyssinia*. London: Methuen, 1937.

Badoglio, Marshal Pietro. *Italy in the Second World War* (*transl by Muriel Currey*). London: Oxford University Press, 1948.

Balabanoff, Angelica. *My life as a Rebel*. London: Hamish Hamilton, 1938.

Balbo, Italo. *Stormi in volo sull'Oceano*. Milan: Mondadori, 1931.

Balbo, Italo. *Diario 1922*. Milan: Mondadori, 1932.

Balbo, Italo. *La centuria alata*. Milan: Mondadori, 1934.

Banchelli, Umberto. *Le memorie di un fascista*. Florence: 'Sassaiola Fiorentina', 1922.

Bandini, Franco. *Tecnica della sconfitta*. Milan: Sugar, 1963.

Bandini, Franco. *Claretta*. Milan: Sugar, 1960.

Bandini, Franco. *Le ultime 95 ore di Mussolini*. Milan: Sugar, 1959.

Baravelli, G. C. *Land Reclamation Schemes in Italy*. Rome: Novissima, 1935.

Barbagallo, Corrado. *Lettere a John*. Naples: Fiorentino, 1946.

Barbagallo, Corrado. *Napoli contro il terrore nazista*. Naples: Morano, 1944.

Barbieri, Orazio. *Ponti sull'Arno*. Rome: Editori Riuniti, 1958.

Bardi, Adelmo. *Dall'Etiopia selvaggia all'impero d'Italia*. Sanremo: privately printed, 1936.

Bargellini, Piero. *Il pastore angelico, Pio XII*. Florence: Sansoni, 1948.

Barnett, Corelli. *The Desert Generals*. London: William Kimber, 1960.

Barros, James. *The Corfu Incident of 1923*. Princeton, N J: Princeton University Press, 1965.

Bartoli, Domenico, *La fine della Monarchia*. Milan: Mondadori, 1947.

Bartoli, Domenico. *Da Vittorio Emanuele a Gronchi*. Milan: Longanesi, 1961.

Barzini, Luigi. *The Italians*. New York: Athenaeum, 1964.

Baskerville, Beatrice. *What next, O Duce?* London: Longmans, 1937.

Basso, Antonio. *L'armistizio del settembre 43 in Sardegna*. Naples: Rippoli, 1947.

Bastianini, Giuseppe. *Uomini, cose, fatti*. Milan: Vitagliano, 1959.

Battaglia, Roberto. *Story of the Italian Resistance* (*transl by P. D. Cummins*). London: Odhams Press, 1958.

Baxter, Beverley. *Men, Martyrs and Mountebanks*. London: Hutchinson, 1940.

Beales, A. C. F. *The Pope and the Jews*. London: 'Sword of the Spirit', 1945.

Beals, Carlton. *Rome or Death!* New York: Century Press, 1923.

Bedeschi, Edoardo and Alessi, Rino. *Gli anni giovanili di Mussolini*. Milan: Mondadori, 1939.

Begnac, Yvon de. *Vita di Mussolini* (3 vols). Milan: Mondadori, 1936–40.

Begnac, Yvon de. *Trent'anni di Mussolini*. Rome: Arti Grafiche Menaglia, 1934.

Begnac, Yvon de. *Palazzo Venezia*. Rome: 'La Rocca', 1950.

Bell, Edward Price. *Italy's rebirth*. Chicago: 'Chicago Daily News', 1924.

Bellini Delle Stelle, Count Pierluigi and Lazzaro, Urbano. *Dongo: The Last Act*. London: MacDonald, 1964.

Bellotti, Felice. *La repubblica di Mussolini*. Milan: Zagara, 1947.

Beltramelli, Antonio. *L'uomo nuovo*. Milan: Mondadori, 1923.

Benedetti, Arrigo. *Paura all'alba*. Milan: Il Saggiatore, 1965.

Benelli, Sem. *Io in Africa*. Milan: Mondadori, 1936.

Benini, Zenone. *Vigilia a Verona*. Milan: Garzanti, 1949.

Benjamin, René. *Mussolini et son Peuple*. Paris: Plon, 1937.

Berardi, Paolo. *Memorie di un capo di Stato Maggiore*. Bologna: ODCU, 1954.

Beraud, Henri. *Men of the Aftermath* (*transl by F. Whyte*). London: Grant Richards & Humphrey Toulmin, 1929.

Beraud, Henri. *Ce Que J'ai Vu à Rome*. Paris: Les Editions de France, 1930.

Berio, Alberto. *Dalle Ande All'Himalaya: ricordi di un diplomatico*. Naples: Edizioni Scientifiche Italiane, 1961.

Berio, Alberto. *Missione segreta*. Milan: Dall'Oglio, 1947.

Berlinguer, Mario. *La crisi della giustizia nel regime fascista*. Rome: Migliaresi, 1944.

Bernhart, Joseph. *The Vatican as a World Power*. London: Longmans, 1939.

Berretta, Alfio. *Amedeo d'Aosta.* Milan: Beretta, 1956.
Bertoldi, Silvio. *Mussolini tale e quale.* Milan: Longanesi, 1965.
Bertoldi, Silvio. *I tedeschi in Italia.* Milan: Rizzoli, 1964.
Bertoldi, Silvio. *La guerra parallela.* Milan: Sugar, 1963.
Bevione, Giuseppe. *Due settimane di passione.* Milan: Poligr. degli Operai, 1930.
Beyens, Baron. *Quatre Ans à Rome.* Paris: Plon, 1934.
Bezençon, Marcel. *La vie apre et aventureuse de Mussolini.* Paris: La Petite Illustration, 1938.
Biagi, Enzo. *Il crepuscolo degli dei.* Milan: Rizzoli, 1961.
Bianchi, Gianfranco. *25 luglio, crollo di un regime.* Milan: Ugo Mursia, 1963.
Bianchi, Lorenzo. *Mussolini scrittore e oratore.* Bologna: Zanichelli, 1937.
Bianchini, Giuseppe. *The Work of the Fascist Government and the Economic Reconstruction of Italy.* Milan: Unione Economica Italiana, 1925.
Biggini, Carlo. *Storia inedita della conciliazione.* Milan: Garzanti, 1942.
Binchy, D. A. *Church and State in Fascist Italy.* Oxford: Oxford University Press, 1941.
Biondi, Dino. *La Fabbrica del Duce.* Florence: Vallecchi, 1967.
Biondi, Serafino. *Le tappe della Marcia su Roma rievocate un anno dopo l'evento.* Como: La Provincia di Como, 1923.
Birkby, Carel. *It's a Long Way to Addis.* London: Frederick Muller, 1942.
Blasco Ibáñez, Vicente. *In the Land of Art.* (transl by Frances Douglas). London: T. Fisher Unwin, 1924.
Blumenson, Martin. *Anzio.* London: Weidenfeld & Nicolson, 1963.
Böhmler, Rudolf. *Monte Cassino.* London: Cassell, 1964.
Bojano, Filippo. *In the Wake of the Goose-Step.* London: Cassell, 1944.
Bolitho, William. *Italy under Mussolini.* New York: Macmillan, 1926.
Bolla, Nino. *Processo alla Monarchia.* Rome: Nardini-Nobel, 1964.
Bolla, Nino. *Dieci mesi di Governo Badoglio.* Rome: La Nuova Epoca, 1944.
Bolla, Nino. *Colloqui con Umberto II – Colloqui con Vittorio Emanuele III.* Rome: Fantera, 1949.
Bonacci, Giovanni. *L'Italia d'oggi e le forze economiche mondiali.* Florence: Arti Grafiche, 1931.
Bonavita, Francesco. *Mussolini svelato.* Milan: Sonzogno, 1933.
Bonavita, Francesco. *Il Padre del Duce.* Rome: Pinciana, 1933.
Bond, Harold L. *Return to Cassino.* London: J. M. Dent, 1964.
Bond, John. *Mussolini the Wild Man of Europe.* Washington: Independent Publicity Co, 1929.
Bonino, Antonio. *Mussolini mi ha detto.* Buenos Aires: Ed Risorgimento, 1950.
Bonomi, Ivanoe. *From Socialism to Fascism: A Study of Contemporary Italy* (transl by John Murray). London: Martin Hopkinson, 1924.
Bonomi, Ivanoe. *Diario di un anno.* Milan: Garzanti, 1947.
Boothe, Clare. *Europe in the Spring.* New York: Alfred Knopf, 1940.
Bordeux, Henri. *L'air de Rome et de la Mer.* Paris: Plon, 1938.
Bordeux, V. J. *Benito Mussolini – The Man.* London: Hutchinson, 1927.
Bordeux, V. J. *Margherita of Savoia.* London: Hutchinson, 1929.
Borgese, G. A. *Goliath.* London: Victor Gollancz, 1938.
Borghese, Junio Valerio. *Decima Flottiglia Mas.* Milan: Garzanti, 1950.
Borghi, Armando. *Mussolini Red and Black.* London: Wishart Books, 1935.
Bortolotto, Guido. *Storia del fascismo.* Milan: Ulrico Hoepli, 1938.
Bosca, Quirino C. *Cronistoria della campagna italo-etiopica.* Rome: Guanella, 1937.
Bosis, Lauro. *Storia della mia morte.* Turin: De Silva, 1948.
Bottai, Giuseppe. *Vent'anni e un giorno.* Milan: Garzanti, 1949.
Bova-Scoppa, Renato. *Colloqui con due Dittatori.* Rome: Ruffolo, 1949.
Box, Pelham H. *Three Master Builders.* London: Jarrolds, 1925.
Bozzi, Carlo. *La tragedia degli italiani vissuta da un italiano.* Rome: Leonardo, 1947.

Bragadin, Cdr Marc'Antonio. *The Italian Navy in World War II* (*transl by Gale Hoffman*). Annapolis, Maryland: United States Naval Institute, 1957.
Breve storia di cinque mesi. Rome: Quaderni Liberi, 1944.
Brighenti, Angelo. *Uomini ed episodi del tempo di Mussolini.* Milan: SEN, 1938.
Brizzolesi, Vittorio. *Giolitti.* Novara: Istituto Geografico De Agostini, 1921.
Bruttini, Alessandro and Puglisi, Giuseppe. *L'Impero tradito.* Florence: La Fenice, 1957.
Buckley, Christopher. *The Road to Rome.* London: Hodder & Stoughton, 1945.
Bullock, Alan. *Hitler.* London: Odhams Press, 1952.
Burns, Emile. *Abyssinia and Italy.* London: Gollancz, 1935.
Businelli, Alberto. *Ottobre 1922.* Rome: Novissima, 1932.
Butcher, Capt Harry C. USNR. *Three Years with Eisenhower.* New York: Simon & Schuster, 1946.
Butler, Nicholas Murray. *Across the Busy Years* (*2 vols*). New York: Charles Scribner, 1935–40.
Cabella, G. G. *Testamento politico di Mussolini.* Rome: Tosi, 1948.
Cadorna, Gen Raffaele. *La Riscossa.* Milan: Rizzoli, 1948.
La caduta del fascismo e l'armistizio di Roma. Rome: Azione Letteraria Italiana, 1944.
Caetani, Vittoria. *Sparkle Distant Worlds.* London: Hutchinson, 1947.
Caimpenta, Ugo. *Il Maresciallo Badoglio.* Milan: Aurora, 1936.
Calabrese, Arnaldo. *25 Luglio.* Naples: STEM, 1962.
Calamandrei, Pietro. *Uomini e città della resistenza.* Bari: Laterza, 1955.
'Calibano' (pseud). *Le ultime ore di un dittatore.* Milan: PWB, nd.
Cambria, Adele. *Maria José.* Milan: Longanesi, 1966.
Campanelli, Paolo. *Mussolini.* London: Pallas, 1939.
Campini, Dino. *Mussolini, Churchill, i carteggi.* Milan: Italpress, 1952.
Campini, Dino. *Strano gioco di Mussolini.* Milan: Studio Editoriale PG, 1952.
Campini, Dino. *El Alamein Quota 33.* Milan: Italpress, 1952.
Cancogni, Manlio. *Storia dello squadrismo.* Milan: Longanesi, 1959.
Canevari, Emilio. *Graziani mi ha detto.* Rome: Magi-Spinetti. 1947.
Caniglia, Renato. *Razzismo italiano.* Milan: Italia Industriale, 1938.
Cantalupo, Roberto. *Fu la Spagna.* Milan: Mondadori, 1948.
Capozzi, Gennaro. *Venti giorni di terrore.* Naples: 'La Floridiana', 1943.
Caracciolo, Filipop. *'43–44: Diario di Napoli.* Florence: Vallecchi. 1964.
Caracciolo di Feroleto, Gen Mario. *Sette carceri di un generale.* Rome: Corso, 1947.
Caracciolo di Feroleto, Gen Mario. *E poi?* Rome: Corso, 1948.
Caravaglios, Cesare. *I canti delle trincee.* Rome: CCSM, 1934.
Carboni, Gen Giacomo. *L'Armistizio e la difesa di Roma.* Rome: De Luigi, 1945.
Carboni, Gen Giacomo. *La verità di un generale distratto sull'8 settembre '43.* Bologna: Beta, 1966.
Carboni, Gen Giacomo. *Memorie Segrete, 1935–48.* Florence: Parenti, 1955.
Carell, Paul. *The Foxes of the Desert.* London: Macdonald, 1961.
Carli-Ballola, R. *Storia della Resistenza.* Milan: Avanti!, 1957.
Carver, Michael. *Tobruk.* London: Batsford, 1964.
Cassinelli, Guido. *Appunti sul 25 luglio 1943.* Rome: SAPPI, 1944.
Castellani, Aldo. *Microbes, Men and Monarchs.* London: Victor Gollancz, 1960.
Castellano, Gen Giuseppe. *Come firmai l'armistizio di Cassibile.* Milan: Mondadori, 1945.
Castellano, Giuseppe. *Roma Kaputt.* Rome: Casini, 1967.
Castelli, Giulio. *Storia segreta di Roma 'città aperta'.* Rome: Quattrucci, 1959.
Caudana, Mino. *Il Figlio del Fabbro* (*2 vols*). Rome: CEN, 1960.
Caudana, Mino. *I Fucilati di Verona.* Rome: CEN, 1961.
Cavallero, Carlo. *Il dramma del maresciallo Cavallero.* Milan: Mondadori, 1952.
Cavallero, Marshal Ugo. *Comando supremo.* Bologna: Cappelli, 1948.
Caviglia, Marshal Enrico. *Diario (1925–45).* Rome: Casini, 1952.

Cerruti, Elisabetta. *Ambassador's wife*. London: Allen & Unwin, 1952.
Cersosimo, Vincenzo. *Dall'istruttoria alla fucilazione: storia del processo di Verona*. Milan: Garzanti, 1949.
Cesarini, Paolo. *Elena, la moglie del Re*. Florence: 'La Voce', 1953.
Cetti, Carlo. *Cronaca dei fatti di Dongo*. Como: privately printed, 1959.
Ceva, Bianca. *5 anni di storia italiana, 1940–45, da lettere e diari di caduti*. Milan: Comunità, 1964.
Ceva, Bianca. *Storia di una passione*. Milan: Garzanti, 1948.
Chabod, Federico. *A history of Italian Fascism (transl by Muriel Grindrod)*. London: Weidenfeld & Nicholson, 1963.
Charles-Roux, François. *Huit ans au Vatican (1932–40)*. Paris: Flammarion, 1947.
Child, Richard Washburn. *A Diplomat looks at Europe*. New York: Duffield, 1925.
Chiurco, G. A. *Storia della Rivoluzione Fascista (5 vols)*. Florence: Vallecchi, 1929.
Churchill, Winston Spencer. *The Second World War, Vol I 'The Gathering Storm' Vol II 'Their Finest Hour' Vol III 'The Grand Alliance'*. London: Cassell, 1948–50.
Cianfarra, Camille. *The War and the Vatican*. London: Burns, Oates & Washbourne, 1945.
Ciano, Galeazzo. *Diary, 1937–8 (transl by Andreas Mayor)*. London: Methuen, 1952.
Ciano, Galeazzo. *Ciano's Diplomatic Papers (ed Malcolm Muggeridge) (transl by Stuart Hood)*. London: Odhams Press, 1948.
Ciano, Galeazzo. *The Ciano Diaries, 1939–43 (ed Hugh Gibson)*. New York: Doubleday, 1946.
Ciarlantini, Franco. *Mussolini immaginario*. Milan: Sonzogno, 1933.
Cilibrizzi, Saverio. *Pietro Badoglio rispetto a Mussolini e di fronte alla storia*. Naples: Conte, 1949.
Cione, Edmondo. *Storia della Repubblica Sociale Italiana*. Rome: Latinita, 1950.
Cipolla, Arnaldo. *Da Baldissera a Badoglio*. Florence: Bemporad, 1936.
Cippico, Count Antonio. *Italy, the Central Problem of the Mediterranean*. New Haven: Yale University Press, 1926.
Cirillo, Giuseppe. *Casi e cose*. Naples: Ala, 1948.
Clark, Gen Mark. *Calculated Risk*. New York: Harper, 1950.
Clough, Shepherd B. *The Economic History of Modern Italy*. New York: Columbia University Press, 1964.
Cocchia, Admiral Aldo. *Submarines Attacking (transl by Margaret Gwyer)*. London: William Kimber 1956.
Colleoni, Angelo. *La verità sulla fine di Mussolini e della Petacci*. Milan: privately printed, 1945.
Colleoni, Angelo. *Claretta Petacci: rivelazioni sulla vita, gli amori, la morte*. Milan: Lucchi, 1945.
Collotti, Enzo. *L'amministrazione tedesca dell'Italia occupata*. Milan: Lerici, 1963.
Comandini, Federico. *Responsabilità di Graziani nel ripiegamento libico del 1940*. Rome: Quaderni Liberi, 1944.
Cooper, Alfred Duff. *Old Men Forget*. London: Hart-Davis, 1953.
Cooper, C. S. *Understanding Italy*. New York: The Century Co, 1923.
Corsini, Vincenzo. *Il capo del governo nello stato fascista*. Bologna: Zanichelli, 1935.
Costamagna, Carlo. *Storia e Dottrina del Fascismo*. Turin: Unione Tipografico – Editoriale Torinese, 1938.
Craig, Gordon A. and Gilbert, Felix. *The Diplomats, 1919–39*. Princeton, NJ: Princeton University Press, 1953.
Crispoldi, Filippo. *Politici, guerrieri, poeti*. Milan: Treves, 1939.
Cucco, Alfredo. *Non volevamo perder*. Bologna: Cappelli, 1950.
Cuddihy, R. J. and Shuster, G. N. *Pope Pius XI and American Public Opinion*. New York: Funk & Wagnalls, 1939.

Curina, Antonio. *Fuochi sui monti dell' Appennino toscano.* Arezzo: Badiali, 1957.
Currey, Muriel. *Italian Foreign Policy, 1918–32.* London: Ivor Nicholson & Watson, 1932.
Currey, Muriel. *A woman at the Abyssinian War.* London: Hutchinson, 1936.
D'Agata, Rosario. *Mussolini, l'uomo, l'idea, l'opera.* Palermo: Sandron, 1927.
D'Agostini, Bruno. *Colloqui con Rachele Mussolini.* Rome: OET, 1946.
Dalla Costa, Cardinal Elia. *Storia vera su Firenze 'città aperta'.* Florence: Rinaldi, 1945.
Dalla Torre, Giuseppe. *Memorie.* Milan: Mondadori, 1965.
Damiano, Andrea. *Rosso e grigio.* Milan: Muggiani, 1947.
D'Andrea, Ugo. *La fine del regno.* Turin: SE Torinese, 1951.
Danese, Orlando. *Mussolini.* Mantua: Paladino, nd.
Danese, Orlando. *Il Re Fascista.* Mantua: Paladino, 1923.
Danese, Orlando. *Mussolini, il Papa e la Massoneria.* Mantua: Paladino, 1923.
D'Annunzio, Mario. *Mio padre comandante di Fiume,* Genoa: Siglaeffe, 1956.
D'Aroma, Nino. *Mussolini segreto.* Bologna: Cappelli, 1958.
D'Aroma, Nino. *Vite Parallele.* Rome: CEN, 1962.
D'Aroma, Nino. *Vent'anni insieme.* Bologna: Cappelli, 1957.
Deakin, F. W. *The Brutal Friendship.* London: Weidenfeld & Nicolson, 1962.
Dean, Vera Micheles. *Fascist Rule in Italy.* London: Nelson, 1934.
De Bono, Gen Emilio. *Anno XIII.* London: Cresset Press, 1937.
De Felice, Renzo. *Mussolini il rivoluzionario.* Turin: Einaudi, 1965.
De Felice, Renzo. *Mussolini il fascista.* Turin: Einaudi, 1966.
De Fiori, Vittorio. *Italia incandescente.* New York: English Book Shop, 1937.
De Fiori, Vittorio. *Mussolini: Man of Destiny.* London: J. M. Dent, 1928.
Degli Espinosa, Agostino. *Il regno del Sud.* Rome: Migliaresi, 1946.
De Gruchy, F. A. L. *War Diary.* Aldershot: Gale & Polden, 1949.
De Jaco, A. *La città insorge: le quattro giornate di Napoli.* Rome: Editori Riuniti, 1956.
Delaney, John P. *The Blue Devils in Italy.* Washington: Infantry Journal Press, 1947.
Delcroix, Carlo. *Un uomo e un popolo.* Florence: Vallecchi, 1928.
Del Vita, Alessandro. *La Marcia su Roma con la centura scelta di Arezzo.* Arezzo: FPF, 1924.
Delzell, C. F. *Mussolini's Enemies.* Princeton, NJ: Princeton University Press, 1961.
De Renzis, Raffaello. *Mussolini musicista.* Mantua: Paladino, 1926.
De Vincentis, Luigi. *Io sono te.* Rome: Cebes, 1946.
De Wyss, M. *Rome Under The Terror.* London: Robert Hale, 1945.
Diamond, William. *Industrial Rehabilitation in Italy.* London: UNRRA European Regional Office, 1947.
Di Benigno, Jo. *Occasioni Mancate.* Rome: Edizioni SEI, 1945.
Dies, Luigi Maria. *Istantanea Mussoliniana a Ponza.* Rome: Messaggerie Romane, 1949.
Dinale, Ottavio. *Tempo di Mussolini.* Verona: Mondadori, 1934.
Dinale, Ottavio. *La rivoluzione che vince.* Rome: Campitelli, 1934.
Dinale, Ottavio. *Quarant'anni di colloqui con lui.* Milan: Ciarrocca, 1953.
Documents on British Foreign Policy. London: HMSO, 1946–
Documents on German Foreign Policy, 1918–45. London: HMSO, 1948–
I Documenti Diplomatici Italiani. Rome: Ministero degli Esteri, 1952.
Dolfin, Giovanni. *Con Mussolini nella tragedia.* Milan: Garzanti, 1949.
Dollmann, Eugen. *Du Càpitole a la roche Tarpéienne.* Paris: Presse de la Cité, 1957.
Dollmann, Eugen. *Call Me Coward.* London: William Kimber, 1956.
Dollmann, Eugen. *The Interpreter* (transl by *J. Maxwell-Brownjohn*). London: Hutchinson, 1967.
Dombrowski, Roman. *Mussolini: Twilight and Fall.* London: Heinemann, 1956.

Domino, Ignazio. *Italo Balbo*. Florence: All'insegna del Libro, 1940.
Dongo. Milan: Edizioni 'A', 1951.
Donosti, Mario. *Mussolini e l'Europa*. Rome: Leonardo, 1945.
Dorso, Guido. *Mussolini alla conquista del potere*. Turin: Einaudi, 1949.
Dower, K. C. G. *The First to be Freed*. London: HMSO, 1944.
Due anni di guerra. Rome: Ministero Cultura Popolare, 1942.
Dulles, Allen. *The Secret Surrender*. New York: Harper & Row, 1966.
Dumini, Amerigo. *17 colpi*. Milan: Longanesi, 1958.
Durand, Mortimer. *Crazy Campaign*. London: George Routledge, 1936.
Ebenstein, William. *Fascist Italy*. London: Martin Hopkinson, 1939.
Eckhardt, Carl C. *The Papacy and World Affairs*. Chicago: University of Chicago Press, 1937.
Eden, Anthony. *Facing the Dictators*. London: Cassell, 1962.
Edwards, Kenneth. *The Grey Diplomatists*. London: Rich & Cowan, 1938.
Eisenhower, Gen. Dwight D. *Crusade in Europe*. New York: Doubleday, 1948.
Ercole, F. *Storia del Fascismo*. Milan: Mondadori, 1939.
Ercoli, E. M. (pseud Palmiro Togliatti). *Inside Italy*. New York: Worker's Library Publishers, 1942.
Etnasi, Fernando. *Cronache col mitra*. Milan: Giordano, 1965.
Ettlinger, Harold. *The Axis on the Air*. Indianapolis: Bobbs-Merrill, 1943.
Faenza, Liliano. *Comunismo e Cattolicesimo in una parrochia di campagna*. Milan: Feltrinelli, 1959.
Falco, Mario. *The Legal Position of the Holy See before and after the Lateran Treaty*. Oxford: Oxford University Press, 1935.
Faldella, Gen Emilio. *L'Italia e la seconda guerra mondiale*. Bologna: Cappelli, 1959.
Farago, Ladislas. *Abyssinia on the Eve*. London: Putnam, 1935.
Farago, Ladislas. *Abyssinian Stop Press*. London: Robert Hale, 1936.
Farina, Salvatore. *Le truppe d'assalto italiane*. Rome: FNAI, 1938.
Farinacci, Roberto. *Squadrismo: dal mio diario della vigilia*. Rome: Ardita, 1933.
Farinacci, Roberto. *Storia del Fascismo (3 vols)*. Cremona: 'Cremona nuova', 1937.
Farinacci, Roberto. *Da Vittorio Veneto a Piazza San Sepolcro*. Verona: Mondadori, 1933.
Farinacci, Roberto. *In difesa di Dumini*. Rome: Libreria dell'Ottocento, 1945.
Farinacci, Roberto. *Un periodo aureo del partito nazionale fascista*. Foligno: Franco Campitelli, 1926.
Favagrossa, Gen Carlo. *Perchè perdemmo la guerra: Mussolini e la produzione bellica*. Milan: Rizzoli, 1946.
Federzoni, Luigi. *Italia di ieri per la storia di domani*. Milan: Mondadori, 1967.
Feiling, Keith. *Neville Chamberlain*. London: Macmillan, 1946.
Feis, Herbert. *Churchill, Roosevelt, Stalin: The War They Waged and the Peace They Sought*. Princeton, NJ: Princeton University Press, 1957.
Felletti, Leonida. *Soldati senz'armi*. Rome: Donatello De Luigi, 1944.
Fermi, Laura. *Mussolini*. Chicago: University of Chicago Press, 1963.
Ferrari, Santo. *L'Italia Fascista*. Turin: Ed Libraria Italiana, 1942.
Ferraris, Efrem. *La Marcia su Roma veduta dal Viminale*. Rome: Leonardo, 1946.
Ferrero, Guglielmo. *Four Years of Fascism (transl by E. W. Dickes)*. London: P. S. King, 1924.
Ferrero, Leo. *Diario di un privilegiato sotto il fascismo*. Turin: Chiantore, 1946.
Festa Campanile, Raffaele and Fittipaldi, R. *Mussolini e la battaglia del grano*. Rome: SNFTA, 1931.
Fifteenth Army Group. *Finito!: the Po Valley campaign*. Milan: Rizzoli, 1945.
Finer, Herman. *Mussolini's Italy*. London: Victor Gollancz, 1935.
Fino, Edoardo. *La tragedia di Rodi e dell'Egeo*. Rome: EICA, 1957.
Flora, Francesco. *Appello al Re*. Bologna: Edizioni Alfa, 1965.
Flora, Francesco. *Ritratto di un ventennio*. Naples: Macchiaroli, 1944.

Florinsky, M. T. *Fascism and National Socialism*. New York: Macmillan, 1936.
Foerster, Robert. *Italian Emigration of our Times*. Cambridge, Mass: Harvard University Press, 1919.
Fontenelle, Monsignor René. *His Holiness Pope Pius XI*. London: Burns, Oates & Washbourne, 1933.
Forrest, Alan. *Italian Interlude*. London: Bailey Bros. & Swinfen, 1964.
Forti, Raul and Ghedini, Giuseppe. *L'avvento del Fascismo*. Ferrara: Taddei, 1922.
Fortini, Franco. *Sere in Valdossola*. Milan: Mondadori, 1963.
Forzano, Giovacchino. *Mussolini, autore drammatico*. Florence: Barbera, 1954.
Fox, Sir Frank. *Italy Today*. London: Herbert Jenkins, 1927.
François-Poncet, André. *The Fateful Years*. New York: Harcourt Brace, 1949.
François-Poncet, André. *Au Palais Farnese, 1938-40*. Paris: Fayard, 1961.
Francovich, Carlo. *La resistenza a Firenze*. Florence: La Nuova Italia, 1961.
Franzero, C. M. *Inside Italy*. London: Hodder & Stoughton, 1941.
Frullini, Bruno. *Squadrismo Fiorentino*. Florence: Vallecchi, 1933.
Fuchs, Martin. *A Pact with Hitler* (transl by *Charles Hope Lumley*). London: V. Gollancz, 1939.
Fuller, Maj-Gen J. F. C. *The First of the League Wars*. London: Eyre & Spottiswoode, 1936.
Fusco, Giancarlo. *Le rose del ventennio*. Turin: Einaudi, 1958.
Fusti Carofiglio, Mario. *Vita di Mussolini e storia del Fascismo*. Turin: S.E. Torinese, 1949.
Gafencu, Grigore. *The Last Days of Europe*. (transl by *Fletcher Allen*). London: Frederick Muller, 1947.
Galbiati, Maj-Gen Enzo. *Il 25 luglio e la MVSN*. Milan: Bernabo', 1950.
Galli, Giorgio. *Storia del Partito Comunista Italiano*. Milan: Schwarz, 1958.
Gambetti, Fidia. *1919-45: inchiesta sul fascismo*. Milan: Mastellone, 1953.
Gardini, T. L. *Towards the New Italy*. London: Lindsay Drummond, 1943.
Garrat, G. T. *Mussolini's Roman Empire*. Harmondsworth: Penguin Books, 1938.
Gasparotto, Luigi. *Diario di un deputato*. Milan: Dall' Oglio,1945.
Gatto, Alfonso (ed). *Il coro della guerra*. Bari: Laterza, 1963.
Gavagnin, Armando. *Vent'anni di resistenza al Fascismo*. Turin: Einaudi, 1957.
Gay, H. Nelson. *Strenuous Italy*. Boston: Houghton Mifflin, 1927.
Gay, Vicente. *Madre Roma*. Barcelona: Bosch, 1935.
Gazzaniga, Rodolfo. *Mussolini come l'ho visto io*. Mantua: Paladino, 1927.
Genoud, François (ed). *The Testament of Adolf Hitler: The Hitler-Bormann Documents*. (transl by *Col R. H. Stevens*). London: Cassell, 1961.
Germino, Dante L. *The Italian Fascist Party in Power*. Minneapolis: University of Minnesota Press, 1959.
Gessi, Leone. *Roma, la guerra, il Papa*. Rome: Standerini, 1945.
Ghezzi, Raoul. *Comunisti, industriali e fascisti a Torino, 1920-23*. Turin: Botta, 1924.
Giachetti, Cipriano. *Fascismo liberatore*. Florence: Bemporad, 1922.
Gianeri, Enrico. *Il cesare di cartapesta*. Turin: Vega, 1945.
Gianeri, Enrico. *Il piccolo re*. Turin: Fiorini, 1946.
Giannini, Alberto. *Le memorie di un fesso*. Milan: Corbaccio, 1941.
Gibbs, Sir Philip. *Since Then*. London: Heinemann, 1930.
Giglio, Giovanni. *The Triumph of Barabbas*.London: Gollancz, 1937.
Gilbert, Felix (ed). *Hitler Directs His War*. New York: Oxford University Press, 1950.
Gillet, Louis. *Londres et Rome*. Paris: Bernard Grasset, 1936.
Giolitti, Giovanni. *Memoirs of my life* (transl by *Edward Storer*). London: Chapman & Dodd, 1923.
Girace, Piero. *Diario di uno squadrista*. Naples: Rispoli Anonima, 1940.
Gobetti-Marchesini Prospero, A. *Diario partigiano*. Turin: Einaudi, 1956.
Godden, Gertrude M. *Mussolini*. London: Burns & Oates, 1923.

Goebbels, Josef. *Diaries (transl and ed by Louis P. Lochner)*. London: Hamish Hamilton, 1948.
Gomez, Laureano. *El Cuadrilatero*. Bogota: Libreria Colombiana, 1935.
Gonella, Guido. *The Papacy and World Peace*. London: Hollis & Carter, 1945.
Gorresio, Vittorio. *Un anno di libertà*. Rome: OET, 1945.
Grandi, Count Dino. *Memoriale*. Bari: Edizione Documenti, nd.
Gravelli, Asvero. *Mussolini Aneddotico*. Rome: Latinità, 1951.
Gravelli, Asvero. *I canti della rivoluzione*. Rome: Nuova Europa, 1926.
Gravelli, Asvero (ed). *Marcia su Roma*. Rome: Nuova Europa, 1934.
Graziani, Marshal Rodolfo. *Graziani*. Rome: Rivista Romana, 1956.
Graziani, Marshal Rodolfo. *Ho difeso la patria*. Milan: Garzanti, 1948.
Graziani, Marshal Rodolfo. *Processo Graziani (3 vols)*. Rome: Ruffolo, 1948.
Graziani, Marshal Rodolfo. *Il fronte sud*. Milan: Mondadori, 1938.
Grazzi, Emanuele. *Il principio della fine*. Rome: Faro, 1945.
Greco, Eugenio. *Il Ministro Alberto de'Stefani*. Milan: Ceschina, 1959.
Greenwall, Harry J. *Mediterranean Crisis*. London: Nicholson & Watson, 1939.
Gregory, J. D. *Dollfuss and His Times*. London: Hutchinson, 1935.
Gribaudi, Piero. *La piu' grande Italia*. Turin: SEI, 1925.
Grindrod, Muriel. *The New Italy*. London: Royal Institute of International Affairs, 1947.
Gualerni, Gualtiero. *La politica industriale fascista*. Milan: Istituto Sociale Ambrosiano, 1956.
Guariglia, Baron Raffaele. *La Diplomatie Difficile*. Paris: Plon, 1955.
Guerin, Daniel. *Fascism and Big Business (transl by Frances and Mason Merril)*. New York: Pioneer Publishers, 1939.
Guerin, Thomas. *Caps and Crowns of Europe*. Montreal: Louis Carrier, 1929.
Gunther, John. *Inside Europe*. New York: Harper, 1936.
Gutkind, Curt (ed). *Mussolini e il suo fascismo*. Florence: Le Monnier, 1927.
Gwynn, D. R. *Pius XI*. London: Holme Press, 1932.
Haider, Carmen. *Capital and Labor under Facism*. New York: privately printed, 1930.
Haider, Carmen. *Do we want fascism?* New York: John Day Co, 1934.
Haight, Elizabeth Hazelton. *Italy Old and New*. London: Stanley Paul, 1923.
Halifax, Lord. *Fullness of Days*. London: Collins, 1957.
Halperin, S. W. *Mussolini and Italian Fascismus*. Princeton, NJ: Van Nostrand, 1964.
Hambloch, Ernest. *Italy Militant*. London: Duckworth, 1941.
Hamilton, Cicely Mary. *Modern Italy as seen by an Englishwoman*. London: J. M. Dent, 1932.
Hamilton, Edward. *The war in Abyssinia*. London: John Heritage, 1936.
Harding, Bertita. *Age Cannot Wither*. Philadelphia: J. B. Lippincott, 1947.
Harris, C. R. S. *Allied Administration of Italy, 1943–45*. London: HMSO, 1957.
Hassell, Ulrich von. *Diaries 1938–44 (ed Hugh Gibson)*. London: Hamish Hamilton, 1948.
Hemingway, Ernest. *By-Line (ed William White)*. New York: Scribner's 1967.
Henderson, Sir Nevile. *Failure of a Mission*. London: Hodder & Stoughton, 1940.
Hentze, Margot. *Pre-fascist Italy*. London: Allen & Unwin, 1939.
Herron, G. D. *The Revival of Italy*. London: Allen & Unwin, 1922.
Hibbert, Christopher. *Mussolini*. London: Longmans, 1962.
Hilton-Young, Wayland. *The Italian Left*. London: Longmans, 1949.
Hitler e Mussolini: lettere e documenti. Rome: Rizzoli, 1946.
Hoare, Sir Samuel. *Nine Troubled Years*. London: William Collins, 1954.
Hodson, James Lansdale. *The Sea and the Land*. London: V. Gollancz, 1945.
Horowitz, Daniel L. *The Italian Labor Movement*. Cambridge, Mass: Harvard University Press, 1963.

Höttl, Wilhelm. *The Secret Front: the story of Nazi political espionage* (transl by *R. H. Stevens*). New York: Frederick A. Praeger, 1954.
Howard, Milford W. *Fascism: a challenge to democracy*. New York: Fleming H. Revell, 1928.
Hubbard, Wynant. *Fiasco in Ethiopia*. New York: Harper Bros, 1936.
Hughes, H. Stuart. *The United States and Italy*. Cambridge, Mass: Harvard University Press, 1953.
Hull, Cordell. *Memoirs* (2 vols). New York: Macmillan, 1948.
Hullinger, Edwin Ware. *The New Fascist State*. New York: Rae D. Henkle, 1928.
Hunt, Sir David. *A Don at War*. London: William Kimber, 1966.
Icardi, Aldo. *Aldo Icardi: American Master Spy*. Pittsburgh: Stalwart Enterprises, 1954.
Italy's Fighting Forces on Land, Sea and Air. London: Sampson Low, 1940.
Italy's Struggle for Liberation. London: International Publishing Corporation, 1944.
Italy's War-Crimes in Ethopia. Woodford Green: New Times & Ethipoia News, 1945.
Jachino, Adm Angelo. *Gaudo e Matapan*. Milan: Mondadori, 1946.
Jachino, Adm Angelo. *Tramonto di una grande Marina*. Milan: Mondadori, 1959.
Jemolo, A. C. *Church and State in Italy, 1850–1950.* (transl by David Moore). Oxford: Basil Blackwell, 1960.
Jevons, H. S. *Italian Military Secrets*. London: privately printed, 1937.
Jones, S. Alfred. *Is Fascism the Answer?* Hamilton, Ontario: David-Lisson, 1933.
K. S. *Agent in Italy*. London: Hutchinson, 1943.
Keene, Frances. *Neither Liberty nor Bread*. New York: Harper, 1940.
Keitel, Field-Marshal Wilhelm. *Memoirs* (ed *Walter Gorlitz*) (transl by *David Irving*). London: William Kimber, 1965.
Kemechey, L. *Il Duce* (transl by *Magda Vamos*). London: Williams & Norgate, 1930.
Kennedy, William Sloane. *Italy in chains*. West Yarmouth, Mass: The Stonecroft Press, 1927.
Kenworthy, J. M. (Lord Strabolgi). *The conquest of Italy*. London: Hutchinson, 1944.
Kersten, Felix. *The Kersten Memoirs, 1940–45* (transl by *Constantine Fitzgibbon and James Oliver*). London: Hutchinson, 1956.
Kesselring, Albert. *The Memoirs of Field-Marshal Kesselring* (transl by *Lynton Hudson*). London: W. Kimber, 1953.
Keun, Odette. *Trumpets Bray*. London: Constable, 1943.
Killanin, Michael (ed). *Four Days*. London: Heinemann, 1938.
King, Bolton. *Fascism in Italy*. London: William & Norgate, 1931.
King-Hall, Sir Stephen. *Three Dictators*. London: Faber & Faber, 1964.
Kirkpatrick, Sir Ivone. *Mussolini*. London: Odhams Press, 1964.
Kirkpatrick, Sir Ivone. *The Inner Circle*. London: Macmillan, 1959.
Kogan, Norman. *The politics of Italian Foreign Policy*. London: Pall Mall Press, 1963.
Kogan, Norman. *Italy and the Allies*. Cambridge, Mass: Harvard University Press, 1956.
Konstantın, Prince of Bavaria. *Der Pabst*. Münich: Kindler & Schiermeyer, 1950.
Kubly, Herbert. *Italy*. New York: Time Inc, 1961.
Lagardelle, Hubert. *Mission à Rome*. Paris: Plon, 1955.
Lancellotti, Arturo. *D'Annunzio nella luce di domani*. Rome: Staderini, 1938.
Lanfranchi, Ferruccio. *La Resa degli ottocentomila*. Rome: Rizzoli, 1948.
Langmaid, Rowland. *'The Med': the Royal Navy in the Mediterranean, 1939–45*. London: Batchworth Press, 1948.
Langsam, W. C. *Historic Documents of World War Two*. Princeton, NJ: D. van Nostrand, 1958.

Lapide, Pinchas. *The Last Three Popes and the Jews.* London: Souvenir Press, 1967.
Lazagna, G. B. *Ponte Rotto.* Genoa: Edizioni del Partigiano, 1946.
Leahy, Fleet Admiral William D. *I Was There.* New York: McGraw Hill, 1950.
Leonardi, Dante Ugo. *Luglio 1943 in Sicilia.* Modena: Soc Tip Modenese, 1947.
Leone, Mario, and Pasetti, John. *Inchiesta sulla morte di Mussolini.* Rome: Aletti, 1962.
Lessona, Alessandro. *Verso l'Impero.* Florence: Sansoni, 1939.
Lessona, Alessandro. *Memorie.* Florence: Sansoni, 1958.
Leto, Guido. *Polizia segreta in Italia.* Rome: Vito Bianco, 1961.
Leto, Guido. *OVRA, Fascismo e antifascismo.* Bologna: Cappelli, 1951.
Liberati, M. *La Repubblica di Salò.* Rome: Nuova, 1952.
Lischi, Dario. *La Marcia su Roma con la colonna Lamarmora.* Florence: 'Florentia', 1923.
Lombardi, Gabrio. *Il Corpo Italiano di Liberazione.* Rome: Magi-Spinetti, 1945.
Longhitano, R. *La politica religiosa di Mussolini.* Rome: Cremonese Libraio Editore, 1938.
Longo, Luigi. *Un popolo alla macchia.* Milan: Mondadori, 1947.
Luciano, Celso. *Rapporto al Duce.* Rome: Società Editrice 'Giornale del Mezzogiorno', 1948.
Ludecke, Kurt. *I Knew Hitler.* New York: Scribners, 1937.
Ludwig, Emil. *Three Portraits.* London: Alliance Book Corporation, 1940.
Ludwig, Emil. *Talks with Mussolini (transl by Eden and Cedar Paul).* London: Allen & Unwin, 1933.
Luraghi, Raimondo. *Il movimento operaio torinese durante la Resistenza.* Turin: Einaudi, 1958.
Lussu, Emilio. *Diplomazia clandestina.* Rome: Nuova Italia, 1956.
Lussu, Emilio. *Un anno sull'altipiano.* Turin: Einaudi, 1964.
Lussu, Emilio. *Enter Mussolini (transl by Marion Rawson).* London: Methuen, 1936.
Macartney, Maxwell H. *One Man Alone.* London: Chatto & Windus, 1944.
Macartney, M. H. H. and Cremona, Paul. *Italy's Foreign and Colonial Policy 1914–37.* Oxford: Oxford University Press, 1938.
MacGovern, William. *From Luther to Hitler.* London: George Harrap, 1946.
MacGregor-Hastie, Roy. *The Day of the Lion.* London: Macdonald, 1963.
Mack Smith, Denis. *Italy.* Ann Arbor: University of Michigan Press, 1960.
Macmillan, Rt Hon Harold. *The Blast of War.* London: Macmillan, 1967.
Macmillan, Richard. *Twenty Angels over Rome.* London: Jarrolds, 1945.
Magistrati, Count Massimo. *L'Italia a Berlino 1937–39.* Milan: Mondadori, 1956.
Majdalany, Fred. *Cassino.* London: Longmans, Green, 1957.
Majdalany, Fred. *The Battle of El Alamein.* London: Weidenfeld & Nicolson, 1965.
Malaparte, Curzio. *Technique du Coup d'Etat.* Paris: Bernard Grasset, 1948.
Malaparte, Curzio. *Kaputt (transl by Cesare Foligno).* New York: E. P. Dutton, 1946.
Malgeri, Gen Alfredo. *L'occupazione di Milano e la Liberazione.* Milan: Editori Associati, 1947.
Manetti, Dante *Gente di Romagna.* Bologna: Cappelli, 1924.
Manunta, Ugo. *La caduta degli angeli: storia intima della RSI.* Rome: Italiana, 1947.
Manvell, Roger (with Heinrich Fraenkel). *Doctor Goebbels.* London: Heinemann, 1960.
Manzini, Carlo. *Il Duce a Verona.* Verona: Albaretti-Marchesetti, 1938.
Marchetti, U. *Mussolini, i prefetti e i podestà.* Mantua: Paladino, nd.
Mariani, Pietro. *Le tre giornate di Roma.* Rome: Studio Romano, 1922.
Marinoni, Antonio. *Italy: yesterday and today.* New York: Macmillan, 1931.
Marriott, Sir J. A. R. *The Makers of Modern Italy.* London: Oxford University Press, 1937.

Mariotti, Giulio. *Verità sugli avvenimenti del 25 luglio e' 8 settembre 1943*. Leghorn: Pozzolini, 1946.
Markevitch, Igor. *Made in Italy (transl by Darina Silone)*. London: Harvill Press, 1949.
Martelli George. *Italy Against the World*. London: Chatto & Windus, 1937.
Martelli, George. *Whose Sea?* London: Chatto & Windus, 1938.
Martienssen, Anthony. *Hitler and his Admirals*. London: Secker & Warburg, 1948.
Massock, R. G. *Italy from Within*. London: Macmillan, 1943.
Matteotti, Giacomo. *The Fascisti Exposed (transl by E. W. Dickes)*. London: ILP, 1924.
Matteotti, Giacomo. *Matteotti*. Rome: ANPPIA, 1957.
Matteotti, Giacomo. *Reliquie*. Milan: Corbaccio, 1924.
Matthews, Herbert L. *Two Wars and More to Come*. New York: Carrick & Evans, 1938.
Matthews, Herbert L. *The Fruits of Fascism*. New York: Harcourt, Brace, 1943.
Matthews, Herbert L. *The Education of a Correspondent*. New York: Harcourt, Brace, 1946.
Mattioli, Guido. *Mussolini aviatore*. Rome: Pinciana, 1936.
Maugeri, Admiral Franco. *From the ashes of Disgrace (ed Victor Rosen)*. New York, Reynal & Hitchcock, 1948.
Maurras, Charles. *Promenade Italienne*. Paris: Flammarion, 1929.
Mazzucchelli, Mario. *I segreti del processo di Verona*. Milan: Cino del Duca, 1963.
McCormick, Anne O'Hare. *Vatican Journal, 1921–54*. New York: Farrar, Straus & Cudahy, 1957.
McGuire, Constantine E. *Italy's International Economic Position*. London: Allen & Unwin, 1927.
Megaro, Gaudens. *Mussolini in the Making*. London: Allen & Unwin, 1938.
Mellini Ponce de Leon, Count Alberto. *Guerra diplomatica a Salò*. Bologna: Cappelli, 1950.
Mellini Ponce de Leon, Count Alberto. *L'Italia entra in guerra*. Bologna: Cappelli, 1963.
Melograni, Piero. *Corriere della Sera*. Bologna: Cappelli, 1965.
Mennini, S. (ed). *Le tre giornate di Roma*. Borgo San Lorenzo: Toccafreddi, 1922.
'Micromegas'. *I 7 responsabili del Fascismo*. Campione: Pagine di Campione, 1943.
Miller, Webb. *I found no Peace*. London: V. Gollancz, 1937.
Miller, Henry S. *Price Control in Fascist Italy*. New York: Columbia University Press, 1938.
Missiroli, Mario. *L'Italia d'oggi*. Bologna: Zanichelli, 1932.
Missiroli, Mario. *What Italy owes to Mussolini*. London: John Heritage, 1938.
Misuri, Alfredo. *Ad bestias!* Rome: Catacombe, 1944.
Modigliani, Vera. *Esilio*. Milan: Garzanti, 1946.
Möllhausen, E. F. *La carta perdente*. Rome: Sestante, 1948.
Momigliano, E. *Storia tragica e grottesca del razzismo fascista*. Florence: Mondadori, 1946.
Monelli, Paolo. *Mussolini: An Intimate Life (transl by Brigid Maxwell)*. London: Thames & Hudson, 1953.
Monelli, Paolo. *Roma 1943*. Rome: Longanesi, edn of 1963.
Monroe, Elizabeth. *The Mediterranean in Politics*. London: Oxford University Press, 1939.
Montagna, Renzo. *Mussolini e il processo di Verona*. Milan: Edizioni Omnia, 1949.
Montanelli, Indro. *Le Bonhomme Mussolini*. Paris: Francoy, nd.
Moorehead, Alan. *African Trilogy*. London: Hamish Hamilton, 1965.
Morgan, Thomas B. *Spurs on the Boot*. New York: Longmans, 1941.
Mori, Cesare. *The Last Struggle with the Mafia*. London: Putnam, 1933.
Mowrer, Edgar. *Immortal Italy*. New York: D. Appleton Co, 1922.

Munro, Ion, S. *Through Fascism to World Power*. London: Alexander Maclehose, 1933.
Munro, Ion, S. *Beyond the Alps*. London: Alexander Maclehose, 1934.
Muratore, Giuseppe and Persia Carmine. *I dodici giorni di Mussolini a Ponza*. Rome: STEB, 1945.
Murphy, J. T. *A Manual on the Rise and Fall of Italy's Fascist Empire*. London: Crowther, 1943.
Murphy, Robert. *Diplomat Among Warriors*. New York: Doubleday, 1964.
Mussolini as Revealed in his Political Speeches (*ed and transl by Baron Bernardo Quaranta di San Severino*). London: Dent, 1923.
Mussolini, Benito. *La mia Vita*. Rome: Faro, 1947.
Mussolini, Benito. *My Autobiography* (*transl by Richard Washburn Child*). London: Hutchinson, 1928.
Mussolini, Benito. *Il mio diario di guerra*. Rome: Imperia, 1923.
Mussolini, Benito. *Je Parle avec Bruno*. Montreux: Editions de l'Aigle, 1942.
Mussolini, Benito. *Storia di un anno*. Verona: Mondadori, 1944.
Mussolini, Benito. *Vita di Sandro e di Arnaldo*. Milan: Hoepli, 1934.
Mussolini, Benito. *Fascism: Doctrines and Institutions*. Rome: Ardita, 1935.
Mussolini, Benito. *The corporate state*. Florence: Vallecchi, 1938.
Mussolini, Edvige. *Mio fratello Benito*. Florence: La Fenice, 1957.
Mussolini, Rachele (with Michele Chinigo). *My Life with Mussolini*. London: Hale, 1959.
Mussolini, Rachele (with Anita Pensotti). *Benito il mio uomo*. Milan: Rizzoli, 1956.
Mussolini, Vittorio. *Vita con mio padre*. Milan: Mondadori, 1957.
Mussolini, Vittorio. *Due donne nella tempesta*. Milan: Mondadori, 1958.
Navarra, Quinto. *Memorie del cameriere di Mussolini*. Milan: Longanesi, 1946.
Nenni, Pietro. *Ten Years of Tyranny in Italy* (*transl by Anne Steele*). London: Allen & Unwin, 1932.
Nenni, Pietro. *Vent'anni di Fascismo*. Milan: Avanti!, 1964.
Newman, E. W. P. *Ethiopian Realities*. London: Allen & Unwin, 1936.
Newman, E. W. P. *Italy's Conquest of Abyssinia*. London: Thornton Butterworth, 1937.
Newton, D. and Hampshire, A. C. *Taranto*. London: William Kimber, 1959.
Nicotri, G. and Nicotri, F. *Freedom for Italy*. New York: Italian-American Press, 1942.
Nitti, F. F. *Escape*. New York: Putnam, 1930.
Nolte, Ernest. *Three Faces of Fascism*. London: Weidenfeld & Nicolson, 1965.
Ojetti, Ugo. *I Taccuini, 1914–43*. Florence: Sansoni, 1954.
Orano, Paolo. *Mussolini da vicino*. Rome: Pinciana, 1928.
Orano, Paolo. *Rodolfo Graziani, generale scipionico*. Rome: Pinciana, 1936.
Origo, Marchioness Iris. *War in Val d'Orcia*. London: Jonathan Cape, 1947.
Orlando, Francesco. *Mussolini volle il 25 luglio*. Milan: SPES, 1946.
Orlando, Gen Taddeo. *Vittoria di un popolo*. Rome: Corso, 1946.
Ottaviani, Giovanni Battista. *La politica rurale di Mussolini*. Rome: Littorio, 1929.
Owen, Frank. *The Three Dictators*. London: Allen & Unwin, 1941.
Packard, Reynolds and Eleanor. *Balcony Empire*. London: Chatto & Windus, 1943.
Padoan, Giovanni. *Abbiamo lottato insieme*. Udine: Del Bianco, 1965.
Palazzeschi, Aldo. *Tre imperi mancati*. Florence: Vallecchi, 1945.
Pansini, Edoardo. *Goliardi a scugnizzi nelle quattro giornate*. Naples: Cimento, 1944.
Pantaleo, Paolo. *Il fascismo cremonese*. Cremona: 'Cremona Nuova', 1931.
Paolucci, Raffaele. *Il mio piccolo mondo perduto*. Bologna: Cappelli, 1947.
Papen, Franz von. *Memoirs* (*transl by Brian Connell*). London: André Deutsch, 1952.
Pascal, Pierre. *Mussolini alla vigilia della sua morte e l'Europa*. Rome: L'Arnia, 1948.

Patti, Ercole. *Roman Chronicle*. London: Chatto & Windus, 1965.
Pellizzi, C. *Italy*. London: Longmans, 1939.
Perone Capano, Renato. *La resistenza in Roma (2 vols)*. Naples: Gaetano Macchiaroli, 1963.
Perticone, Giacomo. *La Repubblica di Salò*. Rome: Leonardo, 1947.
Petacci, Clara. *Il mio diario*. Milan: Editori Associati, 1946.
Petrie, Sir Charles. *Mussolini*. London: Holme Press, 1931.
Petrie, Sir Charles. *Lords of the Inland Sea*. London: Lovat Dickson, 1937.
Phillips, Sir Percival. *The Red Dragon and the Black Shirts*. London: 'The Daily Mail', 1923.
Phillips, William. *Ventures in Diplomacy*. Boston: Beacon Press, 1953.
Pini, Giorgio. *Filo diretto con Palazzo Venezia*. Bologna: Cappelli, 1950.
Pini, Giorgio. *Itinerario tragico*. Milan: Ed Omnia, 1956.
Pini, Giorgio. *Mussolini (transl by Luigi Villari)*. London: Hutchinson, 1939.
Pini, Giorgio and Susmel, Duilio. *Mussolini: l'uomo e l'opera (4 vols)*. Florence: La Fenice, 1953–55.
Piscitelli, Enzo. *Storia della Resistenza romana*. Bari: Laterza, 1965.
Pistelli, Ermenegildo. *Eroi, uomini e ragazzi*. Florence: Sansoni, 1927.
Pitigliani, Fausto. *The Italian corporative state*. London: P. S. King, 1933.
Pitt, Roxane. *The Courage of Fear*. London: Jarrolds, 1957.
Pius XII, Pope. *The Pope Speaks*. London: Faber, 1940.
Pius XII, Pope. *Selected letters and addresses*. London: Catholic Truth Society, 1949.
Platt, Sir T. C. *The Abyssinian Storm*. London: Jarrolds, 1935.
Pozzi, Arnaldo. *Come li ho visti io*. Milan: Mondadori, 1947.
Prezzolini, Giuseppe. *Fascism*. London: Methuen, 1926.
Price, G. Ward. *I Know These Dictators*. London: Harrap, 1937.
Price, G. Ward. *Year of Reckoning*. London: Cassell, 1939.
Price, G. Ward. *Extra Special Correspondent*. London: Harrap, 1957.
Pugliese, Gen Emanuele. *L'esercito e la cosidetta marcia su Roma*. Rome: Tipografia Regionale, 1958.
Puntoni, Gen Paolo. *Parla Vittorio Emanuele III*. Milan: Aldo Palazzi, 1958.
Quazza, G., Valiani, Leo and Volterra, Eduardo. *Il Governo del CLN*. Turin: Giappichelli, 1966.
Rafanelli, Leda. *Una donna e Mussolini*. Milan: Rizzoli, 1946.
Raffalovich, George. *Benito Mussolini*. Florence: 'The Owl', 1923.
Rahn, Rudolf. *Ambasciatore di Hitler a Vichy e a Salò*. Milan: Garzanti, 1950.
Raushenbush, Stephen. *The March on Fascism*. New Haven: Yale University Press, 1940.
Re, Emilio. *Storia di un archivio: Le carte di Mussolini*. Milan: Milione, 1946.
Repaci, Antonino. *La Marcia su Roma (2 vols)*. Rome: Canesi, 1963.
Revelli, Nuto. *La guerra dei poveri*. Turin: Giulio Einaudi, 1962.
Rhodes, Anthony. *The Poet as Superman*. London: Weidenfeld & Nicolson, 1959.
Ribbentrop, Joachim von. *Memoirs (transl by Oliver Watson)*. London: Weidenfeld & Nicolson, 1954.
Riccardi, Raffaello. *Pagine squadriste*. Rome: Unione Editoriale d'Italia, 1940.
Richelmy, Carlo. *Cinque Re*. Rome: Casini, 1952.
Rintelen, Enno von. *Mussolini l'alleato*. Rome: Corso, 1952.
Roatta, Mario. *Otto Milioni di Baionette*. Milan: Mondadori, 1946.
Roberts, Kenneth. *Black Magic*. Indianapolis: Bobbs-Merrill, 1924.
Robertson, Angus. *Victor Emmanuel*. London: Allen & Unwin, 1925.
Robertson, Angus. *Mussolini and the New Italy*. London: Allenson, 1929.
Robinson, Vandaleur. *Albania's Road to Freedom*. London: Allen & Unwin, 1941.
Romualdi, Pino. *L'ora di Catilina*. Rome: TER, 1963.
Rosenthal, Eric. *The Fall of Italian East Africa*. London: Hutchinson, 1942.

Rossi, A. (Angelo Tasca). *The Rise of Italian Fascism, (transl by Peter and Dorothy Wait)*. London: Methuen, 1938.
Rossi, Cesare. *Mussolini com'era*. Rome: Ruffolo, 1947.
Rossi, Cesare. *Personaggi di ieri e di oggi*. Milan: Ceschina, 1960.
Rossi, Cesare. *Il Delitto Matteotti*. Milan: Ceschina, 1965.
Rossi, Gen Francesco. *Come arrivammo all' armistizio*. Milan: Garzanti, 1946.
Rossi, Gen Francesco. *Mussolini e lo Stato Maggiore*. Milan: Regionale, 1951.
Rovere, Franco. *Vita amorosa di Claretta Petacci*. Milan: Lucchi, 1946.
Ruinas, Stanis. *Pioggia sulla Repubblica*. Rome: Corso, 1946.
Saini, Ezio. *La notte di Dongo*. Rome: Corso, 1950.
Salandra, Antonio. *Memorie politiche, 1916–25*. Milan: Garzanti, 1951.
Salvadori, Max. *The Labour and the Wounds*. London: Pall Mall Press, 1958.
Salvadori, Max. *Brief History of the Patriot Movement in Italy (transl by Giacinto Salvadori-Paleotti)*. Chicago: Clemente, 1954.
Salvatorelli, Luigi. *Vent'anni fra due guerre*. Rome: Italiana, 1946.
Salvatorelli, Luigi (with Mira, Giovanni). *Storia d'Italia nel periodo fascista*. Turin: Einaudi, 1956.
Salvatori, Renato. *Nemesi*. Milan: Baldassarre Gnocchi, 1945.
Salvemini, Gaetano. *The Fascist Dictatorship in Italy*. London: Cape, 1928.
Salvemini, Gaetano. *Under the Axe of Fascism*. London: Gollancz, 1936.
Salvemini, Gaetano. *Prelude to World War II*. London: Gollancz, 1953.
Salvemini, Gaetano. *Italia scombinata*. Turin: Einaudi, 1959.
Saporiti, Piero. *Empty Balcony*. London: Gollancz, 1947.
Saragat, Giuseppe. *40 anni di lotta per la democrazia*. Milan: Ugo Mursia, 1966.
Sardi, Alessandro. *La Marcia su Roma*. Rome: Istituto Poligrafico dello Stato, 1932.
Sardi, Alessandro. *. . . Ma, non si imprigiona la storia*. Rome: CEN, 1958.
Sarfatti, Margherita. *Dux: The Life of Benito Mussolini (transl by Frederic Whyte)*. London: Thornton Butterworth, 1925.
Schellenberg, Walter. *The Schellenberg Memoirs (ed and transl by Louis Hagen)*. London: André Deutsch, 1956.
Schiano, Pasquale. *La resistenza nel Napoletano*. Naples: CESP, 1965.
Schiavi, Alessandro. *La vita e l'opera di Giacomo Matteotti*. Rome: Opere Nuove, 1957.
Schmidt, Carl T. *The Plough and the Sword*. New York: Columbia University Press, 1938.
Schmidt, Paul. *Hitler's Interpreter (ed by R. H. C. Steel)*. London: William Heinemann, 1951.
Schneider, H. W. *Making the Fascist State*. New York: Oxford University Press 1928.
Schneider, Herbert and Clough, Shepard. *Making Fascists*. Chicago: Chicago University Press, 1929.
Schneider, Herbert W. *The Fascist Government of Italy*. New York: Van Nostrand, 1936.
Schonfield, Hugh J. *Italy and Suez*. London: Hutchinson, 1940.
Schuman, Frederick L. *Europe on the Eve*. London: Robert Hale, 1939.
Schuschnigg, Kurt von. *Austrian Requiem*. London: Gollancz, 1947.
Schuster, Ildefonso. *Gli ultimi tempi di un regime*. Milan: 'La Vita', 1946.
Scorza, Carlo. *Il segreto di Mussolini*. Lanciano: Carabba, 1933.
Scotellaro, Rocco. *L'uva puttanella*. Bari: Laterza, 1955.
Scrivener, Jane. *Inside Rome with the Germans*. New York: Macmillan, 1945.
Secchia, Pietro and Moscatelli, Cino. *Il Monte Rosa e sceso a Milano*. Turin: Einaudi, 1958.
Seldes, George. *The Vatican: yesterday, today and tomorrow*. London: Kegan Paul, Trench, Trubner, 1934.
Seldes, George. *Sawdust Caesar*. New York: Harper, 1938.

Senise, Carmine. *Quando ero capo della polizia*. Rome: Ruffolo, 1946.
Settimelli, Emilio. *Mussolini visto da Settimelli*. Rome: Pinciana, 1929.
Settimelli, Emilio. *Colpo di stato fascista?* Milan: Facchi, 1922.
Settimelli, Emilio. *Edda contro Benito*. Rome: Corso, 1952.
Sforza, Count Carlo. *L'Italia dal 1914 al 1944 quale io la vidi*. Rome: Mondadori, 1944.
Sforza, Count Carlo. *Noi e gli altri*. Milan: Gentile, 1945.
Sforza, M. C. *Gli attentati a Mussolini*. Milan: Mondadori, 1965.
Shapiro, Lionel. *They Left the Back Door Open*. London: Jarrolds, 1945.
Shaw, G. B. *Bernard Shaw and Fascism*. London: Favil Press, 1927.
Sheridan, Clare. *In Many Places*. London: Jonathan Cape, 1923.
Sherwood, R. E. *Roosevelt and Hopkins: An Intimate History*. New York: Harper & Brothers, 1948.
Shirer, William. *The Rise and Fall of the Third Reich*. New York: Simon & Schuster, 1959.
Silva, Pietro. *Io difendo la Monarchia*. Rome: De Fonseca, 1946.
Silvestri, Carlo. *Turati l'ha detto*. Milan: Rizzoli, 1947.
Silvestri, Carlo. *Matteotti, Mussolini e il dramma italiano*. Rome: Ruffolo, 1947.
Silvestri, Carlo. *Contro la Vendetta*. Milan: Longanesi, 1948.
Silvestri, Carlo. *Mussolini, Graziani e l'antifascismo*. Milan: Longanesi, 1949.
Silvestri, Carlo. *I responsabili della catastrofe italiana*. Milan: CEBES, 1946.
Silvestri, Giuseppe. *Albergo agli Scalzi*. Verona: Neri Pozza, 1963.
Simiani, Carlo. *I giustiziati fascisti dell'aprile 1945*. Milan: Omnia, 1949.
Simoni, Leonardo. *Berlin, Ambassade d'italie (transl by C. D. Jonquière)*. Paris: Robert Laffont, 1947.
Sirghebo, Arcese. *Edda Ciano e il 25 luglio 1943*. Leghorn: Moderna, 1945.
Skorzeny, Otto. *Skorzeny's Secret Missions (transl by Jacques Le Clerq)*. New York: E. P. Dutton, 1950.
Slocombe, George. *The Dangerous Sea*. London: Hutchinson, 1938.
Slocombe, George. *A Mirror to Geneva*. London: Jonathan Cape, 1937.
Slocombe, George. *The Tumult and the Shouting*. London: Heinemann, 1936.
Soleri, Marcello. *Memorie*. Turin: Einaudi, 1949.
Spagnuolo, Giovanni. *Ceka fascista*. Rome: Ruffolo, 1947.
Spampanato, Bruno. *Contromemoriale (2 vols)*. Rome: 'L'illustrato', 1952.
Sperco, Willy. *L'Ecroulement d'une Dictature*. Paris: Hachette, 1946.
Sperco, Willy. *Tel fut Mussolini*. Paris: Fasquelle, 1955.
Spivak, J. L. *Europe under the Terror*. London: Victor Gollancz, 1936.
Sprigge, Cecil J. S. *The Development of Modern Italy*. London: Duckworth, 1943.
Starhemberg, Prince Ernst Rüdiger. *Between Hitler and Mussolini*. London: Hodder & Stoughton, 1942.
Starkie, Walter. *The Waveless Plain*. London: John Murray, 1938.
Steer, G. L. *Caesar in Abyssinia*. London: Hodder & Stoughton, 1936.
Steiner, H. A. *Government in Fascist Italy*. New York: McGraw Hill, 1938.
Stimson, Henry L. and Bundy, McGeorge. *On Active Service in Peace and War*. New York: Harper, 1948.
'Storicus'. *Le ultime giornate di Mussolini e di Claretta Petacci*. Edizioni dell'Unione, privately printed, nd.
Susmel, Duilio. *Vita sbagliata di Galeazzo Ciano*. Milan: Aldo Palazzi, 1962.
Susmel, Edoardo. *Mussolini e il suo tempo*. Milan: Garzanti, 1950.
Susmel, Edoardo and Duilio (eds). *Opera omnia di Benito Mussolini (23 vols)*. Florence: La Fenice, 1951–57.
Susmel, Edoardo and Duilio (eds). *Scritti e discorsi di Benito Mussolini (12 vols)*. Florence: La Fenice, 1934–39.
Sweet, P. R. *Mussolini and Dollfuss*. London: Victor Gollancz, 1948.
Tamaro, Attilio. *Due anni di storia, 1943–45*. Rome: Tosi, 1948.

Tamaro, Attilio. *Vent' anni di storia (3 vols)*. Rome: Tiber, 1954–55.
Tamassia, Mirella. *L'attesa nell'ombra*. Padua: Zanocco, 1946.
Tarchi, Angelo. *Teste dure*. Milan: SELC, 1967.
Tarsia in Curia, Angelo. *La verità sulle 'quattro giornate' di Napoli*. Naples: Genovese, 1950.
Tarsia in Curia, Antonino. *I Moti Insurrezionali al Vomero*. Naples: Industria Grafica Puteolana, nd.
Taylor, A. J. P. *The Origins of the Second World War*. London: Hamish Hamilton, 1961.
Terraneo, Sacr Ecclesio. *Il Servo di Dio, Cardinale Ildefonso Schuster*. Milan: Daverio, 1962.
Theodoli, Alberto. *A cavallo di due secoli*. Rome: La Navicella, 1950.
Thomas, Ivor. *Who Mussolini Is*. London: Oxford University Press, 1942.
Tiltman, Hessell. *The Terror in Europe*. London: Jarrolds, 1931.
Tompkins, Peter. *Italy Betrayed*. New York: Simon & Schuster, 1966.
Torsiello, Mario. *Settembre 1943*. Milan: Cisalpina, 1963.
Toscano, Mario. *Le origini diplomatiche del Patto d'Acciaio*. Florence: Sansoni, 1948.
Toscano, Mario. *Pagine di storia diplomatica contemporanea (2 vols)*. Milan: A. Giuffrè, 1963.
Tosti, Amedeo. *Pietro Badoglio*. Milan: Mondadori, 1956.
Trabucchi, Alessandro. *I vinti hanno sempre torto*. Turin: Francesco da Silva, 1947.
Trabucco, Carlo. *La prigionia di Roma*. Rome: SELI, nd.
Tregaskis, Richard. *Invasion Diary*. New York: Random House, 1944.
Trentin, Silvio. *L'Aventure Italienne*. Paris: Les Presses Universitaires de France, 1928.
Trevelyan, Janet. *Short History of the Italian People*. New York: Putnam, 1929.
Treves, Paolo. *What Mussolini Did to Us*. (transl by Casimiro Isolani). London: Victor Gollancz, 1940.
Trevor-Roper, H. R. *Hitler's Table Talk, 1941–44*. London: Weidenfeld & Nicolson, 1953.
Trizzino, Antonio. *Navi e poltrone*. Milan: Longanesi, edn of 1966.
Trizzino, Antonio. *Settembre nero*. Milan: Longanesi, 1959.
Tuninetti, Dante Maria. *La mia missione segreta in Austria*. Milan: CEBES, 1946.
Turchi, Franz. *Prefetto con Mussolini*. Rome: Latinità, 1950.
Tutaev, David. *The Consul of Florence*. London: Secker & Warburg, 1966.
Tuzet, Helene. *The Education of the Italian People*. London: Friends of Italian Freedom, 'Italy Today', October, 1931.
L'Università di Napoli incendiata dai Tedeschi. Naples: Gaetano Macchiaiolo, 1944.
Vailati, Vanna. *Badoglio racconta*. Turin: ILTE, 1955.
Vailati, Vanna. *Badoglio risponde*. Milan: Rizzoli, 1958.
Valera, Paolo. *Mussolini*. Milan: La Folla, 1924.
Valeri, Antonio. *La lotta politica in Italia dall'unità al 1925*. Florence: Le Monnier, 1945.
Valeri, Antonio. *Da Giolitti a Mussolini*. Florence: Parenti, 1956.
Valiani, Leo. *Tutte le strade conducono a Roma*. Florence: La Nuova Italia, 1947.
Valle, Giuseppe. *Pace e Guerra nei cieli*. Rome: Volpe, 1966.
Vansittart, Lord. *The Mist Procession*. London: Hutchinson, 1956.
Varè, Daniele. *The Two Impostors*. London: John Murray, 1949.
Varè, Daniele. *Laughing Diplomat*. London: John Murray, 1938.
Vaussard, Maurice. *La Conjuration du Grand Conseil Fasciste Contre Mussolini*. Paris: Editions Mondiales, 1965.
Veale, F. J. P. *Crimes Discreetly Veiled*. London: Cooper Book Co, 1958.
Vené, Gian Franco. *Il processo di Verona*. Milan: Mondadori, 1963.
Vento, G. and Mida, M. *Cinema e resistenza*. Florence: Luciano Landi, 1959.

Verné, Vittorio. *Quello che deve conoscere ogni camicia nera.* Rome: Libreria del Littorio, nd.
Viana, Mario. *La Monarchia ed il fascismo.* Rome: L'Arnia, 1951.
Vicentini, R. A. *Il movimento fascista veneto attraverso il diario di uno squadrista.* Venice: Acc. Stamperia Zanetti, 1938.
Vicoli, F. *Il condottiero di una flotta vittoriosa.* Milan: 'La Prora', 1934.
Villari, Luigi. *The Awakening of Italy.* London: Methuen, 1924.
Villari, Luigi. *The Fascist Experiment.* London: Faber & Gwyer, 1926.
Villari, Luigi. *Affari Esteri.* Rome: Magi-Spinetti, 1948.
Villari, Luigi. *Italian Foreign Policy under Mussolini.* Appleton, Wis: Nelson, 1956.
Villari, Luigi. *The Liberation of Italy.* Appleton, Wis: Nelson, 1959.
Vinciguerra, Mario. *Il fascismo visto da un solitario.* Florence: Le Monnier, 1923.
Vinciguerra, Mario. *I Partiti Italiani dal 1848 al 1955.* Rome: CEO, 1955.
Vivian, Herbert. *Fascist Italy.* London: Andrew Melrose, 1936.
Volta, Sandro. *Graziani a Neghelli.* Florence: Vallecchi, 1936.
Wagnière, George. *Dix-huit Ans à Rome.* Geneva: A. Jullien, nd.
Webster, Richard A. *The cross and the fasces.* Stanford, Calif: Stanford University Press, 1960.
Weizsäcker, Ernst von. *Memoirs (transl by John Andrew).* London: Gollancz, 1951.
Welles, Sumner. *A time for Decision.* New York: Harpers, 1944.
Westphal, Gen Siegfried. *The German Army in the West.* London: Cassell, 1951.
Whitaker, John T. *Fear Came on Europe.* London: Hamish Hamilton, 1937.
Whitaker, John T. *We Cannot Escape History.* New York: Macmillan, 1943.
Wilson, Sir A. *Walks and Talks Abroad.* London: Oxford University Press, 1939.
Wilson, Hugh. *A Diplomat Between Wars.* London: Longman's Green, 1941.
Wilstach, Paul. *An Italian Holiday.* New York: Harper, 1930.
Wiskemann, Elizabeth. *The Rome-Berlin Axis.* London: Oxford University Press, 1949.
Wiskemann, Elizabeth. *Italy.* London: Oxford University Press, 1947.
Zachariae, George. *Mussolini si confessa.* Milan: Garzanti, 1948.
Zanetti, Francesco. *Nella città del Vaticano.* Rome: Sallustiana, 1929.
Zangrandi, Ruggero. *Il lungo viaggio attraverso il fascismo.* Milan: Feltrinelli, 1962.
Zangrandi, Ruggero. *1943: 25 luglio – 8 – settembre.* Milan: Feltrinelli, 1964.
Zanussi, Gen Giacomo. *Guerra e catastrofe d'Italia (2 vols).* Rome: Corso, 1945.

Periodicals

Abbagnano, Marian Taylor. *The Collapse of Fascism in Italy,* in *Forum,* New York, July, 1949.
Adelfi, Nicola. *Lo sbarco delle truppe alleate in Sicilia fu l'ultimo colpo al regime già fradicio,* in *La Stampa,* Turin, 10 July, 1963.
Agnoletti, Enzo Enriques. *Il primo convengo nazionale del PDA; le giornate del crollo del regime a Firenze,* in *Avanti!,* Milan, 11 August, 1963.
Alatri, Paolo. *Roma tradita,* in *Aretusa,* Rome, October, 1945.
Alvaro, Corrado. *Quaderno,* in *Mercurio,* Rome, December, 1944.
Amicucci, Ermanno. *Mussolini respinse il piano Tamburini,* in *Tempo,* Milan, 13–20 May, 1950.
Andrea, Ugo d'. *Il lungo e drammatico regno di Vittorio Emanuele III,* in *L'Elefante,* Rome, February, 1950.
Gli archivi segreti di Mussolini nelle mani della commissione Alleata, in *Corriere della Sera,* Milan, December 15, 1946.
Arpino, Luigi. *Badoglio parla del 25 luglio,* in *Corriere d'Informazione,* Milan, 28–29 December, 1955.

Artieri, Giovanni. *Il Re si oppose alla soppressione di Mussolini*, in *Epoca*, Milan, 27 February, 1955.
Artieri, Giovanni. *I militari e il 25 luglio*, in *Il Borghese*, Milan, 12–26 March, 1959.
Artieri, Giovanni. *Nuovi documenti per interpretare più giustamente il 25 luglio*, in *Il Tempo*, Rome, 21–22 July, 1960.
Bovi, Vincenzo. *Un pecoraio del Gran Sasso*, in *Tempo*, Milan, April, 1954.
Bracker, Milton. *The Last Days of Mussolini*, in *The New York Times Magazine*, 24 April, 1955.
Brown, David. *The Inside Story of Italy's Surrender*, in *The Saturday Evening Post*, Philadelphia, September 9–16, 1944.
Bugialli, P. *Roma sotto le bombe*, in *Corriere d'informazione*, Milan, 19–20 July, 1963.
Cacciapuoti, Salvatore. *25 luglio in carcere*, in *Unità*, Milan, 25 July, 1959.
Cadorna, Gen Raffaele. *La Resistenza in Italia*, in *Storia Illustrata*, Milan, April, 1965.
Campana, Michele. *Un incontro segreto Mussolini-Hitler*, in *Meridiano d'Italia*, Milan, 11 October, 1951.
Canevari, Emilio. *Il Re, Grandi e Pietro Badoglio*, in *Meridiano d'Italia*, Milan, 12 October, 1952.
Canevari, Emilio. *Roberto Farinacci, l'uomo che ha detto la verità a Mussolini*, in *Meridiano d'Italia*, Milan, 15 July–12 August, 1958.
Canova, Giordano. *28 luglio 1943*, in *Unità*, Milan, 30 July, 1963.
Capozzi, Gennaro. *Quattro giorni di epopea*, in *Mercurio*, Rome, December, 1944.
Caudana, Mino. *Edda mi ha detto*, in *Oggi*, Milan, 24 June–22 July, 1947.
Cavalli, F., S. J. *Documentazione dell' opera di Pio XII per preservare l'Italia dalla guerra*, in *Civiltà Cattolica*, Rome, 16 June, 1945.
Cavallotti, Giovanni. *La caduta di Roma*, in *Oggi*, Milan, 28 August–11 September, 1958.
Cavicchioli, Luigi. *L'Impero fu fondato grazie all' Inghilterra*, in *Domenica del Corriere*, Milan, 23 January, 1968.
Cella, Gian-Riccardo. *Le ultime ore di Mussolini a Milano*, in *Il Popolo*, Milan, 2 May, 1945.
Ceroni, Guglielmo. *Parla Don Chiot*, in *Il Messaggero*, Rome, 11–16 September, 1948.
Cesarini, Mario. *La vita difficile del Maresciallo Badoglio*, in *Settimo Giorno*, Milan, 20 February–20 March, 1962.
Cesarini, Mario. *Il 25 luglio a Regina Coeli*, in *Il Mondo*, Rome, 31 July, 1962.
Cesarini, Paolo. *I misteriosi rapporti fra Vittorio Emanuele III e Badoglio*, in *Gazzetta del Popolo*, Turin, 14 December, 1958.
Che cos'era la 'Spia Acustica', in *Il Tempo*, Rome, 11–18 November, 1945.
Ciano, Countess Carolina. *Il mio Galeazzo*, in *Gente*, Milan, 23 October–11 December, 1957.
Ciano-Mussolini, Countess Edda. *La Mia Vita*, in *Insieme*, Rome, 6 February–19 March, 1950.
C. L. *Edda Mussolini a Lipari*, in *Italia Libera*, Rome, 21–22 September, 1945.
Cocco-Ortu, Francesco. *Il 29 Ottobre al Quirinale*, in *Il Ponte*, Rome, September–October, 1951.
Cohen, Israel. *Mussolini and the Jews*, in *The Contemporary Review*, London, December, 1938.
Come finì Mussolini, in *Corriere Lombardo*, Milan, 24 October–9 November, 1945.
Come fu che non giunsi in tempo per essere fucilato a Dongo, in *Meridiano d'Italia*, Milan, 1 December, 1946–16 February, 1947.
Le confessioni di Mussolini, in *Risorgimento Liberale*, Rome, 22 August, 1944.
Curti Cucciati, Elena & Angela. *Un' amica di Mussolini racconta*, in *Oggi*, Milan, 10 November–29 December, 1949.
De Benedetti, Giacomo. *16 ottobre 1943*, in *Mercurio*, Rome, December, 1944.

De Feo, Italo. *La preparazione del 25 luglio*, in *Il Resto del Carlino*, Bologna, 30 December, 1955.
Del Massa, Aniceto. *Gli ultimi giorni di Mussolini*, in *Settimana Incom*, Rome, 23–30 April, 1949.
De Mattei, Rodolfo. *Ingrato interregno*, in *Mercurio*, Rome, December, 1944.
De Vecchi, Cesare. *Mussolini Vero*, in *Tempo*, Milan, November, 1959–March, 1960.
Di Brizio, Giuseppe. *Della paura*, in *Mercurio*, Rome, December, 1944.
La difesa degli Ebrei, in *Il Tempo*, Rome, 15 September, 1945.
I Documenti segreti dell' archivio di Stato, in *Gazzetta Sera*, Turin, 13 September, 1955.
Dollmann, Eugen. *Diciotto mesi a Salò*, in *Storia Illustrata*, Milan, April, 1965.
Ducci, Roberto. *Morte e rinascita di una diplomazia*, in *Mercurio*, Rome, December, 1944.
Faiola, Lt Alberto. *Campo Imperatore: l'ordine fu di 'cedere senz'altro'*, in *Rinascita*, Rome, 20 July, 1963.
Ferruzza, Alfredo. *Le sensazionali rivelazioni del Duca d'Aosta*, in *Gente*, Milan, 19 February–12 March, 1969.
Fisher, Thomas. *Allied Military Government in Italy*, in *The Annals of the American Academy*. Philadelphia. Vol CCLXVII, January, 1950.
'Flavio'. *Gli anni decisivi: dal Fascismo alla Repubblica*, in *Corriere d'Informazione*, Milan, May 1959.
Floreanini, Franco. *Il 25 luglio in provincia*, in *Avanti!*, Milan, 28 July, 1963.
Fontanges, Magda. *My Love Affair with Mussolini*, in *Liberty Magazine*, New York, 10–24 August, 1940.
Fortuna, Alberto. *Incontro all' Arcivescovado*, in *Giornale di Bordo*, Florence, April–September, 1968.
Fossati, Luigi. *Quando i prefetti e i federali fascisti 'collaboravano' spiandosi a vicenda*, in *Avanti!*, Milan, 28 January, 1960.
François-Poncet, André. *Ciano et les derniers mois de l'avant-guerre*, in *Le Figaro*, Paris, 17 July, 1945.
François-Poncet, André. *François-Poncet rievoca la sua missione a Roma*, in *Corriere della Sera*, Milan, 16–25 October, 1960.
Gabrieli, Vittorio. *Settembre 1943*, in *Mercurio*, Rome, December, 1944.
Gonella, Guido. *Rivelazioni di Guariglia: il tragico agosto, 1943*, in *Il Popolo*, Milan, 24 November, 1945.
Gorla, Giuseppe. *Come si giunse al 25 luglio*, in *Il Tempo*, Rome, 6 January, 1959.
Grandi, Dino. *Dino Grandi Explains*, in *Life*, New York, 26 February, 1945.
Grandi, Dino. *Ecco Mussolini*, in *Epoca*, Milan, 18 April, 1965.
Gravina, Gino. *Ecco l'uomo che arrestò Mussolini*, in *Settimo Giorno*, Milan, 4 July, 1961.
Hazen, N. William. *Italian Agriculture under Fascism and War*, in *Foreign Agriculture*, Washington, Vol IV, No 11, November, 1940.
Hegner, H. S. *Dietro le quinte della cancelleria del Reich*, in *Il Giorno*, Milan, 13 September–24 October, 1959.
Hitler al convegno di Feltre, in *Il Popolo*, Milan. 28 October–4 November, 1945.
Invernizzi, Gabriele. *Dino Grandi tra il fez e la feluca*, in *Historia*, Milan, November, 1967.
L'Italia di Claretta Petacci, in *Il Giorno*, Milan, 24 February, 1968.
Josca, Pino. *L'uomo che arrestò Mussolini fa adesso il notaio a Catania*, in *Corriere della Sera*, Milan, 18 December, 1962.
Lajolo, Davide. *26 luglio, 1943*, in *Unità*, Milan, 18 November, 1962.
Lanfranchi, Ferruccio. *Clara Petacci al giudizio della storia*, in *Oggi*, Milan, 19 December, 1948–24 March, 1949.
Lazzero, Ricciotti. *Un passo verso la verità sulla morte di Mussolini*, in *Epoca*, Milan, 11–25 August, 1968.

Levi, Carlo. *25 luglio in prigione*, in *La Stampa*, Turin, 25 July, 1959.
Livi, Augusto. *Il nuovo motto è: 'Sganciarsi'*, in *Paese Sera*, Rome, 23 July, 1963.
Longhi, Oreste. *Il conto della spesa di Valerio*, in *Visto*, Milan, 15 June, 1957.
Longo, Giuseppe. *Giornate bolognesi*, in *Mercurio*, Rome, December, 1944.
Lualdi, Maner. *La parte dei militari nel 25 luglio e nell' 8 settembre*, in *Corriere della Sera*, Milan, 11 March, 1955.
Luraghi, Raimondo. *Incontro col Gen Ambrosio*, in *Unità*, Milan, 22 October, 1953.
Magini, Manlio. *La pupilla del Duce*, in *Il Mondo*. Rome, 26 March, 1957.
Maria José of Savoy. (with Giacomo Maugeri). *La Mia Vita nella mia Italia*, in *Oggi*, Milan, 13 November, 1958–1 January, 1959.
Massola, Umberto. *Premesse e sviluppi degli scioperi di marzo–aprile 1943*, in *Mercurio*, Rome, December, 1944.
Meissner, Hans Otto. *A Milano con Mussolini*, in *Il Nazionale*, Rome, 29 August, 1951.
Minardi, Alessandro & Di Lorenzo, Carlo. *La verità sul processo di Verona*, in *L'Europeo*, Milan, 9 October–4 December, 1955.
Monelli, Paolo. *Documentario di Piazzale Loreto*, in *Epoca Quotidiana*, Rome, 21 May, 1945.
Monelli, Paolo. *La Favorita*, in *Tempo*, Milan, November 1947–January, 1948.
Monelli, Paolo. *L'arresto di Mussolini a Villa Ada*, in *La Nuova Stampa*, Turin, 28 December, 1955.
Monelli, Paolo. *Mussolini da Milano a Dongo*, in *Storia Illustrata*, Milan, April, 1965.
Monelli, Paolo. *Le previsioni segrete di Mussolini sulla guerra*, in *Epoca*, Milan, 27 March, 1955.
Monicelli, Franco. *Doppio gioco*, in *Mercurio*, Rome, December, 1944.
Monicelli, Franco. *I processi del dopoguerra*, in *L'Espresso*, Rome, 24 January, 1960.
Monicelli, Mino. *1938*, in *Il Giorno*, Milan, 4–13 February, 1968.
Montagna, Gen Renzo. *Cento colloqui con Mussolini*, in *Oggi*, Milan, 19 June–17 July, 1958.
Montanelli, Indro. *Rivelazioni di Dino Grandi sull' arresto di Mussolini*, in *Corriere della Sera*, Milan, 9 February, 1955.
Mors, Hans. *Le SS Otto Skorzeny a menti*, in *Curieux*, Berne, 14 December, 1950.
Nicolosi, Salvatore. *La verità sull' arresto di Mussolini*, in *Visto*, Milan, 1 August, 1959.
Nozzoli, Guido. *9 miti e figure del Ventennio*, in *Il Giorno*, Milan, 11 September–7 October, 1963.
Nozzoli, Guido. *Roatta: Attraversò la bufera senza bagnarsi mai*, in *Il Giorno*, Milan, 10 January, 1968.
Ori, Angiolo Silvio. *Perchè gli Americani non riuscirono a catturare Mussolini*, in *Visto*, Milan, 28 April, 1956.
Orlando, Ruggero. *Che cosa vogliono, questi inglesi?*, in *Mercurio*, Rome, December, 1944.
Pancino, Don Giusto. *Tentai di riconciliare Edda Ciano e Mussolini*, in *Oggi*, Milan, 22 September, 1954.
Parini, Piero. *La giornata del 28 ottobre nei ricordi di un cronista*, in *Roma*, 28 October, 1933.
Pecci, Corrado. *Mussolini, il Re, e Badoglio*, in *Il Borghese*, Milan, 17 February 1956.
Pellegrini-Giampietro, Domenico. *Colloquio in agosto, 1943, con Umberto di Savoia*, in *Il Secolo d'Italia*, Rome, 15 September, 1960.
Pellegrini-Giampietro, Domenico. *La convulsa e vibrante vigilia che porto alla fondazione della RSI*, in *Il Secolo d'Italia*, Rome, 24 November, 1960.
Pellicano, Italo. *I superstiti del Gran Consiglio si sono decisi a parlare*, in *L'Elefante*, Rome, 13 October–17 November, 1950.

'Penelope'. *Dal bombardamento di Roma alla congiura del 25 luglio*, in *Il Secolo d'Italia*, Rome, 24 April, 1962.

Pensotti, Anita. *Edda Ciano parla per la prima volta*, in *Oggi*, Milan, 3–25 September, 1959.

Persico, Giovanni. *Giornate di settembre*, in *Mercurio*, Rome, December, 1944.

Petacci, Myriam. *Dopo sedici anni una testimonianza definitiva*, in *Oggi*, Milan, 2 March–18 May, 1961.

Polverelli, Gaetano. *Dalla campagna d'Etiopia al colpo di stato* in *Tempo*, Milan, 27 September–29 November, 1952.

Radius, Emilio & Cavallotti, Giovanni. *Dino Grandi racconta*, in *Oggi*, Milan, 7 May–4 June, 1959.

Roberto, D. *26 luglio a Ventotene*, in *La Voce Repubblicana*, Rome, 25 July, 1956.

Romersa, Luigi. *Sull' arresto di Mussolini tutta la verità è ancora da dire*, in *Tempo*, Milan, 19 July–2 August, 1956.

Romersa, Luigi. *J'ai vu exploser la bombe atomique de Hitler!*', in *L'Intransigeant*, Paris, 19 November, 1955.

Rossi, Cesare. *I retroscena della marcia su Roma*, in *Epoca Quotidiana*, Rome, Nos 25–28, 1949.

Russo, Luigi. *La nascita del Fascismo*, in *Bellagor*, Messalina, 31 March, 1961.

Saini, Ezio. *Operazione Albania*, in *Settimo Giorno*, Milan, 5–26 May, 1960.

Saini, Ezio. *Una tragedia Italiana*, in *Settimo Giorno*, Milan, 30 July–27 August, 1959.

Saini, Ezio. *I documenti segreti del Maresciallo Caviglia*, in *Settimo Giorno*, Milan, 27 March–17 April, 1962.

Salvadori-Paleotti, Massimo. *The Last Hours in Milan with the Resistance*, in *The Commonweal*, New York, Vol LXIII, 1946.

Salvemini, Gaetano. *Pietro Badoglio's Role in the Second World War*, in *Journal of Modern History*, Chicago, Vol XX, 1949.

Salvemini, Gaetano. *Mussolini e l'oro francese*, in *Il Mondo*, Rome, 7 January, 1950.

Savinio, Alberto. *Uomini bianchi*, in *Mercurio*, Rome, December, 1944.

Scaroni, Gen Silvio. *Confidenze segrete di Vittorio Emanuele III*, in *Epoca*, Milan, 19 July–6 September, 1953.

Scorza, Carlo. *La notte del Gran Consiglio*, in *Tempo*, Milan, 11 June–3 September, 1968.

Serena, Maria Antonietta. *Mussolini a Trento, 1909*, in *Historia*, Milan, June, 1968.

Serra, Franco. *L'Italia è restituta a Dio*, in *Oggi*, 19–26 December, 1968.

Smyth, Howard McGaw. *Italy: From Fascism to the Republic*, in *The Western Political Quarterly*, Salt Lake City, September, 1948.

Soleti, Gen Fernando. *Come Mussolini fu liberato da Campo Imperatore*, in *Avanti!*, 19 July, 1944.

Storia segreta della guerra, in *Milano Sera*, Milan, 11–14 September, 1945.

Susmel, Duilio. *Un uomo ebbe le confessioni di Claretta Petacci*, in *Visto*, Milan, 6 October–10 November, 1956.

Susmel, Duilio. *Mussolini al telefono*, in *Oggi*, Milan, 12 November–3 December, 1959.

Susmel, Duilio. *Processo a Benito Mussolini*, in *Oggi*, Milan, 2 June–28 July, 1960.

Susmel, Duilio. *Il 25 luglio raccontato dai protagonisti*, in *Tempo*, Milan, 8–29 June, 1963.

Susmel, Duilio. *Mussolini non fu tradito*, in *Domenica del Corriere*, Milan, 5–19 March, 1968.

Susmel, Duilio. *Nuovi documenti sul tentato suicidio del Duce dopo l'8 settembre*, in *Domenica del Corriere*, Milan, 17–24 September, 1968.

Susmel, Duilio. *La storia d'amore di Claretta Petacci*, in *Gente*, Milan, 9 October–27 November, 1968.

Susmel, Duilio. *L'infedelissimo fedele*, in *Domenica del Corriere*, Milan, 18 February–18 March, 1969.
Tarchi, Angelo. *Cronaca inedita del 25 luglio*, in *Secolo XX*, Milan, 30 July–7 August, 1963.
Tedeschi, Rubens. *A Dongo l'ultimo atto*, in *Unità*, Rome, 25 April, 1965.
Tedeschi, Rubens. *I retroscena dell' insurrezione che gli alleati non volevano*, in *Unità*, Rome, 25 April, 1967.
Tiberti, Enzo. *Tutta la verità sulla cattura e sulla morte di Mussolini*, in *Visto*, Milan, October–November, 1956.
Tomajuoli, Gino. *La difesa tradita*, in *Mercurio*, Rome, December, 1944.
Traglia, Gustavo. *Il gioco delle sorti nel processo di Verona*, in *La Patria*, Florence, 7 September–18 October, 1947.
Traglia, Gustavo. *Dal 25 luglio al carcere degli Scalzi*, in *Libertà*, Piacenza, 18 January, 1956.
Travi, Colonel. *Agonia di un regime*, in *L'Italia Libera*, Rome, 17–28 February, 1946.
Trionfera, Renzo. *L'orecchio del Duce*, in *L'Europeo*, Milan, 29 April–27 May. 1956.
Trionfera, Renzo & Frascani, Arnaldo. *Come uccidemmo Matteotti*, in *L'Europeo*, Milan, 11 January, 1968.
Trionfera, Renzo. *Addio alla corona*, in *L'Europeo*, Milan, 15 February–7 March, 1968.
Trionfera, Renzo. *Castellano spiega il 25 luglio*, in *L'Europeo*, Milan, 1 August, 1968.
Vaccaro, Nicola. *Le ultime ore di Mussolini sul Lario*, in *Il Popolo*, Milan, 24–26 October, 1945.
Vailati, Vanna. *Ingiuste le accuse dell' ex Re Umberto*, in *Gazzetta del Popolo*, Turin, 27 December, 1958.
Valori, Aldo. *Perduti 120 mila uomini nella difesa della Sicilia*, in *L'Europeo*, Milan, 29 May, 1955.
Vergani, Orio. *Davo del 'tu' a Ciano*, in *Omnibus*, Milan, 15 July, 1948–31 March, 1949.
La verità sul processo di Verona, in *Avanti!*, Milan, 11 September–12 October, 1945.
La verità sull'ultima seduta del Gran Consiglio, in *Italia Nuova*, Rome, 9–24 July, 1944.
La verità sul 25 luglio, in *Vita*, Rome, 11 July–29 August, 1963.
Vené, Gianfranco. *L'homme qui exécuta Ciano*, in *Le Figaro Littéraire*, Paris, 18–25 March.
Vianini, Italo (with Anita Pensotti). *Dopo diciannove anni rompe il silenzio l'uomo che fu costretto a prendere la decisione suprema*, in *Oggi*, Milan, 24–31 January, 1963.
'Waverley'. *Viaggio in Spagna con Ciano*, in *Il Borghese*, Milan, 27 March–10 April, 1958.
Wolff, Gen Karl. *Ecco la verità*, in *Tempo*, Milan, January–February, 1951.

Manuscript Sources

(Unless otherwise stated, these are microfilms furnished by US National Archives.)

Abyssinia: Dispute Between Italy and Abyssinia. British Foreign Office Records, FO 371/18847 and 19113. (*Public Record Office, London*).
Albonetti, Col Fortunato. Narrative of Rome on 8 September, 1943. (Job 141, Frames 040223–28).
Alfieri, Dino. Letter to Benito Mussolini, 15 September, 1943. (Roll T 586, Frames 000644–48).

Badoglio, Marshal Pietro. Confidential Police Reports Concerning. 1934–43. (Job 132, Frames 036804–945).
Balbo, Marshal Italo. Secret Police Reports Concerning. 1934. (Job 109, Frames 029987–8).
Balbo, Marshal Italo. Secret Police Reports Concerning. 1937–8. (Job 129, Frames 035467–584).
Bruni, Gaetano. Narrative of 25 April, 1945, in Milan; unpublished MSS. (*Courtesy Gaetano Bruni.*)
Castellani, Father Armando. Narrative of the San Lorenzo bombing, 19 July, 1943; unpublished MSS. (*Courtesy Father Castellani.*)
Chirico, Lt-Col Ettore. Narrative of the Proceedings at Legnano Barracks, 25 July, 1943. (*Courtesy Lt-Col Chirico.*)
Ciano-Mussolini, Countess Edda. Correspondence with Benito Mussolini, and confidential police reports concerning. 1929–44. (Job 109, Frames 029647–686).
Costa, Vincenzo. Diary, 1944–5: unpublished MSS. (*Courtesy Comm. Vincenzo Costa.*)
De Bono, Marshal Emilio. Police reports concerning. (Job 126, Frames 035047–66.)
De Bono, Marshal Emilio. Documents concerning the Scalera scandal, 1937. (Job 125, Frames 034620–799).
Della Pietra, Ettore. Mussolini in Carnia, 1906–7; the Carnia Redoubt; Mussolini as a combatant in Carnia: unpublished memoranda. (*Courtesy Sra. Maria Della Pietra*).
Dumini, Amerigo. Memoirs: unpublished MSS. (Roll T 586, Frames 010606–756.)
Dumini, Amerigo. Secret Police Reports and Correspondence Concerning. 1926–37. (Job 222, Frames 056795–057048.)
Farinacci, Roberto. Police Reports on and Intercepted Telephone Calls, 1935–43. (Job 122, Frames 033870–956).
Farinacci, Roberto. Correspondence with Benito Mussolini and Reports Concerning. 1924–33. (Job 111–13, Frames 030746–031415.)
Gay, Silvio. Memoranda to Benito Mussolini, 1943–4. (Job 262, Frames 072908–073104.)
Grandi, Count Dino. Miscellaneous Correspondence with Benito Mussolini and Count Ciano, 1924–41. (Job 15, Frames 006832–84; Job 54, Frames 026710–999.)
Graziani, Marshal Rodolfo. Private Diary, 21 January–28 April, 1945. (Job 118, Frames 032161–032333.)
Gueli, Inspector Giuseppe. Narrative of Events at Gran Sasso, 31 August–12 September, 1943. (Job 103, Frames 027703–717.)
Iraci, Agostino. Autobiography: unpublished MSS. (*Courtesy Hon. Agostino Iraci.*)
Kayser, Bruno von. Narrative of the Liberation of Mussolini from Gran Sasso, 1943. (Job 170, Frames 050138–46.)
Matteotti, Giacomo. Letters and Documents Concerning. 1924–7. (Job 33, Frames 016616–754).
Matteotti, Giacomo. Police reports and witnesses' depositions concerning assassination (5 vols). (*Courtesy, Chief Librarian, London School of Economics.*)
Mussolini, Benito. Memorandum Concerning the Strike of 1944. (Roll T 586, Frames 000730–756.)
Mussolini, Benito. Memoranda and situation reports concerning the situation in Valtellina, 1944. (Roll T 586, Frames 000893–946.)
Mussolini, Benito & Petacci, Claretta. Miscellaneous Correspondence, 1938–43. (Job 53, Frames 026456–026491).
Mussolini, Benito. Schedule of Bonds and Private Shareholdings, 1930–41. (Job 227, Frames 058910–944.)
Mussolini, Benito. Miscellaneous Expense Accounts, plus Stocks and Shares, 1942–4. (Job 108, Frames 029729–738.)

Mussolini, Benito. Financial Statements and Securities, Banca d'Italia, 1943–5. (Job 103, Frames 027677–702.)

Negri, Ada. Letters to Benito Mussolini, 1923–42. (Job 252, Frames 068738–97.)

Parini, Piero. Memoranda of the Prefect of Milan to Benito Mussolini, January-August, 1944. (Job 328, Frames 112475–506.)

Pavolini, Alessandro. Letters to Benito Mussolini, 1944–5. (Job 221, Frames 056377–493.)

Rahn, Ambassador Rudolf. Letters and Memoirs exchanged with Benito Mussolini, 1944–5. (Job 231, Frames 060969–061413.)

Renzetti, Major Giuseppe. Reports from Berlin on Adolf Hitler and the National Socialist Party, 1931–3. (Job 170, Frames 050253–276.)

Rosso, Ambassador. Rome Diary, September 1943: unpublished MSS. (Job 306, Frames 097831–857.)

Turati, Augusto. Confidential Reports Concerning. 1932. (Job 109, Frames 029837–57.)

Vaselli, Giuseppe. Letters to Benito Mussolini and Police Reports Concerning. (Job 252, Frames 068836–850.)

Not listed above are battle orders, stenographic reports of Palazzo Venezia conferences, selections from interrogation reports and OSS records and other extensive documentation supplied to the author by the US National Archives and the National Records Centre.

The Eye-Witnesses
and what they do today

The 454 men and women listed below provided the hard core of fact on which this book is based. While some furnished contemporary letters and diaries or specially-written accounts, most of them submitted themselves patiently to question-and-answer interviews. To avoid confusion, ranks, and in some cases, names, are those which pertained during the specific period which he or she described.

Occupations listed are as at time of going to press. Where a name is placed in square brackets, it indicates that a contributor has died since this list was compiled.

The Italians

Parri, Ferruccio ('Uncle Maurizio'). Joint-Commander, Volunteer Freedom Corps: 1944–5. *President of the Council of Ministers: 1945; President of Senate, Italian Socialist Party, Rome.*

Abbate, Lieut Giovanni. Naples, Campo Sportivo: 27 September–1 October, 1943. *Railway inspector, Naples.*

Albini, Umberto. Under-Secretary for Home Affairs, February–July, 1943. *Real-estate administrator, Rome.*

[Alessi, Rino. Forlimpopoli Municipal College (Romagna): 1900–1. *Newspaper proprietor, Trieste.*]

Aliprandi, Capt Giovanni. Chief of Cabinet, Minister of Navy: July, 1943. *Admiral, retd, Rome.*

Almirante, Giorgio. Chief of Secretariat, Ministry of Popular Culture, Salò Republic: March 1944–April 1945. *Secretary, Italian Social Movement, Rome; Deputy, Rome.*

Amendola, Giorgio ('Giorgio'). Regional Organizer, Committee of National Liberation, Emilia: June 1944–April 1945. *Directorate, Italian Communist Party, Rome; Deputy, Naples.*

Amici, Mario. March on Rome: Fascist Party HQ, Piazza Barberini, Rome. *Bookseller, Rome.*

Amici, Michele. March on Rome: Fascist Party HQ, Piazza Barberini, Rome. *Accountant, Rome.*

Amodeo, Galliano. March on Rome: 39th (Neapolitan) Legion, Caserta. *Marine Engineer, Ancona.*

Antonioli, Federico. March on Rome: 'Me ne strafrego' Squad, Cremona. *Clerk, Cremona.*

Antonioli, Mario. Cremona: Private Secretary, Roberto Farinacci, 1922–45. *Retd., Cremona.*

Arenare, Luigi. Naples, via Salvator Rosa: 27 September–1 October, 1943. *Municipal employee, Naples.*

Argenton, Maj Mario ('Pollini'). Milan, Palazzo Cusani: Volunteer Freedom Corps, 25–29 April, 1945. *Lawyer, Rome.*

Armellini, Gen Quirino. Supreme General Staff, Rome: 1940. *Gen, retd, Rome.*

Arnone, Antonio. Milan: 'Avanti!': 1912–14. *Journalist, Palermo.*

Arpesani, Giustino ('Alessandro Giovannelli'). Milan, Palazzo Cusani: Liberal

Party Delegate, Committee of National Liberation, April 1945. *Ambassador to the Argentine Republic: 1946-55; Ambassador to Mexico: 1955-60; advocate, Turin.*

Arpinati, Giancarla. Bologna: Villa Malacappa, 1923-32. *Housewife, Milan.*

Ascione, Sgt Maj Emilio. Nembo Parachute Division, Reggio Calabria: 25 July, 1943. *Occupation unknown, Naples.*

Astoli, Giulio Agostino. Milan, Piazzale Loreto: 29 April, 1945. *Lawyer, Milan.*

Baglia-Bambergi, Count Mario. Director, Italrayon: 1923-43. *President, Institute of Italian Brewers, Varese.*

Balbo, Countess Emanuela. Tripoli, Libya, Governor's Palace: 1934-40. *Independent, Rome.*

Balella, Giovanni. President, Fascist Federation of Industrialists: May-July, 1943. *Financier, Milan.*

Balzerano, 2nd Lieut Antonio. Naples, San Potito: 27 September-1 October, 1943. *Director, municipal publicity, Naples.*

Barberini, Ennio. March on Rome: 1st Grosseto Legion, Civitavecchia. *Agricultural administrator, nr Grosseto.*

Barbieri, Ezio. March on Rome: 'Francesco Gozzi' Squad, Ferrara. *Municipal employee, retd, Ferrara.*

Bartoli, Novello. March on Rome: 'Giuseppe Salvestrini' Action Squad, Monterotondo. *Tractor tyre salesman, Pontedera (nr Pisa).*

Barzini, Luigi. Rome: 'Corriere della Sera', 1934-43. *Deputy, Italian Liberal Party, Milan; author.*

Bassi, Mario. Prefect of Milan: May 1944-April 1945. *Lawyer, Rome.*

Bega, Ferruccio. Milan, Pirelli Factory: 25-29 April, 1945. *Factory fireman, retd, Milan.*

Bellinetti, Pino. March on Rome: Commandant, Polesana Legion, Rovigo. *Art gallery proprietor, Rovigo.*

Bellini delle Stelle, Count Pierluigi ('Pedro'). Dongo: Commandant, 52nd Garibaldi Brigade, 25-29 April, 1945. *Public relations officer, petroleum company, Milan.*

[Benedetti, Giulio. Milan: Chief of National Union of Journalists, Salò Republic, 1943-45. *Journalist, Sanremo.*]

Benigni, Gino. Rome, San Lorenzo: 19 July, 1943. *Housepainter, Rome.*

Benigni, Tagliola, Rosa. Rome, San Lorenzo: 19 July, 1943. *Hospital nurse, Rome.*

Benso Civitelli, Loris. Chieri: 25 July, 1943. *Electrical inspector, retd, Turin.*

Benzoni, Marchioness Giuliana. Rome: Palazzo del Quirinale, 1942-43. *Independent, Rome.*

Beolchini, Lieut Col Aldo ('Col. Bianchi'). Milan, Palazzo Cusani: Intelligence Department, Volunteer Freedom Corps. *General, War Graves Commission, Rome.*

Berti, Ezio. Naples, Central Police HQ: 25 July, 1943. *Hairdresser, Udine.*

Bertozzi, Capt Renzo. Valtellina: Italian Security Services, 22-29 April, 1945. *Insurance executive, retd, Venice.*

Besi, Delia. Rome, San Lorenzo: 19 July, 1943. *Housewife, Rome.*

Betteri, Luigi. Verona Trial: Defence Counsel: 8-11 January, 1944. *Lawyer, Verona.*

Bicchierai, Don Giuseppe. Milan. Archbishop's Palace: 24-29 April, 1945. *Monsignor, Milan.*

Bignardi, Annio. President, Agricultural Workers' Federation: December 1941-July 1943. *Executive, Alfa Romeo, Ferrara; Deputy, Italian Liberal Party, Bologna.*

Bonelli, Gerardo. March on Rome: Chief of Action Squads, Genoa. *Industrialist, Milan.*

Bonetti, Lieut Vittorio. Como/Milan: OSS 'Daddario' Mission, 27-29 April, 1945. *Real estate developer, Elba.*

Bonfantini, Corrado ('Corrado'). Milan: Commandant 8th Matteotti Brigade, 25–29 April, 1945. *Doctor, Milan.*

Boni, Brigadier Alfredo. March on Rome: Central Police HQ, Bologna. *Marshal of Police, retd, Bologna.*

Bonomo, Maria. Rome, San Lorenzo: 19 July, 1943. *Widow, Rome.*

Boratto, Ercole. Rome: Presidential chauffeur, 1922–43. *Retd, nr Pinerolo.*

Borghese, Prince Junio Valerio. Commandant, 10th Torpedo Boat Flotilla, Lonato (Lombardy). *Political organizer, Rome.*

[Bottelli, Giorgio. March on Rome: Brufani Palace Hotel, Perugia. *Director, Brufani's, Perugia.*]

Bottiglieri, Capt Sabatino. RIN La Spezia/Malta: 'Italia', 8–9 September, 1943. *Admiral, retd, Rome.*

Bozzello, Mario. Naples, Ponte della Sanità: 27 September–1 October, 1943. *Film distribution executive, Naples.*

Brambilla, Luigi. Milan, Magneti Marelli Plant: 25–29 April, 1945. *Aircraft engine inspector, Ravagnate (Lombardy).*

Brandimarte, Lieut Piero. March on Rome: Chief of Action Squads, Turin. *Gen of Militia, retd, Turin.*

Brivonesi, Admiral Bruto. Taranto: Officer Commanding, Naval Base, September 1943. *Retd, Rome.*

Bruni, Gaetano. Milan, Archbishop's Palace: 25 April, 1945. *Executive, Snia Viscosa, Milan.*

Bruni, Capt Pio ('Paolo Bardi'). Milan, Piazzale Loreto: 29 April, 1945. *Banker, Milan.*

Brunialti, Antonio. March on Rome: 'Giovanni Berta' Squad, Genoa. *Ship's furnisher, Genoa.*

Bruno, Enzo. Naples, Vomero: 27 September–1 October, 1943. *Baker, Naples.*

Bruno, Renato. March on Rome: 'Cantore' Group, Milan. *War disabled, Milan.*

Bruschelli, Galliano. March on Rome: 'La Panni lunghi' Squad, Siena, Monte-rotondo Column. *Rural administrator, Siena.*

Buronzo, Vincenzo. President, International Federation of Artisans, 1927–43. *Senator, retd, Recco.*

Caccese, 2nd Lieut Francesco. 33rd Battalion, 11th Bersaglieri Regt: 1915–17. *President of Chamber of Commerce, retd, Gorizia.*

Caddeo, Brigadier Giovanni. Zagreb: Counter-Espionage Service, Italian Consulate, 1943–45. *Retd, Salò.*

Cadorna, Gen Raffaele ('Valenti') Milan: Military Commander, Committee of National Liberation, August 1944–April 1945. *Senator, Pallanza (Novara).*

Calza-Bini, Gino. March on Rome: Fascist Party HQ, Piazza Barberini, Rome. *Poet, Frascati.*

Caneschi, Maria. March on Rome: Arezzo. *Housewife, Arezzo.*

Canzi, Egidio. Milan, Piazzale Loreto: 29 April, 1945. *Factory employee, Milan.*

Capozzi, Gennaro. Naples, Museum district: 27 September–1 October, 1943. *Municipal assessor, Naples.*

Capuozzo, Anna. Naples, Materdei: 27 September–1 October, 1943. *Housewife, Naples.*

Carboni, Gen Giacomo. Rome: Chief of Military Intelligence, 1939–40. *General, retd, Rome.*

Carell, Ghitta. Rome: 1922–43. *Portrait photographer, Rome.*

Carpineti, Anita. Rome, San Lorenzo: 19 July, 1943. *Unemployed, Rome.*

Castellano, Ferdinando. Naples, Ponte della Sanità: 27 September–1 October, 1943. *Butcher, retd, Naples.*

Castellano, Gen Giuseppe. Rome, Palazzo Vidoni: Assistant Chief of General Staff, January–August, 1943; Cassibile (Syracuse): September 1943. *Gen, retd, Rome.*

Castelli, Aldo ('Aldo'). Dongo: 52nd Garibaldi Brigade, 25–29 April, 1945. *Hotel-keeper, Domaso.*

Cencelli Orsolini, Count Valentino. Rome, Commissioner for Reclamation of the Pontine Marshes: 1930–35. *Vice President, General Confederation of Italian Agriculture, Rome.*

Cenedella, Maria. Brescia: 25 July, 1943. *Housewife, nr Udine.*

Cerasuolo, Maddalena. Naples, Vico Trone; Ponte della Sanità: 27 September–1 October, 1943. *Tobacco factory worker, Naples.*

[Cersosimo, Vincenzo. Verona Trial: Instructing Judge, 8–11 January, 1944. *Lawyer, retd, Ausonia.*]

Chiappa, Carlo. Milan, Borletti Factory: 25–29 April, 1945. *Factory operative, Milan.*

Chirico, Dr Aldo. La Maddalena (Sardinia): August 1943. *Doctor, La Maddalena.*

Chirico, Lieut Col Ettore. Rome: Vice Commandant, via Legnano Carabinieri Barracks, 25–29 July, 1943. *Cavalry instructor, Cagliari.*

Chiurco, Lieut. Giorgio. March on Rome: Siena Legion, Monterotondo Column. *Professor, Pre-cancer research Institute, Rome.*

Cianetti, Tullio. President, Fascist Confederation of Industrial Workers, 1938; Minister of Corporations, 1943. *Import-export, Mozambique.*

Ciano, Raimonda ('Dindina'). Ponte a Moriano: 25 July, 1943; Schloss Hirschberg, Germany; July–November 1943. *Independent, Rome.*

Ciano, Spartaco. March on Rome: Pistoia Legion, Monterotondo Column. *Occupation unknown, Lucca.*

Cibelli, Arturo. March on Rome: 'Falcons' Squad, Caserta. *Postal Worker, retd, Naples.*

Cimini, Anna. Rome, San Lorenzo: 19 July, 1943. *Housewife, Rome.*

Cirillo, Giuseppe ('Cirillo'). Milan, via Moscova: Communications Section, Volunteer Freedom Corps, 25–29 April, 1945. *Shipyard representative, Genoa.*

Cirincione, Marshal Damiano. Naples, San Potito, Carabinieri Barracks: 25 July, 1943. *Carabiniere, Naples.*

Ciurlo, Luca. March on Rome: 'Benito Mussolini' Squad, Genoa. *Lawyer, Genoa.*

Coltellini, Rodolfo. Rome, San Lorenzo: 19 July, 1943. *Petroleum executive, Rome.*

Cominotto, Furio. 49th ('San Marco') Battalion, Rome: 19–25 July, 1943. *Commercial syndicate, Venice.*

Comuzio, Capt Angelo. 27th Battalion, 11th Bersaglieri: August 1915–17. *Railway employee, retd, Lecco.*

Conti, Luciano. Milan, Innocenti Factory: 25–29 April, 1945. *Free-lance technologist, Milan.*

Conticelli, Gen Giuseppe. Deputy Chief of Staff, Militia HQ, Piazza Romania: 25–26 July, 1943. *Newspaper proprietor, Rome.*

Corbino, Epicarmo. Minister of Food, Badoglio Government: 1943–44. *Professor of Political Economy, retd, Naples University.*

Cordazzo, Giuseppina. Giulino di Mezzegra, Villa Belmonte: 28 April, 1945. *Small-holder, nr Udine.*

Corradi, Rosalino. March on Rome: 'Tenace' Squad, Cremona. *Janitor, Cremona.*

Corsi, Fausta, Rome, San Lorenzo: 19 July, 1943. *Factory accountant, Rome.*

Coscelli, Progresso. Milan, Pirelli Factory: 25–29 April, 1945. *Janitor, Milan.*

Costa, Flaminio. March on Rome: Deputy Chief of Action Squads, Genoa. *Lawyer, Milan.*

Costa, Giuseppina. Milan, Face Standard Plant: 25–29 April, 1945. *Socialist Party organizer, Meda (Lombardy).*

Costa, Vincenzo. Federal Secretary, Milan: 1944–45. *Charity Organiser, Salò Republic Ex-Combatants Association, Como.*

Craighero, Umberto. March on Rome: Lendinara Legion, Verona. *Banker, retd, Milan.*

D'Aloia, Capt Temistocle. Genoa/Malta: 'Duca d'Aosta', 9 September, 1943. *Admiral, retd, Rome.*

D'Aroma, Nino. Federal Secretary, Rome: 1929–33. *Author, Rome.*

Da Mondovi', Don Nicola. Rome, San Lorenzo: 19 July, 1943. *Franciscan Priory of San Lorenzo, Rome.*

Dal Torso, Count Germanico. Berlin: First Secretary, Italian Embassy, 1940–45. *Estate owner, Udine.*

Dal Verme, Count Luchino. ('Maino'). Milan, Palazzo Cusani: Battalion Commander, Outer-Po Pavese Division, 26–29 April, 1945. *Broiler chicken expert, Milan.*

De Majo, Giuseppina. Milan, Piazzale Loreto: 29 April, 1945. *Hospital nurse, Naples.*

De Maria, Lia. Giulino di Mezzegra: 28 April, 1945. *Smallholder, Giulino di Mezzegra.*

De Marsanich, Augusto. March on Rome: Bottai Column, 1922; Under-Secretary of Communications: 1935–43. *Senator; President, Italian Social Movement, Rome.*

De Marsico, Alfredo. Minister of Justice: February–July, 1943. *Lawyer, Naples.*

[De Stefani, Alberto. Minister of Finance: October 1922–25. *Senator, Rome.*]

Del Gatto, Pte Bruno. 8th Engineering Battalion, Settebagni; July 25, 1943. *Occupation unknown, Rome.*

Del Giudice, Riccardo. Under-Secretary for National Education, December 1939–February 1943. *Legal adviser, shipping company, Rome.*

Del Prete, 2nd Lieut Dino. Naples, Ponte della Sanità: 27 September–1 October, 1943. *Lawyer, Naples.*

Della Pietra, Maria. Brescia: 1944–45. *Widow, Tolmezzo.*

Dellera, Erminio. ('Pierino'). 52nd Garibaldi Brigade, Germasino, Finance Guard Barracks: 27 April, 1945. *Publisher's representative, Como.*

Di Nardo, Ferdinando ('Il Cappellano'). Fascist Underground Movement, Naples: 1944. *Deputy, Italian Social Movement, Naples.*

Di Pasquale, Alfredo. } Rome, San Lorenzo: 19 July, 1943. *Oil and wine shop owner, Rome.*

Di Pasquale, Clara. } Rome, San Lorenzo: 19 July, 1943. *Housewife, Rome.*

Divisi, Col Giulio. March on Rome: 'Rino Moretti' Action Squad, Ferrara; Tripoli: ADC, Governor of Libya, 1934–40. *Gen, retd, Ferrara.*

[Dolfin, Giovanni. Chief of Presidential Secretariat, Salò Republic: 1943–45. *Lawyer, Rome.*]

Elia, Lieut-Cdr Emilio. ('Nemo'). Milan: 'Operation Nemo', 1944–45. *Bicycle manufacturer, Milan.*

Evola, Giulio Cesare. Rastenburg, East Prussia, Führer HQ: 8–17 September, 1943. *Author, Rome.*

Fadda, Capt Stefano. Naples, Prefecture: 27 September–1 October, 1943. *Doctor, Italian Red Cross, Naples.*

Falconi, Vittorio. March on Rome: 1st Florentine Legion, Monterotondo Column. *Typographer, Florence.*

Faldella, Gen Emilio. Milan, Palazzo Cusani: Town Major, 25–29 April, 1945. *Gen, retd, historian, Pinerolò.*

Fantoli, Ferdinando. Milan, Face Standard Plant: 25–29 April, 1945. *Factory inspector, retd, nr Sassari.*

Farinacci, Adriana. Cremona, 1922–45. *Housewife, Cremona.*

Fasciolo, Arturo. Rome, Palazzo Chigi: Personal private secretary, Chief of Government, 1923–24. *Retd, Bologna.*

Ferraguti, Mario. Milan, 'Il Popolo d'Italia': 1921–22; Secretary, General Permanent Committee for Wheat, 1925–38. *Fruit farmer, nr Naples.*

Ferrari, Emilio. Milan, Piazzale Loreto: 29 April, 1945. *Occupation unknown, Rome.*

Ferretti, Count Lando. March on Rome: Adjutant-General, Santa Marinella Column; Chief Government Press Officer, 1928–39. *Senator, retd, Rome.*

Finzi, Enzo. March on Rome: 'Francesco Gozzi' Squad, Ferrara. *Stationer, Ferrara.*

Finzi, Lieut Gualtiero. Fiume, 1st Alpine Artillery Regt: September 1919–December 1920. *Municipal official, retd, Ferrara.*

Fioravante, Stell. Milan, Borletti Factory: 25–29 April, 1945. *Factory operative, Milan.*

Fioravanti, Angela. Rome, San Lorenzo. 19 July, 1943. *Seamstress, Rome.*

Fioravanzo, Rear Admiral Giuseppe. Taranto: Military Commander, 8 September, 1943. *Chief of Archives, Ministry of Marine, Rome.*

Formisano, Maria. Naples, via Roma: 27 September–1 October, 1943. *Housewife, Naples.*

Forzano, Lieut Vincenzo. Naples, Parco CIS, Vico Trone: 27 September–1 October. 1943, *Doctor, Italian Red Cross, Naples.*

Fraccari, Cesare. Milan: President, 'Balilla' Youth Organization, 1928–43. *Industrialist, Milan.*

Franciosi, Capt Crescenzio. 8th Machine-gun Battalion, Messéné, Greece: 25 July, 1943. *Schoolteacher, Brescia.*

Frattari, Ettore. President, Confederation of Agriculture: 1939–43. *Agricultural periodical proprietor, Rome.*

Freddi, Luigi. Milan. 'Il Popolo d'Italia': 1919–22; President, Cinecittà, 1937–43. *Author, Sabaudia.*

Furlotti, Maj Nicola. Verona Trial: Chief of Federal Police, 8–11 January, 1944. *Unemployed, Messina.*

Fuzzi, Arnaldo. Federal Secretary, Forlì': 1929–32. *Engineer, Forlì'.*

Gaddi, Col Otello. Verona Trial; Judicature, 8–11 January, 1944. *Lawyer, Milan.*

Galbiati, Maj Gen Enzo. Rome, Palazzo Chigi: 31 December, 1924; Rome, Commandant of Fascist Militia, Piazza Romania: 25–26 July, 1943. *Gen, retd, Bordighera.*

Galeazzo, Ottavio. Rome, Regina Coeli Prison: 25 July, 1943. *Hospital doctor, Genoa.*

Galignani, Guido. March on Rome: Grosseto Legion, Civitavecchia. *Brick factory owner, Grosseto.*

Gatti, Gian Luigi. Chief of Fascist Party Press Office, Milan: 1944–45. *Professor, Advanced Health Institute, University of Rome.*

Geninazza, Giovanbattista ('Titta'). Giulino di Mezzegra: 28 April, 1945. *Chauffeur, Milan.*

Gentile, Brig Oreste. Rome: via Legnano Carabinieri Barracks, 25–29 July, 1943. *Retd, Rome.*

Gerevini, Palmiro. March on Rome: 'Cremona' Squad, Cremona. *Labourer, Cremona.*

Ghioldi, Carlo, Como: National Republican Guard HQ, 25–29 April, 1945. *Union organizer, Como.*

Ghisetti Cancarini, Capt Giuseppe ('Gamma'). Milan: 'Operation Nemo', 1944–45. *Travel Agent, Milan.*

Ghizzoni, Capt Lorenzo. 5th Infantry Regt, Bobbio: 25 July, 1943. *Retd, Salsomaggiore.*

Giaccaglia, Sgt Emilio. 11th Bersaglieri Regt: 1917. *Railwayman, retd, Ancona.*

Giampaola, Leonida. '(Commandant Pino'). GAP unit, Como: April 1945. *Technical draughtsman, Como.*

Giancotti, Elvira. Rome, via Tibullo: 25 July, 1943. *Journalist, retd, Rome.*

Giannini, Vincenzo. Naples, Campo Sportivo: 27 September–1 October, 1943. *Post Office worker, Naples.*

Giordani, Fernando. March on Rome: 'Cesare Battisti' Squad, Bologna. *Electrical installation shop, Rome.*

Giordano, Nicola. Rome, San Lorenzo: 19 July, 1943. *Real estate expert, Rome.*

Giorgi, Arturo. March on Rome: 'Giancarlo Nanni' Cohort, Bologna. *Calendar salesman, Bologna.*

Giovanni, Vincenzo. Naples, Campo Sportivo: 27 September–1 October, 1943. *Post office worker, Naples.*

Giovannini, Umberto. March on Rome: 'La Giustiziera' Squad, Zagarolo. *Clerk, retd, Ostia.*

[Giuriati, Maj Gen Giovanni. March on Rome: 4th Blackshirt Zone, Udine; Secretary, National Fascist Party, 1929–31. *Lawyer, retd, Rome.*]

Goldoni, Carlo. March on Rome: 'Franco Gozzi' Squad, Ferrara. *Driving Instructor, Genoa.*

Golisano, Francesco. March on Rome: 'Sempre Pronti' Squad, Palermo. *Accountant, Como.*

Gonella, Giuseppe. March on Rome: 'Disperata' Squad, Genoa. *Lawyer, Genoa.*

Gonella, Guido. Vatican City: 'L'Osservatore Romano': 1939–44. *Minister of Education, 1946–48; Minister of Justice, 1953; 1957–62; 1968; President, National Council of Journalists, Rome.*

Gori, Gino. March on Rome: 'Franco Gozzi' Squad, Ferrara. *Clerk, retd, Ferrara.*

Gorreri, Dante ('Guglielmo') Como: Regional Inspector 52nd Garibaldi Brigade, 27–29 April, 1945. *Deputy, Italian Communist Party, Parma.*

Grancelli, Luigi. Mayor of Verona, 1943–45. *Lawyer, Verona.*

Grandi, Count Dino. March on Rome: Chief of Staff, Quadrumvirate; Under-Secretary, Home Affairs: 1924–25; Under Secretary, Foreign Affairs, 1925–29; Minister of Foreign Affairs, 1925–32; Ambassador to Great Britain, 1932–39; Minister of Justice, 1939–February 1943. *Livestock breeder, Modena.*

Graverini, Bruno. March on Rome: Arezzo Legion, Monterotondo Column. *Hotelkeeper, Arezzo.*

Greppi, Antonio ('Arnaldo'). Mayor of Milan: 27–29 April, 1945. *Lawyer, Milan.*

Grossi, Domenico. Milan, Alfa Romeo: 25–29 April, 1945. *Factory operative, Milan.*

[Guariglia, Baron Raffaele. Rome, Palazzo Chigi: Political Director, Ministry of Foreign Affairs, 1920–32; Ambassador to Spain, 1932–35; Ambassador to Argentine Republic, 1936; Ambassador to France, 1938–40; Ambassador to Turkey, 1943; Minister of Foreign Affairs, July 1943–February 1944; Ambassador to Spain, 1943–44. *Diplomat, retd, Rome.*]

Guilitto, Bruno \ Rome, San Lorenzo: 19 July, 1943. *Plumber, Rome.*
Guilitto, Maria / Rome, San Lorenzo: 19 July, 1943. *Housewife, Rome.*

Ianni, Gaetano. Rome, San Lorenzo: 19 July, 1943. *Engine-driver, retd, Rome.*

Illuminato, Anna. \
Illuminato, Giovanni. | Naples, Piazza Montesanto; 27 September–1 October,
Illuminato, Rita. } 1943. *Bicycle repair and rental shop, Naples.*
Illuminato, Salvatore. /

Ingangi, Vincenzo. Naples, via Chiaia: 27 September–1 October, 1943. *Lawyer, Naples.*

Iommi, Mario. Naples, Campo Sportivo: 27 September–1 October, 1943. *Newsstand proprietor, Naples.*

Iraci, Agostino. Chief of Secretariat, Under-Secretary for Home Affairs, 1928–33. *Landowner, Perugia.*

Jachino, Admiral Angelo. Commander-in-Chief, Royal Italian Navy, 1940–43. *Admiral, retd, Rome.*

Jacini, Filippo ('Pini'). Milan: Committee of National Liberation (Liberal Party), 25–29 April, 1945. *Lawyer, Milan.*

[Klinger, Umberto. March on Rome: Polesana Legion, Rovigo/Verona/Milan. *Aircraft repair factory, Venice.*]

Lampredi, Aldo ('Guido'). Milan: Vice-Commandant General, Garibaldi Brigade, April 1945. *Directorate, Italian Communist Party, Rome.*

Landi, Leo. March on Rome: 'Michele Ponzi' Squad, Lucca. *Engineer, retd, Lucca.*

Languasco, Col Aurelio. Officer Commanding, Apennine Pursuit Division, Salò Republic. *President, Salò Republic Ex-Combatants Association, Rome.*

Laterra, Milly. Rome, San Lorenzo, 19 July, 1943. *Free-lance translator, Milan.*

Lauretani, Linda. Rome, San Lorenzo: 19 July, 1943. *Unemployed, Rome.*

Lavini, Claudia. Rome, San Lorenzo: 19 July, 1943. *Housewife, Rome.*

Lessona, Lieut Alessandro. March on Rome: 'Francesco Ferrucci' Squad, Florence; Under-Secretary for Colonial Affairs, 1929–36; Minister for Colonial Affairs, 1936–37; *Senator, Florence.*

Leto, Guido. Rome: Director-General, OVRA, 1938–45. *Hotel executive, Rome.*

Liberti, Maj Egidio ('Collino'). Milan: Chief of Staff, Town Major's Dept, 25–29 April, 1945. *Lawyer, Milan.*

Lisa, Don Matteo. Naples, Church of Santissimo Sacramento: 27 September–1 October, 1943. *Priest, Naples.*

Lizzani, Deira. Rome, San Lorenzo: 19 July, 1943. *Accountant, Rome.*

Locarno, Elena. March on Rome: 28 October, 1922. *Designer, London.*

Lombardi, Riccardo ('Gilberti'). Prefect of Milan: 25–29 April, 1945; Minister of Transport, 1948–49. *Deputy, Socialist Party, Milan.*

Longo, Luigi ('Gallo'). Milan: Vice-Commander, Volunteer Freedom Corps, 1944–45; Commandant-General, Garibaldi Brigades. *Secretary General, Italian Communist Party, Rome; Deputy, Milan.*

Lucci, Assunta. Rome, 40, via Pisanelli: June, 1924. *Retd, Rome.*

Luciani, Lieut. Bruno. March on Rome: 'Franco Gozzi' Squad, Ferrara. *City Police Chief, retd, Ferrara.*

Lucitero, Marquis Falcone. Minister of the Royal Household, 1944–46. *Criminologist, Rome.*

Ludergnani, Mario. March on Rome: 'Franco Gozzi' Squad, Ferrara. *Executive, retd, Ferrara.*

Lussi, Tullio ('Landi'). Milan, Palazzo Cusani: Communications Section: 26–29 April, 1945. *Director, plastics company, Milan.*

Lussu, Emilio. Rome, Chamber of Deputies: 1919–24. *Senator; Author, Rome.*

[Magistrati, Count Massimo. Berlin: First Secretary-Chargé d'Affaires, Italian Embassy, 1934–40; Minister, Italian Legation, Switzerland, 1943–45. *Director General of Political Affairs, Foreign Ministry, 1954–58; Ambassador to Turkey, 1958–61; Ambassador, United Arab Republic, 1961–65; Diplomat, retd, Rome.*]

Maione, Capt Vincenzo. Naples, San Potito Finance Guards Barracks: 27 September–1 October, 1943. *Col, retd, Bologna.*

Malgeri, Col Alfredo. Milan: Officer Commanding 3rd (Lombardy) Finance Guards Legion, April 1945. *Gen, retd, Milan.*

Mancini, Margherita. Rome, San Lorenzo: 19 July, 1943. *Typographer, retd, Rome.*

Mandolini, Angela Maria. Milan: Falck Steel Plant, 1922. *Housewife, Varese (Como).*

[Manes, Capt Giorgio ('Fiore'). Milan; 'Operation Nemo': 1944–45. *General; National Vice-Commandant, Carabinieri, Rome.*]

Manno, Fernanda. Rome, San Lorenzo. 19 July, 1943. *Accountant, spaghetti factory, Rome.*

Manunta, Ugo. Ministry of Labour (Socialization Dept), Salò' Republic: 1944–45. *Journalist, Rome.*

Manzini, Carlo. Verona: Editor-in-Chief, 'L'Arena', 1932–43. *Journalist, Verona.*

Maragnani, Lieut Lino. Arbe Island Prison Camp, Dalmatia: 25 July, 1943. *Retd, Milan.*

Marasco, Francesco. March on Rome: Chief of Staff, Santa Marinella Column. *Doctor, retd, Florence.*

Marchesi, Maj Luigi. Rome, Palazzo Vidoni: General Staff, Army High Command, February–September 1943. *Orchid-grower, Rome.*

Marchetti, Romano. Tolmezzo (Veneto): 1913–43. *Occupation unknown, Tolmezzo.*

Marchi, Corrado. March on Rome: Piazza Corvetto, Genoa. *Journalist, retd, Milan.*

Marras, Lieut Gen Efisio. Military Attaché, Italian Embassy, Berlin: 1936–39; Military Attaché and Chief of Military Mission to Supreme Command, 1939–43. *President, Chancellery of the Italian Republic, Rome.*

Martini, Virgilio. March on Rome: Corso Umberto/Piazza del Popolo, Rome. *Editor, Lido di Jesolo.*

Masini, Clara. Rome, San Lorenzo: 19 July, 1943. *Seamstress, Rome.*

Mastromattei, Giuseppe. March on Rome: General Staff, Brufani Palace Hotel, Perugia; Prefect of Bolzano, 1933–40. *News Agency director, Rome.*

Matteotti, Isabella. Rome, 40, via Pisanelli: June, 1924. *Independent, Rome.*

Matteotti, Gianmatteo. Rome, 40, via Pisanelli; June, 1924. *Directorate, Italian Socialist Party, Rome; Deputy, Venice.*

Maugeri, Admiral Franco, Chief of Naval Intelligence; 1941–43. *Import-export agency, Paris.*

Mazzello, Mario. Ponza: August, 1943. *Fisherman, Ponza.*

Mellini Ponce De Leon, Count Alberto. Chief of Secretariat, Ministry of Foreign Affairs, Salò' Republic. *Diplomat, retd, Rome.*

Menin, Count Alessandro. March on Rome: 'Friulana' Legion, Udine. *Cattle breeder, Udine.*

Mepelli, Antonio. Milan: Archbishop's Palace, April 1945. *Chauffeur, Archbishop's Palace, Milan.*

Merlini, Paolo ('Cartone'). Milan, via Telesio: April 1945. *Cardboard box manufacturer, Milan.*

[Mischi, Gen Archimede. Chief of Staff, Army of the Salò Republic: 1944–45. *Gen, retd, Forlì'.*]

Missiroli, Mario. Bologna: Director, 'Il Resto del Carlino', 1918–21. *Journalist; President Italian Press Federation, Rome.*

Monaci, Niccolo'. Rome: 'M' Battalion Barracks, Trastevere: 25 July, 1943. *Tax-office official, Poggibonsi, (Siena).*

Monaco, Giorgio. Rome: Villa Camilluccia, 1937–38. *Architect, Rome.*

Monelli, Paolo. 'Corriere della Sera': 1926–29, 'La Stampa': 1929–35; Lieut Col, Italian Corps of Liberation, 1944–45. *Special correspondent, Author, Rome.*

Monga, Felice. Monza: Breda Aeronautics Plant: April, 1945. *Personnel officer, retd, Milan.*

Montagna, Gen Renzo. Verona Trial: Judicature, 8–11 January, 1944; Chief of Police, Salò Republic, 1944–45. *Vineyard proprietor, nr Pavia.*

Montanari, Remo. March on Rome: Cremona Legion. *Institute of Italian Graphic Arts, Bergamo.*

Montanelli, Indro. 'Corriere della Sera': 1935–43. *Columnist, Rome.*

Morelli, Irma. Rome, Villa Torlonia: 1931–43. *Dressmaker, Forli'.*

Morgese, Salvatore. Naples, Piazza Cavour: 27 September–1 October, 1943. *Factory operative, Naples.*

Morreale, Eugenio. Vienna: 'Il Popolo d'Italia' Bureau, 1927–37. *Historian, Madrid.*

Motta, Stefano. Federal Secretary, Mantua: 1943–45. *Broiler chicken expert, Bologna.*

Murialdi, Paolo ('Paolo') Chief of Staff, Outer-Po Pavese Division: April 1945. *News editor, 'Il Giorno', Milan.*

Murolo, Ezio. Naples, Piazza Dante: 27 September–1 October, 1943. *Gambling club manager, Naples.*

Murru, Lance Sgt Paolo. Anzio: 25 July, 1943. *Magazine editor, Genoa.*

Mussolini, Donna Rachele. Forlì', via Merenda: 1909–15; Milan, Foro Bonaparte,

1919–29; Rome, Villa Torlonia: 1929–43; Gardone, Villa Feltrinelli: 1943–45. *Restaurant proprietor, nr Forlì'.*

Mussolini, Romano. Rome, Villa Torlonia: 1929–43; Gardone, Villa Feltrinelli: 1943–45. *Jazz pianist, Rome.*

Mussolini, Vittorio. Milan; Foro Bonaparte: 1915–29; Rome, Villa Torlonia: 1929–43; Gardone, Villa Feltrinelli: 1943–45. *Newspaper proprietor, Buenos Aires.*

Musumarra, Luigi. March on Rome: Catania Legion. *Occupation unknown, Catania.*

Nadi Ferralasco, Roma. Padua-Rome: 25 July, 1943. *Publicist, Rapallo.*

Nencini, Roberto. March on Rome: 'Fiorentina' Legion, Monterotondo Column. *Delicatessen proprietor, Florence.*

Nicosia, Angelo. Palermo: 1934–43. *Political organiser, Palermo.*

Nozzella, Carmine. Naples, National Museum: 27 September–1 October, 1943. *Occupation unknown, Naples.*

Olcese, Piera. Rome, San Lorenzo; 19 July, 1943. *Pasta factory worker, Rome.*

Oliva, Capt Giovanni, RIN. 'Camicia Nera', 1941–41. *Admiral, retd, Rome.*

Onnis, Lieut Col Anacleto ('Uncle'). Milan: Piazzale Loreto, April 29, 1945. *Col of Carabinieri, retd, Milan.*

Orbitello, Mario. Naples, Vasto district: 27 September–1 October, 1943. *Lawyer, Naples.*

Orlandi, Vittorio. March on Rome: Headquarters Staff, PNF, Bologna. *Insurance, Rome.*

Orlando, Carlotta. Rome: Via Nomentana, October 1922. *Dog breeder, nr Milan.*

Ortona, Egidio. Feltre: Palazzo Chigi Diplomatic Mission, 19 July, 1943. *Ambassador to the United States, Washington.*

Pagani, Ester. Milan: Piazzale Loreto, 29 April, 1945. *Housewife, Milan.*

Pagliani, Franz. March on Rome: Igliori Column, Monterotondo; Verona Trial; Judicature, 8–11 January, 1944. *General Surgeon, Perugia.*

Paladino, Gen Francesco. Inspector-General of Works, Salò Republic, 1943–45. *Gen of Militia, retd, Piacenza.*

Palermo, Carolina. Naples, Piazza Gesù': 25 July, 1943. *Occupation unknown, Naples.*

Palestra, Capt Gino. March on Rome: 'Pavese' Action Squad, Milan, Palazzo Marino. *Col, retd, Pavia.*

Palombo, Col Vittorio ('Col Pieri'). Milan, Palazzo Cusani: Chief of Staff, Volunteer Freedom Corps, April, 1945. *Gen, retd, industrialist, Rome.*

Pancino, Don Giusto. Gardone, Villa Feltrinelli; 1944–45. *Country Priest, nr Pordenone.*

Parente, Alfredo. Naples, Santa Teresa district: 27 September–1 October, 1943. *Principal librarian, Institute of Italian History, Naples.*

Parini, Piero. March on Rome: 'Il Popolo d'Italia', Milan; Secretary-General for Fascists Abroad, 1927–38; Mayor of Milan, 1943–44. *President, Italo-Egyptian Chamber of Commerce, Milan.*

Pasanisi, Capt Mario, Capri: 23 September–1 October, 1943. *Director, Association of War Disabled, Rome.*

Passerone, Lieut Giovanni, March on Rome: Commander, Casale Monferrato Legion; Rome, Palazzo Chigi: 31 December, 1924. *Gen of Militia, retd, Turin.*

Patti, Ercole. Rome: 1921–43. *Author, Rome.*

Paviotti, Attilio. March on Rome: 'Me ne frego' Action Squad, Udine. *Electrical engineer, Milan.*

Pellegrini Giampietro, Domenico. Minister of Finance, Salò Republic: 1943–45. *Banker, Montevideo.*

Pelliccioni Di Poli, Luciano. Rome, San Lorenzo: 19 July, 1943. *Director, Institute of Heraldic & Genealogical Studies, Rome.*

Perlini, Lieut Roberto. March on Rome: 7th Artillery Barracks, Siena. *Land surveyor, Arezzo.*

Perrone, Capt Franco. Rome: Trastevere Military Hospital: 25 July, 1943. *Lawyer, Naples.*

Pertini, Sandro ('Nicola Durano'). Milan, Palazzo Cusani: Committee of National Liberation (Socialist Party), April, 1945. *President, Chamber of Deputies, Rome; Deputy, Genoa.*

Pesaresi, Plinio. March on Rome: 'Benito Mussolini' Squad, Forlì'. *Hospital administrator, nr Forlì'.*

Petacci, Marchioness Myriam. Rome: 1932–43; Lake Garda and Milan: 1943–45. *Actress, Rome.*

Petronio, Ilio. March on Rome: 'Giornale del Friuli', Udine. *Wholesale Newsagent, Udine.*

Piaggesi, Giulia. Rome, San Lorenzo: 19 July, 1943. *Pasta factory worker, Rome.*

Piccardi, Ciro. Naples, San Potito: 27 September–1 October, 1943. *Schoolteacher, Naples.*

Piccardi, Leopoldo. Civil Commissioner for Corporations, July–September, 1943; Minister for Industry, September, 1943. *Lawyer, Rome.*

Piccoli, Vittorio. Rome: Villa Savoia, 1928–43. *Caterer, Rome.*

Pietra, Italo ('Edoardo'). Milan: Commander, Outer-Po Pavese Division, April, 1945. *Director, 'Il Giorno', Milan.*

Pietromarchi, Count Luca. Rome, Palazzo Chigi: Ministry of Foreign Affairs, 1922–43. *Ambassador to Turkey, 1950–58; Ambassador to Soviet Republic, 1958–61; diplomat, retd, Rome.*

Pini, Giorgio. Milan: Editor, 'Il Popolo d'Italia', 1936–43; Under-Secretary for Home Affairs, Salò Republic. 1943–45. *Lawyer, Bologna.*

Piscanc, Ellas. Trieste, Borgo S. Sergio: 25 July, 1943. *Embroiderer, Trieste.*

Pisenti, Piero. Minister of Justice, Salò Republic, 1943–45. *Lawyer, Venice.*

Pistone, Eraldo. Rome, Villa Torlonia: 1937–43. *Post-office employee, Rome.*

Pitea, Oscar. Lissone, Milan: Ercole Marelli Plant, 25–29 April, 1945. *Computer-technician, Milan.*

Pollini, Col Giovanni. Officer Commanding, National Republican Guard of Genoa: Como, 26–27 April, 1945. *Gas-petroleum executive, Milan.*

Porfirio, Giorgio. Abruzzi Mountains: 25 July, 1943. *Librarian, Rome.*

Pozzi, Dr Arnaldo. Rome, Villa Torlonia: 1942–43. *Consulting Physician, Rome.*

Previtera, Capt Gialma. Lucca Motorized Regt, Ariete Division, Casalfiaschetti (Bologna): 25 July, 1943. *Officer, Italian Army, Rome.*

Pricolo, Gen Francesco. Under Secretary for Aviation, 1939–41. *Gen, retd, Rome.*

Provini, Giorgio. Venice: 'Gazzettino del Veneto', 1922–43. *Parliamentary correspondent, Rome.*

Pucci, Marquis Emilio. Rome-Ramiola-Verona-Varese-Sondrio: September 1943–January 1944. *Fashion designer, Florence.*

Raganella, Don Libero. Rome, San Lorenzo: 19 July, 1943. *Director, Oratorio Maschile S. Paolo, Rome.*

Ravegnani, Cpl Cesare. 6th Supply Group: Granatieri Division, 1915–17. *Pensioner, Ferrara.*

Recchioni, Guido. March on Rome: 'Sempre Pronti' Action Squad, Nationalist Party, Rome. *Electrical engineer, Milan.*

Renzi, Anna. Rome, San Lorenzo: 19 July, 1943. *Market stallkeeper, Rome.*

Renzetti, Baroness Susanna. Berlin: Italo-German Chamber of Commerce, 1929–35; Italian Consulate-General, 1937–41. *Independent, nr Pisa.*

Renzulli, Maj Raffaele. Naples, via Cesare Rosserol: 27 September–1 October, 1943. *Mathematics teacher, Naples.*

Riccardi, Raffaello. Under-Secretary for Communications, 1928; Under-Secretary,

Ministry of Aviation, 1929–33; Minister of Currency and Exchange, 1939–43. *Landowner, Varese.*

Ricci, Paolo. Naples, Parco Lamaro/Vomero: 27 September–1 October, 1943. *Artist, Naples.*

Romano, Aldo. Naples, Villa Haas: 27 September–1 October, 1943. *Professor of Modern History, Paris.*

Romersa, Luigi. Peenemünde–Rügen Island; October 1944. *Journalist. Rome.*

Romualdi, Pino. Vice-Secretary, Fascist Party, Salò Republic, 1944–45. *Journalist, Rome.*

Roncallo, Sgt Alfredo. 571st Infantry Regiment. Casalione (Corsica). 25 July, 1943. *Journalist, Genoa.*

Rossi Chiesa, Clementina. March on Rome: Trento Legion, Trento. *Postmistress, retd, Castelrotto (Bolzano).*

Rotella, Antonio. Viterbo: 25 July, 1943. *Unemployed, Genoa.*

Ruffilli, Mentore. Rocca delle Caminate, 1936–43; Gardone, Villa Feltrinelli, 1943–44. *Hotel waiter, Forlì'.*

Rustici, Gino. March on Rome: Siena Legion, Monterotondo Column. *Agrarian administrator, Siena.*

[Ruzzini, Giovanni. March on Rome: 18th (Osimo) Group, Monterotondo Column; Milan; Corso Porta Romana, 29 April, 1945. *Accountant, Milan.*]

Sabadei, Alice. Rome, San Lorénzo: 19 July, 1943. *Housewife, Rome.*

Sala, Ambrogio. Milan, TIBB Factory: 25–29 April, 1945. *Electrical mechanic, Milan.*

Saldarelli, Jole. Naples, Fish Market: 25 July, 1943. *Occupation unknown, Naples.*

Salvadori, Lieut Col Max. Milan: No 1 Special Force Mission, March–April, 1945. *Professor of History, Smith College. Northampton, Mass.*

Sampoli, Aldo. March on Rome: Siena Legion, Monterotondo Column. *Timber executive, Siena.*

Sandrini, Enrico. March on Rome: 'Fiume' Action Squad, Udine. *Registrar of Births and Deaths, Udine.*

Sanges, Giuseppe. Naples, San Ferdinando-Museum Region-via Roma: 27 September–1 October, 1943. *Haberdasher, Naples.*

Sardagna, Col the Baron Giovanni. Como: Town Commander, Volunteer Freedom Corps, 25–29 April, 1945. *Racecourse starter, Milan.*

Sassi, Lino. Milan: Chief Conductor, Municipal Tramways, 25–29 April, 1945. *Tramway official, Milan.*

Scala, Gen Alessandro. Deputy Chief, Army General Staff, Salò Republic, 1943–45. *retd, Rome.*

Schettini, Giulio. Naples, Materdei/Fontenelle: 27 September–1 October, 1943. *Insurance representative, Naples.*

Schettino, Don Rocco. Naples, Church of Gesù e Maria: 27 September–1 October, 1943. *Priest, Pozzuoli.*

Schiano, Pasquale. Paestum (Salerno): September, 1943. *Lawyer, Naples.*

Schiappe Ferrari, Laura. Genoa: 25 July, 1943. *Charity Worker, Genoa.*

Schiff Giorgini, Nini'. Rome: 25 July, 1943. *Housewife, Rome.*

Sechi, Mario. Rome, San Lorenzo: 19 July, 1943. *Farm director, Rome.*

Semadini, Gen Tommaso. Rome: Militia HQ, Piazza Romania, 25 July, 1943. *Auto spares exporter, Rome.*

Sereni, Dolores. Rome: Villa Camilluccia, 1938–43. *Dressmaker, Rome.*

Sereni, Emilio ('Aldo'). Milan, Palazzo Cusani: Committee of National Liberation (Communist Party), April, 1945. *Deputy, Naples.*

Seveso, Pietro. Milan, Breda Aeronautics Plant: 25–29 April, 1945. *Secretary, Provincial Metalworkers Association, Milan.*

Sforni, Oscar ('Osvaldo Scudieri'). Como: Secretary, Committee of National Liberation, April, 1945. *Car Hire representative, Como.*

Silvestri, Ofelia. Trieste, via Pagliaricci: 25 July, 1943. *Housewife, Trieste.*

Solari, Fermo ('Somma'). Milan, Palazzo Cusani: Volunteer Freedom Corps (Action Party), April, 1945. *Clock manufacturer, Udine.*

Solaro dal Borgo, Marquis Alfredo. } Rome: Palazzo del Quirinale 1938–43.
Solaro dal Borgo, Marchioness Ippolita. } *Landowners, Rome.*

Sorice, Gen Antonio. Chief of Secretariat for the Service Ministries, 1934–41; Under-Secretary for War, 1943. *Counsellor of State, Rome.*

Sotis, Giuseppe. Rome: 1937–43. *Lawyer, Rome.*

Spampanato, Giuseppina. Rome, Piazza Mazzini: 25 July, 1943. *Journalist, Rome.*

Spinelli, Giuseppe. Minister of Labour, Salò Republic, January–April, 1945. *Managing director, engineering, Cremona.*

Spoto, Capt Aurelio. Naples, Capodimonte: 27 September–1 October, 1943. *Doctor of medicine, Naples.*

Storoni, Enzo. Rome: Attorney for the Royal Estates, 1940–43. *Lawyer, Rome.*

Strino, Umberto. March on Rome: Florentine Legion. *Hotel-owner, Florence.*

Stucchi, G. Battista ('Noris'). Milan, Palazzo Cusani: Volunteer Freedom Corps (Socialist Party), April, 1945. *Lawyer, Monza.*

Suvich, Fulvio. Under-Secretary for Finance, 1926–28; Commissioner for Tourism, 1931–32; Under-Secretary for Foreign Affairs, 1932–36; Ambassador to the United States, 1936–39. *Insurance, Trieste.*

Tabellini, Col Dino. Chief of Staff, Carabinieri, Rome: July–September, 1943. *Bank security official, retd, Rome.*

Tailetti, Alberto. March on Rome: Siena Legion, Monterotondo Column. *Professor of economics, Siena.*

Tambara, Cirillo. Milan, Foro Bonaparte; 1920–22; Rome, via Rasella, 1922–24. *Jeweller, Milan.*

Tarchi, Angelo. Minister of Corporations, Salò Republic, 1944–45. *Chemical consultant, Milan.*

Teodorani, Countess Rosina. Rome, Villa Torlonia: 1936–37. *Independent, Rome.*

Terraciano, Nicola. March on Rome: 'Falcons' Squad, Caserta. *Agrarian scientist, Naples.*

Terraneo, Don Ecclesio. Milan, Archbishop's Palace: 24–29 April, 1945. *Monsignor, Sanctuary of Santa Maria del Bosco, Imbersago.*

Thaon di Revel, Count Paolo. Minister of Finance, 1935–43. *Political economist, Turin.*

Tommasi, Siro. Milan: 25 July, 1943. *Business executive, Milan.*

Toni, Vittorio. March on Rome: Lucca Cohort, Civitavecchia. *Lottery clerk, Lucca.*

Tozzi, Gino. March on Rome: Siena Legion, Rome. *Doctor of medicine, Siena.*

Trevisani, Chiara. March on Rome: Ligurian Women's Fascio. *Housewife, Genoa.*

Trombetti, Capt Mario. Rome, Passeggiata Ripetta: 25 July, 1943. *Accountant, Rome.*

Valeri, Nino. Catania, Sicily: 25 July, 1943. *Professor of Modern History, Rome University.*

Valiani, Leo ('Federico'). Milan, Palazzo Cusani: Committee of National Liberation (Action Party), April 1945. *Author, Milan.*

Valle, Gen Giuseppe. Under-Secretary, Ministry of Aviation, 1933–39. *Gen, retd, Rome.*

Varenna, Enrico. Milan: Administrative Director, 'Regime Fascista,' 1923–45. *Industrialist, Milan.*

Varo, Sergio. Forlì', Central Post Office: 25 July, 1943. *Post Office worker, Forlì'.*

Vecchietti, Giorgo. Rome: Editor, 'Primato', 1936–43. *Broadcasting Executive, Rome.*

Ventura, Luigi. March on Rome: 'Oberdan' Action Squad, Lodi, (Lombardy). *Slaughterhouse Veterinary Surgeon, Cremona.*

Versari, Nerina. Rome, Villa Torlonia: 1937–40. *Housewife, Rome.*

Vianini, Col Italo. Verona: Inspector, 5th Zone, National Republican Guard, January, 1944. *Occupation unknown, Verona.*
Vigneri, Capt Paolo. Rome. San Lorenzo: 19 July, 1943; Villa Savoia, 25 July, 1943. *Notary, Catania.*
Villarini, Amalia. Rome, 40, via Pisanelli: June, 1924. *Portress, Rome.*
Vinciguerra, Mario. Rome: 1937–43. *President, Society of Italian Authors, Rome.*
Violani, Tullio. March on Rome: 'Benito Mussolini' Squad, Forlì'. *Typewriter shop, Forlì'.*
Virnicchi, Paolo. March on Rome: 'Serenissima' Action Squad, Quagliano. *Journalist, Naples.*
Vita, Enrico. Milan, 1916–39. *Engineer, London.*
Vitetti, Count Leonardo. Rome, Palazzo Chigi: Director, General Affairs Division, Ministry of Foreign Affairs, 1936–43; Director Political Division, 1943. *Ambassador to France, 1956–61; Diplomat, retd, Rome.*
Volta, Alfredo. March on Rome: 'Franco Gozzi' Action Squad, Ferrara. *Retd, Ferrara.*
Zamboni, Mario. Rome: Director, General Confederation of Armaments Manufacturers, 1927–39. *Legal adviser, insurance company, Rome.*
Zametta, Ermanno. March on Rome: 'Audace' Action Squad, Trento. *Marshal of Traffic Police, retd, Cremona.*
Zannerini, Emilio. Rome: Vice-Secretary, Unitarian Socialist Party, 1922–24. *Deputy, retd, Grosseto.*
Zoccoli, Antonmaria. March on Rome: 'Tonino Torrisi' Action Squad, Cremona. *Retd, Pozzaglio.*
Zonta, Giovanni. Castelfranco Veneto (Treviso): 25 July, 1943. *Journalist, Castelfranco Veneto.*
Zvab, Federico. Naples, San Lorenzo: 27 September–1 October, 1943. *Translator, Naples.*

The Germans

von Braun, Freiherr Sigismund. Third Secretary, German Embassy to the Vatican, 1943–44. *Ambassador to France, 1968.*
Dollmann, Standartenführer Eugen, SS. Personal representative, Reichsführer Himmler, 1933–45. *Author, Munich.*
Gerlach, Hauptmann Heinrich, 11th Air Corps. Pratica di Mare/Gran Sasso, July–September, 1943. *Industrial engineer, nr Kassel.*
Gumpert, Gerhard. Commercial Attaché, German Embassy, Rome, 1940–43; Chief of Secretariat, German Embassy, Fasano, 1943–45. *Director, Volkswagen, Bologna.*
von Halem, Gustav Adolph. Consul-General, Milan, 1944–45. *Member, German Board of Film Censors, Wiesbaden.*
Holldach, Heinz. Press Office, German Embassy, Fasano, 1943–44. *Cultural Attaché, German Embassy, Rome.*
Höttl, Obersturmbannführer Wilhelm, SS. Chief AMT VI, Rome, February–September, 1943. *Headmaster, Bad Aussee, Austria.*
Kappler, Obersturmbannführer Herbert, SS. Police Attaché, German Embassy, Rome, 1939–43. *Life prisoner, Gaeta Jail.*
von Kessel, Albrecht. Protocol Department, Foreign Office, 1932–43; Acting-Counsellor, German Embassy to the Vatican, 1943–44. *Diplomatic correspondent, Bad Godesberg.*
Krutoff, Leutnant Leo, Medical Staff, 11th Air Corps, July–September, 1943. *Doctor of Medicine, Frankfurt.*

Langguth, Hauptmann Gerhard. Intelligence Staff, 11th Air Corps, July–September, 1943. *Brigade-General, Bundeswehr, Munster.*

von Mackensen, Frau Winifred. German Embassy, Villa Wolkonsky, Rome, 1938–43. *nr Stuttgart.*

Meyer-Wehner, Leutnant Elimar. 1st Airborne Wing, Rome, Pratica di Mare/Gran Sasso, 12 September, 1943. *Manager, woodwork machine factory, Hamburg.*

Möllhausen, Eitel Friedrich. Consul-General, German Embassy, Rome, August–October, 1943; German Embassy, Fasano, 1943–45. *Chemical manufacturer, Milan.*

Mollier, Hans. Press Attaché, German Embassy, Rome/Fasano, 1943–45. *Literary critic, Munich.*

Overbeck, Karl Kuno. Consular and Legal Dept, German Embassy, Fasano, 1944–45. *Cultural Director, Foreign Ministry, Bonn.*

von Plehwe, Friedrich-Karl. Assistant Military Attaché, German Embassy, Rome, 1940–43. *Western European Union, London.*

Radl, Obersturmführer Karl, SS. *Friedenthal* Formation, Waffen SS, Rome, Pratica di Mare/Gran Sasso, July–September, 1943. *Textile mills representative, Frankfurt.*

Rahn, Dr Rudolf, Ambassador to the Republic of Salò, 1943–45. *President, Coca-Cola, Dusseldorf.*

von Rintelen, Gen Enno. Military Attaché, German Embassy, Rome, 1936–39; Military Attaché and Chief of Military Mission to Supreme Command, 1939–43. *Gen, retd, Heidelberg*

[Schmidt, Dr Paul. Chief Interpreter, Foreign Ministry, 1933–45. *Author, nr Munich.*]

Skorzeny, Hauptsturmführer Otto, SS. OC, *Friedenthal* Formation, Waffen SS, Rome, Pratica di Mare/Gran Sasso, July–September, 1943. *Engineer, Madrid.*

Spögler, Obersturmführer Franz, SS. Lake Garda: Villa Fiordaliso, 1943–45. *Guesthouse-keeper, nr Bolzano.*

Student, Gen Kurt, OC, 11th Air Corps, Frascati/Pratica di Mare, July–September, 1943. *Gen, retd, Bad Salzuflen.*

Westphal, Gen Siegfried, Chief of Staff, Wehrmacht, Commander-in-Chief, Southern Command, Frascati, September, 1943. *Chairman, Rhine Steel Works, Bonn.*

The Americans

[Eisenhower, Gen Dwight David. Allied Commander-in-Chief, North Africa, 1942–43; Supreme Commander, SHAEF, 1943–45. *General of the Army; President of the United States, 1952–60. Gettysburg, Pa.*]

Clark, Kenneth. Rome: Hearst Press Bureau, 1930. *Motion Picture Association of America, Washington, DC.*

Clark, Gen Mark Wayne. Commander, 5th Army, January, 1943–November, 1944; 15th Army Group, November, 1944–April, 1945. *Pres Emeritus, The Citadel Military College, Charleston, SC, 1966.*

Corvo, Maj Max. ('Marat'). Chief Operations Officer, OSS, Italy, 1943–45. *Newspaper proprietor, Middletown, Conn.*

Daddario, Capt Emilio Q. ('Mim'). OSS, Lugano-Como-Milan, 25–29 April, 1945. *Congressman, 1st District, Hartford, Conn.*

[Dulles, Allen W. ('Arturo'). Chief, OSS Mission, Berne, Switzerland, 1942–45. Deputy director, CIA, 1951–53; Director, 1953–61. *Diplomat, retd, Washington, DC.*]

Murphy, Robert. Presidential representative, Mediterranean Advisory Commission, AFHQ, September, 1943. *Chairman, Corning Glass Int, NY.*

Norton, Howard. ('Baltimore Sun') Milan: Piazzale Loreto, 29 April, 1945. *US News and World Report, Washington, DC.*

Poletti, Col Charles. Military Governor of Lombardy, Milan: Piazzale Loreto, 29 April, 1945. *Lieutenant-Governor, NY State, 1939–42; Governor, 1942; lawyer, Marco Is, Fla.*

Roper, James. (United Press) Milan: Piazzale Loreto, 29 April, 1945. *Journalist, Washington, DC.*

Swinton, Stan. ('Stars and Stripes'). Milan: Piazzale Loreto, 29 April, 1945. *Associated Press, NY.*

Taylor, Brig Gen Maxwell D. Chief of Staff, 82nd Airborne Division, 1943. *General: Chief of Staff, US Army, 1955–59; Chairman, Joint Chiefs of Staff, 1962–64; Special Consultant to the President, 1965; Washington, DC.*

Tittmann, Harold H. Rome, Vatican City: Chargé d'Affaires to the Holy See, 1941–44. *Diplomat, retd, Washington, DC.*

The British

Barber, Stephen. ('News Chronicle'.) Milan: Piazzale Loreto, April 29, 1945. *'Daily Telegraph', Washington, DC.*

Hancock, Col Arthur. Deputy Military Governor, Lombardy. Milan: Piazzale Loreto, 29 April, 1945. *Textile executive, retd, Massa Carrara.*

Hoppé, Emil. Rome, Palazzo Venezia: 1934, *Photographer, nr Andover.*

Hunt, Col David. Cassibile, Syracuse: GSO 1, 18th Army Group, September 1943. *Sir David Hunt, KCMG (1963), CMG (1959), OBE (1943); British High Commissioner in Nigeria, 1967–69; Ambassador to Brazil, 1969.*

Mosley, Sir Oswald, Chancellor, Duchy of Lancaster, 1929–30; Founder, British Union of Fascists, 1934–39. *Independent, nr Paris.*

Rennell, Maj Gen Lord, Chief Civil Affairs Officer, Allied Military Government, Middle East, Africa and Italy, 1943–44. *Lord Rennell of Rodd, KBE (1944), CB (1943); director, Morgan, Grenfell; Presteigne, Hereford.*

Roseveare, Edith. Naples, 1920–36. *Languages Professor, London.*

Roseveare, Leslie. Naples, 1920–36. *Retd, London.*

Ruffer, Yvonne. Emilia-Romagna, 1919. *Retd, Norwich.*

Scholes, Walter G. Italy, 1905–34. *Engineer, retd, Leeds.*

Shearburn, Mary. London: 10, Downing Street, 1940–41. *Housewife, nr Fareham.*

Thompson, Inspector Walter. Rome: Palazzo Chigi, January, 1927. *Lecturer, nr Fareham.*

The Austrians

Dollfuss, Frau Alwine. Riccione: 25 July, 1934. *Vienna.*

Mandl, Fritz. Vienna: President, Lower Austria Independent Association, 1938. *Industrialist, Buenos Aires.*

The French

François-Poncet, André. Ambassador to Germany, 1931–38; Ambassador to Italy, 1938–40. *Ambassador to West Germany, 1955; diplomat, retd, Paris.*

Index

Index